Rebel Knight

Rebel Knight

Luiza Dobrzynska

PAPERBACK ISBN: 979-8-9864524-0-1
EPUB ISBN: 979-8-2010135-0-9
***

WRITTEN BY LUIZA DOBRZYNSKA
PUBLISHED BY ROYAL HAWAIIAN PRESS
COVER ART BY TYRONE ROSHANTHA
TRANSLATED BY ROLAND TURNER
PUBLISHING ASSISTANCE: DOROTA RESZKE
***

FOR MORE WORKS BY THIS AUTHOR, PLEASE VISIT:
WWW.ROYALHAWAIIANPRESS.COM
***

VERSION NUMBER 1.00

Table of Contents

The Outlaw

Book One

CHAPTER I

The Nightmare

The year 1360 was to be a year of defeat for war-torn France. Until this year, the French army, although unsuccessful, maintained the illusion of equalization, but the famous Battle of Poitiers crushed this illusion to the ashes. The armed troops of the Black Prince stormed forward, breaking the resistance of the now few desperate defenders. Many French nobles openly supported the invaders, and this number also included a close cousin of King John II, Roger de Valois, commonly known as the Black Knight or the French Black Prince, which better reflected the fright and hatred that this renegade aroused in his countrymen. Even those who agreed with him on political issues and therefore kept close contacts with him did not like him. Cruel and unscrupulous, he made friends with the son of Edward III very fast, with whom during the course of the war he was confronted by a capricious fate, and at a turning point he completely sided with him. Despite the fact that they had a considerable age difference, they understood each other well and liked each other, although neither of them was very inclined to such feelings. Perhaps they did not trust each other all over, but in sufficient measure.

Currently, the Black Knight continued the work of Prince Edward in his own way, eliminating armed groups of knights still resisting and capturing defending towns and individual fortresses. He cut out without mercy all who refused the demand for unconditional surrender, taking the example of his English friend. He was heading towards Paris, not that he wanted to control it, but to expanding the boundaries of English rule, grab as much as possible for himself. Now there was only one stronghold on his way, the last on his list - Bongrais.

It was not a very large stronghold. The town surrounding had few inhabitants, although the property belonging to Bongrais was quite extensive and rich. However, the fortress had a brave and punitive, well-trained crew, commanded by a very young, but already known for bravery and uncompromising attitude, Count Theodoric de Bongrais. He was the main problem because it was known that he would not give up at any cost. He had only been knighted a few months ago, yet the old soldiers listened to him without murmuring, perhaps captivated by the deceptive resemblance of his voice to his father's, which no one ever dared to oppose.

"They listen to him like the Gospel itself, even if he only speaks nonsense," said Don Paulino, steward of Bongrais, to the Black Knight listening to his words. "And we cannot count on his sense. An attack on a castle will cost Your Majesty a lot, too much. I propose a different solution."

"What?" The Black Knight asked. He was actually guessing the answer, but he wanted to give him some time to think. He was known for his openness to other people's ideas, but he usually modified them in his own way. Despite the succinct description of the young knight, he had received from the bribed manciple, he did not want to kill him without speaking to him personally. He knew his mother well, Adelaide de Tourvelle, for whom he had once had a certain sentiment, and he had the quiet hope that he would be able to win her son over to his side. It would not be just any success.

"Go back to the castle and act carefully," he instructed his ally after he had finished speaking. "I accept your plan, but for now I need Theo alive. If he really proves to be too stupid to join me, his death will have to take the spirits of other rebels. This way it will be useful to us whether he wants it or not."

Don Paulino nodded with understanding, bowed, and through a secret passage known to few, returned to Bongrais. He betrayed his master not for the sake of wealth - despite all his faults, he was not greedy and he never misappropriated a thaler from the money entrusted to him. At the root of his deed lay a deep, stinging hatred, born in a time when Theo was not even born. Obsessed with his mother and spurned with contempt, he waited for years for an opportunity that did not come, and finally transferred this bad feeling to the countess's son, unfortunately very much like her. He hated him patiently, for years, and finally had the opportunity to do him permanent harm, and he wasn't going to waste it. He could not openly speak out against his senior, as this would be suicide - no one would support him. Anyone who made up the fortress crew would have been killed for the young count, and besides, although he was indeed very similar to his mother, he had inherited his father's character entirely. And Fabien de Bongrais was not one to be opposed with impunity.

Theo did not require respect for himself and his orders, not supporting this demand. He himself worked for three, repairing and strengthening the fortifications, he was the first on feet before sunrise, and the last lay down. He saw everything himself, looked at every corner, personally counted the supplies and was always present when something was happening. He talked to anyone who wanted it, and when he heard doubts about the chances of defense, he announced that anyone who mentioned the surrender of the castle to him would be hanged on a palisade. Nobody doubted that these were not empty promises.

"This one never hesitates and knows what he wants," had been said of him in and around Bongrais, but it was not entirely true.

Nobody knew those nights full of the worst dilemmas and fears that he would not confide to anyone. After all, he had no combat experience yet, and yet the fate of several hundred people depended on him. It was a burden far too heavy for his less than twenty-year-old shoulders, but he had to bear it, and he believed that he could do it. The worst part was that he had a small squad and only seven archers, but there was no help for that. Peasants who, with his permission, took refuge in the castle were willing to defend it, but could not be worth much in a clash with a regular army. Ironically, he confided in Paulino about his worries and doubts, whom he considered to be an intelligent man with a sober view of the world. He was right about that, but he was not aware of what the stewardess was using his intelligence and cunning for. Don Paulino did not dare to openly oppose him and quietly admitted that, despite his young age, Theo was able to impose his authority on others, but he hated him all the more. When he looked at him, he saw in him an image of a woman who had rejected and humiliated him long ago.

The young knight did not see the hatred in his gaze and did not even sense the impending misfortune. His gloomy gaze glided hurriedly over his subordinates, not lingering longer on any of them, for his head was occupied with something else: the army that was already under Bongrais. There were quite a few, at least two hundred and fifty regular soldiers, a dozen or so heavy-armed knights and a lot of henchmen, who usually did not count, and who could be very dangerous in a combat clash. The date of the first real combat test for the young knight was approaching.

*****

Don Paulino climbed slowly up the winding stairs to the top of the tower, from where Theo watched through the narrow window of the army camped under the fortress walls. He was clearly concerned. The Black Knight contented himself with the surroundings of the Bongrais on all sides, and had done nothing more so far. He did not attack or send parliamentarians; he simply guarded the castle in ominous silence. It was something Theo hadn't heard of before. Was he going to starve the defenders to surrender? It could take months. Lost in his merry thoughts, he did not look back at the sound of the footsteps behind his back, and he knew that it was his former tutor, and now the steward of his goods, coming. He reported him every morning at this point, at the best vantage point of the entire castle

"I don't know what they're waiting for..." said the knight softly. "I do not like this."

"And you, Don Paulina?"

"I do," came the unexpected reply, and several pairs of burly hands seized the count, overwhelming him in the blink of an eye. Surprised, he did not have time to reach for the sword. He was dragged, resisting fiercely, into the courtyard, already overrun by soldiers admitted by the traitor. The screams of the murdered and the futile cries for help of the raped women created a terrible cacophony in which it was impossible to hear your own thoughts. Soon the stone slabs drowned in blood. Held in a firm grip by several pairs of hostile hands, Theo had almost gone mad at the sight of this carnage, disarmed and helpless in the face of the terrible scenes unfolding before his eyes. In his consciousness, people whom he had known since childhood were ruthlessly murdered, not allowing even adolescents and old handmaids to pass.

When he was finally dragged into the dark dungeon and the wrought door behind him, he still had the impression that all hell was still going on around him, and he himself, condemned in life, could not get out of it. He senselessly clasped his hands over his ears and groaned softly as he tried to contain his frenzied heartbeat. When he finally managed to catch his breath, he crouched helplessly against the stone wall. He couldn't say how long the massacre he had witnessed lasted; he had the feeling that it was ages. Judging by what he saw, no one seemed to have chances of surviving, except maybe for a few young girls the winners probably kept to please their desires. And... what happened to Bellette?

He did not see her among the abused women in the courtyard, but that does not mean that she did not share their fate. Theo gritted his teeth tightly to keep from crying. He wouldn't forgive himself for something like that, he had always thought that crying was good for women or children, not for adult men like him. He probably wouldn't have realized that he wasn't quite an adult yet, and would not be offended if he shed a few tears. Especially now... Bellette was everything to him, though he hadn't really realized it so far.

She was the daughter of one of the maids, and as long as he was a boy and she was a little girl, he paid no attention to her. But later... When he was sixteen and she was thirteen, he came home for Christmas like every year. Bellette was already working as a maid by then, and for the first time he looked at her not as a toddler curling up under his feet, but as a little woman awakening to life. This was not surprising - and younger than she was married during this era, and at the court of the King Navarra, where Theo stayed as a page and later as Duke de Candall's squire, even twelve-year-old girls were seasoned certain matters coquettish. Bellette captivated him with her innocence and sweetness, and her sunny beauty with a subtlety rarely found in peasant women. Slowly, timidly, they got to know each other, from the first kisses, stealthily, behind the curtains, the touch of hands to... Young lovers hid their love from the old count, and therefore from everyone else, fearing even to look at each other in the presence of outsiders. This love was a treasure given to both of them by a capricious fortune, and now, as he envisioned that precious body in the paws of Roger de Valois's soldiers, he only gritted his teeth in impotent rage. He didn't want to think about it, he couldn't think about it, if he wanted to keep a clear mind.

"God, if by some miracle I make it out alive, I swear I'll strangle Paulino with my own hands," he whispered.

He could not forgive himself that he allowed himself to be approached by a vile creature. Who would have foreseen that someone who had served his father for so many years would now betray him so wickedly? He thought of Berengard, and a second time his throat tightened. Slow in movement and speech, the rough-hewn block of a tree, a typical French peasant, was for him more a brother and friend than a servant he was meant to be. He looked after the Viscount from the day of the snowstorm which took one of the boys from his mother and the other from his father. Joaquin was a coachman, a simple and uncouth man, raising his son alone. Since the death of his wife, who died in childbirth, he had not any woman, and the malicious said that he was hopelessly in love with the countess. Whether it was true, no one knew, because the coachman had never exceeded his mistress's line of origin and work. However, after the traces discovered in the snow, the course of the tragedy was read. It was clear from them that if Joaquin had left his mistress at the mercy of the storm after the horses had carried away and smashed, he would have been able to get home and save his life, but he would not have done so. He carried the wounded countess until he was completely exhausted, then wrapped his cloak around her, and they were both found dead under the tree. Apparently, there was a frozen smile of happiness on the unshaven face of the coachman.

Whatever the case, it was commonly expected that an orphaned boy would be given up to learn some craft, as was customary, but the old count had other plans. On the day of the funeral, he called Berengard over and told him briefly:

"Your father served me well. I hope you have inherited a sense of duty from him as you will be my son's personal servant from now on. Serve him and look after him as best you can, and you will be able to count on my kindness. You can go."

It was widely believed that the frisky six-year-old would take its toll on Berengard, but these fears were somewhat exaggerated. The boys became friends very quickly, so much so that when Fabien de Bongrais took his son to the court of the king of Navarra, he had to take Berengard, without whom Theo did not want to go anywhere.

Now the young count only hoped that his friend had not had time to return from the village to which he had been sent in time. If he came back, it was probably already over. If Don Paulino had found his body among the fallen, he probably would not have denied the pleasure of throwing his head against the feet of the prisoner, since his hatred devoured him went so far as treason.

"And why does he hate me so?" Theo thought helplessly.

He couldn't remember hurting the steward, and he couldn't have known that the story had started long before he was born...

The massive dungeon door creaked and two silent soldiers dragged him outside. Walking under their watch over the half-ruined corridors, Theo could see through the passing windows a mess of the courtyard and the few surviving peasants who bustled about putting the bodies of the fallen-on carts to bury them in the common grave. The destruction inside the castle eloquently indicated that the defenders did not succumb to the attackers immediately and not without a fight. But now the winding corridors and high chambers stood silent and dead, as if deserted. The exceptions were those in which knights, fighting in the colors of Roger de Valois, were accommodated. Theo had known some of them from his days as a squire, so it was even more unpleasant for his eyes to see them.

The guards ushered him into the knight's hall, where the conqueror of the castle sat in a place of honor at the table and, accompanied by two bodyguards, drank wine poured on them by an apparently battered and terrified maid. The young count felt idiotic relief seeing that it was not Bellette, but Jeanne, one of the kitchen maids. The look of relief on his face did not escape the Black Knight who was staring at him, leaning back in the carved armchair. Indeed, as he noticed, the boy was very similar to his tragically deceased mother. He had her hair, black with a navy blue sheen, her delicate features and captivating beauty, and above all her eyes: large, coal-black, quite wide-set and shaded by black eyelashes. After his father he took undoubtedly heavy, wide eyebrows and the square outline of the jaws, softened by a slightly more delicate line of the chin, and the height and thinness of the figure. The mournful blackness made him even taller and thinner.

"Sit down," he invited him. "You want a drink?"

"Thank you, but I won't sit or drink in your company," said Theo angrily.

The Black Knight disgusted him with insurmountable disgust especially that behind his evil actions there was a lake of blood poured out, including the blood of his countrymen.

The prince smiled coldly.

"Why is that?" He asked. "I have an honest offer for you: join me. The Prince of Wales, my cousin, is a generous and gracious lord, and I'm his closest ally. You will not suffer any harm in this alliance."

"I have a certain respect in the province for my name," Theo said slowly. "You want to take advantage of it, right? None of this, traitor. I'll have no part of this hideous trade with my own homeland. Go to hell."

The Black Knight didn't seem moved by his words.

"And now I'm gonna break your heart. You're probably counting on someone's help? Here no one will help you, my cockerel," he said, turning the silver goblet over in his fingers. "Nobody will stand up for you, because there is no such reason. I'm very happy because you do not deserve any consideration. And you know why no one will speak up for you? Recently, King John signed peace with England, so you are not a heroic defender of the motherland, but an ordinary, gallant-worthy rebel against legally exercised power."

"Not true," Theo whispered through his whitened lips.

"Yes, it is," Roger de Valois sipped his wine and set down the cup. "And since you are rejecting my protectorate, you will be beheaded the day after tomorrow morning in the market in Bongrais. When people see your corpse, they will refuse to rebel. Take him back."

Locked back in the dark and cold dungeon, Theo paced from wall to wall, unable to calm down. He had known before that King John II had been taken prisoner by the army of the Black Prince in the Battle of Poitiers, but he had not expected that such a shameful document would be signed. The king, even in captivity, remains the head of state and should strive for freedom for the country, and not consent to be handed over to his enemies. On the other hand, who knows what methods the victors used to persuade the monarch to sign the treaty. After all, along with him, the young

Prince Philip fell into the hands of the English and did not give up his father even in the heat of the greatest battle. A brave knight of this adolescent, it must be admitted, the more the king could fear for him. The Black Prince had no qualms, he was an unpredictable and extremely dangerous man, and in addition he was friends with probably all French renegades. More than one of them would certainly be happy to remove the brave one of the royal sons. Maybe not even just this one...

Theo had only recently been knighted, his head was full of ideals, and he believed the king as he had been taught. He couldn't have done otherwise, even mentally, not yet at least. Tired to the ground, he finally sat down against the stone wall. Only now did something clear to him that he had not thought of before, absorbed in something else: that he had less than two days to live. He did not want to die, although death on the scaffold, not in a fight, was a guarantee for him to keep his good name. He knew that he would be remembered as a brave defender of the fortress until his death, and this thought was a certain encouragement to him. No one could see the last descendant of the Bongrais shivering for fear of an executioner's ax, and that was the last task he set for himself. He rested his cheek against the wall and closed his eyes. Then suddenly fear came, squeezed the throat, and chilled the heart into a small, frightened ball. Locked in the dungeons of his own castle, the young count fought the most difficult fight - with himself - until exhaustion took over.

It was the sound of hammers that broke him from his restless sleep. For a moment he wondered what it might be, then realized that they were building a scaffold for him. The thought passed unimpressed. He was sore, as if after heavy blows, he had the feeling that his head was about to burst, and what he had witnessed left him with a feeling of insurmountable disgust. There was one other thing that plagued him - guilt. After all, he had failed the people who believed he could protect them, and while he wasn't really guilty of what had happened, he reproached himself bitterly. He scornfully dismissed the food he had brought, and drank only a few sips of the water from the jug. He did not want to eat, he knew that on the way to the scaffold, convicts would often vomit everything they had in their stomach, and he preferred not to have the opportunity to make a spectacle of himself. No beam of light reached the deep dungeon, so he didn't know whether it was day or night, only the incessant clatter of hammers outside let him know that it was still daytime while the workers were working. When the clatter subsided, the prisoner fell asleep again, because at twenty he falls asleep easily, no matter how heavy the heart is.

Only the creaking of the door hinges woke him. Two guards with torches and an unfamiliar, heavily built man in red clothes entered, by which he guessed the executioner.

"Is it time?" he wondered, rising hastily. It flashed through his mind that perhaps the Duke de Valois had abandoned the public execution and had him simply strangled in his cell like any other thug. It was to be expected of him. But headsman only brushed the hair back from his neck with a hand the size of a loaf of bread and surveyed his neck.

Then he left and Theo heard him say to someone in the hallway:

"One cut is enough."

The knight shuddered. Those impassive words were worse than anything he had ever heard. So, this was how all his dreams and plans would end? After all, he was just returning from Paris, where he was knighted, and he was returning to family goods. His father was waiting for him there, rough and withdrawn but admired and adored nevertheless, all the people he had known from his early childhood, and above all a beautiful being so devoted to him. Who could have foreseen it would all end this way. He rested his throbbing temple against the wall, the cold and slightly damp stone seemed to ease the pain, dull his angry grief.

If he had had enough civil courage, he would have admitted to himself that he was simply afraid - the road to the scaffold, pain, death at the hand of an indifferent executioner, in the presence of the foul winners and intimidated townspeople who, now he knew it well, would not even refrain from compassion. They'll be glad it's not one of them, and it's hard to blame them. He had failed them, it was an indisputable fact. It had not occurred to him that he might judge himself more severely than the others.

A hard tug on his arm woke him. In the low light of the torch, he saw a soldier in full gear and jerked back in a senseless defense reflex. The gloved hand closed his mouth in a commanding gesture, then the soldier threw an armful of clothes on his lap, a breastplate, helmet, greaves and the most precious thing: a sword. He grasped it firmly in his hand as soon as he put on the clothes brought by the mysterious savior. He immediately felt more confident, armed and covered with metal plates, and the tension that choked him eased, giving way to readiness to fight. Should it occur, he was determined not to be taken alive a second time.

He and his companion passed the corridor and out into the courtyard, where sentries wandered apathetically, sleepy and yawning. They were too tired to control people in the same colors as them, so they paid no attention to the fugitives.

Only when using the tiny gate, known to a few, found themselves outside the castle walls, the count's companion took off his helmet.

"Berengard! So, are you alive?!" Theo shouted, catching him in his arms.

"Louder, they didn't hear you in the castle," Berengard firmly freed himself from his embrace. "Save those affections for later.

The sooner we get to the hideout, the better. I left my horses behind these trees."

"But where did you get those rags and guns?" the knight asked, barely controlling his mad heartbeat. Berengard waved his hand.

"Trifle," he muttered. "Bellette got a sedative, and what was difficult was to sneak up and pour it into the bowl from which the private soldiers were drawing beer. When they slept, the rest was easy."

From all this, Theo only received information that Bellette was alive and well, since she decided to take an active part in organizing a rescue for him. He felt so relieved that he staggered and almost fell.

"Do you know what torment I experienced in the dungeon thinking about what could happen to her and you?" He whispered in a choked voice. "That thought was worse than anything else for me, and it was quite a lot."

Berengard looked at him sympathetically.

"I know, they made you look at this whole massacre," he said. "But now forget it and hurry up. In any moment they will discover who is missing in the dungeon."

The friends untied the horses hidden behind the trees, threw off their heavy half-armor and climbed into the saddles. They had to hide in the woods before the pursuit began, so they put aside all explanations until they found themselves in a place where they had to dismount from the horses, so as not to smash their heads against the low branches of trees in the dark.

"Bellette found out about the attack on the castle right when she was at her brother's place," Berengard said, walking forward and shoving through the branches. "As you probably know, Pierre is an outlaw for his participation in jacquerie. Bellette tried to persuade him to join you when Colas, the groom who had escaped, found them. The poor girl almost went mad with anxiety. She begged Pierre to save you, but this boy harbors a morbid hatred for all the nobility of the world and has stated that he does not think to risk his life for any bloodsucker who exploits his subjects. Then Bellette furiously shouted at him what you have in common. What he replied is by no means suitable for public repetition."

"I can imagine," Theo muttered. Pierre was known for his vulgar language and his reluctance to follow any social forms.

"However, Pierre's gang was in favor of doing you this favor," his friend continued. "They're good boys, basically, they like Bellette a lot, and you haven't had time to give yourself a hard time. They thought it might be worth getting you out of trouble and poking the Black Knight's nose."

The young count was silent. Pierre's views were well known to him and they could not be surprising for the former participant of jacquerie, but he never thought that they would be troublesome for him as well. He had treated them rather like a harmless quirk until now. Harmless... jacquerie took the lives of two of his uncles and their families, and he could not be sure if Bellette's brother had their blood on his hands, but he decided not to answer. The rebellion was caused by factors he knew, and thanks to Bellette and Berengard he understood, so he could not ruthlessly condemn its participants.

"If a baron takes revenge on an entire village for some nonsense, that's okay, and when the peasants start to bite back, is something wrong?" Bellette asked him when they talked about it once, and he couldn't help but agree. He still had a pure, unadulterated heart and a deep-seated sense of justice. Now he was about to face people who would normally be his opponents, and now they were the only allies he still had. He didn't even know them, he only heard about them, and what he heard was not encouraging, but it was hard to say that he had any choice.

Berengard led him through the forest until they came to the edge of the lake where a small fire was smoldering. Several men and one woman sat around the fire in whom he recognized Bellette despite the darkness. She also recognized him. She sprang to her feet and, sobbing, fell into his arms. He hugged her, dipped his face in her hair, which smelled of hay and herbs, then he felt her lips in the dark, and for a moment everything but them was gone.

Pierre looked at them for a moment with restrained anger, then exclaimed angrily:

"Maybe there will be enough, no? Not enough of hugs?"

He was a tall, muscular man with a disheveled blond hair and a long face, definitely strong and springy. Despite the prevailing darkness, it was obvious that he was very dissatisfied with his sister's behavior.

"Be quiet," Bellette said, and she cried aloud.

Her brother shrugged.

"And why are you buzzing? After all, you've got your count back," he said reluctantly, correcting the fire. "They didn't hurt him. And they should."

"Why do you think so?" Theo asked, trying to soothe the sobbing girl.

"Because I have reasons, and I'm not going to explain myself to you," replied Pierre sharply. His companions did not support him, they only muttered something reluctantly. They had lived with him in the forest for two years, and although they were not outlaws themselves, they felt outlawed. Pierre led them, but they didn't always agree with him, as in this case.

"You'd give it up. You promised help, and don't shirk it now," Berengard reminded him.

"Am I weaseling? Don't just ask me to love one of those who think all the rest of people exist for their enjoyment," Pierre grunted.

"I don't think so," Theo protested.

"You know, Pierre, you would close your mouth, because you really talk trash," said one of those sitting by the fire, a little redhead with a rat-faced face and a tiny mustache. "Come to us, Count, feel free."

He held out a stick with a piece of toasted meat at Theo, which reminded the knight that he had eaten hardly anything in two days. He accepted the meal with poorly masked eagerness. Bellette sat down next to him, her fingers gripping his elbow as if afraid she might lose him again.

"Jean is right," said the second, older and gray-haired peasant. "He is a brave young man, since he did not give up to those bitch sons even in the shadow of the scaffolding. Do not pay attention to our leader, my lord, he is such that he cannot help but make similar remarks."

Theo waved his hand discouraged.

"What does it matter now? Let him say what he wants, I have more worries," he said. "A king in captivity, the country is flooded with enemies and traitors, and I should worry about someone's stupid remarks. But... have you heard about something called the "Treaty of Bretigny"?"

The outlaws exchanged glances.

"Yes," said Jean finally. "All France is talking about it. I don't know why the king signed it, maybe the captivity confused him, but he signed it. The Black Prince will rule here as if he were at home."

The young count frowned and stopped eating.

"That's not good," he whispered after a moment. "Is it all lost?"

Berengard patted him on the back.

"We'll see," he said. "For now, you will rest in the woods until it dies down, and then we can both try to make our way to Paris, to Prince Charles. He is now regent."

"Yes, and apparently he ran away from the battlefield until it was dusting behind him," Pierre interjected contemptuously. "Only his younger son stayed with the king. Shame and disgrace, as if asking me."

"But nobody asks you," said Bellette coldly. "Come on, it will be dawn soon."

Her brother stood up and stretched, then glared at his unwelcome companion.

"Put the blindfold on him and let's go," he ordered.

"Are you crazy?!" Bellette jumped up from her seat as if bitten by a viper. "For what?"

"Because. I don't trust him," Pierre fired sharply.

"You can drown in our swamps without an armband," one of the outlaws supported the girl. "Besides, it's not an enemy."

"Francois, don't be too smart, it'll hurt you! You want to take my place, go ahead, and give it a try!" Pierre shouted furiously, clenching his fist with an eloquent movement.

"Are you going to argue for a long time? I'm not protesting, do what you want," Theo sighed wearily, hiding his face in his hands. He wished with all his soul that it would all be over, or that this man would stop treating him as if he was infected. He didn't deserve it.

"You're not in charge here, so shut up, okay?" Pierre blindfolded him with a rag and helped him to his feet.

Bellette's warm hand grasped the knight's hand, and she led him stumbling over tree roots and some stones, he could feel the damp moss under his feet and the smell of marsh herbs. These swamps were dangerous even during the day, during the periods of spring thaw hardly anyone dared to come close to them, but these people seemed to be close to this place and confident. In other circumstances, he would have been afraid, for even the bravest had feared death in that stinking mud, but now he was too tired and too sore to think about it at all. Finally, they reached their destination and Bellette's hand tore the armband from the knight's head. They were in a large clearing crossed by a stream bubbling over the stones with, surprisingly, pure water. A wooden hut stood a little further, old and twisted in places.

"Go to the attic," Pierre said harshly. "I don't want you to hang around between us."

Theo nodded indifferently and stumbled in the direction indicated. The rest of the men disappeared into the cabin as well, but Bellette stayed, looking at her brother seriously and resentfully.

"Don't look at me like that," Pierre growled, sitting down on the edge of the stream. "I won't change my mind. Do you want to be his toy all your life? After all, he will not marry you."

Bellette sat down next to him.

"You don't understand, little brother," she said softly. "I don't want Theo to marry me at all. I know that it cannot be so, because I'm a peasant woman and he is a noble, but it is enough for me to be happy when he likes me a little. I love him since we were both kids. You don't know how many nights I haven't slept worrying about how I'll grow up to be an ugly girl he won't want. Or that I will get smallpox or burn myself in a fire. I just wanted to give myself to him when I grew up enough to do it, I didn't demand anything in return. And he gave me happiness, my first love, because it's love, what would you say about it. Theo, despite the years spent at the royal court, isn't corrupt or cynical and is able to pay back affection for affection."

She stroked her brother's head and stood up, heading for the cabin.

"She's going to see him," Pierre thought, almost despairingly. He had a feeling his sister would be unhappy with the man, but he didn't have the strength to stop her.

Bellette climbed a well-known loft. Theo was sitting against the wall, his knees tucked up to his chin, his eyes closed, his head resting on the frame of a small window. At the sound of the girl's footsteps, he didn't even move.

"Why don't you sleep?" she asked quietly, sitting down next to him.

"Whenever I try, I can see that hell in the courtyard of my castle," Theo replied without opening his eyes. "What happened there...? I did not even suspect that I would witness something like this and I wouldn't be able to prevent anything. I don't know if I'll ever fall asleep again."

Bellette hugged him sympathetically.

"I know what you've been through," she whispered. "But it will stop hurting someday. I'll pray that as soon as possible."

The young knight shuddered.

"I willn't," he said hollowly. "I don't believe anymore. I lost my faith there in Bongrais. What God could have allowed what was going on there?"

"Stop, don't say that," the girl hastily covered his mouth with her hand. "Don't blaspheme. You're sick, you don't know what you're talking about..."

She pressed the knight's head to her chest, mentally praying for mercy, terrified at the vision of eternal damnation for the man she loved so immeasurably. Theo paused. Always been like that. When he could not do anything, he was silent, stubbornly silent, and that silence was worse than cursing and inventing, stomping and throwing things, as happened more than once to noble boys when something happened against their will. Now, too, a silence grew between them, in which Bellette could clearly hear the echo of his last words, as if being repeated by some malicious troll.

"I'll go to Father Prospero tomorrow," she thought. "Maybe he can do something about it, because I'm not smart enough to help him. And if someone does not, he will finally lose his soul and be damned."

And in despair, she began to say silently one prayer after another, hoping that this would ward off the evil spirits she believed the knight's words must have drawn near.

CHAPTER II

Dead-end

I don't know, my daughter. Father Prospero stopped rubbing the herbs in the mortar and stroked the girl's fair curls. "If God were to punish people for every word spoken in anger or despair, three-quarters of humanity would go up in smoke. Trouble is, he could really lose faith. This has happened to many people, and the war is hardly conducive to conversions. What you sometimes see on it would confuse the healthiest person's mind. Not good, girl. You see, if your beloved had a fever, I would have given you some herbs for him, if he had broken his arm, I would have set it for him, but I know no other remedy for the wounds of the soul other than prayer. You have to trust God and wait. Time is the best doctor. Come on well child, I have to go now."

Father Prospero, although he was the prior of his monastery, he worked the hardest of all his brothers. He was forbidden by religious rule to ride horses, so he carried the herbal mixtures around the area on foot, often traveling long weeks and venturing as far as the neighboring provinces, wherever Carmelite medicines were needed. These herbs were said to heal everything from hangovers to typhus, and everyone was willing to buy them.

After abbot had left, Bellette went to the convent chapel for a moment to pray, then walked slowly back to the woods. Prospero's words did not cheer her up, although she counted on it a lot and she needed it very much. Many days had passed since Count de Bongrais had escaped from the dungeon. Military patrols sniffed all over the area, preventing him from trying to break through to Paris, so he still made use of the forced hospitality in the forest. It was not convenient for him or Pierre, although Theo tried his best not to disturb anyone. Pierre treated him like air, the others showed him the respect he deserves to a person of high birth, but made no attempt to approach him. In fact, only Bellette and Berengard talked to him, and he also bitterly reproached Pierre for his behavior.

"Don't preach me anymore," Pierre answered him. "You were born with a chain around your neck."

"Perhaps," Berengard replied. "But you are not only unfair, but also stupid."

If he had been able to formulate his thoughts better, he would have told this country bully how, at the age of ten, he had been cared for by an abandoned boy and had to grow up in no time to protect him from impunity, in the absence of the old count trying to exploit his advantage. The orphaned six-year-old fell to the only human being that showed him kindness and, contrary to general predictions, did not try to "walk over him". Though at times obnoxious and self-willed, he had no malice in him, and Berengard quickly liked him as much as he liked his little brother.

Even now, years later, he felt responsible for the young knight, although Theo was actually an adult, and his father was dead and he could not order anyone else. It cannot be said that either of the two missed the old count whom they had seen very rarely and briefly since the countess's funeral. Theo could not love his father who treated him indifferently, so while he respected him and admired him uncritically, he did not despair over his mysterious death too much. Busy with the affairs of the king and the country, Fabien de Bongrais somehow did not think about leaving his son at the mercy of service. Admittedly, perhaps that was why Theo was doing much better at the court of Troyes than his peers, brought by their fathers to the court of the king of Navarre. First as a page, then as the squire of the Duke de Candall, he was without a doubt the bravest and most hardened boy of them all, and his fencing and riding skills foreshadowed him as a future champion.

Berengard had no doubt that if Theo had tried, he would certainly have mastered the art of archery more than any of the archers he knew. The young knight did not possess this skill so far. The French nobility considered the bow a good weapon for the common people and did not teach their sons how to use it. Now he was trying in vain to persuade him to go on a hunting trip, on which he could practice. Theo was in a state of mind that did not want to learn anything, and for the time being, there was no hope that his attitude would change. He shut himself up, did not want to talk about what had happened in Bongrais, neither about the Black Knight, nor about the inexorable advancing army of the Black Prince, nor about the betrayal of Don Paulino. If he ever talked about it to anyone, it was only to Bellette, and she didn't want to tell Berengard anything. When he tried to press on her, she almost slapped him.

Berengard looked forward to the day when they could get out of the woods and finally disappear from this place. In silence of spirit, he also hoped it would be the end of the love affair with Bellette, who he hated in full reciprocity. As time passed, however, he changed his mind about her. This girl definitely had something in her, something that average peasant women did not have, and her beauty went hand in hand with quite unfeminine intelligence. Like most men of his time, Berengard considered women much stupider than men and remained, at best, all their life on the mental level of a child. Bellette wasn't like that, he had to impartially admit it. With patience and kindness, she managed to get Theo slowly getting interested in the world again, instead of sitting in the attic all the time, as he had for the first few days. The massacre he witnessed would break many older and stronger people, so it is no wonder that he was shocked and could not recover for a long time.

The hostile atmosphere did not help him either. Fortunately, the outlaws spent most of their time away from their hideout, chatting with wealthy passers-by or hunting, so they had some time to themselves. Usually, the three of them would sit by the fire, roast whatever was at hand - pieces of meat, onions, wild apples, and bread when there was nothing else - and talked about nonsense, carefully avoiding sensitive topics. These moments of respite were worth their weight in gold.

That day, there was something in the air since morning. Theo was less tense than usual, but gloomy as night nonetheless, and nothing could brighten him up. Bellette tried to make a Provencal shashlik by alternating small onions and pieces of venison on the makeshift spit, sprinkled with dried herbs, but hadn't had time to put the spit on the supports when Pierre's companions burst into the clearing, badly bruised and out of breath.

"What happened?! Where's my brother?!" Bellette shouted, jumping up from the grass.

They stared at her, gasping for breath with their half-open mouths, nudged each other with their elbows, and were clearly trying to blame one another on the nasty obligation to speak about something. Finally, Francois, the boldest and most outspoken, mumbled pathetically:

"It's not our fault, Bellette, I swear. There was nothing we could do. Pierre saw the English squad and went mad by the point. He shouted that they would pay him for everything and pounced on them. The second squad came from behind, we barely escaped alive, but Pierre stayed in their hands.

"You left him, you gang of traitors!" the girl screamed desperately and wanted to pounce on her friends with fists, but Theo grabbed her tightly and held her. Were it not for the seriousness of the situation, the fear of four strong men at the sight of the fury of one girl would even have looked comical.

"Stop," said the knight sharply. "Nothing would help if they died heroically. They did very well to withdraw. Go back to the village, Bellette, and try to find out as much as possible. I will wait for the information you get."

Bellette turned her head to look at him in disbelief.

"How is it, you...?" she asked with tears in her eyes.

"Yes, me," he replied brusquely. "Come on, run away and remember, nobody can guess anything."

The stunned girl nodded and ran, wiping away tears as she went. The outlaws were silent, staring at Theo with a mixture of humility and distrust. He looked back at them hard.

"I don't want to hear any excuses," he said sharply. "No circling or walking around the yard. Will you help me save Pierre or should I do it without your help?"

The friends looked at each other uncertainly, and finally Martin dared to ask:

"Lord, can it be done at all?"

"Don't call me 'lord', you know how they gave me it," interrupted the knight. "And answer yes or no."

His black eyes burned so much that no one dared to ask any further.

"I will," whispered Martin

"Me too," Olivier, his inseparable companion, joined him.

"And me."

"And me," the others added hastily.

Theo nodded.

"Okay, then we're waiting for what Bellette finds out," he said brusquely. "If they want to arrange a public execution for Pierre, this will be our chance. It'll be up to us how we use it. Put yourself in order and wait."

The four robbers nodded meekly and vanished with relief into the cabin. They were glad that someone else had made the decision for them and would not have to think about it themselves.

Left to his own devices, Theo sat down on the grass and stared out at the glistening stream. Berengard approached slowly and stood behind him.

"You seriously want to do this?" he asked softly.

His friend looked up.

"I think I owe him that," he replied. "And I certainly owe it to Bellette. Anyway, enough of this shuffling in place, I have to finally pull myself together and this is probably the best time."

Berengard smiled mournfully.

"I recognize you now," he muttered. He knew very well that what his friend was thinking was extremely dangerous, but he understood him.

"I hope you're not trying to prove something like that," he said after a moment, sitting down next to him. "It's true Bellette loves Pierre, but I think she loves you more. Did you know that she never mentioned mother once when we waited for the right time to free you? She thought only about you, talked about you, at night she would scream because she dreamed that they were torturing you... Don't get me wrong, I'm not trying to dissuade you from your decision, but please try to let this poor girl she didn't have to cry for both of you."

With these words he got up and went to the hut so that the young count would not notice how devastated he was, especially since he was of the same opinion as he was. Pierre could not be left in the hands of the English and traitors. On the other hand, trying to save might have cost them all lives.

"You, were your count serious?" came Jean's frightened whisper.

He looked around. The little redhead stared at him with wide open eyes begging for some confirmation.

"Maybe he'll change his mind overnight?" Martin added hesitantly. Berengard sighed heavily.

"No, Martin, he won't," he replied. "His father was like tattoo, with all his faults. He used to say that none of the Bongrais breaks a word once, and it really is. I know you guys are looking at Theo through Pierre's eyes, but Pierre is blinded by hatred, and I've known this boy for a long time. I have accompanied him everywhere and I know what he is capable of.

He ran a hand nervously over his hair and his voice stuck in his throat. It was difficult for him to convey to these people in a few words his attachment to the young count and explain to them that Pierre was thoroughly wrong about him. He thought it would be best not to say anything - time will show these people what his friend really is. It didn't seem that they had any doubts like that. They were simple, uneducated people, glad that someone had taken the responsibility and the obligation to organize help for a friend in need from their heads. And strange as it may seem, they slept soundly that night.

The next morning Bellette came to them with the news.

"They're going to halter Pierre at noon tomorrow," she said. "The execution is to take place in the market square in Bongrais. The city is full of Englishmen, we can't make it."

Theo listened as he ran his fingers through his wet hair. At pale dawn, he went for a swim in the forest lake and had just come back.

"On the contrary," he replied. "Don't forget that no one is expecting us there, which already gives us an advantage. If it's indeed full of Englishmen, they will not expect anyone to dare to take any action. Again, Pierre is hardly anybody important, so there will probably only be a few soldiers for his execution. We need horses, take care of it. Without horses, and good ones, any attempt to help would be sheer suicide. Now let no one bother me, I have to make a sensible plan and draw it out."

He took a piece of unburned blade from the ashen, white-tanned deer skin, and lay down under a tree, drawing intersecting lines on the skin.

"What are you waiting for?" Bellette huffed. "Run for the horses, now!"

The men obeyed her immediately, though they had no idea how drawing lines with an unburned wood on a scrap of leather might help. They knew Pierre would blame them for allowing the young count to take over in his absence, but they did not care. Despite the specific approach instilled in them by the leader of certain matters, they felt that this knight could be trusted and began to like him. Certain unconscious and innate respect for the people of the upper class, pleasant workmanship and sympathetic appearance of this knight, barely out of a boyish age, and his mutual affection for Bellette, who was one of them, played a role here. His decision to help the rebellious peasant who displayed a profound, bordering on contempt for him impressed them greatly.

According to the order, they did not interfere with activities that they did not understand, which lasted almost until the evening. It wasn't until supper that Theo explained everything to them.

"I already know what we should do to make our plan a success. The difficulty is to set up properly. Two of you will have to fire your bows at the guards, two of you will make a fuss on a side other than the one we are running to, and one will be waiting near the gate. I will take Pierre from the gallows and when the two of us get closer to the gate, you will attack the sentries from behind. We will have very little time for all this, literally moments. If any of us screw up, the rest will pay for it with their lives.

"You are in charge, make orders," said Martin shortly, pouring him wine.

Theo drank, took a bite of roast, and continued.

"Those of you who shoot better bows will take up positions on the roofs of two houses by the market square. From there, they will shoot the soldiers as soon as the wagon with the convict will be on the market. Those who stay in the streets nearby, at the first sounds of commotion, have to start their own row, and then disappear as quickly as possible."

"Jean and Francois will go to the roof, me and Olivier are better at hand-to-hand than shooting," Martin decided.

Theo nodded.

"May be. Berengard lurks near the gate. Remember to withdraw behind the city walls as soon as possible. Don't think about your friend, I will take care of him, just follow what I've told you."

"You left yourself the hardest part of the task." Francois remarked.

"For this you need a good horse-riding skill, and this is what a real champion taught me... No offense, but it should be me, if it's to be successful, besides, it'd be advisable to fight with a sword in case of a clash with soldiers," the knight explained to him.

He was telling the truth. His preceptor of horse riding at the court of the king Navarra was a certain Turk, faithless, as it was said, but an excellent horseman, and during his short stay at the Louvre - Captain Larouche, who was well-deserved as the best rider in the kingdom. Theo, with innate equestrian skills, rode excellently at the age of ten, better than any of his peers. The action he planned required the effort of all these skills, full commitment and proverbial dumb luck. It couldn't have happened without it.

Contrary to appearances, his plan was not as crazy as it appeared to be, but it was risky enough that it would take a dose of madness to implement it. And that's what he needed to break out of apathy. On his orders, Bellette stayed in the village with her father and older sister. He wanted her not to be around when the heat started to get hot, not only because she would be in immediate danger then, but also so that she wouldn't be distracted. She, too, chose to withdraw, for she was afraid that at the last moment she would fall at her knight's feet, begging him not to risk his life just now that she had regained it. Somehow, she did not believe that this action could succeed, unlike Pierre's companions who trusted him completely. They equipped their bows with new strings, selected the best arrows, and waited.

Theo, who had spent the time remaining until he set out for action, sharpening his sword and the captured dagger, hardly spoke to them. That morning he'd gone to Bongrais was to decide his destiny forever, and he felt it somehow as he approached the city. In a simple, sleeveless leather jacket and a hooded cloak, he was able to safely cross the gate without being afraid of recognition. He did not stand out from the crowd of peasants and poor townspeople, busy with their own affairs. He was sure that his assistants had taken their seats, but he had to act as if they weren't there. He had to be careful and think only about his task, about nothing else, although the memories the city and the castle towering over him made him feel cold.

Trying not to attract anyone's attention, he examined the market square and the gallows on it, and then the surrounding alleys. Even at best, when Jean and Francois distract the soldiers, he will be left with the executioner and his assistant, and perhaps those soldiers who will guard the condemned wagon. A plan began to crystallize in his mind, but it required an element that he couldn't get at that point. Nevertheless, the plan was good, he felt it, so he began to think hard about its implementation.

Wandering around the side streets with his eyes fixed on the ground, he noticed a linen scarf, probably lost by some townswoman, and his heart beat harder. It was just what he needed.

When he was still an unfledged adolescent, Berengard had taught him to throw stones with a Roman sling, which was a very useful skill. A slingshot, made of a strip of strong leather, is easy to hide with you, and the stones are everywhere, so it is a treacherous weapon and very effective. Wasting no time, Theo folded the scarf so that it could be used as a slingshot, and threaded a noose at one end.

It's enough for one-time use, he thought smugly, and began looking for a position to observe the market from.

His choice fell on a small woodshed with a flat roof, on one side falling very low. He led the horse under this eave, and he hid himself on the roof, waiting for the development of events.

There was still some time until noon, but he preferred not to go anywhere. Here, behind the protruding boards, he remained invisible to passers-by and to the soldiers patrolling the city, and he had a nice view of the market square and surrounding streets. His thoughts drifted to Pierre. He liked him, despite the lack of any reciprocity, valued him for his courage and steadfastness. He hoped that he could be saved and that the torture he had undoubtedly suffered in prison had not crippled him. Certainly, the awareness of who organized help for him will be an additional shock for him. Theo smiled to himself with involuntary malice and then reflected. So far, there was no reason to rejoice yet, and he would not be there until they were safely in their hideout in the marshes. And that might not be easy at all. Their undoubted advantage was that the English did not expect this action. And the Black Knight probably had no idea Pierre had anything to do with a fugitive from his dungeons. The moment of surprise should have been seized. Theo was a good tactician, which he himself did not know, because he had no opportunity to use these abilities. This one was the first, and there would be many more.

Suddenly the young knight shuddered and abandoned his sterile deliberations. There was traffic in the street leading to the castle. Wheels rattled, horses' hooves clicked, and people began to hurry to the square. Soldiers in armor with the marks of the English king surrounded the gallows, leaving a free passage for the wagon with the condemned man and the executioner. Theo got to his feet slowly and uncoiled his makeshift slingshot, looping the noose around his left wrist. He was left-handed. In his early youth, succumbing to pressure from the environment, he trained his right hand so that he could write with it without any problems, but in combat he still preferred to use his left. It was definitely more efficient, despite all the exercises.

At the end of the street a cart appeared, on which Pierre was tied, supported by two executioners. The executioner himself, a stout man in black robes and a black mask, rode alongside on a scarred horse. Theo smiled grimly to himself. It was just an appointment with his henchmen, and indeed, with the soldiers' biting arrows rained down, spreading confusion and disorientation. The knight spun the slingshot. With the first stone he knocked down the executioner, with the second he reached the commander of the soldiers, who was trying to bring some order among them with little success. Then he slid down the sloping roof, jumped on his horse and ran towards the gallows, scattering the townspeople and soldiers along the way.

Before anyone could find out, he grabbed Pierre, threw him over the horse's back, and made the horse first leap over the cart, then gallop frantically across the township's streets. Three or four horse riders blocked his way. He managed to draw his sword and bumped into them without even stopping his horse. The sword curled in his hand like a living creature, biting the Englishmen mortally surprised by this insane attack. The knight, heated by the fight, urged the horse to run faster. He still had to get out of town and hide in the woods, and Pierre, half unconscious, hanging limp on his horse's back, did not make this task easier for him. The mount, burdened with a double burden, had to run slower, which could cost them dearly. If Pierre had been in better shape, he might have just gotten a second horse for him, but now...

It was still necessary to break through the guard at the gate. As soon as the guards, alarmed by the screams and the row at the market square, noticed the fugitives, they grabbed the halberds placed under the wall. Two knights in the colors of Roger de Valois came to their aid. Theo fought them fiercely, out of the corner of his eye to see if someone was coming from behind, but unnecessarily - Berengard attacked as planned, distracting the sentries' strength and attention. After breaking through the guards, Theo urged the horse to a gallop again. He knew that the double loaded steed might finally die, but ultimately their lives were perhaps more important than that of this noble animal. He could feel the warmth of the blood running down his forearm. One of the knights reached it with the very tip of his sword, tearing the skin from elbow to wrist, thankfully quite shallow. Gritting his teeth, he reached for the scarf still hanging from the wrist of his left hand and wrapped it around his wounded arm. It was a makeshift dressing, but for now it had to be enough.

Reaching the lake, the knight jumped off the tired horse and dragged Pierre to the grass. With the pull of the dagger, he cut open his bonds and set it gently on the ground. The young reaver suffered much more than it seemed at first glance, but the knight's cursory examination failed to detect anything in his wounds that could not be healed. It calmed him down. He moistened Pierre's face with lake water, washed some of his wounds, and wiped the clotted blood from his fair hair. Now, as he lay there on the grass with his eyes closed, his likeness to his sister tightened his heart.

"It'll be all right," Theo whispered, wanting to convince himself.

He had witnessed death as a result of torture even as a child, and had the dark awareness that it would not be unusual. He wished with all his heart that it would not happen now. Despite the vigorous resentment shown him from the very first moment by this rebellious peasant, he felt that they could become friends, and he had some strong inner conviction that Pierre felt it too. His participation in jacquerie should be a sufficient reason for mutual enmity, but there was something about this young man, which assured the young count that he had nothing shameful on his conscience, although he undoubtedly did not fall asleep in the ashes during the rebellion. Much later he found out that his guesses were correct. Despite the fact that Pierre, like other participants of jacquerie, shed noble blood, he did not murder the defenseless, he did not participate in rapes and did not abuse anyone. He was honest in his own way and believed in the rightness of the common cause. The defeat of the rebellion was also a personal one for him. He did not want and could not accept the relationship of the younger sister with the representative of the hated nobility, but Theo understood his feelings and did not reciprocate.

Absorbed in treating the unconscious outlaw, only at the last moment he heard a rustle behind his back and turned abruptly, grabbing his sword.

"Relax, it's just us!" cried Berengard, avoiding a cut from a sharp blade. Theo was relieved to find that all five of his assistants had not been reached by the soldiers somehow, they were safe and sound, though Martin had a torn straitjacket and Jean was a little limping.

"We have confused the pursuit by setting the horses the other way," Berengard said in an explanatory tone. "What's with him?"

"Do I look like a medic to you? I do not know. Let's take him to your hideout and have someone bring Father Prospero," Theo replied, a little sharply.

He would probably have confused the way in these swamps himself, so he had to wait for them by the lake instead of taking Pierre right away where he would be safe. The outlaws obeyed him with an eagerness that their leader would undoubtedly displease if he were conscious.

In their hideout, a shaky Bellette waited.

"What did they do with him?!" she cried desperately, throwing herself at her brother being carried by her friends.

"Well, they choked him a little," Jean replied. "But be calm, it's a strong bull, and Olivier has already run for Prospero."

Like almost everyone in the area, he also believed in the medical skills of the old monk. It was not without reason, Father Prospero had vast experience and knowledge that amazed the monk. He knew herbs, knew how to adjust broken bones and sew wounds, and never refused to help anyone. Now, too, he had arrived as soon as he could, and to the indescribable relief of all those present, declared that Pierre would no doubt recover. He poured a few drops of some elixir into his mouth, after which Pierre recovered conscious immediately.

"How are you?" Jean asked quickly.

"Like someone after a long torture, you stupid bastard," growled Pierre. Then he looked at the silent knight and turned his head. Theo knew the bitterness of humiliation was flooding him now, and smiled with secret satisfaction. Somehow the thought pleased him. Pierre touched his head with his hand and cursed in pain as he tried to get up.

"You better not try," the monk warned him as he felt his arms and legs twisted by torture. Finally, he ruled that except for the right shoulder, all bones would heal on their own. Then he added a dozen drops of something brown to the water and with the resulting mixture he washed the wounds and the harpy marks on Pierre's skin. He then added five drops of the potion from another wine flask and forced the man to drink them.

"What is it, Father?" Bellette asked, bravely holding back her tears.

"It relieves the pain, unfortunately for a short time," Prospero explained to her. "After ten drops, even a bull like your brother would sleep all day.

"And after fifteen?" Theo asked. The monk glanced at him.

"And after fifteen he wouldn't wake up at all," he replied, rolling up the sleeves of his habit and showing muscles that were impressive for a monk. "Hold him now."

He thrust one hand into Pierre's shoulder and the other jerked his arm so hard that it snapped, and Pierre howled in pain and fell back on the bed, gasping for air.

"Let him eat well, get a lot of rest, and now show your hand." the monk asked Theo.

"Why? It's just a scratch. The stupid soldier reached me with the very edge of his sword," the knight protested, hiding his wounded arm behind him.

"You're not too smart either," Prospero, in spite of his objection, pulled his hand towards him and brushed it away, a scarf stiff with blood. "Don't you know the wound needs dressing?"

He took a roll of white linen and a jar of herbal ointment from his bag. He worked in silence for a while, treating the wound, then suddenly asked:

"What are you going to do now?"

"I think I should go to Regent Charles," Theo replied, gritting his teeth as the ointment burned him mightily. "I've waited too long on this anyway. I'll be useful to him."

The monk shook his shaggy head.

"I wouldn't advise you to do that," he said, wrapping a clean cloth around his hand. "I don't know how to say it delicately, but your situation is blurry to say the least. Roger de Valois announced that you had deliberately breached the terms of the Bretigny Treaty, thereby defying the will of both the King of France and the King of England. You have been declared a traitor, your goods have been confiscated, and you are an outlaw, my dear. Everyone knows about it already."

Berengard made a noise between indignation and despair, and Bellette shuddered violently.

"Yeah... what are you gonna do now?" Pierre asked, without a trace of malice anyway.

Theo was silent for a moment, biting his lips nervously. From what he had witnessed so far, the news had a less electrifying effect on him than might have been expected, but he was shocked enough to be silent for a long time. The Black Knight and Don Paulino acted quickly and ruthlessly, effectively cutting off his rescue.

"If I had reached the regent's court or Navarra, I would certainly be able to..." he began hesitantly.

"Say one more word in this taste, and I will have you bound as insane," Prospero interrupted him. "You couldn't do anything. Are you well on your mind? They'll catch you and cut you up, and then they'll probably burn you. It's out of the question at all, come up with something else."

"Something else? Well! They want war with me, they will have it. I'll gather a team like me and fight the English as I can!" The knight shouted violently. "I will find those who will follow me, and then...!"

"Stop yelling, my head hurts," Pierre interrupted. "You don't have to look for anyone. We'll have enough to start with, right? Because when it comes to fighting the English, we will follow you even to the scaffold."

Theo looked at him in surprise.

"No, it's not what you think," Pierre replied to his gaze. "I still don't like you, but I already know you can be trusted and I admit that I've gained respect for you. No, not because you pulled me out of the undertaker from under a shovel. Because you, Count, risked your life for an ordinary peasant. I doubt if there would be another nobleman capable of it, for we are not even men to these lords.

Anyway, I would ally myself with the devil himself, as long as he harassed the English."

"This is just a real Christian remark for me," Father Prospero remarked wryly. "You won't ask your people for their opinion anymore?"

Pierre grimaced reluctantly.

"I don't have to. Father will notice how they look at him," he replied. The monk looked at the knight sidelong.

"How old are you actually, young monsignor?" he asked sharply.

"Twenty... I'm finishing next week," Theo replied, flushing a little because he didn't like to admit he was so young.

"No offense, but the prints on my heels are older," muttered Prospero. "But that's not the point, after all, during the crusade, I saw full-fledged knights who hadn't even shaved yet. My point is that at your age it is easy to do all sorts of nonsense, and times are dangerous, and just a minor mistake can cost you dearly."

Theo laughed.

"I promise to be a model of caution," he said. "Besides, it's not that bad. These English soldiers are a bunch of bunglers, only one of them ever knew how to hold a sword.

He stepped outside the hut and took a deep breath. He felt like a man who regains consciousness after a hard hit on the head with a stick and is surprised that the world still exists around him. His mind was clear now. The decision reassured him, he felt again that his life had some meaning, and he knew at last what he really wanted to do. He had to be alone with his decision for a while. Lost in his thoughts, he did not even hear Prospero standing behind him, and for a moment he stared at him, chewing on his own bitter thoughts. He knew his family well, he remembered the day when he blessed the relationship of the beautiful Adelaide de Tourvelle with Fabien de Bongrais, and was a little surprised that this young man, who wanted to fight and kill, was so externally like his mother. It would have been better if he had inherited his father's austere features, and the gentle heart of his wife, while the old count's ruthless character, hidden under his charming exterior, made himself known again and again. He had them all characteristic features of his family, including vengefulness and a tendency to cruelty. Maybe if not for these terrible times, it would have been less important...

"Did you know that in the fight you just started, you will probably die?" he asked softly.

Theo turned his head slightly.

"I know," he replied. "But before that, I'll do as much damage to the English and their allies as possible. I'll make their teeth chatter at the sound of my name and turn gray on the spot. And even if I die, my name will not perish."

Prospero nodded in sad understanding and reached into his bag.

"When your father went to war, he had a feeling he wouldn't be back," he said. "He made me give it back to you, if his gut feelings come true."

He handed him a heavy object wrapped in a piece of dark blue velvet. The young knight unwrapped it, and he saw a very old, flat, forged silver medallion on a wide chain of ornamental links. The Bongrais coat of arms was engraved on the surface of the medallion: three ears of rye. Each successive Count Bongrais wore this heavy gorget day and night, succumbing to the old superstition that the longevity of the family depends on it. Now it was in the hands of Theo, the last of the family.

"Thank you, father," the young man whispered, hanging the locket around his neck with understandable emotion.

* * * * *

The rat-faced redhead Jean, thin, cheerful and insolent, felt unusually intimidated by the young aristocrat. The barely grown young man who had so unexpectedly found himself among them was too different from them to be at ease with him. He was going to be their leader from now on, even Pierre recognized it, because he was so reluctant to him. Frankly, it was Jean who did not understand this reluctance, and Pierre's social views were rather vague to him. He liked Theo from the very first moment, but it was not easy for him to address him directly with a few words from himself and his companions.

A young knight was sitting on a fallen tree trunk and painstakingly cut something with a knife from a long strip of tanned leather. At footsteps, he raised his head and shook hair from forehead.

"Lord..." Jean began shyly.

"Come on, not lord," Theo interrupted. "I told you by name."

"I just wanted to say," the little redhead stuck for a moment, looking for words, "that we are all very grateful for what... you did.

You will not be disappointed with us. Pierre will be faithful to you too, but he won't say it out loud, that's the way he is."

"It's okay," Theo smiled.

He looked at Jean kindly, with no trace of superiority whatsoever, and Jean felt his embarrassment fade away.

"Who would have thought the Count de Bongrais would lead us," he said.

Theo darkened.

"Count de Bongrais is dead. He died in slaughter that day in the courtyard of his castle, along with the others," he said, tugging angrily at the unfinished slingshot. "I'm Theo le Vengeur, and that will be called by those who will not like the name "English Nightmare". Desiring to destroy me, these traitors, Don Paulino and his protector, handed me a weapon, and I will be able to use it. Paradoxically, if I had remained in the regent's service, I would have hurt them less than I'm now."

Jean nodded approvingly.

"We'll get under their's skin together," he assured him. "And you know what I heard in the inn yesterday? Such a joke: a hundred Englishmen are running, and one Frenchman is chasing them with his sword drawn. One Englishman asks another: 'Why are we running away? He is one and a hundred of us.' 'Indeed', the other replies. 'But you not know who he wants to knock with this sword'."

Theo was laughing so heartily that Bellette, who was just approaching him, felt her throat tighten.

"Oh, my one," she thought. "And I was afraid that I would never hear you laugh again..."

She came over and threw her warm hands around his neck, smelling of milk after morning milking.

"My heart hurts that you were hurt so much," she confessed. "But I'm glad you stayed."

* * * * *

The task looked trivially simply: to commandeer some provisions in the village of Kamienisko and punish the peasant who evaded paying the taxes imposed on the village. The decade, sent to the village with his unit, did not expect any problems, so he was even more painfully surprised by what had happened. The intimidated villagers hid wherever they could, as was the rule in occupied territories, where no one dared to oppose the soldier with the lion on his shield. This young man, who suddenly appeared on the road, may have been lured by the desperate scream of the young people, at first glance he did not differ from other villagers. However, even simple clothes could not hide his innate pride and noble features. Tall, black-haired, with pale skin, only slightly golden with the sun, he struck the decade with the hateful look of his black eyes.

"Stop your men," he demanded.

"Why is that, boy?" the Englishman asked contemptuously.

"Because I'm asking you," replied the stranger. "Hurry up or I'll stop being polite."

"Take this audacious man!" The commander shouted to his men.

As if in response to these words, arrows and stones fell from everywhere, and then men armed with daggers and clubs appeared, ruthlessly killing those of his men who had not been hit by the previously fired projectiles. It all happened so quickly that the commander did not even have time to realize the situation.

When he finally regained consciousness and grabbed his sword, the black-haired youth knocked it out of his hand with a quick, incredibly strong cut.

"The only reason you will survive is because I need a messenger," he hissed. "You'll return to the castle and tell Don Paulino and the Black Knight that these goods are under my personal protection and that any rape of these people will be punished without mercy. Understand?"

"Who are you?" The Englishman gasped breathlessly.

The young man scowled in a malicious half-smile.

"Tell your master that Theo le Vengeur is bowing to him," he replied. "He better remember that name so that he knows whom to curse."

He motioned to his men and walked away without looking back at the wreckage left behind.

It took a long time for the commander to gather enough to return to the castle, where he would meet Captain Moore, the commander of the English garrison in Bongrais. The captain was afraid of all the soldiers, especially when it came to one of them to report that he had not complied with the order, so no wonder he was in no hurry. When he finally got to the castle, it turned out that his misfortune had been sprinkled with some good luck: Captain Moore was talking to Don Paulino and the Black Knight in the castle courtyard. The captain generally held back a little in their presence. In a choppy voice, commander reported what had happened and, hanging his head, waited for a lightning strike. Instead, Don Paulino asked in a voice not of his own:

"How did he say his name was?"

"Theo le Vengeur," the commander replied, not understanding.

"Le Vengeur... that doesn't suit me somehow, but Theo's name is not that common again. Not among the villagers, anyway. Could it be him?" said the manager as if to himself. "What did he look like?"

"Very young, of the right height, skinny, black hair," replied the commander. "Face as smooth as a young lady's, dark eyes."

Roger de Valois laughed.

"Our boy is trying to bite back," he remarked sarcastically. "Going to be fun. I'll be happy to hunt him down."

"And he will butcher my soldiers?" Captain Moore asked with restrained anger. The prince shot him an amused look.

"If they are such bastards to succumb to a few yokels, they deserve nothing better." He said.

The captain fell silent. He respected this dark man, and not only because he was the prince of blood and a close friend of the Prince of Wales, under whose orders he was directly subject. He just feared him a little, like anyone who knew him. Always dressed in black, with black curls down his collar and a black chin, with one single gray strand on his left temple, he cynically used his diabolical appearance to overwhelm people and gain an advantage on the spot. He usually succeeded.

Don Paulino followed the captain into the corridor.

"Announce among the soldiers that I'm paying two thousand scudos for the head of this cub," he said quietly. "No matter the rank of whoever brings it to me."

The captain looked at him curiously.

"You must hate him a lot," he said lightly. "Fine, I'll tell them again, but keep your mouth shut before the prince. He wants him for himself."

"May he not regret it," said the old Spaniard prophetically.

* * * * *

It all happened almost a year ago. Now, in late spring, the fame of Theo and his company of outcasts was well established throughout the province. He was told about him at fires, songs were sung in taverns about his clashes with the English, his advantages were often exaggerated and details were added that none of those directly concerned could somehow recall.

The gang had new people: Gwidon, who played the zither as well as he threw a lead ball on a long thong, and Alain, a country blacksmith of extraordinary strength. They were completely different, but both were accepted just as quickly by the gang.

Gwidon, called the Weasel, was an unstable, moody, explosive, but still very liked by all bard from Paris, from where he had to flee after some love adventure. He loved love for the sake of love and was in love practically all the time. Alain, a slow and reticent giant with a huge mop of curly hair on his head, had one major flaw: he didn't wash at all. It didn't bother anyone too much, as cleanliness was not the strongest point of the outlaws hiding in the forest. One Theo was taking a daily bath in the lake, regardless of the weather, unless the lake was frozen. Jean and Pierre were quite clean too, Gwidon looked after himself too. However, the rest felt that it was a waste of time for something so useless and only washed up on major holidays. Theo did not try to correct them in this regard, emphasizing what was really important.

Slowly, without much effort, he transformed the unruly crowd into a punitive unit which, under his orders, quickly took its toll on the English occupiers. The Black Prince's soldiers who came in this direction to support Roger de Valois could never be sure whether they would be inundated with arrows and slingshot stones during requisitions, searches or punishment. Usually, an armed gang led by a dark-haired youth with a sword in his hand appeared next to them. His name was spoken with fear and hatred: Theo le Vangeur, the Avenger. Nobody could feel safe on his premises. He was a bloody revenge for the past and present offenses of the English army, and well-thought-out and well-planned actions strengthened his fame as a defender of the oppressed. He adopted the tactic of a tug of war - his men inflicted quick, precise blows designed to do as much damage as possible, then disappeared like ghosts.

"Not bad, not bad," Father Prospero would say with reserved admiration. "Only by going against the provisions of the Bretigny treaty you put yourself at risk for both sides."

The old monk did not condemn or approve of them, although he himself experienced a kind of internal tear: he could not support bloodshed, but as a good French nobleman he was upset at the mere sight of an English helmet. As a result, he said nothing - perhaps it was for the best, as Theo calmed down slowly and regained his ability to reason clearly. He was still at an age when it is relatively easy to heal the wounds of body and soul, and he became fond of the life he lived now. It had its charm, although it was tough and would break many young men of his condition. It would seem that it was Theo, brought up at the court of the king Navarra, knighted by John II, should have succumbed to the pressure of the signed treaty, but it was not so, on the contrary: he considered the treaty shameful and did not intend to respect it. He knew well that if the English caught him, he would be hanged, and if the French caught him, he would be beheaded, but he was too young to care.

"At this age one dies easily and without regret," Prospero said to Berengard the other day. "If he lives longer, he will know what attachment to life and fear of death are, but I don't think that even then he would change his behavior. I'm worried about him."

"And I'm not? He's like a brother to me. If I have the opportunity, I will strangle Paulino with my own hands for what he has done to him." Berengard gritted his teeth in helpless anger.

The traitor kept him awake at night. He could not understand how one could, without a trace of remorse, put to death people who had lived under the same roof for so many years and from whom no harm had ever been suffered. How can you choose a bounty on your suzerain's head? Another thing is that this award could safely be doubled and tripled without fear that someone would take it. At first, a few soldiers and a few mercenary thugs wants it, but they all gave their heads against the outlaws, and the enthusiasm in this direction cooled. Don Paulino gnawed at it immeasurably, especially since the youngster he disregarded had grown up in the eyes of the people as a defender sent by heaven, and without him it was not easy to maintain order. The rebels did not lack the opportunity to plunder the English, and if they found the French dissenters serving the Black Prince, it ended in a ruthless slaughter.

"What the hell? Is there no way to approach one outlaw?" Don Paulino thought glumly. "Is he enchanted or what?"

Undoubtedly, Theo's successes would have been much less if he had not been supported by simple peasants. Oppressed by everyone, they saw him as their defender from heaven. Theo's gang did not torment them and loot them, on the contrary, they helped and protected as much as possible against the brutalities of soldiers and vagabonds demoralized by the war. Don Paulino had no doubt that if he ever fell into the hands of a count, he would not survive, so he would not leave the castle, unless under heavy guard. At first, Captain Moore and his troops mocked secretly what they thought was excessive caution, but soon they found it hard to laugh. The exiled knight became a formidable opponent who could strike from everywhere and at any time.

"If he ever gets my hands, he'll regret not getting in my way, but being born at all," the captain swore, counting how many people he had already lost to the elusive outlaw.

"You'd better be careful, Captain, lest he cut your hands first. With him it goes quickly: one, two and have no mercy," said the Black Knight ironically, pausing for a moment writing a letter to the Duke of Auvergne.

"We'll see," muttered the captain.

One of the sentries peered into the room.

"Sorry, my lord," he said to Roger de Valois. "There is one knight here, he says he comes from the Prince of Wales."

"So, what are you waiting for, you fool? Let him in," the Black Knight ordered, frowning severely.

Don Paulino looked up from the list he was making, and a hint of unease flashed across his unshaven face. He well knew that taxes and tributes from the provinces did not arrive regularly, and he was not sure that the notorious Black Prince would understand the reason for this. There was a clink of spurs in the corridor, and a knight in full armor, with a red rose symbol on his breastplate, entered the hall. The helmet was held under his arm, so that his pale blond head with noble features and iron-gray eyes was exposed. He was quite young and not handsome at all, but his thin lips had an expression of contemptuous superiority and were certainly not inclined to smile.

"I'm Reynold Plantagenet of Winslow, esquire," he said in good French. "I came to Bongrais on the orders of the Prince of Wales and Lord of Aquitaine, Edward Plantagenet. Apparently, as a result of trouble with some forest thug, you aren't able to send all the tributes due to my noble cousin, and a large number of soldiers die, attacked from an ambush. I have to remedy it."

"Next candidate for dead body." Captain Moore muttered into his mug of beer.

"Captain, when I want to know your views, I will just ask," the knight pointed out. "On the way, I collected some information about this outlaw, whom you are so afraid of here, and I admit that he is an extraordinary figure. I'm going to challenge him to a duel."

Don Paulino put down his pen and stood up.

"With all due respect, think about it again," he said. "That would be the last mistake in your life. Theo wields the sword better than anyone I know, and he doesn't even know pity by hearing. I don't know who taught him fencing, probably the devil himself, because it is impossible to teach such tricks from a man. Do you think that bold and ruthless people are missing here? After all, none of those who wanted to hunt this outlaw came back alive. He ripped the guts out of each one."

"Perhaps, when he was forced to look at his service massacre, he discovered that he liked the sight of blood," said Sir Winslow coldly. "But I don't care about your personal scores, I'm to restore peace in the province and I'll do it, but according to chivalrous customs. After all, we aren't dealing here with a random robber who can be hung without ceremony on a dry branch. I don't need your help, I only expect one thing: tell me everything you know about him, without missing a single detail."

Don Paulino looked helplessly at his protector. The man shrugged slightly.

"Talk, I don't know as much about him as you do," he muttered.

The Spaniard therefore told everything he could remember about the leader of the gang that was troubling him, trying not to miss anything. He had no idea how his messages could help catch a dangerous outlaw, but he felt so uncomfortable under the knight's cold gaze that he dared not ask. When he finished, Sir Winslow nodded and donned his helmet.

"I think two days will be enough," he said. "I'll bring his head over here soon. It'll be possible to stick it on a palette, this should silence the local rebels. From what I've heard, there will be nothing extraordinary about this job."

"Congratulations, my lord, I will hold off on your return," Captain Moore said harshly, giving the knight an unfriendly glance.

Sir Reynold looked at him briefly and left.

"I remembered they called him the Winslow Butcher. He fights for fun, sets out on his own against the worst robbers. I think he is insane," said Moore.

The Black Knight smiled slightly.

"And I know him," he said. "This is King Edward's favorite. If Theo kills him, half the English army will collapse into these woods, so anyway... the end of a beautiful legend. Though this freak seems damn confident."

Moore poured himself a beer.

"Others were too. We found them later with their guts ripped out," he reminded him sourly.

"We'll just have to wait and see, Captain..." Roger de Valois was still smiling awful looking out the window at the nearby woods.

The arrival of the knight in this direction was very convenient for him.

CHAPTER III

A sting in the tail

Berengard, out of breath, burst into a clearing where the rest of the gang were practicing knife throwing at the target, the one who missed being thrown at himself with unrefined jokes. This and other similar activities filled most of the outlaws' free time. There were times when they attended a country wedding or went to an inn to drink and watch the girls, but mostly they honed their skills as if they were actually a regular army unit. As a result, they became better and more efficient.

"Do you have any idea what I found out?!" Berengard shouted to Theo.

"In a minute!" His friend shouted cheerfully, pointing his knife at the square of white bark pinned on the trunk of a large maple tree.

Berengard shrugged angrily and sat down against the wall of their hut. He had known for a long time that there was no point in trying to convince himself that there were more important matters, he had to wait.

After a while, Theo threw the knife, hitting the center of the square without fail, and sat down next to his friend.

"Well, what's bothering you?" He asked, nudging him to the side. Berengard made a vague gesture with his hand.

"I don't know," he said. "You are much more interested in this childishness than my words, so maybe it is not worth beating a dead horse?"

"That you must always grumble... Come on," Theo was used to the fact that the slightly older Berengard still considered himself a guardian and treated him a bit like his younger brother. He had to do him justice: he was great in his role when an orphaned boy needed a kind soul so badly among the reluctant castle servants.

"Well?" He urged him cheerfully.

The friend looked at him from under the big mane falling over his forehead.

"They say some English knight is looking for you in the village," he said. "Don't laugh, that's not all. He's some extraordinary bachelor, and of high blood too. His name is Reynold Plantagenet of Winslow. I had to repeat three times before I remembered that the tongue could be broken on it. He says he wants to wring your neck."

Theo waved a hand carelessly.

"Then there will be one less. Few of them rot in the woods here. Though, truth be told, neither of them were knights."

He thought.

"Winslow, Winslow," he repeated. "I've heard that before. Maybe I'll remember later. We'll wait for now, and if he don't find me, I'll look for him myself and there will be one more dead Englishman."

"May you not miscalculate," muttered Berengard, without much hope of being heard. Theo looked at him mockingly, then stood up and returned to his companions still competing at aiming a knife.

In less than a year since the events at Bongrais Castle, these simple people taught him a great deal: to move silently through the woods, to hunt with a bow, to braid ropes (in winter it was so boring that they would even do embroidery if they could), making arrows yourself, setting traps, as well as "boorish" fistfighting. Pierre was his teacher of the latter, assuming that each of them must be able to do something like that, let alone the leader. It was not without significance that he finally had the opportunity to get to his skin.

"I don't really understand him," said Francois, sitting with his friends on the edge of the stream, watching the struggle. "If I wanted to punch the face of my sister's every boy, I would have no time for anything else. And here because of one lover such a row."

"My sister is a hussy too," said Olivier, looking up from his sandal being repaired. "With women, the devil himself will not come to terms, and why is our poor leader guilty?"

"It's not about the fact, it's about with whom. Pierre's hurts that Theo is a count and should be his enemy as such," Jean explained.

Olivier nodded solemnly.

"He should," he admitted. "He just somehow doesn't want to."

Martin, returning with an armful of broken wood, stopped beside them.

"It will be useful to him," he said. "There are many situations when you cannot draw a sword and knightly rules do not apply somehow. If only he would learn before Pierre bludgeons him to death."

"Don't worry, he's a resilient boy. He can't seem to know anything yet, and at a Manette's wedding from potters, who threw the bench like an old man? You know what smashed your head with the picket," Jean reminded him.

Martin grimaced reluctantly because he didn't like being reminded of such things. However the fact was that he was right. The ability to fight fists was often a matter of surviving in this utterly unchallenged world and could not under any circumstances disregard. Theo, skillful and strong, quickly mastered this art and, in return, taught his new friends to throw stones from the Roman slingshot and the basics of fencing. As non-nobility, they did not have the right to carry swords, but in the heat of battle it was easy to get this weapon from an opponent, and then it was good to know how to use it.

Winter passed for them with similar activities, and it must be admitted that during those snowy months they became very close to them. They have become true comrades-in-arms. Of course, Theo was very different from them, both in appearance and behavior, even in rags he looked like "someone better", but nobody except Pierre did not mind.

"If he didn't arouse such sympathy, it'd be easier for me," Pierre once confided to Father Prospero.

"Then let go of this matter," the monk advised him. "Like him as we all do."

"Never," Pierre growled implacably.

Berengard smiled to himself. Bellette's brother clung to his radical views with stubbornness worthy of a better cause, and rivaled Theo at every turn. It was the same now. Others had gotten bored of playing long ago, while the two continued throwing knives, trying to defeat each other until it was dark. In this state of mind, it was not worth interrupting them. Berengard decided to resume the interrupted conversation the next morning, but when he awoke, the knight was gone. He followed him to the lake where he suspected his friend was taking his morning bath. He was right. When he reached the lake, Theo was kneeling on the shore, tying his sandals. Drops of water dripped down his tanned shoulders and neck, his wet hair flashing black and navy blue in the morning sun. The mere sight of it could get cold, because the mornings at this time of year were still really cool, and the water in the forest lake chilled by the night - ice cold.

The young knight tossed his damp fringe aside and looked at Berengard.

"I have already remembered why I know that name," he said without preamble. "The Englishman who is so interested in me is Winslow the Butcher, the insane knight. Since nowadays it is difficult to find dragons and virgins to be released from lonely towers, as well, he is looking for fame by chasing and killing people like me. The same fun as any other. Sir Winslow is of the princely lineage of the Plantagenet, and the truth is, he could do something else, but I won't convert him anymore. It's worth finding him because if he will look for me too he could intensely hurt someone along the way. I don't want this."

"Could he do that?" Asked Berengard through a lump in his throat.

Theo shrugged.

"I don't know. However, I prefer that he doesn't have the opportunity, it isn't known what will go to his head. He is a strange man."

He thought. He had to instruct the villagers how to behave in case of meeting this man, and that meant going to the village. He visited it more than once, Bellette lived there, and he was almost as often in the Two Sheaves and the Lower Escarpment. He visited his other villages only sporadically, for they were much further away and he only went to them when he really had to.

"And what will you do when some troops catch you in the open space? Maybe it'd better when I go with you," suggested Berengard, alarmed by the idea.

Theo laughed with some pity.

"After all, I'll not go out into such an open space. Besides, a squad of soldiers can be heard a mile away, I always have time to hide. Go back to the hideout and don't worry about me. I'll be here before noon."

He patted him on the shoulder and walked away towards the village, whistling one of Gwidon's playful songs.

Without telling anyone about it, Berengard was very worried, but unnecessarily because his friend kept his word and actually returned by noon.

"Peace everywhere," he announced happily. "These English dogs are a bit calm and do not stick their nose out of the garrison. Bellette will be here tomorrow and bring us some loaves of bread as well as some fresh news."

Pierre frowned.

"Don't use her like that. Do you want her to come to the gallows because of you?" He said sharply.

Gwidon clinked into the strings of his zither.

"You always see in black," he said. "Women are much better in these matters than peasants. In Paris, pretty prostitutes are traditionally used to collect news, and the result is always sure."

"Watch your nose, you weird disguise!" Pierre shouted at him.

"Why weird? All the colors match, and since there are a lot of them, I'm sorry, my business," Gwidon replied with dignity.

"If I have to look at you, mine too," growled Pierre.

The poet took his hips.

"If I like, I'll put on a woman's skirt, a pink checked jacket and a wreath on my head, and what will you do to me?" He asked aggressively.

"I'll make a bowstring for my bow from your bowels!" Pierre screamed, and launched himself at him with his fists.

Theo wanted to separate them, but he couldn't because he was laughing so hard that he couldn't get up from the grass. The rest of the gang were too in love with this kind of show to intervene. They loved it, and such chaos was the order of the day, as perhaps the only entertainment available to them. Gwidon, though shorter and thinner than Pierre, knew how to fight and his favorite weapon, an elongated leather bag filled with sand, was a very dangerous tool in his hand. Pierre quickly found out about it. Gwidon nimbly slipped out of his hands, bit his shoulder and pressed him against the back of his head so that he squatted.

"He bit me," he said resentfully. "He's probably furious, he needs to be drowned. I refuse to fight on such terms."

He shook his sore hand and stood up.

"Either way is good as long as it leads to the goal," said Gwidon victoriously.

"Really?" Martin asked doubtfully.

"Chief, you are so well-versed in matters of honor, so enlighten us: does the end justify the means?" Jean asked his leader.

"Never," Theo gasped between bursts of laughter.

"If I had known you would be so pleased with this pesky weasel, I would have slapped him before," Pierre said furiously, which of course only made matters worse.

"I'll compose a ballad about it: How a Parisian weasel defeated a forest wolf," Gwidon laughed aggressively, looking around for his lemon.

The fun was excellent, but Bellette broke it when she ran into the clearing. Her hands and apron were sprinkled with flour, apparently what had happened tore her away from kneading the bread dough. She fell onto the trunk of a fallen tree and gasped for a moment with her half-open mouth.

"Colas was at my place," she choked finally. "That knight you were talking about accosted him on the road and he told to send a message to you, by word of mouth."

"An unreliable method," Gwidon interrupted her. "It was once used to send a message from Paris to Fontainbleau that the king would be accommodating there for a few days with two troops. When the message arrived, it read: "The Queen has an enormous croup."

"Stop it, Parisian phantom! This is important!" Bellette shouted irritably. "Theo, you are to report to Devil's Crossroads by evening and take up a knightly fight with him, otherwise he will declare you a filthy thug with no honor. The end."

"He talked a lot. And they say the English are reticent," Theo chuckled as he finally got up from the grass. "All right, let's get it over with."

"You forget that Devil's Crossroads are off the beaten track and are a great place to set up an ambush," Berengard said tartly.

Theo shrugged.

"What is it, we are blind and deaf?" He said casually, "If it's a trap, we'll figure it out before those rats have time to move. But I don't think so. Apparently Sir Winslow is an honorable man, but on the other hand, who knows these Englishmen."

"Exactly. We're going with you," Pierre decided sharply.

"Am I saying no?" The knight was surprised cheerfully. "Bellette, go back to the village and let Colas keep his mouth shut."

The girl rose heavily from the trunk.

"Don't worry," she said. "The Colas has more brains in his heel than any of you in the head."

She turned and walked away without looking back.

"What's wrong with her?" Theo asked Pierre in whisper.

"A woman's disease, not a word," the other muttered.

"This is how it is with the weaker sex, sometimes they are weaker than usual," Gwidon sighed, humming melancholy on his zither

"If my wife is also a weaker sex, then I'm a sunset on a clear day," said Olivier gloomily. "One day she found me flirting with the daughter of the neighbors, nothing serious, I tell you, just banter... she smashed my head with a stake torn out of the fence that I still remember."

"I will never marry. I prefer the gallows," said Jean, wiggling his red mustache in a funny way. "Prospero said during the sermon that from the gallows you can also go to paradise, and from the wedding it is almost certainly in the opposite direction."

"If you could break it down into an alexandrine and rhyme it, you could compose a ballad," said Gwidon, and, swinging his ball on his rawhide, began to mumble fragments of poems. He thought so much that he did not pay attention to anything and only woke up when they had reached the Devil's Crossroads. It was an almost forgotten crossroads, where an odd number of paths crossed that, in the old days, led to some towns and settlements that no longer existed. It was whispered in the area that it was here that desperate people who wanted to save their souls came at night, even their names or nicknames were mentioned, and the horror of these stories was not altered by the fact that hardly anyone knew how to sign in these pages.

Overgrown with shrubs and trees, situated between hills and treacherous canyons, indeed, there was no other place suitable for an ambush, but there was no indication that it was arranged. A knight in full armor stood under a decaying mile stake, holding a fine milk-white stallion in a rich harness by the bridle. He was alone.

"So you came," he said.

"Were you in doubt?" Theo asked, frowning slightly.

"It depends," replied the knight. "Do you know who I am?"

"Stay behind," the outlaw instructed his friends and turned to the Englishman again. "I know. Sir Reynold Plantagenet of Winslow, also known as the Winslow Butcher. The nickname is not very grateful, but supposedly accurate."

The Englishman smiled contemptuously.

"And you're probably Theo le Vengeur, also called by my countrymen the Mad Dog of Touraine?" He reciprocated.

"Nice name," Theo nodded and glanced at his men. "Can I use it every day?"

"As you wish. Hope you know what I'm here for?" Sir Winslow asked.

Theo narrowed his eyes in an unpleasant smile.

"Let me guess," he said. "You mean the recipe for French pastry? The kind of sour apples?"

"I'm going to kill you," said the Englishman calmly, not being disturbed. "And I will do it, but I will give you an equal chance. It will be an honorary duel according to all the rules of the knightly code. As far as I know, you deserve it... though you may not be brave enough."

The young count shook his head slightly.

"Pure generosity. You want to slaughter me according to the rules. Let me die, if it's not true undefiled nobility," he said. "Well, Mr. English, you will have that honorable duel of yours, which you demand with the courage of a purebred loser. Well, guys, now as far as you are concerned, if any one interjects me in this duel, he will look for his teeth all over the forest. Understand? Probably, if he defeats me, he will want to take my head as a souvenir, but that I won't need it then, don't bother him."

"As you wish," Pierre said reluctantly. "For me, your frills are an insult to God."

He sat down under one of the trees, and, following his example, others also retreated, leaving a free square for the knights. Only Gwidon, in whose poetic head something called about the need to issue the so-called on his own initiative, he climbed a high elm and from there he watched if anyone was approaching.

Sir Winslow tied his stallion to one of the trees, then began to unbuckle the pieces of his armor, placing them meticulously on the grass.

Theo watched him with his arms folded until he finally couldn't stand it.

"Should I know something?" He asked him.

"You aren't wearing any armor, though as a knight you should not part with it," replied the Englishman. "I'm leveling our chances."

"You know, armor wouldn't be very comfortable in my situation," Theo chuckled.

No jokes seemed to reach Sir Winslow. He remained cool and unfazed.

"Besides," added the outlaw after a moment. "You'd be pathetically slow with all this junk. You wouldn't have the advantage you think you are. But if you want, I really don't care."

He stripped his sword and stepped into the middle of the empty square, taking a ready stance. Already after the first moves of the Englishman he guessed the true master in him and redoubled his caution. Only those who were sure of their hand for a reason started the fight. The first assemblies passed without any surprises - they only served to sense the real strength and abilities of the opponent. Then the fight slowly grew fiercer, it turned into a strategic game, a game of endurance, because whoever had a stronger arm and was able to win longer against his own fatigue was usually the winner. Sir Winslow fought clean, even, with a style that was foreign to the French. Theo parried and struck blows, looking in vain for any gap in his opponent's defense, feeling reluctant admiration and even respect for this English knight overwhelm him. He was different from the English he had known so far, that had to be admitted. He was also very effective. On several occasions his sword seriously threatened the young Frenchman's life, once it grazed his neck, and once it passed a hair from his left side, slitting the leather caftan several inches. Theo had to exert all his strength and skill to avoid the deadly blade, and at the same time all his attempts to reach the Englishman had failed. He had to admit that he was indeed very good, even better than he was said to be. What he did not know was that Sir Winslow had similar views on his skills.

As for Theo's companions, they watched this fight with the utmost anxiety which they tried not to show. They were silent, even trying to breathe as quietly as possible, which was a great sacrifice for them, because usually, watching someone's fight, they did not spare malicious comments on both sides. But now the stakes were too high. And the decision came in a moment as short as a flash. Emboldened by the advantages he had gained, Sir Winslow made a sudden lunge-turn charge, revealing his right side for a moment. Theo quickly threw the sword to his left hand, deflected the cut directed at his shoulder, and before the Englishman could shield himself, he struck his favorite blow: the sword, aimed at the opponent's underbelly, avoided the tableware with the top and struck the point diagonally, slicing the unfortunate swordsman from the ribs to the womb. Sir Winslow squirmed in place, desperately trying to deflect the cut, but only managed to change its direction a little. The blade ripped through his side and thigh, plunging into flesh down to the bone. He dropped the weapon from his hand and fell to the ground, pressing his hands against his ripped body.

Theo knelt down beside him, cut his jerkin open with a drawn knife, and smothered the blood with shreds of cloth, carefully tying his severed thigh.

"Aren't you completely crazy, my beloved commander?" Pierre asked him as gently as possible, observing these activities with some surprise.

"Come on, I will not finish the wounded. And if I left him here, it would work for the same. I will take him to the monastery," the knight replied with some irritation.

"It'll be a good ballad..." Gwidon sighed happily, sliding down the tree.

"I'll give you a ballad in a moment... I'll write every word on your's stupid face!" Pierre got on him from above. "Everyone to the forest. And you better leave him. He would kill you right away..."

The last words were, of course, addressed to the Count, who carefully placed the wounded Englishman on the horse's back. He didn't even turn his head at the remark. He knew his people well, and knew that perhaps, except for one Berengard, no one would understand him. He didn't really know why he was actually doing all of this, but he felt strange. Until now, he had killed every Englishman he met without hesitation and thought he had a right to do so, but now it happened as if someone invisible put a hand on his shoulder and said:

"Think a little. You absolutely want to be like them?"

For the first time since the Bongrais massacre, he had doubts, which was very unpleasant for him. He did not want to have them, in his opinion they reduced combat efficiency and unnecessarily disturbed discernment, but this knight forced him to change his way of thinking and he knew that from now on he would not be able to take up weapons so quickly and without scruples. He didn't like it at all.

The injured man moved and whispered:

"Why are you saving me? After all, next time I can kill you."

"You'd better be silent," growled Theo. "I only do what I have to do. You have proved to me that there can be English people who have a sense of honor, there can be English people who can even be liked. Before, I didn't even admit the existence of such a possibility, and maybe that's why I could be so effective. It's hard for me to explain to you what you have destroyed. I... I'll never forgive you for this."

He tugged the horse's reins in impotent anger and said nothing more.

*****

The lake was warm and calm in the evening. Theo swam and dived, washing off the blood and dust from his body, but still unable to free himself from thoughts of the wounded knight left in front of the monastery gate. Until now, he had not even thought that the Englishman might also have a knightly noble heart in his chest, while Sir Winslow's example proved otherwise. It was hard for him to accept it.

"Hey, hey!" There was Bellette's fresh and resonant voice on the shore. "Pierre says that you are completely stupid. What did you actually do?"

"Ah, nothing fancy!" Theo shouted back to her. "Turn around, I have to leave and I'm a little naked!"

"An ass hasn't seen the sun's, so been sunburned by a moon," growled Pierre, emerging from the bushes. "I'm going to the monastery to spy, and when I get back, you have to finish this monkeyshines."

He walked away without looking back. Bellette chuckled.

"He'll never change," she said, sitting on the edge and cupping her knees with her hands. "Come on, go ahead, I've seen more before."

Theo swam to her.

"You're sweet," he said fondly. "You know, I have the impression that because of all this I turned into a wolf for a while and only now I'm slowly becoming a human again. How did you get along with me?"

"Normally. I love you just the way you are. For you, I'll become whoever you want, even a she-wolf. Do you want us to sip it to the moon together?" She replied teasingly.

The knight laughed heartily.

"You are my sun, my life," he said. "It pains me that I can't give you anything except sneak kisses in the hay. Perhaps I'll even become your undoing."

"If so, you can be sure that I'll die blessing you. I love your eyes as black as a starless night, I love your lips when you talk to me, I love your strong arms when you embrace me..." The girl leaned over and kissed him straight on the mouth.

"Good thing Pierre doesn't see it, I suppose he'd kill me," Theo muttered softly.

"And Gwidon would make a poem out of it for the sloppy melody," added Bellette.

"Ah, you lovebirds," Pierre spoke up behind them. "I specially turned back to see what you were doing. Belle, go home! Father cows are already roaring like slaughtered cows, milking time is long past. And you, rogue, are you not ashamed to touch my sister with the same paw that you split that Englishman a moment ago? By the way, why she doesn't detest anything either..."

The sister laughed, smacked him on the back and walked away towards the village.

Pierre took off his jacket and jumped into the lake.

"Leave her alone," he asked, emerging next to his leader. "She's young, she'll forget. Nothing good awaits her with you. You won't marry her after all, what would your sphere say?"

"I assure you, I don't care. I'll marry Bellette, even if the Pope himself has forbidden me to. I know you don't like it, but I end up marrying her, not you," Theo replied seriously, finally stepping out of the water and putting his clothes on hastily.

"Not a chance... What a time," sighed Pierre with resignation. "King in captivity, a ruined country, and the sister is goint to the dogs..."

Not for the first time, the sound of the bell at the convent's gate heralded the arrival of someone who needed help. Father Prospero was not surprised by the mere fact that the wounded man was found at the gate, although he was a little surprised that he was an English knight. The English did not usually use his services.

However, not showing surprise, with the help of two silent brothers he carried the wounded man to one of the free rooms.

"Oh, I can see the mark of our bully," he said, bending over the terrible wound unwrapped from a makeshift dressing. "So he has not yet forgotten how to hurt people. Please don't move."

"I'll try," replied the knight, gritting his teeth against the pain.

"Well, yes," the monk purred. "You won't get on your beautiful steed soon, and you can consider yourself lucky anyway. Usually, any Englishman who has the bad idea of crossing a sword with Theo le Vengeur bites the dust."

He added a few drops of some essence from the bottle to the mug of wine and forced the knight to drink it.

"It'll help you bear the pain," he explained. "I've to sew this wound. From participating in the crusade, I learned that tar thread wounds heal cleanly and quickly. I was still snot, but I remember everything. The sewing itself, however, is unspeakably painful."

"Will I get better?" Asked Sir Winslow, concluding that under the influence of an essence of unknown composition the pain had actually diminished and the prick of a thick needle was dull and distant.

The monk looked into his eyes.

"If the leg doesn't start to rot, then yes," he replied. "But heavily bleeding wounds rarely rot. Somehow, the artery in the thigh has not been cut, so you will probably recover, though not soon. I advise you to stay here, because you'll have to wash the wound with herbal decoctions, and I have everything at hand here."

"I will," said Sir Winslow seriously. "Father, that outlaw who hurt me... I don't understand him. Is he waging a private war? After all, he is not a robber, but a knight of flesh and blood. Why is he doing this?"

Prospero shrugged.

"I don't know? I think he's just having trouble with balance. Not so long ago, he made such a strange oath that he would remain faithful to the crown of France. And since he is honorable and honest to an exaggeration..."

He paused and stared at the window. He wasn't sure how to explain it to an Englishman, surely convinced of the rightness of his king's claims, what for Theo and his ilk was the reassertion of English domination in their homeland. How to convey the pain of thousands of righteous French knights in a few words?

"The tract has been signed," said Sir Winslow, guessing his thoughts.

"Ah, the tract," Prospero sighed. "The tract was signed by kings, and their subjects suffer, especially the commoners who are defended by Theo. You all consider them your working cattle and you don't care what they feel or how they live. Theo has learned to see them as his brothers and friends, so he fights to protect them and will continue to fight. He takes revenge for what your kin do to the poor, and does not mind interfering with kings."

"What do you think, father?" The Englishman asked eagerly. "You're French too."

The monk looked at him severely.

"I am a religious," he said emphatically. "I love my neighbor as myself. I don't do to others what is unpleasant to me. And I don't think I'm not being tried. Even if I were to support this youngster's actions, I'd not tell him. Besides, he doesn't ask for my opinion."

Sir Winslow was silent for a moment.

"Will there be ink, a quill, and a piece of blank parchment?" he asked after a moment in a tired voice. "My cousin, the Prince of Wales, is stationed not far from here. I'd like to send him a message about what's happening to me, because he knows what I'm here for, and if he thinks I've been killed, he might do something very ugly. Could one of the brothers' take the letter? Just don't let him talk too much."

"There will be no problem with that, my brothers have vowed to remain silent," Prospero replied curtly.

He did not like such a guest under his roof very much, but he could not refuse even the enemy of Christian service. The news that the Black Prince was nearby with his army was not auspicious, for this man was famous for his rather barbaric methods of warfare, despite his courtly manners and artistic passion. His charm and wit were celebrated throughout Europe, and at the same time feared like the devil. He was dangerous, amoral and violent, and at the same time he knew how to be a clever diplomat when the need arose.

"I wonder what the hell they brought him here for," Prospero thought as he brought the wounded man's writing instruments. In his mind he was already reprimanding Theo for bringing the uninvited guest on his neck, but he gave it up when he realized that it had given them an important message: precisely that the Black Prince was around.

****

Captain Moore entered the chamber where Don Paulino was working on the inventory lists prepared for Roger de Valois. His expression showed that he was not bringing good news.

"Sir Winslow sent a letter to Prince Edward," he said grimly. "Theo hurt him quite seriously but he spared his life. He's now in the Discalced Carmelite Monastery by the lake. Our friend scratched his side and thigh, and then kindly took him to the care of the monks. Winslow reportedly writes about him in superlatives. In other words, failure again."

Don Paulino nodded and thoughtfully chewing on the end of his goose feather.

"We should have anticipated this," he said after a moment. "That damned outlaw always lands to his feet like a cat. He can be polite and charming, and almost everyone can be deceived by his sweet face... If the peasants had not supported him so unconditionally... Maybe something would be possible then..."

He paused and pounded his fist on the table until the inkwell jumped and deep blue ink spurted out, staining everything around him.

"That I didn't think of it earlier either!" He shouted. "Captain, gather a dozen or so volunteers from among the soldiers, we'll lure this fox out of the burrow."

"How?" Moore was skeptical. Previous attempts to catch the troublesome outlaw had failed and had cost the lives of many of the soldiers serving under his orders. He had no intention of opposing Paulino, although he had no right to order him, even as a substitute for the temporarily absent Black Knight. However, he generally accepted his orders.

"It's as simple as a bonjour," the steward was feverish. "Theo proclaimed himself a defender of the population of these areas and he is consistently implementing it. Certainly, he can be lured by the news of the threat to the lives of those peasants who still consider him their senior. If we announce that when he does not show up, we will let the village burn, and hang the inhabitants on nearby trees, what do you think he will do?"

"Will this news reach him?" The captain asked doubtfully.

"I'm calm about that," laughed Paulino. "These outlaws hear the grass growing. Gather people, preferably those who have not dealt with this cub yet.

"Wouldn't it be better to put pressure on a peasant and reveal the location of the hideout for these outcasts?" Moore gave in.

"Well, Theo is not an idiot." The Spaniard rubbed his retracted chin with a hand and thought. "He wouldn't reveal something so important just a peasant. However, I think they will somehow communicate with him in times of need."

It was something that could work. He had orders not to kill Theo until the Black Knight returned, but there were other ways of taking vengeance.

"Okay. One can try," the captain agreed, "animated by the hope of getting the enemy in his hands.

He hated Count de Bongrais almost as much as Paulino hated him, but he also had a certain amount of reluctant respect for him. After all, as a soldier, he could appreciate both courage and combat prowess, and this outlaw did not lack either. He paused a moment before entering the guardhouse, staring at himself in the polished dial. The polished metal showed him a bulky, mustachioed man with a scarred face and faded strands around a large bald head, wearing a heavy jacket and leggings tucked into long boots and dark metal chain mail. It was an image more suited to a robber than a soldier, but he didn't care. He has served in the army since he was a child, and his appearance does not count, although deep down he sometimes felt sorry for his ugliness, especially when at games girls ignored him, turning to others, more generously endowed by nature.

"I'd like to watch this Frenchman be executed," he muttered to himself. "He won't be helped by his beautiful eyes when he hits my hands. I'll skin him myself."

If someone at that moment pointed out to him that he was caused by envy, he would have probably been indignant and denied it, but it was a fact. He envied Theo's beauty, youth and, above all, noble birth. He himself was the son of a London vendor, and he hated it. Maybe that was why he got on so well with Don Paulino, who, like him, was of low birth and his ambition could not stand it. Though he didn't always accept his plans, they generally agreed with each other as they do now. The captain entered the guardhouse, he chose the best soldiers in his opinion and proceeded to implement Paulino's plan.

About all this, of course, the outlaws had no idea, and no wonder. After all, they did not have "their man in the enemy's camp." That day, they mostly worked to fill the pantry, which was filled with terrible voids. It was getting harder and harder to hunt anything in the woods, and yet they had to eat. Yesterday's dinner, which consisted of a small rodent stew spiced with ground-grass grits, was a bone in everyone's throat and they would have liked to bite it with anything, but the trouble was they had nothing. So from the morning they chased through the woods, and only Martin remained in their "house", guarding the cauldron, so far full of only water.

Gwidon was the first to return, with a little boy blindfolded with him.

"You were supposed to catch fish," Martin pointed out. "We won't get fed up with this skinny."

"Very funny. Where's our chief?" Gwidon asked, unnaturally serious for him.

"Check in the hay. He's probably messing around with my dissolute sister," Pierre said, coming out of the bushes.

"I'm asking seriously," the troubadour said impatiently.

"I answer seriously," Pierre said, tossing Martin two wild ducks. "I don't think it would be otherwise. I came back because my sandal broke, but I managed to shoot those chicks. You will see, he will bring nothing."

"Why you don't like our leader? If he doesn't come back soon, with or without loot, there will be a shambles in the Two Rods," said Gwidon glumly, removing the blindfold from the boy's eyes.

"Did you make it up, or is something really going on?" Pierre asked suspiciously.

The boy began to cry. Meanwhile, other members of the gang slowly dragged into the clearing, mostly empty-handed and sour expressions. Theo was the last to come back with a half-empty quiver, and Berengard brandishing a bunch of shot hares.

"I always said you'd be a good archer if you put your mind to it," Berengard tossed the bunnies to Martin and frowned as he looked at the crying child.

"What's going on here?" He asked.

The little boy ran to the knight and embraced his legs, plunging him into terrible confusion.

"Save me, sir..." he sobbed.

"From what? More synthetically," Theo looked around his people for some explanation.

"Don Paulino brought the English to the village. They beat and rob, they want to hang. They say that if you do not show up alone, they will burn the whole village down and kill everyone," the boy cried, hugging him desperately.

"Ah yes," Theo finally understood what was going on. "Well, Paulino finally had a fresh idea. This cadent rat wants to pick me up, I think I'll give him the pleasure. Let it cost me whatever it wants, I get involved in it."

"Don't rhyme. This is my domain," Gwidon insulted.

"Okay, okay. Take the kid out on the road and come back here quickly," the chief ordered him sternly, soothing the boy as he could.

Gwidon obeyed the order as quickly as possible and, out of breath, returned to the clearing.

"You must be aware that if you go there, you are asking for some misfortune yourself?" He said to the chief.

Theo finished smoothing his tousled and leafy hair, then washed his face and hands in the stream.

"You are terribly down-to-earth for a poet," he observed, straightening up and wiping his hands on his jacket. "How do I look?"

"Like an outlaw without a ratiocination," replied Pierre. "What are you gonna do?"

"I'll surprise Paulino," the knight replied.

"Will you go there alone?" Jean asked.

"Of course."

"So where is the surprise?" Asked Olivier skeptically.

"The surprise is that I'll leave you in hiding behind me," explained his friend. "You count to one hundred and fifty and..."

"Up to a hundred and fifty?" Pierre interrupted him. "Holy God, we can't."

"No? What a bunch of ignorants," Theo sighed, lifting his eyes to the sky.

"Igno... what?" Pierre didn't understand.

"It doesn't matter. Which of you can count to a big number?" Asked the knight, looking around at his very confused companions.

"Me," Alain said and added. "Up to fifteen. I took that for shoeing a horse."

"Well. So you count ten times to fifteen," Theo agreed with resignation. "Then you attack those English dogs from behind. I'll be standing in front and absorbing their attention. Just don't wimp me out or I could lose my head. Literally."

"Come on..." The friends were almost unanimously offended.

"If we play it right, these fools will find out when it is much too late," finished the knight.

"It was nice to meet you, after all," muttered Jean, nervously biting his red mustache.

"Be quiet, squirrel. I actually know what I'm doing." Theo slapped him in a friendly manner on the back, then unfolded his slingshot and examined it carefully for fraying. He didn't think she was needed for this mission, but preferred to be prepared for any eventuality. After all, he did not know exactly how many Englishmen he would find in the Two Rods, but he kept all doubts to himself.

Others no longer objected. Theo was always able to impose his point of view on others, and he did it in such a way that no one dared to oppose him.

Meanwhile, in the village of The Two Rods, Don Paulino and Captain Moore waited for the effect of their actions, looking around impatiently. The villagers, spent in the middle of the village, stood paralyzed with fear, soldiers plundered their huts, dragging from the corners of those who had managed to hide somewhere, and robbing whatever they could. Most of the villagers did not believe that Theo would come to help them, for who would ever see anyone risking their life in defense of complete strangers? That the nobleman would risk his life for the peasants? Still, they looked around with irrational hope, ready to greet with gratitude anyone who would plead for them. And although both looked so diligently, the one they were waiting for appeared quite unexpectedly, as if it had grown out of the ground. He stood quietly, his arms folded across his chest, and from under the wind-blown mane he watched the crowd, calm as if he were watching a street show. A sword in an ornate scabbard gleamed at his belt, and an ancestral wrought silver gorget glittered on its open jacket. Even though he didn't look particularly threatening, they all froze in place, surprised by his sudden appearance between them.

"Are you waiting for someone, did you decide to stand here no reason?" He asked mockingly.

"So you are here! We were looking forward to you!" Don Paulino exclaimed. "The soldiers only dream of getting their hands on you!"

The outlaw smiled coldly.

"Then let them take me," he said with deliberate provocation.

"Oh no," replied Paulino flatly. "I'll not give you an opportunity for a heroic death. You'll come over here politely and hand over your weapon, understood?"

"It's a bad idea," Theo was still smiling, but it made everyone watching him shudder. "If I come close to you at sword length, misfortune will happen, at least for you and for your English friend, whose underlings are hiding so bravely behind the backs of a few scared villagers. What's up, happy England? Get moving. I'm one and you are out of twenty, maybe one will survive, who knows? By the way, have you started playing executioners, or is it an English custom to hang peasants when you are bored? Nice fun, I admit, just sick."

Captain Moore spat and spun his horse, but Don Paulino grabbed his arm.

"No. He's trying to provoke you," he warned him. "Have your men take crossbows, and as soon as this outlaw moves without my permission, let them put an arrow in some less important place for him. I have to take him alive."

"It makes sense," Moore agreed. Indeed, when several crossbowmen aim at a man's chest, his fencing skills lose importance.

It would be really hard to fault this reasoning, except that the soldiers did not have time to reach for the crossbows they had set aside. From nowhere, armed people appeared behind their backs and, before they could realize the new threat, the first killed and wounded fell. Paulino and Captain Moore, terrified and confused by the suddenly unleashed battle, did not immediately realize that Theo, instead of joining the battle, had done something else entirely. Slipping under the bellies of their horses, he jumped onto the Spaniard's saddle, right behind him. The Spaniard screamed in terror as a muscular, weathered arm wrapped around him, pressing his hands against his body, but then he fell silent as he felt the blade of the dagger on his neck.

"Captain Moore," Theo said aloud. "Please order your men to stop the fight or I'll slit that traitor's throat, and I swear I really want it. You captain will be next, and I can assure you that I will be in time before any of the soldiers come to your aid... assuming one of them will be still alive."

"Put your weapons down!" Moore shouted furiously. His soldier's blood was hot at the thought of succumbing to a gang of forest robbers, but he was a bright enough tactician to know that he had already lost this battle, and he did not want to waste his people's lives unnecessarily.

"That's better," the outlaw chief nodded. "Hey, that applies to you too! Alain, leave the soldier behind, not his fault he's a loser."

"Well?" The captain asked him sharply.

Theo smiled.

"Just take it easy, Captain, you don't feel so agitated," he said, and jumped off his horse, drawing Don Paulino with him. "So, first of all, you will leave these people alone, as you did enough damage here for one day. They are my subjects and I'll protect them. Second, let's make a deal: you don't rape on these areas, you don't murder or rob, and I don't kill any more English soldiers unless I have to. Otherwise, I warn you: for each slain peasant from this area and for each enslaved woman, one English soldier will pay me with his life. Is it clear?"

"Moore..." Paulino groaned, feeling the edge of the dagger cut into his neck.

The captain thought for a moment, trying to calm his agitated nerves.

"Agreed, let it be," he said finally icily. "For my part, however, I solemnly promise you, my beloved outlaw, that I'll hang you on any other tree when I finally get my hands on you."

"Okay," Theo said, unshaken by the announcement. "I'd rather hang dead in a French tree than walk alive in English colors, but I understand it's a matter of personal preference. As for you, Paulino... I decided that I wouldn't kill you just yet. And that's not a good idea to decorate this nice village with your guts. I'm going to take my revenge on you a lot more painfully, and that takes time, so for now I'm just going to leave you a souvenir."

He ran the dagger's blade down the steward's left cheek, cutting the skin from forehead to chin.

"It's an advance," he said with a nasty smile. "You'll be paid full payout in a while, but I won't say when. You will then howl for death. Well, Englishmen, get out of here, now, because I can change my mind and the whole deal will go up in smoke."

*****

"Have you seen those yokels? They did not even thank you," Gwidon stopped tuning his zither and looked at the leader returning from his evening bath in the lake.

"And what are they supposed to thank me for?" Theo asked with little interest, for the lack of something better, wiping his face with a Berengard shirt.

"How is that? You saved them," the troubadour said indignantly.

"He is right. If it weren't for him, they would be fine, so they owe him nothing," interjected Pierre cynically.

"Not true! They would be exposed to the attack of the English, anyway, but there would be no one to defend them," said Olivier warmly.

"It would be worth composing a ballad about it," Gwidon sighed.

"Don't you dare. I don't want drunks singing about me by the fence," Theo said dissatisfiedly.

The singer humbly fell silent, but a few days later it became clear that he was still thinking about this. Being in their favorite tavern, "Under the White Swan", they heard a rather pompous and in fact lame ballad about what had happened. However, Gwidon firmly denied its authorship and there was nothing else to do but believe his words.

The Tavern "Under the White Swan" was the favorite inn of the local residents, although it was said that it should be called "Under the Dirty Pig". People in the fullest sense of the word "decent" didn't look at it at all. On the other hand, the outlaws were frequent guests there, much appreciated for the fact that they paid in cash and did not bargain, and moreover, the innkeeper could always count on their help and protection. They also obtained goods that were difficult to find for him. In a province overrun by a hostile army, it was a valuable acquaintance. Of course, the rank and file of the English garrison also drank there, but it was easy to hide from them in the back room, which had a window overlooking the forest and a door through which you could discreetly watch not only the main room, but both side rooms. It had the additional advantage that one could learn more than one from the drunk soldiers. The forest people knew that the innkeeper would not hand them over, and they were on the best terms with his maidservants, so they stayed there whenever they had some time.

"A shoddy ballad," said Gwidon as he listened to the traveling musician singing. "I'd have written a better one, without a doubt, but the chief prohibited. And besides, from those pathetic rhymes it follows that you beat these thugs one by one, which is, after all, the abuse of a truth."

"Empty words, who you think that you would deceive us. You wrote it," Pierre growled.

"It doesn't matter who, it's almost all lies? After all, I have not drawn my sword!" Theo cried, flushing a dark blush.

"This is exactly how fraternization with the nobility ends for us," Pierre continued, nodding sadly.

Berengard, listening to the words coming from the general room, gave a short laugh.

"What nonsense," he said. "Although, on the other hand, in all the poems praising the achievements of great armies, only chiefs are mentioned."

"Exactly," Brother Bellette said. "And yet each of them alone was worth just as much as a camp zip coon."

"Not at all," Francois protested hotly, almost simultaneously with Olivier. "Because to be a leader you have to be careful. A chieftain's head cannot be used only for wearing a helmet, and zip coon can, what's the difference?"

He poured wine for everyone and broke off a piece of bread from the loaf in the middle of the table.

"I will compose a real poem today... It will be about a fight, about harm, betrayal, crazy courage, friendship that breaks all obstacles, uncompromising nobility, as well as love for a sweet girl, delicate as a flower," sighed Gwidon lyrically, resting his cheek on hand. His poetic flair grew in direct proportion to the number of mugs of wine out, and he had already drunk quite a lot that evening.

"Is my sister supposed to be that sweet little girl?" Pierre snorted. "Then you don't know her. You should have seen Bellette chase our village administrator with a pitchfork across two fields, for he had dared to slap her in..."

They all laughed heartily, Bellette's temperament well known to them. It was not for nothing that she was called "Termagant from Kamienisko" - she took the advances of village boys as something she deserved, but when one wanted to go a little further, he would get a hard slap at best. Admittedly, since the news of her relationship with Theo became known, the village suitors had kept away from her, not wanting to endanger the famous robber and at the same time their senior still recognized by them. There was a more difficult matter with the passersby, they were lured by the blooming beauty of an ordinary, seemingly country girl, which sometimes provoked trouble.

"I'll never understand what people see in this witch," Pierre sipped his wine and shook his head.

"It's natural. You can't see it because what if you fell in love with your own sister? Estrus, promiscuity and scandal," said Gwidon.

"Don't worry."

"And I'm telling you I'll lay you flat," Martin argued next to them with Jean, both tipsy enough not to pay attention to the subject of the conversation. "You are telling me nonsense here?"

"I swear, he wants to defeat me! This little kitchen boy!" Jean called, pounding his fist on the table. "He couldn't beat a ten-year-old!"

"Don't yell like that," the leader mitigated them, glad to interrupt the uncomfortable conversation for him. "You'll lure soldiers here. Anyway, what do you have to argue for, sit down opposite each other and we'll see who's stronger in a moment."

Everyone liked the idea, so the half of the table was quickly cleared, and then both friends sat down opposite each other and rested their right elbows on the table. Francois crouched next to Jean, and Olivier chose a place next to Martin, with which he had a greater friendship than with the others. They started to wrestle, encouraged by the shouts of their companions, but the decision was not reached, because Margot, one of the girls serving in the inn, peeked into the room.

"There are some Englishmen here," she hissed. "Already drunk, better one of you listen to what they are saying. It seems interesting."

"I'll go," Berengard offered, standing up. "I know this low language quite well."

"Go," said Theo. "Your good face will not raise any suspicions."

Berengard nodded, took the tray full of mugs from Margot, and walked confidently among the guests. The innkeeper was not too surprised by his behavior - by virtue of his profession he learned not to surprise anything, especially the ideas of his outlawed friends. After all, they had quite a few.

Berengard was moving among the Englishmen, pouring them beer and wine, wiping the table top with a dirty rag and, above all, listening carefully. The moonshine-flavored liquors had already made the Englishmen rush in their heads, talking loudly and cheerfully, paying no attention to anything. They were obviously new recruits, who had come to the area recently and were unfamiliar with the reality here. One could learn a lot from such rookies.

After some time returning to his friends awaiting him and having drunk a lot, he said:

"They are soldiers of one of the Black Prince's banners. They came here straight from Aquitaine to fortify the garrison. The Black Prince got news about us, or rather you, Theo, and he started taking an interest in you."

"None of this, he's not my type," interrupted his friend.

"How do you know, you haven't even seen him yet," Jean snorted.

"This isn't funny. This English prince is to come here for some talks with that traitor who took your castle," Berengard continued. "Someone from the dauphin Charles is also to be present at these talks. If someone asks me for my opinion, something big is being prepared."

Theo scratched anxiously at the top. Indeed, the arrival of fresh troops might indicate such a conclusion, and Prince Edward's interest in him spelled trouble. He was not a man who could get in the way with impunity. The inhabitants of the cities he had captured and the defeated fortresses - those who had survived - knew something about it.

- We only missed him here. You have to warn people and prepare yourself for any surprises - he said. "We're going back to the hideout."

He tossed a few coins on the table and stood up. He knew well that when his men had a little more drinking, they would inevitably provoke a row with the soldiers, and he wanted no one to know that the outlaws would come to the tavern and listen to soldiers' conversations in hiding. After all, it was their only source of information, and very reliable.

Returning to their clearing, the outlaws found Father Prospero chatting with Bellette.

"You're here at last," he said curtly at the sight of them. "Why didn't any of you come to the monastery for so many days? You are irresponsible. First you leave this Englishman on my head, and then you won't even be interested in whether he has healed or what next."

"You go to our commander with these complaints," Pierre answered him firmly. "I was in favor of slaughtering the reptile without too much ceremony, he wanted to be noble and chivalrous."

"All right, you idiot, because this swell is an important figure," the monk growled. "If you "slaughtered him", the consequences would be dire, not only for you, but for the entire province. Theo, come with me."

Moving aside, Prospero reached under his robe and handed the knight a roll of parchment.

"A letter from Sir Winslow," he explained. "He's really impressed, if I can say that, but I don't know if you should enjoy it, as he described the whole thing to the Prince of Wales, to whom he is quite closely related. I'm afraid the Black Prince will haunt you now. Don't laugh so silly, it's not funny. This man is crazy about finding enemies worthy of his blade, and you are considered France's second-best swordsman."

"That's nice, and who's the first?" Theo asked.

"Roger de Valois, he is his ally, so the Welshman will not fight with him," replied Prospero.

"A vile traitor. Don't worry, I can take care of myself." Theo unrolled the parchment and ran his eyes through a dozen rows of letters.

"A court bachelor," he admitted. "But he promises to cross my sword with me again, and this time he won't let me win. It's like asking him for permission... Father, in case you find out anything, tell us. Soon we will have more English people on our heads than before, and they are expecting a special envoy from the dauphin Charles, with whom I would like to have a word."

"I have no idea why, but let it be." Prospero shrugged and walked away.

The knight looked at Bellette and smiled fondly at her. The girl was sitting on a chopped maple stump with her hands folded in her lap and her head bowed. The rays of the setting sun flickered in her pale hair, lighting it with soft reddish flashes. The smooth face seemed to have the delicacy of jasmine petals; long lashes cast fan-shaped shadows across the cheeks. Her hands, though a bit too large, had long fingers and a surprisingly noble shape for a peasant woman. Theo walked over to her and hugged her, his lips pressed against her hair.

"Stay until morning," he asked softly. "It's getting dark."

"Of course," Pierre muttered, furiously watching them. He was still unable to come to terms with the facts and expressed it at every opportunity.

"Go lay an egg! They have the right to be happy," Jean spoke up for lovers, always on their side.

"I'll give them the right, till them hurt. And if you are so conciliatory, you had to give the count your own sister," said Pierre aggressively.

Jean shrugged his thin shoulders.

"I don't have a sister," he said regretfully. "There were six brothers, and all of us misbegotten like me."

"Dear company, he's right, leave this pair of lovebirds alone," Francois joined him. "They don't do anything wrong. As they say in my native Languedoc, no one died from being loved, but there was one who was born."

"Idiotic proverb," Pierre shrugged, yawned a long time, and made his way to his corner, where he settled down on the deer skin and immediately began to snore melodiously.

CHAPTER IV

Where your heart is

Bellette lived in the village of Kamienisko on the main road to Bongrais, with her father, her older sister and her husband. It was a common wonder why such a beautiful girl hadn't yet to get married, but those who knew her better knew that none of the country bachelors stood a chance with her. Despite her seventeen years of age, she reacted violently and insultingly to all matchmaking attempts, so it was initially said that the poor girl was in love with someone who had fallen in the slaughter at the castle. Then, when it was known that she was related to the outlaws, nothing was said. Anyway, she was the most beautiful in the entire property, had a reputation for being the best milker, baked delicious bread and it was known that she was not afraid of work, so every now and then someone tried to win her anyway, but no one managed to do it.

Bellette's father, an old and sick man, did not interfere in the life of his willful daughter. Nor did older sister Marie and brother-in-law, though they were concerned that the stubborn girl was wasting her life instead of marrying and having children. Marie, in particular, gnawed at what was happening, sometimes staying up all night waiting for her reckless sister to return, though she did not dare to point out to her that she was doing something wrong. There was something about Bellette that forced her to be silent and respectful. Years of service in the castle taught her self-confidence and independence, and instilled a certain disregard for rural bachelors. For them, it was yet another allure of an impregnable beauty, so they tried to get close to her sometimes, but always to no avail. Bellette, meanwhile, bloomed and grew more and more beautiful, so that it was impossible not to look back as she walked along the side of the road, straight and slender as a reed, in an always clean blue linen dress and a white apron, with golden curls scattered on her back. No wonder then that the young, richly dressed nobleman, traveling with his retinue to Bongrais Castle, looked after her with delight.

"Who is this field nymph?" He asked.

Don Paulino, riding beside him, looked in the direction indicated.

"She's just a peasant woman with an armful of weed for cows," he said dismissively. "She used to serve in the castle and now lives in the village. Even pretty, but conceited and loud-mouthed. Her name is Mirabelle, but once people thought it was too much of a name for an ordinary peasant girl and renamed it Bellette, and it caught on.

"Beautiful like a pagan goddess. What an attitude, what a hair... I did not think that you can meet such a charming creature in the countryside," the young man was clearly impressed and kept looking.

Don Paulino shrugged.

"If you like, Prince, I'll bring you that girl to the castle," he said. "I don't like blondes, they are kind of insipid, but it's a matter of taste. For now, however, I suggest you rest after the trip and eat a bit. Prince de Valois and the Duke of Aquitaine are already at the castle."

His companion smiled and urged the horse to pace faster. Paulino did not know what exactly the conversation would be about, but the very meeting of three men from such high families must have been interesting and entertaining. He felt honored to be able to participate, even if pushed aside.

*****

Theo was returning from the Carmelite monastery, whistling merrily. He wanted to sing something, but all he could think of was a playful Parisian song: "Soon, father, give me a spouse. No joke with God's will. If you don't do what I'm calling for, I'll be like public wenches..." Somehow it didn't seem appropriate to him to sing such things after the first confession in over a year he had just made. Crossing with Father Prospero, of course it was not easy, especially since there was a lot to confess about, and the old prior was in an extremely harsh disposition that day.

"When in fear, God is near, and when in illfare, Jew is near, yes?!" Prospero roared, making the walls shake. "If I hadn't blessed your parents' union in time and then baptized you, you'd have been thrown out of here! Christ, that you also suffer such heretics in holy land! In your opinion, your blue army has nothing better to do, but they should run to your aid?! If the eyes of Adelaide de Tourvelle, Dalibo, hadn't been staring at me from that wolf's face, I would have hit you so that you would see all the stars, even though it's only noon! Man, your mother would turn in her grave if she could hear you! There was no more pious woman in the whole province, and you... Wait, I'll do penance for you until you learn to hold your ugly tongue behind your teeth!"

There was much more to it, but all this mixing with mud had an unexpectedly good epilogue: the monk had given him absolution by refusing to do penance for the time being, because, as he said, the entire life the knight was now leading could be considered without exaggeration a penance. There was definitely something to it, but on the other hand, Theo didn't feel so bad as a fugitive. He liked the hard life he led and the people who were his friends against all odds.

"Freedom is a wine that quickly hits the head," as Prospero used to say, and yet it was freedom that was the most important part of this new life. Sometimes bitter, sometimes hard to handle, but still wonderful. Theo de Bongrais was used to breathing this freedom, and he himself did not know if he would ever be able to live again as he once did. In the woods he was dependent on no one and owed nothing to anyone, he lived as he wished and did what he wished, or so he thought. Youth easily adapts to circumstances that would have crushed an elderly man, and he was still very young.

He did not return directly to the hideout, although he had originally intended to do so, for thought had come across him that it would be good to visit Bellette. He hoped he could find her somewhere off the beaten track, where no one would interrupt them, and he smiled to himself at the mere thought. He was close to the village when he saw the familiar figure of Marie running across the meadow. The young woman was shaky and terrified.

"Lord, save us!" She cried, taking his hands in a pleading motion. "They took Bellette! Lucky that I met you, because I don't know what would be..."

"Wait a minute," Theo forced her to sit down and he sat down next to her. "Take it easy, Marie. Who took Bellette and where?"

"English soldiers, to the castle," she replied, panting heavily. "They laughed and said she was honored and should be grateful."

"So they don't know about us, that's good," he sighed with relief. "Try to put out the rumors about our relationship, okay? Now go home and I'll try to free Bellette. If she comes back and I don't, tell her I loved her so much. If we both hadn't come back, apologize to Pierre on my behalf for your sister's misfortune. Understand?"

Marie nodded her head so vigorously that she almost fell off her poorly tied bonnet. Before the knight could protest, she kissed his hands and ran back towards the village. Theo followed her until she was out of sight, then got up and headed for the castle.

Until now, he had avoided even walking nearby, he felt cold with the memories that the old fortress, this family seat had been awakening in him for several generations, stained with the shed blood of defenders, betrayal and the presence of English soldiers. But now he didn't think about it. His Bellette at the mercy of a vile traitor and ruthless enemy - it was more than he could bear. He wanted to swear, the nastier the better, but he knew it wouldn't do any good, though he'd come across quite a few foul words over the past year. Gwidon in particular enriched his little team's native dictionary with purely Parisian curses and insults, which he used when drunk with astonishing eloquence.

On the way, he picked up a handful of young mint and thyme. All the outlaws chewed on their fragrant leaves from early spring to late fall, claiming that they were invigorating, sharpening the senses and cooling the turbulent blood. How much truth there was in it, the young count did not know, but he quickly adopted this habit from his new friends and liked to chew herbs like them. He ate whole stalks whenever he came across a cluster of herbs, and soon he could not do without them anymore. The sharp, cool taste seemed to enhance his intelligence, and it was certainly something to do with it, for before he even got to the castle he had already made a makeshift rescue plan for Bellette.

It would be easiest to sneak into the castle through one of the secret passages, but that would be too dangerous - these passages were suitable for escape, but not invasion, and that was their main utility. The heavy closures could not be simply moved away from the corridors, they could only be opened from the side of the castle. It was also difficult to think about entering the castle through the main gate, and in view of the number of guards and soldiers patrolling the courtyard, breaking the walls, even if successful, would help. Death, even heroic death, was not his goal, so he had to be as careful as possible. Having eaten the mint stalks, he walked around the castle from a safe distance and became certain that it would not be possible to enter it in the traditional way, and the only unguarded place was not guarded precisely because it was completely inaccessible. This vertical wall of one of the towers had a window, but it was so narrow that even a child could not slip through it, much less Theo, who was over six feet tall and, despite his thinness, weighed more than a hundred and forty pounds. However, this was the window he was counting on. According to his plan, it could be useful.

He watched the castle and the soldiers for a long moment, biting his nails irritably until he was sure it was his only chance. The sentries did not guard this place, they did not even look in that direction. He dropped the rest of the mint in his mouth, then stepped back and with his momentum, clinging to the ivy overgrowing the wall, climbed to its top. Then, shifting a little so that the bend of the tower protected it from the eyes of the soldiers, he took off a long and very strong rope with a grapple tangled around his belt. Throwing it was no more difficult than firing a slingshot, and he was second to none in that. Swinging the grappling hook, he threw it with all his might, hitting the narrow slit of the window flawlessly. He jerked the rope to check the hook, then began climbing up the hill until he reached the ledge that enclosed the entire lock and passed under all the windows on the gate heights. That was precisely his purpose: by walking on that ledge he could reach one of the open windows and go inside. He had yet to figure out what to do next, but in fact the most tempting prospect would be to reach the Black Prince and take him hostage. Yet even he had to admit that it was unrealistic. The second option was to crush the first soldier encountered and put on his armor - he would then gain relative freedom of movement and temporary safety. For now, however, he had to reach that open window, and to spite the first two were closed. Such a walk along the narrow protrusion of the wall above the heads of the English people who did not even suspect his presence would be perhaps even exciting, were it not for the awareness that the slightest stumble would risk falling onto the stone slabs of the courtyard, and that would result in breaking neck or breaking all bones, which could be even worse. It would have cost him defenseless to the grace and disfavor of his enemies, or rather out of favor. He had to be very careful and, on top of that, quiet not to reveal his presence, because if he had been seen, any archer would have shot him down from this wall like a dove.

The third window he was approaching was slightly ajar, which seemed to favor his intentions. He was there when something he had not foreseen happened - the weathered stone collapsed under his feet so suddenly that Theo barely had time to grab the open shutter. At the last moment, he managed to bounce off the cornice and replant the window sill.

"This castle is almost three hundred years old," he reminded himself, gasping for breath. "It has the right to crush here and there."

The relief that he had avoided the fall was so great that he did not even think into whose window he had managed to jump so successfully. Before he had time to collect his thoughts, the world around him suddenly flashed, and then everything was flooded with dense, roaring darkness.

He did not know how long he had been in this darkness, but consciousness returned to him with a terrible headache. He was lying on his back on a wide bed, firmly tied with strong straps, and the ceiling, which he had to look at, whether he liked it or not, was circling over him like a drunk man. He knew the ceiling well, but he had never expected it to be capable of such evolutions. He stared at him stubbornly until the ceiling, as if embarrassed by his gaze, slowly calmed down. Only now he looked around slightly. He was in one of the guest rooms, freshly cleaned and decorated. There were guards on either side of the door, colors that vaguely reminded him of something, but he couldn't focus due to a mad headache. In any case, they were not the colors of the Prince of Wales. Both guards looked at him with equal interest as at the section of the wall. From behind the door came the raised voices of several men, no doubt including the voices of Don Paulino and the Black Knight. He didn't know why it suddenly made him angry, and then he wanted to laugh. The whole situation was admirably absurd. If Gwidon could see him in such an unfortunate position, he would not fail to compose a ballad about it, after which it would not be possible to show people. Only Gwidon will not see him anymore, none of his friends will see him anymore, unless after his execution they will steal his battered body and bury it. After all, wasn't this what Pierre did when his first leader, Adam of Armagnac, was hanged? Oh, whatever, he could be proud of himself. Not only he did not save his beloved girl, but he also fell as dumb as possible.

The door squeaked slightly, ajar by someone from outside, and he could more clearly hear the angry voice of Roger de Valois, with a slightly softer voice from Don Paulino. It was about him, it was easy to guess, but why hadn't they just entered? It was already interesting. When the voices behind the door subsided, another boy was heard, probably lying to a very young and at the same time accustomed to listening boy:

"Okay, okay, I've heard that before. This outlaw is my prisoner, I have captured him, and no one will come close to him unless it be my will. I'm done."

The door opened wider and a young noble entered the room, dressed in the latest fashion and with intricate curls. He closed it carefully behind him, walked over to the bed and bent his boyish face, barely shadowed by his first stubble, over his captive. It was kind enough, round and bright, but the gray-green eyes were sharp and searching, and a vague threat lurked at their bottom.

"I see your consciousness is back," he said. "I enjoy it. Do you have any questions?"

"Yes, there would be a few," Theo replied, eyeing the boy with a hostile glare. "Who smacked me so on the head?"

"Me," the stranger replied calmly.

"Somehow I was sure of it," he muttered, wincing involuntarily.

The young man smiled apologetically.

"A little too hard? Forgive me," he said. "But I didn't want you to strangle me as soon as you turn around. People talk differently about you, but everyone agrees that you are terrible raptus and choleric. Theo, don't you really recognize me?"

The outlaw looked carefully at the boy's face.

"Should I?" he asked helplessly, knitting his broad eyebrows until something in his aching head cracked. A vague association flashed through his mind, but quickly faded, leaving a void. He shook his head.

"Don't make me think now," he said. "The pain after such a blow is worse than a heavy hangover. I don't remember."

"Your memory is short. And who did you take the flogging for when the stupid puppy cut the tails of all the horses in his father's stable?" the boy asked him.

Theo sprang to his feet and dropped back to the bed, jerked by the restraints that held him.

"Philip!" He exclaimed. "Philip d'Evreux! Holy crow! I wasn't expecting you here! You've changed... It's been a long time since we've seen each other. What an irony of fate."

"Rather, happiness that you don't deserve at all," the Duke of Navarre said sternly, cutting his bonds. "What were you counting on? Do you crawl into the wolf's mouth without any protection, in broad daylight, all by yourself? You haven't grown up."

Theo sat up and slowly removed the straps from his wrists, wanting to postpone the moment when he would have to answer that question.

"I had a reason," he finally muttered.

"Probably, but be glad you only got a broken head. It could have been worse, especially if I and my people had been accommodated elsewhere," Philip sat down next to him and placed his manicured hand on his weathered fist. "Go ahead, what's going on here?"

The count looked sidelong at him and took a deep breath. There was something about the boy, something that inspired you to trust him unintentionally.

"Roger de Valois's men kidnapped a village girl this morning," he said reluctantly. "This girl... is my... my love."

He looked at him seriously. Philip frowned, then laughed.

"Ah, it must be my field nymph," he said. "Sorry, I messed up. I liked her incredibly, I mentioned it to this Spaniard, and he...

Forgive me, but on the other hand, how was I supposed to know? You've never had a tendency for peasants."

"It's more than a tendency... much more," Theo stared at the floor, then stared at the wall. He wasn't very good at speaking about what he really felt and thought, rather he hid it.

Fortunately, Philip did not need many words to understand everything.

"Well, for a fleeting love you wouldn't risk your life... Although who knows with you. You've always been erratic," he sighed. "Do you remember the time you had a fight with Viscount d'Artois over one of the manor houses? You were both unfledged teens then, but even then you had the habit of falling in love without memory. It was not for nothing that your ancestor was Jacob de Molay, the Templar."

"What's the Templar got to do with it?" Theo was surprised.

"How's what? The Templars had a motto that fits you perfectly. 'Your treasure is where your heart is'."

For a moment, Philip remembered those days when Theo was Prince de Candalle's squire, and he was a toddler who was less than ten years old, his father's page, unbearable and willful.

He shook his head.

"You're my prisoner now," he said almost sternly. "And that gives me the right to make some concessions on your part, don't you think? In other words, I have a request: train me in fencing. They say you have no equal, and I don't really good."

"Without a sword, it'll be a bit difficult," Theo muttered with a flash of involuntary humor.

Philip got up and went to the neighboring room, from where he returned after a while, carrying the sword taken from his captive.

"Here," he said. "Without it, you probably feel like without a hand."

The outlaw smiled secretly. This young man was obviously a sly diplomat despite his young age, and knew what words to use in any situation. He took a familiar hilt, and involuntarily breathed a sigh of relief at the familiar touch of carved metal under his fingers.

"So let's proceed to Lesson One," he said, weighing the steel in his hand.

"Now?" The prince was surprised. "You must have a headache."

Theo touched a sore crown with a hand and grimaced.

"I would be lying if I said I felt great," he admitted. "But remember once and for all: your opponent will not ask you what hurts you and how much. You have to be ready to fight at any time."

"Okay, but how are you?" the prince persisted, feeling obviously guilty.

"Like the last idiot," he admitted openly.

"And quite rightly so." Philip stood before him in the prescribed position, sword raised menacingly.

Theo countered his offensive foray with ease.

"Terrible attitude," he said. "Very elegant, I admit, but worth a laugh when faced with a real fight. Make your legs wider and bend forward a little. Wider your legs," I says.

"It's easy for you to talk," Philip grunted, struggling to meet his seemingly light cuts. "You have legs like a deer, and mine are a bit too short for such acrobatics."

He had not finished speaking yet as his sword flew into the corner, knocked off by a sharp slash at the hilt itself.

"Pick up," his friend instructed. "You should strengthen the muscles of your hands and arms, you are holding the weapon clearly too weakly."

He adjusted Philip's fingers on the hilt.

"Go ahead and attack," he instructed. "Don't let your opponent breathe, and when he retreats, force him to the wall."

They clashed again until the sparks went off the blades.

"Watch your posture," Theo made a short foray, as a result of which the young prince unexpectedly found himself on the floor. "And you're done. You must listen to what I say to you. And don't look at the sword, but at the hand that holds it, and you will not be surprised."

Philip concentrated, deciding to go into attack, which was much better than in defense, because he was taught offensive techniques by the country famous Yves d'Ancoille, a great swordsman, considered undefeated. For now, however, Theo had effectively prevented him from making this volte.

"Make your legs wider, or you're about to fall down," he warned, then made a feint and a quick half-turn. "What, didn't I tell you? Get up, unless you've had enough."

"Never enough! I'm up now." Philip picked up his sword and picked himself up from the floor. "You're really brilliant, you know? What a loss that you cannot participate in tournaments."

"That is my least concern," the outlaw laughed. "Come on. Now attack, you can for real."

"I can? Word?" the prince asked cheerfully.

He gripped the hilt of his sword tighter and crouched down, bending his knees slightly. He launched a roundhouse attack, aiming at the opponent's tableware, but in the blink of an eye his sword flew in a wide arc as far as the opposite wall.

"D'Ancoille," Theo commented coldly. "At the end of the world I will know his hand. What the hell were you targeting the tableware for? It's idiotic."

"Well, I didn't mean to hurt you," muttered Philip embarrassedly.

"No worries. You are not a threat to me in any way, but alone, dear friend, you are revealing yourself. In a real fight, it would indeed be a sin not to take advantage of this opportunity."

He touched the boy's neck with the sword.

"Here," he continued. "Seemingly slight scratch and you die. If you fight without armor, you also have to be careful with your thighs and the inside of your arms. You can't do it at all."

"Usually a knight fights in armor..." Philip excused himself in confusion.

He felt that there was a lot of truth in these words, and deep down he was ashamed of his shortcomings.

Theo drew a bow with the blade of his sword.

"Everything has to be caught up," he said lightly. "The most important thing in combat is that you think what you are doing and at the same time act as if you don't need to think at all. Okay, it's over for today, it's starting to get dark anyway."

They both sat down on the bed. They were tired, the lesson was long and exhausting for both of them. Philip watched his prisoner. After so many years, he seemed more mature to him, but most of all changed, as if everything they had been taught at the court of Navarre had changed in him, perhaps even to its opposite. As if he already belonged to a different class of people.

The servants brought candlesticks and platters of gourmet food.

"I have ordered supper to be brought to us here in the next chamber," said the young prince, standing heavily. "There is little equipment there, so maybe we'll do some workouts next time."

"Why not?" he agreed.

He followed him into the adjoining room, which was indeed much more economical and spacious.

"This was my mother's bedroom once," he said, pausing briefly in the doorway.

"Roger de Valois changed everything here," Philip did not seem to sense the sadness in his voice. "Sit down and eat. What they sent me here looks delicious, and there is something to drink."

He set to eat with the healthy appetite of a young boy who has had a busy day behind him. His compulsory visitor followed in his footsteps, assuming that his weakened strength had to be sustained by something, but he was not hungry. Recent events have completely deprived him of his appetite.

"I thought you'd rather dine with those who invited you," he said, nibbling on his portion of roast meat with no appetite.

"They'll wait," Philip replied calmly. "Eat it, it's not poisoned. They would not risk poisoning the royal plenipotentiary, and since I cannot talk about my mission, let's talk about something else. I guess you know your case is very bad?"

"Oh, I know," Theo agreed. "They accuse me of treason, even though I was betrayed and people don't know what to think about it and prefer to stay away from me. It's like the saying: he stole a foal, or maybe they stole it from him, in any case he was involved in stealing the foal and thus he is suspect. Life itself."

"Tell me what it really was," Philip asked.

He had long dreamed of hearing the version of events from his friend's mouth, because what he had been told so far probably did not deserve faith. Despite his very young age, Philip was already an experienced diplomat, he was a minister in various missions for the royal courts of four countries. However, he had never been tempted to express his opinion on any subject, and he had never formed a view of any matter solely on the basis of hearsay gossip and one-sided accounts. Theo told him succinctly and without pitying himself about everything that happened in Bongrais and beyond. Philip listened to him, half-mouthing his mouth, never taking his eyes off his friend. When he finished, the prince nodded his head with cold sympathy.

"You got a really bad blow from life," he said. "How are you doing now?"

His prisoner shrugged.

"Somehow," he replied. "I have a handful of trusty and tested friends, a house in the woods, and a goal in life: hit the enemy wherever I can. I do not complain about the lack of adventures either. It's true that no one comb my hair every morning and does not bring breakfast, I have to take care of myself and serve myself, but I don't think that this is a reason to worry."

"This life work out well for you," said Philip with a hint of envy in his voice. "Your muscles and tendons are like steel, and although you are weather-beaten like a random tramp, you still know your noble birth. I don't know if in your situation I'd be able to adapt so well to the new conditions."

"You could," Theo rested his cheek in his hand. "In the forest, the world simply says to you: 'Live or die', that's the whole philosophy. I chose the first option because I found it much nicer. I lead a gang of thugs who, like me, have little to lose and somehow live their lives."

"Are you okay with that?" Philip asked, not expecting an answer anyway, and looked at the window, behind which was already completely black. After a moment he turned his eyes back to his friend and smiled.

"The servants will clear the table soon, and then you'll have a bedtime surprise," he said.

Theo got up from the table.

"Are you going to keep me here long?" He asked quite bluntly.

"You are my prisoner, and prisoners don't ask such questions," Philip replied, and the outlaw fell silent with resignation.

He didn't know what to really expect from a childhood friend, and he didn't want to insist on bringing him to something he would regret. The situation was indeed unenviable, and he had no idea how to get out of it. The indifferent servants cleared the table while he stared at the dark courtyard and the lights of the sentries' torches, but, engrossed in black thoughts, did not even notice that Philip had left the room and had not heard his soft words addressed to the servants:

"Tell Paulino to bring me this peasant woman."

Then he went back inside. It gave him perverse pleasure that he had in his hand a man considered to be the most dangerous robber in this part of France, and that he managed to trick him into agreeing to this dependence. Thanks to this, he could additionally play on the nose of people he despised, and whom he had to send to. He liked playing with fire so much. Besides... he liked him, and lately he had fewer and fewer people around him that he liked and not one he could trust. It is not easy being so alone when you are so young, and the life of a trusted diplomat in these complicated times was like walking on thin ice.

The door swung open and two servants pushed a young girl into the room, covered only with a sheet twisted around her body. She was pale and desperate, which made her even more beautiful.

"Oh, field nymph..." groaned the prince with delight.

"Don't come closer, my lord," Bellette stepped back against the wall. "Don't touch me."

"Am I that ugly?" Philip asked jokingly, stepping closer despite the warning and enjoying her beauty in spirit.

Bellette looked around desperately, then grabbed a silver candlestick from the bedside table and lifted it menacingly upward, her other hand holding the canvas that covered her. The door to the adjoining chamber opened silently. Feeling her hands grasping her, the girl screamed and delivered a blindly backward blow, the candlestick almost falling out of her hand.

"Hey, come on, watch out a little," came a well-known voice behind her. "Today I got hit in the head and I don't want any more. Once is enough."

Bellette dropped the candlestick and turned abruptly, falling into the knight's arms.

"Oh, how good it is you. I was so scared that I wouldn't see you anymore, or worse, I'll see you on the gallows," she sobbed, hiding her face against his chest.

"You should know by now that it's not so easy to hurt me," Theo stroked her hair soothingly, as Philip watched with a little jealousy. "And that I wouldn't leave you in danger."

"Exactly. And that's what I was most afraid of." Bellette wiped her tears and looked at Philip with apprehension.

"He's my friend," Theo told her hesitantly.

"Oh, that's okay, because I really didn't know what to ask God for," the girl sat down on the bed, trying to calm down.

"Best of wisdom for your knight," prompted the young prince. "It's a real miracle he's still alive. Well, lovebirds, go to the next room for the night, but it's a pity without me. This is my fate already. I won't spy on you, word. Good night."

In the days that followed, things fell in relative order. In the morning, the Duke of Navarre spent long hours in mysterious councils with Roger de Valois, the Black Prince, and several equally mysterious, unidentified guests of the castle. At that time, Bellette, which no one was guarding, helped in the kitchen. She could go wherever she wanted, and since she had successfully pretended to be stupid, no one was embarrassed by her and she could overhear more than one thing, of which she later reported to her lover. In the afternoon, Philip returned to the guest quarters and spent a good time until the evening learning fencing and having friendly chats. This arrangement suited him perfectly, and he was not at all interested in what his prisoner thought about it.

It must also be honestly admitted that he defended him against the Black Prince and his henchmen, not allowing them to enter the guest rooms. He replied to all arguments on their part:

"You could have made an effort, it's too late now."

"But, Philip, he's a dangerous man. Who knows what will come to his mind one night." Roger de Valois argued him.

"Your Majesty, it is true. Better if you hand over your prisoner to us before any misfortune happens," Don Paulino supported him, but it was to no avail.

"That's my concern," Philip said carelessly as he headed for the door. "Not yours by any means. Better accept that you won't get him, and certainly not this time. My people only obey my orders, so don't try to finagle them, because I wouldn't want my pleasant stay here to be spoiled by the sight of chopped up hosts."

At these words, Don Paulino flinched as though an arrow had stung him, and the Black Knight bit his lips angrily.

"There must be a way, dammit," he muttered as Philip disappeared down the hall.

"We have to think."

"If this outlaw has his weapon, he will get chopped up sooner than caught alive," the Spaniard replied, almost despairingly. "And he's damn good at a sword. Perhaps one prince Edward would take offense at him, but he would not descend in pursuit of some thug."

"Someday, I might have the opportunity to try this youngster's hand myself," said the Black Knight thoughtfully, nibbling at his pointy goatee. "His father was killed by my hand, and I can also kill son. Now, however, we cannot openly oppose this pompous brat, because in his person we would offend the regent. What a situation. Listen up, Paulino, how about using this peasant woman somehow? She has access to guest rooms."

The steward waved his hand contemptuously.

"She's too stupid to understand," he replied. "She's an ordinary cow maid, though she used to be a maid in this castle. She isn't able to see the forest because its trees obscure it. Better not to use such a girl as her, because they'll screw up the simplest of jobs. We have to come up with something else."

Bellette pretended to be a pretty idiot with such success that no one was embarrassed by her, not even him. She was safe - no one accosted her, not wanting to expose herself to an influential guest, and she spent the nights in guest rooms, together with her knight. Philip watched their cupids with a bit of jealousy, as he liked Bellette a lot more than he was willing to admit, but he respected her relationship with Theo and did not impose himself on her in any way. He was of the opinion that just looking at a graceful figure and a sweet face was a lot, and he was content with that. He was worried about something else. The artificial situation he had created could not be dragged on forever, with each day increasing the risk of failure. The Black Knight was wrong to think that Philip was unaware of the danger. On the contrary, the young diplomat was well aware of it, but he did not have the strength to part with his childhood friend too quickly, who once taught him to fish with a rope tied to a bow and climb trees. In the end, however, he decided that he could not delay any longer. That day he broke off his fencing lesson earlier than usual and sat down on the window sill.

"Are you tired? So soon?" Theo asked him, smiling as he stood beside him.

Philip looked at him distractedly and shook his head.

"No," he replied. "I only feel anxiety and generally feel bad."

He didn't really look happy and guilt was written all over his face.

"I can't do anything for you. Nothing, do you understand? I'm helpless. I believe your every word, but my hands are tied. You have no idea how complicated our country's affairs have become and what being a diplomat now requires. The regent doesn't believe anyone, and rightly so, because he has only traitors around him. Think, you had one with you and how did you get out of it, and Charles has dozens of them and he has to deal with it somehow. You are safe in your forest, and when he goes to bed in the evening he does not know if he will get up alive in the morning. In this case, it would be really better not to mention you because that would make it worse. You might even lose your knight's spurs."

"I don't wear them anyway," said Theo reassuringly. "I suffered from what happened to me so far, I would have gotten over that as well. Most likely."

"I've no doubts, but a ban is not infamy. Such a disgrace is for a knight to die in life and I'ld very much like to spare you this," said the prince sadly. "That's why I prefer to remain silent. And you have to get out of here tonight. I have bad feelings."

The outlaw looked out the window at the darkening space, where one could guess forests. He didn't mind running away. He had only been here a few days, and he couldn't sleep at night anymore, longing for walls made of rustling trees and a flood of stars flickering high. Here, in the stone walls, he felt trapped and felt as though he was suffocating. He did not understand how he could once have lived here voluntarily. However, apparently, he could as he lived somehow.

"Listen, I have a request for you," Philip interrupted his thoughts, handing him an oblong, small, but heavy package wrapped in velvet. "Take it with you and keep it in a place you only know, okay?"

"Okay. What's this?" Theo asked, weighing the received item in his hand.

"The extremis," replied Philip. "The last resort. I have no one to turn to, only you. Hear me well: if you hear that I have been in some particularly nasty trouble, of the kind you have experienced yourself, go to the regent and give it to him. But remember, only to him, to his own hands."

"Okay, it will happen as you like," Theo tucked the package into his jacket and stretched, straightening his bones. "And you already know how I can get out of here, and not alone?"

"Alone. I'll take the girl away from here, it'll be safer both for her and for you," replied Philip flatly. "I've thought it through well, my dear. Better that no one connects her with you, because it will be a misfortune. Now for you: can you zip down that window onto the courtyard in an instant?"

"And does the cat catch mice?" he replied with an ironic question. He could feel the thrill of excitement running through his veins, and he could hardly stand still.

"I'll be in conference tonight with the Black Prince and Roger de Valois," Philip continued. "By the way, do you know Roger killed your father?"

Theo nodded slightly, and his face hardened.

"It was a duel, so I cannot file an official complaint. Someday, however, I will pay him for it, because since he knew well that my father had been wounded in the right arm two weeks earlier, this duel was one scandal on his part."

"Well, yes," the prince sighed, and changed the subject. "I'll keep Paulino there so that he'll not disturb you, and my men will distract the guards by starting a row in the courtyard. When the guard runs to calm them down, you'll slide down the rope and go over the wall. It won't be too hard for you, isn't it?"

"Are you kidding? It's like walking on the bank of a small river," Theo laughed, looking out the window and mentally calculating the distance to go.

"If any of the guards, especially from the English garrison, block your way, just hit him and don't look how hard," Philip finished, and thought not knowing about what.

"If one of my smart mouth subordinates were in my place, he would say, 'Teach your grandmother to suck eggs'," his friend laughed.

"Tell me one thing: why did you stick your neck on me then? You know when we were both boys?" asked the prince after a moment.

"Your mother asked me to. I couldn't say no to the lady. She knew your father had an even heavier hand than mine, and I was healthier and stronger than you. There is nothing to talk about."

"It's because I should have confessed then, and not let you be punished for my wrongdoing," muttered Philip.

Bellette slipped into the room.

"Lord, I brought a rope," she said to Philip, pulling a coil of strong rope from under her apron.

"Traitors," Theo laughed. "You guys have discussed it all behind my back long ago, right? Nice."

"Nice or not, it doesn't matter, it's important to be effective. Nobody suspects you?" The prince asked the girl. She shook her golden-haired head.

"I'm playing a knothead," she said cheerfully. "And when that rat, Paulino, asked me once if I had anything to do with the young Earl before the conquest of Bongrais, I argued him out of it quickly."

Here she picked up the hem of her apron and began to twist it in her fingers in mock embarrassment.

"How, my lord, how would the master notice such a stupid girl from the middle of the village," she chirped sweetly. "And I wouldn't, excuse me, and would not dare to dream, although the young master was a like a beautiful picture..."

She laughed at her own harlequinade. Don Paulino, being a lowly born himself, at the same time admirably respected and hated the nobility, so Bellette's argument could indeed convince him. By a whim of fortune, he despised the peasants from whom he came himself, unequally more than a native aristocrat, and he could not imagine that any noble would not share his feelings.

"Philip promised to get you out of here himself," Theo said, embracing the girl in a heartfelt hug. "You will be safe under his protection, my lovely girl."

"I don't think so. He is a noble gentleman, though probably somewhat dissolute, but friendly to you. But be careful," Bellette asked, wrapping her arms around him. "You'll have little time."

"Don't worry," the knight reassured her.

That evening neither of them went to sleep. Philip went out to dinner connected with a mysterious meeting, and a pair of lovers sat in the dark, talking in low voices and waiting for the arranged moment to escape. They were comfortable with each other, in the darkness and silence that they were reluctant to think about the moment of separation, and they were very sorry to hear the sounds of a row in the courtyard, which were a signal to flee. Theo kissed the girl, fastened the rope quickly and slid down it from the window into the dark courtyard. He quickly crossed the open space, reached the wall and deftly climbed it, but here a surprise awaited him: the wall had already been cleared of ivy and there was nothing to hold on to going down. He hesitated for a split second, then waved his hand and leapt down into the darkness. The shock wasn't too strong. Happily he landed on the mowed grass and rose at once, running toward the distant line of the forest, for he knew well how dangerous it was to rely on a bold plan to succeed without unexpected obstacles. The night, a moment before moonless, brightened suddenly as the clouds hid the sky parted, giving access to the pale light of the month. The knight quickened his pace until he ran. Having passed the line of trees, he didn't even have time to breathe a sigh of understandable relief when several pairs of burly hands grabbed him and knocked him down on the moss.

"Oh no!" He screamed, kicking and pounding blindly with his fists. "Again?! This is getting boring!"

"Boring?" Berengard's nervous bass sounded over his ear. "Ah, you mongrel, so that you don't get too interesting!"

"Oh, it's you!" Theo rejoiced.

"You know what you're owed for this escapade from all of us? A decent spanking," his friend growled, helping him get to his feet.

Pierre gripped his shoulders tightly.

"Where's my sister, you rogue?" he hissed menacingly.

"Exactly," said Gwidon.

"Don't worry, she's all right," Theo replied calmly.

"I dare to doubt," muttered Pierre sarcastically, but calm.

The knight adjusted the caftan that had almost been torn off during these short wrestling.

"What are you guys doing here anyway?" He asked sharply. "Marie did say?"

"What do you think? She almost went mad, thinking she sent you to certain death," Pierre grunted angrily. "After all, you went and you disappeared. We didn't know what to think about it, because if any of those villains sitting in the castle got you in the hands, he probably wouldn't hesitate to boast about it in front of people, and here nothing. We came here and we sit there, bitten by mosquitoes, geese and the devil know what else, and you grumble at us. Typically noble."

"Do you want a smack in the mouth? Peasant-like?" The chief asked him. "I wouldn't let your sister get hurt. Philip d'Evreux will take her safely from the castle as he continues his journey. He can be trusted."

"How do you know you can?" Martin asked distrustfully. He was almost as ill-disposed towards the nobility as Pierre, and the surname d'Evreux did not evoke good associations.

"I know because I know. We are friends, and if it weren't for him, not only Bellette, but also my own head, I wouldn't take away from Bongrais. Oh Mater Dei, have a little confidence in me!"

"We have a little bit," muttered Pierre. "But not too much."

"Don't be angry, Chief," said Jean soothingly. "Do you have any idea what we went through? After all, to be honest, we went to the castle only to steal your body and bury it in a Christian way. We sincerely believed you were dead."

Theo laughed softly.

"I'll disappoint you, but you'll have to put up with me for a while. And now turn tail, because when dawn they will probably start looking for me. Philip will not be able to hide the fact that I've disappeared like a cloud for long."

"A cloud, damn..." Pierre growled under his breath, but he did not add anything aloud. Despite fear for his sister's fate, he had to admit that Theo would certainly not have left her in the castle if he were not sure of his friend's honesty. Even for him, a former participant in jacquerie, it was clear that this particular aristocrat could be trusted and, paradoxically, this was precisely the cause of Pierre's anguish. The fact that there was one knight like Theo meant there could be more, and that turned upside down his own little world where everything was clearly defined.

Of course, he did not neglect the occasion, and for the next two days, when they chatted at the village waiting for Bellette's return, he taunted his chieftain horribly. He knew very well that he was unfair, for no one was as worried as Theo, who hardly ever left his post and did not leave the vantage point, even when a violent summer storm drove everyone under the roof. It was doubtful whether even a hailstorm would get him out of there, for though he trusted Philip, he knew that often the best calculations could be spoiled by a stupid accident. The young prince, however, did not disappoint his confidence, and on the second day, in the afternoon, his retinue going to Troyes deviated a little from the road to escort Bellette to the village itself. Theo was so glad to see her that he barely waited for the retinue to disappear into the distance, then whistled the prearranged gang system. The girl looked around, then ran towards the voice, and after a while he held her in his arms, kissing her until she was breathless.

"Okay, okay, that's it," disgruntled Pierre turned his eyes away, as if he did not want to look at such profane. "Not enough of fondlings... Let's get out of here, we're too close to the highroad. We'll have the Englishmen on our necks in a moment."

His attention was not without sense - they were too close to the road, any random patrol could discover them at any moment, and it could have ended badly, for them or for the inhabitants of the Kamienisko. After all, the accusation of favoring the outlaws could end up burning down the village. Theo came to his senses.

"Let's go to the lake," he suggested.

He led the way, and the rest of them followed, talking lively and laughing noisily. Now that the tension of the last few days has subsided, they were all overcome by an exuberant joy to which even Pierre, usually in a demonstrative scowl, had to succumb to it. At Lake Theo stopped and took the girl's hands in his.

"Mirabelle, will you marry me?" he asked softly.

"She would finish nice thanks to it," Pierre interjected, but the others shouted at him, for the situation was too interesting to disturb.

Bellette turned pale at first, then blushed.

"Are you serious?" she stuttered.

"We don't know what else awaits us. Let's be better connected toward God and people," he answered her seriously.

"You will hang together on the twin gallows, is that what you mean?" Pierre interjected venomously, ignoring his friends poking at him.

"Will you marry me?" Theo repeated his question, looking into the girl's eyes.

"Oh, yes," she whispered breathlessly.

He kissed her trembling lips and slipped a ring of braided gold onto her finger, in which a dark ruby glittered.

"Let's go to Father Prospero for a blessing. If we still alive, he'll get us married."

The prior was not as surprised by their visit as they had expected, and without much hesitation agreed to bless their engagement.

"I hope you stick with yourselves," he said, almost kindly, placing his hands on their bright and black heads and covering them with a warm gaze. "Love is a gift so precious and rare that when you find it, you should never let it go for any reason. If you give up on it in the name of superstition, bigotry and hypocrisy, you will be unhappy until the end of your days."

He fell silent, staring at some very old memory.

"Love is the most divine of all divine gifts," he finished in a low voice. "That's probably why some people are denied the right to it. Do not let them separate you, and you, Pierre, if you dare to say a single word, you will get hit by the monstrance in the head so much that you will remember natural great-grandmother."

"I don't know what one she was anyway," Pierre muttered rebelliously, but he did not dare to speak.

"You know what? Let's go to celebrate it, I mean the happy rescue of a pair of lovers and their engagement," Gwidon suggested after they left the monastery walls.

"Good idea, Parisian weasel. Let's go to Under the White Swan," Martin beamed. He and Olivier were known to be able to drink whatever amount of wine they were served.

The rest of them agreed to the plan gladly. After such tiring passages, everyone wanted to have fun, and the "Under the White Swan" inn was fit for the purpose like no other. It was dirty and dark, but quite spacious, divided into three rooms connected to each other, the last of which had a window overlooking the forest. They usually sat there. The innkeeper and two girls serving were well-disposed towards the outlaws, paying fairly and defending against robbery if necessary, so they could go there without fear.

"Hey, Damasus, a barrel of wine and a roasted piglet for the beginning!" Jean called as they entered. "We are making a great, scandalous fun, who knows maybe we will even fight."

"As if it were otherwise with you," replied the innkeeper calmly, walking towards the kitchen. The constant brawls did not bother him too much, because although he still had to repair broken furniture, he was doing his best in general, as his tavern was famous for being the happiest in the province and had crowds of guests every day.

The first toasts passed quite calmly, then it got really cheerful and noisy. Gwidon sang playful Parisian songs loudly, Francois and Martin competed in mimicking the voices of different animals, with the rooster crowing loudest, the rest arousing animatedly about the recent events. Bellette joyfully participated in the game, taking a sip of wine from time to time, much more carefully than the men who went beyond measure at the very beginning.

"A beautiful ring," she said, examining her left hand. "I've never seen one like this."

"It belonged to my mother," Theo explained to her. "She liked it so much that she didn't hide with the rest of the valuables in the casket, but behind the sliding stone in her bedroom. When I was at the castle, I wanted to check if it was still there, and, as you can see, it was."

"I wonder what your mother would say about me," whispered Bellette thoughtfully.

He kissed her heartily on the cheek.

"She would love you as everyone who knows you must love you," he assured her tenderly.

"I'll write a ballad about you," said Gwidon. "But she must be sad. People don't want to hear about happy love, they prefer tragic."

"And of course you give them what they want. You should be a grisette, not a bard," Alain jibed at him, getting spiteful.

"Every troubadour resembles a harlot, it is a profession very similar, only less profitable," Gwidon replied, not at all offended by such a comparison.

"Gosh, we really thought you were gone." After a few cups of wine, Berengard was reliving those terrible days of uncertainty. "We were convinced we'd find you hanging in the Bongrais market. And here's silence, no one knows anything, not even in this inn where English soldiers get drunk, Weasel learned nothing. Next time, at least say where you are going and why."

"You would spoil all my fun," Theo poured himself more wine and flashed his black eyes merrily at Berengard.

"You know, there is nothing worse than having a leader who wants to eat up any row and give nothing of it to anyone," said Jean scandalized. "You should be ashamed, that's what."

"After all, if we went there together, damn, we would give them such a fight that they would not forget until the doomsday day,"

Francois supported him, already drunk at least. "What is it, we can't or what?"

"If I called an English soldier like this, he would cover himself with his legs and fly into the manure," Allain added, curling his enormous paw into an imposing fist.

"Next time I want to make some noise, I'll take you with me," the chief promised him, barely suppressing a smile.

He was amused and touched at the same time.

"Gosh, it's gonna be fun soon!" Olivier crowed happily. "Some thugs got in here, and the tavern is full!"

As per the command, everyone looked at the door and saw that a dozen or so tall men in half-armor and helmets with the sign of a lion are walking around one of the smaller rooms. Finally, they headed for the rear room. A reddish bearded man with a conceited and dull expression at his head, leaned his hands on the table top and fixed his little eyes on Theo.

"Get out of here," he said hoarsely. "You can leave the girl, she will need a company of real men."

Theo stood up slowly, smiling broadly.

"You don't know me, do you?" he asked politely.

"No," replied the soldier with a contemptuous scowl.

"Well, then you will get to know me," with these words the knight kicked the table over with a strong kick, which gave the signal for a merciless fight.

Everyone armed themselves with what they had at hand and after a while it was difficult to tell who was beating whom and for what. Other guests joined the fight, mostly woodcutters and vagabonds, who appreciated any form of entertainment, and a few peasants drinking to drink at an undefined successful enterprise.

The innkeeper, already accustomed to such situations, ordered first of all to put out all the torches. And since it is dark outside a long time ago, in the tavern a veritable Sodom and Gomorrah reigned, in which no one knew who or with what he was beating.

When the outlaws found themselves in the forest, their joy at the successful fun was unlimited. It was a good thing that Bellette remembered to get them torches for the road, for neither of them would have thought of it, they were so excited about the wine and the fight that they would love to go back to the tavern. Fortunately, they still had enough common sense not to risk a fight with a regular unit that arrived at the inn, probably notified by an envoy of the attacked soldiers. Jean, who always knew what to do, had pulled a large wineskin off a table at the last moment, and now, on their way back to the hideout, they passed it from hand to hand until they had toomed to the bottom, which they had managed to do before they had even reached purpose.

"This is the best engagement party I've ever attended," Martin said before he collapsed onto his bed and snored loudly. The rest of the gang unanimously agreed with him (as the oldest of them he had the most experience) and followed his example.

It is simple that after such a merry evening everyone slept until noon, except for Berengard, who got up quite early and went to the village. Having returned, he went to the attic and unceremoniously set about waking up his leader. It was only after the fourth shake that Theo opened his eyes and looked at his friend as if he had seen him for the first time in his life.

"Oh, hello," he said amiably. "How are you?"

"Thank you, not bad, and how are you?" asked Berengard.

"Perfect," Theo replied. "Except for the hangover, of course. The whole world is undulating in front of my eyes, and my head... Never mind."

"There is nothing to be ashamed of, we all drank a little too much yesterday," his friend consoled him. "I've bad news."

The knight sat down and began to gently massage his temples.

"Speak," he agreed. "Why don't you shout the bells in my head."

"First, the ones we sprinkled at the inn are support from the Black Prince," Berengard began. "This Englishman is very friendly with Roger de Valois, which is so nasty that he has put his close friend at the head of the squad, and you hurt him badly. Second, Pierre has disappeared. He came back with us, I remember that, but that he drank more than any of us, the hell knows where he went, and with that previous message..."

Theo sighed.

"I hate leaving my friends in danger, but I don't know if I can even get back on my feet," he confessed helplessly.

"Drink some water," Berengard advised him kindly. "Sour milk would be great, but where to get it?"

He himself was not feeling very well, but better than the others, for he was famous for having an extremely strong head, and therefore he was much better than others to bear the effects of his lack of restraint. He helped the chief descend the rickety ladder and poured a bucket of cold water over his head at the well.

"More," Theo demanded, shaking himself like a dog from water. Berengard granted his wish without a word.

"The sun is high... Maybe he went to the village?" The knight wondered aloud, combing his wet hair with his fingers. "He has a girlfriend there, some Fanchette, though I don't know if he would have come to her in the condition he was in."

Bellette appeared in the clearing, fresh and joyful.

"Don Paulino ordered to announce that if he catches you, he will have you torn by horses!" she exclaimed.

Theo grabbed his head.

"Let him tear me apart, if only quietly," he groaned.

Bellette laughed and set the apparently heavy jug on the ground.

"You got under his skin," she said appreciatively. "Are you hungry?"

Theo paled, actually turned green.

"My love, if human life means anything to you, don't mention food to me for the next six months," he asked in a choked voice.

"At least drink some milk," the girl suggested, controlling her smile with difficulty.

"I hate milk. I'm going for a swim," he replied glumly, and trudged off towards the lake.

"Why is he so dogged about soaking in water?" Bellette asked, looking at Berengard. The man shrugged.

"Father got him used to it. From birth, he bathed him every day to toughen the kid. He had four sons with his first wife, all of them died of pneumonia, so he decided to try to save the fifth. The Countess cried every day, certain it would kill the boy, but the opposite happened: Theo never even caught a sore throat. He's so tempered that if he slept naked in a snowdrift, he'd wake up hot as a fresh muffin. If I think about it, maybe the noble children are sick with all sorts of stuff that they are pampered too much?"

"Well, no one spoiled this boy anymore," Bellette sighed, but she did not continue the topic, because other members of the gang began to come out to the clearing, plagued by a terrible hangover after yesterday's drunkenness. With shouts of gratitude, one by one they approached the milk jug, drinking it down in long sips.

"And how did these English strangers know who had hit them?" asked Berengard.

"It isn't difficult. They described the chief and everyone knows. He's hard to mistake for anyone else," Bellette replied cheerfully.

"It's better that they know who they're dealing with," Alain said, splashing his face with water in the bucket. "We hit them once, we can do it again. Where's Pierre?"

"Exactly," remembered Berengard. "Hasn't your brother been to the village sometimes?"

Bellette shook her head.

"I know he didn't fall into the hands of the English," she said, "because Margot from the tavern said they didn't take anyone, all managed to escape using the darkness. He's probably holed up somewhere and sleeping."

"I'm better now," said Theo, who had just returned from the lake, buttoning up his doublet on the way. "And if those pathetic soldiers want another beating from us, we'll give them, won't we?"

His friends nodded eagerly, for despite their hangover, they were still ready to face the whole world.

The bushes rustled around the clearing, and Pierre strode into the clearing hesitantly.

"Where have you been all night, parasite?" his sister asked him sternly.

He looked at her misguidedly.

"I'll give two thalers to whoever tells me," he replied in a harassed voice, then took a bucket of water in both hands and poured the entire contents over his head.

"I woke up in the raspberry bushes," he said after a moment. "You have no idea how well it sleeps there. What I did before, I don't remember. But listen to what happened to me when I woke up: it turned out that a few soldiers stopped next to my bushes. They were swarming in English, but I got a bit of it. Well, the wife of the Black Knight is coming from Orleans, and it's already today."

Theo looked behind him and his eyes lit up.

"From Orleans?" He repeated. "She must go from north. Let us greet the lady on my estate so that she will not complain later that she has had a boring journey."

Pierre grinned.

"Nice thought," he said, rubbing his neck with his wet shirt. "We can ambush her."

"But no violence," the knight reserved. "Just a bit of forced politeness."

He chuckled, ignoring the increased splitting of his temples... The rest of the gang applauded him eagerly, for while they were all feeling the effects of overusing wine last night, the urge to doggy pranks wasn't dampened at all in them, and the thought of letting your enemies know in such a mocking way was immensely appealing. Don Paulino, as the intendant of the Black Knight and faithful henchman of the Black Prince, took his toll on the whole area, so it is no wonder that slowly each outlaw's fight against him was treated as a personal matter by each of the outlaws. It was clear that the banal headache would not stop them from giving the duchess a memorable greeting.

The burden of looking out for the procession was borne by Jean, who, due to his thinness and small height, climbed higher than anyone else on the team, and besides, he had the best eyes. So, climbing up the tallest oak by the road, he made himself a comfortable seat of twisted twigs, and waited while the rest argued on the roadside arguing about their attack strategy. They finally got along somehow, though there was some trouble with Bellette, who suddenly decided to accompany them, and many arguments had to be used before she reluctantly abandoned that intention.

"Do you see her?" Pierre said sarcastically to Berengard. "If I hadn't been watching her, she would have been wearing men's pants soon. Here's what hanging out with forest thugs leads to."

"Don't be so hard on yourself," Berengard laughed, and was about to add something else when a shrill whistle and Jean's voice sounded from above.

"They're coming! A coach and a strong guard squad!"

"All to your seats and wait for my signal," Theo ordered hastily, nudging his companions with his nudges.

They fell in predetermined places and froze motionless, waiting for a sign. When the carriage wheels rattled on the road, arrows and sling stones spilled onto the accompanying retinue, and immediately after that menacing-looking, armed men with taut bows in their hands jumped out onto the road.

"Oh, Captain Moore," Theo said, meeting the commander of the unit protecting the coach. "What a nice surprise. How is it going? The head does not hurt, the tummy does not bother?"

"Give up on it, future gallows, these dubious pleasantries," said the captain with a calm he had learned from more than he would like to contact the forest gang. "Do you really think that your pathetic jumble will defeat a unit five times stronger?"

"Really five times? It doesn't matter, my people don't count," Theo replied with a broad smile. "Indeed there are more of you than us, but which of your men, Captain, is willing to volunteer to die as a hero? My boys' shots don't miss."

The soldiers were silent, not even trying to reach for their weapons. They knew it would be pure suicide as long as the outlaws' arrows were pointing at them. Seeing that he could not count on the active support of his people, Captain Moore changed tactics.

"Well, have you forgotten you're a knight and you're attacking women?" he asked with a contemptuous scowl.

"Perhaps let's not consider it too closely, lest I remind you sometimes of what Richard the Lionheart did after he conquered the Accra Keep with the women and children there," Theo retorted calmly. "Besides, it's not a robbery, it's a courtesy visit."

He opened the carriage door while the captain crumpled and tugged at his gloves in repressed anger, and froze for a moment in amazement.

In the carriage sat Adeline, the daughter of the Duke of Overnia, with whom he had been mated in his time, and next to her was a small creature in velvet, probably not more than eleven years old, looking like a doll with hair tucked in a golden net and tiny hands folded over knees.

"Who do I see," he said with venomous politeness. "Duchess de Valois, I believe. Congratulations on your good marriage, although I will not say that I am jealous."

"If you want to rob us, bandit, do your part and get out of our way," - the duchess said proudly. "We must yield to force, but not bear the company of you and your scoundrels."

"Oh, Adeline, you hurt my heart. Not so long ago, you were inclined to tell me something else entirely..." Theo was seemingly polite, glancing at the Duchesses's companion.

Now he remembered how he knew the little one. She was Adeline's sister, much younger, weaker, and more delicate than she was. Tiny and inconspicuous, she wandered everywhere in the shadow of her older sister, and hardly anyone noticed her. The only thing he remembered about her was that she always had her hair cut short, like a boyfriend, because as soon as it grew longer, she began to suffer from crazy headaches.

"My husband will order to hang you." Adeline snapped. There was pure hatred in her brown eyes, the hatred of a despised woman, and if Theo had known the fair sex a little better, he would have been more careful.

"He has been trying for years and has only achieved so far that the price for my head has tripled," he replied calmly.

Adeline leaned out of the carriage, glaring furiously at it.

"Get out of my way, you dirty, smelly bandit!" she screamed.

The knight looked offended.

"How can you use that language near my people? They are too well brought up to listen to this."

Behind him, Berengard and Pierre choked with laughter at this exchange, and elbows tossed with delight. The Duchess breathed deeply for a moment, trying to contain her agitation, then said calmly:

"If you're not gonna rob us, let us go. I don't want to look at you anymore. Get out of my sight and get out of my life best."

"With the greatest delight. I kiss the hands, fall to the feet. Respect the little princess and convey my contempt to your spouse. Have a nice stay at MY estate, Adeline."

He slammed the carriage door and waved his hand at Captain Moore.

"You can go!" he exclaimed.

"We'll meet again!" the Englishman shouted at him, spearing his horse.

"I don't doubt about it!" Theo shouted cheerfully. "Whether you really want it or not!"

The entire procession moved sharply from the spot, and when it finally disappeared into the distance, the friends could release their taut strings and put their arrows aside.

"Next time hello a little shorter, okay?" Jean grunted, rubbing his numb shoulders. "It was close, and I would have let go of the arrow and I wonder what you would have done then."

"Don't grumble, the fun was top notch. They were shaking, bitchy sons, as if there were half a hundred of us here," Gwidon chuckled. "I wonder what they will tell their master."

"Who is probably waiting for his wife with a longing not known since Henry II waited for the Alienor of Aquitaine," Pierre added cheerfully.

Theo shook his head

"It was hard for me to say it to her eyes, but I feel sorry for the Black Knight," he said thoughtfully.

"That will comfort him," Martin mockedly remarked, to whom Adeline, despite her beauty, made the worst impression.

But Roger de Valois did not need their sympathy, and if he did, he did not know it. He adored his young wife, who could well be his daughter, and had been looking for her carriage from morning, neglecting everything else. It was good for the health of all his surroundings, for which he was a really tough master. When at last a carriage escorted by soldiers rolled into the courtyard, he ran to meet her beaming with happiness, and did not even notice the very rare expressions of the entire retinue. The young duchess jumped out of the carriage without waiting for someone to shake her hand as was customary. She was so agitated that for a moment she only stamped her feet and clenched her fists like an angry child, until she cried violently and fell on the chest of her anxious husband.

"What's the matter, Adeline?" The Black Knight exclaimed. "Has anyone hurt you?"

Adeline pushed him away angrily and looked at his face with bright, teary eyes.

"Theo de Bongrais must die, do you understand that?!" she screamed.

"He? I thought you had a certain inclination towards him..." asked the prince.

"I hate him!" She interrupted him furiously. "I will spit on his corpse! Kill him, do you hear?!"

"I can hear you, darling. He will die, slowly and in pain, I promise you." "Roger de Valois stroked her hair soothingly, but she pushed his hand away angrily.

"You'd better keep your word," she said menacingly. "Because as long as this outlaw is breathing, I will not be able to eat, sleep or play as usual. Come on, Estelle, and stop smiling so stupidly."

The Black Knight helped the girl out, while trying to collect her thoughts. He was well aware that Theo was no longer the same kid with a head full of phantasmagoric ideas, but a formidable opponent the entire province would stand for if he wanted to. But he was not afraid of it, and he wanted with all his heart to bring about a confrontation, now more than ever.

Estelle jumped out of the carriage and looked at him seriously.

"I hope you don't catch him, Uncle," she said in a thin voice.

"Why is that?" asked the prince with involuntary amusement.

The girl closed her eyes for a moment.

"He is beautiful." she said with feeling.

*****

"Linette, you are also a woman, like your sister, tell me honestly, is this outlaw really so beautiful in the eyes of the opposite sex that you all lose your head for him?" the Black Knight asked his wife.

It was dark and silent all around, the silk sheets were pleasant to cool in such heat. Adeline, lying next to her husband, shook her head.

"It's a matter of judgment," she said. "There are certainly more handsome knights than he, with more classic features... although I don't know anyone with such eyes, that's true too... but he has some poisonous charm around him." He has an incredible charm, and I don't think any woman, from the milker to the queen, would resist his charm if he wanted to consciously use it. Why do you ask?"

The Black Knight thought it was lucky that at one time a cheeky squire did not want the pretty flapper she was then for his wife, even though their parents had already arranged this marriage between themselves. If he had bowed to his father's will then, he, Roger de Valois, would have only dreamed about the daughter of the Duke of Overnia."

"No no... I just think we'll have to find a fiancé for your sister quickly," he said after a moment. "It's too exalted a child to protract." She's a little too young, but let's get her at least, we'll be safer. Otherwise, ready to do some foolishness."

"She? She's unlikely to dare," Adeline yawned disdainfully. "But listen: we are both invited to the tournament in Orleans, let's take her with us. Maybe we can find someone there who will do. Why are you so in a hurry?

"I think Estelle has a crush on this outlaw," her husband replied hesitantly. He didn't want to scare or anger Adeline, but Adeline only shrugged.

"She's still in love," she murmured, suppressing another yawn. "Nothing to worry about. Fortunately, she is not capable of inventing some kind of madness. It's a pity Theo doesn't return these feelings, he could be lured into a neat trap."

"He will not miss it," the prince assured her. "And then he will die really slowly. Sleep now, my little gem."

"I'll dream of his execution," Adeline whispered, snuggling against her husband's shoulder and closing her eyes.

She hadn't promised herself anything big after the Orléans tournament, but pure coincidence had Theo found out about it and felt an irresistible urge to participate. He tried in vain to fight this dangerous whim within himself. His friends did not immediately notice that he was somewhat pensive, only when he refused to participate in a wreath shooting competition, cursed Gwidon for some clown show and at lunch sat over the bowl with a face indicating a complete lack of appetite, they became a bit worried.

"Go ahead, eat," said Martin. "I didn't put strychnine on you, my word. What's wrong? Any bad news?"

Theo waved his hand.

"Ergh, no," he said, starting to eat without appetite. "I'm just thinking about something..."

"Tell me what's going on, because you're about to spoil the appetite all of us. What Martin gives us is not very tasty anyway," Pierre urged him.

"You know! Maybe you will cook it yourself? Martin snapped, offended.

Their leader ate as if he did not know what was in the bowl.

"I think so," he repeated thoughtfully after a moment. - I guess you could manage without me for a few days?

CHAPTER V

The Trap

Berengard threw the spoon at the emptied bowl. "What are you going to do again?" he asked sharply. "There will be a tournament of knights in Orléans," muttered Theo. "I would go..."

"Spare me, probably not as a participant..." Jean choked of the soup with the impression and for a long time he could not control his cough.

"I just want to watch, don't worry," his friend explained innocently.

"Hey girl, don't frolic if you don't give me, don't show me!" Gwidon sang at the top of his throat, beating the beat with a spoon on the rim of the bowl.

"Exactly," Pierre said. "You will look once and you will want to. We know you, of course. It's not as good as you want to go there, then you have to take us with you. You must have someone to watch over you, otherwise you will get into something again."

"I'd like to remind you what the deal was," said Jean. "You promised that when you feel like having a bigger fight again, you will take us with you. Was it like that or wasn't it?"

"We're a team, aren't we?" Francois joined in. "Is there justice or not?"

"Is there any soup yet?" Alain asked, holding an empty bowl out in front of him.

"We all deserve a little fun," said Martin, pouring him the whole bowl. "You can get madness from sitting in this wilderness, no kidding. You have to go somewhere from time to time, right?"

"So, it's decided, we're going to Orléans with a whole bunch," Pierre ended the discussion, smiling victoriously. He didn't often win a fight with a chief, even if only verbal, and this time he was the top.

Gwidon stopped humming his song and turned to the chief with a very practical question for a poet:

"And what will you do when someone recognize you there?"

"Who would know me? I'll put on a hooded coat, in the crowd that will be there, no one will notice me," Theo replied cheerfully. "Besides, how would they know if I was going to go over there?"

"It's enough to know you, you can easily guess the rest," Jean muttered, brushing his red mustache with his thumb. He was happy, as were the others, for recently, since the commander's memorable engagement, nothing particularly interesting had happened, and out of boredom they were starting to argue among themselves, just as long as they had a reason to fight.

The life of an exile sharpened the temperaments, warmed the blood, constantly demanding new impressions, as if the outlaws were trying to make full use of every moment of their life, in the conviction that the next one might not exist anymore. Now everyone was looking forward to the tournament as if they were going to play it themselves, so they set off the next morning. So far, they were sticking to the forest paths, but not far from Orléans, they mingled with other travelers. Theo was right: so many curious people came to the tournament that they could hide among them without any problem. They just died in a crowd of almost equally dressed people, where nobody paid attention to anyone. As was usually the case on such occasions, an unusually colorful jumble came to town: jugglers, vagrants, street bards like Gwidon, traders of literally everything, from tacky clothes to cookies of suspected origin. On the occasion of the tournament, there were also smaller competitions, addressed more to the common people. It did not mean that the masses were not passionate about knightly tournaments, but for obvious reasons a livelier emotion in the representatives of the lower classes was aroused by those competitions in which they or the like could take part. Many newcomers from other cities and towns roamed the streets in groups of several people, so the fact that the outlaws stuck together was not dangerous.

The tournaments lasted from time to time to a week, so friends settled in a great inn, which the witty owner called the "Orleans Caravanserai" - perhaps someone in his family had participated in the crusade. The places in the stable were numbered and for each horse left, its owner received a plaque with a number engraved on it. It was an interesting innovation, taken from Parisian night shelters for travelers, and theoretically ruled out confusing mounts. In practice, it was different. Of course, the friends did not think to sit in the tavern, waiting for the main tournament, on the contrary, they used all the entertainment to their heart's content, fasted by a long stay in the forest, together, now separately. For the tournament, however, they gathered in a tight group and fought a real fight on fists and elbows to get the best position for themselves in the part of the audience "for the commoners". Of course, the stands were intended for the nobility, the benches for the townspeople, while the lowest ones crowded behind the railing separating them from the trampled ground on which the fights took place. Even several days were spent like this. Typically, the tournament included horse skirmishes, foot fights and a kind of competition in composing short panegyrics in honor of the love of your heart, and none of the viewers wanted to miss anything.

"Gosh," Theo whispered to his companions, his eyes sparkling over the knights ready to kill themselves for the gracious gaze of their lady. "Who isn't here ...Gaston d'Anjou, Ivor de Brenne, known as the Lion of Dhijon, the other is the famous Montroux, then Joaquin d'Hevri... Oh, there is also Paul de Guish, apparently invincible hewer... None of them would not admit to me now, but I know them all personally. Oh mommy, look at the box of honor, you'll fall in awe."

Everyone looked where he was pointing. In the box next to the Duke of Orleans, his wife, and his two growing sons, was Roger de Valois, accompanied by Adeline, in a white gown trimmed with silver, and little Estelle in green satin. Behind them, friends noticed Sir Winslow, scrawny but with a gaunt face on his thin face.

"Chief, why is the lady of your heart wearing white? I don't think she's a virgin anymore," Pierre whispered maliciously.

"She wasn't in my squire's time," Theo replied. "And she was never my lady, not now too. She wears white because that's the color she chose for herself. Her knight in this tournament is... let me see... oh, Paul de Guish. See, he has her ribbon on his arm."

"He's a good hewer?" Jean asked softly.

Gwidon snorted.

"Good? Nobody can stand him. I heard about him in Paris, he is a real executioner for opponents."

"She knew who to choose," Theo confirmed, biting his lips slightly to keep from appearing to his tormenting desire to compete.

He watched the fights with a hungry gaze, the way a man would look thirsty at a spring full of crystal water. At the same time, he was careful that none of his companions noticed the expression on his face. He had not realized so far how much he missed his old life, which could not come back to him, at least as long as the war was on. Fortunately, none of his friends thought to look at him now, busy with what was happening in the square, and it was very interesting. Paul de Guish turned out to be really as good as Gwidon said, for none of his opponents could keep his square for more than one prayer. Although the tournament was attended by knights who might have fought as well as he was, de Guish was the undisputed king of this struggle.

Estelle glanced from time to time at her sister, whose superior smile seemed to tease her immeasurably, until finally she could not stand it and exclaimed:

"You can smile because you are not fighting! If I had my knight here, I would ask him to knock some sense into this swagger who wears your ribbon!"

They all looked curiously at the honor box, and Adeline burst out laughing.

"You'd better stay quiet," she advised her sister. "For such a jerk, no one will expose to the mighty Baron de Guish."

Estelle jumped to her feet, straightening her entire tiny figure and stamping her feet angrily.

"Will there be anyone brave?!" she exclaimed.

The knights murmured among themselves, but none of them wanted to compromise in the service of a still immature, ugly and inconspicuous young lady.

"Sit down, child," the Black Knight advised benevolently, but disrespectfully. "You can see that no one will take it seriously."

"Or maybe?" Paul de Guish looked defiantly at the assembled knighthood. "Well, who's brave? Who will sacrifice for these beautiful eyes?"

Estelle tilted her head so that no one would see the tears of humiliation running down her pale cheeks.

"I cannot stick it," Theo muttered.

"I suspected so. Guys, grab his neck!" Berengard shouted, but it was too late. Their leader threw off his coat and with one jump he was on the tournament square.

"I take up the challenge!" he shouted.

"You!" Roger de Valois roared furiously, leaping to his feet.

Estelle, as surprised as everyone else, sank into her seat, staring wide-eyed at the haughty, slender figure of the forest knight. She hadn't expected him here, and no one had expected him.

"This man is an outlaw!" Adeline echoed her husband. "He isn't allowed to participate in the tournament! He only has the right to hang!"

Behind her, Sir Winslow stood up and grunted significantly.

"I beg your forgiveness," he began with exquisite politeness. "It is a grave offense to deny what lady say, but the tournament code clearly states that any knight who has not been declared a backbitten can take part in it, and therefore also an outlaw. Theodor de Bongrais is not under the infamy sentence, and I myself can swear before the altar that he is a brave and noble knight. I say this in spite of the fact that we are enemies and that his sword wounds still prevent me from standing on the trampled ground.

The Duke of Orleans nodded. It was evident that he was of exactly the same opinion.

"The Count de Bongrais has the right to participate in the tournament." he said flatly.

Paul de Guish looked at Adeline's blazing fury.

"Oh my lady, shall I kill him?" he asked softly.

Duchess looked at him, and an evil smile lit her face.

"Make it hurt and you won't miss the reward," she replied, ignoring her sister's horror.

"You said, most beautiful of the beauties," Paul de Guish bowed deeply.

Estelle, meanwhile, stood up again, trying to assume a dignified pose that was completely out of place with her childish form and little face.

"Come closer, brave knight," she said in a thin voice, a little hoarse with emotion at the moment.

Theo walked over to the box, ignoring the fury of the Black Knight and his wife. The girl tied a green ribbon on his shoulder, detached from her dress, and, with the solemnity of an adult lady, gave him a hand to kiss. Hiding a smile and some strange, tender emotion, the outlaw touched the tiny paw with his lips, which gave him a slight hug of fingers cold with nervousness.

"I'm happy to be able to defend your colors, my lady," he said, looking up at the girl's rosy face.

Behind the barrier, Pierre struggled in the hands of his companions holding him.

"Let go," he screeched furiously. "I'm going to kill him..."

"Take it easy, old friend, this butcher will probably do it for you," Francois persuaded him, while Berengard tried to twist Pierre's hand.

"Spit that word out, idiot," growled Jean, watching with concern what was happening in the tournament square.

The opponents bowed ceremoniously to each other, then moved to the center.

"Announce a meeting!" cried the Duke of Orleans.

The first assemblies went smoothly, as is usually the case when opponents met with about equal skill and strength. Most of the crowd thought that Theo had no chance against the Baron, especially because of the imbalance in armament: de Guish wore strong armor and a helmet, he also had a light shield of hardened iron, and the young outlaw wore only a leather jacket. Nobody took into account that he also had the strength and agility of a forest animal, forced to fight for survival on a daily basis. His sword and keen senses were to be his only shield, for a leather jacket did not provide any protection against a hardened blade.

"He's about to die, and what, are you happy?" Adeline told her sister, cooling a little with anger.

"Not true," Estelle said. "Theo is the best of all."

"Baby, why are you against me?" Roger de Valois asked reproachfully.

The girl smiled as she watched the struggle with an unusual vivacity such as hers.

"I'm not against you, uncle," she replied. "But my whole heart goes out to him, and I will follow him, even if I remain completely alone in this."

"You're a stupid child," the Black Knight irritated and stopped paying attention to her. What was happening on the tournament square was much more interesting than the conversation with the exalted young lady, who was clearly still poorly informed about what was possible and what was not.

Already after the first assembly, Paul de Guish realized that he had found an opponent worthy of his blade and he was very happy about it. He loved fighting, tournaments were his element, and easy victories did not give him any satisfaction. This poorly dressed youth with a delicate face and long limbs moved like a natural warrior, his eyes blazing with a will to fight that he had not seen in a long time. The baron respected him involuntarily. Just to come out and take the challenge, risking head, it really was something, and it certainly wouldn't have been the first to come. However, the baron's admiration was not so great that he would voluntarily give up the advantage that armor gave him.

Theo did not seem to notice the difference in weapons at all to his disadvantage. He was playing a game calculated to make his opponent tired, to irritate him, and to deprive him of the self-control necessary for a duel. Without his armor, he had greater freedom of movement, and with his agility and strength, he was able to use it properly. He parried the most elaborate cuts without letting himself be reached, and gave the baron no respite. Although he has not yet managed to reach it or the slightest point, he has managed to shake his confidence. It is true that de Guish still did not allow himself to think about losing, but he began to lose his humor as his strength ran out. He decided to go on a contingency plan. At a precisely calculated moment, he allowed the opponent closer than the safety margin and suddenly aimed a strong blow of his shield on the temple. Theo caught his maneuver out of the corner of his eye, a fraction of a second before the strike, and managed to get off the main punch line until the shield barely brushed his cheek. He swayed dangerously, but managed to avoid the blade that flashed dangerously close to his neck. Faithful to the principle that you must strike the iron while it is hot, Paul de

Guish struck again, making the same mistake that had nearly cost Sir Winslow's life in his time: he too confident had failed to protect himself. Theo countered, he stalked from the line of attack, hit his blade with all his might, right next to the hilt, knocking his weapon away. Before the baron could understand the situation, he was kneeling on the ground, his opponent's sword blade pressed against his bare throat.

"Kill me," he hissed through his teeth, wishing he had passed away sooner.

He could not nerve yourself to be overwhelmed with shame, to stare at his lady or whomsoever, so he looked down at the ground and waited for the killing blow. Meanwhile, Theo just shrugged.

"What for?" He asked. "I don't kill my compatriots, unless I really have to."

He grabbed his sword by the blade and with the heavy hilt struck the baron on the back of the neck, stunning and knocking him down.

"Get him!" Roger de Valois roared as he sprang to his feet. "Five thousand scudos to the one who kills him!"

"Just take it easy, duck face, or you'll be freaked out," Theo said amused, involuntarily using the country dialect he was used to.

The knights watching the duel did not even need this encouragement to surround him, for his victory was considered a personal insult.

"It's not right!" Estelle shouted desperately, struggling with her sister's hand holding her sash.

The outlaw stood in the center of the square and ran his black eyes smiling over the menacing faces around him, swinging his sword carelessly in his left hand.

"So, how should it be?" He asked cheerfully. "We fight fairly, one on one or all at one? Because it makes no difference to me."

"It doesn't matter to you, do they make you mince right now, or will it take a little longer, right? Now amen with you, monsieur bandit!" Adeline shouted victoriously.

"It's not right!" Estelle repeated with tears in her voice.

Theo glanced at her and softened his wicked smile a little to cheer her up. He touched the ribbon tied around his arm and recited with feeling:

"If green is your color, oh lady / It is right that you only adorn the chosen ones with it / You are like spring, a defeat of white winter / Light green, gently victorious."

The Duchess turned red with anger when she heard this all-too-clear hint to the color of her sash, and she was speechless.

"Nice, nice, but I would improve the rhythm," muttered Gwidon.

"And I'd break his paws," growled Pierre, and burst into the square, knocking the knights aside without ceremony, stopping only by his commander.

"You know what?!" he screamed.

"Of course I know," Theo replied calmly.

The rest of the gang joined them, making their way with their fists.

"What the hell are you guys doing here?" The chief asked them sternly. "No offense, but this isn't your place."

"Are we supposed to politely stand behind the railing and wait for these noble gentlemen to put you in order? A tempting perspective, but unfortunately we too know what loyalty means," retorted Berengard.

"What does that mean?" Alain asked curiously.

"What do it mean, it mean, but why don't you just go away from here?" Theo suggested. "Only accoladed knights are allowed to enter the matches, and you, well..."

"What do we need accolade for?" Pierre bristled.

"Chase the blackness away and kill him at last!" the Black Knight screamed furiously.

"Blackness? What's that word?" Olivier was upset.

"If we make it out alive, I'll kill you personally!" Pierre was still boiling with anger and didn't care who hears him or not.

"Okay, why not, but it can actually be later, because so far you have provoked a situation in which crossbowmen could interfere. I doubt this is an exhilarating possibility." Theo looked at him pityingly as if he were an idiot.

Suddenly, someone else appeared in the square. He was, to the astonishment of the outlaws, Father Prospero, the last person to be expected at a knight's tournament. The old monk was really furious.

"Disgrace you!" He roared loudly. "And this is supposed to be a knighthood! You are the first to drink, eat and rape captives, but when you have to behave with dignity, it doesn't matter, right!? It's not right, gentlemen knights, did you hear?! It is not right! A knightly tournament is not a country wedding, where one peasant pushes another with a rail! There are some rules here! St. George's Codex! And you guys go ten against one and why else?! Because he fights better than you!"

"Because he is an outlaw," Roger de Valois entered his words.

"Right, I am," Theo agreed. One glance at him showed that he was enjoying himself better than the king.

"This is a matter between him and the dauphin Charles!" Father Prospero did not pause. "He took part in the tournament as a right knight, not an outlaw. You are so brave, because he is one and there are so many of you? I remind you, gentlemen knights, one of the principles of the code: in times of need, each knight has the right to make another knight. There will be almost as many of us as you, because my old hands are still good."

There was so much despairing courage in the monk's voice that the knights surrounding them instinctively stepped back.

"Should I accolade you?" Theo asked Pierre.

"Just try it and I'll break your jaw, right here and now," his friend threatened.

The knights hesitated and looked questioningly at the Duke of Orleans, who in this case had the last word. The clink of spurs broke the silence. Sir Winslow left his seat, still moving a little stiffly but firmly.

"And I'll support you in a good cause," he said to Theo. "I'll not allow you to be treated dishonorably in my consciousness."

Prospero looked at the duke.

"It's a shame that an Englishman would teach us French people to behave in honor!" he exclaimed.

"He won't have to," the Duke said, ignoring the Black Knight's half-furious and half-pleading gaze. "Theo de Bongrais and his men are free. They can go wherever they want."

Adeline wanted to say something, but her husband squeezed her hand significantly. He already had a plan.

* * * * *

"Do you have any idea how to get out of here?" Pierre asked his leader aggressively as the gang, fleeing the pursuit, hid in the tangle of Orleans streets. "And take that ribbon off your shoulder because you look like an idiot."

"Not any more than usual," Berengard added maliciously, this time really angry at his friend.

They managed to lose the pursuit, but the situation remained dire - both the Black Knight's squad and the Duke's soldiers were looking for them around the city, and had it not been for Francois, who knew the city inside out, it would be quite bad with them.

"I don't want to be ambiguous, but if we make it out alive, you'll have to prove to me that you're still fit to be a leader," Pierre said flatly.

Theo took the ribbon off his shoulder and, curling it over his finger, tucked it into a pocket on the inside of his belt.

"I will prove what you want," he said. "That the snow is white, the grass is green..."

Father Prospero stood up and wiped his forehead with the sleeve of his habit.

"I thought I was going to fall," he confessed. "Who taught you to run like that, antichrist?"

"You ask who? The Englishmen," Jean snorted. "The shots are catching up the slower ones."

"Yeah. Listen, if you're not going to put down roots here, then I advise you to think about sneaking out of here, the monk said after a while, Where are your horses?"

"In the 'Orleans Caravanserai' inn," Francois handed the friar a bunch of plaques and a handful of coins. "Let father take them out of the city, although I do not know if father will succeed..."

"Don't worry, I have my ways. I will take them to a Carmelite monastery a mile from the city, look for me there." Prospero took them with a worried look and left, adding nothing else.

"Always so smart, figure out what to do now," Berengard said to Theo.

"To be honest, I did not call you in my defense," the commander reminded him coldly. "There was a need to stay where it was good for you, they would only look for me now."

"You think only you have the right to have fun? After all, we are one team, or maybe we all act on our own?" Francois was offended.

"Normally I'd admit you were right," the chief agreed with him. "Except this time it was entirely my business. Knight tournaments are something that doesn't concern you in the least."

"Speaking of prerogatives, one thing was not so strange," said Gwidon. "Who let you write poems, and in public? I thought we had a deal: I don't shoot my slingshot and you don't rhyme."

"Come on, will you hold a grudge for a few words?" Theo snorted.

"Not only him," said Pierre grimly. "Did you forget you're engaged to my sister? How are you not ashamed?"

"That's what I wanted to say," Martin joined him, glaring at the leader menacingly.

"It mean, you think...? Oh boy, you don't understand!" Theo cried, laughing.

"Not the first time, and not the last time," Berengard snorted, and grabbed his weapon as Sir Winslow suddenly emerged from behind a half-blown coal shed.

"Relax, I don't come as an enemy," said the Englishman.

"How did you find us?!" Jean exclaimed in amazement.

"Very simple," replied the knight calmly. "Everyone is looking for you, and I looked for a monk. Maybe I am asking stupidly, but do you realize that you have no chance to get out of here alive? The people of the Duke de Valois and the people of the Duke of Orleans are looking for you. The whole city is raging."

"And you've been bothering yourself here, sir, just to let us know?" Theo asked with icy politeness.

"No, to save your stupid hot heads. I offer you help, what do you say?" The Englishman looked at them with either superiority or sympathy.

Martin looked at Pierre.

"What do you think?" he asked.

"Nothing," Pierre growled, eyeing the English knight with an unfriendly glance.

"Well, kiss the old woman on the tits," Gwidon offered him innocently and dodged not to get fist's blow on the nose.

"Quiet, guys, don't argue," their leader silenced. "Indeed, if we do not take up this offer, we will be left with a choice between an ax and the rope, which does not fit very much to me. Let's say, sir, we trust you. How are you going to get us through the city?"

Winslow clapped his hands together, and two soldiers in his colors emerged from behind the cupboard. They carried armfuls of English uniforms which they then placed at the knight's feet.

"Change your clothes," said the Englishman shortly. "You will come as my escort and no one will know."

"Someone pinch me," Jean groaned. Alain fulfilled his wish with such commitment that the little redhead screamed in pain.

"I wish it were a dream, too," said Olivier, scratching his crown anxiously. "Chief, you decide here, so what do we do?"

"What we do, what we do... We have no choice. We accept Sir Winslow's help," Theo replied firmly, donning the light armor and all the rest. Others dutifully followed his example, turning into a neat squad of English infantry. Camouflaged in such a way, they could boldly go out into the street, reassured all the more that the soldier's equipment included not the worst weapons, guaranteeing the possibility of an expensive sale of their lives. For Theo, Sir Winslow had brought a beautiful gray horse, the rest had to walk, but that was no obstacle for them as they all had strong legs. Putting on their helmets, which changed them beyond recognition, the friends marched in a tight formation behind the horses, passing soldiers searching the city on the way.

"It would seem that you would rather be on the Black Knight's side," Sir Winslow asked Theo, determined not to abandon the ceremonial form of "you." The Englishman smiled with some contempt.

"They also call him the French Black Prince," he said. "Stealing this nickname from my cousin the Prince of Wales... no offense, but don't you guys have your own ideas? After all, your Order of the Star was a response to our Order of the Garter."

"Which fell from a girl while dancing," finished the outlaw mockingly. "And your king picked it up and put it on... He must have been very drunk, weren't he? Ah, don't get angry, Sir Plantagenet, this remark is nothing compared to what has been said here on this subject. I don't want to hurt your feelings by repeating all of this. As for Roger de Valois, this man steals whatever he can get his hands on, so he could also use someone else's name. That's the character. You don't like him, sir?"

"I don't respect him, so I can't like him," said Winslow. "But politics ignores my personal animosities, and I couldn't go to the battlefield with my leg injured. I had to do something, otherwise I would go crazy with idleness."

"No better with your leg?" Theo asked politely.

"Better, better," replied the Englishman. "I hardly limp anymore, you have seen. On the other hand, it could have been fatal, because if I hadn't blocked at least part of your punch, you would have ripped my insides out. Do you like the smell of blood that you kill like that?"

"It's not aesthetically pleasing, right? But it's effective," laughed the French aggressively. "Most of yours wear armor, and I have to get to them somehow to protect my own skin."

Sir Winslow gave him a hard look.

"Don't be so happy because you don't know everything," he said. "I give you life for life by taking you and your people out of town. The next time we meet, we'll be enemies again, and don't be under the delusion of letting you slap me like this a second time. Now I know and adapt to your combat system, so beware of me, Wolf of Touraine."

They both fell silent as the Duke's guard almost felt at them, followed by the Black Knight himself, surrounded by his guards, apparently conducting his own search. He greeted them casually without even looking.

"If you had any choice, you'd better fall into the hands of the Duke," Sir Winslow said softly as the retinue passed them. "I don't know how to die from a blow to the neck with an ax, but I guess it's nicer than in a torture chamber."

"I guess," Theo agreed.

He thought perplexedly that he might like Winslow, though he shouldn't.

They were already reaching the tollbooths, where a lot of guards were checking people leaving the city.

"Lots of them. If there was a battle, innocent people would suffer," the outlaw muttered, biting his lower lip irritably.

"And what do you care about this rabble?" the Englishman asked indifferently.

"This rabble is also people. I don't blame you for such an attitude, it is rather common... I used to think so myself... and yet in the midst of this rabble I found many intelligent and noble people. I know that I'm not one of them, it is impossible, but they are my friends and I'll not let any of them get hurt because of me."

Sir Winslow looked at him in disbelief.

"You wanna be the second Robin Hood?" He asked. "You'll finish bad, because the so-called the people are incapable of feeling grateful, believe me."

"What kind of character is this Robin Hood?" Theo asked.

"Ah, there was one, a fighter for equality, freedom, justice and the like," Winslow replied. "Not so long ago, because in the time of Richard the Lionheart, he collected over two hundred outlaws and almost led to a civil war. Fortunately, they took him by treason, because it is not known how it could end. But wait, isn't that how the Black Knight captured your castle?"

"Very funny," Theo growled in disgust, and instinctively pulled the reins of his steed down as several halberdiers rushed towards them, their expressions menacing and their weapons ready to attack. Undaunted, Winslow showed them his ring, and the guards stepped back, bowing them through. The friends were able to leave hostile city without any problems.

Having left a safe distance, they could finally get rid of their English uniforms, which almost burned their skin. They undressed hastily, Pierre muttering such words that Sir Winslow finally couldn't stand it and asked:

"Am I mistaken because of insufficient knowledge of your language, or is that dribble insulting you?"

Theo looked at Pierre and spread his hands helplessly.

"I believe so," he replied. "But take comfort, sir, it's only a small fraction of what he quietly thinks of me."

"I don't know how you can endure it, but you are so different from the knights I've known so far..." the Englishman said quite openly.

"If everyone in this world were the same, it would be diabolically boring," the outlaw replied cheerfully.

Sir Winslow wanted to say something, but just shook his head and drove away with his men.

*****

Everyone was curious about the result of the announced fight. Both opponents were known for their heavy hand and no one was able to meet them alone, or even in several. They had fought several times with each other, and although Pierre was a bit heavier and had more experience in fist fighting, he usually lost to the point.

"Why exactly are they still fighting?" asked Fanchette, Pierre's fiancée, sitting under a tree next to Bellette.

"Men are just like that, they have to fight together for the sake of well-being, but it's nothing dangerous, they will fight a little and be good," explained her friend quietly. "But you can see for yourself that today they don't feel like it. They walk around and scowl, and no one attacks. What's up, boys?! Get started!"

"Are we starting?" Theo asked doubtfully.

"What's wrong with you, will you listen to woman?" Pierre was clearly scandalized. "Remember once and for all: if you don't know what to do, ask the woman for advice and do the exact opposite. No, we're not fighting."

"Oh, that's a pity," Theo sighed, clearly disappointed.

"There will be many more opportunities," Pierre consoled him, putting on his jacket.

"Didn't I tell you?" Bellette got up from the grass and pulled down her skirt. "Now I will tell you something, my beloved wack jobs: Father Prospero asked for some venison for the convent."

"And dry bread and water are no longer grace?" Pierre asked aggressively, a fierce anti-clerical, but fell silent under his sister's furious gaze.

"Our pantry is empty too," said Martin.

"We do have a pantry at all?" asked Gwidon in surprise, but Martin, ignoring him, continued:

"I suggest that Theo and Pierre take care of supplying the venerable brothers, and we, I mean all the rest, try to hunt something for us. Whoever agrees, hands up."

"You need an enemy to surrender," remarked Berengard rightly. "But the idea is not bad. We must eat something."

"And let's go home. There is a lot of work to do at this time of year," Fanchette sighed.

When the girls left, the men talked to each other for a while, finally agreeing that they would meet in the hideout around noon. It might seem that hunting in such a crowd is a bit of an exaggeration, but there was so little game in the area that it took a team effort to hunt anything at all, and the outlaws were not picky and took whatever game they encountered. Theo and Pierre were lucky - they stumbled upon a fat deer relatively quickly, which they managed to shoot after a short chase.

"You are invaluable," Father Prospero said appreciatively as he examined the gift they bound. "I know that according to some monks should eat roots washed down with spring water, but I learned while in the Holy Land that a fasted person is susceptible to every disease, so I make sure that my brothers have at least a little meat every day. As a result, I do not have fever or bladder in the monastery. It would be impossible without you."

"All right, Father, you're helping us too," laughed Pierre. Although he generally hated "servants of the church," he was fond of Prospero. "You are our friends."

"Don't slander the people behind their backs," the commander mocked him.

"And as always, you only have jokes in your head. Can't you be serious for once?" asked Prospero, trying to be strict.

"We've tried before, and everyone laughed at us," Pierre replied, and the friends left the monastery as it was nearly noon.

They washed themselves in the lake from blood and dust, then walked along a secret path through the marshes that surrounded the islet that served as their home.

"Those bastards aren't there yet," Pierre remarked, looking around. "Are you hungry?"

"Sure, what about you?" Theo replied, placing the bow and quiver on the deer antlers attached to the wall for this purpose.

"I'd eat something too. A whole ox with hooves, for example, but there's not a bite in the hut," sighed Pierre. "Why don't we go to the inn? Do you have any money?"

"Not even a denarius."

"Such a high birth and you inherited nothing from your ancestors?" He sneered cheerfully. "I have, we will go to

Kamienisko. Bellette will feed us there already, and with which, it doesn't matter. I would even swallow a stone, if it was soft."

The idea was not bad, so Theo attached a blade of dirt to the door, which in the secret language of the gang meant "We went to the village", and the two of them started along the road through the forest. They didn't even get halfway when they came across Marie running from the other side.

"How good that I've met you," gasped the young woman, grabbing her brother's hand. "I was just running to you."

"Would you know where to find us?" Pierre asked cheerfully.

"I knew your hiding place before you even dreamed of it, and thank God that only me and Bellette know it," his sister retorted. "But come with me now, Count. I have to show you something."

"You want to show him too? Get under control, Marie, you're married." Pierre chuckled, but he fell silent as his sister gave him a slap on the cheek until the echo traveled through the woods. She was known for her hard hand.

She led them both to the village, circled the father's hut, and then the eyes of her friends saw a completely unexpected sight: Estelle de Villenueve sat on a bench made of rough boards, sobbing helplessly like a wounded child.

"Miss, please drink some milk, it will be good for you, miss," pleaded Bellette, leaning over the little girl.

They were both in astonished silence for a moment, then Pierre declared aloud:

"That's how idiotic ideas take revenge on you," and he turned his back in a demonstrative way.

"She came here from the castle and wanted to see you," Marie explained to the knight in a whisper.

The man raised his eyes heavenward with resignation, then decided to take matters as they were.

"What's the matter, Miss Estelle?" He asked, sitting down on the bench next to her. "Please confide in your knight."

The girl took a sip of milk and confessed with tears in her eyes:

"My legs hurt. I've never walked that far."

"And these lugs aren't for country roads either," said Theo worriedly. "But, little lady, why did you dare to do something so difficult and dangerous?"

"Don't mock me," Estelle asked him. "Do you know how difficult it was for me to sneak out of the castle? But when my uncle and that twit brought your men, I..."

"My people?" Theo interrupted her, getting serious in the blink of an eye. The girl nodded.

"They want to lure you into a trap," she explained. "They know you'll want to save them, and you don't have to be clairvoyant to figure it out."

"Well, yes," the outlaw sighed. "It's kind of you to care for me so much, but I don't know what to do. Perhaps I can bargain their lives for my own... and I think these two are counting on it."

He felt an unpleasant chill in his chest. One could not expect pity from these people, and he would probably regret being born at all if he was released to their grace and disgrace.

"That's bad idea. Uncle will do something terrible to you," Estelle said seriously. "Better just kidnap me and exchange me for your subordinates."

Theo was speechless for a moment.

"Excuse me?" He said finally. "No, look, let's get one thing clear: I'm not a kidnapper. I wouldn't even know how to go about it."

The girl smiled sweetly.

"It's okay," she said. "I've never been kidnapped before either. We'll manage somehow."

The knight looked helplessly at Bellette, who, however, did her best not to burst out laughing and could not help him in any way. Even though he felt uncomfortable under Estelle's innocent gaze, he had to admit she was right - the naive plan she had come up with was the only logical solution to the problem. Why was there such cunning in this adolescent, frail girl, probably consumptive, so inconspicuous that she was probably considered completely harmless and allowed to go wherever she wanted? Where did her courage come from?

He looked at his deputy.

"Pierre..." he began pleadingly.

"I won't listen to this," Pierre interrupted arguably.

"Yes, you will. Otherwise, only the two of us will stay in our hideout. The Black Knight and Don Paulino have imprisoned our friends."

It took a moment for Bellette's brother to hear what he said.

"I will..! I will...!" he screamed, ignoring the presence of the girl listening to him.

"Maybe, but later. For now, you will lead this young lady to our hideout and stay there with her. I'll have to bargain with whoever needs to be bargained." Theo put a reassuring hand on his shoulder. He wasn't sure if it was the best idea, but he had to settle for it due to lack of time to come up with something better.

"Just if you don't talk to her about nonsense, such as that the nobility are bloodsuckers and enemies of the people," warned his friend quietly.

"Don't worry," Pierre said, offended. "Do you think that when I'm a peasant, I can't behave anymore?"

"If I'm honest, you can't, and why, never mind," Theo replied, then left him and walked over to Estelle.

"So, my brave lady, please go with this man here," he said. "He'll look after you until I get back. Now I have to find a way to communicate with your uncle."

The girl took a small turquoise ring off her finger.

"Show him that," she said. "He'll know you're not fooling him. He gave me this little thing and you know, I think he likes me."

"For sure. Who wouldn't love you," Theo took the golden circle from her and slipped it into a pocket hidden at the waist.

Then he looked at Bellette, who, after Estelle had finally disappeared into the woods, was able to laugh unhindered and enjoyed it full breast.

"What are you laughing like stupid? Nothing funny here," he muttered reluctantly.

"You, silly boy, I'm laughing at you," replied Bellettte, wiping her tears away. "You'll always get yourself into some hopeless story. What an incredible absurdity..."

"Laugh if you like, but also give us something edible in our hideout," Theo sighed, deciding he wouldn't talk her out. "I'm not saying that your brother will lose weight, but this little girl has to eat something. She is terribly weak and fragile."

"And you, of course, like it very much?" Bellette asked defiantly. "She's not a thick-skinned peasant like me."

"How can you say that? Besides, Estelle is a child, do you think I could..." The knight fell silent, embarrassed, feeling that everything he could say would fall out somehow awkwardly. Fortunately, the girl was only joking.

"I don't have a lark pate, but I'll think of something," she promised him, laughing.

Having received that promise, Theo set off on a wander around the neighborhood, reasonably reasoning that Roger de Valois would probably send a message for him to villages and roadside inns, so it would be easiest to pick it up there. He quickly found himself right: he saw a boy relatively nearby, nailing a notice on one of the trees along the road. Coming closer, he realized that this was a message for him, so he tore off the parchment and announced:

"Tell those who sent you that the letter was in the right hands."

"Yes, my lord. I'm running, my lord," stammered the frightened lackey and turn tail.

"He's probably convinced I'll eat him for dinner," Theo chuckled silently and looked at the rows of letters stacked up. As he had suspected, the conditions were severe - he was to appear in the castle by the evening, alone and without bodyguards.

"What the hell do they think I have an army here?" he muttered to himself and thought about doing it.

He would have liked the meeting to take place in some open space, because in this situation, entering the castle was almost suicide, but after a while he concluded that the danger could be somewhat lessened.

Having thought out the course of action, he turned back and headed for the castle, determined to end the matter as soon as possible. On the way, he walked to the clearing where their horses were kept and saddled his grey horse, assuming that in unforeseen circumstances it would be easier to escape on horseback than on foot.

He directed his horse to the highroad and, without hiding, he rode to the castle, astonishing the sentries.

"Let one of you go to your master and say that I will talk to him either at the gate or not at all," he said politely, leaning his hands on the saddlebow.

The sentries whispered among themselves, and after a while one of them ran to the castle, from where he returned, accompanied by the Black Knight and Don Paulino, exhaling triumph.

"He's here, give me ten thalers!" he called aloud.

"Don't be so happy, Judas, you don't know what I'm bringing with yet," Theo chilled him.

"With what?" said the Black Knight. "I know. Either you give up or we slit your people's throats one by one."

"Forcible argument," agreed the outlaw. "But I also have something to say. Hold on."

He tossed the little object that the prince caught in the air and, glancing at it, turned so red as if he were about to collapse in an attack of apoplexy.

"Where did you get this?!" he roared loudly.

"The answer seems redundant to me. Let me just add that I left Miss Estelle in the care of a very violent man and, moreover, very much to me attached, so I wish it hadn't occurred to him that I might not come back."

"And if we don't agree?" Don Paulino asked eagerly. "Well, what will you do then? You, chivalrous and noble?"

The outlaw patted the horse's neck and answered casually:

"I don't know yet. I'm so lonely, so why not marry her? In the morning, it can be very cold in the woods, and I have nobody to hug."

"Ah, you pig!" the Black Knight screeched furiously, making a move as if he wanted to pounce on him.

Theo laughed sarcastically and aggressively.

"Okay, you won this battle. Tomorrow, bring the child to the crossroads of the highroad at first morning mass," said Paulino hurriedly, seeing that he could not count on his protector. "Then we'll make an exchange. And for God sake I forbid you to hurt her!"

"And vice versa. If any of my people are missing something, nothing to do with the whole thing," the outlaw threatened him, then turned his horse and went away into the forest.

Just in case, he wandered a bit along the way to lose a possible chase, but no one followed him. When he was in the clearing, Pierre, sitting by the fire, handed him a piece of bread and cheese.

"Bellette surpassed all of us when it comes to supplies," he said. "What did you do?"

"It's okay," Theo replied, his mouth full. "Tomorrow's exchange. Hope everything goes according to plan, because it doesn't seem like they are going to sacrifice the little one. I must admit that she saved me from a very uneasy situation, because I don't know what I would have done if it weren't for her."

Pierre snorted angrily.

"Of course," he said venomously. "You are supposed to be engaged to my sister, but you are just looking how to get some lady from your sphere. Supposedly, you're right. When your time for banishment is up and nothing lasts forever, you will look for just one like her. You make my sister unhappy, I always knew that."

"Eat me, will you?" His friend got angry. "What exactly do you want? You wish Bellette were married to some country brute who would make her children, starve to death in the pre-harvest season and beat her while drunk with a rake handle. Then you think it would be fine, but I make her unhappy, right?"

"Damn you," muttered Pierre reluctantly. "When you put it that way, it's really hard to argue with you."

"Then don't argue. You want to get rid of me, then stab me with a knife and bury me somewhere in the forest... or leave me alone and never bring up this topic again," the knight finished sternly and went to his attic to interrupt this conversation. On the way, he glanced at Estelle huddled in a pile of pelts, sleeping sweetly and peacefully, as though behind the silk curtains of her maiden bed.

"What a mess." He thought with an involuntary yawn, then threw himself into hay and fell asleep.

When the next morning he was awakened by the rays of sunlight streaming through the window, Pierre was gone, and the arrowhead stuck in the door clearly announced: "I went hunting." Theo washed in the stream, combed his hair, deciding that it would be worth a bit of a cut, and woke Estelle as gently as he could. The girl opened her sleepy eyes and looked at him unconsciously.

"What's going on... where ....Oh, that's you," she sighed. "I'm up now. I was asleep soundly."

Theo handed her bread, cheese, and a cup of wine.

"Sorry, we've got nothing better," he said apologetically, and started to eat himself.

"This is perfectly good," Estelle said, and added shyly. "I like it here, with you. I'd rather stay in the woods than go back to Adeline and my uncle."

The knight looked at her with some surprise. He had not expected it, but rather expected that the night spent in this miserable hideout would hurt the delicate aristocrat.

"This isn't a place for a young lady," he said after a moment. "Not really for me either, but what to do? Here it is all too often cold and hungry and dangerous. People, for your information only, also leaves a lot to be desired.

The girl smiled faintly.

"I know. I'm just saying..." she said softly, like a child who knows she won't get what she asks for anyway.

He looked at her with lively sympathy. She wasn't very pretty, but she was so touching with that helplessness and childish grace that she made him want to hug her, and he barely contained himself.

"Come on, my brave little lady, let's go," he sighed, standing up. "I got my horse right now. We have to be there before them because all this trade may not be successful for me yet."

*****

"Except for a few bruises, they didn't hurt us," Berengard was trying to consume both the bread and the piece of undercooked meat and the big apple at the same time, and he was trying to talk too, so he was not doing well. "Of course, we overcooled too, but that's not news..."

"Oh, sorry, I had cold feet," Francois interrupted him.

"We had all," said Gwidon, his mouth full. "Especially when we heard what they want to do to you, publicly, on the market."

"Really? I'd have terrible stage fright before such a public performance," Theo chuckled, happy to have managed to get it done as planned.

"More or less like the early Christians thrown to lions to be devoured," muttered Father Prospero, who was also attending this victory feast.

"If any lion ate our chief, it would be a pity not him, but the lion, he would poison him," Pierre apparently wanted to argue again, but Theo ignored the petty malice. Nothing could pierce the armor of his satisfaction with a successful rescue mission, and he was used to his friend's viperish tongue a long time ago.

CHAPTER VI

On the way to God's judgment

The spring of 63 came quite late, but it immediately stunned everyone with the warmth and multitude of young plants tearing out of the ground and the unconscious chirping of thousands of birds. The villagers, exhausted by the long winter, greeted it with relief, and the forest people also thanked God that this nightmarish winter had finally ended. It was also very difficult for them. In spite of carefully accumulated provisions, they often starved, they were troubled by the terrible frost, so that in the mornings they gathered at the hearth, trembling unbearably and unable to even speak, but above all they suffered from isolation in snow-covered forests. When spring finally dissolved the ice-bound swamp and the water dropped enough to pass, Theo and Pierre hurried to the village, where, to their immeasurable relief, they found both girls in good health, though skinny and blushing. Under an unwritten agreement, neither of them mentioned those long, horrible months, even though they were all difficult. Marie and Guillome's several-month-old child died of pneumonia, Fanchette's brother drowned under the ice when he was trying to get some fish for his family, and several of Kamienisko's elderly inhabitants also did not live to see spring. It was similar all over France, except for the Louvre, of course, where no one cared about such trifles when there were so many more interesting rumors. You could say that their sources thawed in the spring, and this year the main topic was Theo le Vengeur. Estelle de Villeneuve, whom her sister sent to the royal court, told ladies and maids about her "kidnapping", describing the outlaw as "the most beautiful and noble knight of France", which was enough to light small hearts and heads.

Theo, of course, did not know, and even if he did, he would not care too much, when drunk in the spring he wandered around the woods, or on spring evenings he counted the falling stars with Bellette. Anyway, there were other problems.

Currently, it was pre-season, a period as hard as winter. Quarry did not show up at all and supplies were practically exhausted. It was necessary to think about where to get some money, because what the outlaws had, they had given out to the villagers before winter, and now they were completely wiped out. Soon, however, the ubiquitous Jean learned of a large shipment of supplies to Bongrais Castle, which was to be escorted by a detachment of the English army, due to the presence of a casket with money in it.

"A dream opportunity. It'd be a shame to let this one go," Theo said with satisfaction as he listened to his report.

They left at once. Bellette stayed in their hideout to look after Gwidon, who was a little feverish but was making so much noise about it as if he were dying. The ambush was arranged with particular care, double-checking every point of the plan and examining every arrow in all directions. There was no room for any trouble, not even the smallest - the outlaws were superstitious like all their contemporaries, and a failure in the first heist this year would be fatal for their morale. Contrary to the stories circulating about their exploits, not all ventures were equally successful, it happened that they lost the game and had to hastily withdraw from the fight. The taste of failure was never nice, but now it would be doubly bitter. After all, they had to take care not only of their own supplies, but also that the people who trusted them would not be disappointed in them. It was a big responsibility and therefore they doubly cared about success. Self-love, of course, also played a role here. After all, each of the forest robbers silently believed that they were truly invincible, and if they were losing, it was only by a stupid accident. This way of thinking helped them deal with the main inconvenience, the outnumbering of their opponents. Fortunately, they also knew how to be cautious, and each of their plans was carefully developed and considered the worst variants of the development of the situation. Ideally, a stone-laden fishing net should be used to immobilize part of the ward. They did this more than once, but to spite they were all leaky now, and they did not have time to fix them, so they had to bet on surprise their opponents.

Fortunately, the wagon escorting troops consisted of newcomers to Touraine, unfamiliar with the tactics of the outlaws. When arrows and stones fell on them, they lost their heads and were unable to resist effectively. The young captain who commanded them bravely tried to fight and somehow pull the people after his example, but Theo, already in the second assembly, knocked off his weapon and put the blade of his sword against his throat.

"What do you need this for?" He asked. "Is this all yours or what? Take the survivors and run before I change my mind."

"Who are you?" The Englishman gasped. He was probably even younger than Philip of Orleans, and it seemed clear that he had been appointed by birth, not by combat experience. He stared fearfully at the man who held the sword blade to his neck.

"Theo le Vengeur. And the traitor in my castle will tell you the rest," the knight replied, and he withdrew, realizing that his men had enough time to loot what they could and escape. This was the tactic they used most often - catch what you could and run as fast as possible before the enemy had time to pick himself up and close ranks.

"Any luck?" he asked, reaching the clearing where his friends were waiting for him.

"Not bad," replied Berengard. "Money, weapons, food... and these two..."

He pointed to the young people lying in the grass. The boy was unconscious, and the girl was so shaky that she probably didn't even realize where she was. Their colorful clothes, torn and dirty, indicated that they belonged to one of the gypsy camps wandering around the country, so it was all the stranger what the English wanted from them.

"We have to take them with us," said Olivier firmly. "That boy was tortured, and she probably too, although she is in better shape than he is. If we leave them, they will fall into the hands of the English again."

"What's right is right. We take them. Let's go," Theo decided, not adding any epithets to the English, as much as he wanted to, and postponing any explanations for later.

Just in case, the outlaws tied blindfolds on both Gypsies and as soon as they could, they crossed the marshes to their hideout.

Gwidon sat in the clearing, basking in the rays of the spring sun, grunting lazily on his lyre.

"You're here," he rejoiced at the sight of his friends. "And who is that? Goddamn, Preziosa! What are you doing here, baby?"

He grabbed the sobbing gypsy in his arms and began to calmly stroke her loose hair.

"You know these two?" Pierre asked, relieved to knock off the sack of food.

"Sure," replied the poet. "This is Armando and Preziosa Corti, of the circus troupe that once took me in for a year. They are the children of an impoverished Spanish gang and a little dancer from the Vasilla camp, a banal story. They tour the country with other circus performers... so what the hell are you doing here?!"

He shook the girl with some irritation. Preziosa gasped for a moment with her half-open mouth, then stammered out in a barely comprehensible manner:

"Armando was supposed to deliver the letter... I don't know how they knew he had it... They wanted to know from whom..."

"What letter?" Theo worried.

The mere fact that the English took an interest in both the letter and whoever was to deliver it proved that it had to be important for both sides.

"I don't know," Preziosa sobbed. "Someone gave Amando a handful of silver and had it delivered to Cellient Castle, to Baron de Mercier. It was on our way, so he agreed, and how the soldiers knew I don't know anymore, I swear. They killed everyone and took us first to Meung Castle and then..."

The voice refused to obey her, and she started crying again.

"What was in the letter?" Theo asked, handing her a mug of wine. The girl took a sip and shook her head helplessly.

"I can't read, it was sealed anyway," she replied after a moment. "But they said something might not have succeeded in capturing Cellient Castle through that parchment."

"Damn," Theo muttered, losing his temper completely.

What the Gypsy was saying was all too clear to him, and in the light of his personal experiences it was becoming rather bleak.

"Who is Baron de Mercier?" Alain asked him.

"I don't know him personally, although he was friends with my father once," the chief replied reluctantly. "He's an old freak, but a good French, and that seems to be his main problem now. Cellient Castle is on the verge of influence and it was foreseeable that sooner or later the Black Prince would want to conquer it. And that the baron will not give it up voluntarily... Damn it, what to do?"

"Do you have to do anything at all?" Pierre was surprised.

Theo nodded seriously.

"If I don't warn the baron, they'll make a slaughter at Cellient Castle like in Bongrais, because it won't give up voluntarily, not a chance," he explained, shuddering at the mere mention. Even though he tried to forget that horrible day, it all stuck like a thorn in his memory and made him wake up at night with a lump in his throat and his heart pounding in his chest like mad.

"If you tell us that you want to go there alone, you'll get hit in the head," threatened Berengard. "Then you better not say anything unnecessarily. Guys, in my opinion, there is no point in trying to convince our leader, so I say right away: one of us must stay, maybe Gwidon?"

"Absolutely not," the poet argued, "I'm already healthy and I won't stay anywhere!"

"He's fine, Bellette?" Jean asked the girl who was treating the still unconscious Armando.

"He wasn't sick at all," she snapped.

"Let's not argue," Martin offered conciliatory. "Olivier has a sprained ankle, he certainly won't be able to walk long, and I remind you that our horses are gone."

"Not gone, we just ate them this nasty winter," said Gwidon with a shudder of disgust. As a horse lover, he genuinely felt sorry for this event.

"It's one thing. And when Olivier stays, so do I." Martin concluded his speech, undoubtedly the longest he had ever delivered.

Berengard looked at Theo, who nevertheless had the last word, but his friend twisted the strap of his slingshot in his fingers and seemed to be thoughts a hundred miles away.

"The baron has a daughter," he said after a moment, quite unrelated to the remarks of his comrades. "A pretty girl, apparently, but it's better not to get in her way. The baron wanted a son, so he raised his daughter like a boy. They say that she can knock down a fat peasant with a punch of fists, and it is difficult to keep her field in fencing."

He fell silent as Bellette gave him a look that announced quite a storm. The young Gypsy moved and groaned. He was starting to regain consciousness and was probably in a lot of pain after what happened to him.

"Look after them," Theo ordered. "I'll talk to them when I get back, for now we have to get together if our trip is going to make any sense at all."

He looked more closely at the surviving prisoners. The siblings did not look much alike. He had pale, almost white hair and was built like an athlete, while she was small and dark. Of course, what Gwidon said about them, did not necessarily have to be true, in the Gypsy carts, after all, orphans picked up on the way were often raised in the carts, so that these two might not be siblings at all, but in the end what did it matter? In any case, they had to stay, because they had nowhere to go, and besides, the English soldiers were looking for them.

"It's bad to have to go now, but tough," Theo nodded to his men and led the way to Cellient Castle.

The road was long, even when you knew all the forest shortcuts like them, and they really had to hurry if they wanted to make it before the English army. The only consolation in this situation was that so far, they had not seen or heard of any major troops in the area. A greater concentration of troops would not have escaped the peasants' attention, and since they were not there, it meant that Baron de Mercier still had some time. Either way, they had to hurry, a lot. Fortunately, they all knew how to walk quickly and persistently, which was good for them, for Theo set a sharp pace and held on to it as stubbornly as if he weren't prone to such a common thing as fatigue. Nevertheless, they did not reach the baron's castle until the next evening.

"And what now?" Pierre asked, squinting reluctantly at the walls at a distance.

"We'll spend the night here and talk to the Baron in the morning. And so, before dawn, no one will let us into the castle," decided the chief.

"Another night on the bare ground," Gwidon muttered and sneezed several times in a row.

"You could have stayed. Indeed, you catch a cold too easily for an outlaw," grumbled Berengard.

"He could eat a bowl of hot soup," Jean worried.

"Maybe you want a dried pear?" Alain suggested to the poet. "I've nothing else."

Gwidon wiped his nose with his sleeve.

"Thank you, I don't have any appetite," he muttered indistinctly.

"I unnecessarily let you come with us," Theo threw his cloak over his shoulders and regarded him with some concern. After a while, he concluded that the bard was exaggerating as usual, and he secretly breathed a sigh of relief.

"Everyone go to sleep," he ordered, "I'll take the watch."

"You can take my dissolute sister to hug if she lets you. If you are going to talk to the baron tomorrow, you must be well-rested. I'll do it," Pierre said flatly.

"Don't protest," Berengard joined him. "Tomorrow you'll have to make a push to convince the Baron that you are telling the truth, because you don't expect him to believe you outright?"

"I wouldn't be surprised if he didn't believe it at all," added Francois.

"We'll see," Theo yawned. "As you like, Pierre. I'm actually exhausted."

He stretched out on the moss, placing his bent arm under his head. Others followed his example, falling asleep almost immediately. Living in the forest backwoods, in constant danger, taught many things, including falling asleep on command and the fact that after waking up they were ready to fight. Pierre sat under a tree and set about planing his spare arrows to keep his hands occupied. Still, it wasn't long before he began to be sleepy.

Theo woke up with the unpleasant feeling that something cold and sharp was touching his neck. All his experience so far told him that it was a blade of a sword or a dagger, so he took his time opening his eyes. When he finally did so, they widened in astonishment, absorbing the sight for which he had not been prepared. The hilt of the sword was held by a girl - tall, narrow in the hips, broad in the shoulders, dressed like a man, with straight hair falling in a dark wave over her back. Her oval face, not embellished with any colors, had a hard, masculine expression.

"Who are you and what are you doing here?" She asked sternly, ignoring the existence of his people surrounded by her soldiers.

Slowly he pushed the saw blade away with his hand and stood up.

"I'm Theodoric de Bongrais," he thoughtlessly used his family name instead of the nickname everyone knew him by. "Have I had the pleasure of Baroness de Mercier?"

"You call it pleasure? Interesting. Why are you here?" The girl asked sharply.

"I have my reasons and can only tell the baron about them," Theo replied shortly.

The girl's eyes narrowed.

"I will not bring a band of thugs into my father's castle," she said. "I've heard a little bit about you, honored outlaw, and you won't succeed in this robbery. Choose, should I have you hanged or cut with swords?"

There was a serious threat in her voice, and the expressions of the soldiers accompanying her made it all too clear that she was in charge and her word was an order. Fortunately, at that moment, Gwidon started sneezing again and again and the gloomy atmosphere burst. For some reason it had such an effect on Theo that he burst out laughing, infecting others, even a militant girl.

"Miss, you'll always have time to hang us," he said humorously, when he had mastered himself a bit. "But what I come with is too important. Please take us to your father. You're not afraid of us, are you?"

"Me?" The baroness rose with ambition and changed her mind.

Not letting go of the sword, just in case, she mounted her horse, a beautiful gray mane with a mane intertwined in dozens of plaits.

"Follow me," she said over her shoulder. "And you keep them well."

"Order, miss," one of the soldiers, apparently in command of the unit, replied.

"Weak sex, right?" Berengard murmured to his friends, as they were, dissatisfied mainly with the fact that their unit led by a woman had surprised them.

"They are so cruel," Gwidon sighed, but the looks he was giving the girl on horseback were more fascination than fear.

"What happens now?" Pierre asked helplessly.

"I'll cut your head off for sleeping on watch," Theo growled at him and surreptitiously shook his clenched fist at him.

Pierre felt ashamed, fell silent and lowered his head. He himself knew that falling asleep on watch was not only a shame, it was also a great blame for his company, thus endangered in this way, and he bit off at it. Fortunately, his friends were too busy commenting on what had happened and no one paid any attention to him.

Theo did not take part in the conversation. Absorbed in thinking what he would say to the baron, he did not even see the barons' glance at him stealthily from time to time, attentive, if not inclined, then at least interested. Once in the courtyard of the castle, the baroness jumped off her mount gracefully and, throwing his reins on a boy in a gray jacket, headed for the open door, beyond which was a great dining room. In the middle of it stood a richly set table, and strolled by an old, well-fed man with a reddish beard and apoplectic complexion, judging from his clothes, the lord of this castle. When he saw the girl, he paused, ran his fingers over his thinning hair, and, ignoring the strangers following her, cried out loudly angrily:

"You're finally here, Denise! I already told you that these horse games before breakfast will spoil your stomach, and you're still on this! Who are you get with you?"

Theo hurried forward and made a slight bow.

"My regards, Baron," he said. "I am..."

"I know, I know," the baron interrupted. "As if I saw Adelaide de Tourvelle, the most beautiful lady in the Louvre... although you have these eyebrows after your father... and that square chin too. Welcome to my home, dear boy. You and your people are my nicest guests."

"Thank you very much," Theo said with some surprise, "But... how to say..."

"I know, I know, they are not of noble birth," the baron waved casually hand. "I'm fine with that, I like a merry company at the table and as a recommendation, they are your brothers-in-arms, never mind. Sit down and eat, nice guys."

He invited them to the table with a wide gesture and took his place in one of the chairs himself, unceremoniously starting to eat. Outlaws starved by winter, who in addition to yesterday morning ate the rest of the modest supplies taken on the road, at the sight of platters full of bread and meat, they forgot about the whole world, which their host accepted with genuine satisfaction. He liked his fellow diners to enjoy their appetites.

"I love hearing your stories, boy," he said between bites and bites. "After all, anyone who remembers King Philip's reign will tell you that there were no better friends than Fabien de Bongrais, Julien de Mercier and Guillome d'Artoix. We were together on watch outside the queen's chamber when the king gave her a lacing for, generally speaking, meddling in his affairs. You understand, it would be rather undesirable for someone to see Her Majesty with black eyes. Our friendship and inseparability ended only when Fabien was married to the Countess de Tourvelle. He was three times her age, but I'm telling you, I haven't seen a similar love blossom in the Louvre. You remind me of both of them, and if you've inherited your father's character, it's no wonder the English fear you like fire. Perhaps the plague has choked them out, they rule as at home, and here you have, one youth spoils their ranks and smashes them as he wishes. Do you know what reward they put on your head? Three thousand ecus."

"Nice reward, but I'll need my head for a while," Theo smiled.

"They have reason not to like our leader." Gwidon said proudly, pushed his plate aside, unfastened the zither from his belt and sang "The Ballade of the Defeat of the Black Knight" along with it. He composed the song himself, but half of France has sung it since last year's harvest festival. Denise stopped eating and, resting her chin on her hands, listened to the bard singing with half-childish curiosity.

"Was it really like that?" She asked when he finished.

Theo smiled again, this time embarrassed.

"Actually, yes, only for a shorter time," he replied. "They tried to stop us from playing, so we beat them, that's the whole story. Gwidon always beautifies everything."

Berengard chuckled.

"Colas said that when the heavily torn unit returned to the garrison, de Valois asked them, 'Well, did you see this outlaw in the village?' And they replied, 'It was much worse, because he saw us.' It was funny."

"Your friend sings well," Denise said, looking at Gwidon nicely.

"If I hadn't had a cold, I'd have sung much better," replied the poet modestly, and it was obvious that the baroness's praise gave him great pleasure.

After finishing breakfast, he sat down on the bearskin in front of the fireplace and again began to alternate singing and telling the adventures of the whole gang, which Denise listened to with great interest. Others listened to these stories, occasionally inserting a detail he had forgotten or did not know, or a biting remark, while Theo and the baron moved to a gallery full of family portraits that surrounded the room.

"Well, tell me what you're coming with," said the baron, leaning against the carved railing. "Because I don't think you went all the way to see my beautiful eyes. Not in these hard times."

"No, no. I'm already talking."

Theo thought for a moment and as simply as he could, he told what happened, what he knew and what he only guessed. Baron de Mercier listened to him, his red, balding head nodding thoughtfully.

"So that's it," he said when the outlaw finished. "Well, it will be as it has to be."

"Why does it has to be?" Theo was surprised. "After all, your estates, Baron, are on the Ille de France, so all you have to do is go there. This castle probably does not have any particular strategic importance."

"There isn't," Julien de Mercier agreed. "But, you see, I once swore to the king that I would not give up this fortress. If I'm going to die, so be it."

"But why?" Theo asked dazedly. "Do you know what the fortress captured by the conquerors looks like? I know, and I don't wish such a view even on my enemy. Please think about your daughter!"

"Denise will be able to die with a weapon in her hand," the baron said sharply, but then he brightened and clapped him on the back. "Theo, dear boy, don't worry about it all that much. We live once and die once. Nobody will avoid what is intended for him."

"Wait," the outlaw rubbed the back of his hand on his forehead. "If you've given a word to the king, the king may release you from that word, right? Just send someone to him."

"I've already sent four messengers, and none has returned. Someone is very concerned that the king does not receive my message. Too bad, God's will." The baron shrugged his mighty shoulders in fatalistic resignation.

The knight looked him straight in the eye.

"No will of God, only English or traitors or both," he said emphatically. "Write one more letter. I'll go."

"In your case, it will be pure suicide. If you fall into the hands of the English, they will hang you, and if you dare to stand before the king, you will end up scaffolding before you know it." Julien de Mercier finally grew serious, his voice a faint note of hope, despite the bleak pronouncement of his words.

"And who says it. Faith in destiny proponent," Theo mocked. "I'll take a chance. Denise is worth a better fate than the English would give her," he finished firmly.

The baron struggled with himself for a moment, then nodded.

"I'll write this letter," he said. "I'll put a clause in it that I'll accept the answer from the king only from your hands, maybe it'll help you in something. You're right, I've no right to risk my daughter's life. She's still so young, and I only have her. I'll give you a good horse, but for all holy things, be careful."

He left for his chamber, and Theo went downstairs, where Gwidon was singing another panegyric in his honor.

"Tell the lady more about how we all got drunk after beating the English," he advised him maliciously. "Why are you missing such a nice detail?"

"Was it really like that?" Denise laughed.

"Young wine has this characteristic that it is easy to get drunk with it, and it'd be pity to not celebrate such a victory," he explained cheerfully.

"Was it that good? I don't remember," Gwidon sighed, who was the first to lose touch with reality that crazy night.

"Don't overdo it, you two, it wasn't that bad. When the dancing started, we were all still at least sober. Our leader especially, because he is reserved. He had to be sober because he kept his feet steady and danced with every young girl that was around him," Francois remembered.

"It doesn't mean he was sober, but he's a scoundrel and chases after skirts, regardless of being engaged," Pierre grunted.

"Engaged, that doesn't mean dead," Jean pointed out.

"Exactly," Theo grew serious. "Listen to me carefully, you lunatic, you will go back to Touraine and stay there. I'll go to Paris with the baron's letter, because if he is not ordered to withdraw from the fortress, he will stay here and die. Anticipating your protests, one will slip through more easily than several, and if a squad of royal soldiers would block our way, you wouldn't be helping me anyway. I really must deal with this myself.

Denise shook her head.

"Four messengers haven't come back from this way," she said sadly.

Raised as a boy, she did not know the typical female tricks of fluttering eyelashes and tears on command, but the gaze of her dark eyes was very telling, more than tears. The knight smiled to encourage her.

"I'll be back," he promised. "I've experience hiding and sneaking this way and that. I'm an outlaw and we have our ways."

The baron ran down the stairs, shaking the sand he had just sprinkled on the scribed parchment.

"Here's a letter," he said, rolling the parchment and sealing it with wax heated in a candle flame. "Remember, boy, to the king's hand, if you want to see it through. Come to the stable, I'll give you a horse."

Theo looked at his people.

"See you later," he said. "And don't upset Bellette, I'll be back as soon as I can."

"And if you will not be able to?" Alain asked grimly.

"If I can't, I'll also come back." Replied the knight harshly and followed the baron.

A moment later, the horse was carrying him as fast as he could along the road to Paris, swallowing the road at an incredibly fast pace. It was indeed an exquisite mount, the best of the Baron de Mercier's stables. Theo had cautiously managed the forest, not the highroad, where mercenary killers who had been responsible for the disappearance of the previous messengers might have been lurking, but the uncomfortable trail seemed to bother the horse at all.

Great horse, thought the outlaw, bending over the animal's neck. "Thanks to him, I will be at the Louvre today."

He was not at all sure if he would be able to get out of there alive, but the mere possibility of having a similarly fascinating adventure was something very exciting for him. He loved such challenges, and he was still too young to take seriously the possibility of dying in such an adventure. And... he was supposed to see the king. The last time he saw him before the memorable Battle of Poitiers, when he was knighted by him, he kept in mind the image of a benevolent, kindly monarch with a noble face and attitude. For the people of his time, the king was a kind of demigod, and meeting him face to face made an indelible impression. While contemplating this, it was only at the last moment that he noticed a few soldiers in English colors blocking his way. He urged the horse and stripped his sword. He ran into the soldiers at full gallop, slashing left and right. The soldiers did not expect such a decisive attack and fled to the sides, and when they pulled themselves together, the outlaw was already far away and his horse was tearing from its hoof, leaving the chase far behind.

He stopped his horse only near the city and wondered what had so far escaped his attention: how to get to the Louvre. He was quite famous, even among the guards at the tollbooths there might have been someone who would recognize him, and then it might be wrong. After some thought, however, he waved his hand and decided to take the risk. He was lucky - he managed to unnoticeably join the merchant caravan and thus get to the city without drawing anyone's attention. At the first inn he found, he left his tuckered horse and walked most peacefully to the Louvre. He crossed the bridge over the Seine without problems, but then stopped. Even from this distance, he could see the guards at the gate and the knights training in the courtyard. It was impossible to dream of reaching the king without drawing anyone's attention. He walked around the Louvre and was absolutely sure that the only place where he could risk trespassing was a high wall with iron spikes on the side of the gardens.

Having found this, he decided immediately and unfastened from his belt a coil of leather rope with an anchor, which had rendered him invaluable services more than once. He easily dropped the hook on top of the wall, climbed the stones and covered the spikes with his folded cloak. Using this facility, it was easier for him to break through the security and jump into the garden, straight onto the large flower bed of irises.

"Sorry," he said pointlessly and looked around.

He was alone. A few dozen more steps, a small door in the castle wall and he was already inside, in one of the corridors of the right wing, empty and quiet. As far as he remembered, the royal chambers were in the left wing, so the most difficult thing was still ahead of him. He managed to pass several corridors without problems, but finally, coming around one of the bends, he unexpectedly came across four halberdiers.

"Hey you!" One of them, who looked like a patrol leader, cried. "What are you doing here, loiterer? Who are you?"

"I have a letter to the king and I must see him," Theo replied, hoping that it would do nothing. He knew too well such hardliner soldiers. And indeed.

"You wish!" The halberdier snorted contemptuously. "As if every doggy could get to the king just like that. Anyway, you invaded without permission and you will rot in the dungeon!"

"First you have to drag me there, bastards, and I won't make it easy for you," Theo answered back, upset in both his words and his tone.

"Will you resist the royal halberdiers? Who do you think you are?" The guard commander nodded at his men and all four started to attack the intruder.

He with an ironic smile dodged the blow of the first of them, grabbed his halberd and spun it around like a light pike until the air hissed.

The four sentries backed away in panic.

"Are you crazy, bum? You only make your situation worse!" Cried the commander. "How do you call yourself?!"

"What do you have to do with this?" Theo charged at him and his men, brandishing a halberd.

One against four is never very close, but the outlaw from the swamp was well trained in such a fight and knew how to steer it so that it could not be reached. The only difficulty for him was the halberd - he was not used to such a heavy and bulky weapon. Soon his hands fainted, but he was no less than the sentries, whom this resistance seemed to inflame.

"Who are you, you bold, and what are you doing here?!" Cried their commander, apparently in the habit of not abandoning a question once asked.

"I'm Roland, Margrave of Brittany!" Theo shouted finally, impatient with his inquisitiveness. "I'm looking for a suitable hill here to die!"

"Who's making the noise and claiming to be Roland?" Sounded an imperious voice at the end of the corridor, and the eyes of the combatants saw a man who was no longer young in thick mourning, surrounded by a crowd of courtiers of both sexes.

He was a little taller than average height, with hair tucked in intricate locks and a short dark blond stubble framing his long face. In a word, it was King John II himself, known as the Good. The halberds immediately lowered their weapons and assumed a crude posture, and Theo backed up against the wall, keeping the halberd stick still in his sweaty hands. He preferred not to deprive himself of defense for the time being.

"Honorable Lord, that ragged man entered here uninvited," the guard commander reported. "He doesn't want to say what he's doing here, he doesn't want to introduce himself, he doesn't want to give up."

"Ah," the king nodded, not honoring the intruder with a single glance. "What does he want then?"

The halberdier glanced over his shoulder at the outlaw.

"He wants to fight," he said shortly.

"Oh, really nothing new in his case," came a sarcastic voice, and from behind the courtiers came the Black Knight, somewhat diabolical as ever, with his pointy, pitch-black beard and silver-braided black clothes.

"No, it's really too much!" Theo had barely mastered the urge to throw the halberd against the floor.

"Hello, outlaw. We haven't seen each other for a long time," Roger de Valois smiled politely at him.

"Not long enough," Theo growled.

The king approached him slowly, folding his hands behind his back.

"Theodoric de Bongrais," he said, with subtle pity and rebuke in his voice. "I remember you as it was today: you knelt at my feet and holy fire burned in your eyes when I touched your shoulder with my naked sword. Your skin was noble then white, you were always neatly dressed and combed... and now? Look at yourself what you look like."

"With all due respect, Most Merciful Lord, but in this situation, it is indeed my least of concern," replied the knight calmly.

He himself knew well that his character did not fit in with that of the sleek court regulars now. He was brown from the day's wandering in forests and meadows, he was dressed in a simple caftan and peasant sandals, and his hair, formerly flowing down to his shoulders, now wore unevenly cut below the ears and falling with asymmetrical fringe down to his eyebrows. It was neither fashionable nor elegant, forced by circumstances, but the fact that none of the others was a better setting for his delicate features and wide-set eyes.

"It is good that your late parents cannot see you now," continued the king thoughtfully. "Their hearts would break with regret. But that's it. Put down your weapon and politely follow the guards to the tower."

"I'm sorry, but it's impossible," replied the outlaw. "Although I even like the idea itself, because I'm so bloody tired... I'm sorry, Good Lord, it breaks out. The thing is, it wasn't just for fun, that I had this whole fight. Allow Lord, please accept the letter."

He knelt on one knee and handed the king a roll of parchment. John II broke the baron's seal and, going to the window, began to read. As he reads, his face darkened more and more, and finally he nodded at Theo and asked him softly so that only them would hear:

"Is the situation really that bad?"

"I think so. If Julien de Mercier is not ordered to retreat, there will be a massacre like the one at Bongrais," Theo replied just as quietly.

The king looked at him sternly.

"Bongrais was a rebels' nest," he said emphatically. "Will you deny it?"

"And this will change something?" The outlaw muttered reluctantly. He felt more and more tired and discouraged, and the enemy seemed to have distanced him a few lengths without effort.

"The baron writes to me here that he will only take an order from your hands," continued John II. "I can guess why. So, what? Should I let go of the man accused of treason and rebellion?"

The last words were spoken a little louder that Roger de Valois heard them.

"Don't listen to him, venerable cousin," he said, coming closer. "I don't think he said a word of truth. He is simply trying to shirk responsibility for his crimes."

"I'm not listening to him," muttered the king, not taking his eyes off the parchment.

"Sire," said Theo after a while, having mastered the urge to throw himself down the Prince's throat with an enormous effort of will. "I swear by my knightly honor that after completing the task I'll return here and turn myself over to the royal guard, no matter what the consequences. But then I'll demand God's judgment between me and this man."

John II looked at him sadly.

"You'd better not do that," he warned him. "Even if you win, for what you did as an outlaw, you'll rest your head on the torturer's trunk. And if you lose and survive, you will have to pay the penalty for wretches like you. You'll be wheelbroken, skinned and dismembered."

"Will it hurt?" Theo asked stupidly.

"It's very possible," replied the king dryly.

"I'll take a chance. What is your decision, Sire?" The knight raised his eyebrows slightly and straightened proudly.

The king looked at the letter again and shook his head.

"I can't forbid you," he said. "I take your oath. You'll be back here in two days for nones[1] or I'll disgrace you. Wait a minute, I'll scratch a few words for the baron.

He left, and the Black Knight gave Theo a mocking look.

"You know, I'll just hurt you," he promised him.

"I'd sooner bite my tongue off than give you such satisfaction."

Roger de Valois smiled politely. He liked this arrangement, perhaps even more than all the others, and was not about to prevent the enemy from fulfilling his agreement with the king, though he could not deny himself a veiled hint that he would try to do so.

Theo peered where Estelle de Villeneuve was huddled among the group. He felt sorry for the little girl, obviously frightened by what had happened here, felt that she was wrong here, in this nest of intrigue, but he could not help her in anything. He didn't even want to speak to her now, when he couldn't be sure how the adventure would end for him. Everything indicated that he was rather sad.

"Too bad," he thought. "But at least before he dies, I'll prove that bastard is lying."

It was common in those days to believe that trials by ordeal[2] really did express God's will, and no one dared to oppose their results, whatever they were.

John II left the room, shaking the parchment on which the ink had not yet dried.

---

[1] Nones as a measure of time - the afternoon hour when the monks used to say one of the daily prayers, signaled by the ringing of the bell.

[2] Trial by ordeal - God's judgment.

"Here," he said. "Remember, you have two days, then I'll declare you infamous.

"I'll be back," Theo replied shortly, bowed to the king, and wasting no more time ran out, this time through the main exit.

Two days was not much, he had to hurry. He quickly picked up the horse from the inn, finding that the noble steed had regained his strength, despite a very short rest, and carried almost as well as at the beginning of the road. He felt sorry for this beautiful animal, being forced to a murderous effort, but he had no choice.

*****

Denise de Mercier was on the night watch, not for the first time, for her father did raise her as a soldier, not a lady. And since she did not think long when something surprised her, she attacked now without thinking. The blade of her ax whistled through the air, but at the last moment the shadow dodged.

"Easy, miss!" A familiar voice called out. "First check who you want to smash, okay? Really, are you always so fast?"

"Oh, Theo," the girl sighed. "Sorry, but it's a siege... and you come out of nowhere. How did you get here?"

"Through the window, miss," Theo replied nonchalantly. "In the English camp, the guards are probably the worst bunglers, because I walked through it almost without hiding, but what was I supposed to do later? Knock?"

"Ah, you," Denise laughed, then grew serious. "Have you been to the king?"

"Of course? Wake up your father, I've a royal order in writing... though I don't know what we can do with it now." He finished quieter when the girl disappeared into the corridor.

The castle was now surrounded by a strong detachment of English soldiers, well-armed, at least two hundred men. There were no more than fifty under siege, probably less. He shook his head. Somewhere down the corridor a door slammed and many feet patted, and after a while Baron de Mercier was right next to Theo and literally snatched the parchment from his hand. Shining the torch on himself, he read greedily a few lines drawn in the hand of the king.

"Well, we are alive," he said victoriously. "You are wonderful, boy, you have accomplished the impossible. We'll all be ready in a few moments."

"Uhm. How do we get out of here?" Theo asked quietly.

"Don't worry about that, kid," the baron laughed coarsely. "The only problem is that we have little time, because the English will storm before dawn. They already promised me that. There is a passage beyond those hills but bricked up. It'll be easy to break the wall, it's thin, but they'll figure out where we've gone. In the open field they will kill us all. If only to find something to keep them..."

"I think I saw cannons in the courtyard," Theo said thoughtfully.

"Oh yes. I've four siege towers, two gunpowder barrels, and a whole pile of bullets. And not a single man who knows how to handle it. What are you actually getting at?" Julien de Mercier asked with some surprise.

"Do you really care about this castle?" The outlaw looked around as if to find the answer to this question among the walls and furniture.

"Not really, I have a second, better one," replied the baron, and suddenly understood. "Wait, you want to throw this pile of stones on their heads! Epic! Why I didn't think of it either? Can you do that?"

Theo winced slightly.

"I've never done that," he admitted. "I don't know much about gunpowder, but I know a little spark is enough to blow it like in hell. Let someone help me get the barrels to the room where we ate and get as far away as possible."

"Well, I hope you know what you're doing." Said the baron and ran to give the appropriate orders.

"Not really, to be honest," he muttered, looking after him. "But I've to do something to save these people. They deserve it."

He has seen too much betrayal and cowardice not to value people who are ready to resist the English at any cost. After a time, which was extremely short for himself, the Baron de Mercier reappeared with him, this time buttoned up with a sword at his side.

"Denise is getting everyone out of here, including dogs and horses," he said. "The barrels are in the dining room, which is also where the transition begins."

"Perfect. I'll do the rest myself. Please go, Baron." Theo said, forcing a smile.

"Do your job and run away like a hare. The passageway begins in the dining area and will lead you beyond the hills. I'll throw the signs, so you don't get lost." The baron patted him heartily on the back and walked away.

The knight stood for a long moment, listening to the uninterrupted silence, then took the torch off the handle in the wall and headed for the dining room. In one wall there was a black hole that had not been seen before - a hidden passage, and in the center, where the table had been pushed back, stood two barrels filled with blackish, coarse powder. Theo looked around. Near the fireplace, he noticed a large chest with logs prepared for firewood, and he rubbed his hands with satisfaction. It was just what he needed. He arranged the dry logs methodically around the barrels and made a compact path from them all the way to the secret passage. Now it was left to wait for dawn.

The English kept their word and set off to storm exactly at sunrise. He heard them smash the door in the palisade with a ram, then knock it against the building's door.

"Well, in the name of God," he muttered to himself, tossed the torch on the wood, and then ran through the serpent-like corridor. He had no idea how long it took for the fire to reach powder - in those days the use of these weapons was just beginning, and hardly anyone was familiar with it.

Breathless and wet with sweat, he burst out of the corridor and only stopped far beyond the hills where Denise and her father were waiting for him.

"And what?" The baron asked.

"I don't know..." Theo replied, breathing hard, but was interrupted by a monstrous explosion that made the ground tremble under the feet of pedestrians and horses.

"This is the end of Castle Cellient," the baron said pathetically. "It's coming down already. We can go. What about you, son?"

"I've to go back to Paris," Theo replied, wiping his face with his hands. "I gave my word to the king that I'd come back, but first I'd like to meet my people. They deserve a little goodbye and an explanation from me."

The baron put a hand on his shoulder and looked deep into his eyes.

"If you have given your word, you must," he said. "May the heavens be kind to you."

Denise handed the knight the reins of her mount.

"Your horse is too tired. Take mine, he's strong and very fast," she said.

Theo accepted the gift gratefully.

"Thank you, miss," he said, riding his beautiful horse.

"No, we thank you. Our lives are too short to show gratitude," the baron answered seriously.

"It was pure pleasure, the purest, and in addition I had a chance to meet such a charming lady," replied the knight seriously and set off on his way.

"A pleasure that can cost him his life if the king is in a bad mood," muttered Julien de Mercier. "Come on, Denise, and stop looking for the eyes of this boy. He's not for you."

"I know, but..." Denise sighed and fell silent. She couldn't put into words what she felt, just hoped the forest knight wouldn't forget her.

Meanwhile, Theo didn't even try to think about her. Before he reached the provincial border, he calculated that he would make it to the Louvre in time, if he stayed in Touraine only as much as it took to say goodbye to everyone, would not go to sleep, and give the horse only a short rest. You could feel tired just from thinking it over, and yet he had already had one sleepless night behind him, and in the future, and between them an uneasy conversation with his people. Worse, he had to speak to Bellette as well. He really couldn't imagine the words he would tell her that he was leaving, never to return.

"Sorry, Bellette," he whispered. "I'd sacrifice my life for you, but I cannot honor."

It was well after noon when he reached Touraine. It was not easy to avoid several English patrols and, having found himself in the forest, dismounted from his horse. It was better to walk through the marshes. When he appeared in the clearing, he was greeted with one great roar of joy, and his heart skipped at the thought that he would have to extinguish that joy, which spoke eloquently about how much he was liked in this wild company. For a moment he had to squeeze their hands and listen to the almost incomprehensible shouts of immeasurable contentment, and finally managed to silence his friends and calm them down.

"How are you Gypsie?" He asked, not sure how to begin this speech.

"It's better," Gwidon replied. "Armando won't recover too quickly and is in terrible pain for now, but it'll be okay. I hope you let them stay here, you know they have nowhere to go..."

"Don't bother me now, Weasel," Jean interrupted. "We must make a great, scandalous feast on the occasion of a successful mission and the happy return of our crazy leader."

Theo shrugged.

"Okay, okay," he said reluctantly. "You've nothing to be happy about. To save the baron and his men, I had to give the king my word that I would return to Paris to duel the Black Knight."

"You'll cut it into slices, season it and eat it," interrupted Berengard disparagingly.

"Maybe so," Theo agreed. "But regardless of the result, I'll hit the scaffold. Only my name will be cleared of the mud. I really care about it, and I have given my word anyway. You understand?"

He looked around at his friends' clouded faces and lowered his gaze to the linen-white Bellette."

"You understand me at least?" He asked hopefully.

She looked up at him, her large eyes, blue as the water in the lake.

"Yes, Theo, I understand," she whispered.

"Then you are the only one," Pierre said sarcastically.

Theo wanted to say something else, but his voice stuck in his throat.

"Goodbye," he muttered and turned away.

His people were silent, not knowing what to say in this situation, and not knowing what to do. The most tempting prospect was to bind the mad chief and hold him in his hideout until he sobered up, but they knew he would never forgive them. So they let him go, though it felt as if everything that was best in their lives was going away with him. Theo was more than a leader and more than a friend to them - as befits typical representatives of his time, they felt a subconscious need to have someone they could call their senior in order to feel safer. So their leader additionally played the role of a protector, however indignant they would be if someone pointed it out to them. Now they were going to be left alone, and it was as if their own little world, which they had built so hard, was collapsing. It hurt so much that no one even noticed that Bellette's face was not only plain despair, but also physical pain.

The way back to Paris was more difficult than the previous one, because both the horse and rider were tired, and there was no moment of weakness. For the same reason, he also had to be very careful not to run into an English unit, because now he would not be able to escape or face them in battle. In addition, his eyes were closing by themselves and he had to be very careful not to fall asleep. He had no idea how he would be able to fight the Black Knight, who was considered a master of masters in this state.

"Well, God's will, as Baron de Mercier says," he murmured, pausing his horse on the road near Paris. Something told him it was better not to show up at the turnpikes of Paris just like that, because someone might want to keep him, and he was right about that. While Roger de Valois did not intend to prevent him from reaching his destination, he had other enemies among the court regulars who would have rejoiced greatly at his disgrace. He did not think for long as a group of young aristocrats appeared on the road, returning from hunting. One of them stopped his mount right next to Theo.

"Not too good a horse for you, boy?" He asked haughtily. "You will have foundered horse if you make him make such an effort. He is tired, and it's a pity such a beautiful animal. Wouldn't you sell it to me?"

Theo smiled secretly. A gray hooded cloak concealed his sword and knightly belt, and his weather-beaten face and hands might suggest that he belonged to a low state, especially when someone was not looking closely.

"So mote it be," he replied humbly, in dialect from around Touraine. "I'll get to the city afoot. I'll just take something."

He dismounted and grabbed the pouch thrown to him. He was glad that the noble animal would get into the hands of the horse-lover when he went to meet his destiny, and besides, the whole thing had an additional and useful aspect for him: he joined without question a group numb from the service fatigue of the young noblemen, and unnoticed he entered cities with them. He made his way through the side streets to the bridge over the Seine, but there he stopped, from his hiding place watching the three ladders with stout truncheons guarding the passage. They must have known him, for they were watching closely anyone who wanted to pass. He thought for a moment, then threw off his coat and, quietly, so as not to alert those at the bridge, slid into the water. The passage of the river with a fairly swift current across, in addition with a heavy sword at his side, exhausted his already heavily strained strength. He had to mobilize all his determination to reach the castle gate and cross it proudly, as befits a knight. Nones had already started, he had to hurry.

When he entered the knight's hall, all eyes turned to him, and the noise of conversation was cut off.

"I was late?" Theo asked anxiously.

"Oh no," said Roger de Valois kindly. "Why are you so wet?"

"I crossed the Seine just for fun," the outlaw replied, not looking at him.

John II nodded his head.

"You are very brave, Count," he said appreciatively. "Now you'll go rest and clean up, and the duel will take place tomorrow at noon. You'll get enough sleep and regain your strength, we don't want my cousin to take the unfair advantage that he would now undoubtedly have. You can barely stay on your feet, Count, and tomorrow you will fight for everything that is important in life."

"Whatever is important in life," Theo repeated mentally, and he was close to losing his temper and for the first time he could remember he sought relief in tears. Father wouldn't let him cry. When he was four, he was bitten by bees and burst into tears, and then the old count beat him so hard that the indignant Countess did not speak to her husband for two weeks. The trauma he had left after that meant that he would never cry again, and now he would "fall apart"? Just because he suddenly found that what was most important in life had nothing to do with this bizarre notion of honor, war, killing and even the monarch himself?

He silently bowed to the king and, without protest, allowed himself to be led to a small room on the eastern tower, where the door was replaced by a wrought-iron grate. Not paying attention, he lay down on the leather-covered bed and fell asleep immediately. A young and healthy body, exhausted by extraordinary effort, demanded its rights regardless of the bleak situation. He was sleeping so soundly that neither the footsteps of the guards nor the conversations of the manor house, which came to see the famous outlaw with his own eyes and see if he was really as handsome as Estelle de Villeneuve had claimed, woke him.

"Why do you keep going there?" The girl was indignant. "He's not an animal in the menagerie to be stared at like that."

"Okay, okay, little Jezebel, you've probably already had a good look at it, over there in the forest," replied the manors with carelessly hidden jealousy. Neither of them would mind if she were to be in her place. The forest knight was very different from the courtiers who surrounded them, he moved some hidden strings in their hearts, and he awakened untold desires and dreams. There was not one among them who did not wholeheartedly wish him a victory in tomorrow's match, though few aside from Estelle believed it. At last, however, everything quieted down and the Louvre fell asleep.

Theo was awakened by the first rays of the sun the next day, and for a long moment he didn't know where he was. Then the memories came back and he looked around with the unpleasant feeling that he was locked up in a cage like an animal. However, he immediately found out that it wasn't - the grille replacing the door was ajar, there was no sign of the guards. He went out into the courtyard, washed by the fountain, shaved for lack of anything better with his own dagger and combed his hair carefully, not forgetting to clean his clothes as much as possible. He didn't want to be remembered in some uninviting way, whatever would happen.

He was about to finish when a curly boy dressed as a royal page appeared in the courtyard, sleepy and yawning. At the sight of the outlaw, he sobered up immediately.

"How can I serve you, Count?" he asked uncertainly.

"Thank you, I can serve myself," Theo replied, running his comb once more through his black hair. "When is breakfast here? I'm so hungry."

"I'll get something right now," the boy offered hurriedly. "The king rarely gets up before noon, and he doesn't eat breakfast anyway, so you'd have to wait a long time. Where are you going to eat?"

"How about here by the fountain? And don't bother yourself with some fancy dishes, all I need is bread and cheese," the knight replied, sitting down on the edge of the fountain.

Here, in the courtyard, he felt a bit better than in the prison-like room on the tower. He never liked being locked up, and since he lived in the woods, this reluctance turned into a kind of obsession. The page expedited quickly, bringing him a tray that was set richly.

"The duel will be at noon and I don't like fighting on an empty stomach," Theo said as he started to eat. "It's very unhealthy. How is it said in the Louvre about these trials by ordeal?"

The boy hesitated.

"Various," he replied after a moment. "It isn't known which of you two is actually telling the truth, and there are also those who have a poor opinion of the duel as a judgment of God. Do you remember, Count, the rape case from a dozen or so years ago? After all, because of trials by ordeal, an innocent man died then, so now people are more skeptical. And Duke de Valois is supposedly undefeated."

Theo smiled and took a bite of a cold roast.

"Well, we'll see that later," he said. He liked the frizzy page, he vaguely reminded him of someone he knew, but he couldn't make out who.

"Miss Estelle is very worried about you, Count," the boy said softly.

He did not add that Estelle had pleaded in vain to the king for mercy on the forest knight until late at night, and that she cried in her chamber the rest of the night. She got emotional the whole thing much more than Theo himself. Besides, there was not a single person in the Louvre who would not think about it, even numerous bets were made about the result of the duel, but no one knew what the king himself thought about it, because John II did not confide his thoughts to anyone, especially from the plans made. The Grand Chancellor of the Crown and Bishop Joaquin even tried to convince him to be more gracious to a young rebel who was so sympathetic, but they too did not achieve anything.

Theo spent time until noon sharpening and polishing his sword, sometimes answering questions or comments from those who accosted him. He did so in a polite but casual tone, completely absorbed in the approaching game. When he was finally told it was time to go to the inner courtyard, he got up and walked there freely, as if he were going to a regular tournament. The courtiers, knights, prelates, mansions, servants and, in general, all who were at the Louvre that day were gathered in the inner courtyard. The only thing missing was Adeline, whose doctor recommended absolute peace and a trip to the countryside, necessary in a very poorly endured first pregnancy.

The king waited, seated in a carved armchair on a scarlet-covered platform, grimly chewing on a straw, waiting for the reverend bishop to finish the elaborate ritual that would initiate God's judgments and both of his opponents to take the customary oath. He raised his eyebrows slightly when he saw Theo. Perhaps he himself regretted at the moment that he was a king who would not be fit to approach this outlaw before such an important fight and tell him directly:

"I am on your side and I wish you victory."

He did not like cousin, although so far, he did not believe in the rumors that sometimes reached him and he could not bring himself to wish him a victory. Besides, the Black Knight did not expect this at all. He was standing in his place, wearing a caftan sewn with brass rings, the kind that made the perfect replacement for chain mail, and a light helmet.

"Bring a similar caftan and helmet for the Count de Bongrais," the king ordered with a displeased voice as the bishop fell silent.

"With permission, I'd rather not," Theo said. "I'm used to fighting as I stand, and besides, it's supposed to be God's judgment, isn't it?"

"Well, as you like. Announce a meeting!" The king cried.

Fanfares sounded, and both opponents entered the empty square drawn on the ground, similar in shape to a circle.

"Ready?" Asked the Black Knight, drawing his sword. "I'll tell you something: I'll win. I don't believe in any trials by ordeal, I don't even believe in God, but I'm sure of my hand. So sure I feel sorry for you."

"Don't feel sorry, don't feel sorry, just kiss me, kiss me..." Theo hummed an innocently popular song, struggling to refrain from making one of the often-indecent gestures used by his people in response to the enemy's words.

Without moving from the spot, he countered the first attack and went on the offensive. His opponent fought a style that Theo had never experienced before, very sneaky and certainly effective, and despite his age he was agile and quick. It could not be underestimated.

"Come on? Can't you get any better?" He sneered, parrying another trim of the outlaw. "I can see that the stories about your skills were greatly exaggerated. Your father was good opponent, but when I slashed him over the head, he fell like a log. You won't even threaten me."

Theo did not respond to these taunts, trying to concentrate his full attention on the fight itself, on the two intersecting blades beyond which the world did not exist now. The Black Knight managed to graze him once on his bare shoulder, and once he knocked him off his feet and almost pinned him to the ground. He was really good and the outlaw couldn't afford a moment of distraction. He deliberately kept his best tricks for later when the prince was tired and less confident, for he felt that they were not enough to defeat such a good opponent. They were simply, too simple, too honest, just like the whole of him, tough, strong, adamant, but completely defenseless against dishonesty and dishonorable deception. With the corner of his eye he caught the flash of the dagger with the greatest difficulty, he lunged sideways, striking his shoulder painfully against one of the benches, he narrowly avoided the deadly blade and jumped up just in time to parry another attack. Both opponents were already tired, Roger de Valois more visible when he decided to reach for the dagger hidden in his sleeve. Such actions were not well received, but generally allowed, as they gave the opponent a chance to show reflexes and training. The Black Knight took a step back, then unexpectedly collapsed on his opponent, who was trying to withstand the powerful blow, but lost his balance and fell on his back. He desperately covered himself with his sword, knowing that it was over, that he would not be able to defend himself against this terrible man, but his blade suddenly met some soft resistance. The Black Knight, wanting to take advantage of the unexpected advantage, lunged too quickly towards the lying enemy and literally threw his throat on the blade of his sword.

Theo jumped to his feet, staring in disbelief at his sword, then at his body, lying in a pool of blood like a crumpled rag. There was something almost unreal about it - this formidable and powerful man who had done so much harm to him was so quickly turned into a lifeless object without any meaning. He didn't immediately hear the king's voice, who had to repeat his name several times for the outlaw to finally look up.

"Give back the sword now, Count de Bongrais," John II said gently. "And let the executioners take the corpse of the unworthy one from here. God pointed out the culprit and administered justice. Count de Bongrais, I don't want to be remembered as a heartless king, so in recognition of your courage and righteousness, I allow you to have one request. I will fulfill it."

Theo closed his eyes.

"Merciful Lord," he said after a moment, when he was sure he would take control of his voice. "I'm begging you for grace and forgiveness for my people. It's the leader who is usually responsible for everything anyway, so let my whole band be punished in my person, and they... let them finally live in peace."

John II nodded solemnly.

"They are pardoned," he said firmly. "Take the count out of here and lock him in the tower pending execution."

Theo without resistance allowed himself to be disarmed and led him to the well-known chamber on the tower. He was still impressed of what had happened, for reasons that were not entirely understood, he felt like a man who had experienced some mighty shock. Now the scaffold awaited him, but the thought was distant and somehow colorless, as if it apply to someone else. He was tired, horribly tired. The thought of death enticed him as the thought of a long-awaited rest, a deep sleep without dreams, but he could not even put it clearly. The feeling of being locked up choked him more than ever. He didn't know how long he sat there with his face in his hands when someone tapped lightly on the grid.

"Do you need something?" The curly page asked him, looking at him with sad, luminous gray eyes.

Theo managed a smile and shook his head slightly.

"No, boy," he said. "Now I don't need anything anymore. When will they cut me down?"

"Tomorrow, sir, as soon as they finish putting up the scaffold," the boy replied. He stood still a moment longer and walked away, looking back.

"I wish I would have had it over today," Theo muttered, and lay down with both hands under his head. He really wanted it - let everything be behind him, fight, love, friendship, all this difficult, happy life, full of sacrifices, suffering and joy, which he loved so much. He remembered well how he couldn't understand Martin, who had had a toothache once, and instead of accepting Alain's help immediately, he dragged the case on until he was semiconscious from pain and insomnia. In his opinion, it was better not to delay what was inevitable anyway. Martin had to be tied at last so that Alain could tear that unfortunate tooth out with his blacksmith tongs, and he was not a coward at all. Theo closed his eyes and saw his friends alive, playing dice in the best harmony, arguing and reconciling at the same time, sipping in the tavern and brazenly accosting the girls serving there.

Staring at this image, he fell into a light sleep, from which he was awakened only by the sound of crying by the bars. He opened his eyes. It was almost dark now, but by the light of the lamp hanging on the wall, he recognized the tiny figure of Estelle de Villeneuve. There were no sentries in sight.

"What happened, my little lady?" He asked, rising from the bed.

"How's what happened? You are asking about it?" The girl cried out. "Theo, I won't survive your death. Please, let's both get out of here. I'll get the key to that damn grate and..."

The outlaw came over and put his fingers protectively around the tiny hands clasped on the bars.

"I can't, my brave, sweetest princess in the world, I can't," he said emphatically. "I gave my word of honor, and that means a lot. Understand, I have nothing left: family, friends, property, and tomorrow I will lose my life. Only honor is left for me, I will not renounce it. Be brave, and I ask you for one thing: do not watch my execution. It won't be a pretty sight."

"I couldn't," Estelle shuddered and sobbed more violently than before.

"Go to sleep," Theo said, wiping the tears from her cheeks with his fingers. "Somehow you will come to terms with all this when you understand that we have only minimal influence on certain things in life. It could be worse, my little lady, I might have died disgraced, and this is how they will remember me as a righteous knight. It's a lot."

"I don't understand," Estelle whispered despairingly. Once again, she tried to convince the knight, but to no avail. Theo was kind and gallant to her, but he firmly rejected any possibility of saving his life, and even the hottest pleas could not dissuade him from doing so.

When the girl finally gave up and left sobbing, the outlaw sat on the bed and sighed heavily. This trip had cost him more nerves than a duel with the Black Knight, for he liked Estelle and didn't want to hurt her, but he was sure he had done the right thing. He just had to hold out until noon, which was not easy with his disgust at being locked up.

"The last thing I will see is the boards of the scaffold," he thought, feeling his throat tighten. "And the last thing I will hear is the whistle of a sword slicing through the air above my head. The last thing I will feel is the blade slam into my neck... and the pain, the last in my life."

He rested his head against the bars and softly hummed one of Gwidon's songs, the more romantic one. It was called the "Child of the Night" and was kind of about them, though it would fit into any company of as daring outcasts as they were. He couldn't sleep anymore, but he sat all night by the window, looking out over the garden and the panorama of the city in the distance.

It was going to be his last night in the world, so he wanted it to be calm, filled with only good memories. He did not touch the breakfast that was brought him but drank the few sips of wine that the curly leaf brought him, stating that it was indeed very good, especially compared to the counterfeit moonshine from the White Swan inn. He didn't want to drink too much so as not to be tipsy as he might lose his self-control then. He was left to wait, and this waiting was worse than the prospect of the execution itself.

The Plaza de Greve was surrounded by guards, keeping order among the crowd of onlookers, in the center stood a scaffold covered with black cloth, on which, beside the trunk, stood a muscular man in a red jacket and red mask, holding his folded hands on the hilt of a huge sword. Surrounded by his court, the king was seated on a specially prepared platform, covered with draped gold-head embroidered with lilies. At the sound of a cart rattling down the street, all those who had so far talked excitedly fell silent.

"Did Miss Estelle do what I told her to do?" the king asked the court marshal quietly. He nodded.

"He didn't want to run," he said. "Now I have also given the order not to bind his hands, if he wanted he could escape on the way.

He silently thought what most of the courtiers did, that the king had been unnecessarily cruel to Count de Bongrais, but he did not dare to say it aloud.

A cart, drawn by a coal-black horse, escorted by two executioner helpers appeared on the square. Theo stood on the cart, arms folded, staring blankly ahead.

"Why wasn't he blindfolded?" The king asked in surprise.

The marshal spread his hands.

"He probably didn't want to let that happen," he explained. "And the executioners were not ordered to fight with him. Fix it, Your Majesty?"

John II shrugged his shoulders and left the question unanswered. The convicts were blindfolded not for any merciful reasons, but to prevent them from thrashing, which made it difficult for the executioner to deliver the right blow. In the case of the famous outlaw, it was unlikely that he would not survive worthily to the very end, so eventually the band could be forgotten.

Theo calmly climbed the steps to the scaffolding and surveyed the square and the people gathered there. Somewhere further a commotion suddenly arose, and the guards looked around anxiously, not quite knowing what to do.

"Let us through, we're unarmed!" A group of men roared, elbows and fists making their way through the crowd. They easily broke the cordon of guards, and before anyone knew it, they stormed the scaffold.

"Chief, who is the king?" The broad-shouldered blonde asked the condemned man.

"The one in the crown, idiot," Theo replied unfriendly.

The blond turned towards the platform and did something could be considered a bow with some effort.

"Sire, I'm Pierre, and these are my comrades," he said aloud, then, pointing at them, named each of them. "We came here to die with our commander, because if he is guilty, so are we."

"Nobody invited you here," Theo pointed out.

"Don't be unsociable," Gwidon admonished his leader.

"Oh," the knight snapped. "Sorry to be alive. But it can be fixed." He waved his hand towards the executioner.

"Your proposal is very interesting, outlaw," said John II calmly. "It shows your courage and loyalty, and in the normal situation I would probably agree to it. But, you see, none of this. Your leader, obligated to express one wish, asked for grace for you, and I'm not in the habit of repeating something twice. You are free, whether you want it or not."

There was a puzzled silence for a moment, then Pierre turned to his chief and said bitterly:

"This time you have really outdone yourself."

"What a fool you did!" Jean exclaimed wringing his hands. "Couldn't you wish for something else? Health, happiness, prosperity for example?"

"Maybe I could, but that was my bloody wish!" Theo exclaimed furiously. "Who is going to die here, me or you? Why are you interfering?"

Jean was out of breath, looked around and fixed his eyes on the king as if seeking his help.

"Why am I interfering?!" He exclaimed painfully. "He's asking why I'm interrupting! I don't know any more if Theo is crazy, does he think I'm crazy... or maybe he wants me to think he's crazy?"

"Are you done?" Theo asked him with a dangerous undertone in his voice.

"I'm sorry, but does that mean there's nothing more can be done?" Berengard looked at the monarch staring at them with a mixture of imploring humility and hope. The king shook his head negatively.

"Your chief could have asked for his life and he would have got it," he said. "But he chose your salvation, so come down now if you don't want his sacrifice to go to waste."

There was silence on the scaffold.

"And... could we at least say goodbye?" Pierre asked after a long moment.

"There you go," said the king graciously.

The friends suddenly became sad. Until now, everything looked like their next adventure, after all they had shared so many of them, but now it became clear that this will be the last and the awareness of the inevitable end lay a stone on their hearts. Berengard hugged his friend tightly, muttered a few unrelated words, and ran off the scaffolding so that no one would see his tears. Others cried quite openly, clutching their leader's hand one by one and saying goodbyes, then coming downstairs with a feeling of complete defeat. At last, only Pierre remained, gloomy but calm. Theo looked at him, brushing back the hair that had fallen over his eyes, and held out his hand to him.

"Well, no offense," he said with an involuntary sigh.

Pierre shook his head.

"A simple handshake is not enough here," he said. "Give me the kiss, brother."

They kissed heartily, regretting that they had never managed to tell each other how much they liked each other despite their constant arguments, and now it was too late for that. They couldn't even let this moment of saying goodbye last too long.

As Pierre left the scaffolding, the condemned man looked at the executioner with a silent question. The latter nodded at him with a movement of his eyes, visible in the holes in the mask. Now it was as if everything was gone, only the scaffold, the man in red with a two-handed sword, and that hideous, sick feeling somewhere inside, a feeling that Theo didn't want to call by name and that he had to somehow duly ignore, albeit an unexpected meeting with his friends it had knock him for a loop.

He crossed himself quickly and knelt, bowing his head over the trunk.

"God, be merciful," he thought, gritting his teeth tightly.

Then he heard the hiss of slicing air and felt sharp iron against the back of his neck.

CHAPTER VII

Honor and homeland

Just a touch. Just a cold and sharp brush that disappeared immediately. A moment passed before he decided to raise his head and look at the executioner, who again stood still, resting his sword against the boards of the scaffold.

"Let's not prolong this scene anymore," said John II from his seat. "I pardon the Count de Bongrais and order him to be at my disposal immediately at the Louvre. I don't have so many faithful and brave knights to execute them on the basis of English accusations. Let those who understand this do an examination of conscience."

Theo, uncomprehending the scene, got up, feeling his knees bowed, and mounted the horse he was given. He felt as if he were dreaming, he could barely hold the horse's reins with his numb hands, and his head rumbled as if he had been hit by something heavy. Having reached the Louvre, he followed the monarch into his private chambers, obeying his commanding gesture.

"Do you think the king has a duty to ask his subjects for forgiveness?" John II asked him when they were alone.

"I don't know, I don't think so," he replied helplessly.

He noticed his fingers were shaking, and he clamped them around the high back of the carved chair to keep it under control. The king opened a small cupboard, took out a silver flask from inside, and poured a small amount of brownish liquid into two goblets.

"Have a drink, it'll be good for you after your experience like this," he said imperiously.

Theo obediently drank, and alive fire burned his throat.

"What is it?" He groaned, forcing himself not to cough.

"Scottish liquor. I got a taste for it, being in English captivity," replied the ruler. "Sit down, that's an order, and stop shaking. What's with you? When you thought you were about to die, you were like a rock and now you can't control yourself?"

He poured him another strange drink.

"Somehow I can't, but it's nothing, it will pass in a moment," Theo took a deep breath and took another sip. According to him, the drink was tremendously strong, stronger than anything he had dealt with so far, so he had to be very careful not to go too far.

The monarch sat down opposite him, rested his elbows on the table and put his hands together with the tips of his fingers, a gesture he had taken involuntarily from the English nobles.

"I asked you a question a moment ago and you answered correctly," he began. "I'm under no obligation to ask your forgiveness, but I'm asking you anyway. I put you on a hard test, the crueler that it is actually unnecessary. But I had to see with my own eyes if you were as brave a knight as they say, otherwise I couldn't have entrusted you with the task I had prepared for you.

This is a very important task, although do not expect any honors or awards from it. Can I count on you?"

"Sir, just order..."

Theo wanted to get up and kneel, but to his amazement his legs would not obey him.

"Sit down," laughed the king. "The body doesn't always want to obey man, as you can see. Have another drink."

"Thank you very much, but my head is weak. I've to keep moderation or I'll be drunk soon," Theo replied.

John II nodded and continued:

"If I want you to fulfill your task correctly, I must introduce you to the merits, and it's this: do you know what ransom has been requested for me? Three million ecu. I cannot pay it, although I agreed and left my son as a hostage in Savoy. Do you know how many people would have to starve if I had kept this agreement?"

"I don't know, certainly many... But France needs a king," said the knight helplessly.

"Oh yes, the king," the monarch agreed bitterly. "But not me. Just look at the result of my rule: half the country lost, the other half in ruins, the treasury empty and an English shoe on our neck. I can't handle it, I can't. Charles will be a much better ruler when... I return to England."

"To England? But, merciful Lord, who knows what's going to happen there..." Theo stammered in a daze as he mechanically twisted his cup in his fingers.

The King smiled sadly.

"They'll poison me," he replied calmly, without a hint of affectation. "It's most likely. Only that way they will pave the way for Charles, and he will take care of them. He's a cold, sly fox, and he hates the English. Do not protest, I didn't order this to you! When you receive the message about my death... at the same time, you will also receive a second quest that you can only find out about then. And I will give you the third one now: this letter you will take to Blanka, then, to Navarra. Charles the Bad does not like you, but you seem to be on good terms with his son, so you will find an opportunity to pass on this letter."

It was common knowledge that of all the women who passed through his life, John II loved only Blanka, whom his own father had taken from him, forcing him to marry Joanna, who had recently died.

"And now the first and most important task," he continued. "I cannot make you illusions about Charles, unfortunately he gives a willing obedience to lips that are hostile to you, but nevertheless he will probably be able to appreciate the importance of what you will do for him. And you are to prepare an uprising. A great national uprising that will break out at the sign you give. Robert Deauville is already operating in Aquitaine, but this strutter is too confident that the knighthood alone will cope with the English. Everyone will listen to you: the nobility, peasants and townspeople, therefore I entrust to you the tying of all the strands. Do you understand how much depends on you?"

"Oh," Theo sighed. "I think I'll drink more."

He concluded that the Scottish liquor was not so bad after it had stopped burning, and that it brightened the mind perfectly. The king looked at him with a smile.

"By the way, it's interesting how someone who has blue blood in his veins could get along with the commoners in such a way," he added after a moment.

"Sire, I have seen enough of my blood to know that it is red as it is in other people," the knight replied, and suddenly chuckled. He felt cheerful under the influence of the Scottish drink. "And everyone wants to fight. You have this reason. For example, my fiancée says that every king collects taxes, but somehow it's nicer to pay your own."

"So, you have a fiancée? Whoever she is, she surely supports you in every endeavor," the monarch smiled. "She must be beautiful, brave and strong, other people would not be suitable for you."

"That's what she is," Theo agreed. "And what is this populace, I found among these people as many noble and brave hearts as there are among the knights. In any case, they remained faithful to me when they all abandoned me."

"The only question is whether they are the same or have they become so in contact with you," John II stood up and took from the wall a decorative sword with the coat of arms of Valois on the hilt.

"Take this weapon now and use it only for the good cause," he said. "I'm sorry I can't restore your position in the world to your birth, but it will be better for our cause if you remain an outlaw. You get it, don't you?"

The knight knelt at his feet and kissed the hilt of his sword reverently.

"Lord, please let me go to England with you..." he began pleadingly, but the king shook his head.

"You'll be needed here," he said sternly. "I cannot be saved, and I don't need to. Believe me, it is not worthwhile for an individual to obscure the good of the country. In time you will understand that I was right. Now go away and remember everything I have commanded you."

Theo left the royal apartments confused, though much calmer. Probably it was the result of a drink with an unknown name and unknown power drunk on an empty stomach, but he was still very happy and the whole terrifying adventure suddenly seemed quite funny to him. He had to hold back from giggling along the way.

His friends were waiting for him in front of the Louvre gate, singing some pointless indecency to Gwidon's voice, which made the sentries laugh so much that they covered their mouths with gloves to avoid bursting out with unregulated laughter. At the sight of their leader, the band sprang up from their seats.

"And what?" Pierre exclaimed.

"Nothing," Theo replied. "On the horses and out of here. Anyway, where did you get these animals?"

"And that's a problem?" Jean shrugged his thin shoulders. "There will always be a few Englishmen who, when properly asked, will not deny a man such a small favor."

"Jean, if they don't hang you, you will be a great man," Theo laughed, riding the horse left in front of the gate, given by the king's orders.

Only outside the city limits did the companions loosen up for good, and they spoke through each other for a while, so that it was impossible to understand a word. The knight listened to this cacophony with true delight, feeling that only now was he able to appreciate their devoted friendship that had allowed him to survive amidst a thousand failures. When they finally fell silent, he asked:

"How did you even think of following me to Paris?"

The friends looked at each other.

"It was a shared idea," Berengard said finally. "A long time after your departure, we sat and consulted, and finally Pierre stood up and made a horrible word to us, you do not even know how..."

"Not that much at all," Pierre grumbled.

"He said it is on such occasions that the people allow themselves to be considered as inferior to the nobility," Berengard went on relentlessly. "That all courage isn't assigned to high families and you have to prove it once the hell."

"Then he reminded us all of mum's trade," added Gwidon. "As for me, he even hit the bullseye, but the others took offense. And before we knew it we were on our way to Paris. You know the rest."

"Let's say that," Theo agreed. "What Bellette had to say about this?"

"Of course, we didn't tell her anything. Anyway, she went to the nunnery to get herbs because she was bothering by a female ailment and felt bad," Pierre explained to him. "Do you have any idea what would happen if she found out about our idea? We would have to tie her up or lock her up somewhere, otherwise she would have followed us even on foot."

"You guys are not right in the head, but I love you," Theo laughed.

Before they reached their hideout in the marshes, he managed to tell his friends about what they did not know yet, especially since, to celebrate the miraculous rescue of the chief, they stopped at a roadside tavern. They could celebrate there as much as they wanted, because apart from a half-drunk innkeeper and two maidservants, not the first youth and questionable manners, there was no one there. They continued their journey, refreshed with wine and roasted mutton, and reached their hideout in delicious moods.

At the sight of them, Prezios, who was washing her skirt in the stream, jumped to her feet.

"Thank God you are here!" She exclaimed. "I already thought you were dead!"

"We thought we were dead, too," Pierre replied cheerfully. "Where's my sister? We have great news for her!"

"I see. Bellette, come here! See who's back!" The Gypsy shouted.

The door of the hut creaked and Bellette, sad and pale as the moon, looked out over the clearing without interest. As soon as her eyes fell on Theo, her pale face turned a bright blush, and with a piercing scream of unconscious joy, the girl threw herself into his arms.

"Gosh, she love him more than I thought," her brother shook his head, watching their warm welcome.

"Well, she has already mourned him," said Martin. "It's important that we are all together again. This is true grace of God."

*****

It is not known what ways the news of the Paris adventure spread around the neighborhood, because friends did not even confide it to Father Prospero, and after a few days the whole Touraine was gossiping about it. Theo was looked upon with double respect, as was his companions, who had the courage to follow their leader to Paris and speak to the king himself. The death of the Black Knight made a much smaller impression on everyone, only Don Paulino was concerned about it, who thus lost his protector, and did not get rid of his sworn enemy. Not knowing what to do, he sent Prince Edward a detailed account of the event, asking for instructions, for he rightly reasoned that Touraine should now be ruled by the Black Prince. After all, it was on his behalf that Roger de Valois was in charge of the province. Theo, for his part, planned to visit Bongrais Castle and deal with the treacherous Spaniard, but certain events made him forget about the immediate fulfillment of his intentions.

One day, just as he was teaching the recovered Armando to use the slingshot, Father Prospero appeared in the clearing.

"Theo, someone's waiting for you at the convent," he said. "Just do not answer me with your grace that if he loves, he will wait. Your answers would even put a perfectly healthy person into an asylum for the insane."

"Alright. Practice it yourself, Armando, you're doing great," Theo said, and followed the monk.

He managed to like both Gypsies, endowed with a lively temperament and a very nice disposition, and he did not mind that they would stay with him, especially since they had nowhere to go. Preziosa dressed like a man, believing that in men's company it is much more convenient, and even despite her brother's protests, she cut her hair, and all this was like a salt in the eye for father Prospero. He thundered at "the loosening of morals," but did nothing. Theo thought at first that it was for this reason that the old prior is so silent and strict that day, but, having crossed the threshold of the monastery refectory, he immediately realized that the reason was completely different.

In the refectory, King John, cloaked in a gray mantle, and his favorite page were waiting for him.

"Do not kneel," the king warned him. "I'm here incognito. I didn't think we would meet again so soon, but I had to come here. Something terrible has happened and I need your help."

"If only I can..." the outlaw glanced at the silent page and caught his gloomy gaze. Something about the boy bothered him, but he couldn't make out what.

"My daughter Isabel has been kidnapped by the envoys of the Black Prince," said the king. Edward wants to marry her to his firstborn, who is much younger than she is. Do you understand what this means? If it comes to this marriage, we will never get rid of the English from our land again. Admittedly, under Salian law,

Isabel cannot inherit the throne, but her husband will. I knew about these plans beforehand, so I arranged my daughter's marriage to Gian Visconti, although I don't like the prospect of affinity with this family. Gian's father is a tyrant and cruelty, but Isabel seems to be safe there, and they are not threatening France's future."

"I heard that..." Theo began, and bit his tongue.

The king looked at him severely.

"I guess what," he said. "Nobody escapes slander, as you can see. I'm just surprised someone believed it. Am I Turkish to sell my own daughter? Anyway, never mind that. Please, Theo, save my baby!"

"It's an honor for me, but where am I going to look for her?" The knight scratched his head and thought deeply.

"I don't think she's already been in Aquitaine, my people have protected the entire border, but who knows? I myself have my hands tied by this damned treaty in Bretigny, and I don't know who to trust... Theo, save her..." for a moment John II did not look like the ruler of a large and rich country, but like every desperate father.

"Sire, I'll try. I'll take Her Majesty at the hands of these rogues, or I'll die myself," promised the outlaw solemnly.

However, he returned to his hideout very embarrassed. He really didn't have any fuss about it, and time was working against him. He gathered his people in the clearing and briefly told them about the whole misfortune.

"I think I already know. This ridiculous marriage must be done somewhere, and of all monasteries only the Cistercians favor the English," Armando said calmly after the chief had finished speaking.

"This limits our search points to Amiens and Chateauroux," said Olivier, who knew best about such issues. "But both of these places are equally likely."

Theo nodded approvingly.

"Then we have to split up," he decided. "Preziosa and Armando stay because they are not trained yet, and for the rest, Olivier, Martin and Alain are with me, we will check the Chateauroux. The rest, led by Pierre, go to Amiens. Any group that determines they are in the wrong place immediately turns back to join group two. Is it clear?"

"Like you don't have any sense," Pierre muttered, hardly objecting to a hopeless mission.

Theo looked at him sadly.

"I know it looks bad, but we have to give it a try," he said.

"Of course," said Gwidon. "Something like that, he wanted our princess. This is too god for the likes of you, you rascals."

"Why exactly doesn't the king take care of it himself?" Jean asked.

"It can't be, so we have to do it," the chief replied, without going into any consideration on the subject, which could take up to the night.

Pierre got up from the stump on which he was sitting.

"Here we go," he said. "There is no time to waste, because at any moment they can take her to Aquitaine, which is not our territory, and we would have a hard time working there."

"Right." Theo stood up as well and looked at his chosen squad.

He also thought it was a good thing that Bellette was in the village, because he would prefer not to explain to her that he was again going on a mission, almost to enemy territory.

"Here we go," he commanded briefly, and went on ahead.

They reached Chateauraux, which was their destination, relatively quickly, as they still had horses grazing in a secret clearing in the forest. Otherwise, the journey might have taken quite a long time. Immediately upon arrival, they split up to penetrate the surroundings and conduct a discreet surveillance. The idea was to find out about everything that had happened in the town in the last few days, and in particular, if English soldiers had not come there with an eleven-year-old girl. There was little hope that anyone would have seen them, but nonetheless there was such a possibility. Theo was the first to finish his inspection, and under an imaginary pretext, he got into the Cistercian monastery, but there was nothing unusual there either.

Alain and Olivier also found nothing, only Martin, who was the last to arrive, had encouraging news.

"One of the milkers saw some Englishmen take the haunted house in the early morning," he said. "They didn't see her because she was hidden behind the cows, but she did. She said there was someone short with a brown cloak with them. Maybe it is our doom?"

"Maybe," Theo rubbed his mouth with his hand and thought. "Coincidence a little unlikely. We will try. Where's this house?"

Almost every town and larger village had their "haunted house", an old shack that was avoided from afar. This one stood on the land belonging to the Cistercian monastery, which seemed to confirm Martin's guesses. The friends walked carefully around the old house and found a stable in the back, where several horses were quietly chewing their fodder.

"It has to be here," Theo whispered. "There is no need to wait, there are only a few, but there may be more soon. We go."

They crept up to the window and looked carefully inside, where three English-colored men were playing dice, then split up and ran in together at the sign: Theo and Alain through the door, Marin and Olivier through the window. The rest fled from the second floor, and all hell broke loose in moments. Theo left the soldiers to his friends, even though his heart drew him to fight, and he started for the stairs. He broke through there easily and ran upstairs, laying down another Englishman on the way. There were several rooms upstairs, all closed. To get to them, he had to break down the door, happy as it was made and equipped with poor locks.

It was only in the fourth that he saw a small figure huddled in a corner, dressed in expensive robes, trembling and crying.

"For God's sake," it flashed through his mind. "It's just a child involved in terrible things. What is she guilty of?"

He knelt and kissed the little girl's hand.

"Your Majesty, I'm Theodoric de Bongra and I've come to take you home," he said.

She didn't speak, just stared at him with terrified eyes and gasped for air like someone unconscious from fatigue, but as he took her wrist and gently pulled her behind him, she stood up and pressed against him, suppressing a sob.

He cautiously looked out the door and pulled the little girl with him so that his body was a shield between her and any possible attack. Martin and Olivier lay downstairs, one curled up in an unnatural position, the other leaning his head almost split in half against the stairs. The princess screamed.

"Please don't look, Your Majesty," Theo covered the girl's eyes with his hand and led her through the room as quickly as possible. Outside, they saw Alain lying on the ground in a pool of blood. The barely standing soldier who had fought him earlier now lunged at Theo. He pushed him away and stuck his sword under his arm. The Englishman has fallen.

"You're not getting away," he moaned. "The entire squad will be here soon. They will catch up with you anyway."

Horse's hooves rumbled on the road, Theo spun around, raising his sword, but the male-clad girl who had jumped off her mount next to him was not an English soldier. It was Bellette.

"What are you doing here?!" He shouted in amazement and horror.

"Preziosa told me where you went," she replied. "I thought if I will die, this time, hand in hand."

"What? Over my dead body! But thank God you came. Take the princess and run to Paris fast. You just hand her over to the king, no one else," Theo said frantically, propping the little girl up onto the horse's back. "Get in, I tell you! And take the sword, if anyone blocks your way, cut without mercy."

Bellette was daringly following his command, tears streaming down her eyes.

"Run away with us," she whispered.

"No. There will be more soldiers here soon, someone has to give you time to free yourselves," replied her knight sharply. "Do not cry. My life is only one life, and it is about the future of the country. Your Majesty, please take care of her when I will be gone."

"She will be a lady of the court," promised the princess in a trembling voice.

"Come on, Bellette, come on!" Theo shouted, and slapped the horse hard on the rump.

When the sound of his hooves died away in the distance, the outlaw wiped the sweat from his forehead and knelt next to Alain, lifting his head slightly. The man groaned barely audibly and opened his eyes, already covered in deadly mist.

"Hold on!"

"I'm dying," the smith whispered with effort. "You can't help me. You too will die. Do you hear the soldiers?"

The knight realized that there was indeed the sound of the hooves of many horses on their way towards the monastery from a distance. Alain groaned softly, and his head suddenly heavy in his friend's hands. Theo closed his eyes, took the slain soldier's sword and stood with his back to the large oak so that he could not be surprised from behind. He waited for the Englishmen erect, head held high, and his heart beat faster and faster.

When they appeared, he greeted them with a well-aimed throw of a dagger, aimed at the neck of the unit commander. The surprised man grabbed his throat and fell off his horse. His men grasped the situation at a glance and, finding it clear (all around, a battlefield, the princess disappeared, and one man is standing against them) understood that all their lives depended on whether they could capture this young man with a sword and make him testify. However, it turned out to be very difficult. The young Frenchman defended himself so fiercely that it was only when two of the attackers were dead, and the third was wounded so badly that he was no longer able to fight any more, that the English, obsessed with combat frenzy, understood what he meant. He just wanted to stop them from chasing the princess who had been taken from here, and so far he had done very well. They didn't know who he was, but they began to suspect who he might be, and the more they tried to get him alive. For his part, Theo was doing his best to sell his skin as expensive as possible, though his eyes were already turning tired with exhaustion and he was bleeding from several, not very fortunately serious wounds. To die in battle - that was all he wanted.

As he seemed to reach his goal, a short crossbow bolt whistled in the air and struck him with terrible force on the shoulder below the collarbone. Theo released the sword from his hand and sank to his knees, gasping for breath, no longer able to defend himself from the hands that grabbed him violently, knocking him to the ground. Someone ripped the arrow out of his body without even bothering to loosen the point. He cried out in pain involuntarily and passed out.

When he returned from a pleasant unawareness to the world of the living, he realized that he was kneeling on stones, with his hands twisted backward chained to a pole. At the same time, as if from a distance, he felt a terrible pain in his shoulder, which sobered him. He looked up with an effort.

"Oh, welcome, Lord Count," said a voice he knew well. "Welcome to Meung Castle."

Captain Moore stood above him, striking the top of his left boot steadily with his coiled hunting crop. His animal face twisted with triumph and terrible joy.

"The Black Prince will be very glad to see you," he continued. "It will be a real hot party."

"Have you long believed, you English hog, that you are human?" Theo asked hoarsely.

"Did he say something? I'll teach you respect in a moment."

Moore unfolded his hunting crop and slapped the prisoner on his bare back. After the first blow, there was more, but Theo could barely feel them, the arm pierced by the arrow so badly hurt.

"That's it," came Sir Winslow's unexpectedly familiar, cool and sarcastic voice. "Well, Captain, have you forgotten what the order was? They are all to remain alive until the arrival of the Prince of Wales, so acknowledge that I, who are responsible for the prisoners, will not allow any harassment here."

"Yes, Sir Winslow," Captain Moore muttered, humbling himself in the blink of an eye and backing away.

"Take the prisoner to the guardhouse and bandage," the knight ordered, then went to his chamber to take off the uncomfortable armor.

He was angry and devastated, for capturing the outlaws was a little success compared to failing to find the princess. Having cleaned himself up, he went to the guardhouse. He met his medic in the doorway, deeply angry.

"This French man can't be dressed," he screamed. "He said me such words that I haven't heard anything like it since dealing with drunken sailors in Calais. If I don't dress him, he'll bleed to death, but to tell you the truth, I don't care."

Winslow nodded to the two guards and stepped into the guardhouse.

"If someone acts like a mindless animal, he is treated like an animal," he said emphatically. "Tie this outlaw. And you dress his wounds. That's an order."

Theo struggled furiously with the soldiers, but he had to finally give in, and the mortally offended medic was free to tie his wounded arm with blood stopping bandages. When he finished, he and the sentries left. Theo leaned his head against the wall without looking at Winslow. The latter stared at him for a moment, then asked:

"Why did you do this for? You were so stung in the eyes that the pointless slaughter could finally end thanks to this marriage? Do you even realize what you have done?"

"Let me think... yes," replied the outlaw coldly.

"You're insane. This marriage could save many people." Winslow walked over, regarded his sunken eyes and gray face with concern, a pain in his heart that he couldn't help him. Not this time.

"Better to die standing than to live on your knees," Theo met his eyes relentlessly.

"We speak different languages. I feel sorry for you because you deserve a better fate than what awaits you," the Englishman sighed.

Theo clenched his lips.

"Maybe you're right, but only from your point of view," he said finally, his voice tired. "Could I... get some water?"

Winslow took from the pot in the corner and tilted the metal cup to his lips.

"Give me your word that you will not try any foolishness, and I will have you take off your shackles," he asked. The prisoner's pupils flashed wildly.

"I won't promise anything to any Englishman," he growled.

A young squire in the colors of the Black Prince peered into the guardhouse.

"Sir Essex is asking you to see you, Sir Winslow," he said.

The knight shook his head desperately, as if this meeting was not the nicest thing that could happen to him.

"Take him to the others," he ordered the soldiers, leaving the room.

Theo made every effort not to lose consciousness again as he was dragged into the dungeons. He was a little dizzy, however, because when he regained his clarity of thought, he was lying on stones in some dark, damp, musty dungeon, chained, with vague outlines bending over him.

"He's alive," said Pierre's voice in relief.

"How the hell..." he began, but his voice refused to obey him.

"We followed our plan, but they already took you," Berengard explained to him. "We followed them, we wanted to rescue you... but there were simply too many of them. That's all. And the others?"

"They're dead. Killed." Theo sat up, overcoming weakness and leaned against the wall.

"Rest in peace," Jean sighed, making the sign of the cross. "They died with honor."

"Go the hell," Pierre muttered dissatisfiedly. "What did you get hit with? With a dagger or a sword?"

"A crossbow arrow," Theo replied curtly.

"He would let someone at a distance of a dagger..." Gwidon chuckled merrily.

"I feel guilty. It was because of me they died," the knight said softly.

"Not because of you, but because of those bloody Englishmen. Don't play dumber than you are." Berengard knelt and touched his forehead.

"He has a fever, right?" Francois asked.

"A little for now," replied Berengard with concern. "But I'm afraid it will get worse and we don't have much water."

"There are some barrels here. If you all move a little bit, I'll reach them." Armando stood and tugged irritably at the shared chain.

"And what are you doing here? You were supposed to stay," Theo had only now begun to see in the darkness well enough to distinguish his companions.

"He was determined, comedian," Pierre replied glumly.

"Nothing of that, empty... some old iron in one." The Gypsy said in disappointment, having penetrated the contents of the barrels.

Theo flinched at the words.

"What did you say?" Iron?" He made sure, then he struggled to get up and tried to squeeze to the barrels.

"What are you doing, you crazy? Sit down, you can barely stand on your feet!" Cried Berengard, grabbing his elbow.

"You have to check, maybe there is something that can be used," said the knight feverishly. "If we can get that hook off the wall, we'll free ourselves from the chain, and that will be something."

"Wait a minute, it's not that stupid..." Berengard frowned.

"Theo, my dear commander, you have a fever, something is raging in your poor head," Pierre wrung his hands, convinced the words were unrelated gibberish.

"Check what's in that barrel," Theo insisted.

Pierre put him by force against the wall

"Okay, I'll check," he said resignedly. "But you sit down, because I'll hit you so much that the whips that the English gave will seem like kisses from my sister."

The barrel between the unidentified pieces of iron turned out to be a real treasure - a broken saw. While handling the broken piece was difficult and exhausting, it could be the key to their freedom, so they immediately started sawing the rusty hook that held their chain to the stone. Theo wanted to get involved as well but was not allowed to.

"You'll need your strength to get out of here, so rest and let us take care of this," Berengard said flatly as his friend tried to protest this pact.

Anyway, Theo felt very bad, which he was not used to, because he probably had never been sick before, except that he had once dislocated his wrist and received unimportant scrapes several times. He didn't even get sick as a small child, which was perhaps the result of the extremely strict, Spartan upbringing he had received at his father's request, but that was why the fever from wounds was completely new to him and he didn't quite know how to deal with it.

Fortunately, the day Berengard announced in a voice trembling with emotion that the hook was about to break, he felt a little better.

"Well, shoulder to shoulder," he said, rising from his seat. "In the name of God, on three. One, two and ...three!"

A heavily jerked chain rang, the hook creaked and jumped off the wall, breaking in two. Removing the shackles from the arms and legs of all seven was a piece of cake.

"Okay, then we got rid of that damn chain. What now?" Francois asked after the hard work was finished.

"Now Pierre and Gwidon are starting to argue, just loud enough to be heard in the courtyard," Theo commanded, grasping the coiled chain with an eloquent movement.

His friends caught it in a flash. It was known that it was Pierre and Gwidon who had the strongest voices, so it was to be expected that they would bring sentries to the dungeon with their brawl. So it happened. The deafening and disarming of the unsuspecting guards were a matter of a moment, but then the friends were stuck. They were in the basement, forming a maze of corridors, one of which must have led outside, but the question was which one.

"How can you be sure that there is a hidden passage here at all?" Pierre asked as they walked down the corridors full of dust and cobwebs.

"There is in every castle, you just have to be able to find them," Theo explained to him. "Explore the walls and look for some leverage or whatever..."

"Right," Pierre agreed ironically. "Let's look for anything."

His tone made it clear what he thought about it all.

"In old ballads and poems, the greatest skeptic always finds a hidden passage," said Gwidon.

"Yeah right," Pierre growled, and hooked his sleeve over what looked like a torch handle. Something creaked and a piece of the wall moved aside with a hellish creak.

"Pierre, you are brilliant." Theo took the torch from Berengard's hand and illuminated the corridor, which must have been unused for hundreds of years, and it reeked of mold and rat pellets. It was impossible to see where it was leading, but with the only alternative to return to the dungeon, they plunged into it without hesitation. The corridor was long and winding, partially cluttered with stone fragments, but after struggling through these obstacles for a long time, they suddenly saw light, and a sigh of relief escaped from all their breasts. Armando pushed his way to the front of the procession and was the first to reach the redemptive exit.

The painful disappointment was so great that at first, he didn't even say anything, just stood and stared down the cliff of rock, almost as steep as a vertical wall and smooth that there was nowhere to hammer even a fingernail in. There was a rocky beach below with a great lake undulating calmly behind it. If it had been closer you might have thought of a jump, but it was at least twenty feet from the foot of the mountain.

"We're dead," he said finally, dully. The others stopped beside him and stared down silently.

"If only a rope," whispered Gwidon at last. "One could take a chance."

"Where will I get it?" Theo muttered, trying not to give in to despair and thinking logically.

"The chain may be?" Jean asked shyly. "I took it with me because I thought it might be useful as a weapon."

"Of course, it will! Jean, you are the king!" The chief hugged him and, having snatched the chain from his hand, fastened one end of it to the bracket in the wall, which was once part of the hinges.

"Can you get down?" Berengard asked.

"Sure. Fortunately, I'm basically left-handed," he replied. The newly awakened hope poured into his veins a force he had not expected.

One by one, hurting their hands on the rusted iron, the friends rode down the cliff, and when the last of them stood on the rocky beach, they barely held back to utter a collective cry of joy. They were free. If they manage to escape the pursuit, they will surely follow them soon.

As soon as they could, hiding in the bushes, they left the castle and only stopped when it was out of sight. They were relatively safe now.

"Run now," Theo ordered.

"Of course. Are you okay under that black fringe? You look like death on the banners! You won't get far..." Pierre looked around and cocked his ear.

"Someone's coming," he said after a moment. "A carriage and a few armed men. We carry out requisitioning."

They fell on both sides of the road, arming themselves with larger stones, for lack of something better. They felt a little embarrassed by this primitive weapon, but they had no other. When a four-horse carriage appeared on the road, escorted by several mounted knights, they jumped on them with the courage of desperado. The accurately thrown stones confused the armed men, throwing three from their horses on the spot, the rest did not even have time to take up their arms when Pierre and Jean slipped between them, catching up with the carriage. Others rushed ferociously to the escort, tearing their swords from their hands, dragging them to the ground and overwhelming them like puppets. Pierre, meanwhile, opened the door of the carriage and looked with interest at the young blonde girl in widow's robes sitting in it.

"Forgive me," he said with some rudeness. "Chief, let it come here."

Theo, with the last of his strength, got into the carriage and fell into the seat opposite the young widow.

"Are you crazy?!" The escort commander yelled, pushing Gwidon and Francois away from him. "Do you know who this lady is?! She is Lady Joan Fitzooter, Prince Edward's first cousin! You'll pay your heads for this attack."

"Tell the Black Prince, you fool, we'll give his cousin back to him when we get to Touraine," Pierre replied. "For now, we need it as a guarantee that there will be no pursuit. Exactly like that."

He slammed the door and leapt nimbly onto the trestle beside the terrified coachman, taking the reins away from him.

"What are you gonna do with me?" Lady Joan asked calmly, folding her narrow hands in her lap.

Theo regarded her appreciatively. She was tall and slender, with a fair complexion and gray eyes shaded by dark blonde eyelashes. Her cool beauty was like a mountain lake and flowers growing on the slopes of bare rock. Suddenly he regretted that he hadn't had the opportunity to wash and change during the escape, that he didn't feel any better. Indeed, it is difficult to enjoy the company of a beautiful lady fully when you are sore and consumed by fever and smell like a dungeon.

"We're not going to do anything," he said. "You may be disappointed, Lady, but we are all too tired. You are safe in our company."

"You are bleeding," the lady remarked.

Theo touched the dirty bandage on his arm. Indeed, under the influence of the effort, the barely sealed wound opened and blood soaked through the linen.

"It's okay, it'll heal. Do you care, lady?" He asked with a slight hint of defiance in his voice.

The Englishwoman smiled.

"I wish no one ill," she said. "Besides, I feel sorry for you, because if my brother gets you in his hands..."

"He'd have to get me first. Many have tried this for a long time, and to no avail." He answered her.

He felt somehow strange under the gaze of the young Englishwoman's gray eyes, and he had to admit that he liked her much more than he should. In her gaze he could also read genuine sympathy, and that made the whole situation unnecessarily ambiguous.

"I think I know who you are," she said after a moment. "The news of a brave outlaw has reached England and describes you very accurately, especially emphasizing that you do not harm women, even from the hostile camp."

"No, I don't," he admitted. "I guess I'd have to fall underground out of shame if I... Are they really talking about me?"

Lady Joan nodded solemnly.

"Yes. And not only that. Especially the story describes the gorget you wear around your neck and the fact that you are young, black-haired and very handsome. One with the other... and I already know that you are Theo le Vengeur, exile knight, defender of the oppressed. I didn't think I would get to know you so soon."

"Well, nice to meet you," he said softly. "And sorry to look like this, but that's the merit of your brother's people, deceptions. Well, it happens."

"You're lucky to be alive at all. My brother's people are ferocious." Lady Joan looked at him seriously.

"So, do we," he replied, looking her straight in the eye.

Suddenly he felt the urge to kiss her and was surprised himself. There was something about this young lady that made his heart feel some unhealthy attraction. It was dangerous, and he liked that it was dangerous, so it was good that soon the carriage stopped.

"Okay, chief, the ride is over," Pierre said cheerfully, opening the carriage. "Get out. Goodbye lady, and no offense."

"Let's say that."

The Englishwoman smiled ambiguously and closed the door herself. Pierre pressed the reins into the hand of the shaking coachman.

"Take your mistress to the castle," he ordered him sharply. The boy nodded relievedly and harnessed the horses until they started.

"Thank God, it's all over," Berengard sighed piously, putting his arm around Theo. "How are you, my friend?"

"Poor," the chief replied, and he had never been sincerer in his life.

Now that the tension with which he had lived for the last few days had subsided, he felt terrible, like someone dying of exhaustion, and he didn't care more and more. Supported by his friend's caring arm, he reached the hideout with difficulty and fell on the pile of pelts, losing consciousness. The exhausted body finally surrendered, and for many days the wounded knight felt a fever without recognizing anyone. Maybe for the first time in his life he was really sick, but the loving care and herbs Father Prospero brought had finally won, and Theo began to regain his strength.

"It's about time you recovered," the old monk grumbled as he changed his dressings. "And what was that for? At least you had a good time pretending to be the savior of your homeland?"

"I don't know?" He replied. "Let me think. I lost three friends, got hit with a crossbow, got rehearsed and spent some time in the dungeon... If it's not a fun, I don't know what is anymore."

"You are not right in the head. Try to sit down, we'll see how strong you are," sighed Prospero.

The knight propped himself up on his elbows, then sat down and took a bowl of roast and bread from Jean's hands.

"Bellette isn't back?" He asked.

"No," Prospero replied. "But I know from my sources that she made it safely to Paris, because the princess is now at the Louvre. Don't worry about her, you told her to stay in a safe place."

"I have to go there to get her," Theo muttered, eating greedily.

"I wonder how. You're all in shreds. You look like a herd of bulls trampling you," Pierre sneered as he stood in the doorway. "You wouldn't stay in the saddle even if we tied you up. Recover your strength first, great and mighty Count de Bongrais, if Bellette loves you, she will wait."

"She probably thinks I'm dead."

Pierre patted him on the shoulder.

"She does not think, she does not think, she knows well that devil will not take an old sinner like you to hell," he laughed and left. He was glad that the whole thing had turned out relatively well, although three of his friends paid with lives for the princess's release from the hands of the English. He thought of them now as heroes who had fallen in battle, even though you couldn't find a lot of people just as unfit for romantic legends - ordinary, dark fagots, a little clumsy, superstitious and down-to-earth like hundreds of thousands like them.

Among the outlaws, the death of close people was common, they accepted it with sadness, but calmly and without surprise, he knew it best. He had wandered around with outlaws since the age of sixteen and had seen a lot.

Theo was convinced, but mostly because he was actually too weak for any journey, which infuriated him. He was not used to the role of a convalescent, and he was furious when he was told to lie down, rest and not be nervous, as if he were a lady of the court suffering from migraines, and not the leader of the band of forest robbers, famous all over France. He recovered his strength slowly, or not as quickly as he would have liked. However, the long-awaited day had come when he was able to swim without rest their forest lake to the other shore and back.

"All right," he said, stepping ashore. "I'm going to Paris tomorrow. I'm now healthy as before."

"Yes, indeed... And besides, how do you want to stand before the king in these rags?" Pierre asked skeptically.

"It's not a problem," said Jean. "I've long ago procured something he could wear. There are many people here from whom it would be a sin not to steal something?"

Pierre shrugged irritably.

"Okay," he agreed. "But you won't go alone. There is no way. And if you try, I'll hit you so that you won't get up for the next two weeks."

Everyone liked this idea, including Preziosa, who already considered herself a full member of the gang and behaved like that. With her boyish acrobat figure, with her hair cut short, she did look like a pretty youngster, and because she was making rapid progress in learning archery, she might have come in handy. So the next morning the outlaws tidied up their outfits, shaved and combed their hair more carefully than usual, and set off for Paris, just in case, keeping to the side, rarely used trails. Nobody stopped them at the tollbooths, so it looked as if everything was going smoothly, but it was advised that Theo should go to the Louvre alone.

"It'll be better for all of us," explained Berengard. "Because if somebody tried to push us about, I'm afraid that Pierre would make a pate out of him and there would be a fight."

"I would," Pierre agreed, and no one doubted that he would. Bellette's brother ambition and sense of personal dignity had driven him and theirs into trouble more than once.

So Theo headed towards the palace alone, and this time he officially entered the gate, not hiding from the guards. Dressed noble, he could easily afford it.

"Where could I find the Good Lord?" he asked, jumping off his mount.

"Try it in the gardens at the back of the castle," one of the guards answered him.

It was a favorite place for walks and games of the whole manor in the so-called free time, if only the weather allowed. At present, the garden was full of a disassembled manor house in colorful dresses and attendant court elegant men dressed as for a ball. Some were playing cheese, others were walking or talking, sitting on carved benches. In one corner of the garden, the knight saw Princess Isabel swinging a saffian ball with a maid in a dark blue dress, with pale blond hair and curls. The girl looked happy and confident, unlike the last time they had met, and Theo thoroughly enjoyed the sight. He had the feeling that his companions had not died in vain.

"Your Majesty..." he said, making a ceremonial bow.

"Count de Bongrais!" The princess exclaimed happily.

The courtier in the blue dress turned abruptly and screamed, then fell sobbing into the knight's arms.

"I thought I lost you, I shed so many tears..." she sobbed, clutching him.

"You won't get rid of me that easily, my lovely one," Theo embraced her and pressed his face against her hair, for the first time since he knew her, smelling not of hay and herbs, but some Arabian fragrances.

"She must love you very much," said the little princess. She was smiling at them as she tossed her ball.

"So you came back," the voice of John II sounded right next to them.

Theo knelt hastily on one knee, and Bellette leaned forward in a deep bow.

"Get up, both of you," said the king. "Your merits for the crown of France are so great that it burns me ashamed that I cannot reward them properly. Unfortunately, in this situation it is impossible, but let us not lose hope that better times will come, those in which your courage will be appreciated."

"We are not serving our country for awards or honors," Theo said, inclining his head with due respect.

"If everyone thought the way you do, I wouldn't lose at Poitiers," the king sighed deeply. "You are probably the last of the knight errant... I must warn you that the Black Prince has the worst intentions towards you, but I hope this will not affect your efficiency in fulfilling the task I have entrusted to you."

"What task?" Bellette asked with some concern.

"I'll explain later," Theo promised. "Of course, it will not, Your Majesty. I don't care about any prince, white, black or red, only your command and your will count for me."

"That is very good," smiled John II. "Because I have one more for you."

He walked over to the fiery Bellette, took her hand, and placed her hand in the knight's.

"In the presence of the entire court and the council, I grant nobility to this lovely lady, who hereby command you to marry her, Count," he said formally. "I hope you will be very happy with each other, despite the war and all the evil. Kiss each other. Come on, that's an order."

Even though Theo was a little uneasy under the gaze of the entire court, he obeyed without reluctance, and so hot that Bellette couldn't catch her breath.

"Thank you, Most Beloved Lord." He whispered after a moment, pressing the girl to himself.

The king smiled kindly as he stroked the head of his daughter standing next to him.

"Maybe you will be happy," he muttered softly. He knew what he was saying. Personal happiness is not meant for kings and their families, and they must come to terms with it.

*****

"So, you will get married at last," said Gwidon with satisfaction, who loves happy endings.

The band was returning to Touraine a little later than planned, for the royal court needed some time to organize a farewell feast and a ball for Theo and Bellette, bringing some merriment among the bored courtiers. Her dialect words made everyone laugh, and her personal charm was softened by the awareness that she was after all... an ordinary peasant woman. Eventually, however, the bride and groom could begin their journey back to the place they called home. Bellette, following the example of Preziosa, put on a male costume for this journey, seductively emphasizing her shapes, and sang together with her brother in two voices their favorite since childhood "Cantata about a cat and an owl". This simple song always enjoyed them a lot and they sang it in moments of great joy.

"Though, to tell you the truth, I don't know if there's anything to be happy about," Pierre cautioned. "I have not changed my opinion about your relationship... but let it be."

"Thanks, benefactor," Theo laughed.

"Jean and I will decorate the chapel in the convent," said Francois dreamily. "And Gwidon will compose some nice ballad in honor of the newlyweds... It will be the event of the year in our area."

"Certainly," said Berengard.

Somehow, everyone became silent and thoughtful at the same time, remembering those who would not be able to participate with them in this great celebration.

"Something must be done to save their memory," Theo said finally.

"Exactly," Armando joined him. "We Gypsies do not have cemeteries, so we record the names of our dead by carving them into the rocks. In the middle of our forest there is a huge menhir, maybe on it?"

"Great idea. I'll do it," Theo decided.

He kept his word - even before his wedding, he engraved the names of his deceased friends on a large stone with the date of those events and the sign of the cross. It was everything he could do for them. He could not know what fate would bring to him, but he knew that he would never forget those who had paid for his success with their lives, and he felt guilty towards them that he now feels so utterly happy. It wasn't fair, but there was nothing he could do about it. Life went on with all its sorrows and joys, the war was still going on, and only he knew what an important role he and his band would have to play in it.

And it was a matter of the very near future.

The Renegade

Book Two

CHAPTER I

Family matters

"This is really outrageous," Beregard was saying to Jean as they both removed the extra shutters and other winter protection from the hut that served as a hiding place for the band. "Now that we've prepared ourselves properly, the winter has been mild, and last year we could almost freeze ours butts off. It sucks."

"That's the way it is," Jean consoled him. "It's probably better than the snow cutting us off from the world again. You forgot, how was last winter? We almost died of hunger and cold, and Theo and Pierre used to baste us because they couldn't meet their girlfriends? Yet we too were deprived of female company."

Beregard laughed, although the events Jean remembered were by no means funny and took their toll on them all.

"They finally got married," he sighed after a moment. "You know, I didn't really think I'd live to see this at all. Man learns all his life."

Theo and Bellette wedding were an event for the whole neighborhood, mostly because no one expected it - it was not customary, even in exile, to marry a subject. It was commonly believed that it would end up with a fleeting affair, so that the official wedding was quite a surprise. It was commented on variously, a few wandering bards, including Gwidon, even composed songs to celebrate this unusual event, but slowly they all got used to it. Bellette moved to a cabin in the woods, rightly believing that now her place is with her husband, and even, following the example of Preziosa, she put on a men's garment, much more practical in the woods than a dress. Here, no one minded it, except Father Prospero, who grunted at "the indignation of manners," though perhaps more out of a sense of duty than of genuine indignation. He was a young couple's best friend, and his friendship meant a lot. It was he, the snow had barely melted, who walked around the nearby monasteries, collecting information that might be of use to the band. It was not consoling news.

There was a disturbing concentration of English forces in the area, and rumors were heard here and there that Edward Plantagenet would personally lead his army. In any case, many swore that had seen his black armor with own eyes.

"As soon as I got rid of the Black Knight, I already have the Black Prince on my neck," Theo said as he listened to his account. "And they say that plenty is no plague."

"It's not funny," Pierre rebuked him. "When that Englishman gets your hands on you, he'll probably give you a radical cure for a headache: beheading."

"Not at all," Theo replied. "Because the English prefer to hang, not cut. You understand, cleaner then around. When you cut off someone's head, you have a lot of cleaning up afterwards."

"Possibly," his brother-in-law agreed. "But the beheading is so spectacular... Just think, the head rolling on the boards of the scaffold, body twitching in a pool of blood..."

"Pierre, you're even crazier than Theo, who never really had his head in total order," Father Prospero interrupted in disgust.

"Spring, Father. In the spring, no one complains about being too unreasonable."

"What you talk about? You, after all, suffer from a chronic shortage," growled the monk, thus closing the discussion.

This spring was indeed exceptionally beautiful and made even those forest people who stood firmly on the ground go crazy in romantic raptures. Of course, it was hard to expect that the old monk, like them, would feel this special time of the year, he associated it rather with diseases that plagued the hungry people in the early days, and with the laborious wandering to brother monasteries, where he took herbal mixtures. However, he also stopped sometimes among the trees, listening to the birds sing and remembering something that should have long been forgotten. The heart of this old monk was not as dry as everyone thought, but he kept this kind of thoughts only to himself and did not confide them to anyone. His constant wanderings throughout the province were very convenient for the outlaws, because thanks to this they were always informed about what was happening in the area, and no one, even the most distrustful Englishman, suspected that the humble Carmelite was the informant and helper of France's most wanted man. Thanks to him, Theo established contact with other groups of active resistance to the invaders, especially with the very numerous party of Robert Deauville.

He had the most trouble with the latter, since the proud nobleman did not believe in "fraternizing with commoners" and expressed his blunt surprise that someone as well-born as Theo might consider ordinary peasants as equals. After long talks, they finally came to what could be described as a half-compromise - Robert Deauville agreed to cooperate with the peasant groups at the beginning of the uprising, if he would lead. Conversations with other leaders were also difficult, but Theo was not discouraged by difficulties, and his optimism and youthful enthusiasm finally won over everyone, even the most reluctant.

Father Prospero was an invaluable help to him, without him he would not have been able to do the work ordered by the king, so it is no wonder that he immediately received a call to the monastery, although it made his plans a bit complicated - he was just about to go with his friends for the Bongrais Spring Festival.

"Go without me," he said. "I will join you as soon as I speak to Prospero. Think about me there."

"There will be no time, they will probably drag us into some kind of competition," Pierre laughed, being in a great mood that day, excited by the attractions that await him and the prospect of meeting the beautiful Fanchette.

"And I'm going with our chief. Who the hell knows if he won't get involved in a row," Beregard said firmly.

Jean, who had knocked his thumb out the previous day, joined as the third, so he could neither take part in the competition nor take up his favorite activity - stealing from wealthier passers-by. Under these conditions, he preferred to go with the chief.

Leaving the amused friends of Theo preparing for the journey, he went to the monastery, hoping quietly that he would still have time to party. But as soon as he entered the refectory, he immediately forgot about the feast, and his throat felt a bad feeling. Father Prospero did not say a word, he even left, leaving him alone with a frail boy, in whom the knight immediately recognized John II's favorite page, and even worse, he pushed both his friends in front of him.

The page was in a deplorable condition. His frizzy hair was matted in mats, his clothes torn and stiff from the sea salt, his haggard face and dark circles under his eyes were also evidence of how hard the journey was behind him. His presence in Touraine could only mean one thing, and Theo felt a faint despair rise in his heart. The boy got up and handed him a parchment wrapped in a piece of leather, bearing the seal of King John.

"A letter from the venerable king," he said softly.

"Heavier words than I can bear," the knight replied solemnly, unrolling the parchment. "I will never come to terms with this tragedy."

The words of the deceased monarch were now reaching him like a distant light, like a whisper from beyond the grave, and he had to pull himself together to start reading at last.

Dear, faithful knight. If you have received this letter, it means that I am already in another world," wrote the king. "Don't you dare cry for me and accept these words as the will of a person close to you. The day I ordered you to return to the woods, I did not give you one more reason for this. My infamous cousin had many powerful friends, you would not defend yourself against them in Paris, especially since my son is reluctant to you and you will not have a friend in him. Nevertheless, carry on the work I have commanded you, and one day Charles will be convinced of you. There is one more thing that concerns you in a very special way. Here is the page my letter brought you is your stepbrother...

Theo, a standing reader until now, sat down on the bench as if he suddenly ran out of strength and for a moment felt that he couldn't catch his breath. The curly page sat at the table, stubbornly staring at the top of the table without saying anything. Having rested for a while, the outlaw returned to the letter:

Yes, you read that right. Your father, as you know, spent a great deal of time by my side, and I can confidently say that I did not have such a devoted knight. What happened between him and this kid's mother was not unusual, but it has borne fruit. I kept the boy with me without telling anyone about his origins, but now he only has you. Therefore, take care of him and teach him all you know. Whether you let him bear your name is up to you, I am not ordering you anything about it. Be patient, the boy doesn't like you, and worse, he despises you, but after all, it's your father's son, blood of blood and bone of bone. I made an oath on him that he will obey you absolutely, the rest is in your hands. Goodbye.

Theo rolled up the parchment slowly, wondering confusedly what exactly he should do next. Now that he knew the truth, he recognized the boy's half-childish features as their deceased father - a broad face, deep-set gray eyes, square jaws, a short nose, and brutal, nearly fused eyebrows. Full, sensual lips with the expression of a silent question were softer. He probably took his mother's dark blond hair.

"Do you know the contents of this letter?" Theo asked after a moment, finally wanting to break the heavy silence. The page, without looking at him, nodded, then shook it.

"Yes and no," he said. "I haven't read it, but I know what it contains."

"Well, yeah... And do you have a name, kid?" the outlaw looked at him with unfavorable curiosity.

"Tristan," the boy muttered.

"Yes? And not Isolde at one go?" Unexpectedly, Theo got angry and slammed his fist on the table top. "It couldn't have been better. The venerable father had a sense of humor. Now I understand why he was so rare in Bongrais: he found himself a substitute for a son, and that was enough for him to be happy."

"It's hard to be surprised looking at you!" the boy replied.

There was a patter of feet outside the refectory door and Jean burst in.

"Four Englishmen have entered the monastery," he reported hurriedly. "Twice as many are waiting in front of the gate. Someone saw us."

Theo looked black.

"This is the nicest news I heard today," he said in such a tone that the good redhead froze with his mouth half open.

"They talk to Prospero," Beregard shoved his speechless friend unceremoniously. "Theo, this is a nasty suspicious story. Some larger force under the command of the Black Prince himself is going to Bongrais and intends to stay there. We must as soon as possible..."

"I know," the chief interrupted him brusquely, and cautiously looked out the window. "Dammit! Somehow a lot of them... Which way would it...?"

"Don't ask us, you're the one who thinks," Jean shrugged his thin shoulders.

"Sure, if I had only counted on you, I wouldn't have done too much," Theo growled harshly. "What a fact is a fact... Come on, Tristan, we must, as they say, retreat in English style."

"And is he coming with us?" asked Beregard.

"Yes, and close your mouth," said the leader. "Now is not the time for an explanation, there will be enough time for us to be safe in our wolf den. Now to the cellars, there is a passage behind the walls, Prospero showed them to me once. As in Meung."

"This one's again," Jean flinched. "I still have chills, when I remember, you once led us out of that castle. There were too many rats in this damned maze."

"You could have gone back to the dungeon, I wasn't holding you."

He picked up the hatch in the floor and went down last, closing it behind him.

"What are you so touchy today, for pity's sake?" Jean wondered, trying to discern his way in the darkness of the basement.

"And among such people I'm to spend my life..." Tristan wailed.

"Your life may be short if we come across the English," his brother replied sternly. "And you, Jean, keep your tongue between your teeth."

"I don't think so," the red-haired thief replied. "Since when our band is a monastery school of good manners?"

"Since there is a child with us unaccustomed to such words." Theo replied with such menace in his voice that Jean fell silent, frustrated.

He had never seen his leader like this before, and he didn't know what he had to think about it, and it was hard for him to talk to Beregard about it now.

They walked down the wide corridor until Theo felt for a door hidden in one wall and pushed it open for them to enter the world. They were some distance from the monastery, where the English could no longer see them.

"What now?" asked Beregard uncertainly.

"Me and Jean will rush to Bongrais to warn the people, and you take the boy to our hideout," Theo told him.

"You're right, you have to warn them, let them hide wherever they can, but be careful," his friend asked with concern in his voice.

He knew very well how much Theo liked rowdiness and with what willingness he would get himself into any possible situation with no way out, regardless of the risks or the price he might pay. Besides, he did not like the role of a nanny for the newcomer from nowhere, an adolescent with terrible manners, full of undisguised contempt for the "low born." But he knew his friend was right - if the Black Prince was coming to Bongrais, the townspeople had to be warned. This man had a gloomy reputation as the initiator of the slaughter in captured towns and villages, and his presence in these areas did not bode well. He would have liked to go to town with his friends but preferred not to oppose the chief when he was in such a state of agitation. He knew that both he and Jean could march very fast and that they would surely reach Bongrais in time, but he was very worried about what would happen next.

He was right - indeed, the outlaws managed to warn the amused inhabitants, who immediately gave up their fun and took refuge in their houses, and in addition bolted the door. They were used to hearing the count as their senior, and regardless of that they trusted him immensely. Having accomplished their task, the outlaws found themselves in a difficult position, for they could no longer escape. The city was surrounded by soldiers checking the area carefully and peering into every corner.

"We're running to Agnes," Francois decided for all. "In the event of a search, we'll crawl into the basement and pretend to be grown rats."

"Who is this Agnes?" Theo asked with rather little interest.

"You don't remember? My fiancée, we are spoken for," Francois looked at him scandalized.

"I don't remember everything... Well, come on, before they notice us," said the knight after a short thought, resigning from deliberating on the private life of Francois, who never mentioned any Agnes to him so vividly.

This one turned out to be just a local greener, a cheerful, a bit too plump brunette, very pretty, but badly dressed. Without unnecessary questions, she let her friends into her house, hiding them in the attic, from which there was a passage to the neighboring house. Fortunately, so far, the English were not about to plunder or search the houses, they simply marched in a tight formation through the town and took the empty castle. That was probably what they meant - the seizure of Bongrais Castle, which was, in a way, a symbol of resistance against them in these lands.

"Poor castle of mine," Theo muttered, half to himself and half to his friends. "It has to endure some ragmen all the time."

He bit his fingers nervously.

"Did you notice who was riding next to Prince Edward? That rat Paulino," said Preziosa, who had the best eyesight of them all. "Apparently, he has crept into his favor for good. I don't think that devil will ever die."

She didn't know Don Paulino at all, but she managed to take over the hatred for him from her new friends.

"He's got no reason to die so far," Francois said grimly. "Chief, let's put ourselves somewhere on him and kill the reptile."

"There will be time for that," the chief promised him with a smile. He was starting to calm down a little and his ability to think clearly was returning to him.

"Agnes, check the area, I don't want to meet a patrol right now, which would set off the alarm," he asked.

"Now?" Bellette was surprised. "Why, some special moment?"

"If you only knew how special..." Theo sighed and fell silent, no longer answering any questions.

"Something happened at the monastery?" Gwidon asked Jean, curious about the leader's mysterious behavior.

The man waved his hand.

"It happened, it happened," he said. "And if I knew what, I'd tell you for sure."

Bard looked at him in surprise, but didn't pursue the subject anymore, concluding that if Jean, the most outspoken member of the band, couldn't find the words for what happened, it must be something big.

Meanwhile, Jean was not only unable to find the words, and he was not yet sure if he had the right to reveal something that had led the adored chieftain to such a state of agitation. Agnes poked around for a while, then returned with the news that it was possible to sneak out of the city without any trouble with one of the side gates of which the English knew nothing.

"Glad you warned us," she said. "They could have massacred us. The mere fact that we were having a good time would stick in their craw."

She had a very funny, squeaky voice, but Theo thought as he looked at her that Francois had made the right choice. She looked like a very nice and sensible person at the same time.

"Thank you, Agnes," he said warmly. "You've helped us a lot."

"Always at your service, Monsignor," replied the girl with a smile.

Careful, lest the soldiers guarding the gates not notice them, the outlaws circled the city and fell into the forest.

"Well, that's it," sighed Gwidon, a bit disappointed that he did not have time to take part in the poetry competition. "Why do you think this Englishman decided to crash into Bongrais? There are no other places in the area?"

"He wants to tease me," Theo replied grimly, pushing forward so fast that the others couldn't keep up with brushing away the branches he'd shattered. "But I'll get under his skin, as I am Bongrais, or I'll have to shave my head and put on the habit."

"Don't you dare, my dear brother-in-law. Besides, I think the plan is brilliant, but somehow, we don't have enough to implement it. We won't be able to make it to the whole English army in a few," Pierre noted.

"Your courage is jammed like bad hinges, huh?" the knight hissed unpleasantly.

"Would you like to test my courage the hard way?"

"He said what he knew," Theo growled, releasing the bent branch so furiously that she slapped Armando on the forehead following him.

"Ow, watch out!" the tightrope walker yelled, holding his forehead.

"Oh, forgive me," the knight finally restrained himself and felt ashamed. "Don't be angry. Not every day you find out that the king has died and that he has inherited the ugliest task in the world. And a few Englishmen in my house... just a minor inconvenience."

Everyone was deeply saddened. John II was loved by everyone, while his son did not enjoy human sympathy or respect, mainly because of his cold demeanor and the lack of typically chivalrous qualities. The changes that were going to happen in this connection did not seem to be for the best.

"Er, what to worry about in advance?" Gwidon finally broke the silence. "It's not good, but let's not lose hope, as one thief said when he was led to the gallows. There hasn't been a situation in which we couldn't handle it, right?'."

"This question can hardly be answered yes or no," the chief replied, feeling his good humor slowly returning.

"You talk nonsense, my dear. Every question can be answered with yes or no," argued Pierre.

"Yes? Well, answer: have you stopped dressing up in women's skirts?" Preziosa asked him teasingly.

They laughed and laughed the rest of the way to their hideout. Their exuberant natures eagerly grabbed every opportunity to play, and since there was not much to laugh about in their hard lives, they made it for themselves.

As they entered the clearing, Beregard was turning a piece of roast over the fire and whistling sadly.

"Where's the boy?" Theo asked him, looking around.

"He went wandering in the woods," his friend replied. "Are you hungry?"

"You let him go alone? And if he will get lost?"

"No worries. A fourteen or fifteen-year-old kid himself escapes from the guard in a foreign country, goes on a fishing boat to France and reaches central Touraine without anyone's help, and would lose his way in any forest?"

He reached for salt and added it on the baking meat.

"I don't understand," Pierre muttered dully.

"And what is there to understand? We've got a new one, and it's gonna be trouble with him for sure. Such that I do not wish them to the enemy," Theo plunged into the forest and after a long moment returned, dragging a frail boy with curly hair.

Washed and dressed in a clean caftan, Tristan looked a lot nicer than at the beginning, but everyone was almost speechless at the sight of him.

"Sit down and eat," the chief ordered sharply. "It's getting dark, it's time to sleep. If it weren't for Beregard, we would have gone to bed without supper because of today's nonsenses."

He sat down by the fire, cut off a piece of roast for Tristan, and then another for himself. Others followed his example, only now feeling how hungry they were after this eventful day.

"Oh, I'd forget," Theo said after a moment, cutting off another piece of meat for himself. "This boy is my stepbrother, Tristan de Bongrais, you could say a farewell gift from my late father. Yes, nice daddy! After the king's death, the kid has nowhere to go, so he stays with us. Is that clear?"

Tristan huddled under the eyeing him up, not necessarily benevolent, gazes. The outlaws stared at him for a moment, then Pierre swallowed a large chunk of meat almost without chewing, and asked dimly:

"So how are we supposed to address him? Monsignor, Viscount or Puppy?"

"Control your tongue, yokel," Tristan growled.

"What are you going to do to me?" Pierre laughed unpleasantly.

"Enough," Theo cut in sharply. "No arguments. The kid has a name and that's what you call him. And don't show me your sulk here, understand? There are no nobles, no peasants here in the forest. We are all equal."

"Now I know why the king's court was said that you are crazy," the boy said, and he wrapped himself tighter in a straitjacket that was too big for him.

Beregard smiled secretly. The little one reminded him irresistibly of Theo when he was yet an unfledged adolescent with the worst opinion of any boy in the king of Navarre's court. He kept mouthing, causing fights, which sometimes ended in spanking for him, and it seemed that the frizzy face was his worthy counterpart.

"Congratulations for your little brother," Pierre said, getting up from the fire. "I prefer my stupid sister."

"Ah, bear, come on, he has to tame, and I'll teach him everything he needs to know, including manners," Beregard said agreeably.

"Good luck. It'll be plowing on fallow," Pierre laughed kindly and entered the hut, singing at the top of his throat one of the most impossible lullabies composed by Gwidon: "When my Margot is asleep, nothing is on her... Sleep, baby, sleep and sleep and dream about our frolics..."

"I don't agree to sleep in the same cottage with such simpletons," Tristan said disgustedly.

"Then build your own inn," his brother suggested ironically. "Don't think you're gonna be in charge here. I'll teach you about tossing around people you don't know anything about."

Tristan wanted to say something boisterous to him, but his voice cracked and he turned his head to hide his tears.

"Ah, you crybaby," Theo shrugged angrily and went to his attic. Bellette joined him a moment later.

"You're not too hard on him?" She asked quietly, sitting down next to him, "It's still a child, after all."

He sighed and rested his head in his hands.

"You're probably right, but his mere presence makes me angry," he confessed after a moment. "Nobody cared about me at his age, I was coping without my father, probably because this puppy was already in the world. I was not protected by royal grace, and my only kind soul was Beregard. If it weren't for his cleverness, sometimes I wouldn't even have anything to eat, because between the boys raised at the court of the King of Navarra, there was a fierce competition for literally everything. The chief preceptor would punch me with a thong at every opportunity, and often without it, my father would never show up at all. I thought I loved him after all, until I received news of his death. Then I realized that, in fact, he was a stranger to me, and that I basically loved my image of him, not his... No, I don't say that to complain. If it weren't for the tough school of life, I probably wouldn't have managed to be a hunted animal, outlaw, cursed and slandered. However, I'm angry to see this boy who lived in prosperity and respect, even though I'm the legal son of my father. Everything that went to Tristan there in the royal court should be mine. It should be me!"

He hit his fist on his knee.

Bellette put her arms around him.

"Deal with it," she said gently. "Tristan isn't guilty for what happened. He is a sensitive child, and your word can strike harder than a stone thrown from a slingshot. Not everyone is as hardened as you, my darling. Of course, if you had been more sensitive, you would not have endured all the misfortune that befell you but be more understanding to those who do not have such a thick armor."

Theo glanced up at her from under the black mane falling over his eyes.

"I didn't expect you to think so badly of me," he said with joking resentment. "So, in your opinion I'm callous and insensitive?"

Laughing, she stroked his bare neck.

"Maybe so," she said teasingly. "But that's how I love you. I just ask you to be more understanding with this child. He is now more lost and miserable than you have ever been. And yet he is a brave boy, since he managed to escape from the guards and get all the way here. You have more in common than you think."

The husband embraced her and dragged her to the hay with him.

"You can always disperse dark clouds," he confessed. "You are the greatest gift of fate I could receive."

Meanwhile, Tristan, unable to sleep in a strange and unpleasant place, slipped away quietly from the cabin to the fresh air. Here, under the stars, in the middle of a silent forest, he could finally allow himself a moment of weakness and cry. He wasn't as strong as his brother, in addition, he was painfully aware that he was merely a bastard, a child of illegitimacy, and who knows, whether his father and king wanted to suffer the humiliation associated with it save him by hiding his identity from the rest of the world.

"Father, I miss you so much..." he whispered, touching his lips to the heavy signet ring, the only one the mementoes he had left of his father.

Bushes rustled behind him, and Preziosa's whisper rang out:

"No need to cry, young master. Theo would be angry if he saw. Besides, everything will work out somehow, you will see."

"How can it work out? I hate him, he doesn't like me," he whispered helplessly.

Preziosa unexpectedly embraced him in such a maternal movement that he couldn't control himself, and with muffled sobbing, he clung to her caftan.

"The Lord's brother is a good and noble man," said the Gypsy after a moment, stroking his frizzy hair. "He can be rough, it's true, but it's because he is afraid not to show too sensitive. He just can't afford it, do you understand, lord? Besides, the news that he had a brother was quite sudden and unexpected for him, he must get used to it, and it takes time. You'll see the lord, he's not half like that terrible as it seems at first glance."

These soothing words made Tristan calmer and wiped away his tears.

"Won't you tell anyone?" He asked quietly.

"My lips are sealed," she promised him. "After all, it is better for none of these mongrels to know how easy it is to hurt you. They are good boys, but terribly thick-skinned and vulgar."

*****

After a week or so, everyone got used to Tristan's presence in the woods, and he somehow had better adapt to adverse conditions than might have been expected.

The boy, although sad and withdrawn at first, aroused keen sympathy, and yet, however, they were like no clearer physical resemblance between them they looked as cut from the same cloth. Having got used to the new situation, Tristan first strongly protested against leaving him aside and demanded the right to take part in all expeditions and raids. It was so much troublesome that he could hardly know anything yet, and he had little strength, so Theo told his men how the quickest training of the boy in everything that he might need. Tristan had to learn to throw stones, shoot a bow, fight with a dagger and a club, wrestling and swimming, as it turned out that the boy who sailed alone in fishing boat from Dover to Bordeaux, he can't swim at all. When it came out the whole band had come to respect him and treated him differently. Tristan anyway, he was very careful to make up for his shortcomings. He learned to swim himself, after just taking a boat out to the middle of the lake and jumping overboard. For the first time Jean pulled him out, Pierre the second, and the third the boy swam to the shore by himself. When asked why he did it with his clothes on, he replied that he did not swim for fun and in times of danger, he probably won't have time to shed his clothes. With the slingshot he was doing quite well, but the obstacle in archery was that he was quite weak. Only Millot, the new band member, literally snatched away by his companions from the gallows, he came up with the idea to make a bow for him with a slightly thinner handle, easier to stretch, though not carrying as far as those the outlaws used on every day.

"You see, son," he explained to the boy who was listening curiously, continuing his work. "The first thing to do is to choose the right tree, strip the bark and initially shave. Not every piece is suitable for this either. After the initial sharpening, you need it well soak and bend over the steam in an appropriate way, and when it is dry, warm the tips again and bend them in the opposite direction. Then the bowstring hooks are formed with a knife. Then, using a mixture of resins, the outer side is taped with a horn, and the inner one with properly dried animal tendons. A bow prepared in this way will serve you for years without compromising your lift.

Millot was a skillful craftsman, a cheerful and handsome highlander from Bearn, who by chance wandered this way and immediately exposed himself to an English's patrol. His sonorous voice was almost as pleasing to the ear as Gwidon's and the fast and cheerful highlander dialect sounded particularly nice in his mouth.

Everyone liked him, because it was impossible to remain sad in his company, and moreover, he was an invaluable asset to the band because of his skill of making weapons. Until now, outlaws had to either steal it or go without it.

While waiting for Millot to finish the bow for him, Tristan was learning from Jean how to plan arrows, and from Beregard to operate a Roman slingshot, to which, like his brother, he was congenital abilities. He quickly mastered the technique of appropriate swing and feeling a convenient moment to release the free end of the slingshot held in the hand.

The accuracy was a bit worse, but Beregard consoled him by saying it was a matter of training and that it will come with time. He liked the boy very much.

"He's just like you at his age," he even said to Theo. "And I can bet you that when he comes to years, he will be the same plague as you. You can see it now."

Theo smiled secretly at the words. When the first agitation had passed, he had to admit that this is not a completely bad situation. After all, Tristan was his family, probably the last one left. His father had thirteen siblings, but most of them died before reaching adulthood, while the rest were devoured through the rough tide of jacquerie, or through the war with England. If Theo were to die,

Tristan would be the last of the Bongrais. Until now, the young count, with his attention preoccupied with other things, did not even realize how much he missed the family he was so brutally deprived of. After the first stormy tensions, relations between the brothers turned out surprisingly well, and soon, as Preziosa had predicted, there was no trace of their mutual hostility. Bellette also liked Tristan, who evoked some maternal feelings in her heart even though she was no more than seven years older than him, and she always defended him when her husband wanted to reprimand his brother some more severely. Theo himself tried to educate Tristan sharp, soldierly, but he was not very successful, especially since he noticed that the poor kid took every innocent word in earnest. His over-sensitivity made the knight embarrassed.

"Words fail me," he confided with a sigh to Father Prospero as he arrived at his call to the monastery.

"Just because he's not such a hardened bastard as you, doesn't mean he'll blubber in the face of the enemy. After all, the same blood flows in you, the prior remarked dryly."

Father Prospero has aged and thin recently, but he has not lost his harshness and a sour irony, though he complained of pains in his bones, and it seemed to be oppressing him quickly progressive disease.

"Yes," Theo admitted. "But there's something about this puppy that I don't really understand."

"He's probably not as primitive as you. Maybe he likes music, theater, painting, and it's rather difficult in your vulgar company."

"Thanks a lot, Father. You're terrible and then you wonder why nobody likes you. Alright, what am I here for?"

Prospero sighed.

"Someone was looking for you," he replied succinctly.

The outlaw made a vague gesture with his left hand.

"More details, please," he demanded dryly. "The whole English army is looking for me, and the half of our knights. I've been extremely popular lately."

The monk snorted angrily.

"Hide these jokes for a better occasion. An English lady is looking for you, so don't forget by your grace that you are married," he said.

"In mourning?" Theo asked.

"Do you mourn already?!" Prospero said indignantly.

"Does this lady mourn after all?" The knight explained patiently.

"Oh, that's what you mean... Yes, she is mourning. You know her?" The monk looked at him curiously and with a certain threat.

"It looks. Thank you, Father, maybe you did me a favor," Theo jumped up, somehow unusually animated, and ran out.

Of all English ladies, he knew only Lady Fitzoother, and he didn't mind seeing her again. The description suited her. He still remembered her sitting across from him in a carriage, with fair hair sticking out from under a widow's cap and hands, folded on the lap. What was it about her that he couldn't forget? On addition, it appeared that she, too, remembered the ragged prisoner who was so unceremoniously used her carriage to escape from Castle Meung. It remained a mystery why she was looking him for. Somehow, he couldn't believe she wanted to ambush him, no she looked to him to be capable of such intrigues. Well, you should have found out.

There were no problems with finding the Englishwoman. He quickly learned that she had gone for a ride around the neighborhood in a small carriage, so he had to find her. He did it relatively quickly, and his fondness for easy effects made him jump into a carriage from a roadside tree, instead of just stopping it somewhere on the road.

"Were you looking for me, lady?" He asked with a charming smile, speechless with surprise lady. Her companion, probably a maid, was looking at him round with fear eyes, clearly struggling with the urge to jump out in the middle of the road.

"You really weren't taught better manners?" Lady Joan asked, getting her voice back.

"I see it's good reason why some people call you the Werewolf of Touraine. What is this idea with this tree jumping?"

"It's not an idea, it's not a mistake, it's a necessity," he replied. But never mind me and my tricks. What came to you, lady, to this pretty head to follow me around this area? If I hadn't found out about you, you wouldn't have come across mine trace anyway, and you could be in danger yourself. We are not the only ones hunting here.

It was true. Theo and his band had long been running what father Prospero referred to as a "holy war" with common robbers oppressing residents.

It began with mercenaries hired by Don Paulino to change clothes to discredit the Touraine gang by attacking the peaceful residents on their behalf. It was a disgusting thing and briefly poisoned their lives. And then others showed up, no longer impersonating them, but no less dangerous. Except for the cluster young boys, known as the "band of Falcon of the Pyrenees," Theo had around actually the enemies themselves.

"Big thing. I don't think to be afraid of just any thug," said Lady Joan contemptuously. "And I just had to find you. I know a little about you and I feel sorry for you, because in front of mine brother you cannot defend yourself. So please leave this place, preferably to Italy or to Spain and make a new life there. You're done here. The war is over, but you don't want to acknowledge it, and you won't win anything other than the gallows."

"One priest said something similar to me once," Theo said thoughtfully.

"Son, heroism doesn't impress anyone anymore, but it is a great opportunity to die."

"I'm serious," the Englishwoman looked him straight in the eyes, without squinting.

"If it's a matter of money, I'll get it for you, but you have to leave."

"First, my lady," said the outlaw calmly. "It hasn't happened to me yet to surrender for whatever reason. Second, you are a lady, and ladies are a much better in embroidering pillows than fighting strategies. And third, I can't understand why my miserable fate cares my enemy favorite's cousin so much. You must admit, my lady, it's a bit weird and utterly illogical."

Lady Joan folded her beautiful hands in her lap and looked at them for a moment, then she decided to look up again at the swarthy man sitting across from her with a pretty, cheeky face and a burning gaze. It was completely different from restrained, fair-haired knights with cold eyes and clenched lips like those she is used to in England. She herself could not understand what was in him so attracted to her. She has always been convinced that she hates brunettes, and now...

"You know nothing about women," she said. "I'm a close cousin of Edward, that's true and I even had some influence on him once, but that doesn't mean that... Anyway, he has been taking me lightly since he has a French lover like Adeline de Valois."

"What? Duchess de Valois?" Theo cut her off, taking his eyes seriously and taking his wide eyebrows in a puzzled expression.

"You know this witch?"

"Yes, but otherwise you are right. I don't know anything about women. If I was just a little wiser, I wouldn't make an enemy of this lady."

He was horrified at the thought that perhaps Adeline had become the Black Prince's mistress just to get revenge on him.

Lady Joan looked at him with a smile.

"And I was told that you are not afraid of anything," she said teasingly.

"Maybe not, but the question is, how am I supposed to fight a woman?" Theo shrugged.

"That's why I tell you, go away," the Englishwoman touched his hand with her fingers.

Theo took her hand and held it in hiss for a moment. Lady Joan turned dark blush when he looked her straight in the eyes with a smile both tender and provocative. His smile was beautiful, his teeth even and white.

"You have such a lovely hand, lady," he said softly. "So delicate and small, it is not suitable plotting intrigue. Better for Prince Edward not to find out about ours meeting. Safer. He might have some unreasonable suspicions, what not would be most advantageous. I don't want you to have any trouble because of me."

The Englishwoman nodded, slowly slipping her hand from his.

"The only noticeable unpleasantness is that you don't trust me," she said. "But that's it, I warned you. You will do as you like."

Theo smiled again, suddenly placed a courtly kiss on her hand, and sprang from the carriage to the side of the road without even waiting for it to slow down. He stood for a moment and watched it wandered off towards the castle, then turned slowly back into the woods. It was not pleasant knowing what kind of enemy was on his neck now, but he had to admit that not knowing it would be even worse, even disastrous. Willing to help (why?), Lady Joan provided him with very important messages of invaluable value. It is always good to know who a man is going to fight against, and while Theo had been taught not to trust the English under any circumstances, he had to admit that Lady Joan would have had no advantage in deceiving him into Adeline's presence at the castle. And not the Adeline he knew, the reckless bobbysoxer with empty head, but hatred, capable of anything. He congratulated himself on Bellette living with him in the woods - admittedly Adeline didn't know anything about her, but if she had any rumors... he wouldn't even want to think about it. And Tristan? The unbearable younger brother, still so young and only recently involved in his affairs? Family is all trouble.

He found the horse he had left in the forest and returned to his hideout, where Pierre was teaching Tristan to throw a knife at the target.

"And what?" Pierre asked when he saw the chief.

"Nothing fancy," Theo said lightly. "Only that the Black Prince had it in for me, and he is helped by Adeline de Valois and, of course, Don Paulino, which means that we have all our enemies complete at Bongrais Castle. Poor old walls, ruled by an honest family for three hundred years, and now given up to scoundrels."

"You owe yourself, you should have killed Paulino when you had the chance," Tristan remarked insolently.

"What goes up must come down," answered his brother. "He will die not by someone else, but by my hand, worse with Adeline."

"Why, are you afraid of one skirt?"

"You don't be too smart, because it will hurt you. Fear has nothing to do with it, it's just not an honor to fight a woman. Fighting women is an absolutely hopeless undertaking for a righteous knight, especially since you are on a point of losing position," Theo explained to him.

Tristan shrugged his thin shoulders and threw the dagger at the target, missing it by a few inches.

"How is he making progress?" The knight asked softly.

"Not too bad," Beregard replied, looking up from the new table leg he was just sharpening. "Your blood, it cannot be denied, in throwing stones he will catch you soon, and with the knife he has its ups and downs. But he is weak."

"Maybe he will get stronger over time? I, too, when I got here, I was not Jack the Lad as now."

"The comparison sucks. You were stronger than Tristan when you were eight. Listen, tell Millot that if he wants to fight Pierre, let him watch out for the equipment. We have few of them."

"Okay, I'll tell him," Theo nodded absentmindedly, but not thinking about the constant quarrels between Millot and Pierre, and that by some strange coincidence all of them liked Tristan, even though the character was terrible and the way around it was unpleasant. Slowly, he was beginning to convince himself of the people with whom he was bound by a blind fate.

"You will have to watch out for him," he said, watching Gwidon try to hit the target with his slingshot, without much interest. "It's full of these English dogs now. Actually, why do I offend dogs, after all, God's creatures? Hey, weasel, you'll never hit anything like this. You have to feel at what point to release the handle, otherwise nothing of all the fun."

"I know well," the poet groaned. "Why can you do it and I can't?"

He bit at the fact that he was worse than his comrades, but the more he tried to master the art, the worse he was. He showed no flicker of talent in that direction, though dagger, bow, and bolas did quite well. The problem was that, as a poet, he took this lack to heart and stubbornly trained, generally hitting everything except the right target.

"Don't worry about it so much," Theo told him. "You're like a baby. Apparently, you don't have to sling that, well, knack. It's not a reason to worry."

"But it is," Gwidon insisted tearfully.

The knight tried to calm him down, but Pierre broke his orders, who somehow wound up nearby and shouted:

"What are you doing...?! You better go ripping, because with such a shooter, you are sure that your death is close!"

Offended, Gwidon disappeared into the woods, and Theo tapped his forehead as he looked at Pierre with pity. He could not somehow explain to him that you cannot treat a troubadour like every other band member because he is more sensitive than them and thinks differently.

"Do you always have to scream the place down like this?" He asked reproachfully.

"Oh, there is a defender of the oppressed," Pierre retorted. "You'd better take care of your own brother. He has just stabbed me in the right... buttock, because I noticed him he's been aiming too long. And Gwidon is also nice. Let him not take for what he cannot, because he will kill all of us here."

Theo laughed, got up and walked to the other side of the hut, where Tristan, with the most innocent expression on his face, sharpened his dagger on a stone...

"What is this stabbing people in the back area with a knife?" He asked, trying to be strict, though he still wanted to laugh.

"Why, this is not allowed here?" The boy asked. "So, what finally allowed?"

"You can't be like this. We are all trying to teach you how to survive here, you can't even have a little patience?"

Theo took his shoulders and met his eyes with a gentle excuse. Tristan dropped his gaze.

"I'm trying," he confessed after a while. "But understand, I can't like your companions. They are boorish, uncouth, ignorant... They stink, they don't wash at all, and they talk that ears hurt. How can you even fraternize with them like that?"

His brother thought for a moment.

"I got used to it," he said finally. "I had no choice. If you saw the slaughter in Bongrais as I do, up close, holding by hands twisted backwards so that you wouldn't be able to help anyone, and by your hair so you wouldn't be able to turn your head... I assure you, it would be indifferent to you whether your comrades-in-arms are washing themselves or not, what language they use, and how many of them can count.

The boy grew serious.

"I've only heard of it," he whispered. "I didn't know anyone from the castle, not even you, I didn't realize what a tragedy it was... They helped you?"

"Yes. I would not be alive for a long time if it weren't for this band of rude people."

The older brother looked somewhere above his head, remembering the first not easy months when he had to learn everything from scratch, and he couldn't allow himself to be lost and unhappy. He had to be strong, tenacious, he could not allow himself any weakness.

"Be glad you didn't study with me. And that I would never hear about stabbing my people with a knife in the buttocks," he announced sternly, to break the growing affection he did not like.

"Cut your ears off then," Tristan said insolently. "And in general, you all want to command me, because I'm the youngest here. I should join the Falcon."

Theo laughed mockingly.

"Don't be so smart!" He said. "You know it's Claude de Foix a real chief of band of Falcon, not this youngster."

The Pyrenean Falcon, as it was commonly called, was a distant cousin of Gaston Febus, a seventeen-year-old youth who assembled a team of equally young boys, in most of the orphaned descendants of great families, and tugged at the English as much as he could. Theo liked and valued him, but refused to command him, despite such suggestions. Tristan, of course, liked this bunch of frisky teenagers very much, but his brother tried to limit these contacts, fearing a bad influence on the young boy.

"It's undisputed, anyway," Theo decided it was time to end this conversation, he slapped his brother in the back for goodbye and went to the stream.

Armando came across from him, carrying bottles tied together on his back.

"Where are you coming from?" He asked, though the answer was basically clear.

"From Under the White Swan," replied the Gypsy. "I bought some wine and heard some news! The Black Prince has announced that anyone who helps you will be hanged immediately, without trial. He raised the bounty on your head, and he hasn't forgotten to raise taxes. He had two unfortunates, who were suspected of collaborating with us, to be tortured, and because they really knew nothing, he sentenced them to death out of anger. Several others were trained mercilessly at his command, one of which died immediately. I tell you, chief, we will not be happy now."

Theo gritted his teeth until his muscles were outlined under the smoothly shaved skin on his broad jaws, involuntarily curling his hand into a fist.

"It seems time for a declaration of war," he said after a moment, when he was sure he would have his voice under control.

He felt responsible for those people who would otherwise be his subjects and his service, and considered any harm done to them as a personal insult. Someone must have informed Prince Edward about it, and it was easy to see who.

"But that's not all, my dear," Armando said with a note of sympathy in his voice. "The practiced one who died was Bellette and Marie's father... I don't know if it was a random choice or a deliberate act, but the fact is unfortunate anyway.

The knight snatched one of the bottles from him, drank some wine and wiped his mouth with the back of his hand.

"Collect people," he ordered shortly.

The tightrope walker nodded and ran to the hut while his commander headed for the village. By the time he returned, the band was full and waiting for him, talking lively about the revelations Armando had brought. Bellette was with them, too, pale but calm. When friends tried to express their sympathy to her, she replied:

"Whoever fights suffers losses. My father is no exception to this rule."

She never flaunted what she felt, and neither did it now. When the chieftain returned from the village, he surveyed his little unit with a stern gaze and announced:

"The girls and Tristan stay; the rest go with me."

"Why me?" His brother insulted, offended by such treatment.

Theo looked at him sharply.

"Because I'm going to do something I'm not proud of," he replied. "And no discussion!"

Tristan paused and looked at Bellette.

"Has he been doing something he wasn't proud of?" He asked quietly when they were alone.

The girl nodded.

"It happened, it happened," she replied. "Do you think that everything in his life can be arranged and squeezed into the appropriate fairy tales? I don't know what he wants to do now, but I have some guesses, and you better not see it."

Tristan shrugged.

"What do you know about me? Do you think that I can be removed from everything because I am a child? I've seen many things before," he muttered and walked away.

He generally listened to his older brother, and yet now he was very tempted to break the prohibition and follow him.

Meanwhile, the entire gang gathered near the Bongrais Castle, hiding carefully from human sight, in a place from which they could observe what was happening on the road without any obstacles. Theo was silent, there was a threat in his silence, and no one had the courage to ask what they were waiting for. After some time, a small unit of English soldiers appeared on the road, which left the castle, heading towards the village of Two Bars.

"Pierre, Jean, get them on Elves sacred spot," Theo whispered commandingly.

Elves sacred spot was a large clearing in the forest, for some reason perfectly circular and devoid of all vegetation, located deep on the sidelines. The English soldiers, lured by the vision of easy prey, were easily led there and found themselves surrounded when it was too late. They had been unceremoniously dragged from their horses, but to their amazement they had not been disarmed, on the contrary, it seemed that the aggressors were seeking to fight, not to plunder. It all became clear when they recognized the leader of this gang - they had already heard of him, and some knew him by sight.

"Theo le Vengeur, what a surprise. The last time I saw you at Meung Castle, you looked a little less pugnacious," said the squad leader.

With some difficulty, Theo remembered the man. It was Sir Essex, friend of the Black Prince and commander of most of his troops

"Oh, yes," he said, drawing his sword. "I looked what I could in that situation, but now I feel quite well. You're about to find out, you and your people. By the order of the Black Prince, three peasants were killed, innocent because they had nothing to do with me: two servants from the castle and old man from the village. That is why you and two of your soldiers will die. Well, the rest who will return to the garrison should give his prince my ultimatum: for every killed inhabitant of this area, one English soldier, whatever rank. Since you cannot talk to barbarians in a civilized way, I will use speech that you can understand."

"Are you so sure you can make it?" Essex asked, slowly taking his sword hilt.

"We'll see in a minute," Theo replied calmly.

He took a step back, raising his weapon. Without moving from his seat, he blocked the Englishman's foray and he answered with a biting retort, hitting his wrist. Sir Essex repeated the attack, but all his clever cuts hit the void without reaching the enemy. Theo let him try his hand for a while, then knocked out his weapon with a strong blow from his hand and in a semicircular twist he drew his sword back, cutting the opponent's throat with the very tip of the blade. Blood spurted from the severed arteries. The Englishman for a while longer struggled to stay on his feet, then he slumped slowly to the ground, freezing in a dark puddle.

"Two more," Theo ordered coldly, addressing his men.

The English did not ask for mercy, they defended themselves, not letting go of their weapons until the end, as if they knew they couldn't count on anything. People from the Black Prince's adjutants they were the backbone of the English army, the most trained and the bravest of all what translated into the word "cruelest", but also meant that they did not tolerate any signs of weakness. Theo, trained from early childhood for the role of knight, he could not underestimate these qualities even in his enemies.

"Take the corpses of your comrades," he said to the soldiers, hardly overwhelmed by his men. "Tell the prince they fought bravely until the end, and I know very well what it means not to break down in the face of death. Let it order bury their bodies with the honors they deserve.

He had heard too much about the Prince of Wales not to know that he was even unfair to his own people, if he feels they have failed him. It was rather hard to expect him to read the defeat of those who had failed to shield his cousin and friend from death otherwise. No one of Theo's companions was seriously injured, so they could consider their action a complete success. Pierre was pleased with this turn of events, as he did not support the overly gentleness towards enemies, which, in his opinion, the gang leader had recently shown, and even considered it even harmful to their common cause. The death of his father, of course, had fueled these bad feelings, and the fact that Marie's husband was the second practitioner had a lot to do with it.

"Serves them right," he said to the chief on the way back. "What a mean, torture an old sick man. You know what, Theo, what if it wasn't a coincidence? My father and brother-in-law... they are your family now too... The Black Prince has a black heart and usually works effectively."

"You know what? Shut up," Theo told him shortly.

"But why?" Pierre was surprised. "I'm just glad you got smart."

The chief stopped and grabbed him by the caftan over his chest.

"Listen," he hissed. "It's not my fault that they only recognize the law of the fist. They want war with me, they will get it, and I'm not going to take prisoners, but don't think I like it. I don't want to become like them, you see, doesn't mean I like it!"

"Sure, sure," Pierre agreed, trying to pull himself out of his tick grip.

Theo released him and resumed his position in front.

On the way, they also visited Kamienisko, said a few words of consolation, crying at the bedding of Marie's husband, and warned the inhabitants to flee into the woods, under their protection, if necessary. They did not expect any retaliation at the Kamienisko, in the end even Prince Edward knew some moderation, but they preferred to be prepared for anything.

"I'll take the people through the swamps if necessary," Marie promised them. "You think they'll come here?"

"Not really, but you'd better be prepared for the worst," Theo replied dimly.

Marie looked at him gratefully. The subservience with which she treated the young count often brought her brother's reprimands upon her, but they were to no avail. Perhaps one of the villagers thought that due to the rivalry of the parties, not only the Kamienisko but the entire neighborhood could go up in smoke, but no one revealed it. Due to the constant tension, insecurity, uncertainty of tomorrow, ruining taxes, hunger, plague and bestiality of soldiers, everyone was brought to the extreme, and if someone gave the password to the uprising, everyone would follow, including women, children and the elderly. Once Prince Edward's soldiers had shown how they were going to rule here, there was no point in fearing retaliation for the outlaws. They would always find a reason for cruelty.

Of course, everyone was curious about what the Black Prince said, but he accepted what happened with astonishing calm. Locking himself in his chamber, he thought about everything, then went out and strictly forbade his soldiers to kill any of the inhabitants of the Bongrais area until they could capture the outlaws and hang them in public.

"I warned Your Majesty," said Don Paulino, without any trace of triumph.

The prince looked at him briefly.

"The soldiers swear that this outlaw fought fair and that he gave Essex a fair chance..." he said after a moment.

"When someone fights Theo de Bongrais, the chances are never equal," Adeline interrupted, lifting her beautiful head from her embroidery. "I think Lucifer himself taught him all the tricks, because it is impossible to learn it from a human."

The Black Prince considered these words for a moment in silence.

"Well then. Don Paulino, were these villagers just a convenient excuse for him or did he really care about them?" He asked finally.

The Spaniard made a face of disgust.

"He really cares," he replied. "God knows why. He cares. Like on dogs."

The Englishman smiled coldly.

"So you have to take advantage of it. Essex was a good swordsman, and your Theo cut him up like meat for a stew. Perfect... It's been a long time since I met an opponent worthy of my blade. You just need to get in touch with him somehow..."

He left the room without finishing his thoughts. Adeline looked at Don Paulino doubtfully.

"He can do it?" She asked.

"I don't know," muttered the Spaniard. "But if he can, I'd be drunk with joy. What the hell, there is no one to suppress one outlaw and the king's son has to be bugged."

Adeline and he had long agreed to work together, though the Duchess always disrespected him as a servant and lowborn being. The hope that she would see the fall and death of a man who despised her would push her to ally with everyone. Together with Prince Edward they were a really matched three, though the latter seldom confided in them of his plans, the way he did now, when they had to guess everything in half-words.

CHAPTER II

Duel

Having received the news that, the Black Prince wanted to meet him at the crossroads, Theo first and foremost distrustfully read it a second and third time.

"I don't understand," he said finally obtusely.

"Did you forget the letters from walking in the woods?" Francois asked innocently.

"No, I understand the words themselves, but I can't read the sense," replied the knight. "Why the hell does this Englishman still want to talk to me? It's all clear."

"Maybe not for him," muttered Pierre.

"Exactly," Millot said. "Maybe the English are already like that, nothing reaches them? Explain to him, chief, by hand, like others, he can understand something."

Theo slowly rolled the letter up.

"Well, let's see what he wants," he said with open dissatisfaction. "I don't like the introduction itself anymore, but what to do? War is war. Pierre, Millot and Armando, you will penetrate the area of the crossroads, if they have not been prepared for some ambush, like what Don Paulino wanted to tie us into a bundle and give the prince a birthday present."

"Orders, commander," Armando replied.

"Theo, I don't think it's good for you to go there..." Tristan groaned incredulously.

"I wouldn't count on it. When his eyes shine like this, he usually thinks something dangerous and extremely stupid," Bellette said as she continued braiding her braid.

In the flashes thrown by the fire, she looked like a dryad and tearing her eyes with beauty and freshness, effectively resisting the hardships of life in the forest. She looked sixteen at the most, and the people she sometimes met on the road kept looking after her until she was out of sight. Only Pierre was still amazed at what people saw in his sister, and more than once expressed it baldly. He had no "prevaricate" habit at all and always said what he thought.

"I can't risk being called a coward," Theo said. "Besides, I won't go alone. In case of any betrayal, shoot an arrow and do not look at who, you have my blessing for it."

Pierre shook his head.

"Something stinks in here," he confessed. "This prince is not an idiot either. He had to come up with the fact that you would protect yourself somehow, so what is he really going to do? You know, chief, if I were you, I wouldn't go."

"Exactly. Which is why you are not in my place."

Bellette finished braiding the braid and tossed it on her back.

"I don't expect you not to go," she said. "It wouldn't make sense. I do not invoke your sense also, because there is nothing to talk about here, but please, be careful at least."

Theo hugged her warmly.

"I'm always careful, my beautiful," he assured her. "Don't worry, it takes someone smarter than this English to surprise me. We have to find out what it is about, after all, probably not only about my skin, and these barbarians, apart from the speech of the fist, do not understand another."

"He speaks well, give him some vodka," said Gwidon, giving light applause.

"There is no way," objected Beregard. "He's talking like he's drunk already. Besides, there is nothing to drink."

"Fortunately, there is someone with foresight," Preziosa got up from the grass and brought a bottle from the hut, carefully hidden behind the chest.

"I knew I loved you for something," Jean beamed, eagerly took a long gulp and gave the bottle to the others.

"But I have no idea what I saw in you," said the Gypsy mockingly. "I guess it's your red mustache that's driving me crazy so much, although to tell you the truth you are a bully, a thief and a boozer."

"You both have soft in the head and it brings you closer to each other," muttered Armando sourly and handed the bottle to the commander sitting next to him.

The man shook his head refusingly.

"I'm going to the monastery," he said, standing up. "Let Jean, Francois and Beregard hunt something, because there's nothing to eat again. And take Tristan with you, maybe you'll teach him something. In any case, I gave it up at the very beginning."

"That speaks badly for you rather than me," the boy snapped back at him.

"Take the bow, it's ready," Millot advised. "I'll just stick the bowstring. You should start practicing to get used to it. There is nothing to wait for."

"Exactly," Theo agreed, and disappeared into the woods.

On the way, he managed to hunt a nice roe deer, which made him very happy because he didn't like to appear empty-handed at the monastery. Father Prospero greeted him not as usual in the refectory but in his cell. He was lying on a bunk made of rough boards and looked out very old and miserable.

"It's good to have you here," he said. "I was about to send someone to get you. Nice of you to think about stocking up our pantry, because we've been feeling some shortcomings for a while, but more important is something else. You messed up with the Prince of Wales, I heard, so I tell you be careful. You can fight him in any way you like, but don't you dare touch him. It isn't Don Paulino, nor Roger de Valois, nor any of your lousy companions, and if you do something to him, the entire English army will fall to Touraine. Stone on stone won't stay here."

"Yes, I know. Roger de Valois is, you could say, a spot of bother," the outlaw agreed.

"What?" The monk rose from the impression on his elbow. "A spot of what? Listen, boy, maybe use more elegant language in a holy place. This is not a brothel."

A brother, no longer young, entered the cell, carrying a mug of steaming drink. Father Prospero, frowning a little, drank the liquid served him, then the silent monk took the empty vessel and left.

"He looks a lot like you, Father," Theo said, looking after him. "Is that your cousin?"

"He's my son," Prospero replied dryly.

"Excuse me..."

The old monk shrugged his shoulders emotionlessly.

"For what?" He asked. "It isn't you who broke your religious vows and you are not punished for it. Enough about me, more important is what is happening to you. I'm afraid your exaggerated fame as invincible forest knight has hit you hard, and you're starting to do incredible nonsense. Do you think this pathetic collection of yours will be able to defeat a regular army? After all, the mouse might as well have pounced on the hound."

He paused for a moment and wiped the sweat from his forehead.

"Father Prospero, you are really sick, and this is serious. Let's break this conversation, you shouldn't get tired," Theo pleaded, leaning over him anxiously.

"Leave me alone," the monk muttered angrily. "You cannot even take care of yourself, and you are eager to take care of others. Listen to me carefully: make peace with the new king. You must have him by your side at all costs. Listen: you can beat a hard nut until the end of the world and you won't do any harm to it, but when it gets between two stones... You understand?"

"Man is a little different from a nut, even in that he can think," replied the outlaw with a careless wave of his hand. "I won't go to the dauphin and tell him: Let's make friends, buddy, why don't you give me a cup?" For now, I must play with the dice that fate has pressed into my hand. I understand your objections, Father, but I'll be fine somehow. As for the Black Prince, well... I will follow your instructions and not kill him, although it is a huge temptation. I know my hands are tied, but he doesn't know it. And that means I don't."

"Interesting conclusion, as pointless as everything you do and say," Prospero smiled involuntarily. "Remember what would happen, you can always count on me and my confreres. And if I'm gone, go ahead and speak to my son."

"I don't think I will have to for a long time. Just watch your weakness pass away and you will torment sinners again," Theo laughed.

He couldn't quite imagine that a monk he had known forever could one day disappear from his life, it seemed so far indestructible, but some sediment of these words stayed. After all, he had to admit that the old prior looked very bad and, formerly active and energetic, now reluctantly leaves the monastery. Nobody knew what was wrong with him, as he dispelled all questions briefly and gruffly, so it was commonly believed that it was only a temporary ailment.

Returning from the monastery, he came across Gwidon, who in his absence went to the inn to get a supply of alcohol.

"You really only have one thing in your mind," Theo said scandalized. "On the other hand, the idea isn't bad. Didn't you see the English on the way?"

"If you don't count those who drank at the inn, then no," the troubadour replied, adjusting the heavy load on his back.

"They don't count, they are camp staff members. Too bad, I thought you would find out something else."

"And what else is there to add? I don't think it's a trap because he'd come up with something smarter, so maybe this Englishman just wants to talk? What did our prior tell you?"

"So that I don't fools rush in where angels fear to tread, more or less."

"What now, will you listen to him?"

"I don't think so. If I'm to die, let me die fighting for what I believe." Theo quickened his pace and strode into the clearing where Beregard sat, tending the magnificent boar.

"How was my brother doing?" he asked.

"Wonderful," Beregard replied, continuing his work. "He missed twice from a sure shot position."

"And the third time?"

"And the third time he hit the target. But not a boar," Jean replied angrily, coming out from behind the hut.

He was holding his buttock covered with dried blood and was clearly limping. Theo folded arms.

"No, he cannot hold a weapon, because there will still be a misfortune!"

"No exaggeration." Beregard finally dealt with the peeling of the boar and proceeded to splitting meat. "He needs to exercise. Neither were you as omniscient as you are right now, and he is just getting started. Better think what to do so that this Welsh monster doesn't turn you into a ghost from Bongrais Castle..."

*****

"I really don't think that's a good idea. Sir Winslow said to Prince Edward as he and his bodyguard reached the crossroads.

"A little faith, cousin," the prince said indifferently. "You yourself say that the weakness of this outlaw is his sense of honor and exuberant pride. I don't think he has ignored such an opportunity to build up his fame."

"I don't mean that at all, just that..." Winslow didn't finish and waved his hand in discouragement.

He knew his cousin enough to know that he could not be persuaded. He didn't like Edward, but he remained loyal to him and therefore tried to stop him from carrying out a plan that looked truly crazy. However, the Black Prince remained deaf to the voice of reason. He loved such challenges and for nothing in the world he would not give it up. Perhaps he would not have been so fierce were it not for Adeline, who skillfully fueled his aversion to the rebellious outlaw day and night. The prince's plan was not only sneaky but also dishonest, but Sir Winslow did not intend to betray him, though his heart ached at the thought of being part of it. Besides, it would be useless, Theo le Vengeur probably loved danger as much as the Black Prince, and it would be useless to try to warn him. And yet he knew how to take care of himself despite his apparent bravado, since attempts to use these traits against him had so far yielded no results, and that comforted Sir Reynold somewhat, who waited anxiously for the outlaw to appear at the appointed meeting point.

The Black Prince showed no emotion, as usual. It was only when Theo suddenly appeared in the opening between the trees that the prince's gloomy face brightened a little.

"You came here then," he said. "I must say you don't look too threatening... and not extraordinary at all. It's hard to believe that this is what they say so many cock and bull stories about you."

"Likewise," Theo retorted. "Why did you insist on this meeting, Englishman?"

The prince shifted in the saddle.

"You lack manners," he said dryly. "Well, let me tell you straight, without any embellishments: I want to offer you a certain arrangement. We will fight each other at a tournament that will soon be held in Bongrais. If you win, I will comply with your demands, and if you lose, I will continue to rule my way, which will be indifferent to you, because you will be dead."

"What if I refuse?"

"Well... You didn't think you'd scare me by murdering Essex. If you refuse, I will burn one of your villages with the villagers. Then the second, and so on. Will you take it on your sensitive conscience? Unlike you, I don't care about these villagers."

"I understand the situation," said the outlaw sternly. "When?"

Prince Edward smiled slightly.

"In a week to be exact," he replied. "The most distinguished knights of England and Navarre will be present, so you will have the opportunity to present yourself with dignity. Dress up somehow nice."

"And what am I missing?" Theo shrugged with a clear provocation, turned a deaf ear by the Englishman.

"I still think it's a terrible idea," muttered Sir Winslow, leaning towards his cousin.

The man just smiled. He had already made up his mind about the rebellious French and had no doubts that he would win this duel without trouble. It was a prestigious matter for him. Or at least, that was what he thought of it.

*****

"You're crazy. Nobody in their right mind would do something like this. Don't do this, do you hear?" Pierre said for the tenth time, assisting in the inspection of clothes stolen by Jean and Francois from different places and on different occasions.

"No, why?" Theo replied absently. "After all, I can't go there without good looking, I suppose you will admit it yourself."

He was just trying on another caftan, this time brown, with lighter ornaments.

"Don't play dumber than you are," Pierre said irritably. "You know what I mean! No normal human would go to this tournament. You won't come back alive from there."

The chieftain looked at him with a smile.

"Are you suggesting I come back as a ghost?" He asked mockingly. "Don't worry, old man, I won't let myself be chopped up just because this butcher likes it. There will also be too many high-ranking people there to risk embarrassment, organizing some kind of treacherous attack on me. It would be terribly distasteful. How do I look?"

"Like a dead man," Bellette's brother growled, and walked aside to avoid irritate.

"He wants to beat me with his own hand. Only this will give him complete satisfaction, very chivalrous," Theo continued, ignoring him.

"I hope you know what you're doing," Jean handed him another jacket, this time dark blue. "That son of a bitch must be incredibly confident, and I've heard he's got no equal in England. Perhaps he is preparing something unexpected, or maybe he is only really that good?"

"Perhaps. But overconfidence can end up sad, and for me the stakes in this fight are just too high for me to afford to lose. Oh, this jacket will be good."

Pierre shook his head desperately from a man who knows he was in a no-win situation. He was aware that no words would now convince his well-born brother-in-law, who sometimes acted as if he were the spiritual heir to all the positive characters in Song of Roland. It is true that so far, he had somehow defended himself from all dangers, but it was hard to expect that this series of victories would last forever. And if it stopped right now, the consequences would be fatal.

"I must be getting old," he thought. "I used to be able to enjoy the present moment, and now I just grumble like an old grandpa. If there is any higher justice in this world, Theo cannot fail. He just can't."

This thought reassured him so much that he could more calmly await the tournament, about which was a row now. Presumably Gwidon, the gossiper called, told in the inn about what the stake in the tournament would be, because the whole province was humming like a hive. The message spread like circles on water, and quickly spread beyond the borders of Touraine. Those who knew the Black Prince said that the outlaw had no chance in this clash, and those who had meet Theo vehemently disagreed. By the way, bets were made for quite significant sums. The biggest problem was for those who knew both relatively well - they didn't know which one to bet on. In a word, the confusion about this duel became big, which was not surprising considering that the son of the King of England was going to have a run-in with an essentially insignificant rebellious knight of Touraine, which does not happen every day.

Bongrais, on the occasion of the tournament, organized by the Black Prince, turned into one big fair attracted by circus performers, sellers of everything possible, guests and ordinary onlookers, not forgetting the petty thieves, hoping for a real golden harvest. In the market square, stands were built for distinguished guests, and there was a place for commoners. Such a revival has not been remembered here since the beginning of the war. Prince Edward had been in a good mood since morning, as gracious as ever, and excited about what was about to happen, painfully so. His plan to annihilate the pesky outlaw along with his dangerous legend did not, of course, foresee that Theo might have a completely different vision of ending this story and that he would prepare well for the game that so much depended on. It is true that he was bound by the word given to the priest, but only the two of them knew about it, and the common people expected that his protector would simply kill the invader.

The event, caused by the whim of the English prince, rose to the rank of a symbol. It was no surprising that the tournament square was literally besieged on all sides and the soldiers struggled to keep order.

"I hope your Theo doesn't chick out at the last minute," Prince Edward said, leaning over to Adeline sitting next to him.

"Certainly not," the duchess replied calmly. She was wearing a new deep blue gown with a low waist and white ribbons, and a short hennin with a veil. She looked so beautiful that everyone looked at her with delight. "Anyway, here he is."

She pointed to the lone rider heading towards the square. Despite the distance, it was difficult not to recognize the graceful, slender figure of a forest knight, despite the outfit he usually did not wear - simple, but well-cut and elegant. His steed, a beautiful dun, wore an expensive saddle and a silver-adorned bridle.

A beaming young man ran out across from the rider.

"Hello, old friend!" He called, holding the horse by the bridle.

"Hello, Philip." Theo jumped off his horse and hugged the young man heartily. "I never thought that I'd meet you here."

"My father is Edward's ally, so you know... Do you really want to go to this pointless duel?" Philip looked anxiously at the box of honor.

"It may be meaningless to you, but not to me," Theo answered seriously.

The young prince met his eyes and pursed his lips for a moment.

"I've heard about the stake," he said. "For me it wouldn't be a reason enough, but you are so different from me..."

"I'm not going to get killed, if that's what you mean."

"Oh, yes, I know it's not your intention," sighed Philip. "The problem is that the Black Prince's fame as a swordsman is by no means not exaggerated. Be careful. I know you dealt with Roger de Valois relatively easily, but the Black Knight, though a scoundrel, was at least French, and as such he had this last bit of decency. After that, don't expect any rules to be followed."

Theo shrugged and smiled.

"Do I expect? I have yet to meet an honest Englishman... with one exception, perhaps."

The prince nodded slightly. When his outlaw friend smiled like that, his smooth cheeks were dimpled like a girl's, and his eyes sparkled with such innocent merriment that it was hard to believe what a formidable opponent he could be. The impression of harmlessness was intensified by his tall, but very thin figure, thanks to which, despite the fact that he had already exceeded twenty years, he still seemed to have grown up too quickly. Perhaps the Black Prince was deceived by this innocent appearance when he challenged him to a duel and ignored the stories that circulated about him.

"I'll tell you this first," he said after a moment. "I'm getting married to Estelle de Villeneuve. You are, of course, invited to our wedding with your people and that pretty blonde girl, for whom you almost died then, as you know."

"Are you marrying Estelle? With this kid?" Theo was surprised.

"She is fifteen, no longer a child. She is here with me, but I didn't let her leave the box. No offense, but with your tendency to tease everyone who lives, you are dangerous company for a young lady."

"Probably for the old woman too. Take it easy, I know how to behave."

Philip patted him on the shoulder and left. In fact, he was here not so much at the request of his father as on the orders of King Charles, who ordered him to watch everything closely. Unlike his father, Philip remained faithful to the crown of France, although his policy was in fact treading on very thin ice. This is why he gave a friend in his time what he called "the last resort." Only him he could really trust. For his part, Theo was not thinking about political matters now, preoccupied with his own problems. He felt nervous, something very dangerous about such a situation, and he had to use all his willpower to contain his jittery nerves. He knew he could not afford to do anything that would take away his movements with the necessary speed and precision, but self-directed calm is fragile when a geyser of emotions seething beneath its surface.

The worst part was that he had to wait. If he could fight right away, his mind would be so much clearer and his heart wouldn't be pounding like mad against his ribs. In addition, he always felt bad in the crowd, and now, after spending several years in the forest, his acute senses have been exposed to real torture. Flashy colors, the buzz of many voices, the crush and the mixed scent of roses, myrrh, musk, sandalwood oil with the scent of onions and the natural fumes of many bodies made him sick. Quickly figuring out how much time he still had, he stepped out of the crowd and went for a walk, trying not to lose sight of the honorary box.

He almost ran into a colorfully dressed juggler with a white painted face, tossing four lit torches with monkey dexterity. Nearby, a teenage songstress in a cheesy tunic, clearly too large for her and a huge wreath of wild flowers on her head, was singing something under the second zither, a colorfully adorned minstrel, in a hat with a feather put over her forehead, a dancer with a low neckline, flouncing dress, dancing, rhythm on the tambourine. The outlaw glanced at them inattentive, tossed them some money and walked on, passing similar itinerant actors, clearly more in the place than himself.

"Father Prospero was right, I had gone wild in this forest," he thought. "I would give a month of my life to be back among the trees, and yet I should feel at home here. Wait, I'm at home, that's my property," he added after a moment, and almost laughed out loud.

As always, his sense of humor helped him regain his spiritual balance. The tension eased, now he could wait for the duel without unnecessary nervousness. He calmed down to such an extent that he became interested in the tournament struggles and began to watch them closely enough that he looked for even a better place. People parted in front of him not very willingly, but they did not protest, be getting to know him or simply seeing that they are dealing with someone well-born.

"So you came, well," a sarcastic voice sounded above him at one point. Surprised, he looked up and realized that, in search of a better place, he had ended up involuntarily under the box of honor.

"Did you doubt it, honorable Englishman?" He asked unfriendly, angry at being surprised.

"Let's say I doubted," replied the Black Prince. "Even though the lady here has promised that you are brave enough for that."

He put his arm around his companion.

"Or stupid enough to be one thing," she said. "You won't get out of here alive. You don't know Sir Edward as well as I do."

"Oh yes, we got to know each other very well."

The Black Prince ran his lips caressingly over her hennin hair and swan neck. Adeline succumbed to those cares with a smile, though her eyes remained cold and angry.

Theo stared at them for a moment, then announced aloud:

"I'm sick of it," he stepped aside.

He really felt disgusted. He couldn't understand how a high-born and well-bred lady could do something similar: be the mistress of an enemy country in order to reach out to someone who had offended her long ago by his indifference. It suddenly occurred to him that Adeline was expecting a baby, so what could have happened to him? Even according to the most conservative calculations, she should have given birth long ago. He decided to ask Estelle about the baby at the earliest opportunity. For now, he was waiting for the tournament to end, figuring out a way to get out of town as safely as possible after the fight. He did not think he would be officially attacked, the Black Prince would not risk such an embarrassment, but an ambush was quite another, it had to be reckoned with. Absolutely yes. Like any good Frenchman of the day, Theo did not believe in English honor, though Sir Winslow's example might have taught him entirely something else.

"What must be, must be, let's not panic in advance," he thought, touching his hand to the cool hilt of Valius' sword.

He took it with him for the occasion, deliberately, not for the king's coat of arms, but because it was made of the finest Damascus steel. Usually swords were made of inferior varieties, or even ordinary iron - these were the cheapest, but also cost a lot. Better specimens often cost the price of a good village, but they were worth it, because the quality of the weaponry depended on a knight's life on the battlefield. How much this sword would cost, Theo did not even want to guess, and his former affiliation with the king still doubled this value.

"I will try it on you, English strutter," he promised in his mind.

He was looking forward to his turn, and yet patience was not his favorite virtue. It was well in the afternoon when the trumpeters finally announced the end of the official part of the tournament and the beginning of the most important struggles. Hearing his name, Theo hurried through the crowd around him and stepped out into the middle of the square. At the sight of him, the audience froze at first, then began to whisper among themselves with increasing excitement. Those who already knew him shared their remarks with those who saw him for the first time, and wondered how such a skinny young man with a gentle, over-beautiful face could have the courage to challenge all English power against himself. The viewers were convinced that the stakes of this duel were only a mocking excuse, and in fact this fight is about something completely different, the reasons given for various, sometimes profoundly absurd. Anyway, this is how the Black Prince saw it - the stake was indifferent to him, he only wanted to destroy his opponent and the rest did not count.

"Ready to die?" he asked, baring his sword and wrapping his left forearm in a cloak, which was a commonly practiced cover.

"You're never quite ready for that," Theo replied calmly. "However, I inform you that I'm not going to the other world yet and that I'm not on my way at all. Maybe later."

Oddly enough, this Englishman made a rather nice impression on him. He had long, light brown hair, a little facial hair, and eyes a blue so translucent that you had the impression that you could see all his thoughts through him. He did not look like the heartless monster that was portrayed in France. Yet he was the man responsible for the countless slaughter and pogroms, as well as for the shameful, whatever else, the slavery of King John. Theo unhurriedly stripped his sword and took the fighting position. Out of the corner of his eye, he caught the image of Estelle leaning out of her box and smiled slightly at the thought of how much this exalted young lady must now be concerned, whose ribbon was still in the inner pocket sewn into his knight's belt as a lucky charm.

Without retreating, he withstood the first attack and countered, showering his opponent with a barrage of virulent blows. Both opponents represented more or less the same level of skill, but Prince Edward, though slightly shorter than the black-haired Frenchman, was more muscular and looked stronger than him. It must be admitted that even the English, captivated by the beauty of the slender figure of an outlaw and his sparing elegance in fighting, almost wished him victory and whispered among themselves:

"It's a pity that he has to die."

Theo had that rare, inborn gift of liking even the fiercest of enemies - the only exception was Don Paulino, who hated him with ferocity worthy of a better cause. Those of the French who knew the hand of the Black Prince initially, with their English neighbors, expected the fight to end soon, but to the amazement of both, Theo was doing quite well. Prince Edward, whether he wanted it or not, had to respect his sword. He was beginning to understand why Captain Moore and his men feared him so much, and decided that he should settle this fight in his favor as soon as possible if he wanted to avoid public embarrassment. The French knight, despite the prolonged fight, did not look tired at all. He circled his opponent, tossing his sword from hand to hand, never taking his wolf gaze from the prince. In fact, he felt a lot worse than he showed. Edward managed to reach him in the ribs with the side of his sword. He could clearly hear the crack of a bone cracking then, and now with each inhalation, circles of searing pain were spreading through his body, making him almost breathless. He himself has not yet managed to break the Englishman's defense, which additionally weakened his self-confidence, somehow insufficient this time.

The Black Prince took a step back, then collapsed on his opponent with a combination of a lunge and a feint, so quickly that he did not leave him time to lay down. Theo had managed to raise his sword, but nothing else when he received a powerful blow aimed straight at the head. The Damascus steel did not break under a blow that would break any other blade like a stick, but the hand he had not had time to stiffen failed. The blade fell directly on his head, hitting him with what he thought was monstrous force. He stumbled back, his hand instinctively gripping the wound. Warm blood ran down his hand and face, he couldn't catch his breath, for a moment he had the impression that he was losing his eyesight. Almost blindly, on sharp, forest instincts, he parried the Englishman's thrust and after a desperate parade, he leapt to the side, shaking his head desperately. The fog was passing, he could still see, though dimly. He focused solely on characters with a sword, somehow erasing everything else from the world. As expected, the prince will now make a fundamental mistake: he will believe in his advantage and will want to use it.

He was not mistaken. He knelt down, diving under the blow that should have split his head open, he flipped his sword to his left hand and delivered a powerful blow from below, and inserting it with all the strength he still had.

The Black Prince's sword shot up in a wide arc and fell, plunging the blade into the trampled ground. Before anyone could sigh, Theo was standing upright as a reed, holding the blade of his weapon against the Englishman's neck. In the silence that followed, everyone heard his voice clearly as he said loudly and emphatically:

"You lost, sir."

Then he whistled. There was whinny, and a dun steed burst into the square, scattering the people. The outlaw mounted him and pulled the reins.

"Remember your word of honor, prince, because I will certainly not forget it," he threw over his shoulder and rode away, not letting know that he was already with the last of his strength.

He had to bitterly admit that if he had been attacked now, he would have been unable to defend himself. So he sped the horse along the path he had spotted before, holding his breath, waiting for the sensation of the attack. He still felt the pain with each inhalation, his head felt as if he were going to split into pieces and his vision was blurred. Panic seized him at the thought that he might stay that way. What if he loses his eyesight at all? He could not even imagine something so terrible and he did not want to think about it, and what was worse, he was completely defenseless in the face of this misfortune, he could do nothing. The fact that he knew Bongrais really well helped him get outside the walls now, for the side alleys were a tangle, a maze for someone who had been here for the first time, for example. The fact that he was not being pursued seemed too good, and Theo was so relieved as he left the city that he almost passed out. It didn't come to that, but he weakened so much that he could hardly stay in the saddle.

"Come on, my old man," he muttered to himself. "I don't think you won this fight for now die along the way. Such a small scratch will probably not knock you down..."

The wave of nausea seized him again, and he seized the pommel with trembling hands, trying to gather all his strength. His vision was getting worse, but he could still see soldiers approaching him. He realized with horror that he was gone, and drew his sword to at least die with weapon in hand. Suddenly, a speeding circus car drove between him and the soldiers, turning violently and ramming the surprised Englishmen. The colorful juggler leaned out of the coach-box and with lightning blows of a thick stick knocked two of the attackers off their horses. The dancer in the heavily cut dress and the minstrel almost simultaneously released the triggers of the crossbows they were holding, and two more soldiers were on the ground, and the last survivor turned his horse and sped him into the city, apparently losing his fighting spirit. The juggler made a semicircle around the cart and galloped past the knight, while the minstrel and the singer in the wreath pulled him off the horse, throwing him onto the leather lining the cart so quickly that he did not even have time to realize what was actually going on. A pretty, worried face bent over him. It took a while for him to realize it was Preziosa, though the colorful handkerchief on her head and the big circles in her ears, which she did not usually wear, changed her beyond recognition. He raised himself on one elbow.

"I understand now," he said hoarsely. "The juggler is Armando, the minstrel is Gwidon. But who is the singing girl? Too small for Bellette."

The singer tore the wreath from her head and shook the frizzy hair.

"Guess," she said shortly.

"What? Tristan, get out of that dress right now! Do you want to embarrass me?!" The knight shouted in shock.

"A peculiar way to thank for help, brother. Gratitude is not your strongest point," replied the boy sourly, relieving himself of the gown he had worn underneath it.

"How could you take him?" Theo dropped to his leather again, feeling a wound on his head is bleeding again, and the warm moisture is running down his neck and back.

Preziosa took a handkerchief from her head and moistened it with water from a carefully taken water bag.

She carefully wiped the leader's face and hair with the blood and pressed the handkerchief tightly to the wound.

"Hurry up, Armando!" She screamed. "He's still bleeding! I can't stop it!"

"Let me die," Theo whispered, seeing the world blur before his eyes.

Panic took hold of him, everything went dark around him and he passed out, he did not know for how long.

When he woke up, he was no longer lying on the cart, and was mangy pelt on a wide wooden bench. Above him he could see the faint outline of the old monk's figure.

"How are you?" Prospero asked him brusquely. "Only without lies. During the last crusade, I witnessed a Crusader, severely hacked by the Moors, when asked by the physician what was wrong with him, he replied with a broad smile: "It's all right." And he died."

"Well, I'm not okay," he replied in a barely audible voice. "It hurts like hell... and I don't see well. I could endure the pain, even if it was the worst, but my eyes... Prospero, will I go blind?"

"How do I know? We will see," the monk skillfully dressed his head with ointments and a cloth saturated with herbal decoctions. "It happened after such a blow. We'll know in a few days. You will stay here for now. I'll blindfold you, a few days of strict diet and lying in the dark, and then whatever God gives."

He poured something into his wine and made Theo drink it.

"Now you will sleep until morning."

"Until morning," the knight repeated bitterly. "And if I... Prospero, will you give me enough to sleep... all eternity?"

"No," replied the monk briefly. "Your life is not your property, outlaws. It belongs to God and you will not take it yourself. Certainly not in my consciousness."

Theo said nothing more, especially since the monastic medicine had finally begun act and everything drifted away from him as if he were in a boat on a wavy lake. When he finally fell asleep, the monk went out into the corridor where his friends were waiting for him.

"I don't want to deceive you, it's bad," he said bluntly. "I've seen such cases in the crusade, and they usually end fatally. In about five days we will know more, until then we are doomed to uncertainty. God bless you all, because that's pretty much the only thing we can do for him right now. As for you, stay here overnight, it is dangerous to go by the swamps after a night."

Those few days, spent in absolute darkness, were later remembered by Theo as one great nightmare. Father Prospero would not let him get up, he kept him on the previously announced strict diet, which did not matter that he at the same time drank it with herbal essences, so disgusting in taste that one could not even think about eating after them. Theo swallowed it all scornfully for death and lay as patiently as he could, but the only thought troubled him all the time: what would happen when father Prospero removed the blindfold from his eyes. When the expected day finally arrived, he felt a sudden dread and tried to postpone the moment of removing the dressing as far as possible.

"Okay, okay, we know how to do it," the monk told him sternly. "Sit down and give me that rag. We will know in a minute if everything is okay or if everything is not right. Sit up straight."

He cut the dressing and removed the bandage.

"Open your eyes," he ordered.

Overcoming the trembling of his eyelids, the knight carried out the order.

"Why is it so dark in here?" He asked in a choked voice.

"Because it's night, and I've covered the candle with a jug," Prospero replied. "Look in the direction of my voice."

Slowly, taking his time, he raised the jug and asked, carefully concealing his anxiety:

"And how? Can you see anything?"

Theo took a deep breath.

"It's good... I can see well," he replied. "Sharp and clear. Forgive me, father, if I could get wine? I must drink."

Prospero handed him a coarse clay flask, prepared carefully. Theo took a few sips and wiped the sweat from his brow with a trembling hand, wincing involuntarily as his hand hit the sword wound that was not yet fully healed. Prospero did not even show how relieved he was.

"You can go back to what you call home now," he said with rough indifference. "It will be fine, but be prepared for the fact that you may experience some visual sensations for many more months. Don't be frightened by it, it's harmless unless it haunts you in combat."

"But my whole life is a struggle," the knight laughed, apparently regaining his former spirit.

Prospero opened the door and finally let him out of the stuffy lock into the corridor, where Pierre as gloomy as ever waited. At the sight of the leader, he brightened a little.

"Finally," he said. "We were dying to know if you were alive and... how you live."

"Thank you, not bad. Does it worry you?"

Pierre waved his hand.

"You know nothing," he grunted. "And I will not lie to you? You have no idea what happened while you were lying here. Bellette... Bellette lost her baby."

The knight paused, staring at him in disbelief.

"How is that?!" he exclaimed.

"What how is that? I don't know about these woman's things, I don't know how exactly, but the fact remains the fact," Pierre replied with a shrug. "Didn't you know she was pregnant?"

Theo, confused, shook his head.

"You would know..." muttered Pierre.

"Is it because of me?" asked the knight in a choked voice.

"I'm sure that being upset over you didn't help her... but I don't know. Forgive me, I just love my sister and I fear for her, and nothing good awaits her with you."

"I love her too. If I had let this Englishman kill me, at least she would have been free of me once and for all, and you would have breathed a sigh of relief."

Pierre stopped abruptly and looked at him sharply.

"One more such stupidity, and I will break your jaw to the fullest," he announced, and after a moment his unshaven face was lit by a crooked smile. "You really know how to make someone feel guilty."

He tapped the chief on the shoulder and quickened his pace. Theo struggled to keep up with him, tired of lying down, insomnia, and eating a Draconian diet, and listened silently to his brother-in-law's story. Bellette was for some time under the care of a village herbalist, who was also delivered births. She felt not too bad, but for two days it was very bad, her life was literally hanging in the balance. All this time, Pierre could not sleep, and his wishes for his brother-in-law were not suitable for public repetition. As always, he blamed him for everything. Theo did not even blame him, especially when he entered the hut, he saw a pale woman lying on the bed, aged a few years, with the same look in her eyes as people who are desperate or hard hit by fate.

He knelt down and wrapped his arms around her.

Bellette pressed her face against his chest.

"This is the second time," she whispered despairingly. "I'll never be able to give you a son."

"So what? You think some brat is more important to me than you?" The knight got angry. "What would I do if you died? I wouldn't have anything to live for, you understand? I love you, not what you could possibly give birth to for me. To hell with the baby, Bellette. Why would we have them on such a terrible world?"

His words sounded brutal and harsh, but at least they were meant to be uplifting, so she fell silent and said nothing. She had always dreamed of giving son to her beloved, a little knight, a living portrait of a beloved man - but this child would not be there, and maybe Theo was right in saying it was even better that way. Only that she was choked by the sadness she had to deal with on her own, because she knew that her husband, because he was a man, would not be able to understand her.

After a moment she forced a smile and stroked her knight's cheek with her fingers.

"You are sweet," she said kindly. "But now go. I want to be alone."

Theo stepped outside the cabin and sat down against the wall, resting his head on his hands. After a while his whole band came, talking lively among themselves in raised voices. He got up when he saw them.

"All right," he said sternly. "Someone now explain to me what my brother, the Gypsies, and that pesky Weasel were doing in Bongrais. Come on. Whose idea was it?"

The outlaws nudged each other with their elbows for a moment, looking at each other, then Tristan replied with undisguised embarrassment:

"Mine."

"What?" Theo stared at him in amazement, mixed with indignation, and gasped.

"Yes, Tristan," Beregard said. "And you don't get angry. After all, you announced that neither of us would show up in the city during the tournament, because, first of all, they will hit us right away, and secondly, you will smash each one's head. Was it like that or wasn't it?"

"It was... But I..."

"Silence, now I'm talking," his friend interrupted him sternly. "Well, if so, then went the Gypsies, whom no one in Bongrais has had time to meet, Gwidon and Tristan as the leader, because we all knew that you would not raise your hand against this kid. Mainly because you'd kill him on the spot, he's such a midget."

"Well, well, well," the boy said, offended.

"You'd look nice if it weren't for them," said Millot. "You should be grateful to them, and you are angry as if there was something to do."

"Wait a minute. Does this mean that my brother, on his own initiative, changed into a dress and, in a thin voice, was pulling out romanza?" Theo asked incredulously.

"Exactly. He was even getting on well," admitted Gwidon, humming melancholy on his lyre.

The knight turned his back to his friends.

"It's unbelievable," he said. "I cannot believe it. A puppy without any experience tells you to jump, and you are already in the air asking how high. It's sick! Next time, I want you to strip naked, paint with flowers, and dance the farandole around the castle, and you will listen to it too. Why I had to wait for such a disgrace..."

"You were close, and you wouldn't actually live to see it," Jean remarked scoldingly.

"Exactly," said Armando grimly. "Those soldiers had the worst intentions of you. You're ungrateful, you know?"

Theo nodded melancholy.

"Ah, you two-faced monsters," he said. "Someday, I will... But thank you. Especially you, little brother."

"At your service," Tristan grinned, pleased at the change in tone in his older brother's voice.

He wanted him not only to like him, but also to be proud of him, and now he felt that he fully deserved it. He didn't notice the shadow on his face, but when he later found him alone, behind the hut, he became concerned.

"Why are you so sad?" he asked.

"Whatever," Theo muttered. "You wouldn't understand anyway. You follow me?"

"No, I just wanted to know where you are. I know you don't need a nanny," the boy said, resentfully.

Theo reached out and patted his frail shoulder hesitantly.

"You showed off today, you... the egg wiser than the hen," he said softly. "You're not stupid. Really smart. Too bad there are things you can't help me with."

"I know," Tristan whispered.

He too thought of Bellette, in a pain and despondency that had not left her for many days. Later, however, youth and health overcame weakness, and the girl's blue eyes shone again with the unfettered joy of life. What was not talked about among the outlaws under an unwritten agreement designed to make their uneasy life a little more bearable. This did not apply, of course, to other people. Everything that had to do with a bunch of bold outcasts was widely commented on, so it's no wonder that an event as important as this duel could not be forgotten either. The news of it spread all over France, which rang out with stories of how an outlawed French knight had humiliated the pride of an English prince, and these stories soon reached England as well. The immediate consequence of this was the arrival of the Black Prince's younger brother to Bongrais, Sir John Lancaster of Gaunt, claimant to the throne of Spain and ally of his brother in his claims against France. His arrival was a great surprise for everyone, and in addition not very pleasant, because it was known in advance that he would baste as much as possible on his older brother. The Black Prince would have liked to chew the bitterness of defeat without the participation of anyone in the family with whom he lived in forced accord, but since he couldn't just throw his brother out the door, he accepted him with reluctant courtesy.

Sir John did not seem to notice it, on the contrary, he made himself at home with all ease and merriment. Honorable Adeline gave a lot of courtly compliments which, oddly enough, put her in a terrible mood, and had some rather insignificant conversations with the soldiers guarding the castle. He was kind and elegant to everyone, which the Black Prince found suspicious to say the least, and watched him distrustfully. Finally, during the joint supper, he could not stand it.

"You came here especially from England to shine here, spreading your personal charm?" he asked directly.

Sir Lancaster laughed.

"Always the same," he said. "Well, if so, let's leave all the courtesies. Our father is concerned about your condition here."

"Unnecessarily," his brother replied dryly.

"You don't seem to realize what you are saying," said Sir John pityingly. "All of England knows about your brawls with this outlaw. People are laughing at you for posing as a god of war, and the usual forest thug gave you such a slap that you could hear it in London. For my part, just to add that I do not understand how you could have survived such dishonor at all."

"Oh, with permission," said Adeline. "There is a lot to say about Theo Le Vengeur, but not that he is a random thug."

Sir John smiled charmingly at her.

"My beauty, I know it, and you know it, and half of France knows it," he said. "But for the English it's just an ordinary forest robber and that's it. Some people compare him to Robin Hood, but let's be honest, who was Robin Hood? A fugitive, a robber, a rebel against legally exercised power, and the comparison with him cannot be flattering to anyone."

Prince Edward gritted his teeth angrily.

"I'll skin that outlaw alive if he falls into my hands," he growled.

Lancaster narrowed his eyes with pity.

"Well, what does that get you?" He asked. "Be reasonable, you won't save anything with this. Otherwise, if he were easy to catch, his body would long ago be rotting apart at the crossroads. No, my dear brother, you just won't catch him. This Theo has already managed to prove what he is worth, and by underestimating such an opponent, you are only making fun of yourself."

"Oh, yes, Theo le Vengeur is an enemy worthy of respect," his brother agreed furiously. "I will hang him with all due respect."

"This after you catch him," Sir John agreed. "For now, I would advise you to find someone who will facilitate his escape from Orleans. Someone had to do it, unless you assume that it was the angels who flew with him on a cloud behind the walls, which seems to me, for example, somehow unlikely."

Adeline looked at him with interest.

"Who do you mean, sir?" She asked. "Theo hates the English, and the French, who have come to terms with the current state of affairs, perhaps even more. I don't think he has contacted anyone around us. Anticipating possible suspicions, I will answer that I'm not an option. Theo despised me and killed my husband, I hate him like no one else."

Sir John smiled secretly at these words.

"Where would I dare to suspect such a lady," he said gallantly. "To be honest, my suspicions go in a completely different direction, towards a man who is close to us. Do you guess Edward who I'm talking about?"

The Black Prince nodded grimly.

"Exactly," finished his brother. "Watch out for him, and he may lead you to your enemy faster than you think. For now, let's forget about the troubles and have fun."

With a smile, he raised his cup to the air. He was amused by the sight of his older brother in such pickles, and felt that if it had fallen on him, he would have done better. Being younger and more handsome than Edward, he mastered the art of intrigue, using to this end his personal charm and the innocent expression of his eyes. He was more skillful with poison, denunciation, or an assassin's dagger than with a sword in open combat, and felt that if he could not defeat the impudent outlaw in a chivalrous way, some quite nonchalant should be used. However, he knew in advance that his brother would not agree to it. The Black Prince, after all, had certain rules which he did not deviate from in any situation. Another thing is that, by acting with his methods, John Lancaster could do more damage to the enemy in a few days than Edward and his entire army in three months. This time, however, he did not come here to support him, the visit was rather of a courtesy nature. In fact, Sir Lancaster stayed with his brother for only a few days on his way to Madrid. He intended to lay claim to the Spanish throne, which he had a right to thanks to his marriage to Blanche, the Infant of Spain, and which he did not intend to give up. Of course, he also couldn't pass up the opportunity to tease an older and more famous brother, whom he hated privately. The conversations he had with his people were for fun rather than information, because he should have asked Don Paulino for it, which he did not want to do - he despised people of this type, although he sometimes used their services himself.

Having rested and amused at Edward's expense, he decided to go on his way in the morning, which the Black Prince accepted with genuine relief.

"Calm at last," he murmured, watching the retreating retinue.

"It will be calm when Theo le Vengeur finally dies. I would like to be there."

Adeline pushed a strand of her silky hair from her forehead and sighed deeply. During the recent experiences she has become thinner and paler, but her dazzling beauty has not lost anything on it, on the contrary, she has become more mature and more refined, more subtle, and her hazel eyes acquired a cold shine.

Prince Edward put his arm around her.

"You'll be there," he promised her. "And even if not, at least I will take his head to yours feet."

He had never realized how much he had fallen in love with her, how much he cared about her. He did not know if he could live without her anymore, although in the depths of his black heart he knew that she did not love him at all, he saw in him only a convenient instrument of her revenge. He was even convinced that Adeline still loves Theo, she loves him with a bad, cruel and twisted love, but still. He had experienced similarly violent feelings in his life, and he was concerned with this dilemma much more than the mockery of his younger brother, who was just walking away on a road through the woods.

"A fool," he thought contemptuously. "If he had run into Mad Dog like this, he would have stopped talking nonsense."

Thinking like that, he didn't even know how quickly his wish would be fulfilled. The commander of the entourage had made a timid suggestion to take a detour, a much safer route, but Sir Lancaster only scowled at his words.

"What my father says is true: if you don't slap yahoo mouth in the morning, he walks stupid all day," he said. "I thought you weren't afraid of just any robber. He will probably hide with his people in the mouse hole anyway, and even if not, it will be his last mistake. We're going through the forest."

No one dared to speak at this remark, and although the escort troops were also inconceivable that a handful of ragged peasants would dare to attack the king's son, they had their heart in their mouth.

The forest quickly thickened, it became dark, and the long-worn trail was lost in the bushes. The soldiers, brave on the battlefield, but easily succumbing to superstition, remembered the stories of sorcerers and werewolves reportedly encountered here, so the whole squad was grimly afraid. Many of them wished to meet the outlaws who were at least a tangible reality. It happened very quickly: without warning, a net laden with stones fell on the tightly packed soldiers and ten men armed with clubs and daggers fell out of the bushes. Only Sir John and his two bodyguards were able to take up arms, the rest could not cope with the net entwining them. The attackers acted according to a previously developed plan. They murdered those trapped in the net with daggers strikes, and the knights fiercely defended themselves with clubs.

"So, it's true," thought Sir Lancaster, struggling to fend off the robbers.

He was disgusted with the thought that he would die here, at the hands of rebellious peasants, in a wilderness where even no one would find his remains, and what was worse, he could only blame himself. After all, he had been warned about what was going on here.

Suddenly, a group of other men, not much different from the attackers, grew out of the ground, who unexpectedly came to his aid. They had better weapons and were better trained in combat than the others. In addition, their relief came at the most opportune moment, and for Sir John it was the most important thing. His eyes were caught by the commander of the rescue gang - a tall, dark-haired youth in a simple leather jacket tightened at the waist by a knight's belt. You didn't have to be a clairvoyant to guess the outlaw in him who made a lot of trouble his brother. The sword in his hand twisted and bit. It was easy to understand why the English fear him so much. The rest of the gang were also well trained. In about half the pace most of the attackers lay dead or incapacitated on the grass, and their leader was dying, bleeding profusely from his throat, cut with the very tip of the sword.

"You've done it, Scaramouche," said the leader of the victorious gang in a soft baritone, wiping his sword of blood. "I warned you this was my territory and that there would be no second warning."

Sir John walked over to him.

"Theo le Vengeur, I believe," he began. "I know you, but you don't know me yet. I'm John of Gaunt."

The outlaw glanced at him quite indifferently from under the black mane that fell to the wide forehead. Even if it did not quite match the description, he would settle all doubts a square gorged on a chain of decorative, flat forged links - the Bongrais coat of arms carved on it was all too clearly visible.

"You saved my life, thank you," finished Sir John, feeling awkward somehow.

"I don't know if I'll forgive myself for that," Theo replied with a sarcasm, barely masked by fake politeness. "After all, I dare to note that it was not about you, but about our settlements with this gang. Actually, I should have attacked you myself, but now it would be at least distasteful on my part. Go with God, my lord, and the second time do not go where no one has asked you, because you may be less fortunate."

A teenage, curly boy in a gray jacket approached him and said softly:

"They have four killed and three really badly injured, and many have been hurt a little."

Theo shrugged.

"And what do we have to do with this? Do you think to play medic or gravedigger? Better get our people back, let's go back," he said.

"I hope fate will give me an opportunity to repay you one day," Sir Lancaster sighed, realizing with some bitterness that to this outlawed knight his person meant no more than those whom he had killed in front of his eyes.

"Oh, better not," Theo said. "You, my lord, do not repay me. I'd rather not deal with English courtesy. For us french people, it can be unhealthy. Until now I have traces of your hospitality on my back and I would prefer not to use it again."

He motioned to his men, and they walked off into the woods together without looking back. If not for the killed and groaning wounded on the ground, it would seem that this terrible adventure was only a dream.

"Well, let me write all this to Edward, he'll be surprised," thought Sir John, as he helped his soldiers lay down the wounded and the dead on a stretcher hastily made of coats and branches.

Meanwhile, Theo and his band returned to their hideout, dodging out of habit to confuse any chase.

"Well, Scaramouche and his thugs won't be messing with us here anymore," Pierre remarked, digging up pine cones along the way.

"Stubborn mules. If they had taken my first warning seriously, there would be no such carnage," Theo said with a hint of guilt in his voice.

He did not enjoy killing unfortunate people like him and his companions, only those who were more feral with hunger and mistreatment. But he had no choice - he had to protect the inhabitants of his lands. Such ruthless robbers were no better than English soldiers, he could not indulge them.

"Tell me again that you hate violence and that we are all brothers and we will put you back in the convent," said Millot with subtle pity. "There is also someone to pity."

"I don't pity anyone, and I certainly will not be over you when they finally hang you," the leader snapped at him.

"It isn't known who will be the first one," highlander did not remain without any reaction.

"We didn't have to liquidate them as the first ones, and Father Prospero probably doesn't have any supplies left," Theo said after a moment. "I'm going to the monastery, and you go home, just don't run into the English on the way, because lately there is a lot of them hanging around."

"Likewise," Beregard replied.

The knight turned into one of the side trails. It has not been easy to hunt anything in these forests for a long time, often for months they were condemned to loot them by means of robbery. This time, however, he managed to hunt a small boar, which he could proudly bring as a gift to the Carmelites. Father Prospero accepted this gift with rough gratitude and listened carefully to the outlaw's account of the adventure he had just lived.

"If you think the Black Prince will feel like he owes some gratitude to you now, then you may be confused," he said. "Assuming, of course, that Lancaster will admit what happened to him. People would... although, on the other hand, everyone has different problems now. You have no idea what is happening all over the country right now. Plague is spreading everywhere, just look when it will be in Touraine, people eat dogs and rats, you will not see a cat, how long and wide France, a human meat dealer was hanged in Paris, and here, please, we eat wild game."

"Human flesh? Seriously?"

"Oh yeah. Apparently the folks knew exactly what they were buying. Such things have happened during the Crusades, my love."

The outlaw sat down on a wide bench and his face turned slightly green.

"O Mother of God, ragout from the deceased..." he groaned in disgust.

"You're young, you don't know how it is. Sometimes it's just a matter of choosing the lesser evil," Prospero consoled him.

Theo was barely listening to him. He himself knew well what hunger was, but he had never been so hungry as to view another human being as something to eat. It was a shock to him to realize that he, too, could find himself in such a situation. He had lived on the edge for a long time, tearing out to the inexorable fate each new day of existence, and he was used to living only in the present moment, only in this part of the world, without thinking about what was going on somewhere else. Sometimes, however, this more distant world entered his life - just like it does now. Yet even without it, he already knew that there were things that could humiliate and disfigure a person, that everyone, treated properly, had to bend, and it was a depressing consciousness that questioned everything he had been taught in his early youth, everything he believed in.

"Don't overthink all this," advised Prospero, who could see the storm raging in his friend's heart. "Always be faithful to your principles, and then, even if you die, your name will never perish."

"Thank you for your spiritual comfort, Father, but I'm not going to that world yet," Theo laughed cheerfully.

As usual, his sense of humor allowed him to regain his spiritual balance and to see everything from the necessary distance. He returned to the hideout quite calmly, whistling one of Gwidon's more romantic compositions along the way and not thinking about what he had heard. He always returned from the convent uplifted, no matter how bad it was. Whistling, he entered the clearing, where his friends were sitting at an improvised table, eating something from a wooden bowl, nibbling on bread.

"Sit with us," Bellette called cheerfully. "Pierre picked up some honey from beehives in the woods, you want?"

"Sure, give me!" Theo, who was fond of sweets not available in this backwoods, beamed.

Jean handed him a spoon, and Beregard handed him a large slice of bread. The knight scooped up a slightly thick, dark yellow mass that smelled of meadow flowers and gnawed at it on bread.

"Oh, wonderful..." he muttered with delight.

"Speak up," Millot urged, accustomed to the fact that every visit to the Carmelites means fresh news from the countryside and the country.

"Nothing," the chief replied. "It's just that in Paris they supposedly cook a stew of corpses, for lack of something better, but you can find a gallows for this."

"Corpse soup, chopped worms," said Gwidon cheerfully. "I wrote it in coal once in one inn. Its owner chased me through half the city with a spit in hand."

"Oh, and the plague may still come upon us," finished the knight calmly, and put another batch of sticky sweetness in his mouth.

"What a great idea. Why is it here?" Francois was surprised cheerfully.

"If the Black Prince had caught it, I would give a bit for Mass of joy," Beregard sighed deeply.

Jean shook his head.

"Unlikely," he said after some thought. "The devil will not allow anyone so useful to him to die of any plague."

"There is something about it."

*****

Philip d'Evreux picked up a flat stone from the shore and threw it into the calm waters of the lake.

"You are not easy to reach," he said.

"That's the point, not to be easy," Theo le Vengeur replied. "Any fool will hit the target you can see. And I have to watch out not only against the English, who do not know these forests after all, but also against the scoundrels of entirely native farming. There aren't enough of them, Philip."

The young Navarian smiled.

"Right, there are a lot of them," he admitted. "Some terrorize entire provinces, occupy fortified fortresses and even smaller towns. Bertram du Guesclin[3] has waged a ruthless war on them, but it will take a while to achieve something. There aren't many

[3] Bertram du Guesclin - (born circa 1320, died July 13, 1380), Breton and French knight, considered one of the most outstanding knights of the Hundred Years' War, French constable.

people like you or the Pyrenean Falcon, most think about their pockets. Well, never mind that. Will you be at my and Estelle's wedding? I'm afraid it will be rather empty. My family has already turned their backs on me, many others believe that Estelle should pay for her sister's sins... But the king promised to honor the ceremony with his presence. You know, our friendship seems more and more unreal to me. After all, my father tried to poison him and made pacts with the English..."

He shook his tired head. It was really getting harder and harder for him to understand.

"It happens. And what they say about your fiancée shouldn't matter to you," Theo said warmly. "People are quite often unfair, I experienced it myself. When a mercenary was impersonating me, terrorizing people, everyone turned away from me, everyone believed that it was me... It hurt a lot. However, from now on, I care less about what people say about me and I don't build any locks on their friendly feelings. I got smart."

"You got rather bitter. So, will you be there?"

"I wish, I'm afraid, that there would be no unpleasant confusion because of me," said the outlaw hesitantly.

He really wanted to be at the wedding, but he had the feeling that he shouldn't go there, and a vague feeling that his friend wasn't telling him everything.

"What's the matter, Philip?" He asked heartily, placing a hand on his shoulder.

The young man looked at him with anguished eyes.

"I'm scared," he replied. "Something is happening that I don't understand, and although Charles still shows me friendship, there must be something behind it. Hope you still have what I gave you at Bongrais Castle? One day it may really be my last resort. For now, however, I'm waiting for you in Tours, because I'm to marry my bride there. It's close enough to her family, and far enough from my father, to be calm and without surprises."

"I will be there," his friend promised him.

The young people embraced warmly.

"Tell me one more thing," Theo asked. "What happened to your future sister-in-law's child?"

Philip frowned.

"It was a strange thing," he said reluctantly. "The baby is said to have been born dead, but Estelle swears it's impossible because she heard crying at the night Adeline gave birth. Apparently it was a girl. The next morning, there was no sign of her left, and Adeline acted as if nothing had happened at all. That's all I know. Watch out for Adeline, she hates you and now lives by faith with your worst enemy. And she is a lady from such a good family... It is true that the Black Prince did not show himself by chance, after all, he is the king's son and an excellent knight. Tell me honestly, which of you is better at the sword, you or him?"

"I don't know," Theo shrugged reluctantly.

"How don't you know? You beat him?" Philip was surprised.

"Maybe so, but he reached me twice, and I never really reached him. Wait, that more important: what could have happened to the baby?"

"I have no idea, but if I were you I would look in the country cottages," the young prince said indifferently. "Many unwanted children of great ladies, no matter whether they are bastards or not, are raised by the women who earn money like this. Why exactly are you so interested in it?"

"Oh, I don't know..."

Somewhere nearby, the scythe whistled. It repeated three times, then fell silent. Theo folded his hands to his mouth and chirped like a siskin. From the woods, a turtle-dove coo answered him.

"They're waiting for me," he said. "Something must have happened. Goodbye, Philip."

"Bye," sighed the Navarrian. "I envy you your unfettered life. At the royal court, you have to be careful that you don't miss a word of truth, and keep looking back."

It really was like that. He sincerely wished they could just be friends, be comrades in arms under the same banner, they just had to meet in secret, as they do now, and hide their friendship from the world. Theo cared less about all of this. He nodded to Philip, adjusted the bow slung over his shoulder, and disappeared into the woods.

"Of course you didn't hunt anything because you were busy having affairs with this duke," Pierre told him as he joined him. "It's good that we have some smoked meat left, because you would eat dry porridge. Fly to Prospero after lunch, he has an urgent matter."

"Maybe now...?" the knight wondered.

"Come on, have a bite to eat with us first, or you'll eventually die of non-eating," Pierre advised him in a friendly manner.

As always, he felt that the old monk had nothing really important to do with them.

They quickly reached a clearing where Armando, gloomy as night, with a much disliked "cauldron guard" that day, was pouring steaming porridge into his friends' bowls. Theo set to eat with a healthy appetite.

"I'll find something for tomorrow," he promised with his mouth full.

"Sure, anyone can have a worse day," Tristan agreed with overly hypocritical solidarity.

"Oh my lady, a day without you is worse than death..." sang Gwidon groaningly.

"And what is this graveyard poetry again?" Pierre bristled.

He sometimes composed poems himself, but rather revolutionary ones, and he hated Gwidon's poetry.

"It's not mine, it's Tybald the Singer," the troubadour was offended.

"I wonder if it's true that he and Queen Blanche... hey, Theo?" Francois asked, licking the spoon and nudging the knight on the back.

"I've no idea, I didn't follow them," the chief replied.

"Nobody knows. They still argue about it at the Louvre," Tristan said cheerfully.

Indeed, this old story still fascinated people, although no one knew whether the romance itself actually happened. It was known that Queen Blanche of Castile favored Tybald, who because of her parted with his wife, and even the pope's intervention did not help in this matter. The lower strata of the population believed that the romance was an irrefutable fact, and that the malicious people of Paris, as always, pick the queen and her favorite to pieces. The students from the University of Paris excelled in this in particular, young people who were both playful and unbridled, which the Queen apparently did not pay attention to, for a time. One day, there were riots in which over three hundred students were killed, killed by desperate townspeople who were fed up with their antics (an attempt to rape the daughter of one of the innkeepers provided a direct excuse). The Queen then refused to order an official investigation into the matter[4]. She was not convinced by any, even the most ardent and logical arguments, not even references to the special status and special university rights, always respected so far. The queen said that everyone had the right to defend themselves against unruly youths like schoolboys, and that she even forbade prosecuting the perpetrators of the massacre. It had its good points - the students were quiet for a while.

"Ah, whatever," Gwidon waved his hand, remembering that bloody day, still alive in the memory of the people of Paris. "Whoever plays with fire, usually gets burnt. I also wanted to study, but unfortunately for me I was born in brothel. It would be nice to have a Bachelor of Arts degree..."

"No title will help you, bastard," muttered Pierre harshly.

"No soap will help the raven, nor the incense of the dead," said Jean.

"The cliché is always at hand," Theo grimaced. "You tease the Weasels, because there is something that can do better than you. Okay, I'm going to see Prospero and find out what he wants from me again."

He stretched, tossed the emptied bowl onto the grass, and stood up. As always, after a sumptuous and quickly absorbed meal, he was overwhelmed with blissful laziness and would most willingly stretch out in the sun. But he knew that Prospero was certainly not summoning him for some stupidity. He preferred to make sure what it was about. He made his way quickly to the convent, stopping only to pick up thyme, valued by outlaws as much as mint and pine sap for chewing. He called the monastery gate and, nibbling on the aromatic herb, looked out of habit to see if he was being followed. Brother Michael opened it.

---

[4] Historical fact.

"You are here at last," he grunted. "We're looking forward to you."

"Is it that urgent?" Theo was surprised.

"More than you think."

Brother Michael led him to the back of the building, to a small shed, where to his amazement Theo saw Sir Winslow lying on his makeshift bed - in a deplorable condition. Lady Joan, weeping desperately, was kneeling over him. At the sight of the outlaw, she jumped to her feet and clung to his chest.

"But please don't cry, my lady," tightly embarrassed, he embraced her and tried to calm her down. "Crying won't help. What happened?"

"Edward is crazy. He accused Reynold of collaborating with you and wanted him to tell him where you are hiding," the Englishwoman whispered, choking back a sob. "He had him tortured. I managed to organize an escape, but I have no one to turn to for further help..."

Theo stroked her head absently. He felt indescribably stupid. It seemed ridiculous and absurd for him, an outlaw French knight, to help an English lady on his own lands, appropriated by the English. There was indeed something ironic about it. Meanwhile Lady Joan, having cried out, wiped her tears and moved away from him as if she had only now realized the wrongness of her conduct.

"Help him," she said. "No one else would dare to do this."

"I can't say no to the request of such beautiful eyes," he replied. "Besides, I owe a debt of gratitude to Sir Winslow. He is the only Englishman I like and respect, although if you repeat it to someone, I will deny everything. It can't be done differently, I've to take him to the woods, because here the Black Prince will surely find him. Wait, my lady, I'm running for my people."

Lady Joan wiped away the tears that came back to her eyes.

"You are a great, noble knight. What a pity your king can't see it," she whispered gratefully.

"Ah, this is a matter between the two of us."

Theo waved his hand dismissively and ran out of the convent. He was soon back, accompanied by Pierre and Beregard, their expressions very blurry and, seeing Sir Reynold, stopped dead.

"I thought you were kidding," Pierre said as sweetly as possible, as if he wasn't quite sure his chief was sane. "Don't you think that you are exaggerating a bit with this nobility this time?"

"He's English, if that's what you mean, but exceptional," Theo replied sternly. "Have you forgotten how much we owe him? Well, the day has come to pay off the debt. Get him on a sheet."

Father Prospero approached them.

"Here are herbs for him," he said softly. "Rinse his wounds with the decoction. If he does not regain control of his legs within a week, he will never does."

"Is it that bad?" The knight looked into his eyes with silent terror.

"And how did you want? The value of torture as such is debatable, since it has been so perfected that the innocent will admit everything," the monk replied grimly. "Even though you have already passed your life and you have traces of an English hunting crop on your back, you have been spared this one thing and you don't even know what it means not to break down under torture. May you never know."

"You know very little about me, Father," Theo muttered very softly, and helped his friends move the unconscious Englishman onto the folded cloth and carry him out of the monastery.

They had to hurry, because any moment someone might remind the Black Prince that Sir Winslow had received treatment at this monastery before, and then his envoys would certainly be here.

"My lady, please hide from Prince Edward until his anger wears off. I know it's your brother, but it's still better to get out of his sight for a while," Theo asked the Englishwoman, who followed them into the monastery meadow.

This wise and brave woman fell to his heart, he admired and respected her, and what is worse, he liked her more and more.

"Thank you," she said softly. "Thank you all. I would like you to consider me a friend despite this terrible war."

"Lady, we..." Pierre stuttered, and fell silent, not knowing what to say.

Conscious Beregard prodded his side and pointed sternly at the forest. There was no time to be polite, they had to hide as soon as possible before Prince Edward's soldiers ran into trace of an escaped prisoner.

CHAPTER III

Falcon and cuckoo chick

When Sir Winslow regained consciousness, the first thing he felt was a terrible pain in his whole body. Only after a long moment did he manage to control it enough to pay attention to anything else and look around. His gaze fell on the young man dozing by the bed he was lying on, and he was deeply surprised.

"It's you? Where are we both, in the dungeon?" He asked, struggling to get his voice out of his battered larynx.

Theo, awake, jerked his head up and looked at him with his still-dormant eyes.

"No, both of us free," he said after a moment, rubbing his face with his hands to brush away the remnants of sleepiness. "Thanks to Lady Joan's dedication and courage."

He was very tired. He watched day and night beside his visitor, waiting for him to wake up while his friends circled with gloomy expressions. Although most of them recognized the debt owed to the English knight, Armando, for example, announced immediately that he would not even touch him, not to mention help.

"Joan," Sir Winslow sighed. "To think that when I could get it, tournaments and war were more important to me. It got revenge on me because she married other man. I lost her because of my own stupidity... What a wonderful woman she is... A real lady, and at the same time a warrior with a fearless heart. There is no weakness, except maybe one: she loves children and cannot have them."

"So you are her weakness too," Theo said. "She was crying for you so that our lake almost flooded. What exactly is with Prince Edward that he get you so hard?"

"I don't know," muttered the Englishman. "He is ready to sell his soul to the devil just to get you."

"And I thought he had already sold out. Can you move your legs?"

Sir Winslow tried and groaned.

"They hurt like hell, but I guess I can," he replied.

"So you'll get better with time. Now drink it and sleep."

Theo held a cup of some herbal decoction to his lips. Sir Winslow dutifully drank. After a while, the pain penetrating his body was dulled, and his mind was in a beneficent darkness. Theo breathed a sigh of relief, stretched, and curled up in a ball on the pile of skins beside the bed. Now he could finally get enough sleep, and he needed it badly.

From that day on, the scarred Englishman began to regain his strength, and his wounds healed surprisingly cleanly under the influence of the monastic herbs. Father Prospero's mixtures once again proved their power, as when Jean and Pierre had typhus. Colas, a stable boy who worked in the castle, informed the outlaws that the fury of the Black Prince knew no bounds when they discovered the escape of such a closely guarded prisoner. The prince literally fell into a rage. Penalties fell on the soldiers. He even had the sentries on duty in the dungeons hanged, and in the whole castle everyone hid from him wherever they could. Only Adeline could feel safe, but she, too, preferred to get out of the enraged lover's eyes and wait out his anger, hidden in her chambers.

"You shouldn't bridle," she said finally, when she felt she could now approach him without fear. "It won't do any good. At least you have proof that your suspicions were not unfounded, because an innocent man does not run away."

Prince Edward looked up.

"No, Adeline," he replied wearily. "Anyone would get away, the problem was Winslow couldn't. Someone helped him. Traitors and cowards surround me."

The young woman poured wine into a silver goblet and handed it to him.

"Calm down first, then think," she advised. "Theo le Vengeur is strong, clever and determined, but not wise enough not to fall into a properly set trap. I have an extremely delicate plan on this. You see, my sister is getting married to Philip d'Avreux. The ceremony will take place in Tours, and the mayor of this city is very devoted to you. It must be used."

Prince Edward drank the wine served him greedily and considered her words.

"You think Teo will be at this wedding?" he asked.

"For sure. I myself suggested to Philip and Estelle that they should invite him, and I know from a good source that the stupid Navar did it. He'll be there, Edward, so if he's not caught by wedding day, he'll be able to try there."

"City, wedding, not the best scenery," said the prince thoughtfully. "Let's treat this plan as a last resort. Maybe another matter will work. Moore has just reported to me that his men have surrounded a bunch of youngsters. I've ordered the leader and two others caught alive and slaughtered the rest. They're not from around here, so my deal with this outlaw doesn't apply to them, and maybe they can be used as bait. This outcast has a soft heart."

"I hope it works," thought the Duchess, staring at the window.

She wasn't at all sure if she really wanted it. She did not love her tragically deceased husband at all, she was even glad that thanks to the outlaw he stopped harassing her, leaving all his property in her hands, and thus, great power and complete freedom. So maybe it was really about her hurt feelings? Maybe she couldn't get over the fact that this cheeky outlaw with the face of an angel and the hot eyes of a romantic lover just didn't want her? For the pampered daughter of an influential duke, accustomed to tribute, it was inconceivable that someone would not pay attention to her, and someone she really liked. No wonder, even as an adolescent Theo extinguished his peers with beauty, and his charm and cheerfulness won all hearts. It got to such a point that the proud young lady envied, in the depths of her broken heart, the maids and servants with whom Theo gladly talked, joked and kissed in the corners. When their fathers began to marry their children, she was the happiest girl in the court of the King of Navarra. However, her dream of happiness was short-lived, and the awakening was very brutal. The young squire explicitly stated that he did not think to marry so young, and certainly not to Adeline, which his father would impose on him by force, but to choose his own wife. A terrible row ensued, which was a slap aimed at the pride of the maiden, described as the most beautiful noblewoman and the best party in Auvergne. Fortunately, a few days later disturbing news began pouring in from around Crecy, and everyone had other problems. However, Adeline did not forget. She would sooner forgive the Viscount for even the most brutal rape of herself than for such crushing indifference, and it was a real happiness that she did not even guess the real reason for this state of affairs. And it wasn't just any reason - she had pale golden curls, azure eyes, a delicate nose, and lovely lips that Theo couldn't forget. It is good that the cruel and unforgiving aristocrat had no idea of her existence. The outlaw underestimated Adeline as an adversary, which was the fault of the era's general tendency to consider women a kind of big but weak and silly child. But even if he appreciated, he wouldn't be able to fight against her. He was alien to the cynicism and unconscious cruelty with which women of this era were often treated, but being a knight of flesh and blood, he would not be able to find the strength to take such an enemy seriously. Adeline was well aware of this.

A knock on the door interrupted her thoughts, and Captain Moore peered inside.

"Your Majesty, my squad is back," he reported. "They have prisoners."

Prince Edward brightened a little bit his sullen face.

"Bring them in."

A few soldiers threw three battered, tightly bound youngsters, no more than sixteen or seventeen years old, into the room. The Black Prince rose from his chair and walked slowly towards them.

"Who do we have here?" He said venomously. "Mr. Falcon and his companions. What are you guys doing this far from Bearn, kids?"

The prisoners were glumly silent. They still hoped that their friends had managed to escape from the English into the woods and join Theo's gang, but they did not take into account that none of the young Bearnesians knew these forests and therefore their fate was doomed. The prince looked at their leader, who looked slightly older than the other two. He had noble features, a nice aquiline nose, slightly slanted green eyes and dark blond hair that fell in unruly strands to the collar, and his shapely figure clearly said that he must be strong and resilient. Instead of answering, he only spat at the prince's feet with a contemptuous expression on his face.

"Courage to the end," Prince Edward mocked him, not allowing himself to be led out of balance. "This attitude won't help you, Falcon. I will teach you how to fly on a line, and I promised you that the last time we saw each other. Get them out."

He turned to Adeline, staring blankly out the window. She cared not for Falcon or the more than twenty young people whose remains were being killed off by Captain Moore's soldiers in the hills, but about the possibilities of public execution.

*****

"Do you have a headache sometimes after my cousin's cut?" asked Sir Winslow as Theo changed the dressings on his almost healed wounds.

The outlaw smiled sadly.

"Sometimes," he admitted. "Sometimes I also lose my eyesight for a moment, which is very unpleasant, I assure you, but I'm lucky it is nothing worse. You could say that I got out of this hay oppression. Your cousin has a strong hand."

"Just so you know," Winslow agreed. "There are few who have fought with him and lived, and none of them he hated as much as you. You can be proud of yourself."

"I'm not," Theo muttered, gloomy.

The more he thought about this duel, the more he became convinced that he had done everything wrong from the beginning to the end, because this fight had to be started and conducted in a completely different way. He was actually more fortunate than of sense, because according to his current assessment, he should have died. He mechanically touched the long scar on his forehead and temples beneath his thick mane. He resented himself for allowing himself to be hurt so badly, because if he had caught the Black Prince's intentions a moment earlier, he would have parried that cut smoothly and wouldn't have reached his head.

Pierre's voice interrupted his unhappy meditations, sticking his head inside and saying in a voice that did not bode well:

"Chief, would you please come out? We want to show you something."

Theo got up, wiped his hands on his caftan, and walked out into the clearing where Jean and Millot awaited him, both of them very sullen.

"Come on," they said shortly, and they moved on.

He followed them, more and more intrigued, for his friends had never been so mysterious, and their voices had never heard such hidden hostility. They led him to the escarpment, where the forest turned amphitheatrically into a beaten track, and the knight saw a terrible sight. The whole area was literally littered with the corpses of young boys, often cruelly massacred, and it took Theo a moment to realize that he was looking at his friend from the Pyrenees, though he couldn't see his corpse here.

"It's the work of the Black Prince's soldiers," said Jean, breaking the ghastly silence. "You can see that these boys defended themselves desperately and certainly reached more than one before they died. We will not find out now what they were doing here, instead of being at home in the mountains."

"Yes," agreed Millot. "But we have a request for you, commander: take away from us this Englishman, for neither of us can vouch for himself now, and if nothing happens, misfortune happens."

"You're right," Theo said after a moment. "But someone should go spying on Bongrais now. You have to find out if Falcon escaped or was captured."

"Francois's daughter will take care of it," Jean replied. "She's a clever child, and Francois can show up in town without fear because his face is so common that no one pays attention to him."

"Pierre and Millot, get the villagers and bury these unfortunates," Theo ordered shortly, and ran back to the hideout.

"Tristan, take your horse and go to the castle de la Motte," he told his younger brother. "You will tell Lady Joan that the danger is over and that she must come to the convent as soon as possible. Don't talk to anyone else."

"Okay," the boy agreed. "What happened?"

"Something very bad, but you can't help it," his older brother replied involuntary roughness.

He was terrified of the thought that he might one day find this kid's body chopped with the swords of English soldiers or hanging shamefully on one of the roadside trees, but he kept that feeling under control and kept him from taking any potential danger away from him. He tried to treat him like any other member of his gang, although it was really difficult. Moreover, as unfamiliar to the English face, he was more than once really useful, as now, when he was able to get into Lady Joan's estate without problems, for example pretending to be a messenger from her uncle's brother.

While he waited for Tristan to return, Theo sent his men around on various pretexts so that they would not have to put up with the English company at such a time, and also to spare Winslow their gloomy glances. The latter, however, realized immediately that something bad had happened and had to explain in short words what his countrymen had done this time.

"I'm sorry," said the Englishman when the outlaw had finished. "My cousin does not recognize half measures in pursuing a goal."

"I just saw. That's why I have to get you out of here," Theo replied glumly. "My people are good companions, but discipline is fragile for them, and you are English. Better get out of their sight."

"I understand that," Sir Winslow nodded gravely, adding nothing else.

He still felt very weak, but he chose not to mention it, so as not to put his savior in an embarrassment. Anyway, he believed that by mobilizing all his strength, he would somehow reach the monastery, even if he was to fall later. When Tristan returned with the news that Lady Joan was already headed for the convent in her carriage, Theo had a plan ready. He did not want to wait for what Claire would learn, he decided to visit her in person and penetrate everything with her help. He had no hope of snatching Falcon out of the hands of the Black Prince if he was in Bongrais, as there were too many soldiers there to have any chance of a successful rescue operation. His main point was to see if he was even there. He hoped not.

Blindfolding Sir Wislow, he led him through the marshes.

"I'm sorry it turned out that way," he said, after they had left the hiding place. "I know you aren't guilty, but my people are furious. Watch out, branch! They were all young boys, almost children..."

"I understand, I understand well, and I regret what happened. I also appreciate your help, I'm really grateful," replied the Englishman.

"Unnecessarily, it's just a debt payment. Lady Joan will pick you up from the convent and I don't think we'll see each other again, Theo thought for a moment. He did not want anything to threaten Joan because of him, that sweet creature to whom he had an indefinite warm feeling, forbidden because, first, he was married and, second, they both belonged to hostile nations.

"Talk well of me when they hang me," he finished smiling.

"I hope they don't," Sir Winslow shook his head. "It's such a dishonorable death, and you deserve better."

They were already at the monastery gates. Theo called the gate and left quickly to avoid meeting a beautiful Englishwoman who might already be here.

"I hope he can wash his name off and return to his rightful position in the world," thought Winslow, watching him go.

"I hope the Black Prince has recovered from his stupid suspicions about this man," Theo thought at the same time as he followed the trail to Bongrais and pulled his hooded cloak tighter around him.

He preferred to go alone, without friends who were sometimes hard to control and who now had one more reason to hate the invaders. If Falcon was already in the castle dungeon, it was impossible to help him, but if he was just looking for him, they could be faster than the English.

There were more soldiers in the streets of Bongrais than usual, which was a bad sign in itself, but Theo had already learned to sneak between them so as not to draw attention to himself. There was another thing that bothered him - people seemed to be flocking to the market square, and something like this happened rarely, only during tournaments or public executions. It wasn't easy for him to push his way as close as possible, and then he saw what everyone was looking at: the triple gallows and the platform where the Black Prince and Adeline sat in ornate armchairs, like a royal couple. Three youngsters were being led onto the scaffolding, and Theo immediately recognized them as Falcon and two of his friends. He groaned silently, biting his lower lip. There was nothing he could do, he would not have protected them from such a crowd, even if he had all his men with him, he could only watch, holding his breath, at what was going to happen here.

The Black Prince, meanwhile, rose and silenced the people with a commanding gesture. He literally felt some incomprehensible triumph.

"As all of you here know, these three young robbers have been condemned to death and will be hanged in a moment," he announced aloud. "But I don't care about them, they are spear carriers, posing no real threat to the power of the English army. Now, I give the princely and chivalrous word of honor that I will give them their freedom if Theo le Vengeur takes their place. Somehow I'm sure he's here somewhere."

Theo gritted his teeth tightly. It only took the blink of an eye to hesitate before he made up his mind. He pushed his way through the surrounding soldiers and ran to the center, throwing the hood off his head at the same time.

"I hold you to your word, Englishman!" he called out loudly.

People murmured excitedly, and Prince Edward laughed sarcastically.

"I knew you'd always come," he said mockingly. "I'm not going to break my word, if that's what you mean. Hey, let those three jerks off! We'll catch them another time, and even if we don't, I don't want them when I finally got you."

He spoke the last words almost hissing. There was so much hatred from his whole character that it was really possible to be scared. Adeline was also eager, unconsciously gripping her hands on the armrests of the chair.

Released from his bonds, Falcon escaped from the scaffolding.

"Why did you do that?" He asked reproachfully. "Your life is worth more than ours."

"Remark just for your level. Get out of here before this Englishman changes his mind." Theo unfastened his sword from his belt and handed it to him.

"But you..." Falcon began, but fell silent as the knight shook his head.

"Fabrizio, life sometimes makes us make choices," he said. "It must be as it is, and if you don't want my death to be in vain, continue my work and... take care of my brother. Now he will be the last of the Bongrais."

Falcon met his eyes, but he was speechless. His fingers tightened on the offered to him sword.

"Goodbye, my friend," he whispered sadly, and with his two silent companions, he went into the crowd. Had it not been for them, the two terrified boys he felt responsible for after the death of their parents would have stayed to die along with Theo, whom he adored and admired indiscriminately. Now, however, the most important thing was to escort the two to some safe place. He did not know yet that in the hideout in the swamps he would not find his comrades-in-arms murdered by the Englishmen.

Theo watched them until they were out of sight, then shoved the soldiers who had approached him from both sides and climbed the scaffold, feeling his throat tighten in advance. In fact, he had faced death so many times before that it shouldn't have made any impression on him. Still, he felt that nauseating, disgusting spasm in his upper abdomen he already knew, and his hands were so numb that he could hardly feel the touch of the hangman holding his rope binding his hands. Controlling himself, he climbed a high stool under the noose hanging from the shoulder of the gallows.

"Are you not frightened by the prospect of non-chivalrous death?" the Black Prince asked him venomously, never taking his eyes off him.

"Less than you'd like," he replied calmly. "And even if, I can assure you that I would not cry."

"Oh, yes, you are a real hero," the Englishman mocked.

Theo did not reply to that remark. The executioner was just tightening the noose around his neck, the touch of his hard fingers was unbearable, the stiff, probably fresh rope caught on the stubble on his neck, which was ungainly due to lack of time in the morning, and giving him a taste of what awaited him. Involuntarily, the knight felt the hair on the back of his neck prickle under a blind terror that he could not contain.

"Anything else you want to say before you die?" the Black Prince asked him politely.

"What for? Everything that mattered was said long ago," the outlaw replied, forcing his numb lips to sneer.

"So let's do our job," Prince Edward leaned back in his chair and took his companion's hand. "Master, be gentle with this outlaw and do not break his vertebra. I want to watch how slowly, very slowly, the rope chokes him to death, and I know it will take time. After all, he is strong, he will not die quickly."

He felt Adeline's fingers tighten on his and patted her soothingly with the other hand on the forearm. Theo took a deep breath, savoring that long sip of what he thought would be his last, and mustered his strength for what was to come. When he was a squire he had seen petty criminals hanged more than once, and he remembered well how long the futile struggle for life had sometimes lasted. The memory alone could be enough to take away anyone's courage.

The Black Prince was already opening his mouth to give the final command to the waiting executioner, when suddenly a thin, short boy with curly hair jumped on the dais, where there were chairs, and aimed a crossbow arrow straight at his chest.

"One word and the English court will mourn the fearless son of Edward III!" he called in a thin voice.

"And who is that?!" cried the prince in amazement, more surprised than frightened by this threat.

"He's just my crazy brother," Theo explained resignedly. "Be warned that he is confused and does not listen to anyone, especially not to me."

The boy looked fearfully into the prince's eyes, his thin hand trembling slightly under the weight of the soldier's crossbow. The Englishman slowly spread his lips in a dismissive smile.

"You dare not, puppy," he said and shouted sharply. "Hang him!"

The executioner leaned forward, yanking the stool from under the condemned man's feet.

"No!" the boy cried desperately as he spun in place and released the trigger on the crossbow. A short, wide bolt whistled through the air and hit the rope, breaking it halfway.

Theo landed on his slightly bent legs, gasping for air with his half-open mouth in bewilderment. Exactly at the same moment, a shoulder emerged from behind the back of the prince's chair, and the Englishman felt the point of the dagger sticking into his neck.

"The boy doesn't have to be credible, but I am," a voice screeched right in the prince's ear. "And I swear I'll cut your throat, English dog, if you make one move or say one word without my permission. Order my friend free and let the soldiers drop their weapons."

"Free this outlaw and drop your weapons!" cried the Black Prince, choking on his fury.

The soldiers obediently obeyed, and the mysterious attacker forced the prince up from his chair and left the dais with him. The boy followed, relieved to abandon the heavy crossbow.

"Beregard, you are great," Theo sighed, loosening the noose around his neck with relief and pulling it over his head as soon as the executioner, still indifferent, untied his hands.

He jumped off the scaffolding.

"And I'm not?" Tristan was offended.

"And you not, because you had to shoot the prince, as you promised, and not to think about it," his brother laughed and petted him playfully on his curly head.

Beregard dragged his captive with him.

"We'll let you go outside," he promised gloomily. "Better no one will chase us. We understand each other? Let them make a transition for us."

"Split up!" cried the prince, controlling his bursting fury and resolving to submit himself to the circumstances for the time being. The outlaw's dagger constantly brushed his neck, reminding him of the threat, and a strong hand held his neck, without a trace of respect for the king's son and the commander of the victorious army.

Only when all four were at the edge of the forest did Beregard let go of the prince and sheathed his dagger.

"I advise you from the heart, Englishman, be careful, you may be less fortunate next time," he said grimly.

"You too," Edward replied. "I'll skin you, hick, if you ever get in my hands."

"You better deal with the fact that you're not doing so well lately," Tristan snorted.

The Black Prince looked at him closely.

"I know you," he said. "Last time I saw you in Savoy with your late king. If I knew then whose brother you are... But nothing is lost, you will still fall into my hands."

"Come on. Different with me, but don't you dare, your Englishness, to threaten my brother," Theo warned him menacingly. "Are you looking for glory fighting with children? I didn't know, but that doesn't mean I'm surprised."

"Laugh as much as you like. There will come a day when you won't laugh," Prince Edward promised him, and walked away towards the city without looking back.

The outlaws plunged into the forest with relief. Only after a long moment Theo shook hands with his friends and said softly:

"Thank you. I thought I was gone."

"Me too. I mean, I thought you will be gone," Tristan admitted honestly, not adding that it was only when he saw his older brother on the scaffold that he understood how much he meant to him. Until now, he had rather mixed feelings for him.

"But how did you end up in Bongrais?"

"The boy realized you might want to look there on your way from the monastery," replied Beregard. He confided in me that he would have done so anyway, and that he would go there to check it out. I waited a little and followed him, that's all."

The knight paused for a moment and wiped the sweat from his forehead with a trembling hand. He wanted to say something else, but his sensitive hearing caught the crack of dry twigs broken with many feet and voices.

"Soldiers," he whispered. "We're splitting up, Tristan comes with me."

They used this simple procedure whenever they dealt with the overwhelming forces of the enemy, thus confusing and distracting him. It was not a problem to escape the chase in the forest, but they were separated from the hideout by a long road, some of which ran across the open ground, next to the village of Kamienisko, and through the fields. Beregard chose the second route, a bit longer, leading through Two Rods.

"Could we slow down?" Tristan asked intermittently after a long run.

He was not resilient, and such feats were difficult for him. Theo looked around, then pushed him into a small field basin and covered him with dry branches.

"Don't say anything, don't let know about you, I'll be back soon," he promised and ran along the path he had chosen.

His plan was simple - to lure the soldiers as far away from his younger brother as possible and return by a roundabout route through the Swamp of Three Specters. It was so because three foresters drowned there and they were all avoided from a distance. It had no permanent structure, and it took quite a bit of courage to trust the clumps of marsh grass that protruded from it. Theo crossed the dangerous spot, leaping deftly from clump to clump, left the pursuit far behind him, and returned for Tristan.

"Let's go," he commanded cheerfully, pulling the boy from under the branch. "I left them in the swamp, maybe they will drown. We rush on, we still have to pass Kamienisko."

Tristan nodded obediently. They moved forward, slipping as carefully as possible between the huts. They were already at the end of the village and only a field passage separated them from the forest, when a unit of four soldiers suddenly emerged from behind the huts, most likely sent for a forage. There was no time to turn back. Theo grabbed the broken drawbar of the peasant's wagon abandoned on the ground and charged the soldiers, waving it menacingly. He was grateful now to Pierre, not for the first time, that he had taught him peasant fighting methods, coarse but effective. Before the soldiers could get to the fight, they were already lying, smashed by the blows of a wooden pole, and the two outlaws were hurrying towards the forest with all their strength. One of the soldiers, in a hurry, with less reach, rose on his elbow and grabbed the crossbow. He aimed for a moment, then released the trigger. A short bolt struck Theo in the shoulder above his right shoulder blade. The impact of the blow knocked him to the ground near the tree line.

Tristan cried out in pain and fear, grabbed his slingshot and hit the already rising soldier with a stone straight in the forehead. Then he lunged at Theo, but his brother was already getting shaky, gasping for breath.

"Run," he ordered shortly, grabbing his terrified brother by the hand.

He dragged him deeper into the swamps behind him, dodging so as not to leave a clear trail behind him until he found what he was looking for: one of the little hiding places that had once been prepared, a kind of cavern made of branches of wolfberry and blackberry bushes wrapped around a thick birch trunk. He pulled back a curtain of branches behind them, making the hiding place invisible, and cut a small twig from the birch trunk.

"You have to get that arrow out of my arm. Pry the tip from the bottom and turn it, you will loosen it and..." he said to his brother, stripping the bark of the twig.

"I?" Tristan groaned in horror.

"And do you see someone else here? I can't do it myself. Come on, now."

He pushed the hilt of the dagger into the boy's hand, bit the twig, and knelt, leaning his fists on the ground. Whether he wanted it or not, Tristan proceeded to the ordered operation, and although he was doing it for the first time in his life, he carried out his task with great skill. Despite the fact that his stomach was in his throat and he was afraid of vomiting at the most opportune moment, he extracted the arrow from the profusely bleeding wound and blocked the blood with a cut off piece of his shirt.

When he finished tying the dressing, Theo spat out the broken twig and took a deep breath. He smiled with an effort, trying to encourage his brother.

"You'll get used to this job, kid," he said reassuringly.

"I don't think so," Tristan groaned.

His hands were trembling and his face was chalky as it was just before fainting.

"When you get a little tighter, you'll learn not to faint at the sight of a few drops of blood. It isn't the first wound I have been hit, and it isn't the last one, and you don't die from such a small graze."

He could indeed speak of luck - the arrow pierced the muscles without damaging any of the large arteries and lodged relatively shallowly. Now it was only necessary to reach the hideout, which was fortunately close enough. Just in case, the brothers waited some more time before leaving their safe haven and on their way.

"Finally!" Cried Beregard at the sight of them. "What's taking so long? Show me that arm."

"I'll need it," Theo chuckled despite the pain.

"Funny as hell," Beregard grimaced, unwrapping the makeshift bandage Tristan had been wearing. "Wherever you go, the blood must always be shed. Couldn't you do without it?"

He washed the wound with wine and wrapped it in fresh cloth.

"Ah, that's a minor matter, it could be worse. I'll give this hand a rest for a few days and it will be like new. The point is that I'm alive and thanks to you," his friend said heartily.

"What exactly happened?" Pierre asked. "Falcon said nothing, only that you told them three to come here, and now he's sitting by the stream, crying because we told him what happened to his team."

Theo waved his hand reluctantly and went looking for Falcon, leaving Tristan and Beregard with the trouble of explaining what had happened in Bongrais. He found the Bearnean on the bank of the stream, in a place where it spilled over into a small pond.

"I'm sorry," he said softly, sitting down next to him and putting his hand on his shoulder.

The boy looked up at him swollen and dark circles under his eyes. He didn't even have the strength to be surprised or pleased.

"I couldn't say I left you at the gallows," he said hoarsely. "They don't had similar scruples. After all, these boys were still children..."

His voice broke and Falcon hid his face in his hands.

"I've had something like this, too," Theo said seriously. "Later I saw such and even worse views: children cut in half, adolescent girls with torn bellies, people half-burned, but still alive... This is what war is like. Nothing beautiful. Don't believe the poems and ballads. I know you can't come to terms with it just like me, but you will have to if you want to go on and fight on."

"I want to, of course I want," answered Falcon after a moment. "Will you accept me and my boys? There are only three of us left. I'd love to go back to the mountains, but for now I can't, there are too many English people there, and even my uncle has a hard time dealing with them."

"If you want, of course, but remember that you'll have to accept my discipline. Here I give orders."

"Sure."

The Bearnean nodded apathetically. At the moment he would serve under the orders of the devil himself, so that he could reach the hated enemy. Theo patted him lightly on the back and left him alone, for he knew well that in such a situation everyone would prefer to be alone for a while.

*****

Captain Moore entered the coat of arms with the look of a man ready for the worst.

"They got away, my lord," he muttered, his eyes dropping guiltily.

Contrary to his expectations, the Black Prince did not fall into the unconscious rage characteristic of him, and only waved him away. He thought for a moment, then got up heavy and strode into the bedroom, where Adeline was combing her dazzling hair in front of the oval mirror.

"What did a messenger from your brother bring?" she asked, setting her comb aside and tying the wide straps of a lace night cap under her chin.

"A very strange and rather unexpected handwriting," the Englishman replied, sitting down heavily on the bed and taking off his shoes. "If John had never been prone to such jokes, I certainly wouldn't have taken it seriously. This writing changes everything and complicates matters devilishly... But on the other hand, I understood something when I was thinking what to do with it. Think for yourself, my beauty, what will the death of this outlaw get me? Nothing at all. If I want to take revenge on him, I must not kill him, but humiliate him, deal a death blow to his pride."

Adeline turned to him. She looked delightful in a night cap and satin negligee, but her eyes were blazing with a bad, cold light.

"What do you mean?" she asked.

The prince smiled as he unbuttoned his jacket.

"Let's see what we know about this outlaw? He is brave, he is not afraid of torture or death, he is not greedy or prone to love affairs. His only weak point is his fear of disgrace, and this is where I should strike," he explained casually. "I'm surprised it didn't occur to me before. Suppose today's execution would be completed, and what? And nothing. He would die happy to know well that people would remember him as one who gave his life for friends. A beautiful legend would remain after him. No, I should have acted otherwise and I will use your sister's wedding for that. I will pour such bitterness into this outlaw's heart that even in other world he will remember. And I will kill him on another occasion, in a duel. It must come to it. People cannot remember that the Prince of Wales was defeated by some thug on the trampled ground."

"Charles V will be at Estelle's wedding," the Duchess said.

"Doesn't matter. The son of John II does not sympathize with this outlaw, he will not disturb me," said the prince. And, to finish the case, he hugged Adeline and pulled her to him.

He preferred not to confide in her exactly what his plan was going to be, just in case, not because he didn't trust her, but because he had never liked bragging about a plan beforehand. Better to keep his details a secret for a while.

*****

On moonlit nights, instead of sleeping, Gwidon would walk in the clearing, gazing at the stars, and composing his songs. He couldn't live without it. Now he was doing it too, secretly preparing for the poetry tournament in Amiens. He was going there, although he had cautiously not mentioned it so far to the commander, who might have a completely different view of the importance of this event. If he had strictly forbidden him from this escapade, Gwidon would have to obey, but what the eye does not see, the heart does not grieve over, so Theo knew nothing of his intentions. The poet sighed. He composed most of his ballads for Bellette, though neither she nor anyone else knew it. He had been in love with her for a long time, even though he had the sense not to betray it. Theo could have reacted violently to this. Only Preziosa suspected something, as he thought, but he could count on the Gypsy's discretion, so he did not care. In the mornings, when he was sleepy and distracted, he pondered a project more boldly, a very risky one, and watched Bellette surreptitiously. Her white-pink beauty successfully resisted the hardships of life, and unlike her withered and prematurely damaged peasants from the hard work of her peers, Bellette still looked like a freshly blossomed bobbysoxer. And yet she had had so many bad moments, so many misfortunes that would break down many others in her place.

Theo doesn't appreciate her at all," thought Gwidon rebelliously. "Bellette is a true goddess and deserves the best, and what she gets? Just that shack in the swamps, hunger and cold and cobwebs and brazen cockroaches. This is really not fair."

The more he thought about it, the more he felt angry at his leader and the more sympathetic he felt towards his wife, and it never occurred to him that she might feel completely different about it. Just before the tournament itself, Pierre expressed a sudden desire to participate, which was met with strong opposition by the chief, who called his deputy a complete idiot and advised him to put a wet poultice on his head.

"You obviously got a sunburn from working in the field," he ended a lengthy tirade on the subject.

As it was late summer, all the outlaws helped their peasant friends with the harvest. Due to the war, there were few able-bodied men, and the harvest that year was extremely successful. Perhaps it was because of the exhaustion of the day's toil that none of the outlaws noticed that their troubadour was strange. In addition to helping with the harvest, it was also necessary to defend the local population against the requisitions and whims of soldiers, and all of this together meant that they barely had the strength to eat dinner in the evening and fell asleep, without even putting up a guard. In this situation, no one had the time or the inclination to look at Gwidon. In addition, things turned out as if the poet was favored by some deity of mad bards - on the day of the tournament, early in the morning, the outlaws set off against the collectors of the Black Prince, and only Bellette, Armando, who was "guarding the cauldron" remained in the hideout, and Gwidon, who was prudently he pretended to sprain his arm chopping wood for the fire. This situation was a gift of providence for him. As soon as the band disappeared into the woods, the poet approached Bellette, repairing a torn skirt.

"Would you like to have a little fun?" he asked timidly.

"Depends what you mean by that," the young woman replied, biting the thread.

"I'm going to the poetry tournament in Amiens," he explained to her. "I wrote a beautiful ode in your honor, but without your presence people will not be able to understand it well. It is accepted that the poet brings the lady of his heart with him to such a tournament. You understand, it's just a little trip, no one will even notice and we'll be back soon."

"So I'm the lady of your heart? Weasel, I'm married," Bellette laughed, and became serious.

In fact, she really wanted to go somewhere among the people, not to mention the fact that she was flattered by the adoration of the troubadour.

"Okay," she said suddenly, and ran to change into her finest blue cretonne festive gown and put her hair in a tied back curl, imitating the hairstyle of a high society maid.

"Hey Bellette, where are you going?!" Armando called after her.

"I'm going to Amiens with Gwidon," she replied briefly and without covers.

"Theo will be furious," her friend warned, stirring the kettle with a large spoon.

"Let he be mad. I'm his wife, not private property," Bellette growled rebelliously and got on the horse brought by the poet.

"Okay, go ahead, but you do it at your own risk." Armando reached for a bunch of dried herbs and peeled a few leaves from it.

Gwidon mounted the other horse and he and Bellette set off on the road to Amiens. He did not think at the moment how far his willfulness would anger the impetuous leader, all his thoughts were occupied by the contest and what he was about to sing. He had no doubts that he would win the laurel of the winner and that Bellette's beauty would dazzle everyone present. In competitions of this type, bards rarely brought true beauties with them, and although many well-born ladies were allowed to be praised there, their beauty was often questioned. The regulars of poetry tournaments were used to it, and if they were surprised, it was rather the appearance of a lady really pretty enough to be celebrated. Everyone knew about it, and also about the fact that these tournaments always attracted a lot of soldiers who liked to watch the girls and listen to poetry, which they did not know about. That's why Theo forbade Pierre from driving to Amiens. However, Bellette's brother was deftly lost in the woods on their way back from a successful assault on the tax collectors, a fact his brother-in-law noticed only after reaching the hideout.

"What the hell, where is Pierre?" he cried menacingly, looking around at his men.

"Aren't you interested in time, where is your wife and Gwidon?" Armando asked ironically.

Theo looked at him in surprise.

"Bellette and Weasel? You will not say that..." Here he ran out of breath with indignation.

"Oh yeah. Gwidon took her to a bard's tournament, and Pierre came here only for a moment, took his horse, and rushed after them," the Gypsy replied calmly, throwing the stew with coarse flour.

"WHAT?!" Theo roared furiously.

After a while, he was sitting on the back of his white-haired horse and was racing towards Amiens as if he were chasing by a hundred demons.

Near the city itself, he pulled the reins and dismounted from his tired steed. He couldn't be sure if anyone would recognize him, after all, many soldiers saw him even from a distance, or at least some of them had been in the city that day. So he had to get a disguise. But what disguise and where? Considering this issue, he calmed down completely, and after a while he made a decision to... go to the nearest tavern, where it was easiest to get some information. Just in case, he sat down in the darkest corner and pulled the hood of his cloak over his forehead. After a long moment, a soldier with a mug of beer joined him, clearly angry and resentful about something. He drank the beer in one gulp and wiped his mouth, muttering what sounded like curses. It hit the knight. He called the ministering girl and ordered her to receive a whole jug of wine, for which the soldier apparently had no money, then poured him full. The Englishman gratefully drank greedily and began explaining to him in mixed language that he had bad service and the captain was treating him like a rag. The knight listened to him with an interested face and kept pouring him wine. The English, who drank mostly beer, had weak heads, and the wine sold in such taverns was usually adulterated with moonshine to make it stronger. He counted on it and did not pause. At one point, the soldier's head started nodding and his tongue twisted until he finally fell asleep deeply with his head resting on the table.

Theo, who had been waiting for it, dragged him outside now, to a small alley behind the inn, where he could easily take his uniform off him.

"It's warm today, so he won't catch a cold," he muttered to himself. "That they also take such retard to the army... I feel sorry for him."

His anger was gone by now and he was starting to play with the whole brawl. Soon, disguised from head to toe as an English soldier, he was able to walk calmly to the square where the competition was taking place. He stood in the passage where the artists and their muses were entering the square and began to look around at the audience. He couldn't see his friends anywhere. In the middle of the square a bard was reciting a ballad in honor of his mistress to the accompaniment of his lute, who might even have been considered pretty if she had not been marred by her long, curved nose. Comments that reached the ears of the outlaw could even amuse the corpse. The next show was not any better, as the lady that was to be praised was not the youngest and already definitely ugly, so that remarks about her sprinkled much more bitingly. Theo, although he knew it was not chivalrous, as well as the others, couldn't help but laugh. He grew serious and alerted only when Gwidon came running, tugging Bellette by the hand.

They both almost rubbed against their leader in the aisle, ignoring him. Slightly out of breath, flushed from running, Bellette stopped behind the barrier separating the spectators, and the poet entered the square alone. They both came to the conclusion that it would be better for the girl not to draw anyone's attention. Gwidon stood in the middle of the square in a theatrical pose, struck the strings of his zither and began to sing, without exaggerated affectation, but as sweet and gentle as only he could. Ode was really successful, the music was pleasant to the ear, and the audience listened with full approval. However, the performance ended with an unpleasant screeching: Pierre burst into the square and cast a rebellious gaze as usual at all the participants.

"Enough of this foolishness!" He exclaimed. "Who are you singing to, you fool? Have you no shame?!"

And he gave poor Gwidon such a fierce slap that it almost knocked him over.

"Hold him, he's a famous robber!" Someone shouted from the stands. "Guards! Guards!"

Several soldiers made their way through the crowd of onlookers from the lower strata.

"This way!" Theo called to his friends who were amazed by him.

After letting them pass, he gracefully stepped foot on the first of the soldiers, slammed his helmet between the eyes of the second and pushed it at the others. Taking advantage of the confusion, the friends caught up with the horses and made them gallop.

"You must have spoiled my performance, you country brute?!" Gwidon yelled to Pierre, who was galloping on his horse beside him. "Couldn't you just wait for them to hand out the prizes?! I would definitely take the first!"

"For such a howl, only stocks can be the reward!"

"I'll reward you both, let's just get home!" the leader shouted at them sharply.

There was no sign of any worried about it, and they were still arguing, reaching out to arguments that were certainly not meant for female ears, and they hadn't bothered about Bellette's presence at all. Reaching the hideout, Theo, first of all, tore off his English uniform, then shouted at his friends to be silent. The two, startled, immediately stopped arguing and stood next to Bellette, nudging each other with their elbows. Theo walked over to them and without a word of explanation with a blow on the mold he sent first one to the ground, then the other, then he looked reproachfully at Bellette and, rubbing his sore fist with his open hand, went to the hut. After a moment he emerged from there with a bow slung over his shoulder and, calling for Tristan, disappeared into the woods, ignoring the two friends who sat silly on the ground rubbing their jaws.

The boy happily grabbed his bow and ran after his older brother, jumping merrily.

"Well, this stupid adventure seems to be over." Bellette muttered and went to change.

"Ouch, he hit me..." Pierre moaned, holding his head.

"Good for you," Beregard said sternly, handing him a piece of cloth soaked in cold water. "That Gwidon has a maggot in his brain, it is known not from today, but you supposedly were supposed to be smarter."

"If you believed it, you would believe everything," Preziosa said sourly.

Meanwhile, Theo, at a safe distance from the hideout, sat down on a stump and began to laugh irresistibly.

"Wish you had seen it, little brother," he said, when he was finally under control. "Pierre made such a show that they will not forget it for a long time, and for the first time in a long time I had the opportunity to have a little fun without risking sudden death. Come on, we gotta hunt something."

"You have a weird idea about fun and what's funny," Tristan remarked, keeping pace with him. "You held jokes even under the gallows. Say, weren't you really scared?"

Theo turned serious.

"Now you're making jokes. I was dying of fear, just like any other would-be hangman. I was so confused that I couldn't even pray, because all I could remember were silly poems like 'drunk lady, virginity lost', which Gwidon gives us when he wants to be witty."

"Then you pretended to be fearless," Tristan said appreciatively.

"It was terrible," Theo thought back to those moments, and a slight shiver gave him a shudder. "What does this gloomy realization that there is no tomorrow for you, that you won't see the sun setting again, compare to what? I'm not afraid to die in battle, but for nothing in the world I would not like to hear the words of the executioner again: 'Forgive me, man.' It's worse than anything else."

"But, unfortunate, you yourself get into such nasty situations," the boy said and drew his bow as something rustled in the bushes nearby.

His brother slapped him on the hand.

"Come on, it's Claire," he said.

Indeed, she was Francois' daughter - about fifteen years old, sloppy and clumsy girl with a silly face, much appreciated in Bongrais as an excellent seamstress and embroiderer. Adeline de Valois herself praised her services and kept her with her, which was a very favorable circumstance for the outlaws. Francois as a father was actually quite reckless and mostly absent, but nevertheless loved his illegitimate daughter and tried to care for her. Claire relayed the messages she had picked up at the castle to the outlaws mostly through Agnes, but this time she preferred to go to the woods alone. She didn't have time to search for her father's friend all over town, and the news she got had to get through as soon as possible.

Theo listened to her with an impenetrable face.

"If Adeline's going to that wedding, that just means I'll have to be a lot more careful," he said. "Don't worry about me, Claire. Go back to Bongrais and be careful."

"It's you, be careful. I'm not in danger of scaffolding," the girl replied and turned back.

In view of the revelations she had brought, the knight gave up hunting and returned to the hideout, where his friends were constantly arguing whether participation in the poetry tournament was great fun or simply stupid.

"Please, be quiet!" Theo called. "And gather with me. I want to inform you that I'm going to Tours next week for Estelle and Philip's wedding. I'll be away for maybe two, three days. You observe Bongrais Castle discreetly. If you notice that the Black Prince is also going this way, you must overtake him and warn me in time, otherwise it could be quite bad."

"You know what? You'd better skip this wedding," Beregard advised him.

"Should I chicken out? Never."

"Do you prefer to be a living dog or a dead lion?" Armando asked him.

"One can still be a dead dog," the chief answered him logically. "Don't expect this from me."

"Hold me or I'll hurt him!" Bellette yelled, unnerved.

Since no one had rushed to her call, she looked around and, noticing a heavy bronze jug on the ground, lifted it up in a menacing motion.

"No, no, no, little sister, you will sweat," Pierre firmly took the jug from her and turned to the knight. "Let's talk better like civilized people. What's up, my man? First you hit me and the Weasel on the face for an innocent poetry tournament, then you expose yourself to ten times greater danger, and for what exactly?"

"I won't explain to you, you won't understand anyway," Theo grumbled dissatisfiedly.

"Maybe try it," Pierre encouraged him gently.

"I don't think so."

Pierre handed his sister the jug he had taken from her.

"In the head, baby," he encouraged her with a gloomy gleam in his eye.

"I don't think it'll do any good," Tristan said.

"Slowly," Francois decided it was his turn now. "Let us have a little confidence in our leader. He thought it well, if we keep an eye on this Englishman, he will be safe. After all, a beautiful duchess will probably not grab a sword with her own hands and attack him. In my opinion, the boy is right: he has to show everyone that he will not succumb to the dictatorship of some English robber."

"The prince," corrected Falcon automatically.

"A robber for me," Francois insisted.

"Right," Theo said. "Sir Edward may be the son of an English king to himself, but to me he is a common robber, appropriating someone else's property."

Bellette set down the pitcher with a sigh.

"If I had any hope that you would get a sense of this, you would already be lying with your head smashed," she said and demonstratively hid in the hut.

Theo gave her a tortured look. For some time he had had the feeling that his wife had stopped understanding him, and he was gnawing at it, unable to understand the cause of the change. He probably wouldn't understand that this change was due to a growing fear of losing the closest person. If they were to die together, no, she wasn't afraid of that at all, but the thought that she might be left alone in the world without her black-eyed knight was unbearable for her. She hadn't thought that way before, but now she was more mature and childish admiration for the strength, courage and beauty of her beloved man was replaced by fear for his life. It made her darker and more violent than she used to be, and she often argued with her husband about little things.

Tristan was their constant bone of contention. Bellette did not accept the way Theo was trying to turn this fragile and sensitive boy into something of his own, and he felt that she should not interfere at all. He did not understand why King John had neglected to teach his favorite page at least the basics of knightly craft and tried to make up for this neglect on his own, which was going reluctantly. Tristan was definitely weaker and less enduring than a boy his age should have been, but at least he tried to obey his older brother as he was told by the king. But sometimes he had trouble understanding what he was doing, just like he is now.

"Have you made your mind up?" He asked when they were alone. "You are asking for some misfortune. The Black Prince has his flaws, but he is a devilishly intelligent and madly brave man, you should not provoke a meeting with him on unfavorable terrain. While in England, I heard a lot about him."

Theo shrugged.

"Oh yes, I know that there is the entire English army behind him, and only a few thugs behind me, which disturbs the balance of power a bit, but you don't think I'll be scared of him?"

Tristan crossed his path and grabbed his hands.

"You said yourself that you weren't fearless at all," he said. "Do you remember the torments you experienced while standing on the scaffold? Do you want to go through it again?"

Theo smiled, though his eyes turned sad.

"You're still too young to understand that if I hadn't thrown myself into every danger as I do, I wouldn't have been able to control my own fears," he said seriously. "I have to do this, otherwise it will soon come to a point that I will start despising myself, and then I will not have anything to live for anymore. Okay, enough of these nonsense. Come with me, brother, I need to see Marie now. She was going to do some research for me."

"She?" The boy was surprised, but he followed his brother without objection.

He thought the visit of Bellette's sister was probably just an excuse to get out of the hiding place now before the moods agitated by his statement subsided, but he was nonetheless curious to see how Theo would justify it. To his amazement, however, it was not just an excuse. When Marie saw the knight, she put her broom in the corner and went outside, wiping her hands on her apron.

"As instructed, my lord, I have asked everywhere," she said. "Almost every village has such 'cuckoo children', but probably only one of them will interest you. At the fair, I met Claudette, the wife of a cooper from the village of Big Spikes, about half a day's drive from here towards Clermont Ferrant. She complained to me that a maid of some great lady had left her with a newborn girl a few months ago, for which she had to pay a lot for livelihood. But then she never showed up again. In Claudette's house, poverty squeaks, she has seven children of her own and a drunk husband, no needs such a burden."

"How can I be sure this is the baby I'm looking for?" Theo asked, frowning.

"Well," the woman began. "Time more or less is right, it was the end of May, besides, and the little one was wrapped in a scarf with the coat of arms, which is rare. She was only a day old, and usually such a lady would wait at least a week for the child to be stronger before she was taken to the country. But the most important thing is, of course, time - in the time period you are interested in, I only managed to locate it. The rest of the kids are either much older or younger."

"Well, it doesn't hurt to try. We're going there tomorrow morning, huh, bro?" Theo asked Tristan, who was looking at him with an uncertain expression on his face.

"What is this child?" he asked.

"Maybe I'll tell you... but not now. We come back. Thank you Marie, you helped us a lot."

"At your service," Marie replied, and stood watching him until he was out of sight. Even though she had been married for years, even though she truly loved her husband, with Theo, she would have cheated on him at any moment and without a trace of remorse.

Tristan followed his brother, puzzled. He didn't understand any of this, couldn't understand why Theo had suddenly taken an interest in some foundling, and what that unknown child had to do with him, but thought it would be safer to ask him about it while they were on the way. It wasn't the first time that he was surprised by his older brother's behavior.

When they both got to the hideout, the rest were already sitting at dinner.

"A little more and it wouldn't be enough for you," Armando grunted, scraping the remains of the porridge out of the pot for them.

"Potage, I like it," Tristan said, and began to eat with relish. He hated soups.

"Tomorrow morning, Tristan and I will go to some rather special errands," said Theo, eating hurriedly. "We'll be back tonight. Please do not make any trouble when I'm away. I don't want to hear about any competitions, festivities, or helping me out if I'm late.

"Don't worry," Pierre said ironically, licking his bowl.

"What are you getting into again?" Bellette worried.

"Nothing special this time," her husband reassured her. "Don't worry about me, it won't be a dangerous trip. Nothing's going to happen to me, the only thing I will get tired of is a brisk walk."

"We don't take horses?" Tristan, who did not like hiking, worried.

"Yes, it's easier to sneak around on foot and you don't pay attention to yourself."

"So be it," muttered the boy without enthusiasm.

"Some idiot ideas again. And when will you grow up?" Beregard sighed hopelessly.

After supper, everyone went to sleep, and when the first bird tricks woke their friends in the morning, both brothers were gone. They had left before dawn, and when the sun rose, they were already quite a long distance beyond the marshes, walking rather slowly but persistently.

"Maybe you can finally tell me what kind of child you are looking for?" Tristan asked as they stopped on their way for a short break.

"I'll tell you," Theo broke off a piece of bread and handed it to him. "This is Roger de Valois's child. Adeline left them at the mercy of fate, and I feel guilty about it, because I killed that baby father, who would definitely not let it happen. I don't know why Adeline did that, maybe because it's a girl and she wanted a boy."

"She's nice mommy," Tristan began to eat, looking around him out of habit. "But I don't understand what your fault is in all this. Was it you who made the Black Knight fraternize with the Black Prince? You made him insist on your life? Or do you think you should have let him kill you because he wanted to?"

"You'll understand when you get older, you're too snotty for now."

"Ooh, smart adult."

Having rested, they moved on, avoiding quite numerous military patrols, which would indeed have been impossible if they had gone this way on horseback. Around noon, they reached the village of Big Spikes, ate a small meal at a roadside inn, and went to look for a cooper's house. It was not difficult - it was decorated with an image of a cotter with one stave dropped out, which made Tristan enormously laugh. His brother nudged his side to calm him down, then knocked on the door.

A pale, gaunt woman in a dirty apron opened the door.

"What is going on?" she asked fearfully, moving her eyes from one to the other.

"Are you Claudette, the cooper's wife?" Theo asked politely.

"My husband is not at home as usual," the peasant replied. "Look for him at the inn. I won't give you anything, I don't have a penny at home."

"But we are about another matter." Tristan unceremoniously pushed the door open and stepped inside. "And we came to you, not your husband."

"Don't worry..." Theo looked around the dark and run-down room in which a few ragged children fought.

"But what's the matter?" Claudette stepped back from the door, staring at him with fearful eyes.

"Is it true that you have a child in your cottage, left here by a servant of some kind great lady?" the outlaw asked, regarding her sympathetically. She certainly did not eat enough, she worked too hard, and her husband beat her while drunk. He shivered at the thought that Bellette's life might have been like this, too, had he not been in her way.

Claudette sighed deeply and went back to stirring some miserable food in a pot on the stove.

"Indeed it was," she admitted. "Except that she was supposed to pay me, and she never showed up. I'm not heartless, but my own children are often hungry, how can I look after someone else?"

She shook her head miserably.

"Where's that baby?" Theo asked.

"It's under the window," she replied, continuing her stirring.

The knight turned in the indicated direction and on the pile of old rags he noticed the bundle lying there. He picked it up carefully. The child was as emaciated as all the inhabitants of this poor hut, indescribably dirty and neglected.

"Are you the little Princess de Valois?" Theo asked quietly, lifting the baby to the light so he could get a better look. The girl picked up an indifferent, foggy eye-piece on him, and for some reason he suddenly became sure that it was this baby he was looking for.

"I'm taking her with me," he said firmly. "If anyone ever asked, say that she died of a fever, it could have happened. Take it, I have no more."

He handed Claudette a small bag, which she grasped in her hands trembling with joy.

"God bless you, my lord!" she exclaimed, hiding it hastily in her arms.

Suddenly remembering something, she threw herself into the chest in the corner and took something out of it.

"It was wrapped in this," she said, handing Tristan a large silk scarf with coats of arms embroidered in the corners.

They were undoubtedly family marks of the Villeneuve family, the last proof of who this was abandoned child."

"What is her name?" Theo asked.

"I don't know. I don't even know if they baptized her," replied the peasant woman. "They brought it to me right after birth, still bleeding from the umbilical cord."

"Come on, I'll make her a name. Thank you and I wish you a better fate," said the knight warmly, and then he and his brother left the cottage.

"It's unbelievable," Tristan exploded after they had gone a long way. "That people live like that! What mother can voluntarily leave her child in such a place?"

Theo shrugged and looked at the wrapped baby. He didn't cry, perhaps because he felt safe in his muscular arms, or maybe because he had learned that crying was no good for him.

"Many unwanted children are brought up this way," he said sadly. "God, this little girl weighs almost nothing..."

"What are you going to do with her?"

"I've got some idea. But for now, we have to take her to the hideout, anyway."

"Well, I can imagine what we're both going to hear," Tristan said skeptically, and removed his bow from his shoulder as they had just entered the woods.

Feeding a crowd like their gang was a tough job, so they always looked for something to shoot, and Tristan was not lagging behind the rest. The older brother ignored his actions, lost in his own thoughts. It was hard for him and his heart was bad. After all, he was the cause of the child's orphan hood and misfortune, which no one else in his place would have cared about, but Theo was a knight in the best sense of the word. Which, as was commonly predicted, would eventually be his undoing.

The return journey was very long, they were already tired, but they did not stop anywhere. Tristan, hunting through the bushes, lucky enough to kill two large black grouse, which turned out to be very useful, because when they reached the hideout, they found no one there - they were all in the monastery, where they were repairing the roof, which had been broken during the last storm. Without delay, they lit a fire, plucked the birds and stuffed them on the spit.

"The baby is definitely hungry, too," Tristan said, looking at the sleeping infant.

"She's used to hunger, that's not news to her," Theo muttered, turning the spit. "But you're right. The sooner Bellette takes care of her, the better, I know nothing about children."

The bushes rustled and their friends began to enter the clearing, talking lively and everyone except the girls, covered in tar.

They fell silent at the sight of the brothers.

"You two always know how to get out of the job," Pierre said harshly. "At least it's good that you arranged dinner. It smells delicious."

He walked over to the fire while the others scrubbed with sand by the stream. Just at that moment the baby woke up and whimpered, which made Pierre literally jump backwards.

"What is it?!" He shouted fearfully. "Whose child is this?"

"Mine," said Theo thoughtfully.

"What?!"

"Come on, of course not literally. But don't ask about anything else, okay? Suffice it that I had to look after it," said the knight firmly.

Bellette walked over to him and nodded pityingly.

"She's the daughter of the Black Knight," Theo said, looking into her eyes with a silent plea for understanding. Adeline ditched the baby like old clothes after he died. Nice, isn't it?"

"You're insane," Bellette firmly took the child from him. "And you don't know anything about kids. They need to be washed and changed, and besides, run to the village and have Marie give you some milk for her."

"Now? It's getting dark," Theo protested, but at the sight of her menacing expression, he became acquiescent and stood up.

It was completely dark when he returned with a pitcher full of milk and a small clay flask. Bellette took it from him, poured milk from a jug into it, and covered the neck with a rolled cloth. She slipped a corner of the cloth soaked with milk into the mouth of the child, who began to suck greedily.

"I'm going to sleep, and we'll talk tomorrow," Theo yawned, and dragged himself to the attic.

He was already so tired that his eyes were closing on their own, and he fell asleep like a stone, scarcely fell on the hay.

He woke up when the sun was high and went downstairs yawning.

"You finally got up. I've never seen anyone asleep for so long in my life," Jean greeted him, giving him a piece of yesterday's roast.

"Back off, fox face," Theo muttered reluctantly, digging his teeth into the cold flesh.

Bellette was sitting beside the fire, the infant wrapped in fresh cloth on her lap, and she rocked it gently. When her husband approached her, she looked at him sadly.

"Theo, I want to keep this baby," she said softly.

The knight sighed and sat down next to her.

"We can't do it, you know very well," he said. "We don't have a space in our hut, you know very well how crowded it is on rainy days. Besides, our life excludes caring for babies. Supposing one day none of us returns from another trip, then what will happen to this baby? It will die of hunger alone. You want that?"

Bellette hugged the baby to her in this hard-to-follow, maternal move that only women know.

"I know you're right," she whispered sadly, resting her head on the knight's shoulder.

He put his arm around her. Deep down, he too would have liked to keep the little one in their forest hideout, but would not admit it, considering a similar weakness to be unmanly. He was ashamed of his fondness for children so much and never admitted it.

"I warmed up the milk for the baby," Preziosa said, standing behind them.

Bellette took her flask and fed the baby, so Theo got up and walked over to his friends playing charades. As usual, Beregard led the way, knowing how to arrange charades that no one could solve.

"How's "your baby"?" Pierre asked teasingly.

"If you want to fight, be straightforward, don't look for excuses," Theo replied, and after a while they were both rolling on the grass, sticking together.

It's been a long time since they had a fight so seriously, but this morning they both needed some sort of emotional release. By the time they finally stopped churning and sat down, panting heavily, they were both in a much more agreeable mood.

"And what, will you finally tell us where you got that toddler from?" Pierre asked as he surreptitiously rubbed the various bruised spots on his body.

"I can't, but this is obviously not my baby," replied the knight. "The pain is that it only has me. Don't worry, it'll not be here for long."

"Who do you want to look after it?" Jean inquired.

"I know," the chief answered him sternly. "And you don't have to know."

*****

"I baptize you, Mathilda, in the name of the Father, Son, and Holy Spirit." Father Prospero dipped the screaming infant in the baptismal font and handed it to the godparents.

"I welcome this child into the bosom of the holy church in your name. May Mathilda de Bongrais be a faithful and zealous Christian from today, and may she be saved on the day of her death by baptism," he continued the ceremony while Bellette dressed and silenced the crying child.

"Why did they decide to give this little one their last name?" Pierre asked Tristan in whisper.

"I have no idea," the boy whispered back.

Falcon listening to them shook his head. Not for the first time, it occurred to him that he should rather join Robert Deauville, but he also knew that he would not have the strength to leave that merry gang that had so warmly embraced him and his friends. He, Raoul, and Patrique could not be said to be quite comfortable with the rough peasants, and some of their chieftain's ideas seemed incomprehensible to them at least, but they liked them very much nonetheless. The most important thing was that they shared a common goal, to continue active resistance against the English. It was the most important thing, without a doubt, although in general the nobility fought each other, and the peasants shied away from each other. And Theo had no qualms about brotherhood in arms with the low born.

"I don't understand," Falcon muttered to himself.

"You aren't the first and not the last," Pierre explained his remark completely misguidedly. "Theo and Bellette made the decision together, but they always did their best to spite others. In their time they had even better ideas, birds of a feather flock together. You know when they started romancing each other she was only thirteen and he was not much more? When I found out about it, I wanted to kill him first, then her... or maybe the other way around?"

Falcon suppressed a huff of laughter, very out of place in the church. He liked Bellette, but felt that Theo had committed an unforgivable misalliance by marrying her and could not change his attitude. Nevertheless, he was precisely Bellette's brother who got along best, despite his initial disagreements. For his part, Pierre, with an irreconcilable aversion to the nobility, liked Falcon, though he sometimes dismissively called him the Bearn doll. In response, he was sometimes called Kuba the simpleton or the dark boy, but this did not diminish the sympathy they had for each other.

"You two always act in the chapel as if you were out in the pasture," Beregard grumbled as they left the monastery. "You have no decency."

"Because it is funnier," Falcon answered him, looking at the leader following them.

"You may consider us incorrect if it relieves you," Pierre Beregard offered.

He shrugged impatiently and turned to Theo.

"And what now?"

"Now I have to take this child to the care of someone who will take care of it," Theo replied with carefully concealed sadness.

He threw the hooded cloak over his shoulders and picked up Bellette's still crying child. Once in his arms, it immediately fell silent and relaxed, plunging it into terrible confusion.

"Women adore you passionately," Jean chuckled, drawing the leader's glare at him.

The old monk standing at the door of the monastery smiled slightly. For the first time since he had known Fabien de Bongrais' son, his mother's warm nature spoke to him, and Prospero was glad it was even possible. Bellette wiped her tears lightly and handed her husband some rolled-up scarves.

"Just in case you have to change her on the way," she explained. "Can you handle it?"

Everyone laughed, but then fell silent, as the leader looked at them with fierce, foreshadowing outbursts.

"Don't worry," he grunted. "Kiss me, Bellette, and don't cry. That will be better."

He mounted his horse, holding Mathilda with one hand and collecting the reins with the other.

"Take care of yourself," said Millot with concern. "It would be awkward to fight a baby in your arms, so avoid the English."

"Thank you for the warning. I won't be back until tomorrow, so don't worry about me," Theo said, nodded goodbye to them, and set off.

He knew full well that it was risky to go on such a trip alone, but he preferred that no one but him knew where he was taking the baby, even Tristan, angry and offended that he hadn't taken it. He deliberately chose to drive along forest tracks, which made the road a little longer, but made it much safer. He was in no hurry to part with the child who was trustingly hugging him, but he wanted nothing to endanger it, and that required burning the boats. He wondered how much it hurt him to make such a decision. The girl slept soundly in his arm, wrapped in hastily made swaddling clothes, and Theo felt his heart slowly envelop itself in an idiotic warmth that a man in his situation should really not allow himself to do. He had never before understood the words of Father Prospero, who used to say that man always carries the greatest enemy within him, and now these words became quite clear to him. Suddenly he felt fed up with this stupid, dirty war, hatred, violence, hiding in the woods and slitting the throats of people whose main fault was that they were born on the other side of the border.

"Why can't kings just take a copy and settle it among themselves?" he muttered, shaking his head desperately.

He remembered that John II at the Battle of Calais had proposed to Edward III just such a solution[5], but this one did not accept the challenge. He grimaced in disgust. He was not taught to ponder royal orders and deeds, he was taught to obey, and only now, with the help of a few-month-old girl, did he begin to understand things that had eluded him in the past.

It was late afternoon when he finally reached his destination, la Motte Castle, Lady Joan's estate. He dismounted and tied horse to the open gate in the orchard, and, spotting a young maid picking ripe apples, he beckoned her with a wave of his hand.

"Tell Lady Joan that the one with whom she last saw at the monastery by the lake is waiting in the orchard," he said.

The girl looked at him, meditated for a moment, biting her lower lip, finally nodded and ran to the castle. Theo retreated deeper into the orchard and sat down on a stately plum bench.

"Our paths part here, Princess," he said, rocking the half-awake child. The girl squealed softly, opening her black eyes.

"Hush, hush, you have to."

He kissed the soft fluffed head carefully, then the little hands, feeling his heart flood with a wave of unfamiliar tenderness. He could hardly remember whose child the baby was and how much harm his parents had done to him.

"I swear on Robin Hood I would have expected death sooner than a picture like this," a silvery voice said next to him.

He looked up. Beside him stood Lady Joan, immaculately elegant as ever, in her black dress adorned with purple embroidery and a widow's bonnet.

"Hello, my lady," Theo said, rising to his feet.

---

[5] Historical.

"I'm so glad to see you," said the Englishwoman kindly, placing her narrow hand on his shoulder. "Me and Reynold will never return the favor for what you did for us."

"I didn't do anything out of the ordinary, my lady. But what I want to ask you..." the outlaw stuttered and fell silent, not knowing how to put what he wanted to say. Lady Joan smiled with sad understanding.

"Whose child is this?" she asked softly.

Theo looked into her clear, calm eyes and changed what he wanted to say.

"This is my daughter," he said. "The life that I lead, what is happening here... Understand, I would like her to at least survive when me and my companions... This is a cruel irony of fate, but I have no one to trust, I have only you, daughter of a hostile nation and the cousin of my greatest enemy. Nobody else can help me."

Lady Joan reached out and touched the baby.

"Do you know how much I wanted to have children?" She whispered. "I already thought that God refused me this when it turned out that I was pregnant. A month later, I fell down the stairs. A Moorish medic saved my life but said I would never have a baby again. And now you come here and trust me with your daughter. It's like someone is offering me a star from heaven."

She took the little girl from his hands and started rocking her.

"I will love you very much, little one," she promised tenderly, and looked up at the knight. "But do you really want it? See, me and Reynold will probably get married and then go back to England. This is where it gets dangerous."

"It's even better for Mathilda," Theo said through a lump in his throat. "The war will not move to England, your own country will not be so littering and ruining... sorry, somehow I broke away. I'm a bit shattered by it all."

"I'm not surprised."

The Englishwoman raised her sweet, oval face like in Byzantine paintings to him. It was as if something stronger than the two of them pushed them together, their lips touching in a fierce, hot kiss, as if they were not representatives of two feuding nations, but two lovers from a lyrical poem. It was only after a long moment that they sobered up and moved away from each other.

"Sorry," Theo whispered guiltily as his fingertips touched his throbbing temples.

Lady Joan wrapped the baby tighter in the scarf that wrapped it.

"One thing to you, Franks, impartially: you know how to kiss perfectly," she said without a trace of embarrassment. "Farewell, Theo le Vengeur, and watch out for my brother. He's not exactly a bad man, but it's better not to get in his way. Don't underestimate him, noble outlaw."

She turned and walked away towards the castle - straight, tall, and slender like a dryad.

"No, he's not bad. And I'm not bad. Nobody is bad, although we all do badly. What a world, for God sake." Theo touched his fingers to his lips and smiled involuntarily. The kiss was unexpected and illegal, but it was so enjoyable it cheered him up and made him feel good. It resulted in a genuine puppy freak: having reached Bongrais deep at night, he made a successful image of a gallows on the walls with a piece of limestone, a twig of gorse attached to a loop, from which the Plantagenets derived their surname.

He even wanted to sneak into the castle and scare some superstitious soldiers by pretending to be a ghost, but he gave up the idea. He could not have known that if he did, he would witness an interesting conversation between the Black Prince and his brother John, who was again in Bongrais. It lasted almost until dawn, and the only witness was Don Paulino, who served both knights.

"Well, that's all settled on," said Prince Edward as behind the windows began to turn gray. "Calm our father, I also know where to go and under what circumstances. And I'm indebted to this outlaw, who would have thought."

He shook his head in disbelief.

"Don't overestimate it, any more than overestimate our father's revelations," Sir John warned him. "He can be unnecessarily sentimental. The best thing to do is to say to this outlaw: "Thanks a lot" and stab him in the heart. He is very dangerous, perhaps more than you think."

"Now you overestimate him. Let's go to sleep, it's morning," his brother said dismissively. "Besides, everyone has a price, even him, but I don't know the price yet. Calm down, I will win in our little game."

He was very fond of meeting opponents worthy of himself, and was pleased to think that Theo was one of them. He didn't want to kill him anymore - he wanted to break him, and he even had a plan to do it.

*****

"Theo, do you know an elegant man called Bertram du Guesclin?" asked Falcon.

The whole gang sat at one of the tables set up around the village and enjoyed the harvest feast. As every year, the village has prepared all the best for this game, in accordance with the superstition that what harvest festival will be like this and the next year's harvest. Music was playing, the villagers danced and sipped their new wine, nibbling on honey cakes, spit-roasted meat that they only tasted a few times a year, and this year's fruit.

"I know," Theo replied to his friend's question, watching the couples dance. "By sight and by hearing... Apparently, as a child he was so misfortune that his parents were ashamed of him and treated him like a servant. One day the boy had enough of it, he ran away from home and became the head of a gang of youngsters, like you. Well, everything would be fine if he did not want to fight one day under the mask. He was beating a few recognized masters, the king noticed him and hired him...[6] Oh, the whole story. Why?"

"Oh, nothing. Only that he was appointed commander-in-chief of all French troops and he has just declared war on "great companies"," said Falcon, trying to be indifferent.

Sometimes the "great companies" consisted of several hundred representatives of noble families derailed by the war and terrorized entire provinces, becoming another problem of a tormented country.

"God bless him, but where are we here? Our company is rather small," said Gwidon and hummed a song about a troubadour joining a unit going to war.

"Just don't do such a fool sometimes," warned the chief.

"And who is talking about common sense?" Jean scoffed.

"Quod licet iovi, non licet bovi," said teaching Patrique, who studied at the seminary for six months but then quit becoming a priest and fled to the mountains.

"What does it mean?" Pierre asked curiously.

"What is right for Jupiter is not right for an ox," translated Patrique with a little superiority.

---

[6] Historical.

"Thanks for the deification," Theo laughed. "You can see that an unhappy childhood does not always interfere with a later high-profile career."

"And what was your childhood like? You never talk about it." Millot looked at him questioningly.

The knight smiled dismissively.

"It's nothing important," he said, pouring himself some more wine. "First, I was a page, so you can say a girl with velvet clothes for everything. I ministered and studied, preceptors threw me with a thong as much as they liked, and other pages and older boys called me 'Thierrette' as I looked really terrible with my long hair. After that, I was a squire and worked like a madman to ensure that Duke de Candall always had shiny armor and a clean horse. Instead, he taught me chivalrous customs, the most important of which, in his opinion, was the custom of getting drunk every evening in the good company of friends and hired lovers. Usually in the morning it turned out that I was the only one around him and I had to take care of all of them lying like logs. Finally, I became a knight myself in a traditional rite, and that's it. Boring, huh?"

He drank some wine and reached for another piece of cake.

"I don't know? It doesn't sound that scary," Armando sighed with some vague longing. Perhaps he was thinking that he might have become a knight himself, if he had not been born a bastard, and that life was unfair.

"I prefer herding cows and plowing," Francois said firmly, which made his friends laugh quite a bit.

"It's as if you spent your sinless youth doing just that, and not practicing robbing passersby in a crowd," Jean exclaimed cheerfully.

"Everyone likes other things. However, it is not fair that in France only a knight's son can become a knight himself. In England, the king can match whomever he pleases," Pierre interjected rebelliously.

"Which is why there is so much rude between English chivalries," finished Tristan calmly.

Pierre choked on the plum and gave the boy a murderous look.

"What did you say?" he hissed.

"You heard it," the boy answered him calmly. "Everyone in the world has their place and if we do not stick to it, the whole God-given order collapses. One plows, the other builds houses, the third prays, the fourth swings his sword and that's how it is."

"What about free will?" Raoul asked.

"Exactly," Beregard said. "Who does not like this order, hides in the woods like your brother. Such views don't stand the test of life, boy."

Bellette came over to their table and sat down on the bench next to her husband.

"I thought the English would want to spoil our fun, but they don't show up." She said.

"All right," her brother said, and turned to his brother-in-law again. "By the way, Theo, I've heard knighting is fun in itself, and that's quite a story."

"Oh, I don't know if you'd like it," Theo shook his head doubtfully. "Bath first. Since the other squires knew very well that I was as toughened as hard to handle on cold water, they poured boiling water over my skin that I didn't jump out of my skin. Then I was to pray all night in the castle chapel. Of course, no one really prays, and everyone sleeps as a righteous one, but the younger pages let me have bats in my porch, since they couldn't think of anything worse, and I couldn't pray or sleep. And the funniest thing was yet to come. After the king handed me the knight's belt and said a few kind words, Count Claude de la Rienne screamed: "Now let's count! This will be the shortest knighthood in the history of Christianity! Draw your sword!"

"He really said so," testified Beregard, who had witnessed these events.

"God in heaven, why?" Falcon was surprised.

"And why are two French knights fighting each other? Sure it was for a lady. Liline, the lovely maid, preferred Theo and hence the misfortune," Beregard explained. "But the other one got nasty, and not for the first time. It's a pity you didn't see how he knighted his own squire in order to reckon with him for passing a broken lance to him at a tournament. The boy then chopped the count properly, and our leader is no worse. True, he had little to do. First he stood and listened politely to the words his opponent was throwing at him, then gave him such a dismissal that the man fell straight into the bowl of cream and tarragon prepared for breakfast. All in all, it was probably the funniest knighting I've ever heard of."

"Yeah, and then you went back to Bongrais and seduced my sister," Pierre said to Theo.

"Saints of the Lord, this same again," said Bellette. "If you want to know, it's not then."

"Of course, only much earlier. Nothing to brag about, you little debauchee."

"Okay, okay, enough of these memories, let's have more fun." Theo got up from the table, grabbed Bellette by the half and joined her to the dance parade.

The others followed his example. The fun lasted until the morning, and when it started already dawn, the friends left the village amused and set off to their hideout, singing merrily as the wine rustled well in their heads. Theo and Bellette walked a little back, hand in hand with everyone.

"I love you," Theo said fondly.

Bellette smiled as she looked up at him.

"And will you love me when I'm old, gray and wrinkled like a dried pear?" she asked teasingly.

The knight laughed.

"And you will love me when I'll be bald, fat, bloated man with a dignified goatee?" He asked.

"With your lifestyle? When will you get old?" Bellette embraced him warmly and looked at the castle shining in the first rays of the sun with a certain fear.

She saw a few riders heading for the gate, but from this distance they seemed unable to see the outlaws stalking towards the swamps. She chuckled silently at the thought of how angry another drawing on the walls, this time of a soldier in full armor, with an English lion on his shield but no pants, would make them angry. This way of fighting did not harm the enemy physically, but it was perfect for undermining his morale.

CHAPTER IV

Judgement day

Theo woke up before midnight, hopelessly sober. He had been sleeping irregularly for a long time, and recent events caused him to lose his normal rhythm of sleep at all - he did not sleep all night, but then did not wake up until noon. Now, in addition, he couldn't stop thinking about Estelle and Philip's wedding to which he was invited. He knew it was going to be a risky trip. His mind circled stubbornly around the figure of the Black Prince, his main enemy, whom he knew very little about. The eldest son of Edward III, seated on the throne of Aquitaine (where he was as welcome as the plague), enjoyed a reputation as an excellent tactician and born knight, he had never lost battles, and had no mercy for the defeated. Theo didn't know his way of thinking, unfortunately, which meant he didn't know what he could prepare for him. A few innocent drawings on the walls of Bongrais must have angered him and may have provoked him to make a mistake, but the Black Prince remained silent. Claire only brought the news that he was about to express that Theo would remember his title friend's wedding for a long time, if he dared to show up there. It was not good news. The easiest solution would be, of course, not to go to Tours, but that would mean he chickened out, and he couldn't let people think that. Besides, he really wanted to do it. He liked Philip and Estelle, a tiny, sweet creature with a silly head and a brave heart, and his rebellious nature reared at the mere thought of denying himself this pleasure because of his hated enemy. After all, this wasn't the first time he had ever done something risky.

Unable to stand in the attic, he got up, trying not to wake up his sleeping wife, dressed himself and went out into the clearing, illuminated by the pale crescent moon and high-blinking stars. He couldn't understand how this forest at night could be so calm and quiet as if it hadn't witnessed the worst things during the day. After all, not many years had passed since the day that in this very forest a terrible battle took place between the participants of jacquerie and the royal troops, a battle in which neither side took prisoners and blood soaked profusely into the ground, staining the stream and grasses red. And how many English and French have died here since the beginning of the war, defending their land? It would be impossible to count the bones rotting in the bushes, while the forest was humming like centuries ago and seemed to be an oasis of peace. Theo loved this forest, which, through a series of unfortunate events, became his home, fed him and sheltered him, but sometimes he felt an undefined fear of it, as of a living, powerful and unpredictable being. He did not know that many of his enemies felt a similar fear, being at a disadvantage because they were not very close to him. At the cost of many hardships, in the first year of his exile, the young knight learned to walk in the woods also at night, but it was always risky, because you could fall into a swamp, deadly in late fall and early spring, and dangerous at any time of the year. No one would risk looking for the outlaws' hiding place in these swamps, the forest defended its inhabitants from enemies as best he could.

Theo knelt by the stream and drank the water from his clasped hands. He always wondered why this stream was crystal clear, despite the fact that there were swamps all around, but perhaps the secret was that it flowed in a wide chasm filled with coarse sand.

Gwidon came out from behind the trees, staring at the stars and muttering fragments of some poetry to himself. When he saw the leader, he stopped.

"You what, you became a poet too?" he asked in surprise.

"I'd have to fall on my head first," Theo stood up and wiped his hands on his jacket. "Gwidon, I have a request for you: tell everyone in the morning that I have decided to leave a little earlier, because it's a long way to Tours after all. Let them guard the castle."

"Don't worry, they've been doing it for a few days," the troubadour reassured him, and he looked again at the stars.

The knight left him, took the sword he used every day from the hut and strapped it to his belt. He preferred not to take the one he had received from King John, lest the sight of it angered the current monarch, who might have different views on whom to bestow in this way. He made his way through the trees to the clearing where the outlaws kept their horses, saddled one of the sleepy grass-chewing animals, and led them to the road that led to Tours. He preferred to leave before his friends woke up, to spare himself hearing their warnings and complaints with which they had been treating him for a week.

The rested stallion carried him lightly, the night air tasted sweet like the juice of fresh grapes, and the world around was idyllic, as if there had never been any war on it. The darkness softened the contours and blurred all traces of damage. It was easy to understand why Gwidon needed her so badly to be able to compose his poems. When the day finally got up, Theo was already a long way from Bongrais and headed towards Tours, keeping to the side lanes just in case. He enjoyed the ride, he felt almost as if he were an ordinary young man with no sentence, no slander. He hadn't felt like this for a long time. Perhaps it was influenced by the awareness that he would meet the king, and despite the awareness that the king was ill-disposed towards him, deep down he did not believe in his aversion at all. He simply couldn't realize what he had deserved, and he was sure King Charles would appreciate that he was doing his father's will with such dedication, no matter what. John II appreciated his devotion and entrusted him with an extremely important mission, to free his own daughter from the enemy's hands and the task of establishing a conspiracy. Why would the son of such a father hate a good and faithful knight? It would be illogical. In other words, Theo was sure that when he faced the king, he would have no trouble convincing him whose side he was on and how wrong the wrong opinion was about him. All he had to do was meet him, and the wedding of two friends was the perfect excuse. He remembered father Prospero also suggesting that he try to reconcile with the new king, and smiled to himself. There will finally be an opportunity to do so.

When he arrived near Tours, he was surprised, above all, by the traffic, greater than he had ever seen. At least he thought so, though in fact it didn't have to be that big. Theo simply got used to larger groups of people and they made an overwhelming impression on him, although of course they had their advantages - it was easy to get lost among such a mass of unknown people. More cautiously than out of real need, he pulled the hood over his head and meditated for a moment on what would be better for him: to greet the newlyweds in the cathedral or visit them just before the ceremony in the castle. On reflection, he chose the castle. The cathedral was a public place, too bulky to fight, not to mention the fact that it was not proper to fight there, and it was always necessary to take into account that someone might attack it. The castle, especially on such a day, was a much safer place. Contrary to popular belief, Theo was not an advocate of unnecessary risk, though the main problem was that he understood the word "unnecessary" quite differently from most people. Leaving his horse at the inn, he went to the castle, prepared for the fact that he would have to work hard to figure out a way to get in, but it turned out to be unnecessary. The castle had all the gates open, and a lot of people - servants, vendors, and visitors - hung around the courtyard. There were too many for anyone to notice. Entering the side stairs was not difficult, because no one guarded them on this solemn day. In fact, if Theo wanted to, he could enter the main door without any problems, but he preferred not to tempt fate. He had had situations in his life where everything seemed safe and bright as the sun, and it ended in a total catastrophe, from which he only miraculously finished alive.

The building was adorned with flowers and silk ribbons of various colors even in this side corridor, and it was tidied up clean. The atmosphere of joy and kindness was palpable, radiated by all the people he met, the lowest servants and the elegant ladies alike. Unassisted, Theo searched several corridors methodically, until finally in one of the solemnly decorated rooms he found a young couple: Philip in a festive caftan and Estelle in a white dress and veil, under which her tiny figure was almost lost. Apparently, they both did not believe in the superstition that a groom should not see a bride before marriage.

"Hello, lovebirds," he said, closing the door behind him.

They both turned sharply.

"Theo!" Philip shouted happily. "I was already afraid that you would not come, and I would not be able to fully enjoy this day without you."

The knight hugged him heartily and kissed Estelle's hand, pink with happiness.

"Unfortunately, I won't be staying long," he said. "I came only to wish you both happiness, and perhaps, if you want it, I might hide in the cathedral somehow, so as not to draw attention to myself. I would prefer your wedding not to turn into a tavern brawl, because whatever goes at the shepherd's daughter's wedding, with, say, a brewer's son, will not suit you under any circumstances."

"Have you ever been involved in something like this?" Estelle asked.

"Once or twice... maybe a few," he replied honestly. "At country weddings, it is so, that when a row starts, after a while no one knows who, what and for what. However, it would be out of place for you, and I could unfortunately be the cause of disagreement. It probably comes as no surprise to you that I have enemies on both sides."

"Too bad, I thought you would bring friends with you, especially this lovely blonde shepherdess girl," Philip said with real regret.

"If I had known you wanted an argument, I would have," Theo laughed. It was strange, however, how a politically experienced prince did not understand the simplest of military strategy, and it seemed to him that it was enough to give a few commands to save his guests from an ambush.

"King Charles has promised that he will not be in any way inciting any of my guests," said the Prince, having guessed his thoughts.

"Stay with us," Estelle pleaded pleadingly, smiling beneath her veil.

"Well, I don't know..." Theo hesitated.

He was eager to stay, mainly because he was curious about the reaction of the other guests to his presence, but he realized that it would be at least unwise. But on the other hand, the tiny bride looks at him so pleadingly, and she is so touching in her bridal white. Indeed, it is difficult to imagine her as a sedate married woman.

"I think I could..." he began and broke off, as unexpectedly the chamber door creaked and the young king entered.

He was not much like his father - he had a clean shaven, long face, dark brown hair and eyes, but without any warmth inherent in the color. They were cold and prickly and looked at them without a trace of kindness.

Theo knelt involuntarily, but the king barely looked at him. He was neither surprised nor moved to see him.

"Get up," he said indifferently. "I don't care about your tributes. Honestly, I didn't quite believe you dared to be here, but you are clearly even more insolent than they say. Well, while you're here... Philip, Miss Estelle, leave us alone, and shut the door behind you."

Philip clearly wanted to protest, but he lost the urge to do so as he looked into the king's cold eyes. He bowed silently and left the room with his pale fiancée. Even he did not dare to oppose the new ruler, frail and weak, but with an iron will and not succumbing to any sentiments. He felt an undeniable intelligence, a tendency to cold cruelty and the ability to impose his opinion on others, very useful to any monarch. He must have valued other qualities of body and mind than his father, who died in mysterious circumstances, one of the best knights of his time. It was whispered that he was suffering from flushing to his head and that the physician had to bleed his blood so often that the wound does not heal. However, he was undoubtedly respectable, and it was difficult to oppose him under any circumstances. Looking at him, it was easy to believe that his father's hopes were not in vain. Theo felt very uncomfortable under Charles V's cool, appraising gaze, but he tried to hide it.

The king approached him slowly, folding his hands behind his back.

"I promised Philip immunity to his guests," he said. "But you are not the visitor, but the intruder. Philip forgot, poor fellow, that I was compiling the guest list, and your name, outlaw, is not on it."

"If Your Grace says so, it probably is," Theo replied respectfully, wondering what the king might be aiming for. He knew his name couldn't be on the official guest list - that would be too blatant a provocation.

The king watched him through narrowed eyes.

"Various things say about you," he continued after a moment. "For example, that you are the best in swordsmanship. Why don't you show it to me?"

He took one of the decorative swords hanging there off the wall and examined it carefully.

Theo shook his head.

"I'm serious. Draw your weapons, I order you." Charles V touched his breast threateningly, next to the silver gorget.

"I'm sorry, but I'm forced to refuse," said the knight calmly, not stepping back and not taking his eyes off his hostile gaze. The king pushed his sword lightly until the blade pierced the doublet and scratched the skin on the knight's chest to blood.

"Then you will die, here and now," he said menacingly.

"I'd rather die than raise my hand against my lord," Theo said firmly.

The blade against his flesh twitched, plunging a little deeper. The knight smiled with the corners of his mouth, raised his hand and moved it a little to the side and a little down.

"Better to hit here, Lord," he said in a tone of good advice. "The blade will pierce the heart easily without sliding over the ribs. Go ahead, Sire, go ahead. It is an honor for an outlaw like me to die at the hand of his king."

Charles V did not take his eyes off him.

"So fearless? I hear that you are not afraid of death and that you have managed to trick her more than once," he said. "But you won't impress me with that. It is very easy to die, to live much harder, especially to live with the stigma of disgrace. Surely you know that I escaped from Poitiers and you think I am a miserable coward, just like everyone else, but tell me what is worth more: to die like a hero or live as one who has to pick up the miserable pieces, once called France?"

"First of all, I never thought you were a coward, Sire," Theo replied seriously, still meeting his eyes. "There is the courage to die and the courage to live, and it is very easy to judge someone without knowing his motives. The duties of an ordinary knight are different, the duties of a king are different, especially in such a difficult time. I can allow myself to die when I want to. You not."

The monarch withdrew his sword from his chest and examined the red stain on the shining blade.

"You are strong in your mouth and you can talk to many people. You charm people with these smooth words. My late father also had some inexplicable weakness for you. But I... You know why I hate you?" he asked.

Theo made a quick mental examination of his conscience and shook his head. He couldn't remember anything wrong that would alienate the young ruler.

"I had a favorite," said the king. "Her name was Camille de la Molle, and she was the niece of my cousin Roger, whom you killed. You should be careful with suing people for God's judgment, it is one thing to kill a man and another to disgrace him, because the disgrace also comes on the family. Camille loved her uncle very much and, hearing about what happened, hanged herself. Never, do you hear? I will never forgive you this."

"I'm sorry, I didn't want to. Me and the Black Knight..." choked the outlaw feeling guilty.

"I don't care about your feud or your reasons," interrupted the king. "The effect of your actions counts. After all, I will let you go, because I don't want to spoil Philip's day, but you have to get out of here. Now. Don't irritate me with your sight, as I might not be able to bear it. Go away."

Theo bowed silently and left the room, feeling the unpleasant feeling that the king was serious. He didn't seem like a joke at all. Due to the lack of physical strength, this man could not be a knight like his father, instead he planned and decided, which yielded unexpectedly good results, better than fighting with a sword in hand. Running down the side stairs, he found his friends, who were very nervous, who breathed a sigh of relief at the sight of him.

"I can't stay," he said, squeezing their hands. "Once again, I wish you as much happiness as possible, because if you do not deserve it, I do not know who deserves it."

"I wish you had not to go," Estelle said sadly.

"It'll be really better," he assured her, not to mention the real reasons for his decision. He wanted his friends to know nothing about this unpleasant conversation.

Philip hugged him.

"See you soon, my friend," he said.

"See you," he replied, and left the castle on one of the side gates.

After all, he thought it was good to know what was being accused of him, although he was sorry to hear that he had involuntarily killed a young girl whose existence he had not even known. She must have really loved her uncle very much to take her life on hearing of his poor fate. Sorry for her. In addition, he was plagued by a feeling of undefined defeat and guilt towards Philip, whom he had put in a truly embarrassing position by accepting this invitation. His friends were right, he shouldn't have come here.

Lost in his thoughts, he turned the corner of the street and did not notice how he was cornered by a squad of English crossbowmen who raised their weapons menacingly at him. He reached for the hilt of his sword - a ridiculous, unnecessary gesture, for what could he do with a sword against arrowheads threatening him from all sides?

"Leave that toy, son," a well-known hateful voice sounded. "You'll hurt yourself yet."

He looked back and froze as he saw the Black Prince rushing in with the mayor of Tours and a dozen men.

"My people..." he thought in horror. "What did they do to them?"

It was clear to him that, since he had not been warned in time by someone from his band, apparently the English had approached them just like him, and had either beaten them or imprisoned them.

The Black Prince regarded him with a malicious half smile.

"One move and my soldiers will flood you with arrows," he said warningly. "Moore, take the weapon from him."

The captain obeyed with undisguised satisfaction. The disarmed Theo was dragged to the market square and brutally pushed against the stone pillory. The soldiers closed the hoops on the wrists of his hands, which ended with the rusty chains hanging from the pole, and then stepped back to form a circle.

The Black Prince calmly watched the spectacle from the back of his horse.

"Now, my dear outlaw, let's talk," he said, resting his hands on the pommel of the saddle. "I have an offer for you, which I advise you to take seriously: here you will sail with me to England and take an oath of allegiance to my father. He will accept you for his service and be generous with you, for, unlike Charles, he can appreciate good knights. I don't like you, but I believe that it isn't right to waste talents like yours. Think carefully about what will be better for you and accept my offer or face the consequences, I assure you, very sad."

Theo was trembling with anger, his hands clenched into fists. Convicts from the lower strata of the population were put under the pillory, against whom a shameful punishment was imposed, for a knight it was an unimaginable humiliation that even death could not wash away. He felt the curious glances of townspeople stopping at the market square and passers-by as almost physical pain, stinging like a whip lash on bare skin.

"I will never do it, I think hell will freeze first," he replied, when he was sure that he would take control of his voice.

Prince Edward did not seem to be touched.

"What are you counting on?" He asked calmly. "Nobody will speak for you here. Your compatriots threw you beyond the margins of life, they crossed you. Your king hates you. Such loyalty is stupid."

"I'm not counting on anything. It's just that I don't make my loyalty to my homeland dependent on how they treat me here," replied the outlaw. "If your father relies solely on the traitors you bring him, I await him a bad end, which he fully deserves."

Captain Moore cursed vulgarly and raised his hand to face him, but was restrained by the prince's menacing voice.

"Don't you dare, Moore."

The Englishman jumped off his horse and walked slowly towards the prisoner. Theo noticed that someone else was hiding behind him: Don Paulino in a straitjacket sewn with silver rings. He gritted his teeth in a helpless rage that did not go unnoticed by Prince Edward.

"As always, you are adamant, no matter the cost," he said ironically. "It may not be the most sensible, but it shows not just any courage. My proposal will remain valid for some time to come, but I'm forced to teach you a painful lesson, so that you will be a little self-righteous and learn the right behavior towards higher-ranking people."

He grasped the knight's ancestral gorget with his black gloved hand and looked at its surface characters.

"Your coat of arms," he said after a moment. "Don't make such a face, I will not take it from you, even more, I will add one more sign so that you remember what we talked about."

Still silent, the mayor waved his hand at someone. Two men in red caftans had set up a metal basket full of hot coals near the pillory. A branding iron handle protruded from the basket.

"Everything is ready, Your Majesty," said the mayor dispassionately.

Theo suddenly understood what awaited him and turned pale despite his tan.

"Kill me," he whispered through his whitened lips, abandoning the ceremonial form.

The Black Prince smiled pityingly and turned away.

"And what it would bring to me?" he threw over his shoulder.

"What you have already done to me is not enough for you?! You took everything but my life from me, so finish the job, you bloody Englishman, and let it all be over once more!" the knight shouted, struggling desperately at the chains.

Prince Edward turned to him again and gripped him by the doublet over his chest.

"I won't," he said emphatically. "And because, contrary to what you think about me, I have a little mercy in my heart, so I won't tell you why you won't die today. You won't hear it from me, and you know why? Because once you know, hell will open up to you and you will never find peace again until the end of your days. You can protect yourself from this only by accepting my offer."

"Never!" Theo shouted, pushing him aside in open disgust, as if he had some reptile in front of him.

"You wanted it yourself," said the Englishman, controlling his emotions with force.

He smoothed his hair and turned to the captain.

"Hold his arm, Moore."

The captain walked over to the knight and grabbed his hand, but he let go of him as he got his knee below the waist so that he bent. He cursed, struck the prisoner with his fist in the stomach and pressed him to the pillory with his bulky body, twisting his left arm at the same time. Prince Edward took a wooden handle and drew a red-hot iron in the shape of an English lion from between the coals. He smiled cruelly and looked at the old Spaniard at his side.

"Don Paulino," he said slowly. "I think you deserve this pleasure. A little retaliation, huh?"

The steward's long scarred face lit up in a smile that was scary to look at. He jumped off his horse and took the executioner's iron from the hand of his protector. It was really more than he could have expected.

"I should have killed him when I had the opportunity," Theo thought helplessly, barely able to breathe in the captain's steel embrace, He was crushing him to the stone pillory with all his considerable weight, additionally reinforced by a heavy armor with a breastplate wrought in the shape of a crayfish tail.

There was no point in wasting strength trying to free yourself from his hands, and there was no point in waiting for some help. It couldn't come, and the people who were watching this scene from a safe distance weren't on his side, they just liked to watch such shows. Theo gritted his teeth tightly, but the touch of the hot iron was so horrible that he was momentarily dazed with pain, and the world around him was a blinding white that he already knew and hated. He sobered up only with his own scream, a desperate whine that had nothing human about it. With an effort beyond his strength, he managed to stifle his voice and keep silent, but at the same time he weakened so much that he could hardly keep on trembling legs. Had he not been chained to this shameful pillar, he would have certainly fallen as Moor finally released him from his hard hands.

The Black Prince shook his head.

"Theo le Vengeur, brave and undefeated defender of the oppressed," he said. "So you can look at yourself now... You look like a wounded child, you don't want to believe that someone might be afraid of you. Stupid boy, if you were a little smarter, I wouldn't have to hit you that hard. Now you will stay here until evening so that you have time to think about your mistake. Four stay on guard, the rest with me!"

He mounted his steed, and Don Paulino and Captain Moore did so reluctantly.

Theo could barely see them. The whole city was shrouded in a reddish mist in his eyes, sounds penetrated through a thick wall, nothing was clear except for the pain in a deeply burned arm. After a while, a terrible thirst began to torment him, made worse by the sun scorching from the morning and the lack of even the slightest gust of wind. The world wavered before his eyes, only this woman, watching him from a short distance, was clear and unfazed. Tall and slender, in a blue dress of an unfashionable cut and with her hair tied back in a large knot, she looked at him with her large eyes, shining like torches in her motionless, triangular face. Amazed, he shook his head with the greatest effort, but the lady did not disappear.

Staring at the mysterious spectacle, he did not even notice how a group of street urchins started throwing stones at him, only when one of them hit him right in the mouth, not too painfully, he returned to reality and the red fog disappeared, and with it the ghost. Some adults chased away the bullies, without sparing them nudges.

"I sink so low...," Theo thought bitterly.

The thirst burned his throat so much that it was hard for him to even breathe, but his shoulder and the fever that consumed his body made him suffer. Therefore, at first he did not pay attention to the approaching figure of a woman, considering her to be another delusion, only when she got quite close did he understand that it was Adeline de Valois, quite real to it. She was wearing a festive dress, embroidered with gold and hennin, from which a snow-white veil ran. In her hand she held the reins of a horse that was saddled knightly.

The soldiers hesitantly barred her way.

"You can't, lady," said one of them.

Adeline smiled sweetly before tearing the front of her dress with a sudden tug.

"Shall I tell Prince Edward how you treated me?" she asked venomously.

The soldier stepped back in visible panic. Everyone already knew the duchess enough to know that she was capable of anything to please her whim.

Adeline calmly walked over to the pillory and unfastened the hoops that held the knight.

"Can you go?" she asked softly.

Theo nodded, unable to utter a word. He climbed into the saddle with difficulty, finding that a sword and a dagger were strapped to it, precious in his position as a treasure.

"Why are you helping me?" he asked, concentrating his attention on not falling off.

Adeline shrugged slightly.

"Maybe I just feel sorry for you," she replied. "You are like a butterfly in a spider's web: you thrash, but in vain, because everyone has abandoned you, even those you trusted the most."

"What do you mean?" asked the outlaw with dry lips.

Duchess in a sweet and friendly incarnation seemed even more formidable to him than in the hateful incarnation.

"I don't want to cause you more pain," she said in an almost believable sadness. "But you'll find out anyway. How do you think Edward knew exactly where and when you would be? After all, only one man could tell him about it, I don't count my stupid sister."

Theo stared at her for a moment with wide eyes.

"Philip? But he is my friend..." he finally stammered in disbelief.

"Oh, yes. The point is, he cares more about King Charles's friendship than about yours. Think why he insisted on you being present at his wedding? He knew how dangerous it was for you, and he had no qualms about it."

Listening to these words, Theo felt a string break in his heart. It wasn't about whether they were truthful - it, frankly, didn't matter anymore, what mattered was the result, in his case deplorable, the intentions receded into the background. Something was irretrievably over, and realizing it, he felt even more devastated than he was.

He gathered the horse's reins with his right hand.

"Tell your prince he hasn't beaten me yet," he said.

The whole thing was getting more and more confusing and suspicious, but Theo didn't have the strength to consider it anymore. His shoulder ached so badly that his eyes grew dim. The thirst was becoming unbearable, it permeated his whole body so that he did not even know where he was going. It was a fortunate coincidence, because if he steered the horse on a straight road to Bongrais, he would inevitably fall into an ambush arranged there, and the horse, left to his own discernment, carried him along another, safe route. He relied on him. He was too fuzzy to think clearly, and he didn't care if he was on the right track or not. He could only think of the water, which he looked in vain for. He hadn't realized how terrible dying of thirst must be before, but now it was quite clear to him. He felt worse and worse. He was seized by a desperate urge, known only to wounded animals, to hide in his lair and die there in peace, away from everyone and everything.

Fortunately, the unattended horse, guided by instinct, turned not to the wilderness, but towards the nearest human residence - a tidy house with a large yard and a timbered well in the yard. With the last of his strength, Theo pulled down the reins of his mount and slid to the ground, trying to reach the bucket. He was suddenly seized with a peculiar feeling of relief, of deliverance from the suffering burning his body, and he passed out as he fell right next to the well.

After some time, consciousness returned. On his lips he could feel the wonderful, fresh taste of water that was poured over his face. Opening his eyes, he saw a shapely female head bent over him, wrapped in namit, flowing from under a white cap. The woman tilted the scoop to his mouth. He drank greedily, in long gulps, enjoying the cool and clean water, though his throat was so dry that he could hardly swallow in the first moments. After a while, he recovered enough to feel ashamed, especially as he noticed that the stranger woman kneeling beside him was in a very advanced state of pregnancy.

"Sorry to bother you," he muttered, trying to get up. "I'm going to get on the horse right now and go on."

"Yes, of course. You won't get far," she said. "It will be a miracle if you manage to enter the house on your own. Come on, lean on me, and we try."

Her voice was nice but firm, and the supporting arm was surprisingly strong for a woman. Theo got up, gripping the lining of the well and straining to keep from fainting again.

"Gautier, take care of the horse!" The woman called. "Pierrette, get that cup you can't touch from the cellar, and a roll of linen!"

A boy about ten years old obediently grabbed the horse's bridle, the younger girl ran somewhere. Their mother helped the wobbly knight enter the house, led him to a large, clean and bright room, and sat him down on a wide bench covered with straw and a rug woven from colorful strips of fabric.

"I see you've been in serious trouble," she said, examining his arm carefully. "How do you call yourself?"

"Theodor. Theo le Vengeur," he answered her thoughtlessly, leaning helplessly against the wall.

"That explains a lot," she murmured. "Thank you, Pierrette, now go have fun. I'm Marianne. I warn you that it will hurt now, because before applying the ointment, I have to clean the wound, otherwise it will not work."

She wet a piece of linen cloth in the wine and began to wash the burn carefully. Her decisive movements made it clear that such a job was no stranger to her. She tried to be as gentle as possible, but Theo almost passed out from the pain a second time. Finally Marianne applied a cup of ointment to the burn, and after a while the knight's arm went numb.

"Why are you helping me?" He asked, relieved that the pain had dulled and that he had regained his ability to think clearly. "I can be someone terrible, so much is said about me. Are you not afraid?"

The woman smiled. Despite the fact that she was already over thirty, she was still pretty and, in a maternal way, gentle.

"My dear, the wife of the executioner must know not only about dressing wounds, but also about people, and I'm the executioner's wife," she replied. "That's why I know that you had to get in the way of the English, because you were not marked with French iron. And as an enemy of the English, you must be a good French. Besides, I know your name well, and from the good side. Lie down now."

"No, I'd better keep going. I don't want to cause you any trouble," the knight tried to get up but fell back on the bench as he felt dizzy.

"You're not going anywhere," she said firmly. "Soon you will have such a fever that you will not recognize your mother.

Someone branded you very unskillfully, but as cruelly as he could. And it was definitely not a cat."

"How do you know?" Theo asked senselessly, obediently lying down on the coffee table.

"When an executioner brandishes a condemned man, he only touches his skin lightly with the iron," she replied. "It's more than enough that the mark will remain for life and cannot be removed by anything except with the skin. In your case, the burn is very deep. You can even die from it."

"I wish I had died," he whispered, closing his eyes.

The ointment of unknown composition was truly wonderful, if he didn't move his arm, felt almost no pain at all, and there was unspeakable fatigue. Marianne wiped his forehead carefully with a damp cloth.

"Get some sleep now," she whispered. "And don't think about death. You better be alive, believe me. Life is priceless, the executioner's wife tells you that."

Her voice was soft music. As Theo fell asleep, he was surprised that such a good and beautiful woman had chosen the executor of the most terrible sentences as her husband. Really incomprehensible.

Besides, she was not only kind and pretty, but also experienced - the fever she had announced actually deprived him of discernment for a long time. He lost track of time and place, slept most of the time, and on the rare times he woke up felt nothing but a terrible pain in his head and shoulder. Marianne looked after him with a genuinely sisterly tenderness, even though she had considerable household duties, and in her condition it was not easy for her to fulfill them. She was drinking him with herbals, she changed his dressings, but despite her efforts, the wound was nasty and the fever persisted. In a word, it was bad.

The first thing that reached the knight after a long ignorance were the sounds of the storm raging over the house and the furious drumming of hail on the roof and closed shutters. For the first time he had a good idea of what was going on around him for a long time, though he felt he still had a fever. He was very thirsty. He reached for the jug beside the bench he was lying on and drank greedily, wondering how long he had been lying there. Certainly, taking care of him was very troublesome for a pregnant woman, whose head was in addition to the entire household.

"I have to leave this house as soon as possible," he muttered to himself, and froze, jug in hand, as he heard a groan from somewhere deep in the house, then a scream.

At first he thought he was hallucinating, but the scream was repeated, painful and desperate. Theo jumped up from the bench and grabbed the sword on the table. Never before had a weapon felt as heavy to him as it is now. His legs buckled under him with weakness, but mobilizing all his strength, he opened the door and staggered to the spacious room where Marianne was sleeping with the children. It was dark in the room, it was lit only by one barely smoldering torch, but he noticed the children huddling against the wall and kneeling by the bed, Marianne in a bloody shirt.

He looked around unconsciously, looking for the mysterious attacker.

"What happened?" he asked, seeing no one.

"My child," the woman groaned. "It started. I'm giving birth."

It took a while for the knight to realize this simple truth and that there was no robbery.

"Come out into the hallway, kids," he ordered briskly, put down his sword and helped Marianne lie down on the bed.

"I'll get help from the village," he offered, but the woman shook her head.

"In such a weather? Nobody will come here, and you won't get anywhere," she said, her voice breaking. "Make a fire and heat the water. I will manage somehow, after all, this is my third child, and you are here too."

"I? How can I help you? I haven't even seen the mare getting foal," Theo was frightened.

He blew the fire into the fireplace, added some wood, filled the cauldron with water, and placed the largest bowl he could find on a stool. He didn't know what else to do.

Marianne waved her hand.

"It's enough not to be alone," she whispered.

The outlaw sighed and sat down next to her, taking her sweaty hand in his dry, burning hands. Marianne tightened her fingers on his wrist with a force he would never expected from her, and let out a short groan. Then she alternately screamed and squeezed his hands so tightly he could hardly take it. He felt desperately helpless, more than ever. He could not help this woman, he knew nothing of midwifery activities, and even if he did, he sincerely doubted that he would dare to do anything. As for most knights, the body of a woman was a mystery to him and he would face a hundred Englishmen more willingly than deliver a child. He didn't even want to think about what would happen when Marianne died, so he alternately prayed silently and cursed with despair. Finally, the woman's body twisted in its final contraction, she let out one last, long scream, and fell silent on the bed.

"And it's all over," she gasped, trying to smile. "Take a knife and a piece of leather cord. Tie the umbilical cord in two places, cut it in the middle and tie it tightly to stop it bleeding. Then pour cold water into a bowl, add a little boiling water and bathe the baby, then wrap it in a clean cloth. It's in that chest on the right. And don't turn around until I let you, I have to change."

Theo released her hand and looked around. There was something red, wrinkled and squeaking like a kitten, on the bloodied straw and the scraps of the sheet. He had the impression that as soon as he touched the little one he would do him some harm, but he overpowered himself, cut and ligated the umbilical cord. Then he bathed the baby while Marianne changed her bloody shirt and crawled on her lap to clean her bed. Finally, she pushed a ball of bloody straw into the hearth and, exhausted, lay down on the bed strewn with fresh linen. Theo handed her a baby wrapped in a clean cloth. Marianne smiled fondly at the newborn.

"He's cute, isn't he?" she whispered tiredly.

He sat down next to her.

"I don't know much about children," he said carefully. "It seems so tiny to me."

"Every newborn baby is like that, silly," Marianne laughed kindly. "You were like that, too, though you must be over six feet now."

"Yes, I suppose so," he replied without conviction. "And Father Prospero, who baptized me, said that he had never seen a screamer and uglier baby in his life. Just skin and bones, and I was screaming so loudly that he couldn't hear his own words."

"You know Father Prospero, the prior of the Carmelites? He gave me the ointment that I treated you," said the young mother, hugging the child. "He's a holy man. There aren't many people like him today. Okay, go lie down, I need a little rest, and you're not too strong yet."

"Ah, I feel much better, but you're right, rest now." Theo stood up and covered her carefully.

In fact, he felt quite mean, but the miracle he had witnessed - the miracle of the birth of a new life - was now completely on his mind. It was only now that he realized how much he would like to have children of his own, and he thought that he would have to keep that desire well hidden from Bellette so as not to cause her worry.

In the corridor he found a boy and a girl huddled together in a corner.

"Be good now, because mommy is asleep," he told them kindly. "You have a brother, and everything went smoothly."

The children clearly cheered up and, as silently as mouse, slipped into the bedroom. Until now, the excitement of the unusual situation and the nervousness effectively supported the knight. But now that it was all over, he trudged up to his room and fell down on the bench. As he fell asleep, he thought that he would now have to help Marianne with the farm until the young mother regained strength, then he fell asleep deeply. It was a different, healthy and reassuring dream, after which he woke up feeling very hungry.

He left the house, washed at the well and shaved, using as a mirror polished sheet metal resting on the side of the horse's drinker. The glistening surface showed him a thin face with strongly defined jaws and deep-set eyes, in which the old glow smoldered faintly. The shoulder was still teasing him, but otherwise he felt quite comfortable for what he had been through.

On his return he found little Pierrette, carrying a tray of bread, cheese and a jug of milk with both hands.

"Mum told me to bring you breakfast," she said in a thin voice, tossing her head back a strand of light hair.

"Thank you, baby," he replied, setting to eat. "How does she feel?"

"Good. Baby too. Today I will take care of everything," the girl told him proudly.

"And me." Her brother added, appearing behind him with an empty bucket.

"I will help you. Too much work here for your little hands."

Theo swallowed up his breakfast hastily, not despising the milk he normally detested, then, wonderfully encouraged, set to work. There was no shortage of it in the farmyard, and two children would indeed not be able to cope with it. Marianne had to lie down for a few days, so the outlaw postponed his return project until she was strong enough to be left alone on the farm.

Meanwhile, on the fourth day her husband returned home. He has been absent so far. Not every city could afford its own executioner, many of them simply hired one when needed. It was just like that now. Marianne's husband had just returned and entered the main room just as Theo was using his dagger to repair a shelf in which the pegs had loosened and she fell off the wall.

"What are you doing here?" he asked in surprise rather than anger.

"As you can see..." Theo replied not very wisely, as he shivered at the mere sight of this massive man with a gloomy face, dressed in sullen red. He felt as if he already knew him from somewhere, but that he happened to be faced with an executioner, so any representative of this profession could evoke a similar feeling in him.

"Andre," voice came from the bedroom. "Andre, come over here, I'll explain everything to you."

Executioner gave the knight one more evil look and went to his wife. Theo finished repairing the shelf, then hung it up in its old place and put the various small items on it before they fell. From the bedroom he heard the enthusiastic screech of the children, delighted by their father's return, and he shook his head involuntarily. Somehow he couldn't believe that someone could be a torturer and a loving husband and father at the same time. Suddenly he remembered where he knew him from. He was the same man who had come to the dungeon to inspect his neck after the Bongrais massacre before his expected execution, and he seemed to be as moved by everything as a granite boulder.

"It's small word..." he muttered, contemplating the shelf that did look like new.

After a while, the executioner returned to the main room.

"Marianne told me you helped her when she gave birth," he grunted.

"In truth, she needed no help," replied the knight. "She would be fine on her own. Rather, I owe her gratitude, because if it weren't for her, I would have died like a dog under a fence."

Executioner nodded and sat on a bench against the wall.

"Still, you did well to stay to help her," he said. "Can I repay you somehow?"

Theo smiled. The initial chilling sensation passed quickly.

"Maybe when you cut me, do it in one swing," he said cheerfully.

Executioner shrugged his massive shoulders.

"I always try to do that," he said. "Though I don't understand why you care so much. After all, my first blow, even the most bungling, crushes the condemned man's vertebra and lays him dead. But okay, I'll do my best for you. Worse if it is my chance to take you to torment. Have you ever been tortured?"

"Once," Theo replied, and he shuddered involuntarily as he remembered those awful moments.

It was during the first months of his exile, and the fact that he had managed to survive this misfortune was mainly due to the fact that he was not yet so well-known and that his torturers had no idea who had fallen into their hands.

"So you probably realize that there is no way to help or even alleviate someone's suffering, even worse: in this way only his suffering would be prolonged. But enough of these professional considerations. I want you to know that I am grateful to you," finished the executioner.

"It's a mutual gratitude, but since you're back, it means I can finally go my way," Theo said, staring out the window. "My friends are probably worried about me."

It really was an understatement. The news of what had happened had already flown half of France, and the comments made were not necessarily favorable to the Black Prince. Even among the English knights, the rumors that circulated were quite unfavorable, as in some matters knights, regardless of nationality or ongoing wars, were sometimes in solidarity. This was particularly evident at tournaments, where they could collectively turn against someone who they thought had done something dishonorable. In 1286, this is how the tournament participants colluded against a certain Bavarian prince who, on any pretext, got rid of his wife by sending her to the scaffold. Solidarity of all chivalry, she soon made the prince fall into poverty and end up miserably[7]. There could be no such thing now, but what was said was said.

****

"See, I said he had to be killed." Adeline was saying with concern.

"Believe me, my beauty, I couldn't do that," the Black Prince answered her tenderly. "I know how much it hurt me, but if you knew my motives, you'd judge me less harshly."

Duchess threw her arms around his neck.

"I'm not strict at all," she said fondly. "My only concern is you, my prince, is it a crime?"

Sir Edward stroked her loose hair.

"I'll explain everything to you one day," he promised. "But in the meantime, tell me what do you think, did he believe?"

Adeline considered.

"I don't know," she said finally. "I think he believed. But I don't understand why you are so anxious to quarrel him with Philip. After all, this little swell does not dare to stand openly on his side."

"I didn't mean Philip, but this outlaw. The fortress, besieged and cut off from reinforcements, must surrender one day," the prince replied enigmatically.

Adeline didn't push any further, used to her lover being mysterious and not fully understood.

---

7   Historical

"Let's go to sleep," she suggested. "Tomorrow I want to go to Tours and visit Philip and my stupid sister. Maybe I will know somehow where this outlaw has gone, because I will tell you openly that I do not like his disappearance at all. If so without a trace?"

"Try it, you might actually find out something," the prince allowed her.

Duchess had sincerely meant to leave early in the morning, but her chances had been spoiled by the rain, which had been blowing since dawn, so that she could barely set off at noon. Of course, in such a situation, she had to stop for the night in one of the roadside taverns - it was impossible to travel in the dark on uncertain routes at that time. The tavern was tiny, with only one guest room on the first floor, which, due to its poverty, could be rented to such a great lady, so the servants and the soldiers had to be content with sleeping downstairs and in the stable. Neither of them had a feeling that they were being followed, and it was from Bongrais. Theo's gang had long searched for their leader's footsteps and work themselves into a lather as no one could tell them what happened to their leader after the dramatic events at Tours. In general, it was assumed that he had been murdered, although his body was not found, and there were also voices that he was probably kept in some casemates, but all agreed that the Black Prince and his lover knew what had happened. The Duchess's departure from Bongrais provided a great opportunity to intercept her on the way and force her to confess. Voices rose in the gang as well, to repay her in some painful way for what happened to their leader in Tours, for no one had any doubts that she had somehow had a hand in it, but they were not in agreement as to how. The offers ranged from having her hair cut off to a gang rape, which Tristan and both girls strongly opposed. Finally, the decision was postponed until Adeline was in their hands. For now, the first thing that had to be done was to neutralize the escort. Fortunately,

Bellette had carefully preserved the remnants of the sleeping potion Father Prospero had given her once, so all she had to do was sneak into the inn and pour the essence into the wine.

Colas, who joined his friends in the woods a few days ago, undertake this task when he decided that he was quite old for it. He was only thirteen, but he was taller and stronger than Tristan, the youngest in the team so far, and looked older than he was. Taking advantage of the fact that the soldiers knew him as the stable boy, he slipped easily between them and imperceptibly seasoned the wine they drank with sedative herbs. Now it was enough to wait. However, the outlaws did not count both of the maids traveling with Adeline. Neither of them was drinking wine, so they screamed at the first sound of searching the tavern. Before they could gag them, they woke Adeline, who hurriedly bolted the door to her room from the inside.

"Bad luck!" Pierre said, irritated. "Open up, lady!"

The few soldiers who stayed with the horses rushed inside with their swords drawn.

"Take care of them, we'll get that fox girl out of the hole!" Beregard called to his friends.

"With pleasure!" Falcon answered him, grabbing his dagger.

"Somebody help me! Help!" Adeline shouted, leaning out the window.

"There is no need to scream, no one in this remote area will hear the lady." Millot advised through the door.

"I wish you'd be right, but we'd better hurry up, because no one know what those screams can do." Bellette said angrily.

"No need to think for a long time, we can ram it!" cried Tristan, a little familiar with the art of war.

"Right, we can," Pierre looked around nervously. "Such a puppy would be smarter than all of us. Get a bench here!"

Beregard quickly grabbed the one that seemed to be the heaviest and most solid. Pierre grabbed her from the other end. There wasn't much room in the corridor, but there was enough space to take a swing and the struck door shuddered.

"Come on out, you whore or it will hurt!" Pierre shouted, and waited a moment and gave sign for a second swing.

The re-struck door swayed and huddled in the corner of guest room Adeline screamed shrilly again.

"Again!" Pierre commanded victoriously.

"And what's going on here, for a hundred thousand mindless bastards?!" a voice well known to all suddenly can be heard from the threshold.

Beregard and Pierre turned abruptly, and the improvised battering ram fell from their hands. Their lost leader was beside them in one leap, and his fierce gaze did not promise anything good.

"What's that supposed to mean?" He asked, staring at his deputy. "Will I finally find out? You can't be left alone for a few days, you rabble? Since when is MY team fighting women? Whoa, who has something to say?"

He looked around at his men accusingly. Nobody replied. Everyone froze standing and stared at him without saying a word, eyes dumbfounded, confused, offended and happy at the same time.

"What's up? You've always been so smart mouth, and now shut up as a clam?" Theo went on crazy. "Falcon, Patrique, Raoul, Tristan, I'm surprised by you the most, because you four have known a bit of the knightly code. What is this attack on eleven against one woman?!"

"Fourteen, we two more and Colas," Preziosa corrected him. "Besides, we were looking for you as if you didn't know."

"Where were you going to find me, under the Adeline dress? Did you hit in your heads?" Theo went to the door and pounded it with his fist. "Hey, Countess, don't be afraid anymore, we'll be leaving soon! Sorry about this incident, it won't happen again! Come on, you bastards."

"We're coming," Pierre grunted dissatisfiedly. "Why so angry? Anyway, we ask for such a word 'rabble'. An important dignitary. Anyway, it's your fault. Where have you been all this time?"

"I was a little sick," the knight growled, going downstairs.

"You? How's that? You never get sick," wondered Beregard as he followed him.

The friend gave him a mean look.

"So what? And now yes. What is this, not allowed? The new royal order to put you in the dungeon for illness?" he asked aggressively.

"He has a swollen head now," Preziosa whispered to Bellette in shock.

"The important thing is that he's back, never mind what his mood is," her friend whispered back, measuring her husband with anxious eyes.

She noticed that he was pale and emaciated, and that his left arm was tied with a dirty cloth.

"He suffered from what they did to him," the Gypsy sighed. "No wonder he is a bit rough after such an experience."

"Sure. Just think how much he must have suffered. After all, he is so proud..."

Bellette shook her head, finding no words. On the one hand, she felt inexpressible relief that her husband had finally found himself, but on the other hand, she still feared for him. For a man like him, what had happened was too terrible, it might have pushed him to commit some nonsense, after all it was known for a long time that for this man honor means much more than life. The Black Prince knew it too, which was probably why he chose this way of vengeance. She quickened her pace and, catching up with her husband, took his hand with a confident embrace.

"We were very afraid for you," she said.

Theo gave her a sad smile.

"Seems to be so," he said, looked at the close group of silent friends marching behind him, and added louder. "Although it's all your fault anyway. You've covered me nicely."

The outlaws murmured among themselves.

"Don't be angry, Chief," said Falcon soothingly. "The Englishman predicted that we would be watching him, and gave us a moron in his clothes, and in disguise he slipped away at night. But you're right, we botched and you paid for it. He also led you out of the way, so what, we were supposed to be smarter than our own leader? It's as if your backside wants to be smarter than your head."

"Don't be so smart, and don't fight women," Theo said sharply.

"We know, we know, it's an infamous fight," Millot agreed. "But take into account, by your grace, at my request, that we were going crazy, not knowing what the hell is going on with you. You disappeared without a trace, leaving the entire English army on our heads and the burden of fighting for a better tomorrow."

"I prefer the worse yesterday," muttered Pierre rebelliously.

"We thought that this witch knew something about you," Jean added humbly, in a tone of explanation.

"Nothing of that. And fortunately, because I wouldn't have given a penny for my life if she knew where I am," Theo said glumly.

He disapproved of his friends' actions, but deep down he was glad they had scared Adeline a little, who should get a lesson. Already in the best accord, the gang mounted their horses and returned to their hideout in the marshes.

"How is your arm?" Bellette asked once they were safely in their cabin, away from anything that might endanger them.

"Could be better," Theo replied glumly, sitting down on the pile of pelts. "You know what happened? I am asking stupidly, you surely know. It won't heal, nasty, I'll have to go to Prospero for some herbs."

"Was it very scary?" asked Falcon sympathetically.

He himself could not imagine himself in such a terrible situation, and his skin ached to think of what his friend had to go through.

Theo shrugged reluctantly.

"Initially, yes, but now that I think about it, it just makes me feel weird," he replied. "I don't know what the Black Prince wanted to achieve with this."

"You don't know what? He wanted to disgrace you, and he totally succeeded." Pierre snorted before anyone could stop him.

"You know what, you're an idiot!" Tristan shouted furiously at him.

"I had time to think about it, and I figured that the mark on my arm would just be a visible sign of how far I got under this Englishman's skin," Theo said calmly. "Of course, I don't enjoy wearing this devilishness on my shoulder, and I can assure you that the whole incident was hellishly unpleasant, but I don't intend to drown myself because of it."

Suddenly his voice broke. He hid his face in his hands.

"Who am I kidding? Now even a mentally ill king will not want me among his knights."

"I'm also very unfortunate that you will not become an iron-clad corpse on some battlefield for things that don't concern you anyway," Pierre said contemptuously.

"And the king can be sick in mind?" Jean asked naively.

"Sure," said Falcon. "The English even have sodomite in the estate of the king, and he is the natural grandfather of the Black Prince."

"Are you kidding?!" Colas exclaimed in shock.

"Cross my heart," Falcon struck his fist on his chest. "He had an affair with a certain Hugo, then with his son, also Hugo, until his wife and her lover caught them, they called him Mortimer, if I remember well."

"It doesn't matter what was his name, but what happened next?" Francois asked with unhealthy curiosity.

"Well, nothing. Hugo was sentenced to death in agony," replied Falcon. "First they cut him off..."

"Okay, okay, okay," Theo interrupted him briskly, "There are ladies here."

"Let's say they're ladies. They have heard a lot before," Pierre waved his hand impatiently. "What did the English do with the nasty king?"

"I don't know," the Bearnean spread his hands.

"And I know," Tristan said. "First they tried to lead him in the dungeon to suicide, and if they failed, they attacked him one night and put a red-hot poker in his back, through the cow's horn, so that there would be no traces[8]. It is said that the king was dying for fourteen days in terrible torments, which meant that he was in even worse situation than his lover. In addition, all this was done not only with the permission, but on the express orders of the queen, who was finally able to play with her lover without any problems. When Edward III ascended the throne, first of all, he had Mortimer hanged and locked up mummy."

"Rest in peace poor king," sighed Gwidon devoutly. "The Black Prince has a nice family, I prefer my own, although my mother was a harlot and I don't know my father."

Theo shook his head.

"These English people are not a nice nation after all," he decided. "What did I actually expect for myself? Okay, let's go to sleep, we'll talk tomorrow."

He didn't blame his people for not many of them getting the point. For them, such things were pretty much commonplace, after all. Jean had worn the mark on his shoulder too, burned out when

8   Historical

he was a boy and got caught stealing, and he never made a point of it. Pierre was right - Theo was very different from them, and it couldn't be erased just because they were friends and lived under one roof, waging the same fight against a common enemy. Never before had he felt so strongly that his place was in the royal service, not in those forests where he was hunted like an animal. The memory of the unhappy king distracted him a little from his own troubles, at least enough for him to fall asleep peacefully, cuddled up against Bellette, warm and loving.

"Everything, everything is the fault of this rat Paulino. I should have killed him a long time ago, but what is delayed will not run away," he thought, before a heavy sleep hit him.

He dreamed of something strange and unpleasant, so strange that when he woke up in the morning he couldn't even remember what it was. Yawning and stumbling over the rungs of the ladder, he went downstairs, where his friends were already sitting at breakfast, lively commenting on what else had to be done before the coming winter. It was a lot of it - to face the walls anew, seal all gaps, and supply the pantry.

"We were just struggling with the harvest, and now we're going to sweat with supplies," Pierre concluded gloomily. "And who said we're free as the wind?"

"Me, in my ballad, why?" Gwidon replied aggressively.

"Of course, such nonsense only you could come up with."

"Don't argue," Beregard asked. "It's going to be a harsh winter, we must be prepared for it. Right, chief?"

"Right," said Theo. He broke off a piece of bread and soaked it in watered wine. "But first you will help me with a personal matter. I want Don Paulino to stop poisoning French air at last."

"It's about time," muttered Preziosa.

"I'm going to see Father Prospero now," the knight continued, ignoring her. "When I get my strength I'll deal with Paulino, but this blasted arm must stop hurting me."

"I'm coming with you," Bellette said firmly.

"And me," Tristan joined her.

"As you wish."

He didn't feel like arguing with his family that morning, and he was happy to have their company. It was uncertain whether Prospero would want to perform some surgery on an unhealed wound, which might have been unpleasant, and he was not yet fully fit. The support might have been useful to him. Pleased with the sudden success, Tristan ran for his bow and quiver. Bellette threw a colorful scarf over her shoulders as the morning was cool, and the three of them headed for the convent.

It was only visible in the daylight how much Theo had deteriorated in the days he was gone. Their hearts were squeezed with pain at the thought of how hard his moments were behind him, though at the same time they felt immeasurably relieved that he was with them again. They both did not know how they would have manage without him. Father Prospero, who secretly suffered greatly over what happened to the young count and could not sleep at night because of anxiety about his fate, welcomed them with apparent calmness, and in fact with great joy.

"Sit down, boy," he said with rough sympathy. "I heard what happened, so you don't have to say anything. Show your arm."

He unwrapped the stiff bandage and shook his head. Tristan groaned loudly and turned his head away, and Bellette bit her lip quickly to keep from crying.

"Not good," the monk took a pair of bottles of herbal essences out of a cupboard and set them on the table. "Something like that is called a rose, a pretty name for a nasty condition that can end up badly." How many days have you been feverish?"

"I lost count," the outlaw replied shortly.

"He only came back yesterday." Bellette cut in, her voice trembling.

"And he scolded us terribly right now," Tristan added.

"I had to. I'm driving quietly, and here by the road some screams, quarrels... Does father have any idea that they attacked Adeline de Valois? And I have put in their dumb heads so many times that women are not to be harmed."

Theo hissed involuntarily, feeling the touch of a cloth saturated with herbal essence on his inflamed flesh.

"Have you forgotten how much trouble you had because of that viper?" Bellette asked.

Prospero finished cleaning the wound, placed a dressing impregnated with herbal ointment on it and wrapped it again.

"This is what distinguishes a noble knight from a dishonorable soldier, my dear," he said. "For the former, no situation can be an excuse, and for the latter, each one can. Although, admittedly, there are fewer and fewer true knights in this world. I know also those who considered the enslavement of women in the conquered city to be evidence of a special kind of attention. No, Theo, you don't change. Become the spiritual descendant of Roland, even if you were the last such knight in this lousy world."

"I don't remember Roland being branded with red-hot iron," Theo muttered glumly.

"He didn't stay," agreed the monk with him. "But remember that the hero of "Tristan and Isolde" was disgraced before all knighthood and condemned to the stake. Don't feel as though you are the only one who has been unfairly judged. Don't change, Theo. It is important both for you and for those who will come after you."

He examined and carefully sniffed the removed dressing.

"Someone treated you with my ointment," he observed. "But someone who doesn't know anything about treating burns."

"It was Marianne, the executioner's wife," the knight told him quietly.

"Ah, she," Father Prospero nodded in understanding. "I gave her a pain reliever, a mixture of opium, belladonna, mandrake and hemlock. It will drive away the pain, but it won't heal. It's only to your health and endurance that you didn't get gangrene. You would be dead already. Someone really wanted to cause you a lot of pain."

"Yes, Don Paulino," Theo replied with a chilling smile. "And I ask without preaching about loving your enemies."

"Sermons at your address? Jokes. I know it's a waste of time because you'll do your job anyway. I just wonder how you endured such pain. During the crusade, I witnessed the death of a crusader whose medic burned a constantly bleeding wound, and this physician of ours was certainly more delicate than Don Paulino. You must have some superhuman strength."

Theo glanced at his pale brother and Bellette trembling.

"Father, let you hear me howl," he confessed softly after a moment. "I never thought the day would come when I would lose my temper so much that I couldn't suppress a scream. Paulino had his great moment, a moment of vengeance, a moment of triumph. It burns me worse than the disgrace I have suffered."

He wiped the sweat from his face. Prospero gave him a long look but said nothing. He knew well that the death of Don Paulino was decided and nothing he could say would change it, but he could not bring himself to regret it, and as a noble and a good Frenchman he understood the outlaw's intentions perfectly well. He handed Bellette the essence flask.

"Wash his arm twice a day with it," he ordered. "Make sure that he doesn't strain his arm and that he gives up swimming in our lake for now. Let him wash in the stream, since he can no longer live without it, but no swimming until the wound heals for good. Is it clear?"

"As crystal, Father," Bellette said, taking the bottle from him.

Prospero looked at Tristan.

"And don't follow your older brother's example."

"I'm trying, Father," replied the boy respectfully.

"Tristan isn't a knight, but we are more alike prima facie," Theo looked at his younger brother fondly.

"You're both crazy as far as that is concerned. But watch out for him at least. He's still a child," Prospero said angrily.

"Child, right. If all the children were like him, no one would care about extending the longevity of the family," said Bellette, who felt responsible for Tristan, who did not listen to her by affinity.

"Ah, and one more thing," the monk remembered. "A message that will please you, barbarian. King Charles broke the treaty with England."

"Excuse me? That's wonderful news!" Theo exclaimed a genuinely sunny smile appeared on his skinny face.

For him, these words were like a triumphant fanfare - he probably dreamed of nothing more than that the shameful peace would be finally broken.

"Yeah, you've got your beloved war back," said the old prior sarcastically, running a hand over his gray and thinning hair. "Many thousands will not live to see its end, both ours and theirs... But I see that you are not moved. Don't you be sick of all this killing?"

The knight grew serious.

"You don't even know how much, Father," he said. "But until the war is over, I have no right to put my weapons down. I'm the sworn knight of the King of France, even if he doesn't want to know me, and I'll fight until the last Englishman is banished from our land."

Prospero looked into his burning black eyes and smiled sadly.

"Go now," he said with a sigh. "Because a few more of your words, and I will shed my habit and join your gang..."

CHAPTER V

Retaliation

There were gallows in the square at Bongrais - two solid poles connected by a long crossbar from which hung at regular intervals were loops of woven rope. The crowd gathered around the square watched in gloomy silence at it and the scaffold standing behind it, made of fresh boards. The soldiers surrounding the square looked around at the crowd with a gloomy gaze. A carved armchair on which sat the Black Prince stood on a dais nearby. The bound prisoners were brought to the market by a strong guard unit. Theo went first - straight, proud, showing no weakness or fear, although he knew well that on the orders of the Black Prince he was to die last, so that he would have to watch his friends die. It was supposed to break his spirit, so he couldn't allow himself the slightest weakness, after all, he didn't want to let his enemy fully triumph. Reaching the scaffolding, he turned to his companions.

"Be brave," he said. "We live once and die once. I'm asking for one thing: persevere to the end with dignity and... wait for me there. It won't be long."

"We had a wonderful life," Pierre said heartily. "Don't be afraid, commander, death doesn't scare us. It's important that we die together. It's a pity that you'll have to watch..."

Theo smiled at him, tossing his head the hair from his forehead.

"Courage, friends. Don't let this Englishman think he can scare us."

"Did you say goodbye, you pathetic heroes for the poor?" Cried the Black Prince from his place. "Executioner, do your duty. The one in the black jacket first."

'The one in the black jacket' was Beregard and it was no coincidence that he was chosen. After all, everyone knew how close this particular man was to the unfortunate knight. The knight looked at him closely, but there was no sign of weakness on his friend's rough-hewn, plain face.

"Godspeed, brother," he said, regretting that his hands were tied and he cannot hug him for goodbye.

His friend managed only a faint smile. He had never been good at expressing what he felt, but there was no fear in his footsteps or posture as he stood on a stool under the noose that had been prepared for him. The Englishman, leaning back in his armchair, made a sign, the man in red bent down and tore the stool from under the condemned man's legs, who hung in shaking cramps. Theo bit his lower lip slightly, mobilizing all his strength so as not to show his face and eyes of suffering, forced himself not to look away from the gallows so that no one would think that he was out of strength. Beregard died a cruelly long death. When at last his body hung limply, one of the guards pushed another outlaw, Gwidon, towards the gallows.

"Well, go on," said the poet, pale but unexpectedly calm. "See you soon, chief."

Ah, it was probably the worst of it that he had to stand like this and say goodbye to them one by one, smile and say comforting words while casting contemptuous glances at the Black Prince, when in fact he was dying with each of them, he felt their suffering with every fiber of his body. He could not lose self-control for a moment, allow himself a moment of weakness, because it was this calmness and composure that gave his people the strength to die with dignity, not to break down in the face of the executioner. Colas was the last to be hanged. The young boy had died as bravely as the others, and now that Theo could let his face rest, he felt that she had pulled herself into a motionless mask whose expression he could no longer alter. Pushed by the guard, he walked towards the scaffold, raising his head high. He passed the bodies of his friends dangling from the gallows, the road seemed endless, and he felt a mournful lamentation in him, not for himself, but for them. They believed in him, and he could not save them, he only knew how to make their death so much easier that he did not let them break down, that thanks to his attitude they were less afraid and saw the point that they were dying for their beliefs. He climbed the scaffold up the hastily steps and looked at the face of the Black Prince with hard, unbending eyes.

"Aren't you scared?" the Englishman asked unexpectedly.

"No," he replied. "And those who will come after me will not be afraid, and there will be so many of them that they will flood you like wave of flood."

"Maybe. But you won't see it anymore," growled Sir Edward and made an imperative sign for the executioner.

"Forgive me, my lord," the customary giant in red asked.

"I forgive. Do your duty," Theo replied equally stereotypically, then forced himself to bend his knees. A knight could only kneel before three human beings: a king, a lady of his heart, and an executioner, as he is now. He leaned over the trunk, staring at the overlapping rings on its surface, folded his head, bringing his defenseless neck under the inexorable blade of the broad ax that was raised by the sudden movement of the executioner's mighty arms...

Theo jumped up from his bed, drenched in sweat, shivering as if in a fit of fever.

"What's wrong with you?" Bellette's uneasy voice reached him as though through a wall, he could barely feel warm arms embracing him. There were dissatisfied voices downstairs, and after a while Pierre entered the attic, followed by Jean.

"Have you hit in your head?" His deputy asked sharply. "I think I heard you in Bongrais. We work hard all day, and you give no sleep to others. What is this screaming?"

Theo grabbed his head.

"I had a terrible dream," he said in a voice that was hoarse for some reason. "Terrible. I've seen death mine and yours, oh it was terrible."

Jean shrugged his thin shoulders.

"Dream," he said, struggling to control his yawn. "Listen up, chief, we are really understanding about your madness, but if you don't leave us alone even at night, I give you my word, we'll throw you out of the shack and you'll have to sleep on a tree like a squirrel."

"You're a squirrel." Bellette was offended at him.

Theo still couldn't contain the shivering.

"I don't understand," he whispered. "I never dream of anything, and here is such a terrible nightmare, so real..."

"Go to confession," his wife advised him sleepily. "You must be tired of your sins. Father Prospero always says that a clear conscience is the best pillow."

The knight stared at her with wide eyes that still flickered with his unusual terror.

"My conscience... I don't know what it really wants," he said deafly.

"Let it want what it wants, but silently. One more prank like that, and we'll really throw you on the tree," Pierre threatened him.

"Will you talk like this for a long time?" Millot called from downstairs. "Tomorrow at the crack of dawn I have to go spying on Bongrais, I must be rested, because if I have to run, what will happen? Go to sleep, you lunatics!"

"Ok, ok."

Pierre waved his hand and left, followed by Jean.

Theo embraced his wife and lay down, trying to calm the frantic heartbeat.

"I hope the Black Prince and his men are indeed leaving," he whispered softly. "I'm starting to lose my mind because of this bastard."

"Everything will be fine. Fall asleep now and don't think about anything wrong."

Bellette hugged him tightly in compassion. She, too, hoped the English would leave here, and not only for the sake of a handful of outlaws. The whole neighborhood would breathe a sigh of relief, shedding them. She surely wouldn't have believed it if someone had told her now that the French weren't alone in thinking like this. The English staying here also dreamed of leaving the place where the ground was burning under their feet and death could be lurking behind every bush. The mood among the Black Prince's troops was less and less arrogant, and in no way comparable to those which had been common among them just a few short years ago. The Black Prince's soldiers were secretly delighted to be ordered to leave Bongrais, where they were doubtful about their fate. Recently, even simply going outside the fortress could have ended in the most fatefully way for them, and they weren't safe inside either. Recently, one of them was stabbed to death, two others were secretly poisoned. When the day of the march finally came, many of them said a prayer of thanksgiving.

Don Paulino also set out with Prince Edward. He stayed in the middle of the cavalcade, knowing he could feel safe there, since he had no illusions about what his fate would be if he were caught by his enemies, and preferred to avoid it.

The soldiers rode in a dense formation, aware that from behind every tree, from every cottage they passed, someone was watching them, but they didn't care. And so they drove away from here, and they might not have been afraid of an attack in such a crowd. Millot, watching them from a safe distance, tried unsuccessfully to count the departing people until he finally gave up and started on his way back to the hideout. He was on his way back from the mountains, where he had gone at Falcon's request, and even had a letter for him which he had been ordered to deliver, a letter from the Count de Foix himself, known as the Lion of the Pyrenees. He was the uncle of Falcon, but the proud and impetuous boy did not want his protection, preferring to follow his own path.

"Finally, you're here," Theo greeted him. "And what?"

"You were right, they're out of the mountains as well," replied Millot. "I have a letter for Falcon on this. And our beloved Englishman has just set off to Aquitaine surrounded by probably his entire army. Don Paulino is with them."

"Excellent," Theo said, mending a plan while the summoned Millot Falcon, read the letter from Febus.

"Uncle is telling me to come back," the boy said finally, rolling up the parchment. "He writes that it's time for me to take care of the things that are more appropriate for my birth. What should I do?"

"Listen," Theo said sternly. "Your place is at Bearn. The temporary withdrawal of troops doesn't mean the English won't be messing around there, and I think the end of the war is still a damn long way off. You must go back."

He brought himself a piece of blank parchment left in his cabin and a bottle of ink, and began to write.

"You will take this letter to Robert Deauville on the way," he was saying. "He might not accept the news from a non-noble, he'll take it from you. Now that the treaty is no longer in force, we have a nationwide "to arms" and we'd better all listen to it. You have learned from me how to reduce social differences, use this knowledge to form your troops."

He finished the letter, sealed it and handed it to the confused Falcon, then brought a small box from the hut.

"Here's your share of the prize," he said. "You'll need a new enlistment."

"Gosh, thank you," the boy beamed, just calculating silently how much it would cost. He preferred not to take money from his uncle for this.

The people from Bearn said goodbye to everyone and set off on their way to their own immortal legend, regretting only that they would not take part in the next adventure, which promised to be colorful. However, Theo told them outright:

"Thinking in this way, you wouldn't part with us until the end of the world. You better get out of here right now."

He assembled his team and set off on the trail of the Black Prince's soldiers, who by that time had already managed to push themselves a bit forward. He did not move with his army too fast, because they had with them heavily loaded carts drawn by oxen. Besides, a soldier's cavalcade never moves too fast when it's not really necessary. Theo followed the soldiers with his men all day long, making sure that none of them noticed that they were being followed. Of course, he realized that reaching Don Paulino in the middle of such an army was impossible during the day, so he had to wait until the night when the soldiers will set up camp for the night. He managed to notice that his enemy was sticking to the center of the cavalcade and concluded that he would probably be somewhere in the middle of the camp at night as well. All you had to do was find him.

In order to be able to search calmly, they first had to get rid of the guards, which required a lot of dexterity and a precise distribution of tasks. They did it surprisingly well - quietly, without the slightest noise, they eliminated the guards one by one and reunited together. Now the Spaniard's tent had to be found, which, according to Theo's calculations, would not be too difficult. As it turned out, he had correctly guessed the location of his tent, which stood next to the Black Prince's temporary headquarters, as if hiding in its shadow. By opting for safe anonymity, Don Paulino made a mistake. His tent was distinguished from all others by the lack of any identification marks, a modest gray without any patterns. Theo peered inside, lighting a torch taken from one of the guards, and barely managed to suppress a cry of triumph.

"It's him," he whispered to his friends. "Take him, just block his mouth with something so that he cannot grunt."

Don Paulino did not know what was happening when several pairs of burly hands snatched him from under the rug. Someone brutally pressed a rolled-up rag into his mouth. Sobering up, he understood what was happening and made a hopeless attempt to free himself from the hands of the outlaws. Mad with fear, he jerked and thrashed, trying to spit the gag out until he was brutally thrown at his enemy's feet. Theo picked him up from the ground and rested his back against a mast with an English flag waving.

"Do you remember me? The last time we saw each other was Tours. Did you think you'd get away from me?" He whispered venomously, staring at him with burning eyes. "After all you did to me, did you think I'd let you just leave my lands? No, traitor. Your last moment has come."

Don Paulino's eyes almost popped out of their sockets, his face flushed, vague groans came from behind the gag, sounding like a plea for mercy, but all mercy had already disappeared from the heart of the man he had wronged so many times. The knight plunged the dagger into his stomach, twisted it, and pulled it upwards, ripping open the enemy's body. The rest of the outlaws watched without emotion until the old Spaniard gave up the ghost. Having done his job, Theo looked up at the flag waving in the gentle breeze of the night wind.

"Can you take this rag off?" he asked.

"No problem," said Armando, rolling up his sleeves and climbing the thin shaft with the agility of a monkey.

After a while, he slipped to the ground, holding the flag in his teeth.

"Excellent," Theo said, taking the embroidered silk from him and struggling not to spit on it. "Now let's get this traitor up to the mast instead of the banner. Just right for those bastards."

His friends applauded him and together they dragged the still twitching body with ropes onto the dangerously bending, unadapted mast. When they finished it, they looked waiting for his leader, busy by something strange, he traced his coat of arms with the blood of Paulino on the canvas of his tent: three ears of rye arranged in an even star. He circled the drawing in a wide cartouche, then motioned to his men. It was high time to withdraw from this dangerous place. Without waking anyone, they slipped between the tents and fell into the forest like vengeful phantoms.

"Well, that's it. Chief, let's go to the lake on the way, because you look like a butcher," Pierre suggested when they were at a safe distance. "My sister will faint when she sees you like this."

"You better now?" asked Beregard, patting his friend on the back.

Theo sullenly shook his head.

"I only feel emptiness and disgust," he replied sincerely.

"Indeed, it's hard to please you," said Gwidon.

"Well, we're over the traitor, he got what he deserved, we can start preparing for winter," Francois said after a moment. "As usual, our supplies are weak, and the winter can really be harsh, so we have to dig a decent cellar, buy grain and flour in the village, and start hunting when the first frosts come. Lots of work."

"Does not matter. At least we don't fall into debauchery out of idleness."

Gwidon, as always lofty, expressed his opinion, which was all the easier for him because with great talent he always avoided any harder work, believing that he was created for purposes incomparably higher.

"You just know something about work, lazy," Pierre growled.

Gwidon ignored him.

"Autumn in the countryside is so beautiful," he sighed, kicking a mound of dry leaves. "Purple, gold and brown, you don't see that in Paris. Just cobblestones, rubbish and foul gutters... It's good to be here."

"I wonder what this Englishman will think when he sees our message," Millot wondered aloud.

"Whatever he thinks, it doesn't matter, more importantly, what he will do. Maybe not leave it like that," Jean said admonishingly.

Theo shrugged.

"Let he not leave it. I wonder what else he can do to me."

"Be careful, you may find out and you won't like it," Armando warned him cheerfully, stuffing his hands into the pockets of his straitjacket.

The murder he committed did not spoil his mood, nor did anyone in the gang, only Theo felt what he called, for lack of a better word, "moral hangover." He did not understand where it was coming from, after all, he was not first to kill his enemies, only after a long moment did he understand why he felt like that. He killed a defenseless man for the first time, it did not matter that he was a scoundrel and a rat. After all this act was not chivalrous but on the other hand, it was impossible to do otherwise. Don Paulino has already done too much harm, while remaining completely unpunished. Theo shook his head. Now that the excitement of the difficult game was over, he felt terrible, his arm hurt more than usual, and he would have given half his life to turn it all into a dream. Only the thought of what face the Black Prince will probably make, having discovered the macabre "message", improved his mood a bit. He would have liked to see it, but he had the sense to know that this weakness could cost him a lot.

He was right. Prince Edward, seeing the body hanging on the flagpole in the morning, at the first gust of anger, ordered all the sentries on duty on that unlucky night to be hanged, regardless of the fact that the survivors were tied up and badly mauled. His fury had awakened not so much the death of his faithful henchman as the disappearance of the flag.

"You are all going to Castle Meung," he said, when he could already think clearer. "Captain Moore and his squad are staying with me. We're going back to Bongrais."

Sir John Lancaster paused in his contemplation of the corpse with its entrails disemboweled from the flagpole and looked at his brother.

"What you want to do?" he asked.

"Retrieve the flag, it must be clear. This outlaw took it with him to annoy me and to disgrace our colors. I have to pick it up," Sir Edward replied, trying to remain calm.

"How? Theo is not afraid of you and has reason to hate you," said Sir Lancaster. "One reason, strictly speaking, the one you burned on his shoulder. It was the stupidest thing you've ever done in your life, and you already have a lot of nonsense on your conscience. Like what you did with Reynold..."

The Black Prince waved his hand.

"I lost my temper," he admitted reluctantly. "Oh, well, it happened and that's it. I'll make it up to Reynold and we'll make up somehow, we're a family after all. Oh, I got it, I'll put Limoges under management, and it will appease him."

As it turned out, this was not the happiest idea of the Black Prince as ruler of Aquitaine.

Sir John shrugged.

"As you wish," he said indifferently. "But as for what you want to do now, I'm coming with you. You may need someone to grab your hand at the decisive moment. You are hot-headed, and Theo may provoke you to commit some madness. It would be very similar to him. How are you going to get him to return the flag anyway? After all, it's an important trophy for him, after all, a proof for quite good feat: he crept into the middle of the enemy camp, slaughtered the target, took the flag as his own, and disappeared. You have to admit that it is impressive."

"How am I going to...? I don't know yet, but I'll think about it along the way. You can accompany me if you like, but I don't think you have to hold my hands. I know myself that I have to be smart rather than strong here."

The Black Prince drank from the wineskin given to him by the squire and wiped his mouth with his sleeve. It was a difficult matter, but he had no doubts that he would somehow manage to solve it. He felt that for this purpose he had to use what he already knew about his opponent - his chivalry and his heart sensitive to someone else's harm, he just didn't know how. Driving at the head of his squad the armed men stepped forward a little and lost themselves in thought. He did not hear what Captain Moore and Sir Lancaster were talking about, he did not see the puzzled looks of the occasional villagers, he paid no attention to anything, and he only strained his mind, trying to find a sensible way to bring the enemy nearby.

"We'll stop at Kamienisko," he decided finally. "This village was where Theo always got his messages the fastest, so it will probably be this time too. I just have to lure him to this place, and it probably won't be too hard, just scare these villagers."

"It's really easy, and Theo will probably be furious as soon as he gets our message." Captain Moore said, unhooking his rawhide from the saddle.

He strode forward and entered the village first, and a moment later someone heard a despairing scream from among the miserable huts. Not in any hurry, the rest of the English joined him.

"Enough, Moore." The Black Prince stopped the captain with a wave of his hand. "Enough of this. Hear you folks! Have one of you go to Theo the Avenger and tell him that if he doesn't show up, you'll pay his debt. I won't explain what's going on, he knows it."

He looked around and looked at the pale Marie.

"I saw you talking to that outlaw once," he said. "Run for him now, otherwise your husband and your children will be the first to know that I'm not kidding."

Marie wanted to protest at first, but realized that it was useless and withdrew hastily.

Without dismounting, the English took all the villagers to one of the barns and closed the door behind it, propping it with a heavy stake. Now they had to wait for Theo to come to their summons, for he would do so, they had no doubts. They didn't pause. It was not long before the outlaw they had been waiting for appeared on the road, clearly agitated. He was alone, at least it seemed, but the English had the unpleasant feeling that a few or a dozen sharp arrows were pointing at them from the brush.

"Before you say anything, bear in mind that if I was going to hurt anyone here, I would have done it without waiting for you," said the Black Prince, anticipating the knight's words. "I didn't scare those yahoos just for fun. Being in my camp at night, you took something from there and I want it back. Whatever you have against me, you cannot say that I have ever desecrated your flag or your signs, so don't do it either. Give me the flag."

"Not for nothing," Theo replied, silencing his anger at the news that no one had suffered too much.

"What do you want in return?" asked the prince.

The outlaw looked him straight in the eye.

"Information. The truth. Did Philip of Navarre really tell you that I had accepted the invitation to his wedding?" he asked, and against his will his voice trembled.

The Black Prince struggled to suppress a smirk of superiority. Paulino was right - Theo le Vengeur was painfully predictable, it was strange that this predictability had not yet been turned against him.

"Yes, he said," he said. "Not to me or to Adeline, but he has not kept your arrival a secret, and you will carry the effect of his indiscretion on your skin for the rest of your life. Why was it so important to you to know this? Do you like to drive a knife deeper that hurts your heart?"

"It's none of your business," Theo took the folded flag out of his sleeve and tossed it at him with a contemptuous motion. "You have this rag here, Your English Highness, it won't even be of any use to us to wipe the floor."

It was easy to tell that the prince's answer had hurt him deeply, and he still hoped that Philip was not in any way involved in setting a trap for him.

"Why did you kill Don Paulino, not me? Paulino was only a tool," Sir Edward carefully put away the flag and looked at the young French with interest.

The man looked up.

"You, the prince, are my enemy," he replied after a moment. "I can respect the enemy, despite everything, but I hate traitors. Anyway... your death would be of no benefit to anyone, rather a lot of harm, because vengeance would fall on the innocent."

The Black Prince nodded understandingly.

"You can see what blood is flowing in you," he said. "Someday you will understand my words. Goodbye and let us not meet again, because it may happen that only one of us will survive this meeting."

Something in his gaze disturbed Theo, so that his anger suddenly faded completely, leaving only a feeling of emptiness and strange regret.

* * * * *

Winter hit quite late this year, but fiercely. The oldest inhabitants of the area did not remember such a thing. God must have been angry, they said, and it really looked like it. The frost tightened almost immediately, chilled the marshes and the lake with ice, and at the same time dense snow fell, covering the entire area with a thick layer of white fluff. The stream and the well also froze, so the outlaws were left to the melted snow at the furnace. It was difficult to get through the snowdrifts, so the outlaws hardly left their hideout, inventing various entertainment and activities so as not to get bored in winter. From time to time, on exceptionally clear days, they would go to the "Under the White Swan" tavern, where, as always, it was cheerful and noisy, and the wine flowed. Theo, hardy to the cold, did not care at all about snow or frost. High boots made of several layers of leather by a local shoemaker, thick gloves, and a fur jacket with a large hood made him armor enough against winter, and sometimes he wandered out in the woods with Beregard and Tristan all day long. They picked blackthorn berries, which took on a sweet taste after the first frosts, fought snowballs and organized races. Others joined them when it was a little warmer, but mostly on their own. And the winter went on and on. The faint, as if reluctant gray of the mornings gave way to a brighter morning, quickly turning into an early winter twilight. Little by little, everyone was drowsy and apathetic, ceasing to do anything that was not necessary, and wished they could hibernate like the bears. Luckily, they didn't lack anything, as they had already stocked up. They even had vodka and wine in casks, covered with several layers of straw in the attic, so that they did not really need a permanent connection to human settlements. They did not have to help either, because the English were gone, and the harvest was good enough for the inhabitants of the surrounding lands not to worry about what they would eat. Not every year it happened to them. The only thing they could complain about was the cold and boredom, but soon something happened that provided them with a topic for reflection until spring.

"Where are you going?" Millot asked the chief, seeing him pull on his boots on the heel.

"To the monastery," Theo replied cheerfully. "I haven't been there for a long time, or maybe my brothers need something."

"I don't know if that's a good idea. It's getting ready for another blizzard," Jean said, peering through the open shutter.

"It's still gathering, unless it's snowing," the chieftain replied lightly. "If I had been paying attention to it, I'd never have gone anywhere. Come on, keep warm, and if it does break, don't worry, I'll wait in the monastery."

"If only it wouldn't catch you on the way," sighed Bellette.

He kissed her heartily on the cheek.

"Don't worry," he said. "I always manage like you don't know."

He patted the back of Tristan, who was listening to them, and left, closing the door carefully behind him. The clearing was covered with snow above the knees, but the paths in the forest were relatively easy to walk, as their natural shelter was the dense canopy of trees above, stopping the white fall. It caused a gloomy darkness in the forest, but it was not unusual for Theo - he was used to such things. He trudged through the woods, whistling Gwidon's songs. The Parisian troubadour had, it would seem, countless supplies, and one was better than the other, they were easy to hear and effortlessly memorized. Most of them had extremely playful texts, but there were also those that were true lyrical pearls. Theo liked them very much.

He reached the nunnery, shortening his way across a frozen pool, which saved him about two miles away, and tugged the bell cord at the gate. It was opened by his brother Michael, who was a porter this month, which was a pass-through function.

"The Reverend Prior is sick," he announced gloomily. "Take it easy on him. It's very good that you came, he said he wanted to talk to you before..."

"Spit the word out, Prospero will outlive both of us."

Theo shook the snow off his fur curtain vigorously and hung it from a hook in the hallway. He could not imagine a world without Father Prospero, and frankly did not believe that the old monk would ever die. It seemed to be indestructible. However, the attention of brother Michael made him cross the threshold of the prior's cell and look closely at the monk lying on the bunk and become concerned. Prospero's face was sallow and sunken, the remnants of his hair were completely white, his eyes dimmed and dulled.

"Father Prospero, what's wrong with you?" he asked anxiously, sitting down next to him.

"What's wrong, what's wrong with me... I'm old, that's all," the monk growled. "Old age is not joy, death is not joy. Boy, I'm over ninety, pneumonia is no fun at this age. I should be glad that I'm still alive at all."

He coughed deafly and struggled to lift his head a little higher.

"I've a case for you," he continued after a moment. "First of all, take the deposit you once left me. Second, take care of Tristan. You must draw up a document stating that he is your brother and heir, otherwise, in the event of your death, they may take away his family goods and surname."

Theo slapped his forehead with his palm.

"Why I didn't think about it myself," he muttered.

"You see. With your lifestyle, it could easily happen that a poor boy becomes a nameless orphan. You may find it strange that I, a monk, urge you to do something little better than simple perjury, but you must write that your father and his mother took a secret marriage by order of John II," continued Prospero. "Say nothing, I know it's a sin, but you must commit it if you care about your brother and that in the event of your death he will not be left without his name, title and property."

"Of course, I care. Okay, Father, let's make such a document, if only there is something to write here," agreed the knight.

"Don't worry about that. Get Brother Godfrey here, you'll find him in the chapel, cleaning there every noon."

Prospero coughed again and, grimacing a little, took a sip of some liquid from a mug standing next to the bed on a small table.

Theo did so quickly. Prospero said a few words to the young brother, and after a while he brought parchment, ink, goose feather, sand in a small bowl and wax. Under the direction of the old monk, the knight wrote a corresponding declaration, which he, Prospero and three other monks, summoned by the prior, then signed. He would not have managed without the help of a monk, for he rarely had the opportunity to hold a pen in his hand, his fingers were more used to a sword, a bowstring and a slingshot. He also had no idea about editing documents, especially important ones. He usually wrote with horrendous errors, although when he tried, he traced the letters very neatly. His childhood preceptors neglected the correct spelling, putting a lot of emphasis on calligraphy. As part of this teaching, they ordered their pupils to copy long passages of the Bible after the whole day, which developed patience and handwriting. Now, only with the help of the monks, he managed his task reasonably well. The parchment was rolled up, sealed and deposited among other documents in the monastic chancellery. Then Prospero reached into the glove box hidden behind the headboard of the bed and retrieved a velvet-wrapped package that he had once received for safekeeping.

"You better take it," he said. "My earthly journey is ending, so now let it be with you."

Theo took the package from his hands.

"Oh, whatever," he sighed, weighing it in his hand. "I don't know if I would even like to help Philip now."

"Be a good Christian, forgive the wrongs and do not burn in anger," Prospero rebuked him severely. "How's your arm? Not troubling anymore?"

The knight shook his head.

"It's long ago," he replied. "It healed beautifully, probably under the influence of those father herbs, because before that it was terribly dirty. I now have a successful image of an English lion on my arm, and I have to wear long sleeves... But I still can't understand why Edward adorned me this way instead of slitting my throat? I know there was a reason, but the Englishman wouldn't tell me why, he just said something that if I found out why he had spared me, hell would open up to me. I don't understand any of this."

Prospero looked at him, brow furrowed.

"I understand," he said after a moment. "He overdid it a bit, it's not that scary, but it means he already knows... And if he knows, Adeline will soon find out, followed by all of France, and eventually you may find that you are the only one you have no idea."

"Meaning what?"

Theo leaned in slightly, feverish excitement shining in his black eyes.

"Don't get so excited," Prospero shifted on the bed. "It's not even an honest family secret, it's just a forgotten story. I didn't tell you anything because it didn't matter, and I didn't suppose anyone else remembered it. So listen: at the court of Henry III, an orphan was raised with his sons, the son of one of the royal cousins, a purebred Plantagenet. Roderick was his name. From childhood, there were only problems with him, he was willful, arrogant, he did not want to submit to his uncle. Despite the trouble with him, King Henry liked him and tolerated his excesses, but one day enough was enough. It's not known exactly what it was about, probably for some trifle which, as the saying goes, be the last straw, at least the king, out of anger, chased the boy out of London. Sir Roderick was mortally offended, collected as much money as he could and, together with a devoted squire named Linton, set off to France. He wandered around the country for about two or three years as a knight errant, participated in tournaments and armed brawls, and finally ended up in Bongrais, where your great-grandfather, Antoine, held a big tournament in someone's honor. His bravery and dexterity gained universal recognition, and when he was wounded in combat, your great-grandfather offered him hospitality. Sir Roderick was a very handsome young man, so it's no wonder Antoine's daughter, your grandmother Odetta, fell madly in love with him. Roderick did not know who she was, since Odetta did not appear in public without a thick veil on her face, as she had been disfigured by fire as a child. She had a scar on her forehead and left cheek. After disguising herself as her own maid, she dealt with the wounded knight in secret from her father. Sir Roderick pulled through for quite a long time, and in the meantime, something he had not foreseen happened, namely, he fell in love with the girl serving him, because, apart from a pretty face disfigured by the fire, he saw the intelligence and sensitivity that had captured him. He fell in love not in a chivalrous and noble manner, not poetically and not romantically, but quite simply, in an earthly way. Initially, he persuaded the girl to run away with him into the world, he had no idea who she was, and when she refused, he left alone. He came back two days later like he was not proud and, finding Odetta in the yard, he threw himself at her feet, begging her to marry him. This is how your great-grandfather found them and, as you can guess, he fell into terrible anger. He loved his daughter and feel sorry for her accident, and he couldn't believe that someone like Sir Roderick Plantagenet would seriously fall in love with a young lady with such a scar on her face. He made such a hell that the castle shook from the basement to the attic. Finally your grandmother resorted to the old, tried and tested way of all women, namely, she began to cry, and did not stop until she appeased her father. After long arguments, Count Antoine de Bongrais finally agreed to marry his daughter to an English knight, but he made a rather strict condition. He had no children other than Odetta, so he demanded that Sir Roderick terminate all ties with England, renounce the Plantagenets, and take the surname Bongrais, thus ensuring continuity of the family. Sir Roderick agreed without hesitation, although he made a condition - he wanted to keep the coat of arms given to him. Save anything of his inheritance. That's it. They continued to get married, had a lot of children and were quite plainly happy with each other.

"Oh, yeah. But that means..." Theo began.

The old monk nodded slowly.

"Yes," he said. "It means there is some Plantagenet blood in you, too. You and your enemies are chained together. Have you ever wondered about the coat of arms of your lineage, so different from the others? Those three ears of rye?"

The knight shook his head.

"It is used to saying that it shows the ears of rye, although no one would be able to explain why such a comparison comes from. Have you seen the coat of arms of the Yorks or Lancasters? Check out my books. Unless you see your "ears" similar to the leaves on the Plantagenets' coat of arms, then you are less intelligent than I thought."

The knight pondered, looking at the frozen window.

"All right," he said after a moment. "I understand now why the Black Prince did not want to kill me, but just came out with this idiotic offer. But where is the hell he promised me? Somehow, I don't feel any worse than before."

"Prince Edward exaggerated a bit, or perhaps overestimated your sensitivity," Prospero said dryly. "Anyway, blood issues are exaggerated completely unnecessarily. After all, if you wanted to be logical, then the Black Prince himself has almost exclusively French blood in his veins, and what? And nothing, because his heart is English, and if so, he is English and our enemy. It amazes me, to tell you the truth, he pulled out that old story. Maybe he wanted to break your fighting spirit?"

Theo laughed mournfully. But he don't feel like laughing at all.

"Nothing of that. Dear father, I would have denied my brother if he had betrayed his homeland, though perhaps I wouldn't have tried to kill him. Although, who knows?"

"I don't doubt. You've a skewed concept of right and wrong."

The old prior coughed again. Reaching for the small bottle, he poured a few drops of brown essence into the cup and added some water. Suddenly the alarming sound of the bell at the monastery gate broke into the resulting silence.

"Who the hell is coming here in such bad weather?" Prospero asked, setting the cup aside.

"I will check."

Relieved, Theo jumped up from his seat, taking the opportunity to leave for a moment. He liked the snappy monk very much, but in his presence he always felt like a little boy, which was not nice. In the corridor, he came across Brother Michael, very embarrassed.

"Some nobleman fell off his horse near the monastery," he said. "Looks like a broken leg in the ankle, lucky he somehow stuck here."

"Where did he go in such weather? He couldn't sit on his ass in front of the fireplace and grope the manor house?" the outlaw was surprised.

Brother Michael looked at the cell door.

"What condition is the Reverend Prior?" he asked.

"He says it's better, but I don't believe him," Theo said shortly.

Even though he already knew what the two had in common, he still couldn't work out their relationship. Michael waved his hand.

"Too bad, he'll have to help," he muttered and went to the cell, while Theo went to the refectory, where the sick and wounded were usually brought to the monastery.

Two silent Carmelites helped a rider just stretched out on a bench to take off a torn fur coat stuck in the snow, the third cut open the top of a long shoe to remove it from his rapidly swelling leg. The wounded man was an old man, quite short, with a stocky build and a strikingly ugly face: pockmarked, with a downward curved mouth and an impressive nose. Grayish wisps stuck out around the large bald head, and great, protruding ears completed the measure of misfortune.

Theo paused in the doorway.

"Let lightning burn me in this holy place, if you are not a French connetable!" He exclaimed. "Bertram du Guesclin in person! Am I wrong?"

"Not at all," the injured man replied with a strong bass. "And I'll tell you that I've a famous outlaw in front of me. Theodoric de Bongrais, right? Or would you prefer Theo le Vengeur?"

"Something new, even those who have not seen me in their life will get to know me now. Call me, lord, as you like. What is such a dignified person doing in this forbidden corner?"

Connetable did not have time to reply when Father Prospero, leaning on Michael's shoulder, entered the refectory.

"Prospero de Montargis!" Cried the connetable with amazement and joy. "I mean, Father Prospero, a Crusader! I didn't know the father is here! I'm very happy about it."

"At my age, I'm glad to be anywhere," the monk replied, kneeling with some difficulty and feeling his swollen leg with skill. "What happened?"

"The horse was frightened by a crow that broke from under its hooves. And I landed in the snow. I think broken, right?"

"Only taken out of the pond," replied Prospero. "It's less dangerous. Brothers, hold tight our guest. Theo, come on, your strength will come in handy here."

"Yay, and that's something new. I've never been a medic before."

Theo obediently walked over and took the foot of the connetable in the way Prosper had instructed him. The old monk grabbed the man by the shin.

"When I tell you, pull as much as you can," he said. "Now!"

The knight carried out this command with such vigor that the wounded man screamed out loud and almost fainted from the pain, but at the same time there was an unpleasant crack and the damaged joint returned to its place. Bertram du Guesclin went limp for a moment in the Carmelite hands holding him.

"Something terrible," he said weakly as he recovered.

"You're lucky anyway, my lord, it's not a fracture. At your age, the bones don't want to heal properly anymore," Prospero said sternly. "And these horse frolics in such weather are also not for your years. You will be here for at least a week before you are fit to continue your journey."

"A week? I don't have that much time. To tell the truth, I don't have time at all, I have to be in Paris as soon as possible," the connetable said.

"And why? The whole world will collapse otherwise, or maybe just France?" Theo asked mockingly, handing him a cup of wine for reinforcement.

Du Guesclin looked at him hard.

"Not the world, not even France," he replied, taking a sip of wine. "But the head of Philip d'Evreux, who is awaiting execution, locked in Chatelet, will fall."

The outlaw frowned.

"And what did that sucker do?" he asked with obvious dissatisfaction.

Since the events of Tours, he no longer considered Philip his friend, not even because he believed Adeline's accusations, but because the confirmation he had received from Prince Edward made him aware of a bitter truth - that the outlaws had no friends. The young king's dislike for him could not be balanced by the friendly feelings of Philip, for whom good relations with the king were certainly much more important than friendship with an outlaw.

"This is a very serious matter," continued the connetable. "Philip was accused of participating in a plot to poison King Charles. As you may remember, his father tried it before, but Philip was always on the dauphin's side. This is, now king. His guilt is confirmed by a forged document, but whoever drew the plot did not manage to destroy the real handwriting. If the king got it, he would have proof of Philip's innocence, but it must be done quickly, because if the prince dies, it will be not only his personal tragedy, but also the end of hopes for the alliance between France and Navarre. This is the document."

He took out a roll of parchment, secured with a cloth.

"The problem is that even if you wanted to, I don't know how, you won't get to Paris in this state. You've been badly battered, not to mention your leg," Prospero said sternly.

"I'll go," Theo said firmly.

"Are you crazy? Even if you get there, the king will have you beheaded!" Prospero was angry.

"Maybe not... I have an unpaid debt to Philip, and I don't like being in debt. I will go."

"What? We have no horses in the monastery, and Mr. du Guesclin's steed is bad," Brother Michael remarked soberly.

"No, no, I changed it only a mile away." Bertran du Guesclin looked at the outlaw hopefully.

"Exactly. Give me this document, my lord."

Theo took the parchment and tucked it under his jacket.

"Wait," the connetable stopped him. "I will write a few more words to the king, as long as the venerable brothers have writing instruments."

"Bring it, Michael," Prospero ordered resignedly.

He had learned long ago that when his young friend stuck something in his head, he wouldn't vince him.

"Never mind, wouldn't I have done the same in his place?" He thought, and added aloud, "have you thought it through?"

The knight smiled.

"I thought. And I have to do it. No, Father, not for Philip, for myself. I don't want to avoid mirroring my own face when I pass the mirror. Don't worry, I should be fine. Tell my people that I'll be back maybe soon, maybe in a few weeks... maybe not at all."

"Lovely news, especially for your wife," the monk growled.

"Do you think I don't feel sorry for her? I myself would like to have time to say goodbye to her, but it's impossible," said the knight seriously. "I love her. Father knows, she looks like an angel lately, a real angel. If she were dressed like that in an opulent gown, no one would have guessed that she was an ordinary peasant woman. She's so beautiful... Well, I can't think of her right now."

"You never think about her, especially when you get into another row. That girl has a broken life with you." Prospero sighed hopelessly.

Connetable finished writing, sprinkled the parchment with sand, and imprinted his signet ring in the molten lacquer.

"You can only give it to the king," he commanded. "No one else. And hurry up, don't spare your horse. Let it fall. You are the only hope of preventing a terrible misfortune."

He took the ring off his finger and handed it to the knight.

"Show it to the sentries if they don't want to let you pass," he added.

"Don't worry, I'll be fine."

Theo smiled reassuringly at the wounded man and went out into the corridor. After a while, Prospero joined him.

"Zip your jacket tight and pull the hood over your head," he said, handing him a long piece of woolen matter. "And fold this up and wrap your face tightly. Breathe only through the material. Here you have vodka with the addition of herbs. If it gets really bad, drink a few drops, it will warm you up and give you strength, but be moderate. It is extremely strong."

He handed him a small wineskin.

"Father pray for me," Theo said cheerfully, pulling on his gloves.

Brother Michael led a great steed into the yard, covered with a thick rug with holes for eyes and saddled in a knightly manner.

"Good luck," he said shortly.

Theo mounted his horse, ignoring his angry snorts, and immediately outside the gate urged him to run fast. To undertake such a journey really had to be courageous, and deep down the outlaw wanted to prove that he had no less than du Guesclin, twenty years older senior and yet determined to take the risk. This confirmed the popular opinion of this soldier for whom there was nothing but a duty to the king and to his homeland. It was not for nothing that he was called "the great man", this term best describes the essence of the matter - he was small and ugly in body, he had a great and truly beautiful soul. Theo respected him immensely, but he also wanted to prove that he was no less brave and willing to sacrifice than he was.

An extremely difficult journey awaited him. All the roads were covered with heaps of snow, frozen on top into an icy shell, the horse was sliding, then collapsing. The knight was slowly beginning to realize what madness he dared, but, regardless of anything, he pushed forward bravely. He was most afraid of mistaking the road in the blizzard, which, fortunately, was not yet too strong, but was already starting to sprinkle tiny ice needles as hard as grains of sand. It seemed that the wind was blowing furiously in all directions at once. Every now and then Theo took the glove off his hand and removed the frost that had deposited from the horse's nostrils, making it difficult for the brave animal to breathe. And when he put the glove back on, his fingers were so cold he hardly felt them. The woolen cloth wrapping his face quickly turned into a single sheet of ice, painfully rubbing his mouth and cheeks, but he did not dare to take it off, after all, it gave at least minimal protection against the freezing wind entering his lungs and particles of frozen snow as fine as sand. He did not stop driving when it started to get dark - the road to Paris was wide enough to be followed in spite of the darkness. It was only when the shape of a roadside inn appeared in the snowstorm that he decided to give the horse a little respite, already tired of fighting the blizzard.

The tavern was deserted and half covered with snow, but luckily the door opened enough to allow him to go inside and lead his mount there. It was a little warmer inside, but not warmer enough to do without fire. Theo broke a few stools, struck a fire, and when the fire in the hearth crackled cheerfully, he finally pulled the stiffened scarf from his face with relief. He warmed his hands with delight for a moment by the fire, then filled the old bucket found in the corner with snow and, having melted it, watered the horse. Then he hung a sack with a rim on its head, and he took a piece of smoked meat from the saddle bag for himself. After he had eaten, he sat down, curled up by the hearth and rested his head against the wall. If he wanted to reach Paris the horse needed a rest, otherwise he would not have allowed himself such a waste of time. He was lucky to find this tavern. His first winter in the woods had a worse adventure: he lost his way and was caught by a wind far away from human habitation. He survived thanks to the fact that he built a mud hut for himself and the whole blizzard sat in it. Now it would have been all the more difficult since he had a horse with him. Besides, the frost was much worse now, and the tiny balls of ice that the snow turned into were not suitable for molding. The fire crackled, the horse chewed on its fodder, and the knight, lazy with heat, fell into a light, restless sleep.

The cold woke him. The fire was long gone, daylight shone through the cracks in the warped boards. He jumped up, grabbed the scarf, which was thankfully already dry, and wrapped it around his face again. The rested horse made for the road, his animal instinct sensing that in such a frost stillness was his worst enemy, but the ride turned out to be much more difficult than the previous afternoon. The blizzard grew, and he had to fight the furiously blowing wind. At one point, it turned out that Theo, blinded by the snow, had confused his direction, and it took a long time for him to find the right route. He hoped to make it to the capital before dusk, but upon encountering a mile-post, he found that he had traveled far less than he had anticipated. He almost lost his spirits. He knew well that his horse, though strong and of good blood, would not endure a second such night. And the fact that he still has the strength to fight the blizzard is undoubtedly due to that little diluted booze, which he poured into his mouth by force before they left the tavern. Apart from the cold and the blizzard, he was terrified of the emptiness around him - he had the feeling that he was riding through an extinct country, and he was also awfully aware that if he succumbed in this struggle for survival, his body would only be found when the snow fell. To make matters worse, he was starting to sleep, a dangerous companion of such driving. He drank some herbal booze, which warmed him up and drove away his sleepiness a little, but it soon got worse again. He was freezing more and more, all the time he had the feeling that the road was not getting any less, or that it was going in the wrong direction again. To make matters worse, the blizzard, which had stopped for a while, raged again. At first, snow fell in large patches, then turned into tiny, knife-cutting stars, painfully offending the eyes, already inflamed with frost. The road was blurred, faint in a blinding white that consumed everything, the whole world. Theo was already steering the horse at random, silently praying not to confuse the way and not to fall asleep because it was getting harder and harder to keep his attention tight. The whirlwind, howling furiously near the ears, seemed to have its own personality, as if it were some powerful, unspeakably malicious creature, enjoying playing with human life, but on the other hand it helped to stay awake, direct resistance and hatred against something. Dead silence would be a hundred times worse.

Suddenly, the exhausted horse stumbled over something and, with a desperate squeal, rolled over the slight icy drop, throwing the drowsed rider out of the saddle. Theo was lucky he know how to fall, for this was where the icy snow was pounded to stone - he could break his bones. But the shock made him a little dizzy. As he recovered and stood unsteadily, shaking his head, he saw to his horror that despite his efforts his horse was unable to rise. The poor animal had broken its leg as it fell, and although it felt no pain yet because of the frost, it was clear that it would never get up. For a moment, Theo felt despair overwhelm him. Here he was left alone in a blizzard, far from human settlements, with no one being to help him, no chance of saving him. Then he pulled himself together. First of all, he had to finish off the unfortunate steed so that he would not suffer, and he did it by sticking his sword into his neck. The use of the Valois sword in such butchering work had been disgusting him, but there was no way out. Then he wiped the blade with snow from the blood and sheathed it while looking around. He was somewhere on the height of Fontainbleau, which meant that there was still a long way to Paris, but the only alternative was to stay here beside the horse's body and freeze to death. He did not feel like it. He took another sip of the herbal booze from the wineskin and started down the road to town.

Digging through the icy snow was torment, but he had no choice but to keep going if he wanted that one slim chance of reaching his destination. He never used to give up without a fight, and even less so now he did not want to do so, when it was not only his life that depended on reaching his destination. He knew well that he must not stop on the way that his only chance was precisely in this constant fight against the wind and blizzard. However, he had the impression that the wind blowing directly in his face was penetrating him through, despite the thick veil and hood. When it began to dusk, he lost all hope again, for the road seemed to drag on forever, and there was no sign that he was reaching his destination. He paused to rest for a moment, then, courageously despairing, set off again into the rapidly falling darkness. He had to go forward. He did not care if he was attacked by wolves, the howling of which was clearly reaching him through the sound of the wind - if they torn him apart, at least it would be over, he would stop suffering. Every breath burned his lips despite the woolen cover, his bones ached as if they were about to burst, nightmarish fatigue dulled his mind, made it impossible to think clearly. Nevertheless, he continued walking, fighting the blizzard. He no longer knew how long he was going or where he was. The world became for him a dark space with no beginning or end, filled only with uniformly swirling snow, in which even the goal of this journey through torment melted away. With snow that consumed the skin, annihilated the soul, it even destroyed the awareness of his own existence, it left nothing but pain. Because there was pain, it stuck sharp teeth into the body, did not let him forget about itself and, in fact, exhausted to the limit of his endurance, the knight was satisfied with such a companion, because only thanks to it he felt that he was still alive.

"I'm not giving up," he whispered, gritting his teeth and drawing his last strength to overcome the next bit of a road.

But the moment had to come at last, when "I will not give up" imperceptibly turned into "I give up" and Theo sat helplessly under a tree, crouching and pressing his hands around his knees. It didn't matter to him, he finally wanted to rest, if only for a while. He reached for the flask with the remnant of the booze, but was no longer able to bring it into his mouth. His body, frozen to the maximum, was overwhelmed by treacherous warmth, the pain was blunted, and at the same time the white mist that had obscured his eyes for a long time had thickened imperceptibly. He thought dreamily that all this was a sign of impending death, and, reconciled to fate, rested his head against the trunk of a tree.

He was already falling asleep when someone shook him.

"Get up," he heard a silver urgent voice.

With difficulty, reluctantly, he unstick his eyelids and saw, surprisingly clearly, before him the figure of a young woman in a blue dress. He didn't even have the strength to wonder what this beautiful lady was doing in this wilderness on such a terrible night, in addition in summer dress and all alone.

"Get up," she said in what seemed somehow familiar to him. "If you fall asleep, you won't wake up anymore."

"I can't," he whispered through his frost-numbered lips. "I don't have the strength anymore. I'm too tired."

His head fell on his chest, but a second, stronger shake brought him out of his half-sleep. He remembered he knew this lady: he had seen her that terrible day in Tours, she had been dressed and brushed in the same way. She shook him again, so hard it hurt.

"Leave me alone," he whispered. "It doesn't make sense, and anyway... I want to die. Fall asleep. Die. Go away."

The beautiful lady put her hands on his shoulders, and that shook him out of his shallow sleep again. Small hands gripped his arms with the force of iron claws, and the cold beating from them seeped through the fur covering and scalded his skin like ice.

"Sonny, please...!" she screamed.

Theo jerked his head up, suddenly sobered, and sucked a deep gulp of the frosty air into his lungs.

"Holy God, I'm going crazy..." a thought flashed under his skull, surprisingly clear and refreshing.

The vision was gone. Theo was surprised at how much it hurt him, after all he knew it was an illusion and only an illusion. The blizzard has long ceased, the deep blackness of the night has given way to the gray of the winter morning. Before the eyes of the knight, in the frosty air, the panorama of nearby Paris, lofty and majestic, was surprisingly clear and plain.

CHAPTER VI

Royal prisoner

Paris, the destination of his journey. At first, he thought it was a continuation of the delirium, but the nearby town stood unmoved and did not disappear. He realized that it must be real, just as real as the chill that was penetrating him again with all its strength. He got up from under the tree, brushed the snow off his clothes, drank the last of the booze, and rubbed his face vigorously with a piece of wool not yet stiff from his frozen breath. He had to make his last effort, and he had the impression that he would not get away even a few steps. Fortunately, the wind had stopped, he didn't have to fight it, but instead he had to fight through drifts of freshly blown snow. He had the feeling that he was going on forever and the city was not getting closer at all, but it was an illusion and he finally got to the turnpike. The streets of the capital were already busy and buzzing, churches were ringing, street vendors were praising their goods, everyone was in a hurry to go somewhere, and no one paid any attention to the tired wanderer, unsteadily heading towards the Louvre.

Theo was trying his last strength not to crash on the way. He felt as if he was dying, and all that else was rattling in his aching head was a desperate thought:

"If only I would not fall on the street... If only to come..."

He lost track of time and space, and when the gate of the royal palace finally rose before him, he felt so relieved that he also lost his breath. Sentries barred his way with halberds, and their faces, red from frost, took on a martial expression. The knight paused, pulled the gauntlet from his swollen and bruised hand with his teeth, and showed them the ring of the Beregard du Guesclin. The sentries withdrew their halberds, letting him pass with signs of respect. Theo made his way through the snow-covered courtyard and struggled to open the gate.

The dressed-up servant, carrying something down the corridor, looked at him in surprise.

"Envoy to His Majesty's own hands," grunted the outlaw, not recognizing his own voice.

Without a word, the attendant motioned him to the ajar door of the knight's hall. Theo pushed it open and went inside, no longer caring that he was breaking all etiquette. Over the table on which the map of France had been spread, the king was talking silently to the great chancellor. Probably earlier he had given the order not to disturb them, as he looked at the unexpected stranger with surprise and obvious displeasure. Theo approached the table and, kneeling down in front of the monarch, handed him the documents extracted from his lap and a velvet-wrapped deposit. He could be proud of himself. Despite all the odds, he did something that seemed impossible: he got there and delivered the package to the right hands.

The chancellor, in reaction to the sign given to him by the king, scooped up a map from the table and left.

"Take off your blanket and warm yourself by the fireplace," said Charles V roughly, breaking the seal of the connetable and unrolling the parchment.

Theo obediently removed his outer clothes, unwrapped his scarf from his face, and sat down by the fireplace. He had the feeling that he would never be warm again, and the fire burning so close to him was as frosty as the gusts of the night wind. Instead of getting warmer, he was getting colder. After a while he began to tremble and chatter his teeth like in a fever attack. Charles V, ignoring him, scanned the letter from his connetable twice with his eyes, then unsealed the document attached to the letter, studied it carefully, and looked into the opened package. Only then did he approach the knight huddled by the fire, and he looked up at him with half-conscious eyes.

"There you go," said the monarch. "I didn't think I'd see you here, outlaw. I admit that you don't lack courage. Bertram writes to me that he is injured. You hurt him?"

Theo shook his head painfully, but to his amazement he couldn't get a word out. The impatient king clapped his hands.

"Mulled wine with ginger, quickly," he instructed the page who had appeared at the sign. "You have to warm up this man, otherwise we won't learn anything from him."

The page rolled up quickly, bringing what was requested of him on a silver tray, then left, closing the door behind him.

"Sit at the table and drink it," the king ordered, pouring the steaming liquid into the goblet.

Theo dutifully drank, convinced it would kill him, but the sharp-smelling liquid he swallowed so hard at last warmed him up and restored his ability to speak.

"Where's Bertram du Guesclin?" the king repeated his question.

"In the Carmelite monastery next to Bongrais. The horse kicked him off. He's got a dislocated leg and a bit bruised, nothing serious."

"Where's the blood on your clothes?" Charles V asked distrustfully.

"My steed broke his leg on the ice. I had to pierce his heart so that he would not suffer," the knight explained, still struggling to find his voice.

The king folded his arms behind his back and began pacing the room.

"So Bertram had an accident, and you, as a good friend, of course decided to save Philip d'Evreux by bringing these documents and the signs of our childhood blood pact," he said quite ironically.

Theo looked at him hard.

"My friendship with Philip is a thing of the past," he said with an effort. "But that doesn't mean I want him to be beheaded for something he didn't do. I know very well what it means to be unfairly accused."

"How noble you are," the king sneered mercilessly.

The outlaw did not answer. He took a few more sips of the wine, feeling it slowly warm up to his fingertips. He did not like the king's bad gaze, felt as if he was cornered by an invisible enemy, and he was no longer able to fight. Anyway, he was starting to feel indifferent to everything.

"And... Count, did you finally marry this... shepherd girl or a milkmaid there?" the ruler asked him unexpectedly.

"With Bellette? Of course," Theo replied in surprise.

Charles V nodded with deep pity.

"Where did we get this," he said. "A descendant of an old noble family marries a peasant woman and probably does not see anything shameful in it."

"After all, your late father ordered me to do this and even made Bellette noble, and I..." began the outlaw, but the king interrupted him sharply:

"My unhappy father did and said many things that I don't approve of at all. He was way too good and that's why he ended up so bad. For example, he unnecessarily interrupted your execution... well, it happened. However, I'm not my father and I tell you that I'll not allow my knights to marry peasant girls. And it was not only with this act that you tarnished your name. You fraternize with boons as if you were the last bastard yourself, indeed, you consider them equal to the nobility. In this context, it's no longer surprising that you have allowed yourself to be branded publicly like a man without honor. That you were mercilessly lashed out as if you were a slave peasant yourself. Oh no, I don't want knights like you. In the afternoon, I will gather my advice and take your knightly girdle and nobility from you. If you love peasants so much, you will be one of them."

Theo rose from his chair, resting his hands on the table top.

"Bright Lord," he choked out. "I never asked for mercy and didn't think that it would come to me..."

He paused as he saw the lord's eyes gleaming with cold satisfaction.

"Save it," said Charles V. "I have already made my decision, you will not recover anything. Besides, what are you doing? I just make it possible for you to live the way you want. You will no longer have to follow the code, act honorably, sacrifice yourself for your monarch, or do such boring things. Anyway... okay, choose it yourself."

He poured a little more wine into the goblet, then pushed aside one of the portraits that adorned the walls of the room and took out from a hiding place a small box, half filled with grayish powder. He carefully measured the powder with a tiny wooden spoon and poured it into a silver dish. The wine frothed for a moment and turned a lighter color, then calmed down to its previous color.

"To use an old saying, I give you a choice between sword and scissors," he said, setting the cup on the table. "Think it over carefully and make the right decision. You have time until the sand spills out."

He pointed to a small hourglass, then left the room, leaving the outlaw alone.

Theo sat up helplessly, watching the golden flecks fall and feeling that like them his life is running out. He knew well the saying about the choice between sword and scissors, dating back to Queen Frenegond's time - it meant the choice between death and disgrace. In those ancient times, it was so shameful to cut someone's hair that even a king could lose his throne. After all, this was the case with the heir to the throne, Merovech, who, falsely accused by Frenegonde, begged his friends to kill him, when his hair was cut off as a sign of disgrace[9]. The memory of those customs has survived in the tradition of cutting the hair of convicts before their execution.

Theo slowly picked up the cup and rose from his chair. He moved his gaze over the portraits of the former kings of France hung on the walls, lingering his gaze to the portrait of John II. The artist captured the image of the king in profile, marking an expression of benevolence in the line of his mouth, alien features of Charles.

---

[9] Historical.

"You know, Sire, what's the worst?" He confided in the portrait. "That the goddamn Black Prince was right. I'm a naive, hopeless fool."

He didn't say the words regretfully, rather indifferently. He was too tired to feel anything, even the pain of disappointment, even bitterness. Everything was already distant and so muffled that it escaped his attention. All he wanted was to be able to confess before his death, but he knew it would be in vain to ask for it. In those days, denying the viaticum to convicts was still a common procedure used to restrict their punishment with awaiting condemnation beyond the grave. After all, even King John II did not allow him to talk to the priest before the planned execution, and he was not as badly disposed towards him as his son. He lay down on the bench by the wall and drank the poisoned wine.

"Our Father, Who art in heaven..." he began and broke off.

He couldn't remember what was next, despite his best intentions, so he only made the sign of the cross and closed his eyes. He was slowly losing the feeling of his own body - it was not an unpleasant feeling, especially since he expected more pains and convulsions which, according to his knowledge, always accompanied the poison. He was breathing slower and slower, his heart seemed to stop beating, the world around him was enveloped in a growing darkness. Before it finally closed over his head, he realized in a last glimpse of consciousness that he had been deceived.

*****

"You see? He chose a sword." King Charles V said to a little over ten-year-old boy who entered the knight's hall with him.

"You didn't expect it to be otherwise, my brother," the boy said respectfully. "I feel sorry for him."

The king put a hand on his shoulder.

"Don't worry about him, Louis. He'll be sleep for a while, that's all. Everyone loves him for how fearless he is, so I wanted to test his courage for myself. I admit I also wanted to see the fear and suffering in his eyes... a slim reward for my Camille. I miss her so much."

"So what are you going to do now? Are you really gonna take his belt away?" The boy asked after a moment, looking sympathetically at the sleeping forest knight.

Even now, his face showed determination and courage in the face of death, only his long, shadow-casting eyelashes felt damp - perhaps it was melted frost. It was strange that someone famous for his incredible feats and steely character could have such delicate features and appear to be no more than twenty years old.

"I don't know yet, Louis," the king ruffled his younger brother on the head. "I'll figure out what to do with it. No, I will not deprive him of his nobility. That would be petty on my part and, needless to say, ungrateful, because if it weren't for him, poor Philip would have lost his head. I have already given the order to be brought from Chatelet. I also have to send someone to Bongrais to see the fortune, there must be an indescribable mess right now, and you have to take care of the lands from which you collect taxes. The outcast's father was a Touraine seneschal, but he was unfit for the role. I'm afraid that he will not even be able to cope with his estate if someone does not help him. He's a soldier rather than a steward. We'll have to teach him discipline, teach him to obey, and maybe there will be some use for him. I'll even try to like him, because I know my father would like it, but this will be the hardest part."

"The medic should have seen him for now," said Prince Louis with concern.

"Certainly," the king agreed with him, and left to give the appropriate orders.

In addition to Bailiff, a fortunate chance favorable to the young count due to his former friendship with his father, he also sent people to Bongrais for Bertram du Guesclin, who was in the monastery, and appointed servants to look after the unexpected guest. Theo was transferred to one of the rooms in the right wing, stripped of his clothes soaked in melted snow, and laid, for the first time in so many years, in clean sheets of thin linen. Stunned by the action of the gray powder, he slept without knowing anything, and this dream, as deep as death itself, was for him the best relief from his suffering. However, the effect of the drug had to finally pass.

When he woke up, he didn't know at first where he was or why he was there. All his skin stung unbearably, scratched by a hundred combs, his head almost bursting with pain. He had a sore throat too, so much so that he could hardly swallow some of the wine that was on the table within his reach. He was apathetic and indifferent to everything. The wine lightened his mind enough to remind him of the previous day's events, the king's threat, his own desperate choice, and the sense of defeat he had felt just before he fell asleep. But it didn't matter to him anymore. He gave up. For the first time in his life.

A small page peeked into the room and, seeing that the knight was conscious, he brought the medic.

"You have been very lucky, sir," the medic said, examining him with trained hands. "There are no severe frostbites, and your breath is clean too, so your lungs are fine. There is a slight fever and your whole body is definitely in pain, but it will pass."

"It will. Like everything else in this world," Theo thought impassively, staring at the barred window beyond which the snow-covered branches of the garden trees were visible.

He regretted he had woken up, but there was no help for that, he had to face reality, whatever it was, to accept the king's sentence with all the dignity he could do. The medic left him some drink, disgusting in taste, but certainly effective, and he left, and instead a fair-haired man dressed as a servant appeared. Theo unquestioningly allowed him to drink at regular intervals the nasty recommended by the medic, who apparently believed like Prospero did - that a tasty medicine would not heal, and an effective one scuzz somebody out. This drink must have consisted of ginger, cloves and marjoram, as well as several ingredients not even known to the knight by name, but nevertheless terrible to taste.

The patience with which he took the medicine paid off - the next day he felt much better. Of course, his iron health helped a lot, an immunity that was hardly to match, and the fact that he was neither used to being sick nor to feeling sorry for himself. Along with his better well-being, impatience appeared, and if he hadn't had anything to wear, he would have got up in the morning.

"I don't want to lie anymore," he said as soon as the man looking after him appeared in the doorway. "Where's my clothes?"

"Everything will be in a moment, my lord," replied the servant, without trying to convince him. "One moment."

He left, leaving him alone. Theo could barely lie down, he wanted to be able to move so much, he even forgot that when his fever subsided, he was suffering from an excruciating hunger. After too long for him a servant appeared, accompanied by another.

"I'm Medard," he introduced himself. "I'm to be at your service now with Jacques, Count. Please take a bath."

"Excuse me?" Theo threw back the covers and stood up. "It's nice that I know your name, I won't have to treat you like household utensils, but as for the bath, I don't need any help with these matters since I was six years old."

"Such is the custom," the servants answered him, almost in chorus.

"I prefer to be indecent," sighed the knight, entering the adjacent room, in which stood a large bowl full of warm water.

He plunged into it without enthusiasm, for even the slightly warm liquid irritated his chilled skin unpleasantly, but the love of cleanliness outweighed the desire for comfort. He reluctantly surrendered to the hands of the servants, who tried to be as gentle as they could, and felt terribly stupid, especially when he thought what his forest friends would say at the sight of him. But he knew the protests would be useless - he was a prisoner rather than a guest of the place, and both servants knew it. He felt one of them touch the mark on his arm with fingertips, then run them over the scars on his back. He looked around.

The servant withdrew his hand, clearly startled.

"I'm sorry, my lord," he muttered.

"You're welcome," Theo replied indifferently. "The English gave me a few lashes the other day and there are traces. That's nothing."

He knew Medard and Jacques exchanged startled and scandalized glances behind him, but he didn't care. Slowly, he began to realize that the years of exile had made him a person belonging to no realm, above social divisions and prejudices, and at the same time the loneliest man in the kingdom. Only his companions understood him, but perhaps only because they were outlaws themselves, and the outlaws stick together. The bath refreshed him and made him feel better, and although he still did not know what the king had decided in his case, he already felt strong enough to accept the king's sentence with highbrow.

There was a knock on the door and a little boy with an armful of clothes walked in.

"Hello, Count," he said cheerfully. "By the king's order, I'm to be your page from now on. Here are your clothes."

"It's not mine," Theo finished wiping the sheet handed to him and stared in disbelief at the costly robes. "Should I put it on?"

"I think it would be advisable." Answered him humorously.

He had fiery red hair and a flat face, all freckles, and his gray-green eyes sparkled with cleverness and joy in life.

"I take your word for it, it's hard for me to sit here naked," the knight sighed with resignation. "You name somehow, my boy?"

"Ettienne de Castelle Jaloux, and I'm ten years old. Well, almost ten," the boy replied hastily.

"Oh. At this age, you already know something about life. So I won't say anything new if I find that I don't understand any of what's going on here," Theo took some pleasure in wearing a soft-weave shirt and a high-fashion caftan. "Who am I, what am I... What's this about...?"

"For now, the point is, breakfast is coming soon," said Ettienne. "And the King said that if you feel better, you should be there with everyone. And he added: 'There are people in this world that you can't even kill with an ax'."

"Very accurate statement, but exaggerated," the knight laughed mournfully. "I'll clean myself up in a moment, but all by myself, okay? I feel like the last idiot when someone gives me that."

The two servants exchanged amused glances, the wicked eyes dropped, and Theo realized with embarrassment that he was speaking in Touraine's lowland dialect. He made up his mind to watch his tongue and it was best not to speak unnecessarily at all. After leaving the room, he followed the page trailing behind him to a large hall, where usually the court gathered for joint meals. Although he felt uncomfortable in court robes and saw he was not part of this environment, he was calmer, for everything indicated that the king would not fulfill his threat. Whatever his plans for him, everything was better than the prospect of losing his knighthood.

Right in front of the hall, he literally bumped into Prince Philip heading in the same direction.

"It's good to see you!" Philip cried cheerfully, catching him in his arms. "Are you sure you shouldn't lie down yet? Heard you got here in terrible condition. I will never repay you for what you did for me."

"I did it mostly for myself. Now we're quit." Theo stepped back coolly.

Philip grabbed his hands.

"Friend, believe me, I didn't know there was an ambush prepared for you," he cried fervently, not caring who might hear him. "I had nothing to do with the plot of the Black Prince, nothing."

The friend looked at him coldly.

"What's the difference, did you have?" he asked.

"Very big."

Theo shook his head.

"Not for me," he said, and, pushing him aside, entered the room.

He hesitated at the doorway, so a little hand discreetly tugged his elbow to his place. Some of the revelers were already at the table and gossiping eagerly about various topics, the king was not yet there. The other courtiers hurried to take their seats. Charles V soon appeared and, after greeting everyone kindly, sat down at the head of the table. Soon after, the dressed-up maids began serving platters of various dishes and pouring noble liquors. Although very hungry, Theo only swallowed a few bites, forcing himself to do so. The court dishes were bizarre for his taste, they floated in sweet and greasy sauces, and the smell of spices used in them, mixed with the smell of perfumes present at the table of ladies was unbearable. And there were too many of these spices: saffron, cardamom, basil, and savory were literally floating in the air. The mere sight of the dishes on the table aroused inexplicable disgust in the forest knight, although he ate in the forest at times completely unlikely things, for example a stew made of young crows, spiced with dandelion roots, or a kind of shashlik made of squirrel meat and wild onions. Other revelers did not share his abomination to what was served to them, on the contrary, they ate a lot and with relish, and the sight of them reminded the knight of his companions, left far away, and from that moment he could not swallow anything. Once or twice he caught Philip's sad gaze, but stubbornly averted his eyes from him. The English lion, brutally carved on his shoulder, divided them like a stone wall. After breakfast (at this time in the forest, it was rather lunch, if there was anything to serve), the courtiers did not part, and began social games, without interrupting lively discussions.

"Well, they have nothing to do, they can play all day long," Theo thought sadly, not knowing what to do with himself.

He was tormented by the urge to hide from everyone, for although he apparently ignored him, he knew well that most of the conversation concerned his presence at the Louvre, and he didn't like it at all. He slowly retreated to the side and stood by the window, overcome by the urge to squeeze into the door frame and out of sight, but then Charles V saw him.

The king nonchalantly approached him.

"Having a good time?" He asked. "You must be made of steel to have recovered in two days after all this. My men passed your horse's body near Fontainbleau. If it means that you made it from there to Paris in this blizzard and survived, then you are truly worthy of your legend."

Theo forced a smile.

"It's not my merit. God gave me such a strong body, probably for a purpose," he said. "Maybe in this one?"

"Perhaps," the monarch agreed with him. "Drink now and have fun, you deserve it."

"Thank you, my head is weak. Once I drank too much, the concept broke off, and then I woke up in the dungeon chained and this rat Paulino was standing above me laughing," the knight said unceremoniously. "Sire, I need to know: what's going to happen to me?"

The monarch shrugged.

"You'll stay here," he replied dryly. "You can't leave the Louvre until further notice, but it's probably not a terrible slavery. You have to re-learn what it means to be a king's noble and knight because you have apparently forgotten it. I will not take your sword... although God is my witness, I should. Someone has bailed for you, and this gives you a chance to redeem yourself."

"Who bailed?"

Theo frowned in surprise as his gaze involuntarily searched for the prince of Navarre.

"Not Philip, I assure you," the king laughed. "Gaston Febus, if that interests you."

"Gaston de Foix? He doesn't know me!" The knight really couldn't understand anything now.

"He doesn't know. But his favorite, unbearable cousin, Fabrizio, knows you. Thanks to him, you received what can be described as a limited credit of trust. Very, very limited so beware. You'll be kept informed about your new duties, and for now, you simply have to participate in court life."

He raised the goblet and took a sip of wine. Under the cold gaze of Charles V, known as the Wise, Theo felt defeated and hung his head, seeing with full clarity what awaited him. Here he is, a bold and proud outlaw who trembled English soldiers, who faced the Black Prince as an equal, who feared no one or anything, here in the Louvre, he will be reduced to the role of a tame wolf, a toy of bored courtiers. He didn't dare to go against the king's orders, but he couldn't hide the sadness that choked his throat either. The past was crossed out, everything was decided for him and beyond. Probably none of these colorfully dressed, chipped people would understand him. After all, he was supposed to regain his position in the world, royal grace and, after all, considerable fortune, and he has the feeling as if he was only a lonely and unhappy forest animal, locked in a palace menagerie.

The king shook his head disapprovingly.

"What's that face?" He asked sharply. "What I have commanded you isn't a cause for despair, but an honor which, I testify to God and the truth, you don't deserve at all. You've been running around in the woods for too long and you're in over your head. However, our time is difficult, so it isn't right for your talents to be wasted. I don't like you, but I respect your righteousness and courage, and I believe that once your banner is formed you will surely be a good leader. Of course, this is a matter of the future, for now you must bend you to associate with people more suitable for your comrades. It's a pity that it has to be done by force."

He turned and walked over to a table where several men and two ladies were playing cards, a novelty that was quickly gaining support at the royal court. Theo felt someone nudge his thigh. It was Ettienne, stubbornly sticking to his side.

"Cheer up, sir," whispered the little page, winking mischievously at him. "It won't be too bad. A man will get used to everything if he has to."

This philosophical remark in the mouth of the nine-year-old kid made the knight laugh and had a salutary effect, because thanks to it he found his usual sense of humor, which more than once was his life-raft amid adversities. He felt that he was going to need him badly now.

"Why did the king appoint you?" he asked.

"Because no one else can stand with me, and it is said that you have experience with savages," the boy explained to him openly. "I'm supposed to be a cheeky and unbridled rogue."

"Well, there'll be two of us. And stop this 'you', just call me by name."

He patted a page on the shoulder. His red hair and all manner of being reminded him of Jean, the good thief without whom he could not imagine his band. He sensed that this little boy was in fact the only gentle creature here, lonely for some reason just like he was.

"Tough!" He thought. "I have to play with the dice that fate has pressed into my hand."

Despite this conclusion, he could not bring himself to actively participate in the court games, either that day or any of the following. Court regulars and residents slowly got used to the fact that he remained aloof, although there were attempts to stir him up a bit, and manors, captivated by his beauty and the stories circulating about him, they made goo-goo eyes at him. Theo was nice and polite to everyone, but he didn't take part in gossip or games, he was constantly lost in his own thoughts and hardly smiled.

"Grim Raven," was said of him.

Slowly the case lost its charm of novelty and everyone got used to it. The knights ignored him, considering him a renegade, the servants disregarded him, and the ladies of the court took interest in him only insofar as they tried to seduce him one by one, and as their efforts were in vain, they were very dissatisfied. In fact, it even suited him to be treated like that. He could no longer communicate with these people and did not want to, because what was important to them seemed to him a pathetic clown and he could not hide it. Every day he hated his surroundings more and more, and had it not been for the royal orders, he would have escaped from there in an instant.

Fortunately, he was soon assigned some classes. From morning to noon, he carried out exercises with the select unit of Bertram du Guesclin, and in the afternoon he taught young adepts of the art of chivalry to use the sword. He preferred to spend his free time in his chamber, in the company of a constantly chattering page. Ettienne clung to him from the very first moment. Among the pages and squires, the famous outlaw was an extremely popular figure, he was told about legends they had heard, stories about real, embellished or completely imaginary events, they sang ballads and adored him with childish, uncritical admiration. So the ginger kid felt immeasurably proud to serve him. Plus, Theo was kind to him, like an older brother, and that was new to the boy. He was an orphan of a knight who, in the heat of battle, covered the retreat of the dauphin Charles and died, saving his life. He grew up in the Louvre, but had no official guardian or property, as his father had lost everything through the war. Recalcitrant and willful, gifted with a keen intelligence, he constantly got into trouble, but he did not mind the punishment falling on his back. It didn't matter, and he was a child with no future, doomed to indifference and a complete lack of prospects. Everything changed with the arrival of Count de Bongrais at the Louvre. Without speaking to him about it once, Ettienne felt that the forest knight would not abandon him, since he had already agreed to take him under his protection once, and this sense of security was very pleasing to him.

The more he was worried to see that Theo was unhappy and downcast, though he tried to hide it from people. He followed him on the trail, watching and trying to be close at hand, despite the fact that a group of court pupils called him to their company. Theo quickly got used to this little shadow following him everywhere and only disappearing when the boys were having his lessons and he was doing military training.

"You are good and you are getting better," said du Guesclin the day he appeared on the maneuvers, still limping a little. "A knight like you really shouldn't waste himself in the woods. I'm glad that the king recognized this and that we will be able to cooperate."

Theo smiled faintly as he unhooked his breastplate.

"I got out of habit to all that junk, but apparently whoever can fight it doesn't forget it anymore," he said, taking off his helmet and smoothing his matted hair. "At first, I was afraid of embarrassment."

Connetable twisted his pockmarked face in an ironic grimace. He had just witnessed the young count deftly maneuvering his horse, at full gallop grabbing small rings on the lance's blade, placed in various, often hard-to-reach places in the courtyard.

"You? But you are a natural knight. You have nothing to worry about."

Theo shook his head slowly.

"No, Mr. Connetable," he said. "Nobody is born a knight. You'd be surprised if you knew how many knightly hearts beat in the breasts of commoners. It would be a long time to..."

He broke off suddenly, staring at the figure turned away from him, the woman who had appeared suddenly in the courtyard. Bertram du Guesclin followed his gaze, surprised at him staring at this slender figure with fair curls falling down on a wide collar light blue dress, but he did not manage to ask for anything when the knight rushed towards the girl and he grabbed her elbow with a choked cry. Courtier, surprised, turned towards him with her pretty face, embellished with dyes.

Theo released her elbow and stepped back.

"Sorry," he muttered. "I thought it was Bellette."

"It doesn't matter," replied the courtier coquettishly. "My name is Angelique, but for you I can call myself whatever you like."

The knight did not seem to hear her words at all. With his face hardened and aged, he suddenly finished taking off his armor, gave parts of it to a page that appeared out of nowhere and looked at it with a worried expression, then returned to his chamber without speaking to anyone.

Ettienne followed him in and sat in the corner to clean the armor.

"Will you do something for me?" Theo asked suddenly, never taking his eyes off the window, behind which it was beginning to snowing.

"Anything you like," replied Ettienne cheerfully.

As ordered by the knight, he addressed him directly, though only when they were alone.

"Take the letter to the Carmelite monastery in the suburbs."

The Page raised his head and looked at him sympathetically.

"The king forbade you to write and receive letters," he reminded him quietly. "This is the principle of house arrest."

Theo hit the windowsill with his fist. He hoped Ettienne wouldn't remember it. He felt helpless, trapped worse than a galley keeper, who, at least, was forbidden by anyone to try to escape and send messages secretly.

"You miss your band, don't you?" Ettienne said after a moment, polishing the breastplate with a cloth soaked in vinegar. "And your wife. I hear she is said to be very pretty and kind. Ellie, one of the lady-in-waiting, remembers how she brought Princess Isabel here and spent some time outside. Why don't you want a mistress? Here, everyone has one, some of them has several at once, and conversely, many of courtier has three or four lovers. Okay, I'm not saying anything more, but you know what? Pull yourself together, the king will finally soften and you'll be able to go to her. You are too sad. You should start having fun like everyone else and time will pass faster. I also noticed that you eat almost nothing. You can't, you won't have the strength."

"There's nothing to eat here," Theo muttered glumly, barely listening to his chatter. "Since I'm here, I have been starving all the time, and yet when I see what is being eaten here, I lose my appetite."

He looked at the boy and became suddenly concerned.

"Where did you get that bruise on your cheek?" he asked.

Page shrugged.

"I mistook Latin words and the Preceptor slapped me," he replied indifferently. "And that's good, he did not have time, there were no flogging."

"Son of a bitch!" Theo yelled, and ran out of the room as if someone were chasing him. He hated violence against children, although it was not unusual in his time.

Like the epitome of fury, he ran through the entire left wing and burst into the room where the preceptors usually reported to the king about the progress made by the boys (after all, one of them was his youngest brother), ignoring the king's presence at all.

"Listen up, you ragged paper-pushers," he began sharply. "If any of you dare to touch my page once more, even with the tip of a finger, I will shove all the teeth down his throat, do you understand?"

"Pay attention to your behavior, Count!" the king shouted, more amused at his words in the purest dialect than he would have liked to show.

"I assure you, Sire, I'm very, very aloof," the knight replied. "Because if I hadn't been, I would have screamed so much that the pictures would fall off the walls! And the young prince would have fainted from scandal if he heard how I can speak!"

"I certainly wouldn't have fainted," squeaked Prince Louis cheerfully.

"If any of you have failed at nighttime fool around or something else, do not dare to take advantage of this child, for you will remember me until your dies, or longer," Theo finished his threat, bowed to the king, and left.

This outburst brought him relief, he finally felt like that outlaw whom he had left far behind and whom he missed so much. With a happier and calmer pace he returned to the room, where the page looked up at him with surprised eyes from his work, but he asked nothing.

"Dinner will be soon," he said after a moment, setting his breastplate aside and moving to his greaves. "You probably won't eat anything again. If it goes on like this, you will starve yourself and run into consumption."

"Without exaggeration. If I really have to, I lavish me with anything. I swallow just trying not to look at what I eat, but it's really hard for me to savor the stuff they call a gourmet dish here. I swear it would be easier for me to eat a boiled rat."

He sat up in bed and sighed deeply. He did not like these joint dinners not only because of the dishes served there, but he tried to accept things just as they are. Ettienne finished cleaning greaves, then stood up and opened a drawer from under the table, revealing the writing utensils hidden there that Theo knew well they had not been there before. He smiled and gave his knight a Persian eye.

"Write," he said softly. "I have to run to town today, I'll carry it by the way, and no one will know."

He broke off as Theo spontaneously embraced him and kissed him. Unaccustomed to such symptoms, Ettienne almost burst into tears with emotion, but somehow managed to control himself. He had adored his knight before, but now that feeling had grown into an almost idolatrous worship. He didn't even dare to dream that this unlike any other man would like him, and now he knew he was truly his friend, and he knew he was honest about it.

That evening, when he returned from town, in addition to the news that he had passed the letter in the Carmelite monastery to a friar who was about to go to Touraine, he also brought a large piece of roasted goat and a loaf of black bread from the inn where the rank and file soldiers ate. The gesture meant more to Theo than just food, though for the first time since he had been here, he could eat his fill. It made him realize that he did have a friend, that he was not as alone in this hostile place as he thought. Among the outlaws, what is on the heart is also on the tongue, and in the Louvre everyone wore a mask that was better or worse and did not reveal what he really thought or felt. In such a mendacious company, there really was no place for someone like Theo, whose atmosphere of intrigue and hypocrisy literally choked out, killing every little spark of joy in life. Perhaps that was why he was surrounded by the enemy reserve on all sides. Nobody openly accused him, since provoked by the Marquis de Beauchampierre, he almost killed him in a duel, so he had a relative peace, but he had no one to exchange words with. Most of the time, he had dealt with it somehow, but there were days when he almost wished he had accepted the Black Prince's offer that would at least give him freedom of movement. At such moments of spiritual decline, he asked himself a despairing question, what exactly was the purpose of his stay at the Louvre: so that the king would have someone to torment? He was close to doing a terrible thing, willingly surrendering his sword to the king, and relinquishing his nobility for freedom. But it was a price so horribly high that he still couldn't decide to pay it. And it was even worse, on those nights, when he was digging his teeth and nails into the pillow, unsuccessfully trying to push back the image of Bellette hugging him, when, opening the window, he exposed his naked body to the gusts of icy wind, to cool the somehow choppy blood, he almost decided to take this desperate step - and in the morning he just tried to survive until the evening. Even during the day, there were times when he wanted to throw himself at the king's feet with a plea:

"Kill me or release me!" And what prevented him from doing so was not so much the fear of being ridiculed as the awareness of the futility of such an action. Charles V did not seem to be pitying. In fact, if it were not for a small page, there would be no one to cheer him up in these moments of despair.

*****

Spring came suddenly, melted the snow, made the trees green, and chirped with the sounds of birds unconscious with joy, smelled of violets and lilacs. The courtiers were relieved to throw off their thick winter clothes and spend most of their days in the gardens of the Louvre, from where they returned with glistening eyes and pink cheeks, hands full of snowdrops and anemones. Spring madness engulfed heads and hearts, although everyone knew well that spring really meant a restart of hostilities, which was no reason to rejoice. There were games and activities in the open air, the entire Louvre was divided into teams, competing in friendly tournaments in fencing, horse skirmishes, throws to the shield and even runs, with dozens of bets placed.

Theo didn't want to be part of any of this. Since it got warmer, he completely lost his will to live and spent whole days in his room, sleeping or staring indifferently at the wall. Only the king's order was able to force him to go outside. He was not even interested in the news that the bailiff sent to Bongrais had been summoned to return and report on its activities. It was already known that with an enormous amount of work he had managed to bring order to the count's affairs, so that he could easily take over his property for re-administration, but no one knew the details yet.

Bailiff was really committed to this work with all his commitment, remembering his friendship with Fabien de Bongrais and overwhelmed by a feeling of sympathy for his son, who was so hard hit by fate. Now he was returning to the Louvre, pleased with the work done and that he would finally be able to rest. The first man he saw there was Bertram du Guesclin, talking to the Duke of Navarre.

"Hello, Honore," cried the connetable cheerfully. "How was your trip? Me and Philip have just arrived, and here everyone in the inner courtyard is playing. Are you coming back from Bongrais?"

"Yes, and I would like to give the King a report," replied the Bailiff. "He's probably in the courtyard too? Well, I'll change and go there."

"We'll wait," suggested Philip, glad to postpone the meeting with his friend, who still stubbornly pretended not to see him during the meetings at the Louvre.

In the company of two men twice his age and generally respected men, he just felt more confident. He still felt guilty about what had happened to Theo, though at the same time he felt sorry for him for the fiery resentment with which he had treated him. After all, although he was the perpetrator of his misfortune, he was an involuntary one. He had hoped in his heart that perhaps in the presence of the connetable he could somehow explain it and clear the air. He cared about this friendship, perhaps even more than before.

Bailiff quickly changed his travel attire, and the three of them walked into the inner courtyard, now decorated like a tournament ground. Around the designated circle, there were amphitheatric benches on which dignitaries and ordinary courtiers sat and shouted at the participants of the tournament. Currently, a kind of wrestling competition was held, much liked in this group, although it was not too aristocratic entertainment. The clear favorite today was Hector de Guise, over six feet tall and built accordingly. He easily put on the shoulder of anyone who dared to accept his challenge to fight.

"The chevalier de Guise does what he wants with everyone as usual," said Bertram du Guesclin, looking at the two naked men, one of whom was already kneeling on the ground, shouting:

"I give up, let go!"

"You have to be insane to want to fight this bear," Philip replied, and, nudging him sideways, he pointed to one of the benches, the one on the edge of which his friend, whom he had not seen for two months, sat, accompanied by a little page.

He was changed, and not for the better. His tan had disappeared without a trace, his hair was much longer, his eyes seemed larger in a pale face with sharpened features, and the whole motionless, stooped figure expressed boundless despondency. He was probably the only one who didn't care about the game.

"Wait until the tournament is over," Philip said, stopping the bailiff who wanted to go to the royal couple right away. "The King will not listen to you now, he is too concerned with what is happening here. He likes such shows, and besides, the report can wait."

"Maybe right."

Bailiff sat resignedly on the bench next to him and the connetable, for now giving up the thought of a meal and a warm bath. Meanwhile, Hector de Guise was strolling around the square, proud as a peacock, shouting:

"Who's next? What's up, gentlemen knights, do you lack guts or are you afraid of those few spanks? I promise not to hit hard!"

The knights looked at each other, but no one was eager to take the challenge. The chevalier de Guise had already shown what he could do that day, and no one was in a hurry to become the giant's next victim. After all, those who were considered the strongest among them had already tried it, from which they emerged with a sore body and tarnished with self-love.

"Who?!" Hector continued, undaunted. "Perhaps you, lord marquis No? Or maybe you, young friend? Also not? Gentlemen, gentlemen, have a little shame! Or maybe you, an outlaw?"

Lost in thought, Theo, to whom this last point was directed, hadn't heard it at all, and he probably wouldn't have paid attention if it weren't for Ettienne, who prodded him in the thigh.

"Huh?" He asked absently. "You were talking to me?"

"I don't see any other outlaws here," Hector replied with malicious glee. "I asked if you had the courage to face me. Or maybe you'd rather not take your jacket off? Got it, got it, but you can take your time. And so we all know whose mark you wear on your shoulder and what marks are on your back. Well you were unlucky my friend. I understand that you couldn't help it... although I, for example, have a bit of honor and would rather hang myself than display such trinkets in public. On the other hand, you might think that you really liked the Welshman, since he gifted you before parting with the symbol of his country... Well, it's hard not to like such a beau."

Theo shook his head discouraged and stood up.

"I would like to draw the attention of everyone, from the Bright Lord to the cute maids, that I did not accost that donkey," he announced in a bored voice, unlacing the jacket and pulling it over his head.

Then he took off his shirt and tossed it all to his page, pale with the sensation that his freckles highlighted like blueberries in cream. He wasn't sure whether to be proud of his knight or to fear for his health, since he looked like a harmless, long-legged mosquito next to a heavily muscled cavalryman.

The courtiers, greatly excited, whispered frantically among themselves. Theo didn't really look like an opponent to Hector de Guishe, for though not much shorter, he was thin, even bony, like someone who had been starving for years. It wasn't, of course, the fault of under-eating, which he rarely did, it was just the way he was.

"Gosh, he'll swallow him for breakfast," groaned Bertram du Guesclin.

"I would not be so sure," Prince Philip said in a tone as if he wanted above all to convince himself.

"Three to one for Hector," the queen said to her husband.

"I'm betting three hundred ecus on our outlaw and I'm betting five to one," Charles V replied with a mysterious smile.

Hector looked contemptuously at his opponent's thin, hairy torso, on which gleamed the dull ancestral gorget.

"It will be a short fight," he announced loudly, hitting his right bicep with an eloquent motion.

"If you prefer..." Theo replied calmly, casually assuming a wrestling stance.

Hector attacked with a sudden lunge, the count made a slight feint, grabbed his wrist, knocked him off balance, twisting his arm with a move so strong and fast that there was no question of countering it. Then, with a kick to the knee, he forced him to kneel and plunged his fingers into the muscles of his neck just below the ear.

"Ouch!" The chevalier howled. "Let go!"

"Who won, dear?" the opponent asked him with sweet irony, still holding his grip.

"You! You won..." Hector groaned, barely breathing from the pain.

Theo laughed briefly, released him, and walked slowly to his page, turned from wonder and admiration into a living pillar of salt.

"Stop goggling your eyes like that, because it will stay like that and you will look like a toad after enema," he said, unconsciously returning to the dialect he used on a daily basis in the forest.

"It seems to me that the chevalier de Guise's did not like his breakfast," Prince Philip remarked maliciously, squinting at the speechless connetable.

He closed his mouth open in surprise and swallowed violently.

"Gee, I was kind of expecting if anyone defeated this bear it would be Count de Bongrais, but I didn't expect it to go so quickly."

"Bravo, Count!" The king cried, looking at the knight for the first time with a hint of sympathy in his eyes. "Who taught you this trick?"

Theo, who was now lacing his caftan, stopped in mid-movement.

"Who, Sire?" He repeated. "Friend. A simple, dirty, lousy peasant who smelled of garlic and onions, a farmhouse blacksmith who fell in defense of his sister. He had a purer and more loyal heart than most of the nobility I had come across in my life."

"For the first time since you've been here, you spoke a long sentence in public and you must have offended everyone in one breath," remarked Bertram du Guesclin rebuking.

"Why offend?" The knight calmly finished the lacing of the caftan. "If the cap fits, wear it. All I'm saying is that Alain never let me down, he was as faithful to me as a dog and that he died like a hero. I know that for all of you heroic deeds make sense when they are performed by the nobility, but I don't share that view. It isn't only unfair, but also simply idiotic in the world. Heroism isn't only attributed to high families, and had it not been for the sacrifice of my fence-born friends, Princess Isabella would be in the hands of the English today. I could always count on them, unlike some of my high-born friends."

"Oh God, the same again!" Philip leaped up from the bench, like stabbed with a dagger. "How many times do I have to tell you that I had nothing to do with the Black Prince's intrigues? I didn't even know this Englishman was in town!"

"Let's say," Theo growled, buckling his belt as if he wanted to tighten it around the prince's neck.

The king raised his hands.

"Enough of this," he said firmly, in that voice that made to listen. "You are to stop arguing immediately, understood? Shake your hands, now! That's an order."

The young people, frightened by the threat in his voice, hastily obeyed.

"As for your doubts, Count, Prince d'Evreux really did not hand you over." The monarch rose and slowly left the improvised stands. "If you have anyone to feel sorry for what happened to you, then sooner to me, because I, my brave outlaw, knew what the Welshman wanted to do, and I neither interrupted him, nor even warned you. And what do you think?"

"Nothing," Theo said sternly. "You are my king, Sire. King is not judged or billed."

The King smiled with amusement.

"Clever answer," he praised him and entered the palace.

"Most Bright Lord, Bailiff Honoré de Blois has returned from Touraine and asks to be heard," the marshal of the court caught up with the ruler and looked at him expectantly.

"Oh."

The king turned back to the courtyard where the bailiff was talking to the connetable. When he saw the monarch, he interrupted the conversation and turned to Theo:

"I'm going to the king. And this is for you boy."

He handed him a roll of parchment.

"From Prospero?"

The knight, having recognized the cloister's seal, broke it hastily and started reading. However, the writing was not from Father Prospero.

"Dear friend," Brother Michael wrote to him. "It is with great sadness that I inform you about the death of our venerable prior, dear to both of us, who moved to a better world at the beginning of spring. I know well that he was close to you, but the whole neighborhood mourns him no less than we do. The letter from you was delivered to us after his death, so, according to the monastic rule, I had to burn it without reading it. All I could do was let your people know that you were alive and that the king forgave you, because so much could have been guessed from the very fact of delivering the letter. Your people are waiting for your return, and I think it would be advisable for you to hurry up. Your wife will be giving birth soon, so I don't think you have any more obligation than to be with her in these difficult times. It would not be good for you, having regained your royal grace, to forget about those who love you, although the news that sometimes comes about you is such that it is hard to believe in them. Whatever the case may be, I send you my blessing and ask, son, to speak up as soon as possible. Brother Michael, a Carmelite.

Theo lowered his hand, automatically rolling the letter into a roll. The longing he was trying with all his might to suppress himself suddenly exploded in him with redoubled force, hitting him with such venomous power that it took his breath away. The King, listening with one ear to what Honoré de Blois was saying, looked at him curiously.

"...like an insect impaled on a pin," comparison gloomily flashed through the knight's mind.

"Honorable Lord, I must go home," he said determinedly. "Please understand me. My wife is about to give birth to our first child... Sire, I'll be the father!"

The king looked at him with pity, took the parchments handed to him by the bailiff and left without a word to the palace. Philip d'Evreux followed him.

"A child with a peasant girl, what an event," Charles V looked at the prince with obvious anger. "No, he's completely irreformable. There is no point in wasting time on this madman, because a little longer, and I myself will go crazy because of him! Philip, this is unbearable. I did what I could, but even the saint wouldn't last longer! I can't look at his dead face anymore! This is the first time I see a man for whom the Louvre is too tight, and who prefers the company of rude peasants to the company of the country's highest aristocracy. Philip, do you even know this peasant woman?"

"I know," the prince replied in a dejected voice.

"Pretty though?" the king unfolded one of the bailiff reports and began to read.

"A real goddess. And brave like Diana. Sire, I think... I don't want to say anything against that unfortunate maid who was her mother, but in the Bongrais they say... they say Bellette's father was actually Rene d'Artois, a close friend of the old count, and a frequent visitor to castle. It isn't completely pointless, the girl is nothing like her supposed father and very different from the peasant women I know well.

"Unless so," muttered the king, unrolling another parchment.

"God will forgive me this lie," thought Philip, staring out the window. "I would do a lot for my friends..."

"You can go, I have a lot of work to do," the king interrupted him and shut himself in his chamber.

The prince bowed and walked slowly in search of his friend.

"I care so much about your friendship, Theo," he sighed to himself. "If our life had not been such a hellishly complicated puzzle..."

He knew very well that it would never be between them as before, even if Theo forgave him, for the stigma burned on his shoulder would be a cause of disgrace and suffering for the count for the rest of his life. And there will always be someone to remind him of them. He would have given up whatever to be able to turn back time and save the outlaw from the terrible blow that struck him, but that was not possible and he fussed about it.

Meanwhile, Theo went to his chamber to wash and change clothes before dinner, though he was sure he would not be able to swallow anything. He decided that he would have a decisive conversation with the king that day, but for now he had to hold back and get over this joint meal. They were all a real torture for him, and now it was going to be even worse, because he knew that he would not be able to hide his tormenting feelings, which would cause malicious looks and low-noise remarks.

"You know, Ettienne," he said. "I don't think I've ever changed as much as I do now. Why are you looking like that?"

"I'm sad you'll leave here and I'll be alone again."

The little page tried to speak casually, but the corners of his mouth involuntarily curved downward. Theo stroked his red head.

"Would you like to come to Touraine with me?" he asked.

"Oh yes!" Ettienne called hotly.

The knight laughed, putting his arm around him.

"And you will not mind the company of simpleton?" he asked teasingly. "You will not get to know the most wonderful man in the world, Father Prospero, but others will be there."

The Page, laughing, shook his head.

"Okay, I'll take you with me."

Along the way, he encountered a group of animated gossipers heading in the same direction and stopped to let them pass. Before he knew it, the girls surrounded him in a vibrating circle.

"Ah, dear Count, we are all impressed by your victory," they chattered one by one. "Each of us would like to express our admiration in a slightly more specific way than words. You are worth every sacrifice on our part."

"Wait a minute, my ladies, I'm married!" Theo cried, having understood with some difficulty what they meant. "And what are these ideas, anyway? Have you no shame?"

"But we have," said Ellie, the boldest of the courtiers. "If you wish, Count, I'll be ashamed all the time."

"Ellie! You're only sixteen and such things already? At your age?"

Theo's eyes widened, because even though he had seen many things before, this girl, a plump brunette with always laughing eyes and a razor-sharp tongue, did not stop from surprising him.

"Just at my age," replied the courtier, as if it meant the same thing; "Should I wait until I'm old and ugly? Better to give to the boys than to the worms, dear Count."

The knight ran out of words, raised his eyes in a silent sigh, and hurriedly entered banquet, thus freeing himself from a company that is too casual for his taste.

"Your wife is prettier than Ellie?" asked the little page who was stepping on his heels curiously.

"Ten times," Theo assured him, sitting down in his seat.

The dinner went on and on, he could barely sit down as his thoughts were with Bellette, now more than ever in need of his company. He felt guilty, though there was not a speck of his guilt in what had happened and in the fact that he was imprisoned here against his will. This time he couldn't really eat, he couldn't swallow a drop of wine. After dinner, as everyone else began their usual games, the king finally took pity on him and walked over to him.

"I have read the reports provided to me by Honoré de Blois," he said. "It looks like he has everything in order, and there is no outstanding debt on your estate. You can go back there and start forming your banner which I already mentioned to you... I also allow you to hang any English you find in your hands in Touraine... although I don't think you need such a permit. You always knew what to do when you came across one.

"Oh, my lord, I will not fail your confidence," Theo said with such fervor that the king smiled. Since Count de Bongrais entered the Louvre, he had not seen him so brightened.

Bertram du Guesclin, who passed by, stopped.

"And you see, it all turned out well," he said kindly. "Driving in a blizzard paid off, right?"

"It was close and I would have fallen like your unfortunate horse."

Theo smiled as he remembered that hellish journey from which he only miraculously escaped with his life. He wasn't sure how he had done it himself, and he remembered with horror what he had gone through: the terrible cold, the wind, the blizzard, the incredible fatigue, and the sight that had saved him from freezing in a relieving sleep by his intervention. He did not confide in this one to anyone. He wasn't sure if it was his mother's shadow that had come from the underworld to save him, or if he was delirious with fatigue and fever, but he preferred not to ask anyone.

"Then you will come home, but not soon. You have to stay until the end of the training," said the connetable, patting him on the shoulder amiably. "It's only less than two weeks, you will definitely hold on somehow."

"If necessary..." agreed the knight without enthusiasm, but understanding that he must follow the discipline imposed by the commander-in-chief of the troops so as not to jeopardize his authority.

"Just give up on this fraternization with the peasants. It's not good for your health. And forget your lawlessness and live as befits a loyal knight of your ruler," the king advised him. "Come on, Bertram, we need to talk about the Spanish campaign."

They left, and Hector de Guise approached Theo for a change.

"I just wanted to say you really impressed me," he said cheerfully. "You have hands of steel. I hope you are not angry about these few words, I just wanted to provoke you, but now I would be honored if you would give me your friendship."

He extended his hand as large as a frying pan to him. The count hugged her warmly.

"I have no grudge," he said. "And it's always good to get a new friend."

"Hope you'll be at my wedding. I'm marrying Denise de Mercier." Hector was very pleased, his face beamed with kindness, and he obviously had no regrets about losing. This really impressed the young count, because he knew very well that the ability to lose classy was extremely rare.

"You're going to have a wonderful wife, chevalier, congratulations," he said.

He remembered the male dressed baroness, raised as his own father's squire, yet full of mysterious charm.

"I'll try to come," he promised.

He would not be sure if he would succeed, for he knew well how unpredictable life was and he did not build any castles at the royal grace. It was not important anyway. The important thing was that he would soon return to Touraine, to her friends and beloved wife, and that he would finally be able to offer her everything she deserved.

"Finally." He whispered, relishing the pleasant feeling that a series of misfortunes seemed to be endless, it's over.

And he ignored the little voice whispering in his soul that perhaps this was not the end at all, but only the beginning.

Honor Above All

All

Book Three

CHAPTER I

Return

It was a warm spring day. On days like this, horseback riding is a real pleasure, especially when you've spent the whole winter locked up, even in the Louvre. Theo struggled to control himself not to scream for joy, but the little page riding beside him was screaming without any embarrassment.

"Why are there so many empty villages on the way?" he asked at one point.

"Hunger, plague, war... variously," the knight replied. "It's sad, but you can't help it. Don't lean out of the saddle all the time or you'll fall."

"I can't," Ettienne admitted honestly. "I'm so glad that I'm vibrating. No one has ever wanted to take me home, they said that

I was brazen and disobedient, and that you never really know what I was thinking. And you are different."

The knight smiled at him.

"I'm brazen and disobedient too," he said. "That's why we fit together. But wait until you meet my brother and the rest of the boys. Colorful company, I'm telling you."

"Gosh, do you know how much I've heard about them and you so far?" The boy was feverish. "It would never occur to me that I'd meet you one day, and even more so that I'd become your page. This is the greatest thing that has happened to me in my life."

"Because you live too short," Theo laughed, but he was very pleased to hear something like that.

He hadn't realized how famous he was and how much people talked about him, it was only this kid who made him realize it. He was glad that he had decided to take him. However, most of all he was glad that he had finally escaped from the Louvre, and breathed in the spring air, so different from the atmosphere of the royal court, saturated with dust and fragrances. He did not think about how he would live now that his name had been cleared, he only thought about his regained freedom and reveled in it as if the dark shadow of the Black Prince had never hung over his life. And yet he was somewhere there, he certainly did not give up his intrigues, although in France he was on shaky ground. Now Theo wasn't thinking about him. Traveling in the company of a freckled as turkey egg page was so pleasant that it would be a shame to spoil it by dwelling on the wrongs suffered.

When the well-known inn "Under the White Swan" appeared in the distance, he decided to make a short stop. You could find out what was going on in the area at this inn, and Theo hadn't heard of it for a long time. Having tied their mounts next to the others in the stable, the knight and his page went inside, where a dozen people, most often of suspected condition, were already sitting at the worn tables.

The innkeeper, an elderly fat man with a dark complexion and black hair, lightly flecked with gray, left the drunkards he was serving to his own fate and bowed to the newcomers, wiping his hands with an apron as dirty as holy earth. Knights came here very rarely, mostly peasants and various vagabonds were the whole clientele. Damasus Magyar, as he was called, gladly welcomed the opportunity for better earnings.

"How can I help you, sir?" he asked humbly.

"Come on, Damasus, don't you recognize me?" Theo exclaimed, amused.

The innkeeper finally looked at his face, and his eyes widened.

"Oh, is that you, Wolf? I didn't recognize you in those rich robes," he said finally. "Damn, you've changed... But it's good that you come back. We were wondering what was happening to you and no one knew where you were gone."

Theo waved his hand.

"It would be a long talk," he said. "Don't you know what my people are doing?"

The innkeeper looked at the back room.

"Sometimes I know," he replied. "They've been sitting here drinking since morning. Be careful, they are already stiff."

"Not the first time!" The knight shrugged his shoulders carelessly, pushed the door from the room and went inside. Behind him a small page slipped in like a shadow.

Outlaws sitting at a low table and shouting over something, fell silent at the sight of the newcomers, as if struck by lightning. They did indeed seem to be at least drunk. There were a few empty jugs and overturned cups on the table, a recently served roast goose was smoking on a tin plate - a rarity in the pre-harvest season, certainly very expensive, although at first glance it was obvious that it must be old and hard like a sole.

"Hello guys," Theo said. "Why are you so choked as seeing the devil in hennine?"

"Uhm..." Beregard stuttered, not knowing what to say.

"Who do we see here," Pierre interrupted, softly and venomously. "Finally, my dear brother-in-law showed up, dressed as for some wedding... First, you don't give a sign of life for a number of months, and then he'll show up like nothing happened, right? But hello, welcome, we bow to the ground."

A long knife suddenly flashed in his hand. Jean and Francois, who were closest, rushed to hold on to him.

"Stop it, Pierre, you can't," Francois argued mildly, while Jean tried to remove a murderous tool from his fingers.

"Why the hell I can't?!" his friend screamed, distracted from his reasoning.

"You can't take a knife out at your own brother-in-law."

"My God, why is that?" Pierre was surprised honestly and finally let go of the knife.

"I have no idea," Jean admitted. "But somehow you misbecome to do it."

"Are they always so calm?" Ettienne asked in a whisper.

"More or less," Theo replied, neither surprised nor even less terrified by such a greeting.

"Who is this child, chief?" Millot asked curiously. "Haven't you gotten into some, um, trouble?"

"No, as far as I know," the knight replied calmly. "Meet my page. This is Ettienne."

Gwidon pulled the boy towards him, to an empty seat on the bench.

"Sit down, skinny," he said with drunken affection. "Eat something, you deserve something along such a path, and also in the company of our leader."

The boy eagerly sank his teeth into the goose leg he was given. Indeed, he was already very hungry, so he bit tastefully, although even his healthy young teeth could hardly cope with the hard meat due to age and overcooking. Meanwhile, Theo counted his eyes at the company at the table and frowned.

"Where's my brother and Bellette?" he asked sharply.

"Tristan and Preziosa stayed in the woods," Armando replied. "As for your wife, you... you really don't know?"

"If I had known, Gypsy donkey, I wouldn't have asked, it must be logical," growled the knight, leaning his hands on the table. "Talk!"

"You are naughty. I took offense," said Armando, pouting and turning his head. When he drank a little, he got very offensive.

Theo leaned across the table and grabbed him by the caftan across his chest.

"Talk!" he repeated.

"No," the acrobat insisted.

"Leave him. Bellette wants to join a convent. She's already started novitiate, but don't count on us to tell you where," Pierre said firmly, pushing him away from Armando.

"This is my wife!" Theo yelled furiously.

"Your wife? She was your wife when you were one of us. But you aren't anymore. You are an ugly nobleman again, and you have nothing more to do with us."

"Oh, yes?! Ettienne, out the door, now! I'm the one who lives like a monk all winter so as not to compromise my marriage vow, and she makes fun of me? Do you know what celibacy is at the Louvre? It's like starving yourself in a pastry shop! But that's nothing, I'll bring this clown to the path of the marriage obligation, let me just sort out with you, you rascals. I show you right here!" The knight looked around nervously for something heavy.

"Don't show us, we're not curious," Beregard said before Theo grabbed the oak stool and began to flail it like he did in his best times.

If his former companions had been sober, they would not have experienced such a disastrous defeat, but they were not, so they could not defend themselves against the blows falling on them from everywhere. After committing the massacre, Theo walks out of the inn.

"We're going to the castle," he ordered, untie his horse. "There I will consider what to do next. Something like that, a convent!"

Ettienne could barely keep up with him. He had never seen him like this, though he had witnessed his knight's rage one day at the Louvre and knew what he was capable of then. For the time being, he decided, it would be wise to keep silent and stay in the shadows until the Count will simmer down.

They arrived at Bongrais in the late afternoon. The castle was partially restored, although it was still damaged by the war, servants were bustling in the courtyard, welcoming them with humble respect and taking care of the horses without asking anything. Theo, paying no attention, entered the castle and headed for the knight's hall. Renovated and cleaned at the behest of the bailif, it gave the impression that no enemy had ever resided there. At present, only Philip d'Evreux sat in the armchair behind the table, tapping his fingers on the tabletop.

"Don't get up," Theo said, tearing his cloak off his shoulders and tossing it into the corner. "Let me be under an illusion for a moment that you will be responsible for this whole mess. Ettienne, order us the wine and ask why none of these slackers didn't take care of my guest. Also, make sure we get something to eat."

The boy nodded and left. Philip was staring at his friend through narrowed eyes.

"I see you are in an exceptionally good mood" he noted. "You are bursting with joy like a client of an executioner. Something wrong my friend?"

Theo snorted angrily and lunged into one of the armchairs, nearly crushing the carved railing. When he got angry, he became unbearable even for his loved ones, but Philip did not mind. He knew how to use the emotions of those who could not control them, and he enjoyed discovering them in seemingly composed people. True, Theo was never like this.

A maid in a blue dress and a stiff cap brought a large pitcher of wine and tin cups.

"Here's to you," the count muttered, filling the cups and pumping his in one gulp.

"Slower, or you'll get drunk," said Philip.

"Big deal. It would do me good after all this. Something like that. They treat me like that after all I've been through... They said I'm not one of them anymore, do you have any idea? I can't believe it. And my wife went to the convent, just like that."

He shook his head and poured himself more wine.

The prince took a sip from his cup.

"Cause for concern," he observed calmly. "Prove them wrong. As for yours beloved, don't worry too much. I will get you the address of the convent where she is staying, but you too must do something for me."

Theo shrugged.

"I know, nothing is for free," he grunted.

Ettienne entered, leading a servant behind him with a tray full of bread and roasts.

"Sit and eat," the count ordered him.

"It isn't customary for a page to eat at the same table with its master," the boy protested, glancing at the unmoved prince.

Theo cursed and, seizing him by the edge of his jerkin, forced him to sit in the chair next to him.

"Here I decide what is accepted and what is not," he said. "And you have to listen to me like a father or I'll beat your ass."

"Of course, Dad," Etienne replied hurriedly, moving a copper plate over to him and placing a batch of bread and roast on it. Philip gave a short laugh.

"You're both worth each other."

The count poured himself and him a fiery drink. He liked that brown-haired prince with such a deceptively boyish face and a child's innocent gaze that would deceive anyone who didn't know him but didn't trust him. It was by no means the result of Adeline's intrigues - it was just that Theo had ceased to trust anyone.

"What's your business with me?" he asked, feeling his blood warm dangerously under the influence of the wine.

Philip set down his cup and nipped off a piece of roast.

"It's not all my business," he began. "This is a matter for all of France, my friend. Listen, while you're still sober enough to understand anything: our situation is very bad, no doubt about that. We cannot afford internal quarrels. Remember when the late King John put Count de Foix in Chatelet?"

Theo nodded.

"Sure. After all, all of France fulminated about it. The affair of sir de Bucy, it was a feudal tribute on behalf of Bearn. I just don't understand what that has to do with it now."

"It has. Febus is devilishly proud, though he is actually quite a Frenchman," the prince sighed a little wearily. "He's going to Paris these days to talk to the king. This conversation can end quite badly, as always when two characters like them come into contact. I know from a reliable source that Febus is going to stop at Bongrais on the way. Talk to him from the heart, let him not bring out his old regrets now. King John was impetuous, and he also imprisoned my father for some time, although he had no right to do so."

"No offense, but your father is a truly unique schemer."

Ettienne was busily chewing, twitching his ears and glancing at both men with curiosity about the natural gossip.

"It's not about him now. If Febus doesn't get along with Charles, it will be really bad." Philip lowered his eyes to the table. "Navarra will support France's efforts to regain independence, I also know that the vast majority of dukes are faithful to the crown, but without the help of the Bearnesians we will be seriously weakened. Febus has nothing against you, on the contrary, he likes you because of the help you have given the Blue Falcon. Convince him not to argue with Charles about the past. It's really important..."

"...So, you turn to an outlaw for help," Theo finished sarcastically, squinting his smile.

The prince snorted angrily.

"You are unbearable," he said sharply. "Your good name and property have been restored, are you still not enough? Don't you know we have a war?"

"Oh, that explains why so many armed men are hanging around. And I, stupid, thought they were sick in the head."

The count poured himself more wine and sipped it slower, savoring its taste. Philip stared at him, finding no more words. He felt as if he were speaking to a deaf man, and he barely restrained himself from banging his fist on the table.

A servant peeked into the room.

"Lord, there is a retinue coming to the castle," he said.

Philip groaned silently, clutching his head.

"Theo, for God's sake, it's probably him, he can't see me here," he blurted out in one stroke. "I've to leave this place unnoticed. Someday I'll explain why, but now..."

He jumped up from the table and hurried out.

"It's not a castle, it's a lunatic asylum," Theo laughed, and left too, calling for servants along the way.

The wine was buzzing in his head, he felt unhealthy excitement, and to his embarrassment, he wanted to sing something very playful. Through the open gate, he saw the approaching retinue, a colorful procession of many people, similar to the one he had already seen in the streets of Paris. He smiled to himself - it was so long ago...

Suddenly he shook his head and rubbed his eyes violently. The man who rode at the head of the retinue on a magnificent coach, dressed in expensive robes, was undoubtedly the Count of de Foix, and there was no point in staring at him, but a huge brown bear trotted along beside his horse. A tiny monkey in a red jacket sat on its back and played with a silver bell.

The horse's hooves sounded on the drawbridge, and Febus set his horse down in the courtyard in front of Theo.

"Careful, Avenger, your eyes will fall out of your head," he warned him with a laugh.

Theo shook his head again.

"Oh boy, I see a bear," he said finally. "I admit, I drank a little, but to see the bears?"

Gaston de Foix jumped off the saddle. Despite the already clearly marked carcass, he moved very skillfully.

"Don't worry, it's real," he said. "If you're not sure, touch it, it won't bite."

Theo reached out and tugged the bear uncertainly behind the ear. The animal responded with a guttural grunt, then began lazily scratching its hind leg at the drooping dewlap. The monkey squawked, jumped down onto the stone slabs and climbed onto its master's shoulder.

"I like animals. They are more trustworthy than men," said the Count de Foix, almost defiantly.

"Let the lightning strike me, it's a good thing I've never hunted a bear, but mostly because they've never been around Bongrais," Theo finally shook his head. "Please go to the chambers. Supper has just been served and the servants will prepare the rooms and take care of the horses."

A slender figure of a woman in a dark green dress and a golden tiara on her loose hair stepped out of the shapely carriage. Febus offered her an arm and led her to the castle.

"Please rest, Countess. Ettienne, make sure that we are not lacking anything here," said the host, realizing, not without a certain amount of self-mockery, that the little page would take better care of everything than he did. He had long lost the role of the "master of the estate".

Febus helped the lady sit up and looked at him mockingly.

"Don't strain yourself with this kindness," he said. "We're going to call each other by name, okay? This is convenient. Coming back to the point, this isn't my wife, but a lover. Lady Agnes stayed at home. I prefer to be away from her, while Marguerita is happy to accompany me everywhere."

He kissed his companion's hand, who replied with a shy smile. She was very pretty, although it was known that she did not come from a noble family. Together they followed the confused host to the banquet hall.

"It makes no difference to me," he said, pouring wine to his guests. "I never interfere in other people's private matters. Have some food, lady. They will also give you fruit and sweets."

He himself started to eat, because he had no time for it because of his quarrel with Philip.

The servants, driven by a resolute and indispensable page, rolled up like boiling hot water, the guests ate and drank with relish, occasionally offering a morsel of a bear lying on the floor. The monkey first jumped on the table, then grabbed a red apple from the huge platter and hid with it in the corner.

Theo watched her actions with some surprise. He had never dealt with monkeys before, only magnates like Count de Foix could afford such a domestic pet, immensely expensive and difficult to breed. Then he shifted his gaze to his guests. There was no doubt that Febus was truly impressive: very tall and broad-shouldered, with a wavy mane of coppery gold hair, he did indeed appear to be a lion. That's what he was called: The Lion of the Pyrenees. Perhaps it was a slightly exaggerated nickname, but not too much - Febus had not only a lion-like appearance, but also courage. Although he was quite young, for he was only thirty-five, he was already a kind of national legend, which seemed to spoil his character a bit: he was delicious, willful and half crazy, as was said. Theo had no idea how to start a conversation with him about the king, especially since he was not a born diplomat like Philip, for whom a similar conversation would have been no problem. So why didn't Philip want to talk to him? There was a mystery about it that he didn't even try to find out.

One of the servants peeked into the room,

"Forgive me, Count, but some wretch has broken in here," he said, clearly embarrassed. "He threatens us with a knife and claims he's your brother."

Theo frowned.

"So, he probably is," he said sternly. "Haven't you heard that we're all brothers? The priest did not speak during the sermon? Let him in."

What the servant thought upon hearing this speech he left to himself, but it was probably nothing flattering to his master, judging by the expression on his face. In any case, he was gone, and then a weather-beaten, curly appendage in frayed clothing, a knife tucked in his belt, and a bow slung across his back, burst into the room.

"Why didn't you come for me, you rat?!" He screamed in a thin voice, completely ignoring both guests. "Are you going to disown me now?! You won't succeed that easily!"

Febus and his companion stopped eating, staring at him curiously.

"Oh, not at all" Theo replied calmly, in a rural dialect from around Touraine. "I just knew you'd find me yourself. Dear guests, here is my younger brother, Tristan de Bongrais. Sit down and eat, kid, and don't be in a pother over it."

"We know each other," said the Count de Foix, grinning. "You were the page of John II, right?"

"Old days," the boy replied shortly, sitting down next to his brother.

Febus poured himself more wine.

"Nothing like family, right?" He said. "I prefer my dogs. They are faithful, honest, and most importantly, they don't speak back."

He was a little drunk, but he continued to drink more, ignoring Marguerita's warning looks. Theo had no intention of interrupting him. He could see clearly that his guest had some kind of worry, which he did not want to confide in anyone, and for all worries "there is nothing like get stewed", as his forestry used to say. He was no longer touching the pitcher himself. And so he drank more than he should, since his head wasn't strong and he wanted to stay sober. Unlike him, de Foix made every effort to get drunk, and he succeeded so thoroughly that when Ettienne returned with the news that the guest quarters had been prepared, he could no longer get up from his chair by himself. Marguerita with the knight from the count's entourage led him to the bedroom and returned a moment later.

"I'm sorry about my master, he's in a bad mood lately," she said softly. "He doesn't usually act like that."

Theo smiled at her.

"Don't worry, my lady," he said respectfully. "I understand it well. Sometimes things go wrong for a human being."

Marguerita replied with a shy and a little tired smile.

"He's a good man, he only suffered a lot and that's why he's a bit weird. With permission, I'll go to bed."

She curtsied gracefully and left, followed by a little page. The bear got up and lumbered after her, carrying the sleeping monkey on its back.

"This Febus is crazy about keeping all kinds of pets in the house," Tristan said between one bite of roast and another. "He was in Paris once with this bear. He caused panic in the streets! What is he doing here, other than getting drunk?"

"Oh, brother, I feel he's getting me into some kind of row, but don't ask which one, because I don't know yet," Theo sighed, resting his head on his hands.

Tristan smirked with only one corner of his mouth.

"Because you also have a peculiar gift for various quarrels," he noted. "Anyone can tell you that. Why haven't you made a sign of your life all winter?"

"I wrote to you two times! It's not my fault the letters didn't arrive!" Theo said indignantly.

His brother laughed eagerly.

"How did we know about this? We thought you forgot about us. Poor Bellette finally broke down and went to a convent. She is now a novice and wears a facial habit."

"I'll show her the habit, just let me settle the matter of Count de Foix," the knight promised him gloomily. "And you go to sleep, you loony. Ettienne will show you the room, and we'll have a more suitable outfit for you tomorrow. You are Viscount de Bongrais now, not the brother of a swamp outlaw."

"Hallelujah," Tristan said, drank some wine and left with the page.

"Do you sometimes get the impression that my brother has a bad head?" he asked him on the way.

"He's a bit weird, but I like him. He's a great man," Ettienne replied firmly.

"Probably. He can be liked," muttered Tristan maliciously, scowling at him.

He was curious as to where this freckled boy had gotten along with his brother, but decided to save the questions for later. He really wanted to sleep.

Theo got up very early the next day, but Tristan was on his feet and tried on the clothes brought by the servants. It was a tad too big, but whole and clean and elegant.

"I can finally look human," he said when he saw his brother. "What is this Bearnian doing here?"

"He's going to talk to the king, and I have to convince him to make an alliance with him," Theo replied, sitting down on his bed. "Philip d'Evreux asked me. I have no idea why he won't do it himself."

Tristan shrugged.

"I have an idea," he said lightly. "Everyone knows the Count de Foix hates the King of Navarre and all his family. The thing is that the king's sister fell in love with Febus at first sight, so he poisoned the count's first wife so that Agnes could marry him. Febus only married her to torment and humiliate her. He spills all his feelings on the lover, that Marguerita, who is said to be a living portrait of his first wife, and on the bastards who were born with her. Navarre hates and is afraid to think what would happen if Philip acted as the champion of his alliance with Charles, think, Agnes' own nephew."

Theo stared at him with his mouth open.

"What a fix..." he finally groaned, half in horror, half in admiration. He would never have thought of such a peculiar revenge.

Tristan smirked.

"And you see, younger siblings also come in handy sometimes," he said, fastening his belt.

Washed and properly dressed, he finally looked like a young man in his sphere should look.

Theo sighed and decided to go over the problems of the Lion of the Pyrenees.

"Take my page and the two of you have a look at our new shack," he said. "Don't bother me today. I must have this conversation with Febus, and it might not be easy. Then we'll think about how to have fun in three by taking advantage of the reversal of bad luck. If you are hungry, ask the cook, he will feed you, otherwise I'll talk to him. In general, do what you want, you can even burn down the whole damn castle, I won't tell you a bad word."

"You don't like your ancestral home?" Tristan was surprised.

His brother shrugged.

"The blood of the murdered screams at me from every stone," he confessed reluctantly. "I couldn't sleep. Besides... I don't think I'm fit to be a count anymore. I feel suffocated in these walls and in this role that I have become used to. Okay, run now."

Leaving himself alone, Theo sat for a moment to sort out his thoughts, then went down to the kitchen and ordered a suitably sumptuous breakfast to be prepared for his guests. However, it had to wait.

Count de Foix left the guest rooms when the sun was high in the sky. His eyes were bloodshot and he was clearly struggling with a heavy, persistent hangover.

"For me, only sour milk with tarragon," he asked hoarsely. "Is Marguerita up yet?"

"A long time ago," Theo replied. "The lady of your heart is now looking at the horses in my stables. I wonder what she will find there, I don't know what is in them. I only got here yesterday and I have no idea yet."

Febus took a sip of his milk and grimaced.

"Then you have a lot of nice surprises ahead of you." He remarked, setting the cup aside.

"Come what may," Theo decided to get straight to the point. "They say you're going to talks with King Charles. I would like to know: will you support him? No hedging."

The Bearnian smiled crookedly, feeling the pounding in his head, and reached for salutary milk again.

"You're a real patriot, so you probably want me to do it," he said. "For the sake of France and so on. See, the problem is that one of us will have to submit to the other. Why would it be me?"

"I don't know," Theo replied honestly. "However, you could save these disputes for a more convenient time. The King of France cannot give way to you, as you may understand yourself that he must now have the decisive word. And after the war, you can start over, what the problem?

"You have a fun way to put a case. I'll tell you in secret that I didn't intend to seriously oppose Charles' authority, I understand that in a war there must be one army and one commander, but I'm making a condition. Here is my squire, Ernataun, imprisoned in the royal property not far from here. I want you to release him.

He's not only my squire, he's also my unrighteous brother, and I care about him very much."

"I don't understand. Can't you just demand that the king let him go?"

The Bearnian shook his head.

"Not if there is to be an agreement between Charles and me," he explained. "Officially, I don't even know that he is there and I suspect that Charles would also deny it. So what, will you do it? Can I have your word?

"You have my word," Theo sighed. "I'll set him free. And you will agree with the king?"

"I'll agree, but not immediately. For now, I'll pretend I'm against. But don't worry: I'm just going to tease."

Febus felt better at last and carefully took a bite of one of the apples on the table. He chewed them slowly, noting with satisfaction that the sweet and sour taste had somewhat mitigated the effects of last night's overuse of alcohol.

"By the way," he added. "Don't do political intrigue anymore. You don't have the skillful hand for this."

"I know."

The Count de Bongrais nodded solemnly, glad that Febus had not thought of asking him why he was talking about it. He was truthful by nature, and Beregard even once said:

"Lying yourself out something is really not your strongest point."

He thought that Febus was definitely lovable, and he was pleased to add that he and the Count de Foix were somewhat alike. In any case, they had the same square jaws and wide-set eyes. They had to be chained, although they did not know it, which would not be such a novelty among the nobility. He decided he liked him and smiled warmly.

"Shall we go hunting?" He asked. "A ride in the fresh air will do you good for a headache."

"But not for bears." Febus said.

"Not for bears. And neither for the monkeys," Theo cheerfully agreed. "And to forestall possible doubts, I'll add that I don't shoot dogs or even wolves. As the English say, because like attracts like. They call me the Wolf of Touraine when they want to be polite, of course, because at other times they call me Mad Dog."

"You must have bitten them well," laughed the Count de Foix coarsely.

The Blue Falcon told him about Theo, but only when he was able to judge for himself that he found that this man rarely corresponds to his legend. When he left Bongrais with his men after a few days, he did so with real regret and felt remorse that he had placed such a tough condition on his new friend. But the flip fell, and besides, despite his sympathy for Theo, Ernataun was much closer to him, and as the only family member he trusted and as a friend. Roidon, where he was imprisoned, was not very heavily guarded, but Febus cared much more than he wanted to show, and he could not have erased everything with an ill-considered action, especially since he did not inform Theo about the reasons for Ernotauna's imprisonment, which it was not merely malice on the part of the king.

Immediately after his departure, Theo took the two boys and walked with them to the lakeshore. Then he sent Tristan for his comrades-in-arms, preferring not to reveal to his page the path through the marshes, at least not yet, so he stayed with him under the Tree of Love. Friends, gathered by Tristan, even came quite willingly, because, although they did not want to admit it out loud, they missed the former leader a bit and for the adventures they had experienced together.

"So, what do you want, renegade?" Pierre asked irreconcilably on behalf of everyone as soon as they arrived at the meeting place.

"I need your help," said the knight calmly, dropping the threat lurking in this question. "I have to complete a task that will be impossible without your help. Yes, I could hire someone, but I have found that I don't work with anyone as well as with you. We have always acted as one body..."

"When I listen to such nonsense, I get nauseous," growled Pierre, sitting across from him on a root sticking out of the ground. It was a good sign - if he hadn't considered complying with his brother-in-law's requests, he would never have sat down in his presence.

"I need to release a man from prison," Theo continued. "It won't be very safe, and in addition we may expose ourselves to the king, which is indifferent to you, but to me it means trouble."

"Wait a minute, not so fast," interrupted Beregard. "He just rehabilitated you, and you already want to spite?"

"Not to spite. I cannot tell you what it is about, but although the king will certainly not appreciate it, the success of our action will have an impact on the fate of France," explained his friend as convincingly as possible.

"I don't care about the king," said Millot bluntly. "But France isn't one ruler or another, it is our homeland. It doesn't matter how dangerous this trip will be. If it is to help our troubled country..."

"When will you shut up?!" Pierre shouted at him. "It was said that I'm talking and you are waiting to see what will come of it!"

"Why are you so important?" replied Millot, whose highlander nature hated ruler over him.

"Don't argue, just say, will you help me or not," Theo said impatiently.

He had forgotten how quarrelsome and incompatible his friends were. Like true Gauls, they never missed an opportunity for any dispute, and they could argue on any subject. But it was felt that they really wanted to have another adventure with their leader, and if they did not say it directly, it was only out of pride. He looked at them and suddenly became concerned.

"Where's Jean?" he asked sharply.

"Um..." Francois stuttered. "Jean went to the village next to Lottaire Castle. He has a girlfriend there, a washerwoman at the baron's, and the two of them are silently robbing him. He hasn't figured it out yet."

The Camill de Lottaire estate bordered on Bongrais, and for centuries, neighbors had argued over a piece of land between their estates. Theo remembered this with some difficulty. The baron was, as far as he remembered, a natural bastard, but he could also take matters into his own hands without looking back to the courts. His "castle" actually did not deserve such a name, because it resembled the estate of an enriched merchant, but everyone called it that, not wanting to risk.

"He always came back before dawn, maybe something happened to him?" Gwidon worried.

"Maybe they finally caught him?" Beregard whispered, as if he was afraid to make such an assumption aloud.

Pierre jumped up from his seat.

"Theo, wait until we find Jean," he said. "We will talk later."

"Not a chance," the knight said indignantly. "It's as much my business as yours. I go with you, whether you like it or not."

"We don't want to, but we acknowledge you as leader, so we have to... you know," concluded Pierre awkwardly.

"Come on? What do I know?"

In the heat of the argument, he had completely forgotten little Ettienne, who, keeping prudently behind him, followed them on his ponytail. Soon they were galloping down the road to Lottaire. As it turned out, they made it just in time. Their red-haired companion stood under a branch of a great oak tree, his hands tied behind his back. There was a trial in the village - two peasants were already standing under the branch of a great oak, and people in the baron's colors were putting this noose around his necks. Camill de Lottaire and several of his bodyguards watched the activity with a pleased expression. Jean watched it from the hay attic of one of the shacks, drawing his bow. He aimed straight at the baron, but at the sight of his friends approaching at full gallop, his hand twitched and the arrow hit one of the henchmen. The armed men took up their weapons, looking for an invisible attacker.

There was nothing to wait for. The friends fell on the baron's men like a storm. Within moments their victory was complete, the doomed peasants were freed and Jean found himself behind Francois on his horse in no time at all.

"Thanks, comrade," he gasped. "I couldn't do it myself."

"You had to take a brick first and hit your head," his friend instructed. "Have you lost your mind or what?"

"What was I supposed to do?" Jean said indignantly. " I made friends with these people! I helped them because this village is starving! The baron convicted these two of stealing some vegetables from his field and..."

Francois elbowed him in the stomach so that he almost fell off his horse.

"It would be good if they hung you with them! You couldn't do anything alone!"

"What about your lady?" Pierre wanted to know.

"She managed to hide, and I didn't give her up, what again... I would bite off my tongue sooner!" Jean shouted back, rubbing his stomach. "Besides, she's not my lady, we're just friends. You think I'd be romancing a fourteen-year-old? Who do you think I am?"

"Like master, like man," Pierre grunted, squinting at Theo. It was clear what he was driving at - Belette's romance with Viscount de Bongrais began when, in fact, they were both children.

"She could be my daughter, you have a completely rotten brain," the redhead insulted.

They stopped the horses in front of the "Under the White Swan" inn.

"Damasus, wine and something big!" Theo called, hopping off his horse.

The innkeeper appeared immediately, hearing a familiar voice.

"Oh, I see you guys get back together," he remarked. "A leopard doesn't change its spots, right? Sit down, I'll give you some wine. The lamb is just baking, so you have to wait for that."

The inn smelled of deliciously toasted meat, garlic, onions, and marjoram. It was a mystery how during the raging famine of Damasus, called Magyar, obtained meat, but no one asked about it, just in case, and did not investigate what animal landed in his bowl. Anyway, when Pierre sometimes talked about this tavern "we ate many dogs here together", everyone knew that it was not quite a joke.

"Let's eat, that matter will not escape us. Sit down and... oh shit! Ettienne, are you telling me you got into this row with all of us?!"

the knight roared, only now seeing that the little page was with them.

"Sure. Should I be worse?" the boy barked back at him with all the insolence he could do.

Beregard shook his head.

"It's not that simple," he said solemnly. "You already have another accusation on your back: the Count de Bongrais, barely returning home, attacked a neighbor, beat his people and released the thieves sentenced to death."

He sat down and poured himself a huge dose of wine, as if he thought he could not bear what had happened sober. Others followed his example.

"First-class wine, counterfeited by the noblest moonshine," Theo sighed with poetic emotion. "You won't believe how much I missed it at the Louvre. As for your objections, Beregard, it's nothing compared to what we're going to do next."

"Then I have a suggestion: don't go back to the castle afterwards. Stay with us, at least until we figure out what the king is saying," Beregard said with some resignation.

"He can stay, provided he has an honorable fight with me," Pierre said.

"If you want me to punch your face, go ahead," Theo agreed without smiling.

He had already survived several serious fights with Pierre and a dozen smaller clashes in which he had to prove that he was better than him, so this demand was not new to him. In fact, he was expecting it.

"At least you know what the man we're about to release looks like?" Gwidon asked curiously.

"I accidentally know."

Theo remembered the gloomy, taciturn giant who had come to the Louvre one day with some extremely important letter from his master, a letter that could not be seen to be entrusted to someone less trusted. It would be hard not to recognize him after seeing him once.

The innkeeper brought a tray with pieces of smoky, stringy meat and thick slices of bread. In the pre-harvest it was baked whatever it was possible, and it was also better not to think too much about what exactly."

"Oh, one day you won't get back together," he said warningly, before he left.

"He's right," Beregard said.

"Don't grumble, man. I cannot do otherwise. If I don't free Ernataun, Gaston de Foix, I mean Febus, he won't be willing to work hand in hand with the king. And if he breaks out, other magnates may follow his example, which will have catastrophic consequences for our country," the knight patiently explained to him.

"What does it matter if they beat the Englishmen together or individually?" Millot interrupted. "After all, it's important that they do it at all."

"Exactly," Pierre replied.

"Not at all, you idiots," the knight said impatiently. He looked around and, noticing a solid bundle of splinter prepared for kindling against the wall, reached for it and handed it to Pierre.

"Let one of you try to break it," he encouraged his friends.

Bellette's brother, catching up on his face, took the bundle and strained all his strength to break it. He tried several times, then Millot took the bundle out of his hand and wanted to do the play himself. However, he failed and neither did those who tried to do it after him.

"Perhaps you will do it, smart boy," growled Pierre angrily.

"With pleasure." Theo answered him calmly.

He untied the string and, without haste, began to break the splinters, one by one.

"See how easy it is?" He told stunned friends. "Even Ettienne would do the trick. But when they stick together they will resist anyone. I hope you understood me? By the way, Ettienne, what will happen to you? I can hide in the swamp again, it's okay, but you? Maybe you will come back to Paris, to the royal court."

The boy shook his head vigorously.

"I'd rather be with you," he replied. "The Page is always to be faithful to its knight, and so will I. In a palace or in a swamp, what a difference."

"The difference is big, you'll see. Okay, do as you see fit, but remember that you'll only be blamed for yourself if you get hurt. Colas, Tristan, watch out for him. Now let's end this feast. We have a long road ahead, and at the end of it a horribly nasty job."

*****

"You say it was Theodoric de Bongrais?" Charles IV asked incredulously.

Steward Roidon, standing in front of him, nodded eagerly.

"I know him," he said. "It was definitely him and his gang of outcasts. As I was driving here, I also heard that they had previously attacked sir de Lottaire in his own land..."

The king cut him off and waved him away.

"What am I supposed to do now?" he muttered glumly. The Crown Chancellor, who was there, shrugged.

"I told you, Sire, that it would end like this," he reminded him. "You can breed a wolf, but he will look at the forest anyway."

Charles shook his long curled hair vigorously.

"Whoever rejects an once-in-a-lifetime opportunity was clearly not worth it," he said angrily. "Too bad, he only have himself to blame. There is nothing to meditate on."

"It certainly is like that, Sire," said the chancellor with a bow, and walked away.

The king was alone. He paced the room for a moment, hands behind his back, then paused in front of his father's portrait and stared into his face with challenge in his eyes.

"You were right about him," he confided to the portrait. "But what am I going to do with him now? I know very well who is behind his actions, but he will not confirm it, and they surely will not. It isn't fair for him to bear the consequences of the whole affair, but there is nothing I can do for him. Too bad, you can see this is his destiny."

He paused for a moment, then sighed heavily:

"The poor man enjoyed his regained goods short... There is no happiness in this man's life.... Febus and Philip are cynical rascals, but well, I need them. Such is the fate."

Theo le Vengeur and his band were outlawed again.

CHAPTER II

Never mind the rules

Theo and Pierre rolled on the grass, punching each other ferociously and tearing their clothes. The friends around them watched these struggles, shouting for their enthusiasm and not intending to intervene in any way.

In all robber's gangs, this one principle was respected: the question of leadership was resolved through such a duel. Only the weapon changed. Pierre had challenged his unwanted brother-in-law to wrestling fistfights more than once, which others regarded as a harmless quirk. Neither of them would even think of fighting for leadership, especially with Theo, who is known for his heavy hand. This fight ended similarly to the previous ones: the knight pressed Pierre to the ground, hammered his elbow into his throat and held him until he grunted:

"I give up."

As always, beaten and battered, he had to acknowledge his friend's superiority and relinquish his leadership to him. Theo hadn't come out unscathed from the brawl either, but neither the bruises nor the scratches spoiled his mood.

"Ending as usual," said Gwidon, stroking the zither strings. "Pierre, will you never learn that you will not defeat our leader?"

"Nobody can beat him," said Ettienne proudly.

"Everyone will find a better one someday... although in the case of this lunatic, kindly called our chief, we can still wait for it," said Francois, seated on a branch of a sprawling elm and waving his bare feet in the air.

"Cut me off if I'm wrong, but everything seems to be back to normal." Beregard stirred the soup cooked for breakfast.

"Was it normal here before? I didn't notice," said Millot, looking up from the arrow he had just darted.

Theo dusted himself off the sand and grass, then looked at his companions.

"I won't feel at home here until I have my family complete," he said sternly.

"You're not bothering Bellette again," Pierre growled, trying to get up.

"You bet? She is my wife and her place is with her husband, any priest will tell you that." Theo pushed him so that he sat down on the ground again. "If Father Prospero was alive, he would have knocked her out of this idiocy. I have to do it myself anyway. Where is she?"

"I won't tell," Pierre insisted.

"Should I hit you one more time?" The knight frowned menacingly and accidentally hissed in pain because he had a solid bruise on him.

"You'd both give it up. It's not worth arguing about something that should be decided by Bellette herself," Tristan chimed in soberly. "If she doesn't want to leave the convent, I wonder how you make her."

"Don't ask her at all, throw her over the saddle and that's it," Ettienne advised seriously.

"Stay out, freckle-face! My sister has finally found peace and I will not let it tear it down." Pierre stood up and, pushed again, sat down again.

"The boy is right... And I'll find out anyway," Theo stood over him, fists clenched, ready for the next fight, but this time his friends separated them firmly.

Jean pulled the leader aside.

"Think carefully," he asked him. "Bellette is safe in the convent, here you know very well what could be a threat to her."

"In times of war, even monasteries are not very safe. Besides, I believe Bellette will not renounce our love," said Theo firmly.

He wasn't really sure about it, but he didn't want to talk about it out loud. Influenced by his friends from the forests, he believed in "jinxing" years ago, although he was not superstitious by nature.

"You want to go now? So broken up? Wait, or when she sees you she'll drop dead, clean yourself up first," Millot advised.

"It doesn't look much worse than usual," Jean chuckled.

Theo wiped the blood from a split lip and touched his cheek carefully, which had a large hematoma on it.

"Maybe I'll wait a while," he agreed. "Especially since you haven't deigned to tell me where Bellette is yet."

The outlaws looked at each other uncertainly.

"We don't really know," Francois admitted. "Brother Michael took her away and did not say where. He just said that he was going to the convent and that we didn't need to know any more."

"What a tricky clergyman! He wrote me to come back because Bellette is expecting a baby, and then he's driving her who knows where! I'll show him! I'll talk to him now!" the knight screamed furiously.

"He wrote you that? What a prankster," Pierre laughed, for some reason with satisfaction.

"Bellette wasn't pregnant," Preziosa said. "And she didn't want to wait any longer. She decided that the best she could do for you was to set you free. How could she know the situation was going to develop this way?"

"And as for talk, then you won't talk," added Tristan. "He didn't come back after this trip. And there is a new prior in the monastery, some Iohann. It's impossible to get along with him, he'll hand us all over to the English rather than help us."

"Stop it," the Gypsy scolded him. "We just don't know him yet, and he is a bit reluctant to us..."

Theo choked back his anger and thought for a moment.

"We won't risk," he decided. "Let's stay away now. It's good that no one from the monastery knows the way to our hideout, and I don't think Brother Michael would reveal it to anyone. He is, after all, a living portrait of his late father. I'll miss them both."

He ran a hand nervously through his hair. Things got nasty, and he didn't know what he really should do, and he was getting lost.

Ettienne nudged him sideways.

"Don't worry," he said. "Somehow it will sort out, you'll see. We'll find her, I'll help."

Theo laughed merrily.

"Maybe not you, little one, but someone else," he said. "I'm going to Navarra, to Philip, he'll be first to find out. He knows several bishops personally."

More than a week after that conversation before Theo finally hit the road. During this time, he organized his life in the forest anew, which turned out to be not so easy, because the hut, which had been abandoned for a long time, required thorough repair, and the clearing was overgrown with young tree shoots that had to be cut down. On Armando's advice, they also dredged the well to reach the underground mouth of a deep water source, with complete success. In the meantime, they casually robbed the carriage of a noble and traveling speculator, which gave rise to the news that the famous Touraine band was again in the area. Finally, Theo, accompanied by Beregard, Tristan and Ettienne, set off for Orléans, where he expected to find Philip. Recently, he was often in this city, playing his mysterious political game, and it was from there that he sent his friend a letter, which at the same time was a safe deposit enabling relatively free travel. Minion, who delivered the letter, also said that his master would probably spend the whole summer in Orléans, so it was possible to go there without fear. The rest of the band stayed in the woods, finishing the grooming of their common stronghold. They did not mind going back "to the old neighborhood", because although they spent the winter in more human settlements, they felt that their home was here.

"It is said that a wolf, even raised by humans, always returns to the forest in the end," sighed Francois, glancing contentedly at the new-roofed hut made of fresh wood.

"You're dumb, but you're talking smart," Pierre agreed. "Neither am I suitable for plowing, mowing and spreading dung now. Once a person tries a different life, and this already disgusts him."

"You weren't fit for this in life," remarked teasingly Jean, who knew him best.

"You think?" Pierre looked at him with an involuntary smile. Although he emphasized on every occasion that he was a flesh-and-blood peasant, he hated the typical peasant life. As he himself said, he chose the life of a robber, because he preferred to eat meat and drink wine than to eat flatbread and cabbage washed down with sour milk.

"Then maybe we will go to the 'White Swan' now?" Gwidon suggested, struggling to get off the repaired roof. "I'd like a drink."

"Why not?" Pierre agreed. "My throat went dry too. Come on, boys, let's visit Damasus."

"I'm in," said Millot, followed by the others.

"And our chief? He said nothing about walking there..." Preziosa began hesitantly, but her brother interrupted her.

"He did not forbid, and that's enough. Don't make it difficult, baby. You better come with us, why bother here?"

The girl thought for a moment, then shrugged resignedly. It was hard to resist such an argument. She threw a colored scarf over her shoulders and ran after the men.

There was still little traffic in the tavern at this time of the day, only before evening came peasants exhausted by all day's work, suspicious vagrants and petty stallholders. However, the back room was occupied so they sat down in the main room and ordered a few jugs of wine.

"What are we drinking for? For a new life or for a return to the old place?" Francois asked, taking on the role of cup-bearer voluntarily and pouring blood-red liquor into mugs for everyone.

"For our health. It's the safest toast yet," Pierre decided, and took a long gulp. "Oh good, it tastes less moonshine than usual. Margot, get a bite!"

"One moment, what's the rush?!" the girl shouted back to him.

"What's the rush, what's the rush..." hummed Gwidon.

"Close your mouth or something will really happen," the innkeeper admonished him, passing by with a cask on his shoulder, freshly brought from the basement.

Several peasants entered the tavern, arguing animatedly about something.

"Oh, our village administrator," Pierre rejoiced at the sight of a plump, gray-haired man, slightly better dressed than the others. "What's up, Jaussard?"

The village administrator separated from his companions and sat down with the outlaws.

"You alone?" He asked. "Where's our Count?"

"He went on an important matter, which is neither our business nor yours."

"Oh. I was thinking that he turned back to you," said the undaunted peasant, accepting a cup of wine from Preziosa. "The governor, who is now sitting in the castle, came for tribute with two armed men. When I saw the count, I was shocked, I'm telling you, and then I started screaming why he want to collect taxes, and he said that this is order from the king. Then our count punched him and the poor fellow fell to the ground, and count said that he wouldn't allow to cheat us. And he said that he would beat, whether friend or enemy, when he caught someone looting. Good lord, I'm telling you."

"And what do the armed men say?" Armando asked.

Jaussard drank and explained eagerly:

"They jumped up to him. And the count grabbed one by the head, the other by the neck, and started beating with them until the sparks flew! Soon he beat them so much that they fled. Good he came back to us, he won't let us hurt."

The outlaws looked at each other knowingly and without saying a word. It was only when the village administrator had gone to his companions and Gwidon spoke up, shaking his head:

"Yeah. Now that he has had time to expose himself to everything again, he will probably feel at home here again."

"This isn't funny. It's one thing to oppose an invader and another to oppose your own king," said the innkeeper, setting a bowl with sliced bread and pieces of suspicious roast on the table. "It's called a rebellion and you can hang or go on a wheel."

"Theo's scared right now," snorted Millot. "He is hard to scare, and I remind you, Damasus, many have tried. It's a hero with a capital H."

The innkeeper nodded skeptically.

"Now he's going to be in trouble with a capital T," he said. "I wonder how he will deal with the Black Prince on the one hand and our Charles on the other."

"Don't worry about it anymore. What matters to you is whether he will manage to pay the bill, not whether he will risk the authorities," Francois nudged him in a friendly side.

"And when not. This is my friend as well as yours," Damasus was offended and went to the other guests.

Pierre drank again and sighed deeply.

"I hope he thinks it over and leaves Bellette alone," he said sadly.

"Whether you like it or not, they're married, and what's more, they really love each other," Preziosa pointed out.

He looked at her as if she were stupid.

"You, ladies, think of only one thing: he loves me or he loves me not," he said. "There is more to this world than matters that begin and end in the hay."

"You are disgusting."

Preziosa made a face of resentment. Millot drank and said;

"And I'm curious what our chief is doing now. As far as I know him, he might not even get to Orléans if he gets into a row."

"It's a piece of cake for him," Gwidon muttered and played a fragment of a longing song on his lyre, to which he wrote the lyrics himself. The song spoke of a young exile who dies heartbroken, abandoned by a cruel beauty.

"Jesus, Mary, Saint Joseph!" Pierre exclaimed, covering his ears. "If you have to sing something please not your toss! I feel sick from that ghastly howl!"

"What an expert," said Gwidon, and put down the zither.

Like the others, he was curious about how Theo was doing on the road, but less than they were concerned about him. He was quite right - Theo, firstly, knew how to take care of himself, and secondly, having a safe conduct, he could easily move around the province. The word of Philip d'Evreux meant a lot in France. However, he had reached Orleans without reaching for the letter even once, as he was too proud to take advantage of it. He and his tiny retinue have traveled all the way, avoiding the patrols of guards with a talent acquired over the years in the woods, and sleeping under hastily built city huts in roadside inns. Also, the entrance to the city itself did not present any problems. The guards were not able to check all travelers, so they did not check anyone, limiting themselves to collecting tolls and entry fees.

"Where now?" asked Beregard as they reached the streets of the city.

"Not to the castle, that's for sure," Theo replied, looking around. "I prefer not to show up there, the Duke of Orleans has no reason to love me. And now that a reward has been imposed on my head again... Ettienne, you will take the letter to Philip, but remember, only to his hands."

"As if I didn't know," the freckle-face snorted.

"Where will you schedule a meeting?" Tristan asked curiously.

"In the university yard," his brother replied. "There is such a jumble that no one will notice us. They will think that you want to become a student, and I'm a Chevalier."

Beregard laughed heartily.

"Forgive me, friend, but if you look like Chevalier I'm a bishop," he remarked.

"I'm sorry but he's right," Ettienne agreed.

"Who asked you, puppy?"

Theo jumped off his horse and took a piece of clean parchment, a quill, and a tightly corked bottle of ink from his saddlebags. He quickly outlined a few words, signed himself, sprinkled the parchment with sand and handed the letter to the boy. He grabbed it eagerly and struck his mount with his heels on the sides.

"And we at the meeting place."

The knight mounted his steed again and directed him towards the university. The University of Orleans, founded more than sixty years ago, had perhaps a lesser reputation than the one in Paris, but was known for its much more disciplined youth. While

Parisian students from time to time started riots, and were always known for their extraordinary villainy, the Orleans, future medics, geographers and court clerks, were balanced youth and eager to learn. Even now, under war conditions, lessons were taking place, and in the courtyard there were groups of less and more well-dressed teenagers, repeating in an undertone the formulas they had heard from the teachers.

Theo, Beregard, and Tristan sat under the trees in the corner of the courtyard and, trying not to catch anyone's eyes, gnawed at the carefully taken biscuits. People passed through the courtyard every now and then: students of the supplier, bachelors and attendants, it would be really difficult to see who is a stranger and who is not. It was a public place at the same time, and secluded enough to be safe for conversation.

"You never wanted to study?" Tristan asked, looking longingly at the groups of students.

"What an idea. It's good for the weak," his brother snorted. "I wanted to be a knight, not a barber surgeon or a scribe. Don't tell me you are attracted to it."

"Well, not really, but it looks like they are having fun here."

"Do you want to have fun? Be careful, it gets too funny. How insolent that youth is today..." said Beregard, playfully tugging his ear.

Tristan was almost eighteen, but he looked no more than fourteen. He was quite skinny and frail, and his delicate beauty was constantly being joked by friends and acquaintances. It was hard to blame that he would like to have some kind of contact with his peers, not only with outlaws living like animals, most of them twice his age.

"You see," his brother said after a moment. "I had the company of other puppies until the day I was knighted, but that doesn't mean I had a happier childhood than you were. In such a crowd you have to fight for yours with teeth and claws. Enjoy what you have, it could be worse."

"You are as subtle as a communal tub in a public bath, Theo," Beregard said sarcastically.

From the very beginning, he tried to convince his friend to treat his younger brother with a little more delicacy, but to no avail.

Hooves rumbled in the courtyard, and the Duke of Navarre, cloaked in a modest gray cloak, jumped off the saddle of his mount next to his three friends.

"Theo, you monster, what have you been up to again?!" He cried almost despairingly. "The king said that when you fall into his hands, you will be hanged like a random thief, and before that, publicly disgraced. He's not kidding my friend. I won't be able to help you now, and I might even have to watch you die."

"As if you ever helped me, apart from that story in Bongrais, when you weren't risking anything," Theo blurted sarcastically. "As for my death, it's unknown who to hit on. Before they catch me, the king will get in a bad mood, and also remember who dressed me in all this. First you want me to convince Febus of the alliance, then he wants me to return the squire imprisoned by the king to him first, otherwise he will do it his way. What exactly does His Majesty want from me? After all, he has his stupid alliance."

"Oh, you don't understand!" Philip wrung his hands in horror. "This is no joke. You're in more trouble than ever. Charles received an anonymous letter in which someone wrote that you are of the Plantagenet family and that you are acting on behalf of the Welshman. It's absurd, but the king believed it."

"It's not absurd..." Theo muttered, finally getting serious.

"What?!"

"I mean, with this action, yes, absurd, but for the rest... I'm a righteous French and will remain so, but it's true that I have some Plantagenet blood in me, I don't know, Yorks or Lancasters... so what?! The Black Prince had a French grandmother and a French mother, and he is English! Why are they just sticking to me?!"

"Don't yell like that. If that's true, it complicates things even more," Philip waved his hand in discouragement and sat down next to him on the grass. "I was hoping it was slander. Who wanted to harm you so much, what you think?"

"I don't know? I have some enemies. Better tell me if you know anything about my wife," said the outlaw, a little calmer.

The Duke of Navarre nodded.

"A certain brother Michael took her out of the provinces just before certain people wanted to find her," he replied. "I haven't been able to find out who was looking for her. Then they both turned to Bishop Joaquin, who allowed the girl to be placed in a Carmelite convent near Orléans. I had a lot of trouble figuring out where he had hidden her, but I already know: two miles north of town. She is there under the name of sister Marta, now a postulant."

"She won't be there long," Theo promised him grimly.

"Not enough of war with the king, do you want it with the church? So brave? Anyway, do what you like, I will wash my hands of it," said Prince Philip impatiently. "You've never listened to anyone, so why should it be any different now? You know what? I'm growing up and I've the feeling that you stopped at the stage where we were both in Navarre. You're still a stupid puppy with a high sense of personal dignity, although you are physically a man in the prime of life. I love you like a brother, but I can't understand anymore. You have wasted your only chance to return to normal life, so you will continue to live in the forest like a badger and eventually die under the fence like a dog. Do you think that makes me happy?"

His friend looked at him for a long time and almost tenderly.

"Philip, I like you very much," he said after a moment. "But we both have a different fate. Francois sometimes says: 'Whoever is written in the God's Book of Forefathers will remain a forefather for the rest of his life'. There's something in it, don't you think? Anyway, don't mind me. Even if I end up in the worst possible way, it won't be your fault."

The prince lowered his head. His smooth boyish face tightened with unpleasant thoughts he couldn't utter aloud.

"I think," he said after a moment, without looking up, "that deep down you still hate me for what you have on your arm."

"Oh no," the outlaw replied. "I don't even think about it. It's just that now I have to put on a caftan with sleeves up to the elbow, because I don't want to show the English lion. You see, it is like this: I have already experienced the death of people close to me, hunger and cold, the terrifying closeness of death, pain and disgrace... What else can the king do to me? Kill? This is what I fear the least. After as much as I have gone through, death, even the worst, even the most painful, does not seem terrible at all. By the way, apologize to His Majesty for me. Too bad, I will still be outlawed, but that does not mean that I disobeyed him."

"That will surely comfort him," muttered Philip sarcastically.

His friend was clearly striving for self-annihilation, and he could not help but watch helplessly. It hurt, more than he could have put it in his usual restrained way.

"You must have been cursed by someone before you were born. Well, bye." The prince got up and looked down at his friend.

"You know what?" He said again. "When I look at you, I think I see a moth circling around a burning candle. She pays her temporary fascination with pain and death, but this does not discourage her."

Theo smiled.

"And do you know, Philip, why the moth is circling the candle?" he asked, standing up as well and straightening his arms.

"Why?"

"Because she has wings," his friend replied. "Think it over well. To the horses, boys, we have to find Bellette and bring her home."

"Whatever you order, chief." Beregard replied with a sigh. He had his own opinion on this, but preferred to keep it to himself.

Prince Philip watched them until they were out of sight, then he mounted his horse and returned to the castle, bitten and angry with himself. Earlier he was sure he was right, now he was beginning to hesitate. He was no longer so convinced that he had done the right thing by telling Theo where his wife was hiding. Well, he couldn't undo it anymore.

Similar thoughts troubled Beregard and Tristan, but they both chose not to speak, since their leader was in a mood suitable for a powerful brawl and preferred not to provoke him. Having learned to orientate himself in the woods, Theo easily found his way to the small convent situated just on the Loire River and knocked energetically at the gate.

"Praise the Lord, sister," he said politely to the sister of the porter, as soon as she had opened the door. "I need to talk to one of the postulants, sister Marta."

"And do you have a bishop's permission?" the porter asked.

"No."

"Then you cannot come in," said the nun firmly. "I'll tell Sister Marta that she has an appointment, and if she wants to talk to you, she will go out."

"Yes? Well, please tell her that the husband to whom she swore loyalty, honesty and obedience at the altar has arrived," growled the knight angrily.

"Not so harsh, brother, it's a convent, not an inn," Tristan whispered scandalized, but only got a furious glare.

Nun came back after a while.

"Sister Marta doesn't want to come out to you," she announced. "Unfortunately, you have to go."

"What?!" Theo screamed.

"Please, don't make a fuss here..." moaned Beregard.

"I'll go to her," Ettienne offered hurriedly, and he rolled neatly past the nun before she could stop him.

"I'll catch him," Theo promised the outraged porter, rushing after him.

"Sister, please, sister, let him go, he's ready to beat Saint Zita in that," Tristan said resignedly as he perched on the wall next to the convent.

"Dear sister, listen to the young man, he knows this madman better than you, sister," Beregard joined him. "And yet this lady is his wife. He loves her."

"If the abbess were here... " the doorkeeper began in a raised voice, but Tristan interrupted her.

"Believe me, sister, my brother is violent and has virtually nothing left to lose. It'd better if you sister allow him to go."

"What a time," the nun muttered dissatisfiedly.

There were furious screams from inside the convent, and all three jumped up from their seats. The male voice had quieter and thinner female voices, which, however, clearly began to lose after the first exchange. Finally, someone pushed the door aside, and Theo jumped out of the convent gate, thrown over his shoulder, thrashing and screaming high-haired girl in the habit of a postulant. Before anyone could react, the knight forcibly placed Bellette on the back of his horse and jumped onto the saddle behind her.

"My lady, tell bishop that I take what is mine!" He shouted to the gate. "Don't get in my way, or I'll nail the hat to his head, okay?!"

"What, didn't I tell you?" Tristan rode his horse hastily.

"He wouldn't listen to me," Ettienne complained, hurrying out of the gate.

"I've had this problem with him since he was six," said Beregard, lifting him up onto a pony at the same time.

Theo urged his stallion so hard that the other horses could not catch up with him. Only when they had weaned a good ten miles from Orléans did he shudder a bit and pulled the reins to stop his horse.

"You hopeless, shameless, mindless bastard!" Bellette screamed angrily as she regained her breath. "You jackass! You immoral, godless, selfish pig!"

"My dear, no one is perfect," Theo answered her calmly, setting her to the ground. "You'd like a man to have only good qualities."

"How dare you interfere in this?! It was my decision!" Bellette yelled further, ignoring their friends listening to them.

"Husband's right, you idiot! The law of a lover! By the law of an outlaw, defending captured loot!" Her husband roared at her, perhaps trying to show that his throat is stronger than her. "I love you, you idiot, and I won't let anyone make a laughingstock! And if you tell me that you suddenly felt a calling, I'll hit you with a belt."

"Oh yes, that would be very chivalrous..." Beregard said sarcastically.

Bellette put her hands on her hips.

"Just try to touch me..." she began, but stopped, because her husband started to tear the belt buckle with menacing movements, so she gave up verbal arguments in favor of a piercing scream.

"Stop meowing and take that lousy rag off," said Theo. He left the brace alone and tore Bellette the postulant's veil from her head.

"Take off? That's just a word for you." Ettienne snorted, still unfamiliar with the dialect of central France's social lowlands.

Tristan prodded his side to calm him down. The unfolding spectacle was too interesting to drown out.

"Give it back," Bellette snatched the veil from her husband's hand. "What do you know about the reasons that prompted me to take this step! You always only think of yourself, the fighting with the English and the affairs of the country... in that order."

"You are stupid! Would you like me in the midst of the national misfortune to hold your hand and dream to the moon with a chorus of frogs in a pond?! Leave that rag, I'm telling you one last time or I'll get nasty!"

"Even more than usual?! It is impossible. Besides, I'll do what I want," Bellette replied, albeit with less self-confidence.

"Not this time. Now you will do what I want. We're going home... unless you want war," Theo frowned.

The girl shook her rumpled hair, trying to smooth it a little. They hadn't been truncated yet because she was just a newbie, but it was obvious that she had stopped caring for them.

"But, brother, we have a war already," Tristan remarked uncertainly.

"Then we'll have a second one, what a difference," the knight said, a little calmer. "Plenty is no plague. We're going back to Touraine and not a word more. By the way, Bellette, the gray one is very disgusting for you. I can't wait for you to change into something more normal."

"You're the one who is completely abnormal." The girl huffed, but she obediently climbed onto the saddle in front of him. In fact, she was flattered by her husband's commitment, who, despite a winter spent among France's loudest beauties, still preferred her but had no intention of showing him so. She made a heroic effort to make him free, but since he had shown so emphatically that he did not want it, she felt joy and relief against her will. She really did not feel called to live in the convent where Brother Michael hid her.

*****

"The world is falling apart," Pierre sighed, watching Preziosa just hurl quick stitches around the bottom of skirt for his sister. "And why doesn't she want to wear men's pants anymore if you don't mind?"

"In the convent they persuaded her that it was a terrible sin," replied the Gypsy, not looking up from her work. "I don't quite understand why, but let her be. I'm so used to it that the dress would be an unbearable torment for me. Well, a matter of liking."

She bit the thread and flicked her skirt, examining it in all directions. She entered the hut, from which Bellette emerged after a while, adjusting her clothes, a bit too big, as she had lost weight recently. Theo came out behind her, exhaling triumphantly.

"When I say something, that's what it's meant to be," he said. "The husband is to rule, it is and always has been."

"This is my last concession, you despot," said Bellette resentfully. "You have acquired terrible manners and customs in the royal court."

"Careful, sister-in-law. Don't you remember what Father Prospero said when he married you? That the husband is the head of the house," Tristan reminded her maliciously.

"Maybe," Bellette agreed. "But the wife is the neck. The neck turns this head in its own image."

"I don't understand how Theo can be any head," Pierre interjected. "As long as I know him, his own brain hasn't worked a single time."

He was in a bad mood because he was the one to cook something edible for the band that day, and he hated nothing as much as standing by the cauldron. It might not even be so bad if it were not for the fact that, as usual, there was nothing to put into this it. There was a pre-breeding season, there was hunger everywhere, very few animals remained in the forests, and the edible plants had not yet had time to grow. Getting food supplies for the band was of the utmost importance. Every once in a while they dined at the "Under the White Swan" tavern, but they couldn't do it all the time, it would be too dangerous. They absolutely had to have their own supplies.

"What's for dinner?" Theo asked Pierre, ignoring his spite.

"Clear water so far," Bellette's brother growled. "What can I do, collect snails or maybe a caterpillars? If I were a cat, I would at least catch mice."

"No, it can't be like that anymore," decided the chief. "I know where they keep their supplies in Bongrais. Now there is the royal steward, the one whom I gave a knuckle sandwich, but there aren't many armed men. We'll sneak up and get what we can."

"If you weren't such an idiot, you could sit there and not worry about anything, but no, you had to pretend to be the savior of the homeland..." Pierre grumbled further, but more out of habit than real anger.

Unable to think of anything else, he poured into the water a handful of chopped, dried bear garlic leaves, a little salt and a pot of dried bread crusts, usually collected on bait for smaller animals and birds. He added ground acorns and distributed the soup to his friends.

"Block your noses and just swallow," he advised them loyally. "We will not be able to attack as hungry."

Despite the bizarre ingredients, the soup wasn't even that bad. They were used to acorn meal, they usually sprinkled it on everything throughout the winter, because real flour, a luxury commodity during the war, was saved by them for bread, which is difficult to live without, even in the woods. The same was true of bear's garlic, a common plant in these parts. So the soup for them just tasted a bit bitter bread with garlic and that's it. They swallowed it quickly, drank the wine that Gwidon had arranged earlier, and set out."

The action went even faster than they had anticipated, because the servants were so heartily fed up with the royal steward that, with malicious joy, they made it easier for the outlaws to get into the castle pantries. The booty was surprisingly good - a few bags of groats, flour and plain grain, smoked meat and dried fruit. Out of loyalty to those who helped them, they took only what they really needed, plus a certain reserve. Gwidon, who, as usual, was rather one-sided, also stole several related jugs of wine and vodka, of which he was much happier than with the rest of the prey. He might, as he said himself, eat no more than just crumbs, but without some drink he felt as if he had run out of blood.

"Go back to our place with all this," Theo instructed his friends once they were safely out of the castle. "Me and Ettienne will go look around, maybe hear or see something interesting."

"Always the same. One is working, the other is walking," Pierre growled, adjusting the amount of smoked pork on his back.

"If everyone did the same thing, the world would be too boring," Theo said, and walked away with his page.

Ettienne jumped merrily at his side, overjoyed at the distinction. The knight glanced at him from time to time. He felt responsible for the fate of this boy, an orphan without a fortune, who trusted him so completely in everything, agreeing to the life of a wanderer by his side. Still, he couldn't send him back to the king, as he should have. What future awaited him there, especially now? And with him? What awaits this boy in the company of a gang of outlawed outcasts of his own nation? He couldn't push these doubts away, but he felt in his heart that he had done the boy a favor by allowing him to stay with him.

Together they walked around the area and ventured as far as the village of Hidden, which was off the beaten track and quite far from any trails. He was rare there, though he believed that all the villages in his estate deserved the same help and protection, but in Hidden, the peasants were doing fairly well. As he approached the village, Theo saw a ragged peasant huddled under a tree, muttering to himself in a tearful voice. In the village visible from behind the trees, there were soldiers - about ten, all in the colors of the Black Prince, and a man in plain clothes, sitting at a table, writing something. Hidden, it adjoined the lands ruled by the Prince of Wales, so he must have claimed the right to it.

"What happened?" Theo asked the peasant.

"They came this morning for taxes," he replied without even looking up. "And since we have no money, they made doom."

The soldiers dragged some skinny old man in a brown habit to the square.

"Who is this?" Theo whispered.

"Reverend Father Iohann. He tried to reason with these English devils, but probably nothing of it. They probably want to flog him, because he stood up for us too much, and they don't like Carmelites anyway."

"Flog a monk?" The knight was not so much surprised as scandalized. "And in addition, such an old man?"

The peasant looked at him humbly and helplessly. Theo waved his hand at him and turned to his page.

"Run for ours. Let them be here at once."

Ettienne nodded his ginger head and ran with the strength in his legs. The knight hid his sword, belt and gorget under the bush, then unceremoniously pulled his ragged caftan off the terrified peasant.

"Sorry, but mine is too decent, they would be suspicious," he muttered, tossing the rag over himself, not without a certain disgust.

Having smeared his face and shoulders with dust from the road, he hurried to the village. As he had been able to judge so far, these soldiers were new, so they probably didn't know him, but he preferred not to risk. In fact, it would be safest to wait for meals, but he felt sorry for the old monk, who was thin and insignificant.

"The caning could kill him," he thought, quickening his pace. "But not me."

When he fell among the villagers, the soldiers tore off the Carmelite habit and tied him brutally to a pillar in the middle of the village.

"Hey, leave that brother!" He shouted, pushing the peasants away. "What do you want from him?!"

The commander of the unit turned to face him with a look of surprise at the still young, but ugly and shaggy face."

"Who are you?" he growled hoarsely. The harap in his hand twitched, curling on the ground like a snake. Others had similar whips.

"Man as you are," Theo replied in the purest dialect he could use. Let him free. He is old and weak."

The commander approached him, striking himself with the coiled harap on the top of his long shoe.

"Are you looking for a problem, yokel?" he hissed.

"Stand back, son, I don't want anything to happen to you!" the monk exclaimed, struggling to twist his head.

"This man opposes the orders of the Prince of Wales and will be punished," said the Englishman. "And you... look strong. Book him, Humphrey, he'll be a nice recruit."

So, instead of taxes, they decided to take some peasants into the army. It said a lot about the difficulties with filling in the gaps. Theo rushed between the soldiers and shielded the half-naked friar with his body.

"Oh, so brave. So whip him until he moves away!" the commander called to his soldiers.

"Leave me, son, God will give me strength," the monk gasped. "I don't defend you so that someone will suffer because of me. This is not the land of the Prince of Wales and Aquitaine, they are illegally here, and so let them have one more sin on their conscience. Let His Holiness know how the English deal with his humble servants."

"I think that His Holiness has more serious things on his mind and the fate of father will not bother him at all." Theo muttered wryly and shuddered as the soldiers had just brutally tore off his patched caftan.

A moment later, the first blows hit his back. It was nothing new to him, and Captain Moore's harap cut harder than the whips of these soldiers. He felt indignant at the thought that they had wanted to treat the old man that way. Up close Father Iohann seemed incredibly fragile and delicate as a bird, thin and bent over, his thin, wrinkled skin as slender and translucent as fallen parchment. Completely different than the powerfully built, robust as a market-strong strongman, Father Prospero, and like him, his well-established brother Michael.

"Cowards," the knight thought contemptuously, shrinking under the blows of the whip. Let them look for opponents of their size.

The soldier lashing him suddenly grasped his chest and fell down, bleeding blood. The shots that fell on the English were well-aimed and biting, and completely confused the intruders. Taking advantage of the confusion, Theo rushed to the lying soldier, grabbed his sword and terrorized the unit commander with it.

"And now we'll talk differently, you poor torturer of defenseless monks," he hissed venomously. "Draw your sword."

"I'd love to see if you can hold a weapon at all, you dirty shepherd," the soldier reciprocated, and the swords clashed.

The knight had no intention of prolonging the fight - his bruised back hurt too much, and this weakened his ability and concentration. He knocked the enemy off the weapon already in the third assembly and pressed the blade to his throat.

"What do you say now?" he asked mockingly. He knew well that this man's situation was now unenviable, and it gave him perverse satisfaction. Only two people survived from his unit, others were lying on the ground, dead or dying, and around were menacing looking men armed with bows and daggers.

"Who are you, French devil?" the Englishman choked, staring at him.

"They call me Theo le Vengeur," the outlaw replied calmly, catching the astonished gaze of the old monk out of the corner of his eye. "Tell your master to stick to his lands, or else he will regret it. Tell him that I mock him and all his army, and that I will always defend my subjects. Hey, scribe, don't you show up here either! This is Touraine, not Aquitaine, remember it at last, Satan's offspring!"

He swung the sword, slicing the soldier's face with a wide, oblique wound.

"It's a souvenir. Now get out, because you'll lose those two as well."

The surviving Englishmen hurriedly retreated from the village, chased by the villagers in a barrage of stones. Torn from the pillar, the Carmelite put on his torn habit with trembling hands.

"If you're Theo le Vengeur, I guess that means my information was not accurate," he said helplessly.

"Oh, chief, you got nice blows," Pierre looked at his brother-in-law's back with a mixture of horror and respect.

Theo shrugged and grimaced.

"I think so, because it hurts like hell," he admitted. "And they wanted to beat this old man so much, do you have any idea? I don't know where this world is going."

"Straight to hell," said Gwidon cheerfully.

"Don't say things like that," Father Iohann scolded him. "You have to have better control of the language."

The troubadour bowed courtesy to him.

"Forgive me, Father, but too much of a hassle."

The monk turned to the knight again.

"I owe you a thank you, Count. You are righteous and courageous, yet they talk so much horrible things about you... Please consider me a friend from now on, but before that, tell me what prompted you to intervene so desperately."

The outlaw looked at him warmly. Father Iohann had noble features, a dignified posture despite the slight bend of his back, and spoke French so polished that the vast majority of the villagers must have understood a little. Judging by the accent, he must have come from the borderland of Alsace, and he was undoubtedly a man of high birth.

"Father, what to say?" He said. "They could have beaten father to death."

"Okay, but what did you care?" continued the monk.

Theo made a vague gesture with his hand and shrugged.

"Oh, I don't know," he said absently. "Somehow I don't like it when a few armed thugs bully a helpless old man. But what prompted father to find himself in such a dangerous situation?"

The monk smiled slightly.

"Maybe I don't like soldiers bullying villagers?" He replied. "I've seen quite horrible things. The peasants are the most oppressed creatures on this earth. They are oppressed by everyone: the king collects taxes, the lord tithes, and the foreign army takes what is left, raping, killing and setting fire in the process. And if it somehow calms down, there's either a drought or a flood or a plague. I thought those English people would respect the word of God's servant, after all, they are also Christians... but I broke it off."

"And father almost pay with your life for it," finished Pierre. "Let father remember in the future that it is impossible to talk to these English scoundrels except with a solid stick."

"And so good we made it in time," added Francois. "Ettienne was running like a madman, taking shortcuts, it's good that he didn't drown in the swamp along the way. They're dangerous now. And he was still running us. We barely kept up, this brat was quick like a hare."

A half-naked peasant hesitantly approached the group of outlaws and timidly handed Theo his sword, clothes, and gorget. There was admiration in the peasant's eyes, bordering on adoration.

"Let's go," suggested Beregard. "I know you guys have a nice chat, but we'd better come home. Theo's not in the best shape."

"On the contrary. Nothing stirs a man more than a few lashes," the knight jokingly insulted, but he hissed slightly, putting on his own caftan. He always tried not to show his pain when something was ailing him, but now it was not easy.

"Let's get back before you fall," Beregard whispered softly to him. "You will lose your strength soon."

The old Carmelite smiled at them.

"Let one of you come to the monastery for healing herbs afterwards," he said.

"Oh, like in the old days," said Gwidon, but Millot silenced him with a nudge under the shoulder blade.

Like the others, he did not trust this monk anyway and knew that the chief shared his opinion, although out of politeness he did not speak.

CHAPTER III

Surprise

It took a while for Theo to recover from a daring action in the village of Hidden. Opinions of the general public on the rightness of his actions were divided, some believed that he unnecessarily stuck his neck out instead of waiting for his companions, others praised his courage and dedication, and there were also those who laughed at him.

"Don't do anything about it," Beregard advised him. "You can recognize a stupid one by his laughter. Neither of those half-heads would be so vulnerable even to their own sister. We are all proud of you."

"Yes, except me," Bellette muttered sarcastically. "Because I had to give him cold compresses for ten days and run to the monastery for herbs."

"What were you running for, sister? You could have gone on a broomstick," Pierre told her. "Chief, what now? Shall we now restore good relations with the clergy?"

Theo wondered what was not easy for him. He was terribly sleepy because he couldn't sleep on his stomach, and it is difficult to sleep when the skin on your back aches and stings. For the last ten days he had only been giving off the occasional car, which made him tired even more than if he hadn't slept at all.

"No," he said finally. "Somehow I can't bring myself to trust this Iohann, still and all. Better stay away. I want to get up."

Beregard helped him sit up and examined his back.

"Almost all right," he said. "Indeed, you heal like a dog. Can I get you a straitjacket?"

"Sure, I have to go outside or I'm going crazy."

"Be careful, you're weak and everyone knows this air carries disease," Bellette warned him.

"Yes, that's why you closed my window so tightly that I almost suffocated. But that's enough, I'm healthy now and won't be sitting in this stuffy place anymore," Theo said flatly, got up and staggered, almost falling back on the bed.

"Great and mighty Count de Bongrais," mocked Pierre, grabbing his arm. "Be careful, or you'll break your head. Although in your situation it is a small loss, because you have nothing in it anyway."

"You are the specialist for emptiness in mind," growled his sister at him, who did not like to mock her husband, even if she thought he deserved it.

Despite the attempt to become a nun, she surprisingly quickly adapted again to life in the forest, among the outlaws. One day she explained as she changed her husband's back poultice:

"I thought that as restored to royal favors, you should be free to marry some filthy wealthy countess or baroness and have titled children with her. Why do you need a peasant woman who can't even give you a son, as any girl can do?"

"How many times do I have to tell you that I don't care about the children, I care about you?" Theo was irritated then.

Bellette didn't know if he really didn't care, but she sensed with all her female intuition that he wasn't telling her the truth. She had seen him look after the little page and how friendly they were. She was about to make her husband think about the boy's adoption, but for the time being, she still couldn't decide to do so."

"Ooh, what a lovely air," Theo sighed, stretching on the threshold. "I'm better now, and I'd love to eat something. Do we have anything?"

Jean handed him a piece of smoked meat and a large flatbread, and Gwidon offered a cup of wine. Theo devoured this impromptu meal with a healthy appetite, then went for a swim, despite objections from his friends frightened by the idea. They couldn't believe such insane carelessness, they were convinced that he would just drown. However, their leader did not think to drown, although it was really hard for him to fight the water. He was weak, heavy, though his back hardly bothered him anymore.

The scars would remain, he knew, but such trifles long ago ceased to touch him. He had worse scars on his soul, and now even they didn't bother him. He became hard as steel.

"That would sound ridiculous," he thought, struggling to crawl to the shore. "But when I found out that I was outlawed again, I realized that there were more important things in this world than royal grace, and that disgrace was a relative term. That lion on my shoulder... what does he matter? Was I flogged like a slave peasant? Well then. Who cares? Who does it hurt, other than me? Why do people always meddle in what is not their business?"

He evened his breath and pulled the jacket over his wet body. He was neither proud nor dissatisfied with what he had done, and never once thought of the new Carmelite prior he had known from behind the village. If he had wanted to analyze his feelings, he would have said he resented Father Iohann for being Prosper, but he had not thought about it. Refreshed with his bath, he returned to the clearing, where his friends were just preparing to hunt. Even though they now had a full pantry, they decided not to rely solely on what was in it, but to try to supply the band on a regular basis. It was safer that way.

"And where are Tristan and Ettienne?" he asked, smoothing his wet hair.

"They went spying," Beregard replied. "Apparently your castle has been taken over by someone. At first we thought it was the steward sent by the king, but no, he had moved out, and there is clearly someone living in the castle. Someone rich, because everywhere full of dressed servants and maids, just like a picture."

"And that's really interesting. If only the boys don't get into some kind of trouble," Theo ran his fingers through his hair and thought. "Who can it also be? Could King Charles give my castle to someone?"

"Probably so. The kings think that everything belongs to them, so they rule themselves without moderation," Pierre muttered maliciously.

"And don't worry too much about the boys," said Colas. "Tristan has already proven himself to be reasonable and clever, and Ettienne listens to him like an older brother. Nothing will happen to them."

"Maybe we'll finish this chatter and go hunting? We can talk another day," suggested Millot, who had just finished putting the new string on his bow and was waiting in full alert.

"You're right, you highlander butterfly," Jean agreed.

"Stop, boys," Bellette said flatly as she left the hut. "Theo is staying. He has just risen from his bed of pain and will not be wandering through the woods, tracking hare tails."

The knight took his hips.

"Are you so sure of yours?" He asked aggressively. "Who the hell's in charge?"

"Me," Bellette replied calmly. "Why you ask?"

"Nothing, can't ask anymore?"

Theo kissed her cheek warmly and, turning to the rest of his friends, spread his hands in an eloquent gesture. Bellette rarely tried to force him to do something, and she usually succeeded, and now - what to do - she was right. He was not yet strong enough, especially since Father Iohann, brought in with the prescribed blindfolding, and first of all used the traditional bleeding of him. It was a normal procedure at that time, as it was believed that such a procedure cleanses the body of "venoms". It was not entirely without foundation, and most of the time it produced surprisingly good results, only it was very weakening. Like it or not, Theo stayed in the clearing and started making a new slingshot. Since everything had turned out as it had worked out, he needed her. The Roman (or Gallic) slingshot was an effective and silent weapon, it was easy to smuggle with you, and bullets, that is, stones, could be found anywhere. Though his band mostly used pieces of lead, heavier and farther carrying, they could hardly be taken with them, and pebbles of appropriate size were scattered on the roads, in the woods, even in cities. It was a good weapon if someone knew how to use it, which required quite a bit of skill. Not everyone could learn it, for example, Gwidon never did, and both girls quit after several times. Contrary to appearances, making a good slingshot also required a lot of skill, it was not enough just to cut a strip of the right length and width from the leather. Theo struggled with the job until his fingers ached.

He was finishing when Tristan and Ettienne returned from Bongrais.

"Oh, are you already on your feet? Good, but our news is not very good," Tristan said, then stepped into the pantry, from which he emerged with a large chunk of stale bread and cheese.

"Let me guess... Have you seen the dragon eating virgins?" Theo asked without much interest.

"In Bongrais, he wouldn't have much to eat," his brother remarked calmly, his mouth full. "And the news is that the king donated your castle to Adeline de Valois. She has moved in at full speed and throw her weight about. What do you think?"

The knight meticulously coiled the finished slingshot and looked at it critically.

"What do I say?" He repeated. "Even you are too young to hear such words, much less Ettienne. I think I'm going to go to the castle and talk to Adeline from the heart. Don't let her think she can get away with it."

"But she got away already," remarked the little page soberly. "And you will not fight with a woman? You said yourself it was dishonorable."

Theo stood up and ruffled his red head.

"Who said I was going to fight her? We'll just talk," he replied calmly, but the expression in his eyes contradicted his words.

"You must have gone mad," Preziosa called, who, as it turned out, was sewing in the hut by the window and hearing everything. "First, you're not strong enough yet, and second, even if you were, such a trip is pure suicide, and if Bellette hadn't gone to the village, she would have quickly knocked it out of your head."

The knight looked at her sideways.

"But she's not here," he said. "And besides, a man has to decide for himself."

"Well said, Chief, but if you really want to go, you'd better go before your lovely wife comes back," Ettienne advised him gravely.

"Keep pushing him, you freckle-face." Tristan nudged him sideways in displeasure. Theo laughed.

"Don't worry, I'm fine. But... I thought Adeline was with the Black Prince. Did they quarrel or what?"

Tristan shook his head.

"I don't know," he said. "But I heard from an English envoy who went to Paris and stopped in Bongrais that apparently the Black Prince had changed a lot. During the Spanish campaign he contracted some disease and it was difficult to get out of it. In fact, he did not fully recover."

"Why was he even going over there?"

"And he said that his legitimate wife was to come to Meung Castle. In this situation, it better not shine in her eye with a lover," added Ettienne, to whom such connections were not new. It was the order of the day at the Louvre.

"I'll be fine," Teo said after a moment, and he disappeared quickly into the woods, as if he were indeed afraid of Bellette's return.

That he had decided to go to Adeline now had been an impulse, a decision of the moment, but he had always been driven by those impulses and had no intention of stopping. He knew his castle too well for Adeline's minions to corner him there - not if there were regular soldiers. They were probably not there, with the possible exception of a few guards, but they would be in the courtyard and at the gate. He could have tried without any particular risk, and he even had a good plan.

*****

Adeline de Valois finished giving orders in the castle's kitchen, checked the bills with the steward and went to her chambers. She had not yet managed to settle down for good in this special place with which she had so many memories and, to the great relief of the castle service, did not have as many demands and resentments as she used to. Her appearance with the entire retinue and the act of provisional granting, signed by the king, was shocking enough for everyone. Duchess was aware of this and decided this time not to ill-dispose the people who were to serve her. She was already older and wiser, she knew well that the servants could help and could also do a great deal to a disliked lady.

Closing the door behind her, she sat down heavily in the armchair and thought. Her life was going quite well. Despite her affair with Prince Edward, she not only did not alienate the new king of France, but recently even managed to charm him. Despite the passage of years, her beauty and grace have no equal, although more and more in the morning she peered into the mirror with secret fear, looking for the first wrinkles. For now, however, her alabaster skin has resisted the passage of time. With a sigh, she rested her intricately combed head against the high headrest of the chair and closed her eyes, but then sprang to her feet.

A dark green curtain by the window opened and a well-known man stood in front of her. She looked at him silently for a moment. He seemed more serious to her than he used to be, but his eyes used to be ironically shiny, evil... and very pretty, which she had to admit. His face was as smooth as it used to be, only his lips seemed tighter, more cynical in expression. And that faint scar on the temple, almost completely covered with hair.

"I knew you were coming," she said softly.

"I think you knew." her visitor replied just as softly.

He looked at her coolly but appreciatively. She was more beautiful than before, perhaps a bit more mature, but irresistibly attractive - limp and ethereal, with gorgeous hair and a captivatingly beautiful, classically regular face, illuminated by oblong eyes the color of sun-warmed hazelnuts.

"Have you made yourself at home in my castle?" He asked, not letting the silence last too long. "Are you missing anything? Or maybe try to get something for you?"

Duchess smiled and adjusted the folds of her dress.

"I don't think so," she replied. "Thank you for your good intentions, though. You don't lack courage, which has to be admitted. How did you get past the guards? Anyway, I don't want to know. It won't help me anyway, because next time you'll come up with something else."

Theo watched her closely, and suddenly he capitulated.

"Still wanting your revenge on me? Why? Because I used to not want to marry you?" he asked in a perfectly normal tone, without any ironic or hateful undertones.

Adeline shook her head negative.

"It didn't matter that much," she explained. "But the fact that you did not pay attention to me at all... You scorned me, all Navarra played at my expense. No woman, from the queen to the last peasant woman, would forgive you such an insult, even if she felt nothing for you. And I felt. I wanted you, have this satisfaction, I wanted you so much that often I could neither sleep nor eat. I thought that when I got involved with another man, he would help me forget about you, but it was a deceptive hope. I loved you more and more and I hated you more and more because you were still looking at me as if I was transparent."

"Because you took feelings to me into your's head, you tried to get your revenge for so long? It's sick," he pouted, but he couldn't help feeling an unhealthy fascination. Adeline's entire speech flattered him, for understandable reasons.

Duchess smiled mysteriously.

"I've already got my revenge," she said slowly, examining her manicured nails carefully.

"Yes? I don't know about that." Theo shrugged, though a chill ran up his spine out of nowhere.

Adeline looked up at him with hazel eyes.

"And yet," she said venomously. "I've done my revenge, and maybe it's time you found out what it was all about."

She got up from her armchair and started pacing the room, her silk dress rustling. Theo followed her with his eyes, and the unpleasant sensation he had felt began to deepen slightly.

"Do you remember the harvest festival in 63?" The duchess asked suddenly, stopping in front of him. "You played with your peasants as if you were yourself a peasant born under a fence. You should be careful when you drink young wine, it is tricky. Do you remember that night? You slept like an animal and dragged a random girl to hay, and in the morning you probably didn't even remember what happened."

Theo quickly examined his conscience. What he really remembered from that night was a crazy beginning and an equally crazy headache after waking up, and what was between... some delusion. He drank too much that evening, but everyone was drunk then, including Preziosa. Bellette wasn't with them, so there was no one to stop him from doing some foolishness.

Meanwhile, Adeline continued, more and more frantically:

"I disguised myself as a peasant and waited until it was safe enough to blend in with the celebrating reapers. I did it cold. I already knew my husband was too old to give me a baby, so I could be sure that if this night bore fruit, the baby would be yours. Ideally, you should give birth to your son and teach him to hate you, right? But for anger I gave birth to a girl, worth nothing to my plans. She could only serve me in one way: I gave her to the countryside, far away from me and you. Supposedly she died of the plague. You don't understand yet? This is my revenge. Your daughter, blood of blood and bone of bone, died in poverty in a peasant cottage that smelled of poverty, and you did not even have the opportunity to take her in your arms."

There was such hate in Adeline's eyes and words that even an executioner would frighten, but the knight couldn't reach it anymore. He sat down in the empty armchair, feeling the ground slipping away from under his feet. Such an enormity of perversity was beyond his mind, for the first time he was really frightened of this woman, and suddenly the truth exploded with bright colors under his skull, which he had vaguely sensed, although he had not consciously guessed it.

"Mathilde," he thought dazedly, "Mathilde is my child. So I didn't lie to Joan, even though I meant to."

He looked up at Adeline, who was gaping triumphantly, and suddenly fury took the place of terror. He jumped up and gripped her shoulders tightly.

"You cannot even guess, treacherous witch, how incomplete your revenge is," he hissed. "This child is alive, I took her from the coop's wife to whom your maidservant entrusted her, and gave her to someone who is now raising this poor creature as my own daughter. Of course, don't count on me to tell you who it is. And to think that if it weren't for your idiotic guilt about the baby I killed her father, you'd be fine. What kind of mother are you? What kind of woman are you that you could use a helpless child to just revenge?! I never liked you, but only now do I really despise you, and although I don't fight women, beware of me, because, for the Lord's mercy, if I have the opportunity to trip you, you will remember me until you die!"

He let go the Duchess and stormed out the door like an arrow. The corridor was empty, so he immediately turned to the nearest secret passage, hidden in a niche behind old armor and opening by turning a lever hidden in its base. He wanted to run until he smashed his head against the nearest branch, but he forced himself to first of all cover his tracks and a little punch to confuse any chase. He only stopped when he was in his safe place and wiped the sweat from his face with a trembling hand. He wasn't stupid, but he knew he would never have come up with such refined and cynical vengeance on an enemy. Such cold perversity did not fit in his mind. How could a well-mannered, elegant lady drag a drunken enemy into the hay like a common harlot, and give birth to his child only to abandon it like garbage to his fate to accommodate her vengeance? He was starting to doubt whether Adeline was well in her mind. He shivered, though the day was warm, and tightened his doublet tighter, unable to understand where the feeling of chill was coming from. After a while he understood - he was still under the macabre impression of the duchess's words and the shadow they cast over his life. He remembered the tiny, emaciated creature in his arms and bit his lips. Somehow he sensed a connection between this child and him, though he did not understand and was ashamed of the tenderness this little one, so helpless and so innocent, aroused in him. Somehow he had to get over his boiling agitation before he returned to his friends, so he wandered through the woods until he was exhausted.

It was already dusk when he reached the clearing where his friends were waiting, all of them very sour expressions.

"We already thought you were over," Pierre said when he saw him.

"Disappointed?" Theo looked at him so that Pierre sat down.

"No, why..." he disagreed weakly.

He had not yet seen his brother-in-law in such a state, although he had witnessed his fits of rage, always turbulent and loud.

"How was in the castle?" Tristan ventured. His older brother chilled him.

"Never mind," he growled, and to avoid further questioning, he went to his attic.

He didn't immediately notice Bellette huddled against one of the walls. She didn't say anything, but as he sat down beside her, she rested her head on his shoulder. With all her female intuition, she felt that something very bad had happened that her husband could not and would not tell her. She wasn't going to ask him questions. For his part, Theo didn't know if he could now tell her what he had learned from Adeline, nor did he know how she might react to the news that he had cheated her. He didn't want it, but it had happened, and it was impossible to reverse it, and it was impossible to just forget it for Mathilde's sake.

He knew he would have to talk to his wife about it someday, but he was not yet ready for such confessions. But he had to say something, for he already understood that he was wrong to do something about a completely different matter. He put his arm around Bellette.

"I want you to know something," he said softly. "I was telling you that I didn't care for the children, that I didn't want to have them, and thus left you alone in your pain. I didn't support you when I should have. I understood that now."

She hugged him tighter.

"I know," she whispered. "You suffered just like I did, you just didn't want anyone to see it. You are so proud after all..."

She reached out and stroked his neck. Theo pressed his lips against her hair and said nothing more.

*****

"For God's sake, a hundred thunderbolts and knots of brave devils, how many times do I have to tell you that if you don't know how to do it, don't do it?!" Pierre yelled as he sat on the grass holding his broken head.

"How am I supposed to learn anything when you don't let me practice?" Gwidon retorted with a look of hurt innocence, trying to hide an improvised slingshot behind him.

He was still trying to learn to throw stones, although everyone, including Pierre, told him that you had to have a natural talent for that, "a knack," as Jean called it.

"We have to put an end to this, because that idiot is going to kill us all here," Pierre decided, standing up and glaring furiously at the laughing Millot. "Where's the chief?"

"At the other end of our clearing," the highlander answered him cheerfully. "Armando teaches him to juggle lit torches and to walk the rope."

"Not one right-minded in this forest. Now he went loco too. He wants to join the traveling circus?" Pierre snorted in shock and shook his head.

"Not necessarily, but it won't hurt him if he knows how to do it," said Preziosa with dignity. "Besides, he has been in such a terrible mood lately that any entertainment will do him good. He needs something to keep his mind and hands busy, otherwise he might end up going out to the highroad and strangling the first man to respond to his taunt.

Pierre frowned. He, too, noticed that Theo had been snarling at everyone since his visit to Adeline de Valois, eager to brawl and completely lost his usual humor, but attributed it to the collapse of all his life plans and hopes. Now he was starting to doubt it. After all, his brother-in-law was not one of those who cry over spilled milk, he was more inclined to disregard than to exaggerate his losses, so his current behavior was all the more incomprehensible.

"Someone would have to talk to him." He muttered without conviction. Millot laughed again.

"Who will do it, maybe you?" he asked.

"As a matter of fact yes," Pierre grabbed Gwidon by the neck with a determined movement and dragged him, screaming shrilly, in the direction indicated by Preziosa.

Behind the trees that sheltered the cabin on the south side, Theo, led by Armando, tossed three lit torches, maneuvering them with an agility unusual for someone who had only begun his studies a few days ago. Of course, it would be far less of a surprise to someone who knew that he had actually been studying the play in secret for a long time, under the discreet supervision of a white-haired circus performer, except that he was telling no one.

"Chief, show who's in charge!" Pierre yelled suddenly over his ear, causing the knight to lose control of the torches and barely jump back before they fell.

"What I have to show?" he asked half-consciously.

"Who's in charge," his brother-in-law replied, struggling with Gwidon.

"In front of people?" Armando chuckled, pouring the bucket of water calmly over the smoldering wood and dry grass.

"But what is it all about?" Theo irritated, rubbing his sweaty palms on his jacket.

"Disqualify this miserable poet from playing with a slingshot! He hit me right in the forehead and the target was almost in the opposite direction," Pierre complained, pointing to a large bruise on his forehead.

"Why was he hanging around me?" Gwidon wailed. He had the gift of playing the victim of slander, but the chief knew him from this point of view and was not deceived.

"Weasel," he said sternly. "What was the deal? I don't sing ballads and you don't shoot a slingshot."

"It's not fair," the troubadour pouted, but he dared not openly disobey.

"As a penalty, March to the cauldron free of turn." Theo decided all the more willingly that the next day he was supposed to be 'on guard at the cauldron', and for that day Preziosa was cooking and it was too late to change it.

"I understand that you want to punish Gwidon, but why are you trying to screw us all at the same time?" Francois asked dissatisfiedly. "What Weasel cooks up cannot be eaten."

Theo did not pay attention to this protest, because Beregard, who had been absent for two days, had just arrived from the side of the forest. He was tired and dusty and angry.

"Bad news," he said. "The Black Prince seems to be preparing for an invasion. Robert Deauville told me to tell that the Welshman had imprisoned Philip d'Evreux in Meung Castle, who had come to see him for some diplomatic talks. He wants to restore order by force in Aquitaine, where almost all cities are already rebelling against him. Robert Deauville suspects that Prince Philip is held hostage lest the king support the rebellion of the cities of Aquitaine."

"A sad thing indeed."

The knight frowned and began to think about some way to solve the situation. The taking of a hostage of the rank of Philip d'Evreux could be read either as a declaration of war or as acceptance of that declaration. Theo did not know what talks had been held at such a high level recently and who was the stronger party here politically or militarily, but the hostage-taking by one of the parties could be read quite unambiguously, regardless of the content of the talks. In any case, Deauville and his party had their hands tied - risking the life of Prince d'Evreux would not have been forgiven by the King of France, let alone the King of Navarre, who loved his younger son and was proud of him.

"What to do here, for the God's sake?" he muttered to himself.

Beregard cleared his throat significantly.

"I know I'll be regret to tell you this, but I can't keep silent," he said. "I overheard something else: Lady Joan is coming to Aquitaine with her baby, and she will be following the road near Bongrais."

The knight's eyes flashed so brightly that Pierre gripped his head with a groan.

"Are we supposed to be kidnappers?" he asked.

"Somehow I don't like the kidnapping of women and children," Tristan joined him.

"Lady Joan will understand. We already know each other," his older brother replied absently. There was only one thought in his head:

"Mathilde... I'll see Mathilde again. She must have grown a lot during this time. I'm a stranger to her now, but I must, I must see her, at least once more before I die."

Ettienne nudged his hand shyly.

"You want to kidnap her and exchange her for the Duke of Navarre?" he asked, wrinkling his freckled nose.

"You guessed first time round. You're way too smart for a page," Theo said, and clapped his hands three times. At this sign, the remaining members of the gang flocked to him and froze in anticipation.

"We are starting a very difficult task," the chief said to them. "Two of you will immediately head to the main road to Aquitaine and wait in the tavern there for an English lady's retinue to Meung Castle. When they spot it, one will come running to notify us, the other will follow the carriage a little. In case of doubt: the lady we are interested in will travel with a small child. Are there any comments?"

"Get down to the shadows because your brain has overheated," Pierre offered resignedly.

His brother-in-law crushed him with his eyes and repeated the question. But no one knew what remark he could make, except for a few stronger words, nothing came to mind at all. After a pause, Jean spoke, choosing his words carefully:

"We are outlaws and yet we are to serve the king at the risk of our lives, right?"

"More or less."

"I'm not sure this is the best idea," Jean finished his thought and took a deep breath, squinting in anticipation of the thunder.

Millot interrupted unexpectedly.

"We do not serve the king, but France, which is our homeland and will always be it, no matter what king is on the throne. Theo is right, we need to free Philip d'Evreux before things get completely out of hand. Who knows what this Englishman really wants to use him for."

"He will sell him to a brothel, so smoother..." Gwidon began, but Armando silenced him with a kick to the ankle. Gwidon's jokes were risky to say the least.

Meanwhile, Millot's words, lavish as usual, brought an unexpectedly positive response. They all began to speak one by one, animated by what poets call "the flame of patriotism", screaming support for Aquitaine's libertarian aspirations and hatred of everything English, led by the Black Prince. Suddenly, everyone was ready to die for a good cause, even if they had previously disagreed, even the usually cynical Pierre. They were rarely so unanimous. Perhaps it was already in them before, the belief that France, their homeland, is more important than their own little affairs, and even than themselves, but this belief is usually born in people only when they have nothing to do with it. Lose. This point in their biographies was already behind them.

"OK, OK!" Theo finally silenced them, shouting over the multi-voiced buzz. "I know now that you will support me. Let's go further: I propose Jean and Francois for scouts, the two of them are worth the most together. Do you agree, thieves?"

"And why exactly them?" Armando was offended almost simultaneously with Millot.

"Because firstly, they are the best at blending with the environment, secondly they are the fastest runners in our band, and thirdly, because I want to," Theo looked at them severely and menacingly.

"Sorry, but what's that got to do with them running fast?" Ettienne asked, at least as quickly as the other two.

"Well, one of them will have to get damn fast from the road to Aquitaine here. It'll be best to go now, guys. Take some silver with you, it will be useful if you have to wait a long time. Before such an important action, you better not risk being caught in some kind of theft."

"It's as if they caught us once," Francois puffed out with superiority, and Jean added:

"You can count on us, chief. We won't disappoint you."

They ran to the hut to prepare for the journey, both proud as peacocks that their leader had been chosen them.

"There's also an annex to be prepared," Bellette remarked practically. "Somewhere we will have to accommodate this lady, it is difficult to expect that she will sleep with us on the hay or on a pile of pelts."

"Good point," her husband said, avoiding her eyes. He still couldn't make up his mind to tell her everything, and he was tormented not so much by guilt as for the dirtiness he had committed against her."

"Well, we've got a lot to do," Beregard said sadly.

"So can I not take my watch anymore at the boiler?" Gwidon asked hopefully.

"Repeat it and you will get the punch," Pierre, who from time to time tried as deputy commander to discipline the gang, told him sternly.

The poet sighed and wandered to the fire over which they usually cooked on clear days. Millot, Beregard, and Preziosa set about tidying up the outhouse and repairing its broken windows, Pierre and Armando took care of the damaged roof.

"Actually, everything could be cleaned up. Tristan, Ettienne, help me. Bellette, will you join me?" Theo asked after a moment.

"Sure," said Bellette with dignity. "Of all of you, only I know about cleaning and elegance."

"Go on, go to work, maids!" Pierre called from the roof. "Clean every flea to a shine and don't forget to brush the whiskers of the cockroaches!"

"Shut up or you in a whole mess of trouble!" Theo shook his fist and started cleaning with his group.

Every day, no one in this forest hideout paid any attention to cleanliness and order, sometimes Preziosa or Bellette swept roughly the common room, but that was also the end of it. But now the knight just didn't want Lady Joan to think something bad about him and his friends when she saw the conditions under which they lived. He had not realized so far how much rubbish had accumulated in their hut over the years and what was lurking in the corners in blissful peace.

"What about Foussard?" Ettienne worried, sweeping the entire store of various debris from behind the stove.

"Good question. This lady must be terrified of the little creatures," Tristan agreed.

Foussard was a fat old rat who, on a whim, they had tamed during a boring winter and liked it like a pet. For his part, Foussard found this arrangement probably very beneficial, he crawled out from under the floor with a triple tap, fawned like a cat, and never bit anyone.

"Tough! I'll warn her," Theo said, shoving a swarm of long-legged spiders out of the leather-strewn corner. "He probably won't be shown to her anyway. Every beast has its own mind, and it only recognizes us. For two weeks, Ettienne, he didn't even want to come over to you."

"You will always get a stupid idea. A rat as an equivalent of a bird in a cage on the window of the old maid," Bellette ironized, hiding in her soul a truly feminine fear of mice, rats and other little creatures. "Crap, I never thought it was so dirty here, what a pigsty."

"So tidier suddenly? We clean up, what else do you want?" Tristan muttered angrily.

"Maybe you should try to keep order as such here. Neither of you will pick up the slightest scrap, even if you break your leg against it."

"We have more serious matters on our minds," Ettienne said with a comical serious look on his round face.

"Oh, especially you have a lot of them," Bellette muttered sarcastically, pouring a bucket of water with a lye prepared by Preziosa from wood ash and mostly used for washing on the backwater.

The big cleanup continued until night and all the next day, which was not surprising considering that the cottage hadn't seen such cleanup since it was built.

"It's not even that bad," Pierre said after inspecting the hut afterwards. "At least this Englishwoman will not gossip us that we live like pigs in a dunghill."

"Lady Joan is a lady, ladies don't use such expressions," Theo scolded him.

"They probably don't need to go to the bushes either," said Millot sarcastically. "Some maid's doing it for them."

In terms of social views, the highlander was not inferior to Pierre, and his language was sharper. Theo shot him a look that announced the shift to hand arguments, but Preziosa interrupted the row in the bud.

"Come on!" She exclaimed. "If I'm to be in time with this straitjacket, you must not run away from my measure!"

"Our chief is getting ready for the arrival of this English monkey, it's nice," laughed Millot and was punched on the back of the neck.

"I'm not getting ready," Theo said furiously. "I just don't think showing patches and tatters in front of a lady is a manifestation of refined elegance. And I expect you to look like humans too."

"Not a chance," Pierre said, offended.

"You've endured the tidying up, you will endure a neat appearance."

Theo was quite serious, which upset his brother-in-law even more. Neither he nor any of his friends cared about cleanliness, except for him and his younger brother, both of them bathe every day, and Theo also swam on every occasion. The whole gang thought it a harmless quirk, for their concept of personal hygiene ended with the occasional washing of their face and hands, and a short bath only for occasion. It was hardly surprising. In those days, only in cities where there were baths, more attention was paid to whether someone was dirty or clean, and not in the social class from which the outlaws came. Only Gwidon cared a little about his appearance, though also rather superficially. However, this time the leader was unrelenting - everyone had to bathe, comb, shave and put on specially cleaned and repaired clothes for the occasion.

"I've never seen him become so concerned about anything," Beregard said to his friends, having listened to his recommendations.

"In my opinion our knight has a maggot in his brain." Millot said scandalized.

"Shall we stand up to him?" Armando asked doubtfully.

The friends looked at each other.

"No," Pierre sighed, after a moment with resignation. The last spanking he received from his brother-in-law was more than enough for him.

"Theo is quite right, though," Ettienne chimed in, always taking the side of his knight for understandable reasons. "We cannot let the English laugh at us."

"Huh! They wash themselves maybe once a year," said Preziosa. "And they keep their clothes in castle lavatories, because the stench repels moths. I'd rather moths than such perfumes."

Pierre shrugged his shoulders and said sententiously:

"One man's meat is another man's poison. Anyway, I think that it is a bit like ours there, that is, some people do not bathe, and those loony don't crawl out of the water, like our leader. Baron de la Roche, you know, the one who lives in a castle three miles away has a wife from England, she supposedly had a tin pot in a little room without a window, and every other day she bathes in hot water, and sometimes even supposedly in milk. Do you get it? Divine offense and that's it, the children in the villages die of hunger, and such lady bathes in milk."

"Maybe it's just rumors?" Millot consoled him. "Anyway, we aren't in milk, but we must bathe in water, or the leader will be furious. You know he is crazy about obeying his orders."

"And he's right. Give me your rags, I will take care of them, and you will put yourselves in order," suggested Preziosa.

"Hell knows when this little lady will come our way, and in the meantime we'll be bathed in a bath, like a fool," Pierre muttered with displeasure.

"It's also a great misfortune that you will all be clean once in your life," said Bellette, who had just come from the woods, gathering herbs to season her food. "Theo lasted so long. I'm surprised him that he endured such dirty, licey, and smelly company for so many years. He should have rushed you into the water much earlier."

"Come on," her brother growled furiously.

Being with her mother at the Bongrais Castle, Bellette learned to take care of her appearance, which made her stand out from other village girls. Pierre couldn't understand it. Unable to postpone the matter indefinitely, the friends dragged themselves to the lake, where they scrubbed themselves with sand and clay, and finally decided that they could not be any cleaner. Then they rinsed well in the lake and returned to their hideout, temporarily wrapped up with various rags, as it turned out that in the meantime Preziosa had taken their clothes to be cleaned. Since it had to take time (you had to soak everything in a lye solution for at least half a day), they dabbed in what was in the box - various cloths, saturated with the scent of herbs against moths. Sometimes they came in handy when you had to go somewhere in disguise, but of course no one wore them every day, because the clothes of a wealthy merchant, monk or tightrope walker did not fit the life of a forest robber. Their everyday clothes were color-matched so as not to stand out from the forest background and mask their presence. Only Gwidon always dressed in bright colors.

While they waited for their clothes to dry after washing, the friends pondered the dilemma: what would they do if news of Lady Joan's arrival reached them now, for neither of them smiled at the "public appearance" in what they were wearing now, and that not even because the garments were ill-fitting and exuded a strong scent of marsh herb and lavender. They just didn't belong to them, and that was enough to make them feel terrible in them. Fortunately, nothing happened for the next few days. With great difficulty, Preziosa washed their clothes, rinsed them well in the stream, dried them in the sun, and made the necessary repairs, which she was very skillful at.

Theo hardly spoke during those days of waiting, and that was for the best, for he had become snappy and explosive, the way it always does when things didn't go his way. After days he wandered near the road one of the scouts must have come, looking for his eyes, trying to see what was not there. This expectation was more irritating than the case itself. Finally his patience was rewarded - Francois returned to the hideout, rushing as fast as he could.

"They are here," he panted, bumping into the clearing. "As you predicted, they stopped at the 'Merry Goat' tavern, and in the morning they are to continue their journey. A large retinue of twenty men, and a sixth carriage."

He dropped to his knees and gasped for air with his open mouth.

"You stay, the rest follow me," Theo ordered. "Bellette, you're staying too, and get something ready for dinner."

"Best roasted hemlock. Don't worry, everything will be fine."

"How can you be sure that she will want to eat what we eat?" Colas asked skeptically.

"Not our worry, she don't want to, don't eat," growled Pierre belligerently, cautiously moving beyond the reach of the chief's long arm.

The latter, however, had no time for him now, and he did not pay any attention to his words. In the blink of an eye he organized the march, and he himself was at the head of the gang headed quickly up the road towards Aquitaine. The road was long, fortunately everyone had strong legs and did not complain about the pace imposed on them.

It was only halfway through that it suddenly turned out that Ettienne was following them.

"What's that supposed to mean?!" Theo yelled at the boy as the truth came out.

"Nothing," answered him fearlessly. "My place is at your side."

"Are we going or are we talking?" Asked Beregard matter-of-factly. "You can yell at that spotted chicken later, we're in a bit of a rush right now. Or am I wrong?"

Theo looked at him, then at his page, and, waving a hopeless hand, started forward again. Not for the first time, it occurred to him that, for some reason, he was attracting France's most undisciplined freaks, and that nothing could be done about it. It had to be that way, and in the end, even though his friends sometimes annoyed him with their irresponsible behavior, he liked them all very much.

When they reached the Merry Goat inn, it turned out that Lady Joan's retinue had already left it and well advanced. With little thought, they tied up and gagged the boy cleaning the stables, then took all the horses left behind by mister de Lottaire's guests returning from their unsuccessful hunting, feeding at the inn before setting off on their way back. Having horses, they could easily catch up with the retinue, although this, of course, did not eliminate the numerical advantage of the armed men surrounding the carriage.

Hiding behind trees, they drove as close as they could without catching the eyes of the armed men.

"They have to be clamped," Theo said to his companions. "Where's Jean?"

"Here," a red-haired thief emerged from the bushes. "I follow them from the inn itself. What have you come up with, Chief?"

Theo patted the horse's neck.

"We must convince these Englishmen that there are many more of us than there are," he said slowly. "Get bows and slingshots. Half to the left, half to the right, and when I give you a sign you will start firing. And don't show yourselves until I call you. Ettienne and Tristan are coming with me, none of them can be used to the shooting. So let's think... Yes. Beregard, Millot, Preziosa and Colas to the right, Pierre, Jean, Armando and Gwidon to the left. And the three of us are ahead. Focus... Now!"

The outlaws split up efficiently and, having caught up with the retinue under the cover of trees, began sewing with arrows and stones in escorts. They could do it in such a way that the attacked seemed to be besieged by some overwhelming force, which was not an easy art, but extremely useful in such situations. Taking advantage of the resulting confusion and panic, Theo, in the company of his brother, broke through to the carriage, knocking down a few armed on horses on the way, confused by this way of conducting the robbery. Tristan nimbly leapt from his horse to the front of the carriage and snatched the reins from the young postillion's hands, throwing him off the goat to the ground. He pulled the reins with all his strength, stopping the shafts, frightened by the sudden noise.

"Make them stop resisting, my lady, or my men will kill them all!" Theo shouted as he opened the carriage door.

"Surrender! It does not make sense!" the young woman shouted through the window to the unit commander. Still capable of fighting, the armed men put down their weapons hastily. Fighting the unseen enemy was an experience too terrifying for them to continue.

The outlaws emerged from hiding, their bows still taut, aiming menacingly at them. The soldiers huddled together in a terrified group. Their commander, badly wounded by an arrow, was no longer able to command, and they themselves completely lost their heart to fight.

"Easy!" Pierre exclaimed. "How are you, Chief?!"

Theo, oblivious to anything else, stared at the depths of the carriage with round eyes of surprise, disappointment, and anger.

"You... you are not Lady Joan." He stuttered finally.

A plump, dark-haired woman in a richly decorated dress and a lace scarf hugged a maybe three-year-old boy in a defensive gesture. The two maids huddled in the other seat, sobbing in terror, but their mistress did not cry.

"I'm the Duchess Joan of Kent, wife of the Duke of Aquitaine," she said furiously. "You'll all pay your head for this attack, only let my husband find out about it."

"So far, it's not a good prospect," Tristan remarked calmly, peering inside without asking.

Pierre put down his bow and walked nonchalantly to the carriage. He looked at his brother-in-law, then at the carriage passengers, and put his arm around a small page.

"You know what, Ettienne? I didn't think that I'd see the day when our leader would be tongue-tied," he said. "He's always so smart mouth, and now look, he's completely speechless. Theo, can you hear me? I talk to you!"

"What?" The knight, still impressed by his fatal mistake, though not attributable to anyone, looked at him unconsciously.

"No "what", just move a little," Beregard saw fit to support Pierre. "Why you are so speechless?"

"It's easy. Mistake in the address," Ettienne explained resolutely. "The name is correct, the person is not. This is the wife of the Black Prince."

"So what? That's even better," said Pierre blithely. "Listen, chief, now is not the time for grimaces. We take what is and come back. As you start, you should finish... You don't want to back out now, after all the hardships you've exposed us to?"

Theo finally regained his voice, though not his equanimity.

"Unfortunately, I don't think we have a choice," he said in a subdued voice. "Come on, misses, we don't need you. You, soldier... You look smart to me, so you will tell your master that if he wants his wife and son back, he must release Philip d'Avreux. Where he wants to carry out an exchange, let him think for himself and send me a deliberate reply to "Merry Goat", the day after tomorrow for vespers[10]. Just no tricks, tell him he's dealing with a desperate and rather insane man. Add also that I haven't forgotten the ornament that he gave me in his generosity."

"Ye-yes, sir," the soldier muttered, his expression dumbfounded. Both servants jumped out of the carriage with poorly concealed eagerness.

"Better not try anything," Pierre warned the soldiers with an eloquent gesture and nodded to the rest of the outlaws, still pointing arrows at the survivors of the princess's retinue. They had to withdraw now, so that no one could shoot them in the back.

---

[10] Evening prayer, serving as a reference point in time in the Middle Ages.

CHAPTER IV

Difficult Contest

"Do you realize we've made ourselves in trouble?" asked his friend Beregard, equating his horse with his. "Uhm," said Theo thoughtfully.

"Don't be kidding. After all, if the Black Prince gets us now, he will make English dumplings out of us."

"I'm not going to tell him *bon appetit* there. Besides, I don't want to hurt these two. I know our black friend will take it as a personal insult, that's tough! He's a devilishly touchy man."

He looked at the rattle of the carriage behind them. Tristan on the horseback gave him a reassuring sign. Since no one from the gang could drive six horses, only two were left, the rest decoupled already on the highroad. Ettienne rode in the middle - he was entrusted with guarding the abducted lady and her son, which he took as a great honor. In truth, Theo entrusted him with this role due to the fact that Ettienne was the only one in the gang to have a basic knowledge of etiquette, and besides, due to his underage age, the Duchess certainly felt better in his company than in the company of any other gang member.

"Okay, all off the horses!" Theo exclaimed. "The wetlands begin. Lady, please get off."

"Get your dirty mitts off," growled the Duchess unfriendly, reluctantly getting out of the carriage.

"Just not dirty, lady. Our chief washes more often than you change your shirt," Pierre protested vigorously.

"Watch your tongue, yokel, or you will lose it along with your head!" the duchess cried angrily.

"Certainly not because of you..." Pierre began belligerently, but Theo cut him short:

"Shut up. Let me take the boy, lady, it's hard for you."

"Don't you dare touch my son, you hear?!" the Englishwoman screamed, pushing him away with a force he did not expect from her.

"Not only him, but the four closest villages also heard," said Jean wryly. "Chief, I'm telling you that this lady needs to be blindfolded, and she could use a gag, regardless of whose wife she is. We cannot risk that she will bring the entire English army onto our necks."

"A no-nonsense comment, but without respect for a noble birth," said Millot. He seemed to be enjoying the situation excellently.

"As for the blindfold, okay, but be decent," Theo replied with a heavy sigh. "She's not one of the innkeepers, but a real lady. I'm sorry, madam, but there is no need for a blindfold. If it's your wish to carry the baby alone, I cannot force you to change your mind, but it's still quite a long way off."

"What are you so worried about her? She wants, let her carry the brat."

Pierre shrugged, ignoring the fierce gaze of his brother-in-law. Colas and Millot decoupled the horses from the carriage and masked it with branches, and the horses, along with the others, led them to the enclosure in the middle of the woods, where they usually kept the animals, if they had any. There was a large shed, full of hay in the attic and against the walls, a stream and abundant marsh grass, thicker and taller than the meadow grass. Meanwhile, the rest of the gang led their captives through the marshes. Upon reaching the destination, Theo removed the blindfold from the duchess and said:

"This annex must be sufficient for you, my lady, for the time being for the entire palace. Please don't try to escape on your own, because there are swamps all around here and if you don't know the road really well, you can drown in an instant."

The Englishwoman gave him a contemptuous look and entered the annex, slamming the door behind her with a non-English temper. Theo leaned against the hut wall and wiped the sweat from his brow. All this was very unfortunate for him, although he admitted that from the point of view of their overriding goal, that is, the release of Prince Philip, things turned out better than he had anticipated. A mistake, resulting from the same names, could turn out to be salutary. He thought. This Lady Joan of Kent was so different from the Lady Fitzoother he knew that it would be difficult to confuse them. Unlike her namesake, slender, fair-haired and almost as tall as a knight, the Black Prince's wife was short, somewhat plump, with hair the color of freshly shelled chestnuts, and undoubtedly prettier, or at least more attractive. Her son looked like her - dark, with a round face and large gray-brown eyes.

The knight was struck by the fact that, despite the experience that was certainly terrifying for such a toddler, the boy did not say a word, he did not even cry, he only looked at them with his round eyes, cuddled in his mother's protective arms.

"If I were in the Black Prince's shoes, I would move the earth and heaven to get them back," he thought.

Someone suddenly touched his shoulder, Theo jumped defensively to the side.

"Easy, hero. It's just me," Bellette said. "I heard that not everything went according to your plans."

"It doesn't matter," her husband shook his head resolutely. "The dice have been cast."

"So be it and so that it doesn't end badly. People say this lady is terrible, how am I supposed to look after her?" the young woman asked with some dissatisfaction.

Theo waved his hand. He didn't want to think about it now, although he did have to settle it somehow. He did not want to expose his wife to impertinence and insults, moreover, he believed that she should not serve anyone, but someone forced to be with the princess for the service. Maybe Preziosa? She was skillful and not stupid, maybe a little too direct, and certainly the Black Prince's wife would not be pleased with her company.

"Oh, well," he muttered to himself and went in search of the Gypsy.

He found her by a stream washing her male disguise. For a representative of her nation, she was surprisingly clean and hardworking - perhaps it was thanks to the blood inherited from her father, apparently impoverished Spanish grand.

"Preziosa, I have a request," he said, sitting down beside her on the shore. "As long as we host the duchess, serve her. Women like her can't take care of themselves, you know..."

Preziosa smiled.

"As you like, but I'm not going to grovel in front of her," she replied. "If she tries to insult me, I'll answer her the same."

"Perhaps it will do her good."

He could count on this dark-haired dancer since she joined them with her brother, and sometimes he felt remorse that he was taking advantage of her not as a girl, but as another man from his band. She, for her part, did not mind. She was an excellent horse rider, throwing stones no worse than any of them, she even fired a bow, though she could not fully stretch it like a man. Instead, she put every man of her height on her arm. Theo, accustomed to women "airy and gentle as a lily," often could not bring himself to think of her as a girl. Anyway, she knew how to fulfill each task, also this, although it was certainly unpleasant for her. The Englishwoman treated her the same as the others, that is, contemptuously and in advance.

"Fortunately, it won't be long," Pierre used to say to his friends several times a day, longing for Francois to be sent to the Merry Goat tavern to discreetly await a messenger from the Black Prince. Anyway, everyone was waiting for him as for salvation, because the duchess stinged them from the very first moment, so that they would gladly get rid of her without any conditions. However, their chieftain would not allow them to do so.

*****

Lady Joan ran out of the annex, almost stumbling over Beregard as he was repairing her sandal.

"Where is Richard?!" She screamed hysterically. "What have you done with my child, you bastards?!"

"Relax, lady," Beregard rose from the grass, leisurely finishing the tying of the thong. "Do you always have to roar like that, lady?

We all have good hearing. I haven't seen your kid. What exactly happened?"

"I fell asleep for a moment, and when I woke up, he was gone," the duchess wrung her hands, sobbing so that it was difficult to understand her words. "Where is he? Where could he go?"

"Nowhere, I hope. There are swamps everywhere, but I think someone would have seen him." Beregard put on a sandal and called out. "Hey! Has anyone seen the boy?"

"Don't yell like a donkey, you're not in the woods," said Jean, who had drunk some booze the night before and was just trying to fight it off.

"Yes, he is," said Pierre, attracted to him. "What is going on here? Who are you looking for?"

"That little Englishman has disappeared somewhere." His friend explained to him.

"I didn't see him," Pierre said, worried. "Hey, guys! Drop everything and everyone look for our princess' kid!"

The outlaws dutifully looked around the clearing and the forest, and Lady Joan was running unconscious between them, calling desperately:

"Dick! Where are you?! Come back, Dick!"

The confusion was short-lived, interrupted by Theo, who came from the side of a small pool into which their brook ran nearby. In his arms he carried a boy sleeping like a gopher.

"What's this mess?" he asked sternly.

The Duchess ran up to him and snatched the child from his arms.

"I told you not to touch him!" She screamed hysterically.

"Relax, because we'll have to bleed your blood, and neither of us is a medic," Theo replied resentfully. "He came to me, I didn't ask him."

Preziosa tapped her forehead discreetly, staring at him meaningfully. She embraced the still crying, shaky Englishwoman and led her to the annex with reassuring words.

"You really should be gentler this time," Bellette said with obvious displeasure. "She might have died of anxiety. At this point, she isn't the wife of the Black Prince, but just a mother, don't you understand?"

Theo shrugged.

"Maybe I understand, there reason to make such a row?" he asked reluctantly.

"Did this tinker really come to you?" Gwidon asked curiously.

"Just so you know. He came, got on my lap and demanded that I tell him a fairy tale. Well, I told him the one about the princess turned into an orange, it's the only one I remember in full. Before I finished, he fell asleep and that was it. After that, I was afraid to move, so as not to wake him up, I don't know why."

"He fell asleep, you say? I mean, you are a bore." Gwidon laughed happily.

He willingly admitted his friends superiority in every field and was not jealous of anything, but only he could tell legends or sing.

"Francois is running here!" Ettienne called.

"Thank God, something will finally move." Beregard sighed devoutly.

He dreamed of a moment when the pesky Englishwoman would disappear from their lives and stop bothering them with grievances and fumes.

"Writing from His Englishness," said a short Francois, handing the leader a roll of parchment. "Read, chief, you can."

The knight hastily broke the seal he hated and unfolded the scroll. The Black Prince informed him in a concise courtly style that in three days he would be waiting with Philip d'Evreux at the provincial border, in the village of Garou, from Primary to Vespers. The letter contained, oddly enough, neither threats nor even warnings, although the slightly quivering line of the individual letters showed that terrible anger was boiling in the prince's heart.

"Yes," Theo muttered after reading the letter twice. "We have to go there together in case of an ambush, which I still think is very likely. Let me think... I, Tristan and Pierre will go there officially, the rest will follow our trail and allow us to escape, showering the soldiers with arrows. Immediately after causing a commotion among the soldiers, you also run, and each goes home on their own. In case there is no ambush, we return home separately anyway, as it cannot be ruled out that the villain will follow us. So don't come out. Philip will have to take care of himself, I suppose, moreover, that his retinue will be with him, after all, such as he does not travel alone."

"Right," agreed Pierre with artificial seriousness. "He's a big boy and doesn't need a nanny to wipe his nose."

"What if the Black Prince has us killed as soon as we get there?" Tristan asked, running his fingers through his thick curls.

His brother shook his head.

"I don't think he would go so far as to," he said, rolling up the parchment. "He won't risk that a stray arrow will hurt his wife or son. Only when he will have them... It's my head to play it right. Check all the strings of bows and arrows, nothing can fail us in such a fight. We have enough time to prepare the weapons.

Tristan, do you know English really well? I know a few words, but mostly words that aren't used with ladies."

"I know it well enough. And since when do you need an interpreter and why? After all, the whole family of Prince Edward, even the little one, speaks French as do we." Tristan looked at his brother with interest.

"If our favorite enemy is willing to do something, he will give his men command in English," Theo explained. "That's why you joined my unit, and not, let's say, to Beregard."

Everyone nodded understandingly. Their leader's stepbrother, albeit a good companion, was a poor fighter - he shot accurately and rode well, but his physical strength, hand-to-hand combat skills and fighting spirit left much to be desired. He was not told this, not wanting to hurt the boy, but in armed clashes one of the outlaws always made sure that nothing bad happened to him and came to his aid in more dangerous situations. Anyway, Theo himself always placed him somewhere to the side, where he could act as an observer and watch for any larger unit approaching, and not take on forceful matters himself.

"Not everyone is born to be a warrior, even in a knightly family," he would say, trying to justify his stepbrother. "For example, Prince Philip is perfect material for a knight, and our current king, his full brother, is absolutely useless on the battlefield."

For his part, Tristan did not shirk any dangerous task and even demanded to be treated as equal to others. The fact that his brother had chosen him to join his group, even if only as an interpreter, he considered a great honor and was very proud of it.

As the rest of the band went to their business, Theo walked slowly back to the stream. He was happy with the positive outcome of the case, and although it was not quite settled yet, he did not expect any special obstacles in bringing it to an end. Everything seemed to end well, but he felt some disgust. He has always believed that there is nothing to justify such practices as kidnapping women and children, but he did it himself, albeit under the circumstances. He kept his thoughts back to the boy who was sleeping confidently on his lap. He told himself in vain that he was the son of France's mortal enemy, and perhaps the future executioner of his country, for now it was just a small child, helpless and innocent.

"I shouldn't be doing this," he thought.

He loathed himself for what he had to do and wanted to think things through in private. He didn't even notice when it was getting dark and when Princess Joan approached him. She hesitated for a moment, then coughed shyly. Theo, out of his thoughts, looked at her in immeasurable surprise. When the expression of contemptuous superiority faded from her lips, she seemed really very pretty with that round doll face and big eyes.

"I listen to you, lady," he said, rising hastily with all due respect.

"I was rude to you," said the Duchess, stumbling slightly. "I shouldn't, but understand, I was afraid for my son. Only he was left with me. My firstborn, Edward, died of scarlet fever, and the little girl I was so excited about was born dead. It hurts so much to lose a child, and being a princess is irrelevant."

"I understand that, lady," Theo whispered sadly. "I myself lost my child. There is not a day or an hour that I don't think about."

"If my husband would not agree to your demands..." The Englishwoman hesitated and fell silent, looking at him with concern.

The knight shook his head slowly.

"No, my lady," he answered an unanswered question. "I couldn't hurt you two. Even for France. It would be beyond my strength, but luckily your husband doesn't know it. He has already agreed to the hostage swap, so you'll both be returning to him soon."

The Duchess breathed a sigh of relief. Now that her fear for her and her child's life was over, she looked at the famous outlaw in a different way. He seemed quite different to her from the knights she had known before - bronzed brown, supple and springy, with a mane of shiny black hair falling over a broad forehead. The long, dark eyes had some kind of magical charm. You haven't seen eyes like that in England.

"The stories of the outlaw's beauty weren't exaggerated," she thought. "But why is he so sad? They told me he was happy and never worried about anything. After all, they sing about him 'He is always smiling and does not know what fear is. He is not afraid of depths, storms or hail. Although he does not know is the roof above is safe, he laughs and jokes, and loves the whole world. It's a nice ballad though."

When she heard it singing in the roadside tavern, she just shrugged and made a face of contempt. Later, when she saw the outlaw with her own eyes, she was too afraid for herself and her son to be able to see his beauty and grace. Back then, he was a monster to her, whatever he looked like. Now she had calmed down, so her feelings had softened as well.

"You could have asked a large ransom for me," she said with a bit of coquetry.

Theo looked at her and finally managed a smile that drew seductive dimples on his cheeks.

"I couldn't think of a big enough sum, Lady, so I'd rather give it up right now," he replied.

"Peace between us then, right?" the duchess extended her smooth hand to him, which the knight touched with his lips with due respect.

"I have never fought with women," he said. "The fact that I involved you two in my affairs really did not give me pleasure, and if your spouse, my lady, caught me now, I might have forgotten any pleasures. My death would be terrible... nice to think, huh?"

"You have a peculiar sense of humor," the Englishwoman laughed. "But you are right, my husband does not forgive. May you not fall into his hands."

She turned and walked away to her annex.

Theo stayed by the stream, leaning his back against the trunk of the young elm, staring at the stars lighting up in the sky.

Two days later, Millot and Francois tidied up the carriage left in the woods and harnessed the horses to it, choosing the ones they thought were the prettiest. They were convinced that the prettier the horse, the less useful it was for forest robbers. Beautiful horses, in their opinion, were vicious, sickly, and stupid, so they usually chose clumsy crossbreds for their purposes. The horses selected for the Duchess were carefully brushed and fed with oats, then harnessed to the carriage. The Duchess and her son were led through the marshes with the same precautions that were taken with which they were brought to the hideout, that is, blindfolded. It was impossible to give up these safeguards, though it was highly unlikely that someone who had walked this path only once would find it again. You had to learn to read signs on bushes and paths, signs telling you which direction to take, and yet they changed depending on the season and even the weather. It would be impossible to learn it the first time or the second time. Yet the outlaws never neglected anything to protect their secrets, aware that their lives depended upon it. For the same reason, they made sure that the Duchess did not realize their plan and that she left believing that she was accompanied only by three riders, and that the rest of the outlaws stayed in their hideout. For understandable reasons, they couldn't underestimate her - she could be threatening, but she didn't seem to be at all.

When the carriage, escorted by a group of three, disappeared on the road, the others followed, hiding in the forest thickets. They were already so well trained that they could follow their chosen destination for miles without letting them know until the moment they chose to attack. Nobody had even guessed that he might be followed, and when he realized the situation, it was too late. Along the way, the outlaws made short forays in different directions to penetrate the area, but to their relief and some surprise, they found no traces of any ambush anywhere, as if the Black Prince did intend to keep his word. Of course, this did not weaken their vigilance, after all, constantly tense attention was a condition for the success of any such action. This was to be particularly important, as they would meet France's greatest pain and their greatest personal enemy in one person. Every slightest mistake would be catastrophic. As they approached the village of Garou, they increased their vigilance, but still could not see anything that smelled almost like an ambush. It should have reassured them, but the effect was the opposite - it rather increased their distrust. Oddly enough, someone like the Black Prince did not attempt any ruse. They saw the first soldiers only at the entrance to the village - they were guards, ostentatiously looking for the carriage and those who would escort it.

"Be ready," Theo said softly to his friends, and stepped forward.

After a while he saw his adversary, and next to him a retinue in the colors of the Duke of Navarre and Philip himself, clearly restless.

"Hello, prince," he said aloud as he rode closer. "I see that you kept your word, so I keep mine."

The Black Prince seemed to him changed, aged and emaciated, you can see the rumors about his illness were not exaggerated. He was definitely not the same man with whom he had fought his fateful duel in the courtyard of his castle. But his eyes burned with the same hatred as usual.

"You thwarted my plans for the last time, Bongrais," he said firmly. "From now on you are my number one target and you can be sure that you will not get away."

"So far I've been successful... Philip, take your men and go deeper into the provinces as soon as possible. It's best not to stop until you get to Navarra."

"I'd rather not leave you here." Navarrian said carefully.

"I can take care of myself. I have to be sure you're away before I release my hostage," Theo answered seriously.

With all his heart he wanted his friend to understand as soon as possible that he had no time to tease. Fortunately, Philip was intelligent enough to understand it, so he nodded and with his retinue drove off down the track, passing the duchess's carriage on the way.

"Give me back my wife," demanded the Black Prince sharply.

"Relax, such nerves are not befitting the son of an English king."

Theo jumped off his horse and opened the carriage door. He shook the duchess's hand, helping her out, and looked at her husband with a half-serious, half-drunken look."

"I always keep my word," he said emphatically.

"I do, too," the prince replied glumly, jumping off his steed to greet his wife. "You're dead already."

"I didn't notice," retorted the outlaw without a trace of fear.

The Black Prince looked at him briefly and motioned to his men.

"Kill them," he ordered calmly, as if he were giving the order to change the dishes on the table.

The soldiers drew their swords, but before they could use them, arrows and stones rained down on them, confusing and frightening them. Taking advantage of this, Theo and his companions spurred their horses as they made their way back. They managed to weave a good distance before the English could form a formation and follow them.

"We can now pay for your friendship with this little girl with our lives!" Pierre shouted to his brother-in-law, urging his horse to catch up with him.

"You're right!" Theo shouted back to him. "Well, are you okay with that?!"

"You are really crazy!" Pierre said indignantly.

Arrows whistled around them, Pierre's horse whinnied desperately and stumbled. The man who trained in falling did not hurt himself too much, but the consequences of the accident were so severe that he was rushed. The other two tried desperately to hold their mounts, but the terrified horses broke free from their saddles, barely leaping off their saddles and galloping forward.

"Horses are idiotic bastards after all," Theo said, helping Pierre to stand up. "Just little thing and they literally go crazy with fear."

"The hell with them, let's run into the trees or they'll get us," his friend advised.

They ran into the forest.

"I'm afraid they'll kill our people," Tristan squeaked, running beside his brother. His voice was still childish, and in moments of fear it was as thin as that of a meowing cat.

"Don't worry," Theo reassured him. "The main strength will go to us, after all His English Highness wants to get me."

"What a cheer up," Pierre snorted. "Fortunately, these bastards don't know these woods. Let's run the path of the moose."

Theo stopped and looked around.

"Better the wild boar path," he decided. "It's harder to trace."

The names of the animals were used by the outlaws to define routes that were invisible to the eyes of a man unfamiliar with forests and that could be used to escape. These names come from many years of observations of wild animals and their customs. They had to hurry, their pursuers were not far away, although the densely growing trees made it difficult for them to pursue their pursuit. Judging by the sounds, Theo was right - the main force of the Black Prince followed them, not taking any interest in those who shot at them. The fact that the English did not know these forests made their task difficult, but it did not prevent it. The three fugitives sneaked deftly towards Bongrais, but could not, despite their efforts, lose the pursuit. Slowly but surely, the English followed them, not letting themselves be led out of the way, which gave rise to the suspicion that the Black Prince had chosen people especially carefully for this occasion. They were definitely intelligent and well-trained.

"The chances need to be leveled a bit," Theo decided when, after an exhausting run, they finally found themselves in a familiar neighborhood.

Tristan, completely exhausted, sat down on the trunk of the felled tree.

"I can't go on," he groaned.

"He's really not going to run any further," Pierre leaned forward and rested his hands on his knees, trying to even his breathing.

Theo unrolled the slingshot.

"Wait," he said, and disappeared into the trees.

Assuming that the soldiers were not walking in a tight group (which would be impossible in such a dense forest), he could reach with stones those of them who were walking further away from the others. It required dexterity and a soundless tread, but it could work. It even had to be if they were to survive. He quickly saw the first soldier bouncing off the core of the squad and making his way through the undergrowth, keeping his hunting horn ready. This seemingly small detail confirmed the supposition that the Black Prince had prepared this ambush very carefully. In the event of a meeting with the outlaws, it was enough to blow a horn for the entire unit to rush to help.

Theo smiled grimly to himself and twirled the slingshot. The stone hit the soldier right in the back of his head, knocking him into the moss before he could even think of calling for reinforcements. The outlaw strapped his horn to his waist, as something told him that it would be possible to use this instrument somehow, and began to look for the next victim. He saw what he was looking for rather quickly and repeated his trick. Satisfied with the effect, he eliminated three more enemies, then ran a long distance into the forest and blew the horn. When he made full circle, he returned to his companions.

"Come on," he said. "I dragged them away a bit, but we have to get out of here quickly."

Tristan obediently rose, but at first glance it was obvious that he wouldn't get far. He was pale with exhaustion and swayed on his feet. Pierre took him by the arm and dragged him with him in a gesture that could not be resisted, although he himself had to mobilize all his strength to do so.

"Chief, are you made of iron?" he asked gruffly, trying to keep up with Theo.

The knight did not answer, but looked at them with obvious concern. Although he weakened the enemy's strength a bit, they were still in danger until they found themselves in a swamp through which the English would certainly not pass. He hoped his trick would give them some time, but it soon turned out that the Black Prince's best soldiers were indeed... the best - they weren't long left off guard. In addition, the most difficult part of the road was opening up for the escapees, the space between two forests with two villages, arable fields and a dozen large meadows. It was in their best interests to get through the area as quickly as possible, which, however, seemed beyond the strength of a completely exhausted Tristan. However, there was no other way.

"Buck up, little brother," Theo said warmly. "You can't afford any breakdown right now. Later, you may even pass out or break down like a two-year-old, for now you have to be a man."

"Okay... okay," the boy whispered obediently, wiping his sweat-soaked face with the sleeve of his jacket. Pierre shook his head.

"He can't do it," he muttered to his brother-in-law.

"He can do it. He's my brother." The chief clapped him on the shoulder and led the way. They were far enough when crossbow arrows again whistled near their ears.

"Shit!" Theo swore angrily as he fell to the ground.

He unwrapped his slingshot, looking for rocks and wishing he had a pouch of lead pieces with him. Out of the corner of his eye, he saw his companions following his example. The first missiles were thrown from their slingshots almost simultaneously, as soon as the English soldiers got close enough. They had to aim at their faces, at the mouth line unshielded by nasal helmets, but it was not for nothing that they trained their hands and eyes in such feats for nothing, so it was not that difficult for them. Even so, things looked hopeless - there were just too many soldiers for the three of them, and they were too careful. Neither tried to approach the direct battle, all the time maintaining a relatively safe distance from which they could reach the fugitives with arrows, and not expose themselves to their handguns. There was the dismal persistence of a pack of hounds in their actions, relentlessly chasing bleeding, staggering prey until it fell, becoming easy prey.

"I wouldn't like to be pathetic, Chief, but maybe let's say goodbye, because I think we'll have die here," Pierre said grimly, loading another rock into his slingshot.

"I'll believe it's over when they bury me." Theo hit the soldier with an accurate throw, who leaned too far behind his cover, but the stone bounced off the helmet, doing no more harm to the Englishman.

"Don't boast so much that you have a bonehead, which cannot reach anything," Pierre began, but paused and leaned slightly out of the furrow. "Oh, hell...! Someone came to our aid!"

"Okay, but who?" Theo followed his lead and got to his feet. "They're not ours. But ours or not, they beat the English, so we have to help them."

"Of course," Tristan muttered without enthusiasm, hurrying after them.

There were no more than ten allies, and they fought with the determination of people with nothing to lose. Somehow, the outnumbered opponents didn't scare them away. The three outlaws rushed to their aid, drawing their daggers. The fight against armored soldiers consisted mainly in hitting the armor's slit with the dagger blade and not getting killed yourself, taking advantage of the fact that the opponent in armor is much less agile. Outlaws had such a fight well-rehearsed, although this type of tactic was not always necessary. Most of the soldiers fought in plain clothes, rarely leather ones, only the elite troops were better equipped. Of course, the Black Prince's bodyguards, sent on a mission to kill his enemy, belonged to the latter and had no intention of give up without fight. After a brief moment of confusion, they formed line and faced unexpected attackers.

"Chief, I think it's a Falcon!" cried Pierre, who had managed to spot the relief leader from among the combatants.

"No kidding!" the chief shouted back to him, stopping unconsciously and looking around.

"Watch out!" Tristan, fighting at his side, pushed him aside with all his might.

A second later arrows whirred past them, hitting the ground.

"This is supposed to be targeting?" Theo laughed maliciously but stopped immediately as his brother screamed mournfully and fell to the ground, pressing his hands to his chest. One of the arrows pierced his doublet and stuck in his flesh.

The knight rushed towards him. For a moment he couldn't catch his breath, as if the arrow that had hurt Tristan had pierced his heart. From the side of the fighters came a tall young man in a blue jacket with silver embroidery, leaping over furrows. As Pierre had suspected, it was the Falcon. He saw the situation at a glance and took charge.

"Take him to the monastery," he ordered briskly. "Pierre, run with him as cover. We'll take care of these English bugs."

Theo lifted his brother from the ground and ran towards the monastery, escorted by Pierre, who was recovering from his last strength. Fortunately, the monastery was nearby. Reaching the place, the knight tugged the doorbell and brutally pushed the porter's brother, which he opened for him, then rushed inside.

"Quick, where is Father Iohann?!" he shouted, running to a well-known cell, which in the monastery was used as an infirmary.

"Chief, bloody hell, you told us not to trust that new prior," Pierre moaned, running in after him. "Whew, I'm barely alive... You told us to stay away from the monastery!"

"It doesn't matter what I said," Theo set his brother down on a wide bench and frantically tore open his bloody straitjacket, wanting to evaluate the wound. "He's the only thing that matters now. She..." he added after a moment in a daze.

He felt as if the ground was slipping away from under his feet. He sat helplessly on a stool next to the bench and stared straight ahead with his eyes wide open.

"What?" Pierre didn't understand. His brother-in-law shook his head, unable to speak. He looked like he just got something heavy in the head.

Father Iohann entered the cell.

"Get out of here both of you," he demanded. "I'll take care of him... or rather her," he added, after taking a cursory look at the wounded man.

"Her?" Pierre followed Theo out into the corridor, completely stunned.

"My brother is my sister. I can't stand it." the knight said, leaning helplessly against the wall.

His friend shrugged.

"Having a sister isn't so bad," he said reassuringly. "Let's take me and Bellette as an example... Ugh, that's a bad example."

Theo glared at him.

"It's not that," he explained after a moment. "Only that I'm always the last to know about things that directly concern me. One day someone will say to me, "What are you wandering among people, you have been dead for a week. And I won't know anything about it."

"You're dramatizing as usual," Pierre said. "After all, neither of us had any idea how things were going. She disguised herself well. Clever brat."

The knight muttered something incomprehensible, sat down against the wall and hid his face in his hands. Now many little events had become clear to him, he understood what had eluded him before. Still, it felt as if an entire cart of stones had fallen on top of him.

"Why didn't she tell me?" He thought helplessly. "What's it all about?"

He was dreadfully confused and disgusted with the fact that his own sister didn't trust him enough to tell him the truth. The late John II the Good too... because he certainly knew about everything. Why didn't they trust him?

He did not know how long it was before the monk finally left his cell, wiping his hands on his habit.

"Fortunately, the wound is superficial," he said. "The arrow slid down the rib, which must of course hurt and bleed a lot, but nothing threatened the girl. You can enter her, she is conscious."

Theo got up heavily and entered the cell, carefully avoiding Iohann's gaze. He did not know what he could answer to possible doubts, his thoughts were still swirling in his head like flocks of black birds, even gloomier than ravens or crows.

The girl was lying on a bench, covered with a monastic blanket.

"Do you hate me very much?" she asked softly.

"Oh no," he denied. "I'm just very surprised. I would never suspect... What's your real name?"

She cried out - for the first time without embarrassment.

"I don't know," she sobbed helplessly. "I don't think I have a female name. I've always been called Tristan. When my mother was expecting a child, our father expressed the joyful belief so many times that it would be a son that when she gave birth to a girl, she simply did not have the strength to tell him about it. She pleaded with the late king to help her in this mystification, and that he had a weakness for her... Then it was better to delay it, because it would be foolish if it seemed that the royal page was a girl. And even later it would be dangerous to even reveal that I'm from the Bongrais family... And that's how it stayed. I can't be a girl, and I'm not a man. What was I supposed to do? And... I was afraid that as a sister I would be a burden to you and you would want to get rid of me."

He sat down on a stool beside the coffee table and took his sister's hand.

"What have you done? You could have died pretending to be a boy by my side, and I was still grinding you and forcing you to do military drill," he sighed. "Plus, I don't even know if you were baptized as a girl or just as a boy. Father doesn't a girl baptized as a boy need to undergo some additional ritual?" he asked the monk who was just entering with a cup of herbal infusion.

The latter nodded, which could be interpreted differently.

"Why are you dressing up as a boy, my child?" He asked. "Don't you know it's a sin?"

The girl wiped her tears.

"King John told me to do so, I listened to him," she whispered.

The monk grunted.

"Well, yes," he said hesitantly. "Maybe there were overriding reasons... But now you should stop it and live as God commanded."

It was clear that he did not want to undermine the authority of the deceased king, although he did not agree with his decision.

"I don't even have a name, Father," she said shyly. "I've always been just Tristan, and that's what I call myself in my mind. This is how I was baptized as a boy. It's really not my fault."

Father Iohann looked at the silent knight.

"You must name your sister," he said sternly. "We're going to re-baptize. It is your responsibility to deal with this matter, which, I say it quite privately, is one big scandal."

Theo thought for a moment, then leaned over his sister and kissed her forehead.

"I call you Fabienne," he said. "In memory of our father. You have inherited more qualities from him than you might have imagined: courage, cunning, and loyalty to your king. When you get better, we'll give you a baptism ceremony."

The prior nodded approvingly.

"Now get out," he ordered. "I have to confess this poor, stray soul."

In the corridor, crouched against the wall, Pierre slept with his head resting on the bench and snored until it was heard aloud. The knight sat down next to him and took a deep breath. He slowly began to get used to what had happened, even smiled at the surprise that this revelation would cause among his people, and his aching, stiff body began to come to the fore. If he had been a little weaker, he would have been sick of the enormous effort required of him by the complicated brawl on the border of Aquitaine, but he was almost completely weak now. He already knew the same feeling, and he knew that for the next few days he would be of no consolation to anything.

"I wonder if Philip has made it safely to his lands," he thought wearily.

The door at the end of the corridor creaked and Falcon appeared in a ragged jacket and a fresh scar on his cheek next to Theo.

"What's with him?" he asked.

The knight looked at him heavily.

"He's not him," he muttered.

The Falcon nodded and sat down next to him.

"So you already know," he said calmly.

Theo looked at him, shaking his hair out of his face.

"Did you know?" he asked menacingly.

The Bearnean snorted lightly.

"Why do you think I was sticking to your gang for so long and so stubbornly, letting you command me as you wanted, instead of going back to the Pyrenees?" He asked. "I knew. It was a coincidence that I suspected her, the purest coincidence. She made me swear not to tell you, but now, of course, there is no point in silence. How did you take it?"

Theo's black eyes dimmed.

"I understood so many things," he whispered. "All her initial behavior... This incomprehensible secretiveness and shyness... How she must have felt when I was trapped in the Louvre and she was left with this band of savages..."

"What do you do?" asked Falcon after a long moment.

The knight shook his head.

"I don't know. What hurt me most was this lack of trust. I have no idea why I deserved it."

The Falcon patted him on the shoulder.

"Be understanding with her," he advised. "Can you say hand on heart that you have no secrets from your loved ones? Really any?"

Theo thought of Mathilde and didn't answer.

"How did you know we might need help?" he asked after a moment.

"Well... we found out what the Black Prince did," the Falcon began. "We had been circling Meung Castle for several days, until we suddenly found out that you had imprisoned the Englishman's wife. You know, he has become so furious. He said he'd have torn your skin when he finally got his hands on you. We followed in his footsteps when we noticed that he was going on the road with Navarrean... And you already know the rest."

He sighed and wiped his cheek with his hand, smearing blood from the scratched scar again.

"If it weren't for you, we'd have troubles." Theo admitted. "What about these soldiers?"

"What do you think? They bite the ground. Neither did a single man escape."

The Bearnean glanced at Pierre, who was still snoring, and whistled softly. Pierre shifted his sleep and stopped snoring.

Theo sighed.

"The Black Prince's madness is costing more and more people's lives, on both sides. Are you and my sister...?"

"No, no," said the Falcon vividly. "Who do you think I am? Although I admit that I have more than friendly feelings for her. She's a great girl. What are you going to do with her now? You're not going to distance her from you, are you? She was so afraid of it, I suppose that's why she refused to tell you. The poor girl was raised to be a boy from birth, I don't know if she knows how to be different from the one who followed King John step by step."

"And I was wondering why the king hadn't made sure to teach my brother a knightly trade," Theo muttered, propping his chin with his clenched fists.

He felt as if life had mocked him once again, and the Falcon's question about his honesty with his loved ones was still ringing in his ears. He had no idea whether he should tell his wife the truth about Mathilde, he couldn't figure it out, and he couldn't bring himself to seek advice from that young man in the blue straitjacket. His uncle, Febus, would already be better at this. He asked for nothing.

Father Iohann left the cell, quietly closing the door behind him.

"Your sister is asleep," he said. "In about two days, you'll be able to get her out of here and continue to heal her in your hideout. For my part, however, I would advise you not to involve her in your affairs any further. She's not a country blacksmith, but a gentle noblewoman, and I'm surprised she even survived so long, sharing your hard life."

"I'm surprised too. Okay, if so, we are getting back for now. We'll be back in two days and.... Thank you, Father."

*****

Bellette was lying on her bed, staring at the beams of the ceiling. The attic smelled of hay and wood, and the light of a pale moon fell through the small window, from which the winter protection had already been removed.

"And, how is she?" she asked.

Her husband was sitting against the wall with his knees tucked up to his chin and his hands clasped around his legs. He would only sit like this when the situation was too much for him and he was unable to deal with it.

"Not too bad fortunately," he replied. "She's quite strong after all. And to think that I had so long resented Tristan for taking my place next to my father... how hard it must have been for her."

He shook his head miserably.

"She could have more confidence in you. You mustn't fool someone you love," Bellette said sternly.

Theo rubbed his forehead, feeling the scar from the Black Prince's sword under his fingers, and sighed heavily. He felt that his wife was right, and he resented the cowardice that had prevented him from admitting to her for so long that everything was not his fault, or at least not entirely. He closed his eyes. He gathered all the strength he could and told her what happened that night without trying to minimize his guilt. When he finished, Bellette was silent for a long moment.

"And you didn't know it was your baby?" she asked after a moment without feelings.

"I had no idea, I swear."

"But you cheated on me with the first one you meet."

"Bellette, understand, I was drunk and that's it. I didn't know what I was doing..." Theo wanted to add something else, but he paused, feeling that everything he could say would be artificial and somehow untrue.

Bellette turned to her side, her back to him.

"Get out of here," she demanded. "Go away."

He left the attic obediently, going downstairs to the dice-playing companions. Instinctively, he sensed that this was not the best time to convince his wife to forgive him for her betrayal, and that he did not have the strength to do so either.

"Will you play?" Gwidon asked him cheerfully.

"What are you playing for?" Theo sat down heavily at the table and poured himself some wine.

"For once in the mouth," Jean replied, shaking his cup.

"I should get a couple of times," the chief muttered, tipping the cup in one gulp.

"Slow, you're going to drown in," Beregard warned him.

"Give him a break, it's thin. They had nothing better at the inn today."

Jean tossed the dice and grimaced at the result. Theo played with the empty cup for a while, not looking up at his friends.

"I was so self-righteous," he said after a moment. "A flawless knight, always faithful to the rules... Nonsense. I'm a bastard like other bastards, and I'm stupid and blind because I didn't see what was going on under my side. Anyone who was willing to bend me to his plans was enough to strike the right string. I'm such an idiot."

"Didn't I tell you?" Pierre laughed unpleasantly, taking Jean's cup with dices. He shook them until they rattled like an emergency snare drum and threw them on the table. Not very pleased with the result, he handed the cup to Gwidon, who received it automatically, looking sympathetically at the chief, who was sitting with his head bowed.

"Didn't you take my advice?" he asked softly.

Theo shook his head and rested his forehead in his hands. The poet pursed his lips angrily.

"Then why did you even ask for her?" he tossed and shook the cup of dices.

"She doesn't want to know me now, and I'm not even surprised at her," the chief whispered bitterly.

"What are you talking about?" Beregard asked.

Gwidon spilled the dices into his hand and began tossing them, grabbing deftly between his fingers.

"Our leader, a steadfast knight, a specimen of all virtues, has just confessed to his wife's betrayal," he explained with a smile. "Knowing Bellette, I'm surprised he's still alive."

"I felt you did something like that," Pierre said unexpectedly calmly, pouring himself wine. "And that this betrayal has borne fruit. Mathilde, right?"

Theo didn't answer, just tilted his head lower. His brother-in-law shrugged.

"I'd suspect you of anything but not cowardice," he observed. "You just confessed to her now? It took a long time to take courage."

"Leave him alone, strapper," the troubadour saw fit to defend the leader. "He knew nothing. I mean, he must have known that he had spent the night with the girl he had met at the harvest festival, but he did not know that it was a princess de Valois in disguise, or that she had had a child as a result of that drunken night. Come on, didn't you ever go hay with a girl after you had a little drink? You can't tell me you've always been faithful to your Fanchette."

"Fanchette isn't my wife, first, and secondly, I have never sworn allegiance to her. And thirdly, it's probably better to be a strapper than a dwarf weasel like you."

"Gwidon hit the nail on the head, you are romancing left and right, and you blame others for an innocent mistake," replied Millot supporting poet.

He was right, for Bellette's brother, tall and broad-shouldered, was the type of exuberant peasant beauty that village girls liked and knew how to use it. Still, he did not get confused.

"This is different," he insisted, but contrary to popular belief, he was not angry with his brother-in-law. Rather, he felt satisfied that his long-standing prophecies had finally come true.

"Don't worry," he said graciously, patting him on the back. "Bellette will be in a pet and stops. I guess she realized you couldn't be holy, not as you pretended to be."

"Shut up, Pierre!" his friends shouted at him almost in chorus, seized by the apparent suffering of their leader. They haven't seen him in such a bad shape yet.

Pierre shrugged.

"I know Bellette better than any of you, and I know what to expect from her," he said lightly. "I say that she'll be mad, and she'll get over it, I know what I'm saying. Theo isn't the first or the last husband in this world who procured an illegitimate child, there will be no holes in heaven from that. Let's drink."

The knight pushed aside the mug he had been given and walked outside the hut. Stars winked high above him, distant and indifferent to the little human drama, the night forest rustled around him, and thyme smelled. Despite everything, he felt that he had done the right thing, but his heart ached at the thought of how much he had hurt someone he loved most of all in the world. And how was he going to explain to anyone now that he was silent, not out of cowardice, but for fear of causing her suffering?

"Who am I kidding?" He thought with glum amusement. I was afraid of this conversation with Bellette more than of the Parisian scaffold and the gallows of the Black Prince put together. Ah, the beautiful sex did take more men under the velvet plush, or possibly sabotage not only me."

He curled up on a bench against the wall, putting his bent forearm under his head. He did not mind such an overnight stay. He had fallen asleep in less comfortable places, for example in a prison dungeon. And on a warm night like this, sleeping outside was a real pleasure.

CHAPTER V

Destruction of Limoges

The storm had raged since morning. Friends locked in their hut played charades, Gwidon composed a new ballad, and the girls locked themselves in an annex, motivating it in such a way that they had to take a break from male company so that they would not be completely disgusted. Despite attempts to change into a dress, Fabienne still wore men's clothes, as it turned out that in woman's robes, she was completely unable to move.

"Let's postpone this study," Theo finally decided. "As long as we live in the forest, you can still wear the pants without causing any offense. Then we'll see."

"When "then"? Do you still believe that it will ever be different?" Beregard asked him ironically.

He did not tell anyone about it, but he was very upset that his friend, almost a brother, "missed his chance." He knew all too well that he would not have the second one, no matter what he did now. The king, even if he had the best feelings for him, would not make a fool of himself by granting grace a second time to a man who was unable to appreciate it the first time. Yet Charles V, to make matters worse, did not like the last of the Bongrais. It seemed that Theo had lost his life, and there was nothing to be done about it.

Philip d'Evreux, who had been wandering around the area for several days in the hope of meeting a friend, was of a similar opinion. Lying in a miserable little room rented in the inn "Under the White Swan" and listening to the furiously pounding rain on the roof, he thought with bitterness that King Charles had changed a lot since the two of them played with wooden swords as knights. They were friends then, they understood each other wonderfully and one would have jumped into the fire after the other, and now? When he tried to convince the monarch of how great Theo was doing to France and that he should therefore be treated more leniently, the king became so furious that it was close and the whole thing would have ended fatally for the young prince. It wasn't good anyway - he ordered him to leave the Louvre and not return without being summoned, a sign of a potentially dangerous disfavor. And Philip was right. As a hostage, he was a helpless pawn and could do many harms involuntarily, including dividing France and Navarre. Theo saved him from a terrible condition, risking his life and that of his friends, and demanding nothing in return. He needed to see him. Having some time, he decided to find his savior and thank him. This search was interrupted by a storm that was raging over Touraine with a fierce intensity than the entire English army.

"The wind is blowing through the woods, as if someone had hanged himself," said the fat innkeeper, entering the room with a tray full. "And we just had a hail the size of nuts. Why don't you eat something, sir?"

Philip rose slightly on his elbow.

"I can," he said without enthusiasm. "Until this storm subsides, I'm trapped here anyway. Tell me, good man, does Theo le Vengeur come here?"

"I don't ask anyone's name while he's paying," replied the innkeeper, setting the dishes and jugs on the table.

The prince's squire and his face glanced greedily at the table, not daring, however, to approach it in front of their master.

"I need to see him. If you somehow found out how to get him a message..." Philip broke off and waved his hand in discouragement.

Damasus Magyar glanced at him from under the eye but said nothing. He finished arranging the dishes, then went downstairs and found Margot, busy arranging supplies in the pantry.

"As soon as the rain stops, you will tell the Wolf that a young, very rich gentleman is looking for him," he said. "Maybe it's important? It doesn't look like a trap to me, anyway."

"All right," agreed Margot, who had been on the most intimate terms with the outlaws for years. She hummed softly and remembered something.

"There is that little freckle-face sleeping in the shed that is believed to be our count's page," she said. "He came for the wine and the storm surprised him, so he stayed. Let him talk to this man, it will be known whether it is worth bothering the count at all."

"Oh, that's a very good thought."

He knew Philip well, who often visited the king, and since he also knew about the friendship he had with Theo, he was not at all surprised to see him. Philip, on the other hand, was very surprised.

"Did you stay in these woods, kid?" He exclaimed. "And the wolves haven't eaten you yet? God, how could this Theo let..."

He paused, shaking his head in desperation.

"First, Your Majesty, there are no wolves near Bongrais," Ettienne said cheerfully. "And second, I wanted to stay. The page is next to his knight, even in exile. To the point: should I bring him here so that you can have a chat without interruption?"

"It would be nice," Philip replied cautiously. He felt somehow insecure under the innocent ironic gaze of this prematurely adult child. Page smiled broadly, wrinkling his freckled nose in his own way.

"As soon as it calms down, I'll go get him," he promised. "Is... is the king persuaded?"

The prince shook his head sadly.

"He didn't and he won't, boy. Theo will be executed as soon as he falls into the hands of any of the royal forces, without trial," he said. "I have seen such executions before. Even Bertram du Guesclin has ceased to defend him. I'm his last friend at the royal court, or maybe rather outside of it, because disgrace has come upon me as well."

Ettienne was silent for a moment.

"Not easy times, right?" he said finally with a childlike dignity.

The prince looked at him and smiled faintly.

"Not easy," he agreed.

He liked this resolute boy for whom, apparently, nothing was terrible.

As soon as the storm had subsided a bit, Ettienne set off on his way back through the marshes, laden with wineskins.

"Theo, Prince Philip is waiting for you at the inn," he said, meticulously setting the leather containers in the chest.

The knight raised his head from the string he had just woven and furrowed his broad forehead.

"What is he doing here?" he asked distrustfully.

The boy shrugged.

"He didn't say that. Maybe he wants to thank you?" he gave a brilliant thought.

"And he'd bother in such bad weather? Unlikely. Okay, I'll go to him," Theo left his job, put on his sword and strapped it to his belt just in case with a bag of lead nuggets used as slingshot projectiles.

"Will you be back for dinner?" asked Armando, whose turn was to cook that day.

"I don't know," muttered the chief. "I'll try, but if I didn't come back until tomorrow morning, don't be upset."

"We don't mind," Pierre assured him solemnly. "We know it seems like the wrong ones always survive."

He glanced slightly at the ajar door of the annex and winced slightly. Bellette, although apparently normal behavior, remained intransigent towards her husband, which worried everyone greatly. Theo, usually more militant in the face of adversities, let himself be bullied and terrorized without saying a word, assuming that he should be punished for his offense without protest.

"If I were you, I'd beat her to stop pretending to be an insulted queen," said Colas bluntly, outraged by the behavior of a young woman whom he still considered a common maid, made countess by marriage.

"Well, that's why you're not in my place," Theo replied, trying to smile.

He couldn't believe he could raise his hand against the woman, though he had to admit that during his last conversation with Adeline he had been close to it. Even Pierre, always on his sister's side, thought she was exaggerating this time, but he was unable to reason with her. Bellette stuck in stubbornness and refused to even look at her husband, despite all his attempts to reconcile, she treated him like air, and there was a serious fear that the deaf resentment would eventually turn into hatred. Theo gnawed at it a lot, but slowly rebellion grew in his heart. After all, his guilt was not so great, and the fact that he fell in love with his illegitimate child at first sight could not, after all, be brought against him. He was glad that he had not mentioned to Bellette who he had entrusted the child to and what forbidden feelings Lady Joan evoked in him when he made his "examination of conscience". He couldn't fathom this feeling, or even name it. Sometimes, before he fell asleep, his translucent eyes under long dark blond lashes and a mysterious smile on pale lips loomed in him half asleep, and then all night he was tormented by dreams so perverse that he stood up completely out of tune. He had no intention of admitting to anyone. Now, pushed away by his wife, he had such dreams much more often, and while it bothered him on the one hand, on the other... On the other hand, he discovered, deeply embarrassed, that he felt some perverse pleasure in them. He was not so much in love with Lady Joan as obsessed with her. Her proud, reed-like form attracted him so strongly that he sometimes bit his fingers to make the physical pain drive away his sinful thoughts. As he walked through the forest, wet from the recent rain, he considered whether it would be good to disappear for a few days and thus give Bellette cause for concern. It could help break the ice more than any conversation.

"A childish idea," he finally muttered to himself in displeasure.

Having reached the inn, he penetrated the immediate surroundings out of habit, and not seeing anything that smelled like an ambush from a distance, he went inside.

"Damasus, where is the one who wants to see me?" he exclaimed.

"Upstairs," replied the innkeeper. "His servants are in the stable, so you can talk to each other freely. Only, Wolf, be kind to him by your grace, I earned a lot from him and I would like more."

"Don't worry," Theo laughed as he climbed the rickety steps upstairs.

Prince Philip sat at the table in the guest room, writing something on decorative parchment. At the sight of his friend, he threw down the pen.

"I'm glad you are," he said, standing up. "First of all, I wanted to thank you for what you did for me. A friend like you is rare. Once in a lifetime if you're lucky."

Theo perched on the window sill, which gave him a good view of the area in front of the inn.

"Let's say," he said restrained. "But... Philip, I did what I had to do, what you asked for and what was imposed on me. This is the end. I'm not going to do any more for you. Every time I try to do something for my homeland, I pay for it with suffering, humiliation, false accusations, the devil knows what else. This is the only award I can expect. Not that I expect any profits, but I don't think I should be punished for all of this."

Philip shook his head.

"I did what I could, but I have to wait until the right moment..." he began, but his friend interrupted him immediately.

"You're not do anything. The only thing you can do for me is... When you see my body disgraced and bleeding at the crossroads, bury it Christianly. Apparently, after death, a person does not care, but I'm sorry to think about it while alive."

The prince embraced him warmly.

"Don't say that," he said. "I swear, I'll do my best to make the king change his mind. You are strong and brave, don't give up. Life sometimes brings with it surprises that change everything, no matter how hopeless it is."

The outlaw smiled forcibly.

"And you, Philip?" He asked. "Why are you in mourning?"

"Estelle died last month," the prince replied sadly.

"Rest her soul. She's always been in poor health, poor thing. But her heart was huge. If only the older sister were like her..."

Philip nodded. He himself did not like his sister-in-law, although he admired her beauty, because who would not admire such an extremely beautiful creature? And since under this beauty there was venomous anger that was the second matter.

"Theo, listen," he said with a sigh. "If you were ever in a truly desperate situation, remember that I'll help you, even if it is the last thing I do in my life."

The outlaw patted him on the back.

"If it ever occurs to me that I need help, it will mean that I'm in a hopeless situation and I'll certainly not be able to turn to anyone for help anymore," he said with unintentional, gallows humor.

"Don't be kidding. Move with your people to Navarre, you will be safe there. My father will welcome you with open arms," the prince suggested, without much hope of persuading him.

Theo smiled his most captivating smile as he remembered Sir Winslow's analogous proposition.

"One offers me England, the other Navarre... Are you all in love with me, or something? Let me remind you that there is a stake for gayness.[11]"

"They should pull that mangy tongue out of you," Philip huffed. "What happened to you in these woods?"

"I have no idea. If that's all, then let me go."

Theo got up from the windowsill, pulling down his straitjacket.

"Wait," said his friend warmly. "At least consider my offer. I really do not want you to get paid for all your services as Charles or that vile Welshman is preparing for you. He's vengeful as hell. My squire, who stayed on his property with half of my men and was only released with them three days ago, overheard he was getting ready to launch an attack on Limoges, which is being managed by his cousin, Sir Winslow. He has disobeyed him, so Edward is going to raze the city to the ground and tear his disobedient cousin to pieces with his horses, and I can assure you he will. All the more he won't take pity on you."

"What?!" Theo shouted. "And you're only telling me now that he's going to...?! You have to warn Winslow!"

"Englishman?" Philip was surprised rather than indignant. "Let them settle their affairs among themselves, what's the matter with us?"

"This Englishman saved me several times from a terrible fate. I can't leave him like this. Will you lend me a horse?"

"Anything you want, but only because I know that if I don't lend you, you'll steal it from me. I find the idea stupid," said the prince sternly, and shrugged resignedly.

He knew that he would not convince his friend with any, even the most flowery words, and he pained about it, mentally making up his worst words for having missed the news of the Black

---

[11] Homosexual relations criminalized in the Middle Ages on a par with heresy.

Prince's planned attack on Limoges. On the other hand, could he have foreseen such a reaction?

He followed his friend downstairs to the stables.

"Take the sable one, he's the best," he advised. "And for God's sake, watch out."

Theo didn't listen to him, hastily tightening the girth on the stallion's saddle. He himself did not know why Philip's words upset him so much and why, instead of thinking about the innocent inhabitants of the city, he only thinks of the English knight, managing them on behalf of a man whom he... betrayed, as Don Paulino once did with Count de Bongrais. It should outrage him, but he did not have time to consider the ethical aspects of the case. He hastily mounted his saddled horse and sped him towards the Aquitaine border without even saying goodbye to his friend.

He raced at an awful bat, not caring who could see him. He was ready to ride his horse to his death as long as he could make it to Limoges in time, but he had the sense to stop the black steed and give it a break when his breath grew dangerously rattling. He knew that without a mount, he certainly wouldn't get there fast enough. As soon as the horse breathed a little, the knight forced him to gallop again. Even as night fell, he continued his journey, and it was easy to get confused. He made another stop only when he realized that his steed was already chasing with the last of his strength. He drank from the stream, unhooked the horse, and wiped it well with a handful of dry grass. The animal looked dead tired, and it was clear that it wouldn't last long. Theo patted them apologetically on the neck, he thought for a moment, then started walking towards Limoges, looking around to see if a fresh horse could get somewhere. Luck was on his side. Along the way, there was a dormant inn, in which a few horses were drowsily chewing their stables. He untied one of them and leapt bareback onto its back, without bothering with the saddle. The horse was not very fiery, the name of an old jade would rather fit it, but it was better than walking. When it started to turn gray, the knight saw the signpost at the crossroads and found to his joy that he was taking the right direction. He had only been to Limoges once before, but thanks to his excellent memory, he was able to hit anywhere he had ever seen. He urged the stolen horse to run faster. Slowly it grew lighter, and as the sun rose, the outlaw saw puffs of black smoke on the horizon.

"I'm late," he thought in horror.

The moment of hesitation did not last long - he decisively directed the wretched mount into the city, only deviating off the main trail so as not to come across any troops. He remembered the Black Prince's threats at himself well and preferred to avoid capture. Limoges was not, as he had feared, not one sea of flames, for only the buildings outside the city were on fire, but the gates were open, and within the walls there was not so much battle as slaughter. Theo made his way through the city to the castle, stumbling over the bodies of men, women, and children, feeling his madness slowly sweep over him. He hadn't expected to witness something like this a second time, but he pushed into the castle, driven by a fear which he had not confided to Philip.

"Me and Winslow will probably get married," Lady Joan had told him one day.

Well, if it had already come to this wedding, she could have been here with her husband. He had to try to help her. When he got there, the castle was already conquered, and hundreds of knights in full armor fought against desperate defenders. Theo broke through the fighters and ran into the castle. The narrow corridors were filled with hard-to-breathe smoke, and there were dead and dying on the stairs and on the floors. More than once or twice, the outlaw had to face enemies who took him for one of the defenders of the castle. As he could see, he wasn't the only one looking for the lord of this castle, so it was all the more important that he should get to him first, though it had only now occurred to him that he didn't know what to do next. The city was conquered by the army of the Black Prince, it was probably impossible to sneak out of it, and even in the company of someone who was wanted by him.

When he saw a few knights storming the barricaded door to the tower, already swaying under the blows of an improvised battering ram, he attacked them from behind with little thought, assuming that someone significant had taken refuge in the tower. The sword curled in his hand like a living creature, animated by the desire to take revenge on those who had made a bloody slaughter in this city. He felt a real lust for blood. Limoges reminded him of his native Bongrais, which had been turned into a slaughterhouse of yore, and his blood was raging in it. It broke through the attackers, lying dead two of them and turned, storming into the others. The English abandoned the battering ram and took up their swords, but it was a little too late for that.

Nimble as a snake without heavy armor, the unexpected opponent wasted no time. His sword cut through throats, severed arms and legs, cutting the armor exactly where the iron plates were joined with straps. Having done the work, Theo kicked the swinging door, breaking the lock completely, and, hiding behind it as if behind a shield, looked out over the battlements. At first, he saw nothing, but then he saw a scrap of dark silk behind a bend in the wall. He jumped onto the tower, gripping the hilt of his sword tighter, and an unexpected sight saw his eyes. Leaning against the top of the battlement was Sir Winslow, in whose chest were two crossbow arrows, next to him Lady Joan was embracing the little girl convulsively and pressed herself against the stone wall as if she wished to merge into one.

"My lady..." Theo knelt beside her, afraid she might be hurt, but he couldn't see the blood on her robes.

A shudder shook the Englishwoman's body.

"It's you..." she whispered. "Is it really you or am I hallucinating?"

She was scared to death, she seemed to be blind to everything around.

"I am," he embraced her and hugged her reassuringly. "My lady, we have to get away. I have to get you both out of here, but I don't know how."

"Reynold..." Joan moaned desperately.

He looked around and, noticing the second exit from the tower, closed the door, blocking the broken lock with a dagger. Then he leaned over Sir Winslow and examined his wounds. The arrows, deep in the lungs, were quite short and thick, which meant that their points were wide, with barbs preventing them from being removed and tearing the flesh extensively. The knight was breathing hoarsely without opening his eyes, bloody foam was dripping from the corners of his mouth. Theo shook his head and turned to Lady Joan.

He pulled her aside.

"He's dying, my lady," he said softly. "But he will suffer for a long time, and when he falls into the hands of your cousin..."

Lady Fitzoother sobbed, clutching the silent child in her arms, whose eyes following the grown-up.

"My lady," the outlaw took her by the shoulders with a gentle but firm movement. "Please agree. This is the only thing I can do. We can neither take him with us nor leave him to your first cousin revenge. Agree."

Still crying, the Englishwoman nodded helplessly and turned away, trembling like a leaf. Theo stripped his sword. He had seen too many wounds in his life not to know which one would end, but despite his belief in the rightness of his actions, he felt some disgust at what he had to do. He walked over to Sir Winslow, leaning against the wall, gasping for air with his half-open mouth. He had to fight a hard fight for every breath, every moment harder to catch, and Theo felt a thrill of pity at how this noble man must suffer now.

"Forgive me, my friend," he whispered, delivering a lightning-fast, merciful blow.

Blood spurted onto the stones, and the Englishman's body shuddered and fell limp in the red puddle. It was indeed the best that he could offer him under these conditions.

He wiped the saw blade mechanically, choked back any unnecessary tears, and took Lady Joan's hand.

"We're getting out of here," he said firmly.

The English woman passively allowed him to take her to the second staircase, leading, as it turned out, inside the double walls of the tower all the way down. The heavy iron door was locked, but it was not for nothing Theo had a pair of good thieves in the gang, Jean and Francois, who taught him to open locks with a simple knife and a piece of iron wire. Manipulating a little, he opened the door and dragged the jittery lady out into the courtyard. Lady Joan screamed, unprepared for the sight of so many cruelly mutilated bodies. The girl in her arms began to cry.

Theo looked around and waved his hand toward the path that gave him some chance of getting out of the castle. Holding the Englishwoman's trembling hand in one hand, and in the other, the exposed sword ran across the courtyard and peered cautiously through the ajar wing of the great gate.

"Too many," he whispered, thinking.

His wandering gaze fell on the lying corpse courtyard and lit up. They had armor - this was the chance he needed.

"Quickly, my lady, we have literally counted moments," he said in a voice that could bear no objection as he unfastened the armor straps on one of the corpses. "Take off your dress and hennin, put on your pants and those sheets. I'll help you."

Lady Joan hesitated for a blink of an eye, then without a word she stripped off her gown and, with the help of a knight, pulled on the bloody pants, taken from one of the fallen, and a chain mail slightly too large for her. She put on a helmet with a visor on her head, fastened a dark navy blue cape to her shoulders, wrapping it on an iron glove so that she could hide the girl under it. Theo quickly changed into his second armor and showed the gate with an eloquent movement. The Englishwoman nodded and silently followed him, shifting awkwardly in a manly outfit she had no time to get used to. It was stuffy under her visor, she couldn't see much through the glass, and all the time she was afraid of dropping the child wrapped in a torn cloak.

The outlaw moved more gracefully and faster than she, which was no wonder, since he was a knight, but she constrained and delayed him, which made her despair. She had no idea how they would get out of town, and she prayed fervently that no one would discover she was a woman. Perhaps this was the thought of the knight when he ordered her to change. If she had hit Edward himself, there would have been no misfortune, but she didn't even know if he was here with his army, and the others were too angry to notice who they were dealing with. Anyway, what's easier than to kill after a rape? The corpse won't say anything.

Lady Joan shuddered with an overwhelming sense of shame for her nation.

"I'm surprised someone like Theo helps me at all," she whispered to herself helplessly, turning her head to avoid seeing what was going on in the streets.

However, it was happening everywhere, and it was impossible to escape these views, full of inhuman cruelty[12]. As long as she was wearing knightly armor, she couldn't cry, so she suppressed sobbing, though she felt as if she was going to be losing her mind. Meanwhile, Theo was working effectively. He led his companion through the chaos-engulfed city without attracting anyone's attention, and finally appropriated two horses without embarrassment. They were heavy, chivalrous Tartar horses, maybe not too fast, but sturdy. They were a real treasure in their position.

Once in a relatively safe place, he stopped the horses and gave Lady Fitzoother her gown, which he prudently took with him.

"Change your clothes, lady," he ordered, "a journey in this junk would be too burdensome for a delicate lady. I'll hold the baby, just be so kind as to wait while I take off my armor myself."

Dexterously, he undid his breastplate and pulled off his greaves, disposing of the rest of his gear just as quickly. Lady Joan handed him the little girl and walked behind the wolfberry bush, where she changed into her gown.

Theo touched his cheek against the baby's soft, curled head.

"My Mathilde," he whispered. "My little daughter."

The girl looked much better than the last time he had seen her. It was rounded and visibly smoother, and her eyes reminded the knight irresistibly of those of his deceased mother. They were the same black, in the shape of oblong poplar leaves, framed with curled eyelashes. The shape of her mouth was also reminiscent of the deceased countess, and she undoubtedly had broad eyebrows from her grandfather. After Adeline took a slightly upturned, slightly too short nose, a cute dimpled chin and those shiny curls

---

[12] The slaughter of Limoges, although described in macabre details by the then chronicler, is sometimes questioned by historians. Other documents show that only a few people died during the conquest of the city.

on the head. Theo felt a sudden rush of love for the baby, so strong it hurt his chest.

He hugged the little girl to him and showered her with kisses, all the greedier as he could not be sure if he would ever can do so again.

"You're not going to take her away from me, are you?" said Lady Joan's voice next to him.

He looked at her, confused and ashamed of this outburst of unmanly tenderness.

"Oh no," he reassured her. "You better look in a dress than an armor, my lady."

He handed her the baby reluctantly. The Englishwoman pressed Mathilde to her, and she cried violently.

"It was terrible," she sobbed. "Theo, how can men do this... to women, and even to underage girls? And why? Did we owe them something?"

The knight embraced her warmly.

"I don't know, my lady. Unfortunately, it has happened in every war, it has happened in Bongrais," he said sadly.

He stroked the young woman on her trembling back and shoulders, feeling her frenzied heartbeat against his, and struggled to contain the growing tension within him.

"My lady, we have to run," he said finally, forcing himself to end the dangerous situation. "Where should I take you?"

The Englishwoman wiped her tears and tried to control herself.

"To Castle Meung," she replied. "I left my carriage and part of my servants there. I immediately set off to the seaside and return to England. Nothing keeps me here anymore, and I prefer not to see my first cousin under any circumstances anymore."

"OK."

Theo helped her mount her horse and climbed onto the back of the other himself. Castle Meung was not too far away, but they had to walk a long way through the wilderness, so he could not leave the Englishwoman alone. Apart from the ruined and truncated Limoges, the English army did not pose a threat to her, but there were Robert Deauville's rebels, from whom the Count de Bongrais was enough protection. Both Deauville and the others knew him well and respected him. Traveling with him, she was safe, although it would be difficult to say the same about Theo, who in Aquitaine risked his skin if caught, literally. It was unlikely that Lady Joan would have been able to shield him from the wrath of the Black Prince in such a case. It did not seem, however, that such an eventuality would be able to give the brave outlaw sleep overnight. He rode alongside the beautiful lady, carefully choosing a path that would give some cover to the trees and hills, and though he looked calm, inside he was tense and ready to fight. Lady Joan held the child silently against her, trying to shake off the terrible impression. It was the first time she had witnessed what could happen in a war, and she couldn't understand how it was possible to participate in it all without going insane. She glanced from time to time at the knight escorting her. His gentle face was completely devoid of the cruelty that so often marked the faces of knights she knew, and somehow, despite his beauty and grace, he did not bear any features of effeminacy. This is what an Angel of War could look like. Yet his hands, she knew it well, had already shed so much blood from her countrymen that she should hate him, despite all the extenuating circumstances. She couldn't - she loved him and hid this love deeply in her heart, even without saying in her evening prayers. There was no way they could be together (she didn't know if he wanted it anyway) and it was better to accept it in advance. But she did have something - his baby. She remembered the day again, when he appeared at Meung's castle with a baby in his arms, despair in the pupils of his black eyes, terrified of what he was doing and unsure of the rightness of his decision, yet determined to entrust her with his most precious treasure. A tiny girl, black-eyed like her father, from the very first moment captured the heart of a widowed, childless aristocrat. She loved her like her own child, whom she had wanted in vain for years.

"Theo," she began hesitantly. "Come with me to England. What else is keeping you here? After all, your king could not appreciate you. I'm not persuading you to cheat, but is an ordinary, quiet life away from political turmoil a betrayal?"

The knight looked at her with a sad smile.

"Sometimes yes, confusing," he replied. "And besides, there's something else that keeps me here. I have a wife and friends. But I will escort you to the port, so that you will not have any trouble on the way."

"I have my guards and services." the Englishwoman said, a little proudly.

The outlaw nodded.

"I know," he said. "But I'll be calmer if I walk you away a bit. I'll back off, so to speak, in Bordeaux. You'll be safe there. You both will."

Lady Joan kissed Mathilde on the forehead.

"Didn't your wife protest against putting the little girl in my care?" she asked after a moment.

"Mathilde is my daughter, but she is not my wife's daughter," the knight replied shortly.

The Englishwoman nodded.

"I understand."

"No. You understand nothing, my lady. It's more difficult and tragic than you could have imagined."

The Englishwoman asked no more, overwhelmed by the unfamiliar note in the knight's voice and startled by the gloomy tinge of his voice.

When they reached the vicinity of Castle Meung she stopped her horse.

"Stay here," she said. "My brother's guards better not see you. You will join me on the way, it will be safer for everyone."

"Right, my lady," Theo admitted, pulling off the reins of his mount and hopping to the ground.

"Don't talk to me like that," she muttered angrily. "Call me Joan."

Theo smiled.

"Er, it's not proper," he said, slapping her horse on the rump, urging him to move.

Lady Joan rode into the courtyard of Castle Meung and dismounted with the help of one of the guards.

"Balley!" She exclaimed imperiously. "Order the horses to my carriage! Mary, Bernice, pack your trunks! We're leaving immediately!"

"But lady, are you not saying goodbye to your brother?" asked Balley in amazement, the old soldier in command of Lady Fitzoother's personal force, bursting out of the guardhouse at her voice.

"Why so suddenly, cousin?" the duchess echoed him as she appeared in the courtyard.

"Don't ask anything, or better ask your husband when he's back," Lady Fitzoother replied with forced cordiality. "Ask him in the words from the book of Genesis: "Cain, what have you done with your brother Abel?"

"What are you saying, Joan? You are scaring me. What happened in Limoges?" asked the duchess fearfully.

She knew her husband's violent nature too well not to be frightened by her cousin's words. The latter, however, did not answer her, running to her chambers. Soon after, her four-horse carriage, to which the servants had tied their trunks, went out to the courtyard. After a while Lady Joan appeared, already dressed in traveling clothes, followed by both confused maids and a nanny, carrying the baby in her arms. At the same time, escort soldiers appeared in the courtyard on their mounts, ready to go.

"Joan..." wailed the Duchess.

"Sorry, cousin, I can't stay here after what I saw in Limoges," her cousin said firmly, giving her a cool kiss. "I'm going back to England, to Leafort. I should have done this a long time ago."

She got into the carriage with the nanny and the baby. Her maids mounted horses like soldiers.

"I don't understand," whispered the Duchess, looking after her.

"Well, I do," Captain Moore said grimly, standing next to her. "The real misfortune that she had to visit this city right now, without telling anyone yet."

He shook his head disapprovingly. If he had even suspected who was waiting for the Prince's cousin's retinue not so far from the castle again, he would have followed her, disregarding the very clear orders he had received from his master. However, he couldn't have known it, and it was better for everyone. Theo, for his part, hadn't thought of starting any fights in enemy territory, he was just waiting hidden in the bushes next to the Bordeaux road, nibbling on stalks of field mint and thyme to cheat the hunger that was beginning to take its toll on him. He did not want to leave this place so as not to miss his lady's retinue, which meant that he had to fertilize some more time. It was nothing new to him, but it was always not much fun. Finally, in the distance, the wheels clattered and clattered the horse's hooves. Theo hurriedly mounted his steed and, making sure it was Lady Fitzoother's retinue, rode out from behind the trees.

"Easy, Balley." Lady Joan looked out of the carriage window and stopped the guard commander, ready to chase the intruder away. "This is my friend. He will accompany us to Bordeaux."

"Yes, my lady," stammered the old soldier reluctantly, eyeing the young man in plain robes but with a sword at his side with a distrustful glance.

Theo steered his horse towards the carriage and caught up with it.

"Nobody tried to stop you, lady?" he asked, leaning towards the carriage window.

"No," replied the Englishwoman. "But if we come across any of my brother's troops, you may be in trouble."

"That's my concern," Theo laughed and glanced happily at Balley, who was following him distrustfully.

"How handsome this French is," one maid whispered to the other. "How do our lady know him?"

"I have no idea, Mary," the other whispered back. "But you're right, you can't take your eyes off him."

Being bolder by nature, she rushed her mount and caught up with the young knight.

"I'm Mary," she introduced herself.

"Very enchanted," her knight replied courteously. "Please forgive me, I speak bad English."

"You know our lady well, my lord?" the girl asked, switching to French.

"Call me Theo, beautiful daughter of Albion. I know a little,"

"She's my friend Bernice," said Mary cheerfully as the other girl joined them. "We are distant relatives of our lady, poor unfortunately, so we work as her maids, but we do not complain. She is good and generous."

"I'm not rich either, but it's always easier for a man," the outlaw gave the shy Bernice a sweet smile. "Besides, I do not think that the knights of the court will remain indifferent to your pretty faces for a long time. You surely have hoop fans, you just don't want to admit it."

The girls giggled shyly, pleasantly tickled by his words. English knights were much more reserved in paying compliments and much more elevated in court service, so they were not used to such elegant treatment. So while the English hated the French, the English women had a crazy weakness for them, especially those of a slightly lower status.

Theo entertained the two girls with cheerful conversation until the stop, which was arranged at a roadside inn at dusk. There, to his confusion, Lady Joan categorically demanded that he sleep in the next room, not in the stables, as he had intended, and refused to listen to any arguments.

"Balley, don't say anything," she told the commanders of the guard, shocked by the decision. "If something unexpected happen, only he will be able to protect me. No offense, my friend, trust me this time."

The old soldier looked at her wordlessly and only sighed. He had known Joan since she was a little girl, no bigger than Mathilde is now, who had come from out of nowhere and about whom no one knew anything. He loved her more than he wanted to admit it, and he didn't want to be hurt by that French knight, whom he knew nothing about either, but suspected who she really was.

Unlike the two stupid butterflies, he could associate facts, observe and draw conclusions.

Theo ate the supper he had brought him with poorly masked greed and lay down to sleep in a small pamperage adjacent to the room where Lady Joan and her service slept. He was dead tired, too much to think about the possible danger.

*****

"Our paths diverge here," said Lady Fitzoother sadly, standing by the gangplank of the rented boat.

Theo stared at her with unintentionally dreamy eyes, absorbing her slender figure in a dark purple dress and the veil wrapping her face, flowing from under the widow's cap.

"I will never forget our journey together," he said, taking the English woman's slim hand. "Farewell, noble lady whom I will keep forever in my unworthy heart."

Lady Joan sighed.

"Do something else for me: don't get yourself killed," she asked softly.

"Okay, I'll do my best," he promised her. "And you look after Mathilde. She will only have you."

He looked around to make sure no one could see them and placed a hot kiss on her lips, which she returned with no less fervor. For the blink of an eye, there was nothing for them but the two of them, and they felt indescribably good about it, but it could only be for a brief moment. Then Lady Joan turned and walked slowly up the gangplank.

Theo waited until the ship left the quay, then mounted his horse and steered it towards the provincial border. He still felt the kiss of the beautiful English woman on his lips, and he was not sure which was worse: that he was cheating on his wife in this way, or that he was committing something like a betrayal of his homeland. He touched his fingers to his lips and smiled at his memories.

"Even the gods can't take what they've given," he remembered the Latin sentence and agreed with it fully. Whatever awaits him, no one will take those few moments together. If anyone were to ask him now what exactly he felt about Lady Joan, he would not be able to answer unequivocally. As strange as it seemed, his love for Bellette didn't suffer, as if there were two different people in him, each with their own feelings. He was not, however, dazed enough by romantic rapture as to neglect to direct his mount into the forest. On the main roads, he preferred not to travel even in his own province, much less in enemy territory. He knew very well that his worst adventures were almost always the result of chance, and he preferred to eliminate such dangers in advance. He didn't have to stop anywhere. At his saddle he had a bag with food supplies and a wineskin with wine, and since an overnight stay in the open air was nothing new to him, he could do without visiting roadside taverns. He was also in no hurry to get anywhere. There was no such need - his friends would wait, and in the end he had no more appointments for a day and an hour. He was glad to see Mathilde one more time before the final parting.

How has she grown? He thought as he steered his mount along the forest path. "She'll start talking soon, maybe she's even trying? When do children actually start talking? I'll have to ask Bellette, women know such things. The little one looks a bit like Adeline, well, it's impossible to deny her beauty, unless someone is blind to both eyes. Dear God, this is my child, my own little daughter... I didn't know it was such a wonderful feeling to be a father. Now I understand why Bellette laments her unborn children so much. We absolutely have to try again, maybe this time this small, everyday miracle will be successful?"

He smiled to himself. The sun-warmed forest smelled of marsh resin and herbs, rang with the voices of birds and hummed so reassuringly that Theo almost forgot about the still ongoing war and was carried away by his dreams. He was brought to the ground only by an unknown man in a gray coat with a hood, who suddenly jumped on the path and grabbed his horse by the bridle.

"Stop!" he shouted menacingly.

The knight grabbed the hilt of his sword, but Robert Deauville emerged from the thicket behind attacker and gave him a reassuring sign.

"Oh, that's you," Theo stuffed the half-naked sword back into its scabbard. "What do you want, Robert?"

"Talk," Deauville replied seriously. "Our spy spotted you, so if you are here, not far from one of our camps, why not visit us?"

"Why not?" Theo jumped off the saddle, glad to stretch his legs a little.

Robert Deauville led him through the winding paths and led him straight into a large clearing, lined with tents, between which horses and men watched. Together they entered the largest tent, situated in the middle of the clearing, where there were already a dozen knights, deliberating over something.

"Cavaliers, to those who do not know him, I present the Count de Bongrais, better known as Theo le Vengeur," Deauville said to the assembled.

"Sit down, Count," said a middle-aged mustachioed knight who must have weighed a one and a half quintal. "We have a conference. You know, of course, what happened in Limoges."

"I know," Theo replied darkly. "I was there."

"Exactly. I think it is time to chase the Black Prince away from here until he has managed to organize such a massacre in other cities as well," finished the man with mustache.

"Bernard is right," a gray-haired knight sitting a little further back in mourning supported him. "We have nothing to wait for any longer. If we hit with all our strength, our chances are good."

"It's undoubtedly so," said the outlaw. "But you don't take one thing into account, chevaliers: The Black Prince will not withdraw from Aquitaine until he is officially ordered by his father. Until then, he will defend himself with the ferocity of a cornered wolf, and many of you will not see the end of the war."

There was silence after this statement.

"So what, are we supposed to wait like the Limoges people to slaughter us?" asked another participant in the conference.

Theo waved his hand.

"Limoges paid for the English in charge to come over to your side," he said. "It paid, I admit, a very high price. However, I don't think it will happen again. A general uprising will do you nothing unless one of you finds a way to reach the King of England and force him to order his son to withdraw. Personally, I don't see any chances for such an action to be successful."

The knights looked at each other uncertainly.

"So what, are we supposed to do nothing?" Bernard asked with some resentment.

"And where do you even get such news?" his neighbor wanted to know.

"Maybe I have good informants? As for what you could do, I advise you to coordinate your actions with the actions of our king's troops. War is not a hunt for spring bunnies, gentlemen knights. It cannot be that everyone does what seems most accurate to them without asking anyone's opinion. Remember the old proverb it is better that a deer herd will be led by a lion than a lion herd led by a deer. Send someone to Paris and put yourself under the command of Bertram du Guesclin. It's the only way."

"And this is your advice?" Snorted Deauville, choleric and haughty by nature. "Each of us is a knight with great military experience, we do not have to go to the king with every stupid thing! We can beat the enemy ourselves!"

"Guesclin treats the nobility as conscripts from just any village," the one in mourning joined him indignantly. "He makes slaves of well-born men!"

Theo shrugged.

"Good knights who must consult some outlaw," he said, and left the tent, leaving the conspirators utterly stunned.

"I'm beginning to understand why the English conquered us at all," he confided in disgust to his steed, steering it back to its previous path.

Not for the first time, Robert and his henchmen had upset him. He had never been able to explain to them, for example, what benefits it would bring to cooperate in this war with people of the non-noble state, only those who would like to fight. More than once he was furious at those choked heads where certain things could not quite reach, and at such moments he completely lost all hope of any patriotic insurgency.

"Good thing they didn't attack Joan," he thought suddenly. "We would not defend ourselves against this crowd, and they certainly would not want to listen to me. I guess we were lucky, me and her."

Such a hostage would certainly be a treat for Deauville and his people, they would not let her out of their hands at his word, and the situation could become dangerous, because he would not leave her in danger.

"We're done," he finished aloud with satisfaction.

The ride through the forests of Aquitaine was so enjoyable that he soon forgot about Robert and his iron-clad allies with whom it would be difficult for him to find a common language, even in case of emergency. He arrived at the Touraine border two days later. This delay was caused by a circumstance beyond his control - he had to get a new horse, because the one he was riding suddenly lame for unknown reasons. He bought a new one from a traveling trader and moved on.

Only within the boundaries of his province could he be sure that he would not fall into the hands of one of the English troops, and although he had to avoid native soldiers for a change, he breathed more freely. He rushed his horse cheerfully, deciding to drop by on the way to the Under the White Swan Inn and find out what was going on. After all, he had been gone for quite a long time, and a lot could have happened during that time.

To greet him, the most unexpected man ran out of the door of the inn: Philip d'Evreux.

"You still here?" Theo wondered, relieved, jumping to the ground.

He would spent most of his time in the saddle lately, and he was sick of it. Involuntarily, he grunted with contentedly straightening the old pins.

"What, you feel pain in your ass?" Philip asked cheerfully. "As for your question, I swore to myself that I would not leave this place until you returned. And how was Limoges?"

"Terrible," Theo replied, his face darkening.

"I heard. They say they have three thousand dead in the city itself. Come on, let's have a drink and tell me everything."

"Maybe not everything," thought the outlaw, following him to the inn. Upon seeing him, Damasus dropped the jug he had just wiped, smashing it into dozens of pieces, and Margot and Laura screamed happily.

"Come on, thank God, you are here!" Cried the innkeeper. "Your people came here several times a day asking if I had learned anything about you. They go crazy with anxiety."

"Right," Theo waved a hand dismissively. "They would be relieved immensely if the hell got me. Give me wine and anything to munch on."

They sat down with Philip in the corner, at one of the tables, and poured each other a cup of strong drink.

"Tell me," the prince encouraged his friend.

Theo told him what he had witnessed, deftly avoiding confessions that were too personal, but not forgetting his meeting with Robert Deauville. Philip listened attentively without interrupting.

"In a word, it's starting again," he said as his friend finished. "I have a bad feeling about this. Maybe you will come with me to Navarre after all?"

The outlaw shook his head laughing.

"Everyone follows their own destiny, Philip," he said. "Mine and yours are two different destinations. You will wait out the king's wrath and return to your place by his side, and I will return to the woods and be there until I die, amen."

"You didn't deserve such a fate."

Philip looked sad at the dirty table top. Theo finished chewing on a chicken leg and licked his fingers.

"Don't worry about it," he consoled his friend. "Who knows what else life has in store for us? Maybe it won't be what we think.

Come on, I have to go to my own people and inform them that, unfortunately, I'm still alive, although it could be sad for them."

Philip got up and hugged him heartily.

"Until next time, my friend," he said heartily. "Never forget that you can count on me in any situation."

"Just like you on me," the outlaw returned his embrace and kissed him on both cheeks. "I'll miss you. Maybe next time we will see each other in free France?"

"May you be right, and may it be as soon as possible," replied the prince quietly, looking after him in his wake and trying to suppress the pain of parting, which he knew also penetrated his friend's heart.

Neither of them knew it was their last meeting in their lives - and it was better that way.

CHAPTER VI

Follow your heart

"So, how was it?" the innkeeper asked, setting the jug of wine on the table. Jaussard drank and replied, squinting at the peasants who were listening eagerly:

"Well, yes, when lord found no one, he went to the village. Everyone rejoiced as if they were dumbfounded, and Bellette hit him in the face, and second from the other hand... He lost his breath, and when he recovered, he asked: "What are you doing, sweetheart? Why is that?" And she grabbed her hips... "Why, you ask? Why? What? If I knew what it was for, I would cut your head with a scythe!"

"Yikes... And what lord about it?" one of the peasants asked.

"He must beat her," said the other confidently.

"Oh no," replied the mayor. "He kissed her hands, and he said: "Bellette, my heart, if you must, then cut my head off, but do not be angry anymore, because, I swear for God, I will find the girl in the countryside and will need to confess."

"What about Bellette?" the innkeeper asked, wiping his hands on his apron.

"Already she regains her mind, don't know for real or just for show. Good man, this count, but does not know that you have to keep a woman on a short leash," Jaussard ended his speech philosophically and drank again.

"Well, gentry understands things a little different," said one of his listeners.

"Don't say like that," the other one was impatient. "King Philip beat the divine queens, head is head. Woman is a woman, without a few sticks of the advice she cannot do."

"I can't imagine Theo hitting a woman," Damasus said. "He is like such a knight from a fairy tale for good children."

There was silence for a moment.

"And what she wants?" One of the peasants finally said, shaking his shaggy head. "She can't appreciate happiness. Stupid girl. I would like show her how it should be... for sure she didn't want me for this."

"Lucky for you, that you don't have the witch in the cottage," said the mayor authoritatively.

He himself had tried to court Bellette once, too, but he regretted it a lot later and could not forgive her to this day.

Claire ran into the inn, disheveled and stumbling over her own legs in her customary way.

"Damasus, I don't have time to look for my father!" She cried, "Send him a message that Agnes is to be hanged in the market square in Bongrais! This witch de Valois accused her of stealing one of her dresses!"

"When are they supposed to hang her?" Margot asked vigorously, taking off her apron.

"Tomorrow noon," Claire replied gasping for air.

She didn't like Agnes much, but she didn't mean her badly. At the root of her resentment was jealousy for her father, whom she had to share with the beautiful woman."

The mayor shrugged his shoulders as a sign that nothing extraordinary was happening.

"Did she at least steal that rag?" the innkeeper asked.

"What's the difference? Lady want to hang someone, and we need to help," Jaussard said indifferently. Claire gave him a hard cheek and cried out.

"Go back to town, honey. I'll visit the marshes and let your father know," Margot said, giving her a soothing hug and stroking her hair.

She didn't really know the way through the marshes, but she was hoping for a stroke of luck, as generally you could meet one of the outlaws by the lake or in the part of the forest between the lake and the marshes.

*****

"Don't you understand that men have hotter blood than women?" Preziosa added a measured amount of leaven to the bowl and began to knead the dough into bread. "That's why it's easier for them to forget. Besides, what's the harm when you know Theo only loves you? He's gentle, good, and so handsome, let him have lovers. After all, he is not the first and not the last."

"I don't want him to have any other," Bellette replied glumly.

"Well, he has not. Once it's not a lot, just get over it, because you'll go beyond the mark and then he'll really find a comforter.

And if you don't want it, remember the proverb that flies are lured of honey, not vinegar," said the Gypsy calmly.

There were many reasons for what she said, but Bellette still couldn't forgive her husband for what had happened between him and Adeline. At the same time, she completely ignored the fact that she did not know with whom he was in the hay at that time. She tried to act as if nothing had happened, but it was very difficult for her, and Theo, who knew her well, could see the compulsion. He believed that time would heal the wound, but more and more he resented his wife that she could not understand him and that something was clearly going wrong between them.

Behind the cabin there was a patter of feet and Fabienne burst in.

"Where's my brother?" she asked.

"Somewhere around and something happened?"

Preziosa put the kneaded dough behind the stove where it was to grow warm and left the front porch, wiping her soaked hands on a frayed rag to replace her apron.

"Unfortunately, I think so. Margot from the inn is waiting by the lake," Fabienne said, looking around the clearing.

The outlaws abandoned their activities with apparent relief, flocking to her side, and Ettienne ran for the knight and soon brought him to the others.

"What's the matter, little sister?" Theo asked kindly.

After the first period of surprise, he was used to having a sister, not a brother, and even quietly admitted that she was a pretty, graceful girl. Admittedly, she still dressed like a man, but she had stopped trimming her dark blond curls and looked really good with longer hair.

"Adeline wants to hang Agnes for some alleged theft," Fabienne informed him. "Margot is waiting by the lake, she'll explain everything to you."

"Agnes?" Theo furrowed his broad eyebrows in a grimace of displeasure.

He remembered the chubby brunette with smiling eyes who had never refused to help them, then looked at Francois, terrified.

"We're going," he ordered. "Ettienne, Prezioso, you too, I will need all your hands. Bellette, you are staying."

"Of course," his wife muttered sarcastically.

She had long come to terms with the fact that, as a comrade in arms, she was no help for her husband, and she did not want to be one at all. She was even surprised that Preziosa and Fabienne were willing to take part in such expeditions and that they fulfilled their tasks perfectly.

Taking their weapons, the entire gang headed to the lake where Margot was waiting for them as she strolled nervously along the shore. Theo nodded casually in greeting and ordered her briefly:

"Speak."

The girl repeated what she heard from Claire as faithfully as possible and added:

"Just don't be too rash. This bane in your castle must have already considered that you may want to free the condemned one, if only to emphasize that you have a different opinion. The execution is due tomorrow at noon, so you have some time, but she also has. She's definitely up to something."

"Could she know Agnes helped us?" Jean asked, scratching his red head anxiously.

"I don't think so, but it isn't for nothing that our leader enjoys the reputation of a defender of the oppressed. She might have thought of trying to help the nice peasant woman," Millot said sarcastically.

"Did Agnes actually steal that dress from Adeline?" Fabienne asked.

"Even so, do you think a piece of silk cloth is worth human life?" Theo asked. "But no, I don't think so. I know her enough to know that she is honest."

"But she acknowledged her's guilt..." Margot said doubtfully.

Millot gave a short laugh.

"And you know someone who would not acknowledge his guilt when the executioner politely asks?" he mocked.

"Yes, acknowledge one's guilt is not proof of guilt," Theo shook his head. "But Margot is right, Adeline could have seized the opportunity to set a trap for us, it's very likely. What to do here, for a hundred thousand devils?"

He sat down on the low bough of the Tree of Love and thought.

"You can intimidate that witch Adeline somehow," suggested Jean, unable to think of anything else.

The knight waved his hand.

"She won't be intimidated unless I put a knife to her throat," he said. "You can't imagine me doing this."

"And why not?" Colas were simply surprised.

"Because I'm a man and she is a woman, that's why," the chief explained to him.

Preziosa coughed significantly and spoke when everyone looked at her:

"Chief, maybe you haven't noticed it yet, we've only known each other for a few years, but I'm not a man."

"It's true, Theo, my sister is not a man!" Armando exclaimed with artificial animation.

"She was a master at keeping it a secret," echoed Gwidon.

"Don't make yourself dumber than you are," the Gypsy demanded impatiently. "Me and Fabienne could take care of the Ducess de Valois, that's okay."

Theo shook his head slowly.

"It's too dangerous," he said. "She might not be scared, and that would cost Agnes a head. Hey guys... which side would you expect to see this poor girl rescue if you were in Adeline's shoes?"

The outlaws looked at each other with uncertain expressions.

"Which? From the gate, yes?" said Beregard after a moment.

"Exactly. I think I have an idea, but we're going to need Claire's help. Margot, you're coming with us to Bongrais. You somehow call Claire outside the walls and right after that you can return to the inn."

"Agreed," replied the girl happily. She liked helping outlaws, and she had a secret crush on Gwidon and dreamed of impressing him.

Francois pulled the leader aside.

"Don't think I'm ungrateful," he said softly. "But it will be painful enough to lose Agnes, I can't lose my daughter yet."

Theo smiled and patted him on the back.

"Cheer up, you won't lose any of them," he promised him.

In fact, he wasn't so sure of himself again, but he didn't want his friend to doubt the success of the rescue mission. The plan he had conceived was folly, but he saw no other way to free the poor girl. He was not too indignant at the duchess's decision - in those days the punishment for the slightest theft was usually death or mutilation, and no one saw anything strange about it. However, Agnes was the beloved of one of his friends, and therefore he would try to free her no matter what she did.

The people of Bongrais who knew Agnes did not believe her guilt, but no one reacted other than a shrug and a sigh of sympathy as the news of her impending execution spread. Times were hard, everyone had their own troubles, and no one in the whole town thought of looking for a fight with the lady in the castle. The fact that someone was innocent did not impress people of this era at all, because many more innocent people died than the guilty, whether on the way of troops marching or on scaffolding. However, many rushed to the market square at noon to see the execution with their own eyes. It was immediately noticeable that the duchess was expecting some trouble, as the market square was guarded in advance by her personal soldiers, armed and chained in steel. They were clearly prepared to use weapons, as they carefully looked around at the gathered townspeople and did not weaken their attention for a moment.

The sound of the church bell announcing noon to the city merged into one with the rattle of the wagon in front of which the executioner and his helper were walking. The girl riding the cart, barely covered in a tattered rag, looked so battered that many crossed themselves and whispered a prayer for the dying. Indeed, with these methods of extorting confessions, few have proved strong enough to persevere in stubbornness and fail to confirm their guilt. An executioner climbed the scaffolding and checked the noose. His assistant pulled Agnes from the wagon and pushed her in front of him. The exhausted girl stumbled, and she would have fallen if one of the soldiers had not supported her. Then, to everyone's surprise, he picked it up like a feather and tossed it over the back of his mount, then leaping onto the saddle. As if at an agreed sign, several other soldiers turned against their comrades. After a short tumult, leaving the wounded and dead behind them, they fled, taking Agnes with them. The beaten soldiers gathered up after a while, but the pursuit of the unexpected attackers turned out to be seriously impeded - thanks to their armor and helmets, they did not differ from those who pursued them, so it was not difficult to make a mistake.

Informed of everything, Adeline hurriedly mounted her horse and followed her soldiers to lead the pursuit personally, animated by the hope of catching the enemy. She had no doubts who the author of the audacious robbery was. Only one man in the neighborhood would have risked such a risk for some little thief, and she was sure he was right about the person. Just outside the city, she encountered her soldiers, rising from the ground and cursing violently. The wide track collapsed with bare tree trunks.

"What happened here? Cried the duchess, pausing her mare.

"When we left the gate, a puppy hit the pin blocking those stumps on the cart with an ax and it fell like an avalanche," one of the soldiers replied sourly. "The horses got scared and here is the effect."

"And they, you fool, they?!" Adeline shouted furiously.

"What they? They escaped. Were we supposed to chase them on foot?" her soldier said, too nervous to pay attention to the forms adopted.

Duchess picked up the riding crop in her right hand and slapped it over his head.

"Humbler, because I will have you dismembered, son of a dog!" she shouted sharply.

"Lady, you must not alienate soldiers," whispered the commander of the bodyguard, and added louder. "Shall we pursue them?"

"Yes. And the one who brings me their chieftain's head will get a thousand thalers, no matter what his rank," Adeline replied aloud.

"Wait a minute, and how do you know if this is really Theo le Vengeur behind today's robbery?" the soldier was surprised.

"It is he," cut the Duchess, "I can feel it, and my hunch has never let me down before."

The captain looked at her without a word, then turned to the soldiers and sharply ordered them to pursue the pursuit.

Adeline turned the mare and drove to the castle. Throwing the reins of her mount on one of the bollards, she ran upstairs to her chambers.

"Of all the worst bastards...!" she began with a raised voice, thinking she was alone, but stopped.

In her chamber there was someone else besides her: a girl dressed in a man's garb and, what surprised her immensely, the page of King John, known to her by sight. He was older than the last time she saw him, but he had changed surprisingly little."

"What are you..." she began, but stopped again as the question made no sense, the matter seemed completely clear.

She opened her mouth to call the servants, but she did not have time to cry out, because the page was immediately next to her and gagged her with a rag. At the same time, a girl dressed in male clothes pushed the duchess with some kind of force on the armchair and skillfully tied her with a string of curtains.

"Perhaps Theo should have arranged it himself, but you see, he's too well-raised for that," she explained. "Well, I'm a gypsy, we are not well-raised at all. Sit quietly, it is good for your nerves and your temper."

Meanwhile, the Page was hiding the duchess's jewelry in a small purse and was searching the cupboards. The locked secretary pried open with a dagger and scooped all the money hidden there into a purse, which he then wrapped around.

"That must be all," he said in a thin, girlish voice.

"Well, let's go," said the Gypsy. "And Lady, Duchess, I advise you from the bottom of my heart: next time you want to hang someone for allegedly stealing a silk rag, think twice. And thank God that Theo is in charge of us, otherwise I'd talk to a bitch like you in other way. Come on, Fabienne."

They ran out of the room, leaving Adeline furious and helpless in a tightly knotted bondage. The humiliation was unbelievable. All of the Duchess's jewels and all her stock of ready-made pennies were gone, but worse than that was knowing that Theo had mocked her and made her a laughing stock.

"I'll take my revenge," she thought. "I'll take my revenge cruelly. You won't run away from me."

She didn't know how she would take her revenge yet, but making that decision calmed her somewhat.

Meanwhile, Preziosa and Fabienne ran down the kitchen stairs, where Claire was waiting for them with all her belongings in a bundle. She quickly threw on one and the other an ornate traveling cloak, under which their male clothes were hidden, and taking their time, with a careless step, all three went out through the main gate. Nobody paid any attention to them.

Once at a safe distance from the castle, the girls quickened their pace and turned into the forest. There they might not fear the pursuit anymore, because no one, except the outlaws, knew the secret paths through the thickets and swamps, and no one would dare to venture there without a good guide. And it was extremely difficult to find such a guide, and in addition, none of them would venture into the heart of the forest. According to an unwritten agreement, even the most trusted people "from outside", the outlaws showed only one route, namely, which was accessible thanks to the miniature dam on their stream. In the event of the slightest suspicion of disloyalty, it would be enough to lift the stall and the road would become a slushy drowning place. Other paths they did not reveal to anyone, and there were several more, each of them invisible to the uninitiated observer. The girls got to the hideout through one of these paths.

"It went like went swimmingly," Preziosa reported cheerfully, throwing a bundle of jewelry to the chief. "How's Agnes?"

Theo shook his head sadly.

"She's in bad shape," he replied. "Torture does not help anyone, but I hope she will recover. Bellette took care of her, you can go to her too."

Fabienne handed him the money bag and ran after her companions to the annex. Theo hid the girls' treasure in a chest under the floor of their hut, then went out and sat down next to the distraught Francois.

"Get a grip, man," he said heartily. "It's not easy, I know, but the girl is alive and probably not seriously crippled, as long as I know something about it. She will recover for sure."

Francois buried his face in his hands.

"I should have married her a long time ago and go somewhere far away, but I didn't want to leave my friends," he confessed. "What will I do if she dies now? I will never let it go."

"Come on, it's impossible to predict everything," said the knight a little helplessly, because he understood the guilt that plagued his friend and it was difficult for him to find arguments against him. He wasn't sure himself how he would feel about Bellette.

However, within a few days it turned out that Agnes did not suffer as much as they thought, and she was recovering quickly. Her injuries were rather superficial and healed cleanly, and the aches in the strained joints in her arms and legs were soothed by hot willow bark decoction compresses recommended by father Iohann.

"The worst thing is that I haven't even seen that damn dress with my eyes," she said, when she was able to get up and sit down by the evening fire with everyone else. "I just happened to be in the wrong place and that's it. I don't know how I will repay you for what you have done for me."

"Eh, it's nothing. What an idea. How could we say no to our friend's fiancée?" Beregard handed her a particularly well-done piece of meat.

"How did you ever get mixed up among the soldiers?" the girl asked curiously.

"It's Claire's merit," Theo replied. "It was she who introduced us to the castle disguised as food suppliers and showed us where the soldier's weapons are kept. The rest was easy."

"Glad we did it," muttered Pierre.

Francois looked up.

"I want to tell you something," he said. "Agnes and I decided to get married and together with Claire we would go to Bearn. Millot has already offered to guide us until we find a safe spot in the mountains."

"I've wanted to go back to the Pyrenees for a long time," Millot said, his tone of explanation. "Maybe I'll join the Falcon? Anyway, I miss the mountains like a madman. It is completely different here in the lowlands."

"Okay," said Theo, smiling, not revealing that he was hurt at the prospect of parting with his friends. "Preziosa, you will see a wedding dress for Agnes and we will arrange the wedding. It will be a beautiful event."

Jean scratched his red head.

"Actually, I wanted to marry Preziosa on the same day as Francois and Agnes," he said shyly. "You know, Theo, no offense, but I'd like to live a bit like a normal person too. I'm tired of hiding in the woods."

"Then it will be a double wedding," Ettienne squeaked happily.

"There aren't many of us left," muttered Gwidon.

Theo looked at Armando.

"Will you leave us too?" he asked with a sadness he couldn't hide anymore.

The acrobat shrugged.

"I'm not getting married," he replied. "I love my sister, but I didn't marry her and I don't intend to follow her everywhere. I will stay."

"That's good. There will be not many of us here," Pierre said sourly, and cut off another piece of roast for himself. It occurred to him that Fanchette had been waiting a long time for him to make that decision, but he didn't feel ready yet. He even had doubts whether he would ever look at his friends with a wry eye at all, intending to abandon their bachelor's freedom in favor of a marital treadmill.

Others, however, did not share his opinion, especially Bellette, who was reminded of the preparations for her own wedding. These memories made her visibly soften towards her unfaithful husband and she did not annoy him at every step. It would seem that thanks to this, they somehow rebuilt their bond, because in total agreement they took care of the organization of a double wedding. The newlyweds were married by Father Iohann in the monastery chapel, decorated by Fabienne and Gwidon, who for this occasion also composed a wedding song and played his lyre during the ceremony.

"The Preziosa looked wonderful in her wedding gown and veil," Theo said nostalgically a few days later, as he helped the prior get ready the stately deer. "I've forgotten how girly and cute she is when she's not dressed like a man."

"Women shouldn't wear men's garments at all," said the Carmelite disapprovingly. "Do men wear dresses and hennies? After all, this is an open rebellion against the order given by God. And the Bible forbids it."

Theo sighed, expertly separating the pelt from the deer loins.

"I will miss them... It's sad, though I should enjoy their happiness," he said, trying to smile.

"It's always like that. What is a joyful event for one person may hurt someone else. We are glad that you shot this animal for us, but I think his opinion on this matter would be completely different," the monk noted philosophically.

The outlaw looked at him with the knife held over the torn game.

"You know, Father, I never thought of it that way?" he said after a moment, clearly surprised. He looked at the deer with such obvious guilt that Father Iohann laughed.

"Come on, we all have to eat," he said. "If we took these doubts to heart for good, we would have to chew the grass like oxen. Since good God has arranged this world this way, it is not our business to criticize it."

"And to think that I was afraid I would like this old freak," the knight said to himself, amused.

He finished the job, washed at the well, and, having said goodbye to the prior, set off on his way back to the hideout. He walked, thinking about the recent events with a little less melancholy, even managed a smile, remembering the wedding of his friends when suddenly something bumped into him and threw him over the side of the road. Before he could recover, he was disarmed and terrorized with his own sword. The perpetrators of the attacks turned out to be three soldiers in English armor, who came from somewhere else.

"You'll come with us," said one of them menacingly, in whom the outlaw recognized Captain Moore, his old enemy. "His Majesty Prince Edward dreams of seeing you. Especially for this occasion, he stopped in this dingy inn on the road to Aquitaine."

Theo didn't answer, just looked around slightly to see if there was any way to escape, but the English were watching him with their swords drawn, and if he had made even one sudden move, he would probably have been chopped to pieces. So he shrugged his shoulders in resignation and went on obediently, listening without emotion to the captain's mockery, to which he did not even deign to respond. The situation was unenviable. The Black Prince's revenge announced long ago seemed dangerously close, and all who might have helped him were too far away. He had to find some way to get out of this situation without help from anyone... but the blades of the swords flashed dangerously close to his body, too close for him to have any chance of a successful escape. With each step he was closer to his tragic destiny, and still could not think of anything. The opportunity suddenly appeared where the road turned over high rock cliff, narrowing dangerously. A greenish lake shone below. One of the Englishes stumbled over a stone, trying to fit in the road restriction next to the others, the outlaw pushed him away and, before they could stop him, jumped onto the second path that twisted below. If everything went his way, he could get to the forest and hide in it. But he miscalculated the distance, failed to keep his balance at the edge of the path, and rolled off the bluff, plunging onto the rocky shore of a small lake that glistened below. The shock was so strong that he lost consciousness for a moment.

When he opened his eyes, worried mustache faces bent over him.

"Are you alive? Can you stand up?" asked the commander of the unit. He was clearly worried, even scared, because all his arrogance had visibly gone out of him.

"I suppose so," he replied resignedly.

"You could have killed yourself, you crazy French!"

"So what? I'd meet the Creator a little earlier than your master planned, that's it." Theo pushed the soldier's hand away and stood up without help, gritting his teeth so as not to groan involuntarily. He hadn't broken anything, but he had bruised himself badly, and he could only guess what colors his body would take tomorrow. Especially the back.

"Okay, jokes aside. I should tell you right away that His Majesty is not coming upon your life this time. On the contrary, it would be good for me if I did you any harm," the Englishman quickly explained, fearing that the outlaw would repeat his feat. "I know he has to talk to you. He just has to."

It sounded interesting.

"Why the hell?"

"I don't know that," said Moore, "but I have a letter."

He produced a scrap of parchment from behind the wide cuff of his glove. Theo unfolded it distrustfully and ran his eyes across the row of letters.

"Why didn't you give it to me right now, man?"

"Because I wanted to sting you," the captain confessed brusquely. "Would you be better in my place? You made a fool of me few times! You deserved it."

Theo almost laughed even though all his bones ached, especially his ribs. The whole thing suddenly felt grotesque, even funny.

"Okay," he said, folding the letter bearing the princely seal, "I'll come to that invitation myself. I don't need your guards for this."

"But..."

"No buts. I'm going alone. I guess you all know me well enough to know that I'm keeping my word."

"Prince Edward, too," Moore groaned, wiping the sweat off his brow with his glove, "and if I fail him, he will tear off my head, and before that both legs."

Meanwhile, the one they were talking about was sitting in the tavern, sipping mulled wine as the day was very cold and waiting for the return of his patrols. Time dragged on him unbelievably, and in addition, here in hostile territory, he had to sit in hiding if he did not want to expose himself to detection. Finally, one by one, the patrols began to gather, all empty-handed. At best, they had news of where and when his enemy had struck for the last time, and that was of no interest to him. The commander of the last to arrive even claimed that Theo Le Vengeur had been dead for several months, prompting the prince to explode into passion.

"Get out!" he screamed, hitting the table with his fist. "Tomorrow morning, we return to Castle Meung, we will spend the night here."

He drank the rest of the wine and shuffled upstairs to a rented room. With a wave of his hand, he dismissed the squire who wanted to serve him, and entered the room, locking the door behind him. He wanted to be alone to think things over. He did not immediately notice that there was someone else in the room besides him. On the window sill, partially hidden by a cloth simulating a curtain, sat the one he was looking for. His jerkin was dirty and ragged, and his dark face was twisted with an angry expression.

"Next time, Your Majesty, when you want to hunt me, come your own and don't send your dogs," he said.

The Black Prince instinctively glanced at the door, and a long knife appeared in the knight's hand.

"Be careful, Mr. English," he warned him, his voice as a hiss. "I can hit a squirrel in the eye with it, I certainly don't miss you."

Edward pulled up a chair and sat down.

"I don't think to call anyone," he said calmly. "I have to talk to you, and that's why I sent these fools. I'm glad you're alive, because dead you wouldn't be of any use to me."

"Really, what a news..."

Theo played with the knife, never taking his eyes off his interlocutor.

"Listen to me, then you will mock," the Englishman did not lose his composure. "My wife and son are held hostage by your king. He imprisons them in Fontainebleau Castle, and in exchange for their release, demands my father's absolute surrender."

"That's great."

"Great? My father will never agree to this. Believe me, I know him better than you or your king." The prince rubbed his forehead with his hand and continued. "Apart from me, he has other sons, apart from little Richard, other grandsons, so he will not consider the threats of Charles. And he will fulfill them, I have no doubts."

The outlaw smiled a bad, cruel smile.

"And you're scared, huh?" He asked. "You remember Limoges? And the other cities whose inhabitants have been cut down by your troops? There were also some wives and some sons. Feel what you have been doing to others, it will do you good."

"Think, Theo: this is not only my family, but to some extent also yours," the prince reminded him emphatically. "Listen: if you free them, I swear to you, for the salvation of my soul, that I will retreat to England with my troops, and neither I nor any of my soldiers will ever set foot on French soil again."

The knight jumped to his feet.

"Are you crazy, Englishman?!" He shouted indignantly, abandoning the ceremonial "you" form. "What do you want from me?! Should I go against my king?! This counts as a betrayal, and don't expect it from me. No, don't say anything. I know well what arguments you could list for me here, but I will not listen to them. You, kings, take care of these matters among yourselves. As for me, I will not become a traitor to anyone in the world, and for you, that's completely out of the question.

The Black Prince rested his head on his hand and was silent for a long moment. He looked much older than he really was, and his face was marked with lines that had not existed before.

"Yes," he finally admitted. "I have no right to demand such a sacrifice from you. Go away."

"Then what? The whole regiment will come after me?" Theo asked ironically.

"No. You can go. Nobody will chase you." The Englishman waved his hand indifferently, not looking at him.

There was something in his voice that made the outlaw go silent and walk out the way he came, that is, through the window. Though he looked back cautiously and was prepared for any kind of treacherous attack, no one actually followed him, as if the Black Prince had finally learned to keep his word.

"What a situation," he muttered to himself, quickening his pace to get to the forest as quickly as possible. It was a long walk home, and he was tired now, and every bone ached him. All this meant that he didn't reach the hideout until the morning, and the long, night journey, in addition, brought doubts that he had not had before. Without answering questions from his wife and friends, he ate a little, drank wine, and went to bed.

When he opened his eyes after a long, comforting nap, he was able to think clearly and logically, and the events of the last day did not arouse any emotions in him. As he went downstairs, he briefly told his friends what had happened, as well as the offer made by the Black Prince.

"You didn't believe him?!" Pierre shouted, barely had he finished.

"Of course not," he replied. "But, you see, I realized that if it's as he told me, then they are dead. He will never see his wife and son again."

"Good for him," Fabienne said firmly.

"Yes, for him" her brother agreed. "But not them. They didn't do anything wrong, and besides... It will seem silly to you, but this little boy was sleeping on my lap. He was so trusting, so small and defenseless... Charles orders him to poison or strangle him in his sleep with a pillow to take revenge on the King of England, who would not even mind. And this is just a small child..."

"It would not be the first such accident in the royal family," said Gwidon dryly. "They still murder each other and, more interestingly, they get away with it. Remember how much Lady Mahaut[13] has done? After all, it was a public secret that it was she who poisoned the queen, and then the little prince, who was probably not yet two months old. And what did they do to her? Nothing."

"Even if the life of a close family member means nothing to them, how could we expect a king to suddenly start worrying about his subjects?" Colas asked sadly, who had been most impressed by the story.

"Wait a minute, I'm on the formal point," said Armando. "If I understand correctly, Chief, you want to free the Duchess and that kid, right? Well. So I ask: how do you want to start? It's suicide."

"Not quite." Theo stood up and drew the outline of the castle on the wall with a chunk of coal. "This is the royal estate in Fontainbleau. I know it. A prisoner of the state, which the Duchess undoubtedly is, can only stay in this tower, which is easy to guard and to which only one entrance leads. I assume that the duchess was placed in the best of the chambers here. Notice there is a window here, but the wall is smooth, and there's nowhere to get your fingernail in. No woman in the world would attempt to escape through this window, even if she had a rope, but she has a beautiful view. Well, I think..."

"Don't brag, you can't think," Pierre interrupted, but his brother-in-law shot him a scowl and continued:

"If a sufficiently strong rope ladder is attached to the anchor and if I manage to hook it to the window sill, I will be able to carry the lady and the boy downstairs. Note: the cords must be strong enough to withstand the double load. You will probably ask what to do next. And rightly so. I have no idea. All I know is, if I want to get them both safely to Aquitaine, I'll need a lot of smarts and a good load of luck."

---

[13] The Cursed Kings series by Maurice Drouon.

"You have to change your clothes and theirs," said Armando firmly.

"What a news," Beregard said in exasperation. "He has to give up these crazy plans."

"Which disguise will be the best?" Theo asked the tightrope walker.

Armando got up.

"You're very weather-beaten," he said. "You have black hair and black eyes. Eventually, after a little work, you could be mistaken for a Gypsy. In the chest lies one of Preziosa's old dresses, it only needs to be widened a little, because that lady is much plumper than my sister. And also a disguise for a kid."

The knight put his arm warmly around him.

"Come on, let's go over the details," he said.

Pierre looked at his sister.

"Tell him something," he demanded desperately.

Bellette shrugged.

"What for? Nothing gets to him when he is like this," she said resignedly as she hid her face in her hands.

*****

Duchess Joan was sitting in the armchair, rocking the sleeping child and stared with dull eyes at the flame of the candle, which had already been burned almost halfway through. She knew well that she was in a trap from which her husband would not be able to free her, and she had no illusions about helping her father-in-law. Despite the attention and splendor with which she was surrounded in this place, she felt like the last prisoner. She was afraid not so much for herself as for her son, who was in much greater danger than hers. For the first time, she sincerely wished she had given birth to a girl. Since she was imprisoned in this castle, she was afraid to fall asleep, and when sleepiness overwhelmed her, she kept waking up in fear that her beloved baby had not been kidnapped. This made her constantly sleepy and tired. Now her head was drooping, too, though she struggled to stay awake, but suddenly something happened to pull her out of the dullness. Something rattled metallic against the tower window sill. Opening her eyes, she saw an arrow with a string and a note attached to it.

She went to the window, picked up a stick and read: "Pull it in and fasten it." Surprised, she began to pull the string until an iron hook appeared, which she hooked to the stone ledge of the shutter, as best she could. After a while something jerked, and a man in an excessively colorful outfit and a headscarf tied around his head climbed the rope ladder attached to the anchor. A large golden circle hung from his left ear. Only after a while the duchess recognized him and almost screamed. The man put a finger to his lips.

"There's no time to explain now," he whispered. "Please wake the boy up and explain to him that he has to be alone for a while. I will take you first, lady, then come back for him."

"You can't do otherwise?" Princess Joan asked softly, hugging the already half-awake child against her.

"No, you can't, trust me."

Theo gently shook the boy. The Duchess leaned over and began to whisper him reassuringly in English, then set him down on the floor.

"I'm ready," she said, looking the knight straight in the eye. "What about the guards? Always at least two walks under my tower."

"No worries, I've put them to sleep, and we've got some time before they find out."

Theo adjusted the hook.

"Please climb onto my back and hold on well," he said, a little harshly.

He was not at all sure that the pampered lady would behave as she should when descending the rope ladder from a very tall tower, and any unforeseen behavior from her could have catastrophic consequences. She was heavy, far too plump, and for fear of falling she held him so tightly he could barely breathe. At least the ladder tied together by Colas, who had been apprenticing to a rope-maker the other half a year, was trustworthy, but having finally put his foot on the ground, Theo had to rest for a while to catch his breath. Duchess Joan released him at last, feeling the hard ground beneath her feet, and stood beside him, trembling like a leaf.

"Wait, lady," he whispered to her, and climbed the ladder again to the window somewhere above.

The little prince stood politely where his mother had put him and waited for him, his mouth twisting into a horseshoe with fear. Theo held out his hands to him.

"Come on, baby," he said fondly. "I'll take you to your mommy."

He put the child on his back and secured the children to who piece of cloth had been taken for this purpose, then went back downstairs. This time it went much faster and easier.

"I'm not sure if I just saved my nation's future executioner, but never mind," he said, unfastening his belt and freeing the boy.

The duchess grabbed her son and hugged him tightly, almost crying with relief. Theo left the ladder to her own fate and dragged the Englishwoman with him into the woods, where a small carriage waited for them, harnessed by a mouse-like horse.

"Quickly, my lady," said the knight, pulling a bundle of clothes out of the carriage. "Please, put on that gown and beads. The set also includes tambourine and castanets. And with this liquid from the water bag, carefully smear your face, neck and hands."

"What is it?" the Duchess asked a little distrustfully.

"Brown oak bark paint and something else. Fortunately, lady, you are brown-haired, so you can pretend to be a gypsy. We have a long way to go to Aquitaine, better not to be suspected. Certainly, the chase will start literally at any moment."

The Duchess fell silent and obeyed his instructions as quickly as possible.

"Very good," Theo said, tying her hair with a scarf after it had been undone and combed. "Please, put on those earrings."

"You have one too," the Englishwoman remarked, putting large wheels in her ears. He winced slightly.

"Armando pierced my ear," he explained. "He thought that this way I would be more credible and maybe even I am, but I feel like an idiot. Okay, now boy."

He pulled out a colorful skirt and a black caftan sewn with sequins from under a bench in a carriage.

"What?" Princess Joan stared at him indignantly.

"Lady, the little prince is in danger, we must hide him," he explained patiently. "As a girl, it will be easier to escape the attention of your pursuers."

He quickly stripped the non-protesting boy naked, smeared him thoroughly with the coloring liquid from the water bag and dressed him in colorful cloths, and tied a red handkerchief on his head.

"Say nothing, babe," he said to him. "Remember if they ask you, do not answer. We'll play that you're a little girl who can't talk."

"Yes, yes," the little boy whispered.

"Hope he listens," Theo sighed. "We will say that our daughter is mute and that's it. Come on, to the cart."

He folded the clothes of the lady and the boy into a tight bundle, which he tucked under the bench.

"So we're traveling as a gypsy couple. It's good that my husband does not see it," the duchess climbed into the carriage and sat down under a canvas booth with a disguised child on her lap. She covered him and herself with a blanket, as the night was cold, and said a prayer just in case. She was aware of the risks, but also that it would be a greater risk for her to remain in Fontainbleau.

Theo clucked at the horse as it trotted up.

"The legend is that my wife was seriously ill during the performances in Paris," he said. "So when the camp went on, she had to stay, and we stayed with her... I mean, with you, lady. As you have finally recovered, we want to join our fleet in Spain. My name is Amargo, you are Xana, and our daughter is Esmeralda, this must be remembered. Do you know any gypsy songs?"

"I know a few ballads in Spanish, it must be enough," Joan said harshly.

"May be. Of course, just in case, because we might not be able to attract anyone's attention," he adjusted the earring, painfully hurting his newly pierced ear. "Just don't be nervous. The king's army will look for a refined lady with a ducal boy in her arms, not a gypsy woman with a girl in colorful rags, traveling under the care of her husband. Even if you die of fear, my lady, you must not reveal anything. Smile and hug me like nothing has happened and may your son not betray us."

"Richard is very taciturn by nature," said the Duchess, looking tenderly at the baby asleep with his head resting on her lap. And he always obeys my orders, which may not be a desirable trait in a royal grandson, but a very nice trait in a son of a loving mother.

Edward is crazy about him. He poured out on him all his love that remained for him after the death of our older son."

"The one he wanted to marry Princess Isabella? I'm sorry that this happened. I know what it means to lose a child, but here in France, I'm perhaps the only one who will not say that your husband has finally felt the pain he is making to others."

In fact, he did not want to say that to this sensitive lady, who was not guilty of anything after all, perhaps sorry for the secret of her husband's conduct, but he had the impression that someone or something was speaking for him.

The Duchess was silent for a long moment.

"I know," she whispered finally. "I hate this war, I hate dynastic conflicts and all this talk: this or that is mine, is it my right, so I will condemn thousands of innocent people to death that I don't even know. I feel complicit with all this, although I neither started it nor could have prevented anything. You overestimate my importance, Theodore."

The French knight looked at her with a sad smile.

"I don't think you can be overestimated, Duchess," he said softly, and these were not just casual polities. He really began to admire this extraordinary, brave woman and it was already the second Englishwoman who made such an impression on him.

CHAPTER VII

Thin ice

For two days, 10-man units of the royal army searched roads, villages, forests and towns in search of valuable prisoners. The anger of King Charles was terrible - it seemed that no one would survive, but finally it ended with the degradation of the entire guard and the promise that if no escapees were found, the commander of each unit would be beheaded. The task was so difficult that whoever freed the hostages did it very intelligently, leaving no traces, except for a rope ladder, woven in a way unheard of in the representatives of the French guild of rope-makers.

"I don't want to make the accusations empty, but I only know one man determined enough to dare," the king said, staring accusingly at Philip d'Avreux.

The latter grimaced reluctantly.

"And what does the Brightest Lord want from me?" he threw. "I didn't put a match to it."

"Probably. I believe you because you spent that night playing cards with me," said Charles V severely. "Otherwise, I wouldn't have given a penny for your innocence."

Philip kept his face unreadable, but silently prayed desperately:

"Oh God, make it not be him..."

He had little hope because, like the king, he knew why the Count de Bongrais might get involved in this matter. However, for the time being, messengers on all sides returned with nothing, as if Princess Joan and her son had either vanished without a trace or the ground swallows them up. All routes to Aquitaine have been staked out, travelers, whether on foot or on horseback, carefully checked, especially those who seem to belong to a noble family. The inns, taverns and homesteads located along the routes were also inspected in detail. It seemed impossible for even a mouse to slip through the meshes of this dense web, and yet the manhunt yielded no results.

Among the confusion, hardly anyone noticed a Gypsy family, a traveling poor girl harnessed to a mousy horse with a shapeless figure and very dubious genesis. Gypsies were that part of society that was tolerated, a little out of must, a little out of curiosity and for the entertainment they provided to villages and towns. The carriage was searched twice, but fortunately no one found a hiding place with clothes under the bench on the coach-box. The joint journey brings people closer, so it is no wonder that the Duchess liked the French knight more and more, who looked after her with all his commitment and was so tender towards her son.

"They tell terrible things about you, and you have so much delicacy," she said as the carriage rattled slowly along the wide road. "I don't understand this."

"I just can't be gentle with everyone," Theo laughed. "Especially since we have a war, and this nasty thing doesn't foster better feelings."

"I thought you knights love war," the duchess whispered thoughtfully.

She smiled provocatively at the passing party and drummed her fingers lightly on the tambourine in her lap. Theo waited until they were away from the soldiers and replied:

"Only those of us who do not know her personally, unless they have not only an arm but a heart of iron. Nobody should love killing, especially a knight who, according to the code, should first and foremost defend the weak and be a good Christian."

"Saracens and Turks were murdered during the crusades by these good Christians," noted the Englishwoman, not because she felt sorry for the infidels who offered this blood tribute, but to be in harmony with logic."

"Yes," replied the outlaw hesitantly. "I don't like that either. I don't want to pretend to be a sainter than the Pope himself, but I've never believed in converting with the sword. I don't like Mohammedans and find their religion repulsive and blasphemous, but ultimately what do I have to do with it? As Martin, my deceased friend, used to say, everyone has the right to live, unless he lives at my expense. Yes, I agree, we should convert infidels, but why aren't we doing this by setting a good example? What example do we, ministers of Christ, set for them? Two Christian nations bite each other for years like dogs on a bone and throw millions of thalers down the drain to please someone's exuberant ambitions.

"You're a philosopher. You sit so long in the woods away from people, and you have time to think, as you can see."

"I'm hungry," squeaked Prince Richard tearfully.

"He's right, the stage was long, we're going to that inn," Theo pulled the reins and steered the horse towards the wide shack with a big sign "Wine Pot".

"Hey, hosteler, do you have milk?" he called as he entered.

"And you have money to pay?" the innkeeper asked distrustfully.

"We have, we have," Theo showed him a handful of change, which made the man a little calmer.

"Sit down in the corner," he muttered. "Just let this Gypsy girl not steal here."

"Xana, did you hear? Don't steal here," Theo said cheerfully to the indignant "wife."

They sat down in the indicated corner, at the dirty table. After a long while the innkeeper brought them a loaf of bread, a jug of bad wine, a smaller jug of freshly milked milk, and, unexpectedly, a few eggs baked in the ashes.

"Little children like it," he explained grumblingly, nevertheless looking at the gypsy girl with obvious kindness.

"Thank you, host." Theo said with a smile, spilling most of the coppers he had on his hand, and a few silver coins flashed between them. It was this much more than was necessary for the innkeeper to like them.

In the corner where they were sitting, they were hardly visible to visitors entering and exiting. They ate calmly, sipping their wine in moderation, so as not to overpower themselves before continuing their journey.

"I have to be doubly careful," Theo said, explaining. "My head is so weak that I need a little to be drunk like a fish. That is a shame."

"Drink with milk," the duchess advised him, laughing.

"I already did," the knight replied sourly. "And finally, I understood why babies cry all the time."

He poured the white liquid into the cup of the child, who drank greedily.

"You have an appetite for this stuff..." He laughed, but then he became serious and his hand shook.

"Keep calm. The king's soldiers are coming in," he warned in a whisper, the Duchess, who paled despite the brown paint on her face.

Several royal-colored knights entered the inn and loudly demanded wine.

"Right now, dear gentlemen," the innkeeper bowed and sent a solid prick to the side of the serving boy. "I dare to ask if you have found the missing lady yet."

"Don't be too curious, boy," one of the knights said. "If we had found her, we would be returning to Paris now, not sitting in this pigsty with vagrants."

He drank solidly straight from the jug and wiped his mouth with his sleeve.

"We'll find her," added another, tall and shapely, but with a flat, pockmarked and strikingly ugly face. "They will not transport her outside the province, it will be guarded along its entire length."

His ragged eyes stopped on a pair of Gypsies.

"Hey, dog sons, what are you guys sitting around like?" He exclaimed. "Where are you from?"

"From Caril's camp, sir," Theo replied, squeezing the duchess's icy-frustrated hand under the table. "Ours are probably already in Spain, we want to join them as soon as possible..."

"Amuse us, or we'll send you straight to the nearest gilt for hanging around honest people," the knight interrupted brutally.

Theo got up hurriedly from behind the table.

"Forgive me, my lord," he said humbly. "My wife has just got up from a serious illness and she cannot dance for you, because she is still very weak, and she is expecting our second child, but we will do what we can. Xana, take a tambourine and sing something for the noble lords."

The Duchess stood up, her legs buckling under her, and with a smile glued to her face, stepped in the center, tapping her fingers on the top of the drum, which was unfastened from the belt. Meanwhile, her companion took three flaming torches from the wall racks, choosing the longest ones and began to juggle them with the skill of the born vagrant. The spectacle engaged the knights, sipping wine and constantly demanding new shows. Theo's range of circus skills was quite slim, fortunately the knights, tired and angry with their fruitless search, quickly got drunk and stopped paying attention to them. As soon as it could be done, the fugitives withdrew from the inn and got into their carriage.

"God, I thought we were all over," sighed the Duchess, wiping the sweat from her forehead and embracing her son with a defensive gesture.

"We have to be far away before they sober up," Theo quickly untied his horse from the railing in front of the inn and removed the sack of oats from his head. "Fortunately, it doesn't look like it, because they're not finished getting drunk yet. Relax, my dear, no one will associate us."

"I hope so," Lady Joan didn't seem convinced at all. The performance in front of sworn enemies tired her and irritated her so much that she shook like a dab attack.

"Keep calm. I said that I would take you to the place and I would keep my word," the outlaw jumped on the trestle and slapped the horse on the back with the reins. The animal started at a clumsy trot, chewing on the last oat grains.

"How?" The English woman wailed, unable to control herself any longer. "Did you hear what they said? The border is fixed, we won't slip through."

"We'll see that yet," Theo muttered, urging his horse.

He tried to stay calm, but he was disturbed by this confrontation at the inn, and the news of the Aquitaine borders being laid up was indeed highly unsuccessful. He needed to rethink his plan as soon as possible, and he wasn't the best at improvising, although in fact he did it all the time.

"Vianna!" He suddenly exclaimed, awake from a dream. "They probably didn't guard Vianna, because what for?"

"How?" the Duchess asked helplessly.

"Vianna," he repeated, "It's a little river on the border of Touraine and Aquitaine, flowing at the bottom of a nasty ravine. One of the smaller tributaries of the Loire. It would be madness to try to cross this road, the abyss, rocks and eddies, and on top of that, a waterfall that has already cost the lives of a few careless daredevils. The joke is that I know how to get there safely. Me and Beregard discovered this path while we were both still unfledged adolescents and kept it a secret. Keep your heads up, princess, everything will be all right."

He did not add that they still had to reach the border safe, which could be problematic, and that in Aquitaine itself they would not be safe either until they reached Meung Castle. Encountering one of Robert Deauville's troops might end badly for them, but he decided to worry about that later, once they had crossed the border.

He directed his horse to one of the less traveled routes leading to the provincial border in the episode of her that interested him.

"You, men, are fine," said the Duchess after a long moment, a little calmer. "I wish I was as strong and unshakable as you. Your life is like walking on thin ice, even when you don't have to save trapped ladies and yet you are like a rock. How do you do that?"

Theo smiled slightly.

"Oh, lady, we are just as nervous, afraid and even despairing," he said. "But it isn't proper for us to flaunt it. Who is this man that is shaking and crying? A woman is different, it good for you and causes compassion, not laughter and contempt. In fact, it is kind of easier for you in this world."

"Maybe in a way... But somehow I have not heard of any man being enslaved by soldiers in the captured city."

"Maybe no one is just bragging about it?" chuckled the knight, who found this conclusion immensely amusing.

After a while, he decided there was nothing to laugh at, and he frowned. Unlike the Duchess, for whom it was not appropriate to know such details, he had heard of such incidents, surrounded by a conspiracy of silence. The war turned many into a savage.

"You know," the Duchess said softly, stroking the child crouched in her lap. "Regardless of how our escape ends, I'm glad to meet you."

"I fully reciprocate it, and I don't think our escape will be a fairy tale, which ends badly," Theo replied with a certain emotion.

*****

The Duchess finished changing her clothes and stepped out from behind a curtain of rose bushes. She looked like the great lady she was now, especially when she curled her hair in coils over her ears and tied it up with those pins she hadn't yet lost. She was still brownish in the hands and face, but there was nothing they could do about it now. Theo, finishing dressing up the little prince, looked at her appreciatively.

"Now you look as you should, lady," he said, buttoning the clothes of a politely standing child.

"You, too, are better in these modest feathers than in the bright rags of a gypsy acrobat," the Englishwoman replied. "How do you feel in your own skin?"

"Much better. Especially since I got rid of that nasty earring. I'm not a gypsy. Come on boy, you are an English prince again, not a gypsy dancer."

Little Richard looked at him seriously, probably not understanding much of what he had heard. The Duchess put her hand on the outlaw's shoulder.

"I will never repay you for what you did for me," she said softly. "Even though you consider us enemies, you have done more for us than any friend. Will you tell me now why you did this?"

Theo smiled slightly.

"There is some blood of the Plantagenets in me, Lady" he explained reluctantly. "We are very distant, but still related, so how could I leave you in danger? As you can see, I'm not that selfless."

"And I think you underestimate yourself," said the Duchess, and then picked her son up in her arms and walked slowly towards the drawbridge of Meung Castle.

Theo followed her for a short while, hiding from the gaze of the soldiers, then, having made sure that she had been admitted into the castle with signs of vigorous obedience from the sentries, turned back. He had already done his job, he was free to walk away. Now he was already sure he had done the right thing, no matter what King Charles V might think of it, probably still raging with rage after losing such precious hostages.

"It remains to be hoped that he will never find out who is the author of this feat," he thought, unhitching the horse from the carriage.

The weak hack wasn't like the horses he usually rode, but it could get him there as well as they could. Now he didn't have to worry about the lady or the little child anymore, but he knew he still had to be careful if he wanted to get back home safe. Just in case, to return to Touraine, he used the same passage he had used to lead his companion to Aquitaine. He preferred not to run into the soldiers, probably still guarding the borders in the hope of catching the escapees. Theo was the only one on this side of the border who knew how futile this waiting was. He even felt a little sorry for these iron-clad men, on whom the royal anger would probably be a spill when it became clear that the escape of Princess Joan and her little son had been successful. He almost felt like sending them a message that they had nothing to wait and could go home, but he steadied himself and slipped past them unnoticed, hiding into the woods. He no longer wandered off the beaten track, not wanting to stumble upon an armed force now that he had no gang with him, though it was likely that the soldiers, busy searching for the duchess, would not have paid any attention to him.

Driving through forest wilderness, after a long journey, he reached his hideout, where he was greeted with an outburst of wild joy. Although the outlaws firmly believed in their leader, they feared for his life, and when he was gone, they did not leave their hiding place at all, waiting for him almost idly. Of course, at first everyone was telling him that he would not let them accompany him on the dangerous expedition, but Theo explained to them that a large group would be much less likely to travel safely to Aquitaine.

"If we came across a regular army, we could only die heroically," he said firmly. "In this case, success depends not on strength, but on cunning."

"And what?" Pierre asked now. "Did this cleverness of yours help you free the beautiful lady? Or maybe in something else?"

"No foolishness, Pierre," Theo said, glancing somewhat apprehensively at his wife. "I don't even know if this lady is really beautiful, maybe at most pretty. It wasn't that..."

"It's all right, all right," Bellette interrupted. "I'm not jealous. I'm glad that you came back alive, because when we heard how many troops were chasing on the roads, our head was suffering. Will you eat something?"

"Sure, what's up?"

"Squirrel shashlik and honey flatbread," Fabienne informed him, licking her deliciously.

"We haven't eaten yet, either," Ettienne added mournfully. He was growing fast lately, and his appetite was enormous, though no one could tell where those mountains of food fell into such a thin body.

Bellette and Fabienne rushed to light the fire under the makeshift spit, and after a while the shashliks sizzled appetizingly, exuding the scent of fried meat and onions. The friends shared the first shashlik and started eating while the girls were preparing the next one. The feast continued until they had satisfied their appetites, then lay down on the grass, eating flatbreads and honey for dessert. Urged by his friends, Theo told them briefly what the escape and the way to Aquitaine looked like, without coloring, though he was tempted to do so. When he was done, Armando spoke up, nodding his head.

"I told you it was a good way. Do you have my earring?"

The knight reached by his belt and pulled a golden circle from a secret pocket.

"Here," he said. "I don't know how you Gypsies can stand it. My poor ear has been throbbing to the rhythm of the bells for vespers."

"You weren't supposed to rhyme," Gwidon admonished him.

Theo smiled.

"Your zither is gone," he said. "I left it in the carriage. But don't worry, I'll get you another one."

"No worries, Chief, I have the other," said the poet carelessly. "I gave you the worse one, a little distorted, but still good. You think I'd risk such a good instrument?"

"Your sacrifice has always touched me," Theo laughed, shoving another flatbread into his mouth.

Gwidon rolled over on his back, put his hands under his head, and hummed, looking up at the sky:

"A fiery-colored rose, your petals delight me. I dare not bring my mouth close to their scented cloud. I bend my knee in humility at your doorstep. Crazy stars race above us..."

Pierre blocked his ears.

"Mercy, Weasel, enough of this poetry!" He exclaimed. "If you want to write the next "Roman de la Rose"[14], it's away from me. My nerves are too weak to listen to something like that."

"Envier," said Gwidon with offended dignity, but stopped reciting.

Beregard nudged his leader aside.

---

[14] Roman de la Rose - actually "A Tale of a Rose", a late-medieval French allegorical poem in the dream convention.

"Don't you have the feeling that this time you have overdone this chivalrous nobility?" he asked.

The friend looked at him absently.

"I don't know!?" He replied after a moment. "Possible. However, I had my reasons. But I could not explain it to the king, so I hope he never finds out who do the dirty on him."

"I hope so too, or you'll have to learn to live without a few rather important parts of your body," Beregard said seriously.

"I don't care. They'd have to catch him first," Ettienne said dismissively. "It's not easy, is it? Theo, and you know that while you weren't here, a messenger from the Falcon came?"

Fabienne gave him a scolding tapping on the back of the neck.

"Oh," the knight wondered. "What is this about?"

The girl lowered her eyes.

"I got a letter from him," she said softly. "The Falcon is asking for my hand."

"And what the hell does he use your hand for? Let it take you whole."

Fabienne pulled a small roll from her sleeve and unrolled it.

"My beloved," she began to read. "I've been away so long, and I can't help but think of you. I want you to be my wife. I confided my love to my uncle, and he only smiled and said: "Get married then, boy, and as soon as possible, and I will give you some of my goods, since the shameful peace has already been broken and you do not need to hide in mountains." So if your brother doesn't mind, let's get married."

"The affinity with the de Foix family is not just anything. If this boy is close your heart, I agree," Theo said heartily, stroking his sister on the curly head.

"Very," she whispered, hiding her blush.

"There will be a wedding," rejoiced the little page.

Theo sat up and rubbed his hands.

"I'll take you to the Pyrenees then," he decided. "Bellette will come with us, and Ettienne too... Actually, we'll all go there. We aren't so many that it makes a significant difference."

Fabienne smiled gratefully.

"You agree then?" she asked timidly.

"Of course. The Falcon is a wonderful young man and I could not have dreamed of a better husband for you," replied her brother, then got up and went to the cabin.

After a while he returned with a heavy, silver-forged casket.

"You'll get it as a dowry," he said.

Jewels and money were stolen from Adeline de Valois in the box.

"Is it alright?" the girl asked doubtfully.

"In love and war, everything is fine, and yet we have war, right?" Gwidon interrupted. Theo patted his sister on the shoulder.

"Let's take this as a prize of war," he said with a hint of cheerful cynicism. "Adeline lost to us, so she had to pay a contribution. We did not establish such a mode of warfare. You can take it with a clear conscience."

Deep in his heart he felt a great deal of relief. Ever since it turned out that Tristan was in fact a girl, he lived in a constant tension and fear, which he tried not to show. There was no question that the girl brought up as a squire would let herself be guided more than she saw fit, and so many dangers lurked around, dangers to which the young bride was exposed much more than the boy. Fabienne, arbitrary and accustomed to freedom, was nevertheless made of a different mettle than, for example, Bellette. First of all, she was far too thin and too delicate for life in the forest, everyone could see it, and unlike Preziosa or Bellette, she did not have a fighting spirit at all. She did not allow herself to be moved away from participating in the normal life of the band, but in fact she always stayed a bit aside. The bloodshed terrified her. More than once, Theo wondered how King John could have allowed this fragile girl to be raised in the tough school of future knights, but he himself kept her gender a secret to all but him. The fact that she was about to enter the de Foix family was a real relief for her brother, for it meant that she would be in the care of one of the most influential and illustrious figures of the kingdom from now on. Gaston Phoebus loved his cousin dearly, and he would certainly not have let his chosen wife fail in any way. Theo was right about him - Febus as he was, he was: half mad, eccentric, and cruel, he seldom paid attention to what was lost and what was not (in later years he condemned his own son to death for trying to poison him, to the poor boy dared at the instigation of his uncle the King of Navarre, the brother of Febus' rightful wife.) But if he already had affection for someone, he was willing to do anything for him. He hated his wife, and with her all of her family, and he did not even want to look at the sickly boy born of her. That is why, in his time, Philip did not want to talk to him personally... but he had a real fatherly affection for Fabrizio de Foix, the Blue Falcon. This handsome, tall and flexible as a steel blade, the young man was hard to dislike.

*****

After returning from Bearn, the outlaws first had to hunt the envoys of Adeline de Valois, who in their absence took a heavy toll on the local population. Duchess, not knowing why the gang did not respond to her provocations, concluded that the outlaws must have been cut down by the troops seeking Princess Joan and began to rule in the county as she wanted. The peasants welcomed the return of their defenders with relief and gratitude. After several successful raids, Adeline's soldiers respected their arrows and fists and, whether they like it or not, admitted to their mistress what they could not cope with. Contrary to their fears, the Duchess did not get an attack of fury, rather she accepted the news with incomprehensible satisfaction. Everything returned to normal, and she could again seek revenge for the insult the memory of which was stuck in her heart like a scratch. Of course, her feelings were of no concern to the handful of outlawed killers who still lived in their hideout in the swamps and felt obligated to defend the local peasants from exploitation, regardless of who was the exploiter. There are only a few left, only eight, including Ettienne and Bellette. The hut, usually crowded on rainy days, now seemed oddly deserted to them, and it didn't help that Fanchette had moved in, who, having become pregnant with Pierre, preferred not to be exposed to human mockery in the village. Tiny, pretty, cheerful as a bird, a girl with pale blond, glass-smooth hair could not fill the void that suddenly appeared in this place, although for Bellette she was a very welcome company.

Theo, though he missed his sister left in Bearn, did not show it after himself, trying to keep the good mood in the band who had to pick up and organize their lives anew anyway. Despite their greatly depleted strength, the outlaws continued their work, not refraining from helping with the harvest, as they do every year. They returned to each other at dusk, exhausted, and literally fell on their beds, so they had to settle among themselves the duty of hunting and preparing meals for each one in turn. Such a duty hunter and cook in one person, of course, did not take part in the harvest that day, but he had to take care of everything else. Naturally, the turn had to come and the leader, who was very talented in avoiding this duty, had happened at the end of August. The knight, of course, preferred to work in the fields, where he was at least among people, to wandering alone with his bow in the woods, and then to grind to prepare what he hunted, but he couldn't think of any excuses. The work in the field was very hard, but fun nonetheless, which drove away from him that strange melancholy that had been darkening his heart for some time and making life even harder than it was. Here, in the backwoods, which gave the impression of being untouched by human feet, he felt as if he had been abandoned and forgotten by everyone. It was absurd, but he couldn't help it.

This time he was exceptionally unlucky. The hunt was dragging on, as in spite of his anger he could find no game except small birds, not worth the effort, and squirrels, too agile at this time of year. At one point, his sensitive ear caught the distant crack of broken branches and a rustle. He hid in the bushes, gripping the bow tighter in his hand. He knew the sounds of the forest too well to confuse the noise made by humans with the sounds made by wild animals. They were people, no doubt. After a while, a thin, short figure ran near his hideout, and a little later two men in peasant rags, but with swords drawn. Theo had no intention of waiting for further developments on the assumption that if two armed thugs were chasing one, judging from his stature, a child, it was not fair under any circumstances. He ran silently behind the trees and jumped out after thugs looking for the victim.

"Peek-a-boo!" he exclaimed.

They turned abruptly, and then he collapsed on them, sword raised. He was just going to scare them away, but to his amazement they were not peasants or forest robbers, but trained soldiers. Upon discovering this, he redoubled his vigilance. They attacked him too ferociously for him to think of a bloodless solution to this case, and in the end, enraged to the brim, he struck at them with all his strength and technique. It took a while, but eventually he managed to kill first one, then another. Having done this, he took a deep breath and rested for a moment, leaning against one of the trees, until he remembered the fugitive being chased by these people.

"Hey you!" He exclaimed, looking around. "Where are you?! You're not in any danger anymore!"

He started looking on the right assumption that if a kid who had not been with the forest ended up in the swamps, it could be bad with him, and the swamps were not that far away again. He remembered the little figure that flashed before his eyes and decided that it was definitely no peasant, for his outfit was too colorful. Some kind of noble child, a very young boy or girl in men's clothes. He searched the forest methodically, listening for and looking for anything that seemed unusual to him in some way. He was beginning to think it was futile when he spotted a greenish-violet caftan behind the wolfberry bushes.

"Come out, I'm not the enemy!" he exclaimed impatiently, tired of this game of cat and mouse, but the startled fugitive jumped up at the sound of his voice to run away again.

Theo caught up with him easily and overpowered him, knocking him to the ground.

"Let go, you wretch, let go!" A thin voice shouted desperately. "If not, then... Count de Bongrais!"

"Oh, I beg your forgiveness, Your Majesty..." Theo helped the boy to stand his feet, barely concealing his astonishment at the sight of the youngest son of John II the Good here, in his lands, and in such a situation.

Prince Louis looked good, though he was terrified, exhausted and covered with dirt.

"How good it's you," he gasped, gasping for breath. "I thought I was gone."

"I happened to be around by accident. I hate to be nosy, but what exactly happened?" asked the outlaw, unable to understand any of this.

"Oh, something terrible has happened," groaned Prince Louis. "My brother, Count, set up camp near Bongrais, because Bertram du Guesclin ordered maneuvers and Charles wanted to observe them... He took me with him. Duchess de Valois, when she found out that he was there, came to see him on what she called it a faithful visit. They talked for a long time, then she said that a boy like me was probably bored at maneuvers in which he could not participate and suggested that I go hunting. And so as not to distract the army from maneuvers, she offered me her own escort, in addition to the few knights who always accompany me. Once deep in the woods, the Duchess's soldiers began murdering my guards. One of them ordered me to run away, but two chased after me, changing clothes on the way."

"But why are they...?"

"They were supposed to kill me. That it would be upon you," whispered Prince Louis softly, trembling like a leaf.

"Ah, what an adder," the knight muttered, thinking.

"Do you have any idea what would happen if they succeeded?" the prince wept suddenly, like any ordinary, mortally terrified child

"I have an idea," Theo said absently. "Well, I wouldn't like to be in my own skin then. We must reach the king's camp, Your Majesty. I'll do the best for me, because Adeline's plan must have included an emergency exit, so you can get on with some of her people. Please calm down and don't cry. I will lead Your Majesty to your place, outlaw word."

The boy laughed through his tears. There was something about the man's soft baritone that was trustworthy, and he felt he was no longer afraid.

"If we succeed, I'll ask my brother to forgive you," he promised, walking by his side.

Theo put an arm around him.

"Better not," he said. "My sins are too serious."

"I guess not that much."

"As much. You just don't know everything. And you'd better stay out of this, Monseigneur."

The prince was silent for a moment as he walked by his side.

"They say you freed the wife of the Black Prince and his son from Fontainbleau," he said carefully.

"What if it were so?" The knight asked him seriously, as if he were talking to a grown man. "Is it such a crime to save a little boy and his mother from a death trap? After all, King Edward would have sacrificed them without hesitation in the name of his politics."

"You think my brother would hurt such a little child?!"

"If he thought that the interests of France required it... that by doing so he would prove to the enemy that he would stop at nothing..." said Theo slowly.

The boy fell silent. He knew his eldest brother too well to ignore that possibility. Charles V always reasoned coldly and emotionlessly when it came to state matters and made the right decision in his opinion, disregarding its social costs. Just in case, he didn't ask anymore. He had grown to like the exiled count, as his father called him, and preferred not to know anything that would harm him. He felt safe by his side, the shocking impression passed, and giving way to anger at his brother's mistress, whom he had let himself be so dazed with. He was just thinking, not without satisfaction, as he would tell his brother what had happened when he felt Theo's hand tighten on his shoulder.

"Down to the ground and no words," whispered the outlaw, pushing him into the bushes.

They both lay down among the grasses and dead leaves. There were more than three armed men nearby, looking around carefully.

"So, there are more of them... It complicates the matter for us. Is the king far away?"

"Not really. On the other side of the road to Paris, but without horses we won't get there any time soon." the young prince whispered back to him.

"She secured herself, a fox of hers." Theo waited a moment longer and stood up. "I underestimated this woman and now I serve one right. Good for me, donkey. Here we go, Your Majesty, but please stay close to me. I don't know what else will get out..."

He broke off, feeling that he was starting to speak involuntarily in a rural dialect that the youngest prince may have never heard in his life, but the latter barely paid attention to his words - something else he was thinking about.

"Well, as soon as I tell my brother about this reptile..." he said after a moment with deep conviction.

"He may not believe it," warned the outlaw. "Or Adeline will convince him that I got you crazy and you, as a stupid child, were led astray. Forgive me, but she can really use that argument."

He shook his head until the side-swept black mane fell over his eyes. He felt sorry that this still unspoiled boy, fed with ideals, had to turn into a cynical politician, no better than hundreds of others. Now he was a straightforward, honest boy with bright eyes and a knight's soul, and then what? He shook his head one more time, chasing away the dark thoughts.

"I didn't believe once that you could be seriously afraid of a woman, but now I do," he continued after a moment. "This lady is capable of anything, and so perverse that the bald man will show the absolute necessity to buy a dense comb. Do not fight it, but beware of it and protect your brother, because it is possible that Adeline will turn into another Mahaut d'Artois with time. It wouldn't surprise me at all."

Louis felt a shudder of horror and disgust. He never liked Adeline. Being too young to be seduced by her beauty, he was too penetrating to hide her true nature from him, but he did not think she was so perverse.

"Do you think she could turn against my brother, Count?" he asked.

"It depends. If she could see a significant advantage in this... Perhaps I am exaggerating."

Theo looked around at the crack of a twig breaking but calmed down when he saw the feral dog peek out of the bushes for a moment and then back away. There were quite a few of them in the woods, skinny and decayed; ravaged and much more dangerous than wolves, especially when gathered into a pack.

"You see, the wolf is a wild animal, it is afraid of people," Prospero had once explained to him. "And the feral dog is not afraid of people because he knows them, and that's why he hates them. God forbid you come across one like this, especially in winter."

It was true - on the first winter of his stay in the woods, Theo had a hard time escaping a pack of feral mongrels, and it was only because he had saved his skin by keeping consciousness and throwing them a goat he had hunted, which the dogs had dealt with greedily, allowing him to escape. But now, at the end of summer, the dogs weren't dangerous, too many easy-to-hunt games were running in the woods.

"How can we get to the road when there are so many Adeline minions here?" asked the little prince.

"Where?" Theo turned his eyes away from the bushes to see armed figures flashing between the trees.

"For a hundred hell, she didn't have any more?" he growled, placing his hand quickly on the hilt of his sword.

The soldiers searching for them were happily too far away to hear them, rather than looking in that direction. The outlaw waited for them to disappear in the distance.

"These took the road to the marshes," he said finally. "Even if they drown, it is good for them. Come on, Your Majesty."

"Aren't you afraid, Count?" the boy asked curiously.

Theo shrugged.

"I would be afraid if there were, for example, the Black Prince in their place, but these rags can only harm themselves," he replied contemptuously.

"Well, you must be safe from the Black Prince," said Prince Louis after a while, not easily keeping up with him. "He returned to England with all his men."

"Seriously?" Theo almost shouted, taken aback by the news.

He had long forgotten the promise he had received from his enemy's lips, not to mention the fact that he had never believed it for a moment, so that the news was completely unexpected to him.

"Perhaps, involuntarily, I have served my country more than I could by following the king's orders as closely as possible?" he thought, but at the same time his heart ached. A knight's duty, especially in times of war, was to obey his ruler blindly, and not to follow his own calculations, no matter how right.

It was very sad to know that, while remaining in harmony with his own conscience and the principles instilled in it, he had denied obedience to his king and was no longer worthy to be called his knight. The young prince watched him out of the corner of his eye and slowly grew certain of his suspicions. He did not like it very much, but he decided not to mention them to his brother a word, seeing clearly that this was no traitor, but a hapless knight against whom everything had conspired, even his own blood. The silence of their mutual silence was broken by a close cry:

"Here it is!" and the patter of the feet of a few people. Theo swiftly impaled the prince with himself and grabbed his sword, ready to fight in an instant. With momentum he slashed through the temple of the first attacker and slashed the throat of the other with a dagger in the other hand. He pondered the thrust from the lunge, kicked his opponent in the knee and thrust his sword blade under his chin, almost at the same moment lunging to the side to avoid the treacherous blow from behind. The sword passed an inch from his left side, but the soldier managed to keep his balance and with all his strength gripped the outlaw with his arm by the throat, choking him with an iron grip. For a moment his fate was in the balance when the young prince suddenly joined the fight, hitting the attacker with all his strength on the back of the head with a stone raised from the ground. The released knight gasped for a moment, then wiped his face with his sleeve and looked at the boy gratefully.

"It seems, Your Majesty, we are even in terms of saving lives," he said.

"Nonsense. Let us go now, because there may be more of them here," replied Prince Louis, trying in vain to hide that he was trembling like a leaf in the wind.

They moved forward, but this time along the path marked by the outlaw, where you had to wade through blackberries and nettles, but they were less likely to meet sent murderers.

"How does he not get lost?" the boy thought admiringly, watching Theo lead him without hesitating on a path he would not even see. It was difficult for the not hardened prince, who was not used to long walks, to keep pace with the hardened outlaw, but he made every effort not to be left behind, for he was afraid of losing himself in this thicket. Theo was aware of his difficulties, so deliberately he stopped his pace and looked slightly. He did not know how many more Adeline de Valois men were hanging around in the woods, and he knew how easy it was to make an unexpected turn when surrounded by enemies. He felt responsible for this boy and wanted to bring him safely to a safe place, he also knew that his fate was also at the stake. Adeline's plot was cleverly thought out and worked out in detail, pure coincidence allowed the prince to escape and on the way he came across a famous outlaw hunting in the forest. If he had failed to lead the boy to the camp of the royal army, his situation would have been doubly dire. Therefore, he pressed on, almost ignoring the tiredness of his companion. Finally, after a tiring march through the prickly brushwood, they managed to reach the road.

"There's no help," Theo said. "Now we have to go out into the open. May they not dare to attack us in plain sight."

"Horsemen!" Louis cried desperately, clutching his elbow tightly.

The knight seized his weapon again, but did not bare it, recognizing Bertram du Guesclin, who was riding at the head of the armed sub-unit. He also recognized him.

"You're under arrest, outlaw!" he shouted sharply, jumping off his horse.

"I forbid, Connetable!" Exclaimed Prince Louis, stepping forward and straightening his tiny figure proudly. "The men of Princess de Valois set an ambush for me, and this noble knight saved my life, at the risk of his own."

Theo felt admiration and respect, seeing how in the blink of an eye, from a frightened child, Louis turned into a young prince, accustomed to obedience.

"Your Majesty, I heard..." Bertram du Guesclin choked out with obvious surprise and a sense of guilt for his lack of thought.

"You've heard nothing but vile lies and nonsenses," interrupted the prince and turned to Theo, ignoring the connetable and his men. "I renew my proposal, Count. Come with me to my brother and I promise to obtain his grace for you."

The outlaw shook his head slowly, regretfully.

"I can't," he said. "That wouldn't be fair of me. Whatever a man does, he should be consistent."

He unbuckled his sword from his belt and kissed its hilt reverently.

"I got this sword from Your Majesty's father," he said. "But now, please take it. Let it fall into more worthy hands than mine."

The prince looked deep into his eyes. He wanted to say something, but remained silent, struck by the enormity of the painful mystery that was emerging from those black pupils, and took the sword with trembling hands. Connetable stepped forward.

"Take mine," he said softly. "It's not good without a weapon these days..."

He handed his sword to the knight, who accepted it without saying a word. They shook hands, then the outlaw bowed to the king's brother and left, disappearing into the woods.

Bertram du Guesclin looked at Louis, still watching his savior.

"Has he really become unworthy of this honor?" he asked softly.

The Prince gripped the sword of Valesius in both hands.

"He's a very worthy knight," he replied hollowly, overcoming the emotion that choked him. "I don't know anyone worthier than him."

*****

"Not much," Pierre frowned, sweeping his portion of stew from the bowl. "We were working all day, and of course, instead of hunting, you wandered in the woods and whistled."

Theo smiled.

"You're right, unlike you, I had an exceptionally quiet day," he replied. "Don't be angry, I wasn't lucky. Ettienne, how was it working?"

The Page examined his rubbed hands.

"No offense, but it really isn't a job for the nobility," he said. "However, I must admit that it's very funny."

Ettienne was unable to reap, but he helped raise the sheaves, and quickly learned to twist the grass returns to bind them. It was not so easy to do here, and the nettles and thistles tangled between the grasses' could be a real nuisance to untrained hands.

"He was doing brilliantly," Bellette said, adding her brother some of her portion.

Finishing her meal, she stepped outside the cabin and stared at the darkening sky.

"What are you thinking about?" Theo asked, standing behind her imperceptibly. He embraced her tenderly and pressed her pale head against his chest.

"I think about what is and what will be," the young woman sighed. "Will we ever be really happy? Maybe we just don't deserve it."

"We will, Bellette, I promise you," the knight whispered.

She was silent for a moment, then pressed her cheek against his.

"I'm scared, Theo," she said suddenly. "I'm afraid of what awaits us. Can we make it this time?"

"What can we make it?" her husband asked in surprise.

"I'm expecting a baby," whispered Bellette, so softly he could barely hear her.

"This is great news! It must work this time, my sweet. I will pray for this daily, and we must both have faith that God will hear us."

Theo kissed his wife and wrapped his arms around her as if he wanted to protect her and the baby to be born from the whole evil world. They stood together, in peace and quiet, as if there was no one in the world except the two of them, listening to the murmur of the night forest and staring at the black sky, interspersed with flickering lights. It was late summer, the time of shooting stars.

EPILOGUE

"And what happened next, auntie please?" the boy asked, propping his chin up with his curled fists.

The old lady shifted in the chair.

"What would you like to know, Will? There is not much I can add to what I have told you," she said after a moment. "You probably want to hear that your grandfather lived happily ever after, or that he was pardoned and died a knight's death. Unfortunately, none of that. Two years after Edward returned to England, a wave of red moor swept over Touraine. It was a terrible plague. It started with an innocent cough, then the man vomited blood, lost consciousness, and on the same day it was over. When it started, Theo tried to take his wife and a few-month-old son to the mountains, but they both got sick and died on the way. He buried them in the forest, then returned to Bongrais and helped the monks of the Carmelite monastery to nurture the sick until the plague struck him down. It is said that in the morning he had his first coughing attack, and in the evening, he was dead, despite all his strength and endurance. It was a terrible epidemic, few survived, so it is no wonder that he too... His body was burned together with dozens of other unfortunates who died on the same day, the ashes were blew by the wind and everything ended once and for all. Only my memory remains alive and it hurts like it was yesterday."

She closed her eyes, pressing her dry lips tight together tightly. The boy was silent for a moment, staring out the window.

"Auntie loved him very much, didn't you?" he said finally.

"Very," replied the old woman forcefully. "I loved him like I never loved anyone. And I think he also... liked me a bit, but if we tried to be together, it would be read as a betrayal of the motherland. We couldn't, even if he were free."

"Am I like him?" Will asked timidly.

The old lady smiled with an effort.

"You have his eyes and lips; your hair looks the same..." she said. "I think when you get older, you'll be more like him than your brothers, though Robin looks like him too. And your character... That hand movement as you brush your hair from your forehead... Come on, go play with your brothers, I'm tired."

The boy reluctantly got up from the low stool on which he usually sat at his aunt's feet.

"And how does you know all this, aunt?" He asked suddenly. "After all, aunt was not there."

Lady Joan thought about it.

"From Lancey, of course," she said after a moment. "Before he died, Theo asked him to bring me the family papers for Mathilde... he thought they might be useful someday. And the act in which he officially recognized her as his rightful daughter and heiress to the Bongrais family. Lancey did his last wish and stayed here. He had no reason to return to France."

"Why?" Will asked, surprised.

Lady Joan smiled bitterly.

"He watched all his friends and loved ones die," she said. "He experienced the worst loneliness that can be experienced by a human being, he lost almost everything... except his life. What he once considered important has lost its meaning."

"But then he can't be called Lancey. It's an English name, after all." The boy pushed his hair away from his face and frowned.

The old woman nodded slightly.

"Good point," she praised him. "But think about the times... We didn't want anyone to know that one of my people was French, because that would create unnecessary perturbations. It didn't matter, he says, then many Englishmen, born and raised in France, were returning to the country... Lancey did not want to assume a role more appropriate to him, nor to live in a castle. On his own initiative, he started to help my then gardener, lived with him in an annex, and after his death took over the care of the gardens. More than once, I offered him another job, but he didn't want to. Perhaps he feels best in contact with plants."

"Mother says aunt indulges him too much for an ordinary gardener. Now I understand why aunt likes him so much," the boy said seriously.

"Yes, I like him very much," nodded Lady Joan, barely audible. "And I'm sorry that Mathilde treats him badly, despite my admonitions."

"But Mom's not bad for him, just a little dry," Will said hastily. "I heard her tell my father that without Lancey, this house wouldn't be a full house. And she told us how for her sixth birthday he made her a swing entwined with blooming morning glory and ivy... how he taught her to ride her first pony and made sure that she did not fall... so she probably has a heart for him too but thinks that it is inappropriate to show it to a lowly rise."

"The measure of true nobility, Will, is the way servants are treated and those below you in general," said the old lady with an incomprehensible smile. "Not to mention the fact that Lancey... it's irrelevant anyway. Now really go. The brothers are waiting for you."

The boy kissed his aunt's hands and ran out of the room, jumping merrily. After he had left, Lady Joan sat in the armchair for a long moment with her eyes closed, then stood up and, leaning heavily on a silver-wrapped cane, went down to the garden. Around the bend of the sand and pebble alley she saw a tall man in a sun-faded long-sleeved shirt and a straw hat, trimming the branches of dwarf cherries with a huge knife.

"What's up, Lancey?" she asked in a low voice, pausing.

The gardener turned to reveal a dark, wrinkled face framed by long wisps of gray, almost white hair. Despite these signs of old age, he moved with the ease of a man in his middle years at best.

"The last storm must have damaged my lilies a lot," Lady Joan continued.

"Not so much, my lady," the gardener replied, smiling at her with quite inappropriate familiarity. "Fortunately, most survived, and so did the rose bushes on the north side."

Despite the passage of so many years, he spoke with a strong French accent. The old lady was silent for a moment, her walking stick tapping against the pebbles.

"Aren't these boys bothering you?" She asked finally. "They can be obnoxious and do more damage than any storm."

"Just as kids are," Lancey replied warmly. He was their confidant and friend, since they learned to walk and talk, he always defended them when they did something wrong and he hid for them sweets smuggled from the kitchen.

"You spoil them, and they are unlikely savages without it," Lady Joan sighed. "At least it's good that the twins are becoming real ladies so far. There are not many of such polite and unruly girls now."

The gardener restrained a smile. He could also say something about it, but he did not intend to betray the trust of similar to himself as two drops of water, a few-year-old half-devils who could be themselves only in his company.

The old woman was staring at him keenly, though with a kind expression in her pale eyes.

"By the way, it's puzzling how these kids cling to you," she said thoughtfully.

Lancey closed his eyelids for a moment.

"My lady, children always cling to a man who allows them to do everything, is not angry for anything, and knows how to soothe their little sorrows with stolen sweets," he said with gentle indulgence, very out of place with a servant talking to his mistress.

"Maybe. Perhaps so," agreed Lady Fitzoother. "All children like sweets... As far as I know, you also like them... you just prefer to give them than eat yourself."

"With permission, lady," said the French after a pause. "I'd like to finish pruning the trees before sunset. Now is the best time, spring."

"Yes, of course," she admitted absentmindedly, and turned with difficulty, propping her emaciated body on her cane. She looked at the gardener for a moment, her eyes blurry with some long-forgotten emotion. The rays of the setting sun illuminated his weather-beaten face and gray hair, slid down the blade of the knife held by the calloused, clawed fingers, and did not cut sudden short flashes of light, falling into the cut of his carded shirt. Lady Joan started toward the castle again but paused a moment longer.

"Lancey," she said over her shoulder, turning her head. "It's rude to be so undressed in the company of a lady. Lace up your shirt..."

The gardener, surprised, looked down at his torso and, noticing a gleam of silver from under the parted canvas, hastily obeyed her instructions, pulling the straps at the cut of his shirt. He glanced at his mistress, who was still looking over her shoulder at him with a knowing half smile.

"AS you wish, my lady," he said, inclining his head slightly, then returned to his work.

The old lady slowly, leaning heavily on her cane, walked away towards the castle. At the bend of the alley, she turned once more, but Lancey trimmed the cherry branches with calm, measured movements without looking in her direction, very inconspicuous and gray in his plain clothes from this distance.

Just an ordinary old gardener.

THE END

www.ingramcontent.com/pod-product-compliance
Lightning Source LLC
Chambersburg PA
CBHW020604040726
47498CB00003B/623

* 9 7 9 8 9 8 6 4 5 2 4 0 1 *